Tangl
& Twi

Margaret Dickinson is the author of nineteen novels including most recently *Without Sin*, *Red Sky in the Morning*, *Twisted Strands*, and *Wish Me Luck*. She is married with two grown-up daughters, and lives in Lincolnshire, where the majority of her novels are based.

Also by Margaret Dickinson

Plough the Furrow

Sow the Seed

Reap the Harvest

The Miller's Daughter

Chaff upon the Wind

The Fisher Lass

The Tulip Girl

The River Folk

Red Sky in the Morning

Without Sin

Pauper's Gold

Wish Me Luck

Margaret Dickinson

Tangled Threads & Twisted Strands

PAN BOOKS

Tangled Threads first published 2002 by Pan Books.
Twisted Strands first published 2003 by Pan Books.

This omnibus first published 2008 by Pan Books
an imprint of Pan Macmillan, a division of Macmillan Publishers Limited
Pan Macmillan, 20 New Wharf Road, London N1 9RR
Basingstoke and Oxford
Associated companies throughout the world
www.panmacmillan.com

ISBN 978-0-330-45783-5

3 5 7 9 8 6 4 2

A CIP catalogue record for this book is available from the British Library.

Typeset by SetSystems Ltd, Saffron Walden, Essex
Printed and bound in the UK by
CPI Mackays, Chatham ME5 8TD

Tangled Threads
&
Twisted Strands

Tangled Threads

For Dennis

Acknowledgements

The area to the west of Grantham around Barrowby and Casthorpe, the village of Ruddington and, of course, Nottingham are the places of inspiration for the settings in this novel although the story and all the characters are entirely fictitious. The siting of a factory and warehouse on Canal Street in Nottingham and the homes of all the characters within the city in 1900 are also my own invention.

I am deeply grateful to Mr Jack Smirfitt, Miller and all their colleagues at the Ruddington Framework Knitters' Museum for all their wonderful help. I also wish to thank the staff at the Lace Market Centre, Nottingham, for answering my questions and, in particular, Peter Mee, a former twist-hand in the lace industry, who so kindly and generously shared his knowledge and experience with me.

My love and thanks as always to my family and friends for their constant support and encouragement especially those who read and comment on the script in its early stages; my sister and brother-in-law, Robena and Fred Hill; my brother and sister-in-law, David and Una Dickinson; my friends Linda and Terry Allaway and Pauline Griggs. Thank you all so much.

One

1900

'I saw you with him near Bernby Covert,' Jimmy Hardcastle teased his sister when he brought the cows into the byre for evening milking. 'Wait 'til I tell our mam.' He paused for greater effect and then added, 'and Dad.'

Eveleen grabbed hold of him, her fingers digging into his skinny arm. 'Don't you dare,' she hissed.

Jimmy laughed disdainfully as he twisted free of her grasp. 'Stephen Dunsmore'll never marry the likes of you. Oh, he might get you into trouble, but then he'd be off like a rabbit with a ferret on its tail.'

Eveleen's eyes narrowed. 'What about you getting some poor girl into trouble? I've heard about you chasing after Alice Parks. I don't think Mam'll be best pleased to hear about that either.'

'She wouldn't believe you.'

The brother and sister glared at each other. They were remarkably alike. Seeing them together for the first time, strangers could be forgiven for mistaking them for twins. They were equal in height, even though Jimmy, at sixteen, was a year younger than his sister. They had the same dark brown eyes and the same well-shaped nose that on Eveleen was maybe just a fraction too large for true beauty. Their mouths were wide and generous and usually stretched in ready laughter. They even had the same curly hair, a rich chestnut colour, but while Jimmy's was cut short, Eveleen's was a cloud of tangled curls about her face. Though she brushed it one hundred times every night in front of the speckled mirror in the privacy of her bedroom, she could never quite tame it into neatness.

'But I have got nice eyes,' she would murmur. Eveleen's soft and gentle eyes, fringed with long dark lashes, belied a mischievous spirit which her mother, however hard she tried, could not quite quell.

'Besides,' Jimmy went on, 'if anyone said I'd fathered a child—' he stepped back out of her reach as he added, 'I'd say it wasn't mine.'

Eveleen gasped. 'You wouldn't!'

''Course I would. It's what all the lads'd do. Ted told me.'

Ted Morton was twenty and, in Eveleen's opinion, not a good influence on her brother. Ted flirted with her, but Eveleen kept him at arm's length. Literally, for he had never been able even to steal a kiss. She never gave him the chance though she always managed to answer his saucy comments with good-humoured teasing. She had no wish to fall out with Ted. They had grown up together and their fathers, living and working on the same farm estate, were good friends. But Ted Morton was not for her.

Now Stephen Dunsmore, she was thinking, he's a different matter. Her knees trembled at the mere thought of him.

Jimmy's voice broke into her daydreaming. 'It's different for a girl. If you got in the family way, Mam'd go daft. 'Specially if it was with *him*. You know what she's like about "knowing our place".' The youth gave a fair impression of their mother's prim tones. 'And she wouldn't think you walking out with our employer's son was "seemly".'

'Why ever not?' Eveleen flashed back. 'Stephen's father and our dad used to work side by side in the fields and their fathers before them.'

'I know all about Dad's tales,' Jimmy mocked. 'But now we work *for* 'em, not *with* 'em.' There was resentment in Jimmy's tone and it deepened as he went on. 'You don't see Mr Dunsmore getting his hands dirty nowadays and as for Master Stephen, all he's good for is riding about the estate all day in his posh clothes handing out his orders. I bet he doesn't even know *how* to milk a cow. He's never had to work from morning 'til night like our dad.'

To that, Eveleen had no reply. What Jimmy said was true. Ernest Dunsmore, his wife and their son Stephen lived in a large mansion, Fairfield House, just across the fields from the Hardcastles' home. They had live-in servants and all the men employed on their farm lived in tied farmhouses or cottages. And yet Eveleen had always thought of Stephen as one of them. As a young boy, home for the holidays from boarding school, on warm summer evenings he had joined the games of the children living on his family's farmland. In the field behind the big house leading down to the beck he had run races with them and played tiggy-off-ground, leaping onto tree stumps or hanging from the branches of trees to avoid being caught and tigged. Then, as the balmy evenings had shadowed into dusk and the younger children had been called in, he had held Eveleen's hand and walked her home.

But now they were grown and when they met he held her in his arms and kissed her. He did not walk her home any more in case they were seen. By mutual, silent consent, their recent meetings had been secret.

Until this moment.

'We were only talking,' she said now to Jimmy, mentally crossing her fingers.

'Oh aye?' Jimmy sneered. 'Why were you hiding in the trees then?' He shoved his hands in his pockets and walked away, a swagger in his step. He called back over his shoulder. 'You wait 'til I tell 'em at suppertime.'

His shrill, nonchalant whistling echoed round the yard as he walked towards the barn.

Eveleen stared after him. There was nothing she could do. If Jimmy carried out his threat then she was going to be in trouble.

Two

At the supper table, Eveleen pushed the food around her plate. Her appetite had deserted her. Was Jimmy really going to carry out his threat?

'What's the matter, love?' Walter Hardcastle asked his daughter. 'Aren't you hungry?'

At their father's tender concern for her, Eveleen saw the spark of jealousy in her brother's eyes and before she could answer, Jimmy said, 'She's in love. That's what's up with her.'

Mary, coming in from the scullery carrying a plate of buttered plum bread, heard only her son's remark. 'What's that? Some girl got her eye on you, Jimmy?' She sat down next to him and nudged him playfully. 'Well, I'm not surprised. A handsome young man like you. She'll be a lucky girl to get you for a husband.'

Eveleen, despite her growing fear, exchanged a glance with her father and they both had to control their laughter as they saw the horrified expression on Jimmy's face. 'Married? Me?' he spluttered.

'Give the lad time, Mary,' Walter said.

Mary smiled at her son, reached out and smoothed back the hair from his forehead. 'I'm only teasing, love. I don't want to lose you yet a while.'

Playing up to her as always, Jimmy said artfully, 'I'll never find anyone who can cook as good as you, Mam.'

'Oh, go on with you,' Mary said, but her cheeks were

pink with pleasure. It was only as she turned to her daughter that her tone sharpened. 'Eveleen, eat your supper.'

Beneath the table, Eveleen swung her foot to kick his shins, but Jimmy kept his feet tucked under his chair. He said no more and, as the meal ended and she began to clear away the dishes, Eveleen thought she had escaped.

With the sigh of a weary man at the end of a long working day, Walter Hardcastle lowered himself into the wooden chair at the side of the range. He leaned his head against the back of the chair and closed his eyes. Eveleen watched him for a moment, concern in her dark eyes.

Her father was a tall, thin man with a slight stoop. At forty-three his once dark hair was prematurely grey and deep lines gouged his weather-beaten face. He had removed his heavy boots but still wore the striped shirt, black trousers and waistcoat that were his working clothes. As he warmed his aching feet against the fender, he gave another sigh, but this time it was one of contentment.

Eveleen smiled fondly and quietly began to stack the dishes.

Mary fussed around her husband, setting his pipe and tobacco tin within easy reach before she took off the long white apron she had worn all day and sat down opposite him. Then she picked up her pillow lace and bent her head over her work.

Mary looked much younger than Walter although only three years separated them. Her brown hair, pulled back into a neat bun, had only wisps of grey at the temples. The blue and black striped blouse fitted her still slim figure, assisted to even greater shapeliness by her tightly laced corset, and her neat waist was accentuated by a wide belt fastened with silver clips. But there were lines of strain around her blue eyes and her mouth was often pursed with disapproval. Eveleen, carrying the dishes out into the scullery, knew she was often the focus of this disapproval.

As she passed Jimmy, still hovering near the door, Eveleen hissed, 'Well, go if you're going.'

Jimmy glanced at her out of the corner of his eye. 'When I'm good an' ready.'

'Jimmy,' came Mary's voice. 'Close the door, dear. There's a draught round my feet.'

'I'm off out, Mam. To Ted's.' He knew there would be no objection to him visiting the Mortons just down the lane.

Mary glanced at the clock on the mantelpiece above the range. 'Half an hour, then.' She smiled indulgently at him. 'Make sure you're home by ten.'

Jimmy would take no notice. Eveleen knew she would hear him creeping up the stairs at midnight or later, but she would not tell tales of him. She was holding her breath now, willing him to say no more and go. But her brother was not so loyal.

'I reckon Master Stephen is sweet on our Eveleen,' he said into the comfortable peace of the room. 'Can't think why. I've seen better clothes on that scarecrow Ted's put up in Ten Acre Field.'

Mary's fingers were suspended, momentarily idle, above the pillow lace. Eveleen held her breath as her mother glanced at her. Mary's mouth was suddenly tight.

Eveleen laughed nervously and said quickly, 'He's teasing, Mam.'

'I hope so.' The creases between Mary's eyebrows deepened.

'So why's this part of the farm suddenly needing a great deal of Master Stephen's attention these days?' Jimmy asked.

'Could be he's keeping an eye on you,' Eveleen countered. 'Just making sure you're not slipping off to flirt with one of the milkmaids. Alice, for instance.'

'You're the only milkmaid in our crewyard,' Jimmy pointed out. 'And it's not me doing the flirting.'

'Thanks, Jimmy,' Eveleen muttered. He had deliberately ensnared her in a web of trouble.

'I'm off,' Jimmy said airily. 'I'll let you know, Evie, if he's lurking about the cowhouse waiting to catch sight of you.' Then he was gone, slamming the door behind him. They heard his whistling fade as he walked across the yard and out into the lane.

Walter opened his eyes and lifted his head. 'Dun't that lad know how to shut a door quietly?' he murmured, but without real irritation. He began to close his eyes and lean back again, but Mary had no intention now of letting him rest.

'Did you hear what Jimmy said?' she demanded and then snapped at Eveleen. 'And just you put those plates down, miss, and come back here. I want an explanation.'

Eveleen set the plates near the sink in the scullery and, taking a deep breath, returned to the kitchen.

She heard her father's deep sigh as he said, 'What's the matter now?'

'Jimmy says Master Stephen's sweet on Eveleen.' The words were repeated scathingly, as if such a thing could not, should not, be possible. 'I won't have it, Walter. I won't have her getting ideas above herself. It'll all end in tears.' Mary leant towards him, her gaze holding his as she added meaningfully, 'You know it will.'

Walter leant forward in his chair, his kindly, concerned

glance upon his daughter. 'Has Stephen Dunsmore been bothering you, Eveleen?'

Now Eveleen could laugh with ease and say, 'Of course he hasn't, Dad. Master Stephen's too nice to do that.' She ran her tongue around her lips that were suddenly dry as she said carefully, 'But I can hardly ignore him if he – if he wants to – to talk to me, can I? We've been friends for years. Remember how he used to play with us when we were kids?'

'Only because there were no other children from his own class nearby.'

'Oh come now, Mary love,' Walter remonstrated gently. 'The Dunsmores aren't snobs. You can't accuse them of that. Why, the old man used to work alongside us in the fields. That was Stephen's grandfather, of course. George. I was only a lad then. Miles and miles he'd walk behind the two shire horses at ploughing time.'

'That's as maybe,' Mary snapped, for once impatient with Walter's reminiscing. 'But now his son and grandson ride around the estate on a horse instead of walking behind it.'

Walter shrugged, his kindly, placid nature ready to accept change without a trace of bitterness. 'Ernest worked hard as a lad, I'll say that for him, but they've done well for themselves, Mary, that's all. They've a big estate to run now.'

'And you really think that the Dunsmores would allow their son to court the daughter of their gathman?' Mary asked.

Eveleen felt her father's gaze upon her. He smiled. 'Why ever not? She'd make a grand wife for him. Stephen's a fine young man.'

Mary leaned forward. 'I shouldn't think for a moment that marriage is what the "fine young man" has in mind.'

Now Walter swivelled his gaze to meet his wife's angry eyes. The smile left his face and he frowned, concerned now at Mary's insinuations. He glanced worriedly back to his daughter. 'Eveleen, has Stephen suggested anything – anything that's not – not . . .' he seemed to be struggling to find the right word, 'proper.'

Mary too was watching her, awaiting her answer. Eveleen trembled at the memory of Stephen's kisses beneath the shadows of the trees in Bernby Covert. The way he held her close and murmured in her ear. 'Oh, Eveleen, how I want you.'

She ran her tongue around her lips once more but was thankful that she was able to meet their eyes steadily and say, quite truthfully, 'No, Dad, he hasn't.'

'Well, mind you never give him the chance,' Mary snapped.

'Eveleen won't – what I mean is – she's . . .' Walter began.

A long look passed between her mother and father, a look of mutual understanding and something even more. Memories, perhaps, that their daughter could not share.

Walter reached across the hearth to touch his wife's hand in a tender gesture. 'She'll be all right, love. Eveleen will be all right.'

For a moment Mary held his gaze, then she nodded and lowered her head over her work again, but not before Eveleen had seen unshed tears glistening in her mother's eyes.

Three

Pear Tree Farm, the Hardcastles' home, was larger than the cottages occupied by the other workers on the estate. It had a large crewyard and cowhouse, two barns, a henhouse and two pigsties. The weekly wash was done in the washhouse attached to the end of the house where a brick copper built into the corner boiled the clothes, and where Eveleen laboured over the rinsing tub and the mangle. The back door of the house itself opened into the scullery and then into the kitchen where the family ate their meals and sat at night near the range which provided heat and hot water and cooked their food. In this one room Mary cooked and baked and ironed. In the centre of the room was a plain wooden table and to one side stood a dresser holding the pots and pans they used every day. In the drawers Mary kept her lace-edged table linen. Down two steps out of the kitchen, the pantry shelves were lined with bottled fruit, home-made jams, chutneys and pickles, and from hooks in the ceiling hung cured hams wrapped in muslin.

In the far corner of the kitchen, a door led into a small hallway and then into Mary's best room – the parlour – only used on Sundays and at Christmas. This room, by any farm labourer's standards, was grand. The walls were papered with heavily patterned green paper and pictures adorned each wall. In a corner cupboard was Mary's prize possession, a willow-patterned tea service. Above the fireplace was a mantelpiece draped in green fabric to blend with the wallpaper and above that an oval mirror with an elaborately carved wooden frame. A dining table covered with a plush green cloth and four chairs stood in the centre of the room. From the hallway between the two rooms, the staircase led up to the master bedroom, a second smaller room that was Eveleen's and, beyond that, a long, narrow room with a sloping ceiling where Jimmy slept.

Only Eveleen ever heard her brother creeping up the stairs late at night and tiptoeing through her room to reach his own.

Not knowing what had transpired, it was ironic that Stephen chose the very next morning to visit Pear Tree Farm quite openly. Eveleen was in the warm barn, gently turning the eggs in the incubator. Dust floated in the shaft of sunlight slanting through a hole in the rafters and the rays highlighted her chestnut hair with golden tints.

'What a pretty picture,' he said softly. Though she jumped at the sound of his voice from the doorway and her fingers trembled, Eveleen managed to carry on moistening the eggs, inspecting each one for the first sign of a hairline crack that would herald the arrival of a fluffy yellow chick. She closed the incubator carefully, checked that the paraffin lamp at the side was still alight and turned to face him.

'Master Stephen,' she said, managing to keep her voice level though her heart leapt at the sight of him. She felt dishevelled in her plain brown skirt, cream blouse and rough hessian apron. She tried to smooth the wild halo of her unruly curls, mortified to think that there might be wisps of straw tangled in her tresses. If only she could have been dressed in her best blue dress and new bonnet, with a parasol to protect her face from the sun. That was the sort of girl Stephen Dunsmore would court, she thought, not some poorly clad milkmaid employed on his father's farm.

And yet he was here, smiling down at her as he leaned nonchalantly against the door jamb, idly slapping his riding crop against his soft leather boot.

'So formal, Miss Hardcastle,' he teased, but his eyes caressed her.

Eveleen thought him the most handsome man she knew. Gently curved eyebrows above blue eyes, a long straight nose, high cheekbones and a chin that was delicately rounded. The early morning sun behind him glinted on his fair hair, the white collar of his shirt gleamed against his lightly tanned skin and the tightly fitting riding jacket outlined strong shoulders. Whenever she saw him, Eveleen would feel the breath leave her body and her limbs tremble.

She glanced out of the barn door but the yard was deserted, except for his horse tethered at the gate. Then, drawing back into the shadows, she whispered, 'They know. Jimmy saw us yesterday in Bernby Covert.'

Stephen's laugh was unconcerned. 'So?'

'He told Mam and Dad at suppertime last night.'

Stephen's left eyebrow arched a fraction. He lifted his riding crop and tapped the ivory handle thoughtfully against his lips. 'Did he, indeed? That was very foolish of him, wasn't it? I think you'd better warn your dear brother not to tell tales in future.'

'Warn him?'

For a brief moment, his blue eyes were steely. 'If he values his job.'

Eveleen's dark brown eyes widened in alarm. 'Oh, you wouldn't?'

Then he was laughing as if it had all been a joke. 'Of course I wouldn't, darling. But Jimmy doesn't know that, does he? And we'll just have to be more discreet, won't we?'

Relief flooded through her. He wanted to go on seeing her. He did love her as much as she loved him.

He was reaching out towards her, his fingers almost touching her hair when, from the back door of the farmhouse, her mother's voice floated across the yard. 'Eveleen? Eveleen, where are you?'

Stephen let his hand fall and pulled a wry expression. Standing aside for her to pass he murmured, 'You'd better go.'

As she hurried across the yard, Eveleen was acutely conscious of his gaze following her and knew that her mother had seen him too.

It was not until suppertime that Mary chose to mention Stephen Dunsmore's visit.

'He was here this morning,' she informed her husband in front of both Eveleen and Jimmy. 'And she's been less than useless ever since.'

His fork suspended halfway to his mouth, Walter glanced at Eveleen. Slowly, the fork continued its progress then, chewing the mouthful, he appeared to be thinking.

'And?' he said at last.

'He was in the barn with her. Goodness knows how long he'd been there. I only saw him when I called her in to help me fold the sheets.'

'I told you so,' Jimmy put in smugly, but for once his mother took no notice of him.

'Have you anything you want to tell us, Eveleen?' Walter asked, his face sombre.

Her heart hammering inside her chest, Eveleen swallowed painfully. 'No, Dad,' she whispered. 'There's nothing to tell. Honestly.' It was the truth, at least about their meeting that morning.

Walter pushed his plate away, his supper only half eaten, as if his appetite had suddenly deserted him.

Eveleen dropped her gaze, avoiding his. She could no longer meet those loving, anxious eyes knowing how she was deceiving him.

Mary stood up and crashed the plates together, scraping off Walter's uneaten food on to the topmost plate with swift, angry movements.

Then she leant across the table and wagged her finger in Eveleen's face. 'You'd better come to your senses, miss, and be quick about it. You've been in a dream all day ever since he was here. You burnt a hole in a sheet doing the ironing. Then I found you sitting idly on the hearthrug gazing into space when you should have been polishing the fender. Now you can take these plates into the scullery and wash them. Don't forget to put the meat away in the meat-safe and then you'd better get yourself to bed. You've an early start in the morning if you're going to the fat stock market with your father.' She put her hand on her husband's shoulder and her tone softened as she added, 'And you'd better go to your bed, too, Walter dear. You're looking tired.'

Already Jimmy was sidling towards the door to escape before Mary could send him to bed too.

'I think I will, love.' Walter heaved himself up from his chair and, wishing each member of his family goodnight, he hauled himself up the narrow stairs to the bedroom above.

As she washed and dried the dishes and put everything away, Eveleen's pulse quickened. Stephen often went to the cattle market. Perhaps they would see him. Tomorrow she would wear her best bonnet to ride in the pony and trap to Grantham.

As she returned to the kitchen to say goodnight it was as if her mother, sitting once more with her pillow lace, had read her thoughts.

'And don't you be thinking you can wear your Sunday best tomorrow,' Mary said.

Thankful that the comment made no direct accusations, Eveleen was emboldened to protest. 'But, Mam, I can't go to town in my working clothes. What would people think?'

'Of course I don't mean you should go looking like a ragamuffin.' Mary Hardcastle bristled with indignation. 'But your second-best dress and shawl will be quite serviceable.' She pursed her mouth primly. 'I don't want anyone to think you're getting ideas above your station.'

A spark of rebellion made Eveleen ask, 'And what is my "station", Mam? Because I'd really like to know.'

'Eveleen! Don't you dare to answer me back. Now, get to bed and I'll have to decide whether I even let you go tomorrow.'

'But, Mam—'

'Not another word.' Mary flapped her hand, dismissing her daughter.

Eveleen bit her lip to still an angry response. Her mother knew full well that one of the harshest punishments she could inflict upon her daughter was to stop her weekly trip into town with her father. Silently she left the kitchen to the sound of her mother's mutterings about ungrateful children and climbed the stairs.

Sleep deserted her. She didn't like upsetting her mother, but sometimes retorts sprang to her lips and were out of her mouth before she could stop them. In the darkness Eveleen sighed. It was her biggest failing, she knew. But her mother was a difficult and complex woman to understand. Even Mary herself did not seem to know exactly what it was she wanted in life, so how were her children expected to know. At times she would be exhorting them to work harder, to "make something of themselves"; at others she was castigating them for "getting above themselves" and warning them that they should "know their place".

Now their father . . . Eveleen smiled to herself at the mere thought of him. He was easy to understand. Straightforward, placid, loving, and generous as far as his meagre wage would allow him to be. His generosity of spirit went much further than monetary gifts. More than anything, he gave of himself. He gave time and patience to his children. He always had done so, as far back as Eveleen could remember, even helping her as a small child to learn to read, though hardly a scholar himself. He would painstakingly write the letters of the alphabet on to her slate with a piece of white chalk and point to each one, guiding her hand as she traced the outlines of the letters herself.

Even then her mother had grumbled. 'An education's wasted on a girl. What she needs to learn is how to cook and wash and sew and look after a family. What good's fancy learning going to be for her?'

But Walter Hardcastle only smiled indulgently at his wife and said gently, 'You're right, of course, my dear. Eveleen must learn all those things and who better to teach her than you.' Then he would pause and add quietly, but with a firmness that even his wife could not ignore, 'But it will do her no harm to learn her letters and go to school. One day, it might come in useful.'

Despite a restless night, Eveleen was up first the following morning. The fire in the range had been stoked up and the breakfast laid before even her father appeared. When her mother came down, Eveleen went back upstairs to her bedroom to wash in the china bowl and to put on her pink dress with a high neckline and leg o' mutton sleeves. Today Jimmy would cope with the early morning milking, so Eveleen made her bed and then laid out the only two bonnets she possessed. Biting her lip, she stood looking down at them. The newest, the one she had only had since the previous Easter, was by far the prettiest, but it was her best one. The older one was becoming shabby, although her mother declared there was plenty of wear left in it yet.

Deciding suddenly, Eveleen snatched up her best bonnet and pushed the other one back into the wardrobe. She would have to get past her mother without Mary seeing it. She crept down the stairs and into the kitchen. Her mother, clearing away the breakfast things, looked up.

'Look sharp, Eveleen, your father's waiting for you in the yard.'

Hiding the bonnet beneath the cream shawl she carried, Eveleen hurried forward to kiss her mother's cheek and then flew out of the house. Picking up her skirts she ran across the yard and climbed into the pony and trap borrowed each market day from the big house.

Only when they were safely out of the gate and a short distance down the lane did Eveleen breathe a sigh of satisfaction and put on her bonnet.

'Oho,' Walter Hardcastle chuckled. 'I wondered why you came out of the house at a gallop. Now I know.'

Eveleen laughed aloud and then tucked her arm through her father's. 'But you won't tell her, Dad, will you?'

''Course not, love. Our secret, eh?'

Eveleen hugged his arm to her side, her love for him spilling over as they laughed together.

Then Eveleen lifted her face and breathed in the sharp air. An early morning frost silvered the ground and turned trees and hedges into gossamer threads as delicate as her mother's pillow lace. A mist hung over the land and shrouded the trees. But the sun, rising palely before them, would soon warm the earth, melt away the frost and disperse the mist. It was going to be a lovely day.

And today she might see Stephen.

Four

The village of Bernby lay on a hill to the west of Grantham. Even further west, down the steep, narrow lane twisting beneath the overhanging trees of Bernby Covert and over the footbridge across the bubbling beck, lay the Dunsmores' 700-acre farm and the homes of their employees.

George Dunsmore had been born in Pear Tree Farm and at the age of twenty had inherited the house, forty acres of arable land and a herd of cows. But George was ambitious. He chose as his wife a girl from good farming stock and together they determined to build a future, not only for themselves, but also for the next generation.

Ann Dunsmore bore five children but only three lived to adulthood. George Dunsmore focused his hopes and dreams upon his only surviving son, Ernest. With Ernest's birth in 1855, George added more acreage to his farm and built a grand mansion, Fairfield House, just across the fields behind his former home.

Ben Hardcastle had worked on the land from the age of twelve and at fifteen had been the first farm labourer George Dunsmore employed. They worked shoulder to shoulder, just the two of them, from dawn to dusk and beyond. A year after George's son's birth, Ben married Emily and George offered them the tied dwelling, Pear Tree Farm. Soon George employed other men on his expanding farm, but he made Ben his head stockman and

Ben Hardcastle was always the man the others looked up to.

George Dunsmore was a lucky man. By the time he died in 1890 at the age of sixty-five, he had lived long enough to see his ambitions realized and he died happy in the certain knowledge that his son would continue his life's work. By that time, the farm had already grown to five hundred acres and he had seen Ernest marry and present him with a grandson, Stephen, who would one day inherit all that George had striven for.

The Hardcastles had not been quite so fortunate. A year after their marriage Emily gave birth to a son, Walter, but that same night his birth had caused her death. Within a year, however, Ben married a kindly woman who, unable to have children of her own, had lavished affection on her stepson. Neither Ben nor his son Walter had been ambitious and were content to live on in Pear Tree Farm and work for the enterprising Dunsmores. As the years passed and the estate grew, the Hardcastles, while being liked and respected, no longer held the unofficial position of the boss's right-hand man and confidant. A farm bailiff, Josiah Jackson, now administered the day-to-day running of the estate and while Walter carried on his father's work as gathman, he no longer held a privileged position.

'That Josiah Jackson would turn us out of our home, if he could,' Mary would often say, only to be placated by her gentle, unassuming husband.

'Oh come now, Mary love, I'm sure that isn't so.'

Mary would shake her head and smile and say, 'Oh, Walter, what am I going to do with you? Sometimes, I think you're just too good to be true. You don't see wrong in anyone, do you?' And she would pass the back of his chair and plant a kiss on his thinning hair. Walter would only chuckle and his eyes would twinkle. 'Well, I've my stepmother to thank for that, love,' he would say.

'She was a lovely woman,' Walter, speaking of Elizabeth, his stepmother, would tell Eveleen often. 'It's my only real sorrow in life that neither my dad nor my stepmother lived to see you and Jimmy. How she would have loved you,' he would murmur, reaching out to touch his daughter's wild halo of hair.

Then Eveleen would hug her father. 'I wish I'd known her too, Dad, and your father.'

'He was a nice man, such a kind man.' Her father's voice would soften as he remembered. 'Such a shame he died earlier than he should have done. He was only in his forties. I – I found him you know. Collapsed in the field next to our house. A heart attack, the doctor said. No one could have done anything, even if we'd been with him when it happened.'

Eveleen would always shudder when her father recounted this tragedy. She could feel her father's sadness and share his helplessness. The poor man, dying alone in the middle of a field and no one even there to hold his hand.

'What happened to your stepmother?' Eveleen knew the answer, but also knew instinctively that her question helped her father to talk about it. It did him good to talk about one of the saddest days in his life.

'She was distraught, devastated by my father's death. Couldn't come to terms with it at all. She blamed hersen, although that was nonsense, of course. The doctor – everyone – tried to reassure her but she wouldn't listen. She just went downhill afterwards. So fast. I wouldn't have believed it if I hadn't seen it with me own eyes that anyone could go from being a happy, laughing, healthy woman to skin and bone in a few weeks. She didn't live many months after he went.'

Sorrow and guilt were in her father's voice. 'It wasn't your fault. You mustn't feel responsible, Dad,' Eveleen would try to reassure him, but her father's answer was always the same. 'But I do, love. I do. I can't help thinking that if only I'd looked after her better . . .'

Now, sitting together in the trap bowling their way to market, Eveleen asked, 'Dad, how did you and Mam meet? I know you lived alone in our house after your parents died, but you've never told me how you met our mam.'

Joining the lane at the end of the track leading from their home, Walter turned to the left and then after a quarter of a mile or so took another left turn. They passed the wrought-iron gates leading into the sweeping drive of Fairfield House. Eveleen risked a glance and found she was holding her breath, but there was no sign of Stephen.

The pony trotted on, splashing through the ford beside the footbridge across the beck and labouring up the hill towards Bernby Covert. The road passed beneath the trees, cold where the sun had not yet penetrated the shadows, and on towards Bernby village and then Grantham. Eveleen loved these trips with her father, loved having him all to herself for a few precious hours. They talked about all sorts of things and she soaked up his knowledge, his wisdom and revelled in his obvious love for his family.

But now he was not answering her immediately. He was sitting, holding the reins lightly in his hands and staring straight ahead.

'Dad?' Eveleen prompted.

With her arm still through his, she felt, rather than heard, his heavy sigh. His words came hesitantly, reluctantly. 'She came to work for the Dunsmores one potato-picking time.' Walter cleared his throat and seemed to be choosing his words very carefully. 'The work was very hard for her. Not – not what she had been used to. She was – er – ill and, because I was living on my own, I took her in and looked after her. Mrs Dunsmore – the old lady that is – heard about it and said it wasn't seemly.'

Father and daughter exchanged a knowing smile. It was the sort of phrase that Mary herself now used constantly.

'So you married her?'

'Not straight away.' Again, Eveleen could detect that Walter was being careful to select his words. 'Mr Ernest had been married just over a year and his wife had just had Master Stephen and she needed help about the place. In the house and with the dairy work. So when ya mam felt well again, she went to live in for a while at Fairfield House.'

Eveleen could not keep the surprise from her tone. 'Mrs Rachel used to work?'

Her father's expression lightened a little as he said, 'Oh yes. I remember the time when they were first married, Mr Ernest still used to plough fields himself and his bride, Rachel, used to help milk the cows. That was when the old man, Mr George, was still alive. After he died, it began to change and now, of course, like your mam always says . . .' without a trace of resentment or envy in his tone, Walter said, laughingly, 'the Dunsmores can afford to employ others to do all the work while the master and his son ride around the estate on their horses instead of walking mile after mile behind them.'

'But where did Mam come from? Did her family live near here?'

'No – no, she came from a little village just south of Nottingham.'

'Nottingham!' Eveleen could not keep the surprise from her tone, and yet this revelation did answer a question that had been in her mind as she had been growing up but had never been voiced. Aloud she murmured, 'So that's why she talks different to you.'

Walter Hardcastle spoke with the broad Lincolnshire dialect of the area, but Mary's speech was different.

Walter was chuckling softly to himself. 'I'm sure your mother would be delighted to hear you say that. She has tried so hard to erase dialect of any sort from her own way of speaking. And from you and Jimmy. 'Fraid she hasn't managed it with me, though, much to her disappointment.'

They travelled for a few moments before Eveleen took a deep breath and asked, 'Did you know her family?'

There was a long silence and when her father did answer he was now noticeably hesitant. 'Eveleen, love, it's not for me to tell you. If your mother wants you to know, she will tell you in her own good time.'

For a moment Eveleen held her breath, restraining the tumult of questions that threatened to spill out. Then she released her breath slowly, but her mind was racing. So, there was some mystery surrounding her mother's early life. Her mother never mentioned her family and Eveleen did not know if she had grandparents, aunts, uncles, or even cousins. Whatever could have happened to make Mary lose contact with her family so completely?

She risked one more tentative question. 'Are her

parents still alive? Have I got a grandpa and granny somewhere?'

There was genuine sadness in Walter's tone. 'I don't know, love.' Then, more firmly, he added, 'Please, Eveleen, don't ask me any more.'

The remainder of the journey passed without either of them speaking. A shadow had passed across their day.

They came to Westgate in the town close to the cattle market.

'It's busy today,' Walter remarked. 'I'll have to leave the trap here.' They climbed down. 'You can go and look around the shops, Eveleen. Don't get lost.'

They smiled at each other and the constraint that had been briefly between them fled. Eveleen laughed. She knew this part of Grantham almost as well as the lanes around her own home.

'I won't, Dad. Besides, I've a list of things to buy for Mam. I'm not going to have much time for dawdling.'

'Well, enjoy yarsen, lass. You don't get into town very much. Now,' his attention turned to his work, 'I must find Master Stephen. We're here to buy a bull today. Mr Ernest wants to start breeding shorthorns, so I must be sure to find him a good one.'

'You will,' Eveleen said, confident in her father's knowledge of cattle. Walter was reputed to be the best cowman in the area and while the modest man would never speak of it himself, the knowledge filled Eveleen with pride. 'If I see Stephen, I'll tell him you're looking for him.'

At the mere mention of his name, her foolish heart began to beat a little faster and she could feel the colour creeping up her neck. She turned away before her father should see the sparkle in her eyes and her smile of anticipation.

She wove her way through the throng, nodding and smiling at acquaintances and then she was brought to a sudden halt by the tall, lanky figure barring her path.

'If it isn't the lovely Eveleen in her best Sunday bonnet.'

She smiled up at the young man. 'Hello, Ted. What brings you to town on market day?'

'All the pretty girls, of course. But there's none as pretty as you, Evie.' Before she could protest, he had grabbed hold of her hand and pulled it through his arm. 'When are you going to start walking out with me properly?'

Eveleen looked up at him, threw back her head and laughed aloud. 'When the sun shines on both sides of the hedge at once,' she teased.

Ted pretended to be heartbroken and pressed his hand against his chest. 'Oh, I'll die of love for you,' he clowned. Then, dropping to one knee, he clasped both his hands together in supplication as if proposing.

His tomfoolery caused a ripple of laughter among the passers-by and Eveleen had to wipe tears of merriment from her eyes. 'Get up, you idiot. What will people think?'

'I don't care,' he proclaimed loudly, with feigned passion. 'You're breaking my heart, Eveleen Hardcastle.'

A voice spoke behind her. A voice that made her legs tremble and her heart feel as if it was doing somersaults. As she turned to face him, Eveleen caught her breath. On Stephen's face there was an unmistakable look of jealousy as he glanced away from her to glare at the young man who was scrambling hastily to his feet and, for once, looking embarrassed himself.

'Sorry, Master Stephen. Only having a bit of fun with Evie.'

'I see,' Stephen said slowly. 'And have you been given time off from work to "have a bit of fun" with Miss Hardcastle?'

'Oh – er – well, sir.' Ted was fumbling now. He, like his father Bill Morton, worked for the Dunsmores.

Smoothly, Eveleen intervened. While she had no time for Ted as a prospective suitor, she did not want to see him in trouble. 'You were looking for my father, weren't you, Ted?' she asked, and Ted, quick on the uptake, glanced at her gratefully as she went on, 'He's gone to look over the bulls. You'll find him there.'

'Thanks, Evie.' Ted pulled off his cap, gave an awkward gesture, something between a nod and a bow, to Stephen Dunsmore and hurried away, pulling his cap back on his head as he went.

Eveleen turned back to smile up at Stephen. Now she could say quite truthfully, 'And my father was hoping to meet up with you, too.'

Stephen looked down at her, but there was no responding smile. His eyes still glittered with angry resentment. 'Was he?' He raised his hat and bowed his head in a tiny, stiff movement that implied condescension rather than courtesy. 'Then I had better find him. I'll bid you good-day, Miss Hardcastle.'

'Stephen—' she began, reaching out trembling fingers towards him. But he turned and was gone, striding away from her through the crowds that seemed to part for him as if recognizing his position of authority.

Eveleen watched him go, her heart heavy with disappointment.

Five

Eveleen's mind was not on the shopping list her mother has given her. She had been to Boot's Cash Chemist in Market Place and to Mr Crow's, the linen draper's shop, on High Street. Coming out, she paused to consult her list, but her eyes hardly focused on Mary's spidery handwriting. All she could see was Stephen's angry face.

There had been no hint of friendliness towards her. He had not even smiled at her. He had acted as if they were strangers.

Eveleen sighed. Her joy in the day's outing was spoilt and now she was hungry and thirsty too, but she could imagine her mother's tirade if she were to spend precious housekeeping money on the luxury of a cup of tea and a bun.

She folded the piece of paper in her hand and was about to set off in search of the next item on the list when she felt someone grip her elbow and a voice say in her ear, 'Here you are. I've been looking all over for you. You've led me a merry dance.'

Eveleen twisted round and looked up into Stephen's face. He was smiling down at her now and his earlier hostility had evaporated.

'I – I thought you didn't want to be with me,' she murmured.

Stephen released her arm and glanced up and down the street. 'Of course I want to be with you, but we must be careful.' Then, almost as a hasty afterthought, he added, 'I don't want you to be in more trouble with your parents.'

Again he glanced to right and left and then he crooked his arm and offered it for her to take. Self-consciously, Eveleen wiped her trembling hand down the skirt of her dress before putting it on his arm.

'You're looking very pretty today,' he said as they walked along together. 'But I expect young Morton has already told you that.' Again, there was jealousy in the words and in his tone.

Eveleen's heart leapt at the thought that he minded about Ted Morton. Yet she did not want him to think there was anything between them. 'Ted and I have grown up together. We're more like brother and sister than – than anything.'

Stephen smiled at her as he leant towards her, his mouth close to her ear and said softly, 'I'm very glad to hear it. Now, we'll go in here and I'll buy you a drink.' He nodded towards the dim interior of the Horse and Jockey public house.

'Oh, I couldn't. I – I . . .' she said in a squeak. She could almost hear her mother's voice saying, "It wouldn't be seemly, Eveleen. You should know your place."

'It's just a drink. I'm sure it's hours since you had breakfast. I know it is since I had mine. Come, I won't take no for an answer.'

Eveleen glanced around, her pulse racing with excitement and sudden daring. Her father was busy over at the cattle market, engaged in business for his employer. It would be hours yet before he was ready to go home. Eveleen felt a spark of defiance. Why shouldn't she? If he didn't think it was proper, then Stephen wouldn't be asking her, she reasoned. Where was the harm?

She pulled in a deep breath and felt suddenly calmer.

'Thank you, Master Stephen,' she said politely and, to her surprise, found that her voice was strong and steady now. 'I'd be delighted.'

Inside it was dark but certainly not dismal for a bright log fire burned in the grate and the small round tables were polished until they gleamed. Farmers, leaning against the bar and sitting at the tables, glanced at her curiously for a moment and then looked away.

Stephen ushered her into a chair in the farthest corner of the room from the entrance and went to the bar. He had not asked her what she would like to drink but returned with a pale, frothy liquid in a tall glass for her and a tankard of beer for himself. When Eveleen took a sip she found it rather bitter, but at this moment, in Stephen's company, water from the beck would have tasted like nectar to her.

He sat down beside her and, beneath the table, reached for her hand, holding it between both his own. 'Oh, Eveleen, you don't know how I long to have you to myself. Do you know that I ride past your home every day just in the hope of seeing you?'

'Really?' Eveleen felt a thrill run through her and then her sense of humour rose to the surface and she laughed. 'My mother would say, "Haven't you anything better to do with your time?" '

He glanced over his shoulder, but there was no one else nearby. With a courtly gesture, Stephen raised her fingers to his lips. 'I can't think of any better way to spend my time,' he murmured.

He took a long drink, almost emptying the tankard. 'Another?' he asked her.

Eveleen smiled and shook her head. 'No – no, thank you.' She had drunk only half the contents of the glass and already she felt strangely light-headed.

As Stephen went to the bar again she noticed another young man enter.

'Dunsmore, old chap,' he boomed in greeting, slapping Stephen on the back. 'What are you drinking?'

Stephen smiled but shook his head and leaned closer to speak into the newcomer's ear. The young man, dressed in plus fours, turned and looked directly at Eveleen. His loud guffaw echoed around the bar above the buzz of conversation, causing some of the other men to glance again in her direction. Then, as Eveleen saw him nudge Stephen and wink, she felt the colour begin to rise in her face. Her glance flickered around the room and she saw to her utter dismay and confusion what she had not noticed when she had come in. She had been so overwhelmed by Stephen's attention and the excitement of being with him, she had failed to realize that she was the only woman in the public bar of the Horse and Jockey.

'You're late home, Walter. Is everything all right?'

Mary appeared out of the back door of the house as her husband manoeuvred the trap into the yard. Drawing to a halt, Walter climbed down and then held out his hand to help his daughter alight, laughing as he did so. 'It's thanks to this little minx if we are late, Mary. She says you gave her so much shopping to do, I was hanging about for her for over half an hour after I'd finished my bit of business in the market.'

Mary's eyebrows drew together in a frown as she looked keenly at her daughter. 'I didn't give you that much,' she began and then, before Eveleen could think of a reply, Mary pointed to her head. 'And what, miss, do you think you're doing wearing your best Sunday bonnet? I told you to wear your second-best dress and bonnet.'

In her excitement at being with Stephen and then the flurry of being late back to meet her father, Eveleen had completely forgotten that she had deliberately disobeyed her mother.

'I'm sorry, Mam,' she began, 'but my other bonnet is beginning to look shabby and—'

'Don't scold the girl, Mary,' her father interrupted, coming to her rescue. 'Where's the harm?'

'She deliberately disobeyed me,' Mary insisted.

Walter tried to adopt a disapproving expression but his eyes twinkled. 'You shouldn't have done that, Eveleen. Now say you're sorry to your mother and we'll say no more about it.'

'I'm sorry, Mam.'

'Very well, then.' Mary was a little mollified. 'But don't let it happen again or I shall stop you going into town.'

As they began to unload the packages from the back of the trap, Jimmy sauntered into the yard. With a calculated air of innocence, he said, 'Ted says to thank you for saving his bacon with Master Stephen.' Then he glanced slyly towards their mother.

'What's this about Master Stephen?' Mary missed nothing, as Jimmy had known full well.

Eveleen glared at her brother, but was obliged to explain at least part of it. 'I was talking to Ted in the market place. He was acting the fool as he always does, but he meant no harm. Master Stephen came up to us and asked him straight out if he had permission to be off work.' She shrugged. 'All I could think of was to say that Ted was meeting Dad.' She looked to her father, hoping he would feel able to back up her story. 'So I told him where to find you.' Mentally she was crossing her fingers that no one had seen her in the Horse and Jockey.

With gentle remonstration, Walter said, 'I can understand why you said it, but it wasn't entirely true, was it, Eveleen?'

Eveleen bit her lip. 'No, Dad. I'm sorry.'

She seemed to be saying nothing but 'I'm sorry'.

'And then what?' Mary was not about to let the matter drop.

Eveleen trembled but managed to say calmly, 'I went and did your shopping and then – and then I happened to meet Master Stephen again. Completely by accident. Honestly, Mam.'

Mary's face was like an ominous thundercloud. 'And?'

Now she was floundering. 'Well – we just talked.'

'Ted saw you with him,' Jimmy said, and as he turned and began to move away, he threw the words back over his shoulder. 'Coming out of the Horse and Jockey in High Street.'

'He – what?' The scandalized expression on her mother's face would have reduced Eveleen to helpless laughter had she not realized that now she was in deep trouble.

'Do you mean to tell me, miss, that you actually went into a public house?'

Eveleen nodded. Mary moved towards her menacingly. 'Do you know,' she said with dreadful emphasis on every word, 'what sort of women go into those places?'

'But I was with Stephen. I thought—'

Without warning, Mary Hardcastle's hand met her daughter's cheek with a resounding slap that echoed around the yard. 'You little trollop! Have you remembered nothing I've taught you, girl? Haven't I always told you to remember your place? What will people think of you if they saw you with him and in a public house too?'

The memory of the stranger's laughter and his suggestive nudge made Eveleen wince. Now she realized what he, and probably all the other men there too, had been thinking about her.

Mary lunged at Eveleen as if to strike her again, but Walter caught hold of his wife. 'Now, now, there's no need for that. Let's talk about this.'

Mary struggled against her husband's grip. 'You keep out of this, Walter. This has nothing to do with you. You wouldn't understand.' Her words were scathing as she added, 'Being a man.'

Calmly, Walter said, 'Of course I understand and it has everything to do with me. She's my daughter too and don't you think a father understands better than anyone what young men are like?' Even in the midst of the quarrel, he smiled a little as he added, 'I was young once, you know.'

The fight seemed to drain out of Mary and she sagged against him. 'Oh, Walter, you were always good and kind and considerate. You would never have taken advantage of any girl.'

Walter allowed himself a grimace. 'Now you're making me sound very dull, Mary.'

'No, no,' she insisted at once, twisting round in his arms to face him and reaching up to touch his face in a tender gesture. 'You know I didn't mean that.'

'No, no, of course you didn't.' Above Mary's head, he glanced at Eveleen. 'But have you thought, Mary love, that it's perhaps my fault if Eveleen is so trusting of all young men?'

'Of course it isn't your fault,' Mary snapped, her anger rising once more. 'Haven't I dinned it into her until I'm dizzy that she should look to her own kind for a husband, not be setting her cap at the gentry? Someone like Stephen Dunsmore is only amusing himself with the likes of her. Taking her into a pub with no thought for her reputation. That tells you a lot, doesn't it?'

Doubt and anxiety crossed Walter's face, but then he said, 'He's only young too, Mary. Mebbe he just didn't think.'

'Didn't think about *her*, you mean. She's just a plaything to him. Nothing more. He'll likely seduce her and bring shame on this family and care not a jot when he does it.' Without allowing Walter time to protest any further, Mary turned back to Eveleen. 'You're not to meet him again. I forbid it. And if I catch you with him, I'll – I'll send you away. Yes, yes, that's what I'll do, I'll send you away from here. Now get to your bed. No supper for you. If you've been drinking with the gentry you've no need of my supper.'

Eveleen glanced at her father, seeking his support, but for once Walter avoided meeting her gaze. Tears smarted behind her eyes and she bit down hard on her lower lip to stop it trembling. Then she turned and fled into the house and up the stairs to her room. Tearing the offending bonnet from her head she sat down before the mirror and in the half-light she stared at her reflection. Her brown eyes were large and round with distress, her cheeks pink, her bosom heaving and her hair flying wild and loose around her shoulders, and she was trembling all over.

Then she buried her face in her hands and sobbed.

Six

Eveleen kept to her room for the remainder of the evening and for the second night running she slept fitfully. By the morning, however, she had come to a decision.

Whatever her mother said, she would not stop meeting Stephen. She was falling in love with him and she did not want to stop herself if there was the slightest chance that he could possibly care for her.

As she dressed, shivering in the sharp early morning air, Eveleen's resolve hardened. She would do her work, she would be dutiful to her parents in every other way, but in this one thing she would not obey them.

Downstairs Eveleen stoked up the fire, set the kettle on the hob and laid the table for breakfast before she went out into the cowhouse to milk the first of the cows her father would already have brought to the crewyard.

As she was finishing milking the last cow, a shadow appeared in the doorway and she heard Jimmy's voice. 'By heck, you're for it now, aren't ya?' There was glee in his voice. 'You ought to have had more sense. And if I catch him round here—'

A sudden spurt of anger made Eveleen stand up quickly. 'Oh aye, Jimmy Hardcastle, and just what do you think you're going to do, eh? Have fisticuffs with the master's son so that you lose your job?'

'Wouldn't bother me. I'd go to sea. Just like I've always wanted.' He glared at her defiantly.

'Then what about our dad? Think about him. Do you want him to lose his job an' all?'

The lad thrust his hands into his pockets and shrugged. ''Course not,' he said, but his tone was nonchalant as if he didn't really care one way or the other.

'And we'd lose our home, don't forget. Have you thought about that?' Eveleen persisted.

'Have *you* thought about what *you're* doing?' he answered her back. 'You could be making as much trouble for us all as anyone.'

Eveleen stared at him, suddenly unsure. 'How do you mean?'

'Stephen's got a hold over you, ain't he? If you don't do what he wants, he can have us all put out of a job. And,' he added pointedly, 'as you've just said, out of our home an' all.'

'Stephen's not like that. He wouldn't do anything so – so . . .'

Jimmy shrugged again as he turned away. 'You think not. He's a man, our Evie, ain't he?'

Eveleen stood still, watching her brother cross the yard, whistling as he went.

'He's not like that,' she murmured to herself. 'I just know he's not.'

Late in the afternoon, Eveleen ran up the hill towards Bernby Covert where she could see him waiting for her.

'There you are.' The delight was evident in his tone as he dismounted and came towards her, his hands outstretched to take hers into his own.

She threw herself against him. 'Stephen,' she began, breathless from running. She felt the familiar lurch of pleasure at the sight of him, at being near him. 'Stephen,' she said again, savouring the name. Then she tilted back her head and looked up into his eyes. 'They know about our meeting yesterday. About the Horse and Jockey – everything.'

His mouth tightened as he muttered, 'Damnation take the fellow.' He looked down at her. 'I presume it was young Morton?'

Eveleen realized suddenly that although she was standing very close to him and clutching at him, he was now making no effort to hold her. She let her arms fall and took a step away from him.

'Sort of,' she said guardedly, anxious that he should not blame Ted. 'Ted told my brother that – that he had seen us together. But he wouldn't see any harm in that. He wouldn't know.'

'Mm. I'm not so sure.'

'Ted doesn't know about us. Only my family.' Before she had stopped to think what she was saying, the words spilled out. 'It's my precious brother we've to thank for that.'

Stephen raised his eyebrows sardonically and drawled, 'Is it indeed? Then we'll have to do something about him, won't we?'

She moved closer again and put her hands, palms flat, against his chest. 'Don't let's waste time thinking about him. I can't stay long.'

As he pulled her beneath the shadows of the trees and into his arms they both heard the sound of a twig snapping. Stephen stared beyond her, over her shoulder, and then he thrust her away from him and plunged towards where the trees grew closely together and the undergrowth was thick. A moment later, Eveleen was horrified to see him hauling her brother out from among the bushes by the scruff of his neck.

Stephen was taller and broader than the younger boy, but Jimmy was wiry and strong. He kicked and hit out at his captor until Stephen, with a cry of pain, was forced to let go of him. But as Jimmy made to escape, Eveleen grabbed him. 'Oh no you don't. Just what do you think you're doing, spying on us?'

Jimmy's face was ugly as he faced her. 'Wait till I tell our dad about this. Just wait till he hears about his precious, darling daughter. You'll not be his favourite for much longer.'

Despite her anger, Eveleen was filled with a sudden sadness. 'This hasn't anything to do with me and Stephen, has it? You're just jealous of me.'

'Huh! I couldn't care less.' Jimmy's tone was deliberately offhand, but Eveleen could see the hurt in his eyes.

As her grip loosened, Jimmy pulled himself free and began to run. Only then did Stephen shout after him, 'You're sacked, Hardcastle.'

Jimmy stopped, turned to face them and shook his fist at Eveleen. 'See? I told you so. See what you've done now?'

Then he was gone, crashing through the undergrowth.

Eveleen turned to Stephen and wound her arms about him, burying her face against him. 'Please don't sack him. Oh please say you didn't mean it.'

He was breathing hard, his chest rising and falling against her cheek. Then he bent his head and began to kiss her hair, her forehead, the tip of her nose and finally her mouth, murmuring as he did so, 'That all – depends on – how nice – you are to me.'

As his mouth came down hard upon hers and he pressed her to the ground, it was not only the sudden breeze rustling through the trees that chilled her heart.

*

'Jimmy? Jimmy, are you in here?' As soon as she arrived back at the farm, Eveleen went in search of her brother. As her eyes became accustomed to the dim interior of the barn, she could see him sitting on a mound of hay, staring into space, a resentful expression on his face.

'Shouldn't you be fetching the cows in?'

'He can fetch 'em himself,' Jimmy muttered.

'Who? Dad?'

'No. 'Im. If he's sacked me, I aren't doing another thing.'

Eveleen crossed the dirt floor and sat down beside him. 'He hasn't sacked you. He was just angry.'

'Oh aye. Persuade him to change his mind, did you? What did you have to do? Lift your skirts for him?'

'No, I didn't,' Eveleen said hotly. 'Don't you dare think such a thing about me.'

'Pull the other one, Evie. You must have done something. Something,' he added maliciously, 'that Dad wouldn't like to hear about.'

Eveleen stared at him through the gloom. Then slowly and deliberately she said, 'As long as you promise not to tell Mam and Dad, you can keep your job.'

'Oho, blackmail now, is it?' Then, surprisingly, he laughed and there was even a note of grudging admiration in his tone. 'Well, I'll say this for you, our Evie. From being a right goody-goody, you're certainly learning fast.'

He stood up and, dusting the bits of hay from his clothes, he glanced down at her. 'Not sure I want his precious job, anyway.' He sniffed. 'I'll be going to sea soon.'

As he left the barn, Eveleen could not stop the words escaping her lips as she called after him. 'And what would Mam do then, without her precious baby boy?'

At once she was ashamed of her own resentment of the closeness between her mother and brother. 'I'm as bad as he is,' she told herself sharply.

Then she hauled herself up and went to start the evening milking.

Later, with their day's work finished and about to go into the house for supper, Eveleen put her hand on her father's arm.

'Dad,' she asked quietly. 'Why is Mam so upset about me and Stephen?'

In the dim interior of the cowshed, she could not see Walter's features clearly enough to read their expression.

'Eveleen, there are things I cannot tell you – it would be breaking a confidence if I did. But you must believe me if I tell you that your mother has good reason to want to – to protect you. She doesn't want to see you hurt.'

Eveleen's sharp mind was running riot and then, with sudden clarity, she began to understand. 'She was hurt like that, wasn't she? Was it before she met you? Was it?'

'Don't ask me, love. And please . . .' He took her hand and gripped it now. 'Please – never, ever, ask your mother.'

'Is that why she's estranged from her family? Did they throw her out?"

'Eveleen,' her father's voice was firm now. 'I've told you – don't ask me, because I'm not going to tell you. I've said too much already.'

But Eveleen could guess enough to understand now. He had not denied her speculation, and if she had been far from the truth, he would have done so.

In a small voice she asked, 'Dad, what do you say about me meeting Stephen?'

'Oh, love, I don't know. I really don't. He seems a nice enough young man, but I can understand your mother's fears. She's afraid, him being our employer – or at least the son of our employer – that he's only – what is it they say?' Despite the gravity of their conversation, there was suddenly a hint of mirth in his tone. 'He's only trifling with your affections.'

Eveleen laughed. 'That's rather a grand expression for the likes of us, Dad.'

'Well, that's the trouble, lass. It is the "likes of us" and the "likes of him" that's the problem. The two don't mix.' His voice was wistful for a moment as he added, 'Not now.'

'Are *you* forbidding me to see him too?'

'I can't exactly do that, can I? You're bound to run into him and he's every right to come here whenever he wants.'

'That's the bit that really worries me, Dad. They could turn us all out of our home if – if . . .' She hesitated to tell him what had happened earlier in the woods when Stephen's threat had sounded so real.

'Don't you worry your head about that,' Walter was saying. 'His father's not likely to give me the sack just because my daughter won't let herself be seduced by his son.' Then his tone was completely serious as he added, 'You won't, will you?'

'No,' Eveleen said firmly. 'Oh no, I won't let that happen.' But she could say no more. She could not give her father the promise he really wanted to hear.

She would not promise to stop seeing Stephen.

Seven

As the spring began to give way to early summer, the two young lovers continued to meet in secrecy, snatching brief moments together whenever and wherever they could.

Taking the cows back to the meadow behind the house after milking one evening, Eveleen heard, through the dusk, the call of an owl from Bernby Covert. It was his signal. He was there, waiting for her.

She took off her boots and stockings and paddled through the beck to race across the next field, up the hill towards the trees and into his arms.

'I can't stay long,' she said breathlessly while he rained kisses on her upturned face. 'It'll soon be our suppertime. They'll miss me. Or worse still, come looking for me.'

'How I long to put you on my horse and ride off into the night with you, my lovely Eveleen,' he murmured against her hair.

She shivered and though it was more with excitement than cold, Stephen wrapped his arms around her.

'The beck was icy cold,' she said. 'It was snowing today. Did you see it? There were snowflakes floating on the breeze. They melted as soon as they touched the ground, but who would have thought it? Snow, in the middle of May.'

He was kissing her again and she forgot the cold. She forgot everything except his lips against hers and the feel of his arms around her.

'Oh, Stephen,' she breathed. 'I do love you so.'

'My lovely Eveleen,' he whispered, his words a caress.

'I must go,' she said at last, pushing against him, but he held her fast and buried his face in her neck.

'No, no, just a little longer,' he pleaded. 'Make up some excuse. Say you were at the Mortons' place.' His grip tightened on her. 'I'm sure your dear mama wouldn't object to you being in young Morton's company.'

Eveleen gasped at his glib invention and her tone was sharper than she meant it to be as she said, 'I'm deceiving them enough without telling more lies.'

'Don't be such a prude, Eveleen. I thought you had more daring than that.'

'Daring's got nothing to do with it. I don't like deceiving my parents at all and lying to them only makes it worse.'

He released her. 'Then you'd better go,' he drawled. 'I don't want to be guilty of your consigning your soul to eternal damnation.'

She began to tremble and now it had nothing to do with the cold. Was he telling her it was over? Was it to finish so soon? All through some silly quarrel?

She put her arms around his waist and snuggled her head to his chest. 'Please don't let's quarrel. We have such a short time together. It's so precious.'

He seemed to hesitate for a moment, to hold back, but then, as he groaned deep in his throat and his arms came about her again, she knew that he could not resist her nearness. It was heady to think she had such power over him.

'I do love you so,' she murmured again, 'but where is it all going to end?'

He did not answer but his eager mouth was searching for hers. The present was enough, she supposed, as she surrendered to the passion of his kiss. The future would take care of itself.

A while later, as she emerged from the woods, Eveleen heard her father's voice calling her name in the distance.

'Oh no,' she breathed. Picking up her skirts, she began to run.

At the beck she pulled off her footwear again and stepped into the water, gasping at the cold. Scrambling up the bank, she called out, 'I'm here, Dad. Over here.'

As she paused to pull on her boots, his shape loomed up in the darkness. 'Eveleen, whatever are you doing?'

The words were slipping off her tongue before she could stop them. 'Looking for Buttercup. She strayed across the beck.'

'Buttercup did? You do surprise me. She's never done that before. I didn't think she liked water. Where is she now?'

'Back with the others, I think.' Eveleen gestured vaguely in the direction she thought the cows would be.

'Come along, then. Let's get you home and into the warm. It's no weather for going paddling, even if it is the middle of May. I don't want you taking cold, love. Here, have my jacket.'

His consideration was almost her undoing. In that moment she hated herself for deceiving him.

As they entered the house with Walter still fussing over her, Eveleen was aware of her mother's suspicious glance. Mary was not so easily fooled.

Eight

The long, hot days of summer blurred into each other as Eveleen sped through her chores, living only for the blissful moments she spent in Stephen's arms.

But, of course, it could not last.

'What's all this?' Walter, weary from a long day's harvesting, pointed to the supper table where only three places were laid. Already Jimmy was seated at the table, leaving only two chairs unoccupied.

Mary Hardcastle banged a stack of plates on to the table with a vehemence that threatened to break them. 'She's still meeting him. Creeping away to that old barn in Long Meadow. Jimmy's seen them. He's just told me. It's been going on all summer. So, as far as I'm concerned, Walter, I have no daughter. For two pins, I'd turn her out.' She leant across the table towards him, her face twisted with anger. 'But I suppose you wouldn't allow that, would you?'

'Mary, love—' he began, but his wife was not prepared to listen. She jabbed her finger towards Eveleen. 'You're blind where that girl's concerned, aren't you? But I'm not.'

At last even Walter was provoked into saying sternly, 'That's enough, Mary.'

Eveleen felt guilt surge through her. Never had she seen her parents quarrel like this. Normally, they were such a loving couple. Indeed, until recently they had all seemed such a loving family. 'Mam, Dad. Please, I—'

Mary whirled around on her. 'Don't you dare to call me that, girl. Not ever again. You can leave this house for all I care.' Her lip curled. 'If I had my way, you'd be gone already.'

Mother and daughter stared at each other, the older woman with a look almost akin to hatred. Horrified, Eveleen felt the colour drain from her face. For a moment the room seemed to spin around her.

'You'd better go to bed, Eveleen,' Walter said harshly. He rubbed his hand across his eyes as if he were weary of the whole unpleasant business.

Eveleen stumbled towards the door leading to the stairs. As she went, she was aware of her brother's gaze following her, a smirk of satisfaction on his face.

Mary was not able to turn her daughter out of the house for her husband would not allow it. But the woman refused to speak to Eveleen and acted as if the girl were not even there. She never served her any food at meal-times and Eveleen's clothes remained unwashed, unless she washed them herself, for her mother would not include them in the weekly wash. All the things that her mother had always done for her were now left untouched. It was as if Eveleen were no longer a part of the family.

Jimmy revelled in seeing his sister out of favour, not only with Mary but with their father too.

'Who's this, then?' he would say as he sat down at the supper table. But his jesting only heightened the tension, for Mary would smile at him and say, 'I can't think who you mean. I see no one else here. At least, no one worth talking about.'

Mother and son would smile at each other. Walter would sigh and shake his head sadly that Jimmy relished stirring up even more trouble. And worse still, that Mary should egg him on.

If Eveleen had believed that her brother would heed her warnings and threats, she was sadly disillusioned. He delighted in giving nightly reports across the supper table.

'I saw her with him today. Down by the bridge,' he would say, or, 'Where were you all afternoon, then? As if we didn't know.'

'Eat your supper, Jimmy, and be quiet,' Walter would say, an unusual sharpness in his voice, but Jimmy, though saying no more, would glance from his mother to his sister and back again, an evil grin on his face.

At last, after supper one evening, Walter got up from the table and stood over them. 'This can't go on, Mary. I don't like the atmosphere in this house. We used to be a happy, united family. And look at us now.'

Eveleen glanced up at her father. He looked so tired beneath his weather-beaten features, but it was the sadness in his eyes that touched her the most.

'And who's to blame for that?' Mary said.

'You all are,' Walter said, his voice rising in anger.

Eveleen and even Jimmy were shocked now. They could not remember their father ever raising his voice to any one of them. 'You, Mary, for not listening to the girl when she wants to tell you what's going on. Wants to confide in you. Needs her mother's guidance.'

Mary, too, was on her feet now, leaning across the table shouting at her husband. 'I've given her a mother's guidance, but she ignores it.'

'No, you haven't, Mary. You've not talked it out with her, explained to her why you feel the way you do. And you, Eveleen.' He pointed at his daughter. 'For disobeying your mother. You should know her well enough to know that she would not be demanding this of you without a very good reason, even if she does not feel able to explain that reason to you. And as for you.' Now he turned to Jimmy. 'You're just enjoying stoking up the fires, aren't you?'

Eveleen now sprang to her feet. 'Oh, Dad, I'm sorry.' She turned to her mother. 'Mam, please—'

'He'll get you with child and then cast you off.' Mary was hysterical now, the words pouring from her mouth in a torrent. 'Leave you to face the shame alone. He won't care whether your family stands by you or not. He'll not care if you have to live rough. In the woods, in a barn, any shelter you can find. He'll not care if you give birth alone in a dirty, stinking ditch at the side of a field when you're tatie picking, trying to earn pennies to keep yourself and your child alive. Only you won't keep it alive. It'll die. There in the ditch and mebbe you along with it.'

Tears were coursing down Mary's face as she painted the tragic picture. A picture, Eveleen realized, that had a dreadful ring of truth about it. She watched as Walter put his arms around his wife and drew her close, resting his cheek against her hair while Mary sobbed against his chest.

'There, there, Mary love. Don't fret.' Above his wife's head, Walter's sorrowful eyes met Eveleen's. Then he asked the question he had to ask, even though he feared the answer. 'Has he – have you let him – touch you?' His tone was stern as he added, 'The truth now.'

She shook her head firmly. 'No, Dad. I haven't. Not the way you mean.'

He stared at her for a long moment, as if trying to read from her expression if she was now telling him the truth. 'No more lies, Eveleen,' he said.

Eveleen bit her lip, not trusting herself to speak. As

she shook her head, she saw his shoulders relax. This time, he did believe her.

Walter led his wife to her chair by the fire. 'Sit there, love, and Eveleen will make you a cup of tea.' He straightened up and turned to Jimmy. 'And as for you, young man, you're going nowhere tonight. You can clear away the supper dishes and wash up.'

Jimmy's face was a picture. 'That's women's work. I aren't washing up.'

'You'll do as I say,' Walter said calmly, but there was a hint of steel in his tone.

Muttering under his breath, Jimmy began to stack the plates, crashing them together as if he would like to break every one to save him the trouble of having to wash them.

'Be careful, else I'll be taking the cost of any breakages out of your wages,' Walter frowned.

Eveleen busied herself making tea for her mother. As she stood over her, holding out the cup and saucer, Mary looked up at her. All the anger and the hysteria had drained out of her now and just a dreadful sadness seemed to have settled upon her. 'So now you know the whole shameful tale. I hope you're satisfied.'

'Oh, Mam,' Eveleen cried with tears in her eyes, 'I'm so sorry. If only you'd said. If only you'd explained, I—'

'It wouldn't have made any difference. You'd have still done exactly what you wanted. You're headstrong and disobedient.' As she took the proffered cup of tea, Mary shook her head sadly. 'Stubborn and wilful . . .' she murmured and a tiny smile touched her mouth. 'Just like I was at your age.'

*

Later, when the supper dishes were washed and put away and Jimmy had stamped angrily up the stairs to his room, Walter followed him wearily to his own bed. Walter hated quarrels and the trouble Eveleen had caused had left him looking white and strained.

Now only mother and daughter sat opposite each other in front of the fire.

'Nothing can come of it, love,' Mary said, surprisingly gentle now. 'Stephen Dunsmore will never marry you. His family wouldn't let him, even if he wanted to.'

'Don't you think he – he would stand up against them? After all, it's his life.'

Mary sighed. 'The Dunsmores now think of themselves as landed gentry. They own a lot of land and Mr Ernest employs other people to do the work while he lives the life of a gentleman farmer. And his wife, Mrs Rachel, she thinks herself a lady now. They won't take kindly to their only son wanting to marry their gathman's daughter. I'm sure they've already got plans for him to make a more suitable marriage.'

'And you think Stephen will – will go along with whatever those plans are?'

Her mother's smile was sad, 'Oh yes, he'll have to. If he wants to inherit the estate.'

'So . . .' Eveleen could not hide the catch in her voice as she said, 'so you think Stephen doesn't really love me.'

Mary reached out and took her daughter's hand. 'I'm sure he does love you, in his own way. But he's only young. Let's see – he's just twenty, isn't he?'

Eveleen stared at her mother. She longed to ask her about her early life, about her family, about what had happened, but she did not dare. This moment between herself and her mother was so precious. She could not bear to break the bond of understanding that was, at last, strengthening between them. Maybe one day . . .

Instead Eveleen said simply, 'Well, I love him.'

Mary's hold on her hand tightened but it was a gesture more of sympathy than joy at her daughter's words.

The silence between them grew but at least now it was no longer the angry silence of the last few weeks. At least now her mother was on her side, even though she could still offer no hope of a happy future for the young lovers.

But you're wrong, Eveleen wanted to cry. You're all wrong. Stephen loves me, I know he does. But the words remained unspoken as they lingered together beside the dying embers in the range.

Nine

The following day, after evening milking, Eveleen paddled through the beck and ran up the hill towards Bernby Covert. Taking the cows back to the meadow, she had heard Stephen's signal from the trees, the soft whoo-whoo of an owl. She felt happier than she had done for weeks for now she had a new resolve, and there would be no reason for their meetings to be secret any more. Tonight, she was going to ask Stephen to speak to her father. If Walter knew that Stephen's intentions were, indeed, honourable – Eveleen chuckled aloud at the prim saying – then perhaps he would be on her side.

Her father was the one person who could persuade Mary. While her mother now no longer treated her as if she did not exist, Mary still said sadly, 'It'll all end in tears. You'd be better off with Ted Morton and that's saying something, because I know what he's like with the girls. But I still say, you'd be better off with him.'

As she neared the trees, Eveleen could see Stephen's horse tethered there. She picked up her skirts and ran the rest of the way, arriving breathless and flushed, to run straight into his arms.

'Oh, Stephen.'

He was holding her and kissing her as if he would never let her go and she returned his kisses with equal ardour.

'Oh darling, darling Eveleen. You're so lovely,' he

murmured against her hair. 'Let me love you. Please, let me love you properly . . .'

Eveleen drew back a little and looked up into his face. Beneath the trees it was shadowy, but she could see enough to see her own love and passion for him mirrored in his face. Oh how she longed to lie with him, to give herself to him. But her mother's warnings were still fresh in her mind and her own instincts were so strong.

'Forgive me, but I can't. You know I can't.'

'You think I wouldn't respect you, wouldn't love you afterwards? Is that it?'

'I wouldn't respect myself. So how could you?'

'Darling, it's not wrong when two people love each other. I swear I'd love you more, not less, knowing you were mine and mine alone. Please, Eveleen.'

He was pulling her closer to him again, holding her tightly, but now she put her palms flat against his chest and pushed him back.

He flung himself away from her angrily. 'You say you love me, but you don't show it.' He grabbed hold of her again and pulled her roughly to him. 'Prove it, Eveleen. Prove how much you love me.'

Eveleen didn't know what to say or do to convince him of her love, short of doing what he asked of her. They were so close that she could feel his breath on her face. His mouth twisted into a sneer. 'I suppose your dear mama has drilled it into you from the time you could walk that you must never let a man have his wicked way with you until you've his ring on your finger. And a *wedding* band at that.'

'This has nothing to do with my mother,' she said hotly. 'This is to do with me. How I feel. I'm – I'm not saying we have to be married first. I'm just saying now is too early. Too soon.' He said nothing so she went on and her tone hardened as she said, 'A few secret meetings in an old barn or in the woods and you expect me to lift my skirts for you.' She was speaking with deliberate crudity, because that was what he was trying to turn their love into: some sordid, clandestine coupling no better than the beast in the field.

He released her. 'You mean,' he said mockingly, 'that if I was to take you out, wine you and dine you, shower you with gifts and take you home to meet my people, then you would?'

'No,' Eveleen said carefully. 'I don't mean that at all. We know each other's "people", as you put it. But this is hardly a proper courtship, is it? Not hiding away as if we're ashamed of our love.' She put her hand on his arm as she went on eagerly. 'Stephen, I want you to speak to my father about us. We can meet openly then. Please, say you will?'

His gaze dropped away from meeting her eyes. He sat down and leant back against a tree, his hands linked behind his head.

'I could,' he said, evenly. 'But I'm going to be busy for a while. I may not be able to see you so much.'

Eveleen felt as if the breath were being squeezed out of her body. She sat beside him. 'Why?'

Stephen sat forward in a quick, eager movement. His face, animated with excitement, was close to hers. 'My father is going to stand for Parliament and he wants me to take on more responsibility for the estate. He's going to be very busy campaigning.'

'But why does that mean we can't meet?'

'I told you. I'll be busy.'

'But you've got Mr Jackson. The estate bailiff. Won't he—'

Stephen dismissed him with a wave of his hand. 'Jackson's all right. But he's still only an employee. It's not the same.'

'Are you . . . ?' Unshed tears caught at her throat. 'Are you telling me it's finished?'

He put his arms about her and pulled her to him. 'Darling, of course not.' He kissed her but beneath his mouth her lips were cold and unresponsive.

'Darling Eveleen.' He kissed her neck and his hands stroked her hair. 'Of course, it's not over. It's only just beginning.'

Won over by his caresses and his whispered endearments, Eveleen wound her arms around his neck.

'Oh, Stephen,' she whispered. 'It's just that I do love you so much.'

Eveleen ran down the hill through the gathering dusk, her heart singing. Stephen loved her, she knew he did. He hadn't actually said it, but she was sure that was because he was shy. She had found it difficult to say "I love you" the first time, but now the words came as effortlessly to her as breathing.

'I love you, Stephen Dunsmore. I'll love you till the day I die,' she shouted to the cattle grazing in the field. They took no notice and Eveleen laughed aloud, throwing back her head and looking up to the stars above that were just beginning to glow. She held up her arms as if to embrace the whole world. 'I love you, Stephen Dunsmore. I love you, love you, love you.'

She sat on the bank of the beck and took off her boots and stockings, drawing in a swift breath as she stepped into the chill water. Reaching the opposite bank, she was about to sit down to dry her feet on her apron and then pull on her stockings once more when she noticed that several of the cows had wandered down to the beck. They were standing grouped in a sorrowful bunch on the edge of the bank. Then she noticed, through the gloom, a dark shape in the middle of the rushing water. Dropping her boots and stockings she ran forward, afraid that one of the beasts had fallen in. But as she neared it, she saw that the mound was far smaller than a cow though larger than any of the rocks and small boulders on the bed of the stream. Eveleen stopped, struck by a shaft of terror.

The shape was that of a person, a man. She leapt forwards, scrambling down the bank and splashing into the cold water once more. The rushing water bubbled its way around the object in its path as Eveleen reached out with a trembling hand. Though she expected it, knew even before she touched it, it was still a shock to feel the rough fabric of her father's jacket.

'Oh, Dad. Dad!' She ran her hand up and her fingers touched his hair. He was lying face downwards in the water. Crying now, she tried to grip his shoulders and heave him upwards, but the inert form slipped from her grasp and splashed back into the beck. She felt cold droplets spatter her face. She took a firmer hold of him this time, turning him over on to his back so that she could grip him beneath his armpits and haul him out of the water. Sobbing, she pulled and heaved his body, made heavier by the water-soaked clothing, on to the bank. Breathless she collapsed beside him and felt for his face. It was as cold as the water in the beck.

'Dad, Dad,' she cried, but knew in her heart already that it was hopeless. She searched for his pulse but her own fingers were stiff with cold, yet trembling with fear.

And then she began to scream for help, the sound piercing the gloom and echoing around the field, but there was no one to hear her cries, no one to come to her aid.

Eveleen buried her face against her father's sodden jacket and wrapped her arms around him, willing the life back into him. But it was the hopeless gesture of a grief-stricken young girl. Tearing sobs wracked her and it was several moments before she was able to force herself to rise and stumble her way across the field towards her home. She reached the gateway leading into the yard and, breathless, fell against it for a moment. At the sound of the back door opening, she looked up to see her mother standing silhouetted in the lamplight.

'Is that you, Walter?' Mary called.

Eveleen straightened up and began to move towards her. 'No, Mam. It's me.'

'Oh, there you are. Where have you been? Worrying your poor father half to death.' In her anxiety, Mary did not seem to be aware of Eveleen's bedraggled state. 'He's gone out looking for you instead of having his supper. He should be sitting in front of the range by now, resting, instead of—' She paused, surprised into silence as Eveleen put her arms around her and buried her face against her shoulder. 'Why, Eveleen, whatever's the matter?'

Before she could answer, her mother's voice hardened as she pushed Eveleen away from her and grasped her shoulders. Shaking her, she said, 'It's him, isn't it? What's he done to you?'

Stupid with grief, Eveleen said, 'Who?'

'Stephen Dunsmore.'

Eveleen shook her head, sending a shower of icy droplets over her mother.

'But you're wet through. Your clothes, your hair—'

'Mam – you don't understand—'

'Oh I think I understand only too well.'

'No, Mam. Listen!' Now it was Eveleen who took hold of her mother's arms. 'It's Dad. I've found him. He – he was in the beck. I – I think he's dead.'

There was a brief, stunned silence as mother and daughter stared at each other in the dim light. Then, sharply, Mary said, 'Don't be ridiculous, Eveleen. Where is he? Let me—'

Eveleen's grip on her mother's arms tightened. 'No, Mam. Don't. Please, don't go down there.'

'Of course, I'm going to him. It's me he'll want to help him. I expect he's twisted his ankle or something, going out in the dark to look for you, you naughty, wilful girl. Look what trouble you've caused now. Get inside and up those stairs this minute. Jimmy!' She raised her voice. 'Jimmy, come and help me. We must go to your father.'

Jimmy came out of the back door. 'I'm off out,' he began, but seeing the state of his sister, he stopped and asked, 'What's up?'

'It's Dad. I found him in the beck.'

'What do you mean?'

Instead of wasting more time explaining further, Eveleen said, 'Jimmy, fetch Bill Morton and *run*.'

Catching her anxiety and distress, for once Jimmy did as she asked him. He was away like the wind, running out of the yard and down the cart track towards the lane leading to Furze Farm, the Mortons' home.

Mary clicked her tongue against her teeth impatiently. 'You needn't have done that, Eveleen. I can go to him.'

'No,' Eveleen said harshly. 'You stay here, Mam. I'll – I'll go back. When Bill comes, send him down to the beck.'

'Perhaps you're right. I'll get some dry clothes ready for your father and a hot bowl of soup.'

Mary went back into the house, leaving Eveleen staring after her, unable to comprehend that her mother was refusing to believe what she was trying to tell her. Then Eveleen turned and ran back to the place where she had found her father.

Ten

Bill and his son, Ted, carried Walter home on a door, with Eveleen and Jimmy walking beside them. They hesitated briefly as they entered the yard and saw Mary waiting. Eveleen ran forward, her boots and skirt still soaking, mud and tears streaking her face.

'Mam, oh, Mam—' she began, reaching out to her mother, but Mary brushed her aside and went towards the two men carrying her husband.

She did not touch him, she did not even begin to cry, but stood there, staring down at him.

Everyone else just stood there too, not knowing what to do or where to take him until Bill said gently, 'Missis?'

Mary sighed heavily and then said flatly, 'Bring him in, Bill. Into the kitchen and on to the table.' She turned and began to lead the way. 'I'll see to him.'

'My Dorothy will come over, if you want, missis.'

Mary shook her head. 'No need, Bill. I'll manage and Eveleen can help me. Now, gently with him. Don't make it worse than it already is.'

Eveleen stared at her mother. What could be worse than what had already happened? Jimmy came to stand beside his sister as they watched the men struggle to manoeuvre their tragic load through the narrow door of the house and into the kitchen.

Bill and his son laid the door across the table and stepped back, pulling their caps from their heads and standing a moment as if silently paying their respects. Then they trooped out, nodding awkwardly to the two youngsters waiting in the yard. When they were gone, Eveleen and Jimmy went into the house.

They watched in amazement as their mother bustled into the scullery to fetch a bowl, soap and flannel. 'He's in a right mess,' she said, almost conversationally, as if her husband had merely fallen in the ditch, dragged himself out and squelched his way home to be met by his wife's berating. 'And you get yourself out of those wet clothes, Eveleen, or you'll catch your death.'

She turned away as if not realizing what she had said. Brother and sister exchanged a horrified glance.

'I don't reckon she's taken it in,' Jimmy murmured, his glance following their mother as she bent to draw hot water into the bowl from the tap at the side of the range. 'She – she's acting like she did when I fell in the dyke that time when I was a kid and came out in black mud from head to foot. I got a right telling off, but she peeled off all me clothes and washed me all the time she was doing it.'

Mary placed the bowl carefully on the table at the side of the still and silent figure. 'Fancy getting yourself in such a mess, Walter,' she said gently as she began to wash his face tenderly. 'There, there, we'll soon have you cleaned up and then you can sit by the fire and have a nice bowl of hot soup. How'd that be, eh?'

Although she clapped her hand to her mouth, Eveleen could not quite stifle the startled cry that escaped her lips.

'She doesn't realize, Evie. She doesn't know.'

Eveleen pulled in a deep shuddering breath, trying to calm her shaking limbs. They both continued to watch their mother as she washed the inert form, murmuring endearments and gentle chastisement in turn.

'I'm off,' Jimmy muttered. 'I can't stand this.' As he made to turn and leave, Eveleen gripped his shoulder.

'Wait,' she hissed. 'We can't leave her like this, we—'

'You can do what you like, our Eveleen. I'm off.'

Mary was crooning, like a mother bathing her baby, smiling and singing to it.

Eveleen took a deep breath and gave Jimmy's shoulder a tiny shake. With a voice that was not quite steady, she said, 'Go and fetch Bill back and ask Dorothy to come too.'

'Right,' Jimmy agreed at once. He turned and fled the house, relieved to have an excuse to get out. But there was no such escape for Eveleen. She moved forward to stand on the other side of the table to her mother.

'Mam,' she began hesitantly.

'Oh, Eveleen, there you are. Help me get these wet clothes off your dad. He'll catch his death, else.'

It was a favourite saying of Mary's and one she had now used twice in the space of a few minutes. Tears sprang to Eveleen's eyes, but she blinked them back furiously. She must be strong. She had to be strong for all their sakes.

'Mam,' she said gently, her voice hoarse with emotion. 'It's – it's no use. Don't you see? He's – he's . . .' She couldn't bring herself to say the words, not even now. 'He's not going to be all right. He's—'

'Don't be so foolish, Eveleen,' Mary answered spiritedly. 'Of course he'll be all right. He's just cold and tired.' She looked down once more at the white face. 'Come along, Walter. Stir yourself. You'll have to help us. Me and Eveleen can't lift you.'

Eveleen moved round the table and put her arm about her mother's shoulders, trying to lead her away now.

'Mam, come away. It's no use. It's – it's too late. He's – he's gone.'

'What on earth are you talking about?' Mary snapped. 'Will you do as I say and help me instead of standing there talking a lot of nonsense?'

Eveleen's voice was a husky croak as she said, 'Mam. He's dead. Dad's dead.'

Beneath her touch, she felt her mother's body go rigid. Mary stared at her daughter and then slowly turned her head to look down at her husband once more. There was a second's silence and then Eveleen jumped physically as her mother let out a heart-rending scream and threw herself across the lifeless body.

She was still trying to prise Mary away when the back door opened and Bill's huge frame stood there. At once he took in the scene, moved forward and lifted Mary bodily. He held her in his strong embrace, stroked her hair and made soothing noises.

Eveleen felt a huge lump in her throat and the tears she had tried to hold back spilled over and ran down her face. To see this big man being so gentle and caring with her distraught mother seemed to emphasize the painful truth as nothing else could have done.

'Bill?' Dorothy stepped into the kitchen and, at her husband's nod towards Eveleen, opened her arms to the girl. With a sob, Eveleen allowed herself to give way to her own grief, leaving, for the moment, Bill to cope with her hysterical mother.

At last they got her calmed down, but it took Bill, Dorothy and Eveleen to coax Mary to sit down by the range.

'Here, Mary dear,' Dorothy said, 'drink this. 'Tis hot sweet tea. Now,' she went on gently, 'Bill and Ted will move poor Walter into your parlour and then I'll see to him. Ted came back with us,' she explained to Eveleen. 'He's waiting in the yard in case we needed him.'

Dorothy was the person the community ran to in times of trouble. A motherly, buxom woman with a round, placid face, she was the unofficial midwife and nurse. She was always there to lay out the dead when a family could not bring themselves to carry out the sad duty.

'Has anyone called Doctor Roper?' Dorothy asked Eveleen. 'I can't do anything until the doctor's seen him.'

'I'm sorry. I didn't think about that. I knew the minute I found him face down in the beck that he – that he . . .' Her voice trailed away and Dorothy put her arm around Eveleen's shoulders.

'It's all right, love. You couldn't be expected to know what needed doing. You leave it to us now. We'll sort everything out for you.' She turned towards her husband. 'Send Ted for Doctor Roper.'

'Jimmy could go,' Eveleen put in.

The two kindly people looked at her. 'He's run off, love. He came to fetch us and then he went off somewhere.'

Anger sparked in Eveleen's dark eyes. 'That's just like him.'

'Don't be too hard on him, dear. He's very young to have to cope with something like this. I know you're only a year older than he is, but you're so much more sensible.' She gave a little gesture with her head towards where Mary still sat huddled in front of the fire. 'You're going to have to be the strong one in this family from now on, love.'

Eveleen felt the burden of responsibility settle like a

heavy weight on her young shoulders. Automatically, she straightened up and lifted her head as she met the woman's sympathetic eyes.

'Yes,' the young girl said solemnly. 'I am, aren't I?'

Eleven

All the legal requirements surrounding a sudden death had been satisfied and the funeral arranged, but still Mary Hardcastle had scarcely moved from her chair in front of the fire. Eveleen had been trying to coax her to undress and go to her bed when Mary hit her and shouted, 'Leave me be. Let me rot. I don't want to live any more.' Then she began to wail. 'What am I going to do without him? Who's going to look after me now?'

Rubbing her arm where Mary had lashed out at her, Eveleen said quietly, 'We'll look after you, Mam. Jimmy and me.'

'You? You, look after me?' Mary's voice was shrill with bitterness. 'You haven't a thought in your head except skipping off to meet that young feller.' She shook her fist at Eveleen, anger rousing her from her apathy for the first time. 'You'll come to a bad end, my girl, you mark my words. Where's Jimmy? I want my Jimmy. He'll look after me. Jimmy'll look after his mam.'

Jimmy would do nothing of the sort, Eveleen thought. There was only one person that Jimmy Hardcastle was ever going to look after. Himself. But aloud she said, 'He's had to go to work, Mam,' as she sat down on the opposite side of the range in the chair that had been her father's.

A wild shriek from her mother made Eveleen jump up again as if she had been burnt.

'Get out of that chair. That's his chair. Don't you dare to sit in it. You aren't fit to sit in his chair.'

Mary struggled to her feet. She swayed a moment and then, regaining her balance, she came, fists flailing, striking Eveleen on the chin and about the head before the girl could even move to defend herself.

Eveleen caught hold of Mary's wrists and held them tightly. From her work about the farm, Eveleen was strong and, once she had a firm grip, she had no trouble in restraining the distraught woman.

'Mam, don't. Look, sit down and I'll make you a nice drink and some dinner.'

Mary thrust her face close to Eveleen's. 'Oh aye. And what'll you put in it, eh? Poison?'

Appalled, Eveleen stared at her. For the past few days Eveleen had had not only to contend with her own grief over her father's death but to be the mainstay in her mother's life. And she had had little or no help from her brother. Early each morning Jimmy left the house and did not return until late at night, leaving Eveleen to cope alone with all the arrangements and with Mary's paralysing distress. She understood the shattering blow her mother had suffered and had been infinitely patient with her. But now, for the first time, Eveleen began to fear for her mother's reason.

She felt Mary's whole body begin to tremble. She loosened her grasp on her mother's wrists so that Mary was able to twist herself free. Eveleen stepped backwards, expecting more blows, but now her mother sank back into her chair. Eveleen too, began to sit down, but realizing she was once more about to sit in her father's chair, drew a chair from the table closer to the hearth and sat down on that.

'Mam,' she began gently. 'You don't know what

you're saying. You can't possibly think I'd ever harm you.'

'Oh no? I'm in the way now, aren't I? A burden.'

'Of course you're not. You'll soon be your old self again and—'

'I'll never be my old self again,' Mary moaned and sank once more into self-pity. 'Not now he's gone. Without Walter, I'm no good.'

Tentatively, fearing to provoke another onslaught, Eveleen reached out and patted her mother's hand where it rested on the chair arm. If her mother was acting like this now, how on earth was she going to behave at the funeral the following day? Eveleen had visions of the hysterical woman throwing herself across the coffin.

Uncannily, Mary seemed to be following Eveleen's train of thought. 'I wish I could die with him.'

'Mam, please,' Eveleen said, feeling utterly helpless. Then making up her mind, she stood up. 'I'm going for Doctor Roper right now.' Perhaps there was some way he could help.

'We can't afford a doctor. We'll be homeless soon enough.'

Eveleen had begun to turn away but now she swung round and stared down at her mother. 'What did you say?'

'I said,' Mary repeated, 'we'll be homeless soon enough.'

Eveleen's legs gave way beneath her and she sank back on to the chair. Her mother's outburst had subsided and now she sounded rational and very serious.

'Whatever do you mean?' Eveleen whispered.

'I mean,' Mary said, 'that now your father's gone, we

shall be turned out of our home. It's only a tied house, Eveleen. Tied to his job.'

'But we still work for Mr Dunsmore. Jimmy and me. And you often help out in the dairy.'

'Huh. Even if he keeps you two, he'll want the house. You and Jimmy'll have to go into lodgings. They'll want this house –' she jabbed her forefinger towards the floor – 'for the man who takes Walter's job.' She sighed heavily, as she added, 'Stands to reason.'

'But it's our home.'

Mary shrugged. 'It has been our home, Eveleen, but the property belongs to Mr Dunsmore and he'll want it vacated. Once the funeral's over, you mark my words, we'll get a visit from Mr Jackson.'

Conjured up at once in Eveleen's mind was a picture of Josiah Jackson, the farm bailiff, a scrawny, ferret-like man with beady eyes and thin, mean lips. She shuddered. Thinking of him, she could begin to believe her mother's words.

She stood up. 'I'll see Stephen. He'll not let us be turned out of our home.'

Mary rested her head against the back of the chair and closed her eyes. Her shoulders began to shake and Eveleen bent down.

'Mam, don't get upset. Stephen's taking on more responsibility around the estate. He told me. He'll help us.' Then with a shock she saw that her mother was not crying, but laughing. But there was no humour in the sound, only bitterness.

Mary opened her eyes and looked up at her. 'Oh Eveleen, if you believe that, then you're more of a naïve fool than even I thought you were.'

*

As Eveleen hurried along the lane towards Bernby village, she muttered to herself. 'She's wrong. I know she's wrong. Stephen wouldn't do that. He'll help us, I know he will.'

She was desperate to find him now, this minute, but knew she must go for the doctor first. Her mother needed help. These irrational outbursts were so unlike her. Eveleen's footsteps slowed of their own volition as the truth slipped into her reasoning. No, she was wrong. Mary Hardcastle had always been unpredictable.

Eveleen felt her face crumple and she pressed the back of her hand to her mouth as the realization came to her. Only her father, her lovely, patient, understanding father, had been able to calm Mary and keep her volatile temperament on an even keel.

And now he was gone.

The girl stood a moment in the lane, missing her father and feeling desperately lonely.

Then she lifted her head. It was up to her now. Up to her to look after her mother and her brother and to hold the family together. She would have to be sensible. She would not be afraid or too proud to ask for help.

She began to walk again. She would do what she had planned. She would see Doctor Roper and ask his advice. And then she would go in search of Stephen.

Her spirits lifted at the mere thought of seeing him again. It seemed an age since he had held her and kissed her and now she needed the comfort of his arms as never before. Her steps quickened and her heart felt lighter than it had done since that dreadful moment when she had found her father face down in the beck.

Stephen, Stephen, her heart sang. He would help her. She must find him.

*

'I'm afraid master Stephen is not available,' the manservant answering the front door at Fairfield House informed her in pompous tones. Then he leant forward and hissed at her. 'And you should have gone round to the back door.'

Eveleen stood her ground. 'Where is he?'

The man, whose name Eveleen knew to be Tomkins, straightened up and adopted his formal manner again. 'I am afraid I am not aware of Master Stephen's whereabouts.' Once more, he dropped the pose. 'And I wouldn't tell the likes of you, if I was.'

'Thanks,' Eveleen said tartly and turned away. She skirted the big house and crossed the yard at the back. Passing through the kitchen gardens she entered the field at the back of the house. Shading her eyes, she scanned the scene before her. Below her to the left, was the beck and beyond it the field leading to Pear Tree Farm. To the right the land rose to Bernby Covert.

Maybe he was there, waiting for her.

Eveleen picked up her skirts and began to run.

She had waited over an hour. The sun had gone and a chill wind rustled through the trees. Eveleen rubbed her arms and emerged from the wood. She would have to go home. She had stayed here too long already.

I should have tried the barn, she thought. Maybe he's there.

She turned and went back through the trees to the road, crossed it into Long Meadow and began to run, stumbling on the uneven ground.

Panting, she arrived at the door, but the only sound that greeted her was the loose board rattling in the breeze. She waited a few minutes and then went back to the road. She crossed the tiny bridge over the beck and turned towards her own home.

'I'll go there this afternoon. Maybe he'll be waiting for me then,' she promised herself.

But Stephen was not at the barn that afternoon either.

After evening milking, Eveleen put on her Sunday best dress and bonnet. She stood in front of her mother, expecting a tirade. Mary, staring into the fire, did not seem to notice and when Eveleen said, 'I won't be long, Mam,' her mother did not even raise her head or speak.

Eveleen sighed inwardly and closed the door quietly. It was starting to rain and by the time she reached Fairfield House, her shawl was soaking and her bonnet ruined. Standing in the warm kitchen, she felt the eyes of the servants on her.

Proudly, she raised her head. 'I wish to speak to Master Stephen, if you please.'

'Not looking like that, you won't.' The manservant she had seen earlier was carrying huge silver salvers into the kitchen, presumably, Eveleen thought, from the dining room after the family's evening meal.

Two maids, scurrying about at the man's bidding, giggled, hiding their smirks behind their hands.

Eveleen shot them a withering glance and said stiffly, 'I can hardly help the weather. My boots, though wet, are clean.' She took a bold step further into the kitchen. 'If you do not show me up, I will ring the bell at the front door again.'

Her glare caught and held the man's eyes.

'Oh very well then. But stay here until I see if he'll see you. Who shall I say it is?'

'You know very well who it is, Mr Tomkins,' Eveleen snapped. 'You've lived here long enough to know everyone on the estate.'

'I,' Tomkins lifted his nose in the air deliberately, 'do not mix with the outdoor servants.'

Adopting a lofty tone herself, Eveleen said, 'Please inform your young master that Miss Eveleen Hardcastle wishes to speak to him.'

As the man gave a sniff of disapproval and left the room, the cook said, 'Sit by the fire, love, and get warm.'

Eveleen smiled at her gratefully.

'I think there's a cuppa left in the pot.' The woman poured out a cup of tea and handed it to Eveleen. 'There, you drink that while you're waiting, 'cos if I know Mr High and Mighty Tomkins, he'll be a while coming back.'

There was a pause before she added. 'I was that sorry to hear about your dad, love. Nice man, he was.'

Eveleen nodded and whispered her thanks. She drank the tea and sat by the crackling fire. By the time Tomkins returned, Eveleen had been waiting so long that her clothes had nearly dried out and she was almost asleep, made drowsy by the heat of the fire on her face.

'Master Stephen has gone out,' he told her shortly.

Slowly, Eveleen rose to her feet. The man was either lying or he had deliberately waited until his young master had left the house.

Eveleen said, 'Thank you,' and then before she could hold her wayward tongue in check, added 'for nothing.'

The man looked her up and down with a sneer on his face, but said no more. As he turned and left the room, Eveleen thanked the cook for the tea and left the house by the back door.

Pausing in the yard she pondered whether to go back

to the barn, but she doubted whether he would be there at this time in the evening. They had hardly ever met after what he called dinner.

I'll see him tomorrow, she promised herself. Tomorrow, he'll come to meet me as usual.

But then she remembered. Tomorrow they would be laying her poor father to rest in Bernby churchyard.

Twelve

Before anyone else was up the following morning, Eveleen left the house, paddled through the beck and ran up the field to the back of Fairfield House.

Already there was movement near the stables and peering round the corner of one of the buildings she saw Ted Morton saddling up the horse that Stephen always rode.

'Ted,' she called softly. 'Ted.'

She saw him look round, puzzled, not knowing where the sound was coming from.

'Ted. Here,' she called a little louder now. 'Over here.'

Now he saw her and, smiling, came towards her. 'Evie. What are you doing here?'

'I'm looking for Stephen. Is he coming out soon? That's his horse you're saddling up, isn't it?'

The look of pleasure that had been on Ted's face when he had first seen her, died. 'I should have guessed it wouldn't be me you were looking for.'

Impulsively, she put out her hand and touched his. 'Oh please don't be like that, Ted. I've enough on my plate without you going mardy on me.'

The young man had the grace to look ashamed. 'Sorry, Evie. Yes, he should be out in a minute.'

'I'll wait here. I won't get in your way.'

'You could never get in my way, Evie,' Ted said softly, but as the back door of the house banged, he moved away and Eveleen saw Stephen, dressed in his riding habit, striding across the yard.

She ran towards him. Startled, he stopped and his tone, as he asked the very same question as Ted had a few moments ago, was harsh. 'What are you doing here?'

'Stephen, I have to talk to you. I tried to see you yesterday, but—'

'I know,' he said, and Eveleen realized that the manservant had not been to blame. Stephen himself had refused to see her. 'I had to go out.'

No apology. No real explanation. Just the bald truth. If, indeed, it was the truth.

He was speaking again. 'And I can't stop now.'

She caught hold of his arm. 'I must talk to you. My mother's worrying herself silly, saying that we're going to be thrown out of the house now my father – since my father . . .'

She stopped and stared at him, her hand falling away from his arm. Where was the young man who had held her and kissed her and said all those wonderful things to her?

'There's nothing I can do,' Stephen said stiffly, his handsome face a mask of indifference. He was standing only a few inches away from her but the chasm that had now opened up between them felt thousands of feet deep and a world apart.

This was the first time she had seen him since her father's death. Whilst she did not expect him to take her into his arms here in the open yard, with a shock that was like a knife in her heart she realized that he had not even said how sorry he was.

'Wh— what do you mean? Can't you speak to your father? Ask him to let us stay?'

'I told you, my father has handed over the running of the estate to me.'

'Then you tell Mr Jackson.'

'I'm sorry, but you will have to move. The farmhouse you live in . . .' – she could sense that he was choosing his words carefully, minding not to say, 'your home' – 'goes with the position of gathman.'

'But it's our home. And we work for you too. My brother and me. Even my mother helps out with the dairy work.'

'You and your brother are single people. You could lodge with other estate workers.'

'We're a family. We're still a family.'

He was shaking his head. 'The positions you and your brother hold don't warrant a house. Your father's did.'

'You mean – you mean you're really going to turn us out when you know we have nowhere to go?'

Not an eyelid flickered. He didn't even flinch at her bald statement but merely said coldly, 'Naturally we shall try to assist you in finding alternative accommodation. But . . .'

'So that's how it is.' She was too angry to weep. The tears would come later, in the privacy of her bedroom.

Her mother had been right. The Dunsmores wouldn't give a second thought before casting them out of their home. And though it broke Eveleen's heart to admit it, Mary had been right too about the young man standing before her. Stephen Dunsmore didn't love her. Not as she had loved him. Eveleen doubted he even knew the meaning of the word.

Thank God, she thought with fervent reverence, thank the good Lord that I didn't give way to this man's protestations of love. For all her weathervane moods, her mother had been right about that too.

Eveleen turned to leave, feeling physically sick. She glanced back at him, just once, still hoping for a sign that he had some concern, some feeling for her.

A few feet away Ted stood holding Stephen's mount. He could do nothing to help her, Eveleen knew, but the look on the young man's face told her that at this moment Ted would like to throttle the young master.

As for Stephen, he stood in the middle of the yard, idly slapping his riding crop against his boot just watching her go, his face expressionless. He made no move towards her, gave her no words of farewell in what he must realize would be their final parting.

A sob rose in her throat but she held it in check until she had passed through the gate and into the field.

Then she began to run and run as if she couldn't put distance between them fast enough. 'I hate you, Stephen Dunsmore. One day, I'll have my revenge on you.'

Those who could take time from work on the estate attended Walter Hardcastle's funeral.

'They'd all have come if they could have,' Bill Morton told Eveleen. 'But you know what Jackson's like.' He had nodded across to where Josiah Jackson was standing. 'He'd dock their pay if they missed a couple of hours to attend. He's only here because he has to represent the Dunsmore family. But him and ya dad never got on. I think Jackson was jealous of your dad because Walter always got on well with Mr Dunsmore. Him and ya dad went back a long way to when Mr Ernest worked as hard as any of the men he employed.'

Eveleen's mind was working fast. How stupid she

had been. It was Mr Ernest, Stephen's father, she should have gone to see. Maybe he would have been kinder, more understanding. But at Bill's next words, her hopes faded. 'But that was a long time ago. Before he got rich and moved up in the world.' He sighed. 'He seems to have forgotten now how they started.' Then he added resentfully, 'And all those who helped him do it. And now with all this Parliament business.' He put his arm about Eveleen's shoulders. 'Ne'er mind, lass. Least we can sleep in our beds at night with a clear conscience, eh?'

'Not for much longer, Bill,' Eveleen said quietly. 'If what my mother says is right, we'll be out on our ears now the funeral's over.'

To this Bill could say nothing.

Josiah Jackson knocked at the door of their house the following morning.

'I've come to see your mother.'

'She's not well enough to see anyone,' Eveleen informed him and, making no attempt to invite him inside, stood in the doorway with her arms folded. 'You'll have to deal with me.'

The man gave a grunt of disapproval but said, 'Very well then.' He held out a long, brown envelope. 'This is your formal notice to vacate these premises by the end of the month. There are lodgings to be had with other estate workers if you and your brother want to continue working here, but there's no place for your mother. We do not require her services any longer.'

Eveleen snatched the envelope from his bony fingers. 'And where do you suggest my mother goes? The workhouse?'

'If your father did not have the foresight to put a little aside, then I'm afraid she has no alternative.'

'On the measly wages the Dunsmores pay?'

Josiah wagged his forefinger at her. 'You watch your tongue, my girl, or you'll find yourself in the workhouse alongside her.'

'That'd be better than working for the Dunsmores.' The words were out of her mouth before she could stop them. Appalled at her own rash stupidity, Eveleen waited, holding her breath, for the axe to fall. The blow was not many seconds in coming.

'If that's how you feel, then you'd better all go there. You're dismissed, Miss Hardcastle.' The man smiled maliciously. 'You and your brother. All of you. And you can be out of this house by the end of the week.'

He turned and walked swiftly away while Eveleen closed the door and leant against it. Now what had she done?

Thirteen

'It's all your fault, Eveleen,' Mary wailed, rocking backwards and forwards in her chair. 'You and that tongue of yours. How many times have I told you it'll get you into trouble one of these days? And now it's got us all into trouble. The workhouse! What would your poor father say if he was still here?' She covered her face with her apron. 'Oh, what will become of us?'

Eveleen bit back the words, If Dad was still here, we wouldn't be in this mess. Her rash tongue had done quite enough damage for one day.

'If you hadn't been so disobedient,' Mary went on. 'So wayward and caused him all that worry, he'd never have had a heart attack.'

Eveleen felt the colour drain from her face. This was a guilt she had tried to keep buried, tried to put from her own mind, yet now her mother was voicing it aloud.

''Tain't Evie's fault,' Jimmy said as he spooned the last of the apple turnover into his ever-hungry mouth.

Eveleen glanced at her brother. It wasn't often that Jimmy took her side. 'Dad's father died in the same way, didn't he?' he went on. 'Was that Evie's fault too?'

Eveleen held her breath, but Mary was not listening to him. She was too sunk in her despair. 'The workhouse,' she was murmuring. 'He saved me from it once, but now . . .' Her voice faded away and she sat staring into the flames and shaking her head, sad and defeated.

Eveleen took a deep breath and stood up. 'We're not going to the workhouse. None of us. Jimmy and me'll find work. There are other farms, other cottages.'

'You're too young,' Mary was refusing to be hopeful. 'No one'll give you a house any more than the Dunsmores'll let you stay here.'

'Then we'll find work in Grantham and get lodgings or a house to rent. There must be work in the town.'

'It'll be hopeless.' Mary was refusing to be optimistic. 'How are you going to find anything by the end of the week? It'll take us 'til then to pack everything up.' She sighed heavily and added, 'But what's the point of packing up anyway, if we've nowhere to go?'

Eveleen bit her lip. 'Bill said they'd help out if they could. Maybe you could stay with him and Dorothy. We could put our belongings in their barn.'

'And get him the wrong side of Jackson, an' all? Get him the sack too? No, no, your dad wouldn't want us to do that. He thought a lot of Bill Morton. He wouldn't want you to bring trouble on him and his family.'

Eveleen thought back to the previous day as the mourners had all trooped away from the graveside. Out of all those who had come to pay their respects only Bill and Dorothy Morton and their son had remained behind to offer practical help. Eveleen had been surprised and touched by Ted's words. He had taken hold of both her hands and looked at her with serious eyes.

'Evie, if there's anything I can do, anything at all, you will tell me, won't you? I heard what *he* said this morning. I wanted to black his eye.'

Despite the sadness of the occasion, Eveleen felt the urge to smile. 'I know you did. I could see it in your face.' That was nothing, she thought, to what I wanted to do to him. She sighed. 'Thanks, Ted. But I don't think there's anything anyone can do for us without putting themselves at risk, and . . .' – there was a catch in her voice – 'Dad wouldn't have wanted that.'

'I don't reckon your dad would have thought for a minute that the Dunsmores'd do this to you though. But don't forget, if there is anything I can do . . .'

As she had nodded and thanked him, a tiny part of her mind was thinking, the only thing you can do is to marry me and get a cottage where we could all live. But she buried the thought deep. She was prepared to make all manner of sacrifices to look after her mother and Jimmy, to keep what was left of the family together, but that was one thing she would not do. Marry a man she did not love.

And the man she had loved with all her heart had turned his back on her when she had needed him the most.

Now, putting all thoughts of Stephen Dunsmore firmly out of her mind, she said, 'Tomorrow Jimmy and me'll walk into Grantham, Mam.' She wagged her forefinger, half-playfully, half-seriously, at her brother. 'And we're not coming home until one of us has got a job.'

'It's market day,' Jimmy observed. 'We'll go there and ask around.'

Eveleen smiled at him. 'That's a very good idea.'

Mary raised her head and looked across at Jimmy. 'There, you see, Eveleen. I knew Jimmy would look after me. He'll look after us both, won't you, love?'

Eveleen did not know whether to laugh or cry.

It was raining the following morning; a fine, steady drizzle that looked innocent enough but by the time they arrived in Grantham had soaked them. But the two youngsters, so intent on finding work, were oblivious to the cold seeping through to their skins as they wove their way among the farmers milling round the livestock pens in the market.

'There's Ted,' Jimmy said suddenly and darted off.

'Jimmy, don't—' Eveleen began but Jimmy had gone. Sighing she followed him.

'Hello, Evie,' Ted greeted her with a smile, but concern showed in his eyes.

Eveleen greeted him but then said, 'Come on, Jimmy, we must speak to as many farmers as we can.'

'He's just been telling me why you're here,' Ted said. 'Try old man Johnson. He's always looking for someone.'

Jimmy pulled a face. 'Aye, an' we all know why, don't we? He treats his workers that badly, no one'll stay with him long.'

Ted grinned. 'He treats his animals well though. To him, his animals are more important than people.'

'We'll leave him 'til last,' Eveleen said. 'We'll see how desperate we get.'

By mid-afternoon, they were indeed desperate enough to seek out Mr Johnson.

'We've no one else left to ask,' Eveleen said. 'Everyone I've spoken to won't take the three of us together. They'll take you or me or even both of us. But not Mam.'

Jimmy scuffed his foot on the ground and muttered, 'Same here. I could have had three jobs easy. And there was lodgings. Just for me, of course.' He looked up at Eveleen. 'Why don't I take one of 'em? It'd be better than nothing, wouldn't it?'

'We agreed, Jimmy. All or nothing. We stick together.'

'*You* agreed, you mean. I don't remember having much say in the matter.'

'Well, if that's how you feel—'

'Don't start, Evie. It's just that it seems daft to be turning down jobs. Why don't I take one and you and Mam get a little cottage somewhere.' His face brightened suddenly. 'Or I could go to sea, just like I've always wanted. I'd send you money each week.'

Eveleen glanced at him sceptically. 'Aye, an' pigs might fly.' She grasped his arm. 'Come on, let's go and find old man Johnson.'

The old farmer was climbing into his pony and trap as they approached.

'Mr Johnson,' Eveleen called. 'Could you spare us a minute, please?'

'Eh? What?' The man, bent with age and hard work, frowned at them from beneath bushy white eyebrows. 'What d'you want?'

Eveleen licked her lips nervously, while Jimmy stood beside her, silent and morose, his hands shoved deep into his pockets.

'We wondered if you needed help on your farm.'

'I allus need help,' the old man snapped. 'But the beggars allus want paying. They want their keep and paying an' all.' He glowered down at Eveleen as if she were personally responsible. 'You young folks don't know the meaning of hard work. Why, when I were a lad, I had to be up at four every morning . . .'

She stood patiently, listening to the old man's grumbling while Jimmy fidgeted beside her and kicked small stones, sending them rattling along the road.

'All we need is somewhere to live, Mr Johnson. My brother and I could work for you on the farm and my mother can even take a turn in the dairy.'

'Ain't no dairy,' Mr Johnson muttered. 'I keep pigs. And me harvest's all in. Don't need no extra help. Not now.'

'My mother's a good cook,' Eveleen tried again.

'So's me wife. Don't need no cook. And I ain't got no cottage, neither.' He picked up the reins and flicked them. The pony began to move, but Eveleen grasped the side of the trap.

'Please, mister. You knew our dad, didn't you? You know our family. We're good workers. Reliable and—'

She was still hanging on to the trap and moving along with it.

'I heard you'd been turned out of your jobs and your house. If the Dunsmores don't want you, then neither do I. Good day, young woman.'

He raised his whip and brought it down across her hands. More shocked by his unexpected action than by the pain, Eveleen let go at once. As the trap moved away she was left staring after him, rubbing her stinging hands.

Jimmy swore loudly and shook his fist after the old man. 'Keep your job, you miserable old bugger.'

'Come on, Jimmy,' Eveleen said forlornly, noticing for the first time how cold and wet and hungry she was. 'We'd better go home.' Then she added sadly, 'While we've still got one to go to.'

'I'm sorry, Mam. We couldn't find anyone to take the three of us.'

'I didn't think you would.' Mary was sitting exactly as they had left her early that morning. There was no supper set ready and the fire, though not quite out, was very low. Eveleen wondered if Mary had moved from her chair at all during the day.

'I could have got a job,' Jimmy put in and glowered at his sister. 'But Evie says we must stick together.'

Mary leant back and closed her eyes. Wearily she said,

'You'd do better to find yourselves a job and put me in the workhouse.'

'We're doing no such thing,' Eveleen snapped. 'And I don't want to hear another word about the workhouse.' She looked down at her mother, trying to rouse her from her apathy. 'Have you any suggestions, Mam? I mean, sensible ones.'

Slowly Mary raised her gaze to her daughter. 'We'll have to go home.'

Eveleen caught her breath. Had her mother's mind really turned? 'This is our home, Mam, and – and we've got to leave it.'

Mary shook her head. 'No. Back home to Flawford. To my family.'

Mystified, Jimmy gave a wordless shrug. Out of sight of his mother, he tapped the side of his head indicating that he, too, thought she was losing her reason.

Anxious not to upset her further, Eveleen bent closer to Mary. 'Mam,' she began carefully, 'is that where you came from? Flawford?'

Mary nodded.

'And – and have you still got family living there, then?'

'Dunno.'

'But you think you might have?'

'Shouldn't think my parents are still alive, but Harry might be.'

'Who's Harry?' Eveleen asked gently.

'My brother. My brother, Harry. Maybe he's still there. And his wife, Rose.'

Eveleen and Jimmy exchanged a glance. An uncle and an aunt, maybe even cousins, they were both thinking. All this time they had had these relatives, close relatives, and they had never known a thing about them. They had not even known they existed.

'Right then,' Eveleen said firmly, standing up. 'That's where we'll go, Mam. Back to your folks.'

But Mary was shaking her head yet again. 'They'll not want us. They turned me out once, disowned me. What makes you think they'd help us now?'

'They're family, Mam. Your family – and ours. Surely they will help us? Surely your own brother won't turn his back on you?'

'Huh!' Mary at last let out a sound that had some spirit in it. 'He was the worst of the lot of them. Very religious, is our Harry. Hell and damnation, that's where he said I was headed. Aye . . .' Once more she began to sink back into self-pity. 'And if it hadn't been for your dad, that's where I would have ended up.'

'That was years ago. Surely, he won't still feel – well – that way towards you. Not now.'

'Oho, you don't know Harry. He's the "if thy right hand offend thee, cut it off" type. So,' she added simply, 'that's what he did. He cut me off.'

Eveleen took her mother's hand. Softly, she asked, 'Was it so very dreadful? What you did?'

Slowly Mary raised her head and looked straight into Eveleen's eyes. 'Oh yes. It was very dreadful. At least, in his eyes. And in the eyes of the whole community. Everyone shunned me. Everyone.'

Tears spilled down Mary's face and Eveleen patted her hand. 'Don't, Mam. Please don't cry.' Once more she silently gave heartfelt thanks that she had resisted Stephen's pleading and his sweet words. She understood her mother so much better now.

With renewed resolve, Eveleen put her arm about her mother's shoulders and glanced towards Jimmy. 'We're going to take you home, Mam. Back to your family. Surely, after all this time, they will have forgiven you.'

'I doubt it,' Mary murmured.

Well,' Eveleen said, 'whether they want us or not, they're going to get us. Watch out, Flawford, here we come.'

Fourteen

'Have we got everything, Mam?' Eveleen asked, taking a last look around all the rooms. 'Are you sure you've got everything you want? We don't seem to be keeping very much. Our trunks and boxes have only taken up half the length of the dray.'

Her mother stood in front of the cold range. It was the first time that Eveleen could remember not seeing a fire burning in the grate. The whole house seemed chilly because of it. Mary glanced about her. 'I've got everything I *can* take,' she said pointedly. 'It's no good taking a lot of furniture. There'll be nowhere to put it.' Then her face crumpled. 'Oh Evie, I don't want to go. I don't want to leave here. It's the only place I've ever been really happy.'

'Weren't you happy as a child? Before – before your trouble?'

Mary pressed her lips together to stop herself weeping and shook her head. 'My father was a hard man. He ruled us all with a rod of iron, and the men that worked for him, an' all.'

'Worked for him? Your father employed people?'

Mary nodded and said airily, 'Oh yes.'

'What doing? I mean, was he a farmer?'

'No. He was a stockinger.'

'A what?'

'A hosier. He ran a workshop making socks and stockings and other knitted garments.'

Eveleen stared at her mother.

'I 'spect it's all still there,' Mary mused, more to herself now than to her daughter. 'I 'spect Harry's got it all now.' She stood for a moment as if the memories of her childhood were crowding in on her. Then she shook her head again. 'I don't want to go back, Evie. I really don't. I love the countryside. I love Lincolnshire. Even though I wasn't born here, it's my home and I don't want to leave it. Oh, Evie,' Mary held up her arms and wailed, 'I don't want to go.'

'Mam.' Eveleen enfolded the older woman in her embrace. 'We have to go. You know we can't stay here. They won't let us. And we have to go somewhere.'

'But they won't want us either. They'll turn us away and where will we go then? The workhouse?'

'I told you, Mam,' Eveleen tried to make her voice playfully stern. 'You're not to mention that again. I promise you, you'll never have to go into the workhouse. Don't even think it.' She hugged Mary harder, noticing with a pang of regret how thin her mother had become even in the short space of time since Walter's death. 'And one day I'll bring you back to Lincolnshire. I swear to you that I'll bring you back home.'

It was a solemn vow, but the young girl, only seventeen, could not possibly know just how difficult that promise would be to keep.

Together they took a last look around the house. They were having to leave so many of their possessions.

Mary smiled pensively as she ran her fingers along the back of Walter's wooden chair and, seeing her, Eveleen had to swallow the lump that rose in her throat. In the parlour, Mary nodded towards the cabinet where her best china tea service was still displayed on the shelves. 'That was our only wedding present, you know.'

'Who from?'

'Your dad said it was from Mrs Rachel Dunsmore, but I reckon he bought it himself, just to make me think that someone, other than him, thought enough about me to buy us a gift.'

'We ought to take it with us,' Eveleen said, but Mary shook her head firmly. 'No, we've got everything we need. Someone else can have it.'

As Eveleen led her mother towards the door she noticed that Mary took one last lingering look at the sparkling willow-patterned cups, saucers and plates that she had so lovingly washed every week of her married life.

'I just hope someone will take good care of it,' Mary murmured.

Eveleen locked the door and slipped the key beneath the loose brick beside the doorstep. Taking her mother's arm, she led her towards the farm dray. Jimmy was already sitting on the back, swinging his legs and chewing on a piece of straw. Ted was standing awkwardly beside him, kicking aimlessly at loose stones while Bill stood near the two huge black and white shire horses. He had been given time off to drive the family to their new home.

'You'd best be back by the next evening, else it'll be the worse for you,' Eveleen had heard Josiah Jackson telling him.

'I'll do my best,' Bill had replied in his deep, placid tones.

'You'll do better than that, else you'll be following them next week.'

Bill had faced the farm bailiff and said steadily, 'And who would manage the horses, Mr Jackson, if you sack me?' At which the bailiff had thrust his gaunt features close to Bill's face and muttered, 'No one's indispensable, Morton. Just you remember that.'

'Oh I will, Mr Jackson. I certainly will.' Bill kept his tone deferential but his expression implied, No, no one is indispensable, Josiah Jackson. Not even you.

Now the day had come to take the Hardcastle family to their new life. The kindly man feared for them. More than anything he pitied the young girl who seemed to have such a burden of responsibility resting on her young shoulders: a mother who was not quite stable, especially since the death of her husband, and a youth who had the makings of a real rascal. Here, in this community who knew, liked and respected the family, Jimmy might have been kept on the straight and narrow. Lord alone knew what would happen to a lad like him turned loose on city streets.

'Now then, missis,' Bill moved forward to help Mary on to the front of the dray. 'Where is it we're headed? Nottingham, is it?'

Mary did not answer. She was holding a handkerchief to her face and sobbing.

Eveleen glanced helplessly at Bill. Her mother was making as much fuss as if they were indeed heading for the workhouse. The girl forced herself to be patient with the unhappy woman. Mary had suffered a most grievous loss with her husband's death and to be cruelly deprived of the only home where she had been truly happy was a devastating second blow.

Eveleen was suffering too, and not only for the same reasons as her mother. Added to her misery was Stephen's callous rejection of her. She glanced back one last time at the farmhouse. In the pale light of early morning the dwelling looked lifeless and lost as if it, too, did not want to see the Hardcastle family leaving. Her gaze flickered around the yard, taking one last look.

The previous evening she had gone alone to the beck. 'Goodbye, Dad,' she had murmured to the place where she had found him. 'For now. But I'll bring her back to you one day. I promise.'

Then she had lifted her gaze. In the far distance to the left, she could just see the spire of Bernby church where her father now lay, high on the hill overlooking his beloved fields. His grave was beside those of his father, mother and his adored stepmother. Walter was at peace and she knew he would have been content with the resting place they had chosen for him, even though it would not have been his wish to leave his family so soon.

As her gaze came closer to home, to the trees of Bernby Covert, the lump of sorrow and disappointment in her throat had threatened to choke her. Her emotions were in chaos. She loved and hated Stephen Dunsmore all in the same moment. She had turned away to walk slowly back to the farmyard. Already the place had a deserted air. There were no pigs snuffling and grunting in the sties. No hens scratching and complaining in the yard. Even the cows in the neighbouring field had been taken away. Bill had come to the farm early that morning, an embarrassed flush on his ruddy face. 'I'm sorry, Eveleen, but Jackson's ordered me to take all the livestock up to the big house.'

In the strange silence, Eveleen had leaned on the gate and looked towards the western sky to watch the red glow of the sinking sun silhouetting the ramparts of Belvoir Castle on the distant hills. It was a sight she had always loved, one that her beloved father had always relished and they had often stood together on this very spot and watched the glorious sunset of a late summer evening. No wonder, Eveleen thought, that her mother had found refuge in this place and could not bear to leave it.

As the sun sank below the skyline, Eveleen had leant her head on her arm and shed tears for her deep sense of loss and loneliness. When at last she raised her head again, a velvety dusk had fallen. Then she glanced back, just once, to the dark shape of trees and tall chimneys of Fairfield House.

'I've shed my last tears over you, Stephen Dunsmore,' she vowed, but as she turned to go into the house, to spend the last night under the roof that had been her only home, the misery was like a leaden weight inside her.

Now, in the cold light of morning, she took a final look round.

'Evie.' Ted came towards her, his face unusually solemn. 'I just wanted to say – I mean, I know me dad and me mam have said it all – but . . .' He was gauche and clumsy, but Eveleen knew he meant well. 'Don't forget us, will you? And if you need any help, well, just send word and we'll come. Wherever you are, we'll come.'

She was touched by his genuine concern and, impulsively, she put her hands on his shoulders and reached up to plant a kiss on his cheek. She was surprised at the colour that suffused the young man's face. 'Thanks, Ted. I don't know what we'd have done without you all these last few days. And no, I won't forget.' Then she forced a smile and punched him playfully on the shoulder. 'And don't you forget us either, 'cos we'll be back. One day, we're coming back.'

Now Ted grinned. 'You'd better,' he said as he helped her to climb up on to the front of the dray beside his father. Bill took the reins and, as the horse began to move, Ted stood in the centre of the yard waving. But only Jimmy, at the back of the dray, waved goodbye in return. Neither Mary, sobbing into her handkerchief, nor Eveleen, who set her face determinedly to the future, looked back.

As they joined the lane at the end of the track and began to turn right to take them to the main road to Nottingham, Eveleen saw a rider on horseback coming towards them, galloping at speed.

Her heart lifted in joyous relief. Stephen. He was coming to her. He was coming to rescue her family, even at this, the last moment. He hadn't meant to be so cruel. He had been obeying his father's orders. He was coming to her. She put out her hand and murmured, 'Stop, Bill. Please stop a moment.'

Bill pulled on the reins. 'Forgotten summat, lass?'

Eveleen, her gaze still on the galloping figure coming nearer and nearer, shook her head. 'It's him. I knew he didn't mean it. It's him.'

Nearer and nearer he came, riding towards her as if his life depended on it. Nearer and nearer, not slowing, not stopping.

Eveleen gasped as the young man neither slowed his horse's pace nor even glanced in her direction but thundered past the dray and rode on round the bend in the lane. Her gaze followed him until she could no longer see him and the hoof beats were a faint thudding sound that echoed the beating of her heart.

Her shoulders slumped, the last vestige of hope gone. He had not been coming to her. He had not even glanced at her as he had passed by.

She felt Bill's strong arm about her shoulders. 'Come on, lass,' the big man said gently. 'Time to go.'

They set off along the lane once more with Eveleen sitting rigidly on the front of the dray beside Bill, staring straight ahead, neither speaking nor looking about her.

But Mary, sitting the other side of Bill, now twisted and turned in her seat, exclaiming, 'I don't want to leave, Bill. It's such a lovely place. Such a peaceful place. Look how pretty the trees are. They'll be turning such wonderful colours soon, gold and brown. And the beck. Oh, how can I leave the place where my poor Walter died? How can I leave him lying there all alone in the churchyard? I can't bear to go.'

But all Eveleen was seeing was Stephen's face, set in disdainful, callous lines. Then anger came to her rescue. It spurted through her, hardening her resolve. Her eyes were dry and her head rose in defiance as she pulled in a deep, shuddering breath. 'Don't fret, Mam. We'll be back. You mark my words. One day, we'll be back.'

Fifteen

'Where is it we're going exactly?' Bill asked.

They had been travelling the road towards Nottingham all the morning and had stopped to eat the picnic that Dorothy had packed into a hamper and insisted Bill brought.

'They'll not have time to be making sandwiches, poor things,' his wife had said. 'So I've packed enough for all of you.'

Now, opening it, Bill chuckled. As he had suspected, his missis had packed enough to feed an army. 'Well, if we don't reach wherever we're going by nightfall, lass,' Bill said to Eveleen, 'I reckon we've enough food here to last us the week.'

Jimmy tucked in ravenously, but Mary only nibbled at a sandwich and Eveleen chewed the food round and round in her mouth, finding swallowing it difficult for the misery still choking her.

Eveleen glanced at her mother as she answered Bill's question. 'It's a place called Flawford. It's where my mother came from.'

'Oh aye,' Bill nodded. 'Can't say I've heard of it, but then, I've never been far from Bernby.'

Tears flooded Mary's eyes again as she said, 'You're lucky.'

Bill glanced at Eveleen apologetically. Eveleen said, 'Are we on the right road, Mam?'

'I don't know and I don't care,' was all the pitiful woman would say.

They finished eating and climbed back on to the dray. Taking the reins, Bill said quietly to Eveleen, 'We'll go a bit further and then I'll ask someone. Don't bother ya mam.' Beneath his breath he murmured, 'Poor soul.'

The sun was a copper-coloured ball sinking beneath the horizon when Bill, following the directions he had been given by a farmer herding his cows turned off the road skirting the south of the city of Nottingham and took the direction towards Loughborough.

'He said it was about a couple of miles down this road, didn't he, Eveleen?'

Eveleen nodded. 'We take a sharp right turn somewhere down here and then straight across at the crossroads, he said, and we'll come to the village.'

They trundled on with Eveleen leaning forward eagerly to catch the first sight of the place that she hoped would be their home. There were houses ahead.

'Is this it, Mam? Is this Flawford?'

Flatly, Mary said, 'Yes, it is,' but a few minutes later, with surprising sureness, she added, 'Keep straight on, Bill, until I tell you to turn left.'

Eveleen and Bill exchanged a glance.

'You do remember the way then, Mam?'

Mary's mouth was a narrow, compressed line. 'Oh aye,' she said, bitterly. 'I remember all right.' In a lower voice, she added, 'As if I could ever forget.'

The dray rattled on and passers-by stared up at the three people sitting on the front and the boy at the back swinging his legs and munching yet another apple.

'Oh my goodness,' Mary exclaimed suddenly and clapped her hand over her mouth.

'What is it, Mam? What's the matter?'

'That's Georgie Turner as I live and breathe.'

'Who's Georgie Turner?'

'A village lad, that's all. He used to work for my father. I wonder,' she added, musing, 'if he still lives in one of our cottages.'

As she watched her mother's gaze fix upon the man standing at the side of the road, Eveleen pondered. Was that all that Georgie Turner had been or had he been her mother's sweetheart all those years ago?

One wheel ran into a deep rut at the side of the road, causing the passengers to clutch each other in alarm and Jimmy to yell from the rear. 'Eh, look out. You'll have me off the back 'ere. I've dropped me apple, now.'

Bill grinned. 'Sorry, folks.'

They travelled for a short distance and then Mary spoke again. 'Turn left.' A few yards more and then she said, 'Now right into Ranters' Row.'

Eveleen gasped. 'Is that what this street's called?'

For the first time, Mary smiled, but it was a grim smile; a smile that did not reach her eyes. 'No, it's the locals' name for it. Its proper name is Chapel Row. It's a dead end and a bit narrow, but there should be room enough to turn the dray around. Pull up outside that gate, Bill, on the left-hand side.'

Bill drew the dray to a halt, but Mary made no move to climb down.

'Is this it, Mam?'

'Yes,' she said but still she did not move. 'You go, Eveleen.'

'Where do I go? That door there?'

To the side of the gate was a long brick wall with windows and a door in the centre, but Mary was shaking her head, 'No. That's the door to one of the cottages.'

As Eveleen looked mystified, Mary explained briefly,

gesturing towards the building. 'This is a row of four cottages. Two at either end and two in the middle that are back to back. The entrance to the one at this side is off the street.'

Eveleen still hesitated.

'Well, get on with it, if you're going,' Mary snapped. 'Ask for Harry Singleton and tell him who you are.'

'And then?' Eveleen asked.

Mary's only reply was a slight lift of her shoulders as if to say, How should I know?

Eveleen sighed and jumped down. Jimmy joined her and they stood looking up at the tall, solid gate.

'Looks like a prison,' he muttered and stuffed his hands into the pockets of his trousers.

'Take your hands out of your pockets and smarten yourself up a bit,' Eveleen said, pulling his cap straight and smoothing her own wayward hair. 'Now, come on. Let's get it over with.'

They opened the gate and walked through, closing it carefully behind them. They had walked into one corner of a rectangular enclosure. At the end nearest to where they were standing was the line of cottages that her mother had described. Now Eveleen could see the doors leading to the other three homes. The street side of the building had looked austere, but on this side a huge peach tree climbed the walls straddling the whole frontage, the fruit hanging heavily on the branches.

As she saw Jimmy's hand creep upward towards a ripe peach, Eveleen gripped his shoulder. 'Don't you dare,' she hissed.

Jimmy grinned roguishly at her, but dropped his hand away.

A brick path ran in front of the cottages and halfway along it was a pump. From this, another path ran the length of the yard, branching off to the buildings on either side and at the far end. There were patches of garden on either side: a few flowers, but mostly vegetables – carrots, cabbage and lettuce – and, entwined in a wooden frame, a trailing blackberry plant laden with juicy black fruit.

'What's that noise?' Jimmy said. 'It's coming from there.'

Eveleen followed the line of his pointing finger toward the buildings standing on either side of the yard. These were obviously not homes. She took a few steps forward, staring up at the two-storey buildings. On each floor there was one long window, with tiny square panes, running the full length of the wall.

Taking the words from her mouth, Jimmy said, 'Them's funny windows.' Then he paused and sniffed the air. 'Evie, do you smell what I smell?'

For the first time in two weeks her smile was genuine as together they said, 'Pigs!'

The smell, and now they could hear the sound too, of pigs, was coming from the buildings across the end of the yard. They tiptoed along the brick path. Next to the pigsty were communal lavatories, presumably for all the workers as well as for the residents of the cottages, Eveleen thought, and a coal store.

'Why are we creeping about?' Jimmy asked.

'And why are we whispering?' Eveleen giggled.

'Because we feel like a couple of criminals, that's why.'

Closer now they could identify the noise as the clatter of machinery coming from the long buildings.

'It must be the workshops or whatever they call them, where our uncle has his knitting machines.'

As she glanced about her, she saw a girl emerge from a door at one end of the workshops. She had her sleeves rolled up to her elbows and she was drying her hands on a piece of rough towelling. Steam billowed from the door behind her and Eveleen recognized the look of someone on washday. It was a bit late in the day to be washing, Eveleen could not help thinking.

The girl was slim with black hair in one long plait, although strands had escaped and lay plastered against her forehead. Her face was thin with high cheekbones and, at this moment, her cheeks were flushed from the heat of the copper. She stared at the strangers for a moment and then slowly came towards them. Eveleen could see now that her eyes were a deep blue and fringed with black eyelashes. Her eyebrows were neat, arched lines, so well defined it looked as if someone had pencilled them in. 'Are you looking for someone?' Her voice, when she spoke was soft and low.

Eveleen nodded. 'Mr Harry Singleton.'

'That's my father,' the girl said. 'I expect you've come looking for work, have you? Well, I'm sorry, I don't think there are any vacancies at the moment.' She glanced at Jimmy, smiled a little uncertainly and then dropped her gaze shyly.

Eveleen's heart fell. If there was no work for them to help pay for their keep, their uncle was even less likely to take them in.

She took a deep breath and said, 'We do need work, yes, but we've come to see your father because – because he's our uncle. Our mam's outside on the dray. She's – she's his sister.'

The girl's eyes widened as she stared at them. 'His sister? I didn't even know he had a sister.'

So, Eveleen thought grimly, the family rift went so deep that this girl did not even know of their existence. And yet, she reminded herself, until a short time ago, she had not known of hers. She forced herself to smile and say brightly. 'Can we see him?'

'Well,' the girl looked about her uncertainly, 'I don't know. He's working and he doesn't like to be stopped. Not until teatime and that's an hour or so yet. Six o'clock, he'll stop.' The girl bit her lip, hesitating. Then slowly, she said, 'I suppose you could see Gran, if you want.'

'Your gran?' Eveleen thought quickly. 'Is she your father's mother?'

The girl nodded.

'Then she must be my gran too,' Eveleen smiled.

'I suppose so.' For a moment doubt crossed the girl's face, looking as if she felt she had offered more than she should have done. 'I'll go and ask her if you like. Who – who shall I say it is?'

'I'm Eveleen and this is Jimmy. We're Mary's children.'

'And your mam is here too?'

'Yes, she's waiting for me. I think she's a bit nervous.'

The girl stared at her, clearly not understanding. 'I'll – I'll go and tell her. You'd best wait here.'

She was gone for what seemed an age to the youngsters who waited. Workers from the machine shops passed through the yard to the communal lavatory and stared curiously at the strangers. One or two nodded and smiled and one young man winked at Eveleen as he looked her up and down with a bold, appraising glance.

Eveleen sniffed and turned her back. She'd had quite enough of good-looking young men to last her a lifetime.

'Gran says she'll see you, but be careful what you say to her. It's put her in one of her moods.'

So, Eveleen thought, as she and Jimmy followed their cousin, our grandmother has moods too, does she?

The girl led them to the end house and in through a green painted door. The small room was dim, lit only through the one window facing out into the yard. It was hot and stuffy and when her eyes grew accustomed to the light, Eveleen could see that an old woman sat in an armchair close to the range where a fire burnt brightly. As her eyes became accustomed to the gloom she saw that the woman wore a high-necked black dress with leg o' mutton sleeves. At her throat was pinned a cameo brooch and her hair was drawn tightly back beneath a white lace cap. Eveleen didn't think she had ever seen anyone with so many wrinkles on her face. Her mouth was shrunken, the lips almost lost, but her eyes were bright and sharp.

'Come here where I can see you.' The voice was high-pitched yet strong and commanding. Eveleen stepped forward and stood on the hearthrug facing the woman, but Jimmy hung back, hovering near the door, ready to escape.

'You too, boy.'

Reluctantly he came to stand beside his sister and submit himself to the old woman's scrutiny. She squinted up at them. 'My eyes aren't as good as they were.' There was a pause as she took in their appearance. 'You don't look like her. How do I know if you're hers? You could be anybody's. Is she dead? Is that why you've come?'

Eveleen hurried to explain. 'No, no. She's outside on the dray. But she wanted us to come in first to see – to—'

'To see if we'd a welcome for the prodigal, eh?' The old woman gave a toothless grin, but the gesture was without humour. 'We've no fatted calf, but I'll see her. Bring her in, girl.'

Eveleen hurried out expecting to leave Jimmy with the old lady but found him following her closely.

'I aren't staying there with that old witch,' he muttered as they reached the gates.

'Shush,' Eveleen tried to scold him but found herself overcome by a fit of the giggles. 'Someone might hear you and then where would you be?'

'I wouldn't care. I don't reckon much to it here anyway.' He glanced around dismally at the narrow street and the terraced houses.

'It's very different,' Eveleen had to agree, her laughter dying. Then, with stout determination, she said, 'Come on, don't let our mam see you looking so glum. Just think how difficult this must be for her.'

Jimmy's only reply was to pull an unsympathetic face and as they reached the dray he said, 'I'll wait here with Bill. You take Mam in.'

Eveleen held her mother's arm as they went back to the house. She could feel Mary trembling even through the thick clothing they had both worn for the long journey on the front of the dray. As they paused outside the door, she was concerned to see that her mother's face was white and she held one hand to her chest as if her breathing was difficult.

'It's all right, Mam. Don't get upset. If they don't want us, we'll go somewhere else.'

'Oh, Evie,' Mary's voice was unsteady. 'But where?'

To that Eveleen had no answer.

Sixteen

'Hello, Mother.'

They were standing side by side, like two naughty children awaiting their punishment, facing the old woman. Eveleen was aware that the young girl was hovering beyond the door leading further into the house, listening to every word.

'So, Mary Singleton,' Bridget, Mary's mother, demanded. 'What brings you back home after all this time?'

'It's – it's Mary Hardcastle now,' Mary mumbled, her head lowered almost to her chest.

'Oh.' The old woman's tone was laced with sarcasm. 'So you did find some poor deluded feller to marry you then?'

Eveleen felt her mother stiffen and her head came up a fraction. 'He was a good, kind man.'

'Oh aye, good enough to take on another feller's bastard. He must have been a good man to do that.' Her screwed up eyes rested upon Eveleen. 'Is this her? Is this Brinsley Stokes's by-blow?'

Mary shuddered and she stumbled over the words. 'No. No. That – that baby died. This is Walter's child.'

'Walter? Who's Walter?'

'My husband. Walter Hardcastle. I – I met him just after . . .' Her voice trailed away, beaten and defeated.

'You've been a very lucky woman to find someone to take you on. A very lucky woman.' Bridget paused and then asked, 'And where is this paragon of virtue? Where is Walter Hardcastle?'

Now Eveleen felt her mother sway and sag against her, so that she put her arm about Mary to support her. She faced her grandmother squarely and said, 'My father died two weeks ago. The cottage we lived in was tied to the job, so—'

'So you're homeless,' the old woman stated baldly. Her gaze returned to Mary, 'And you thought you'd come running home.'

Eveleen lifted her chin. 'If we're not welcome, we'll go. Right now.'

The old woman's eyes were on the young girl's face, now flushed with indignation. She smiled. 'My, but you've a fiery one here, Mary.' The smiled widened. 'I like a girl with spirit. Maybe we'll let you stay a while after all. I reckon you an' me would get on together all right, lass.'

'We aren't looking for charity,' Eveleen said. 'We'll work. All of us. My mother makes pillow lace and—'

'Oho, so you haven't forgotten everything I taught you then?' Bridget's words were heavy with sarcasm again, and Mary's face, from being deathly white, now flushed with embarrassment.

'No, Mother, I haven't forgotten.'

The old woman sniffed. 'We'll have to see what Harry says, mind you. He's head of the family since your father died.'

Mary asked, 'When – when did that happen?'

'Oh years ago,' Bridget said in a matter-of-fact way. 'Fifteen, maybe. Or is it sixteen now. I forget.'

Eveleen was struck by the lack of emotion shown by her grandmother. There had been no show of feelings on meeting her daughter after more than twenty years and now there was not a shred of sorrow in her tone when speaking of her dead husband. Perhaps it was because the event had happened some time ago, whereas their own loss was so recent that each time she even thought about it Eveleen could feel the prickle of tears and the pain in her throat. But the woman sitting before them seemed hard and unfeeling.

What mother greets her long-lost daughter without even reaching out to touch her or rising from her chair to greet her? But this one had. Unless, of course, the hurt went so deep and the bitterness was still so strong that she could not bring herself to welcome her child back even after all these years.

Eveleen sighed inwardly. Her own mother had been right. Her family did not want them. She tightened her hold around her mother's waist and said, 'Mam, I think we'd better go.'

Before Mary could answer, the old woman said, 'Now then, lass, don't be so hasty. I said we'll ask Harry.' She raised her voice. 'Rebecca, get back in here, girl, 'cos I know you're listening at the keyhole.' There was a slight pause before the girl opened the door and slid back into the room.

'Did you call, Gran?' she said innocently.

'You know very well I did. Fetch your father across here.'

'He won't like being fetched from his work.'

'Tell him I sent you.'

Eveleen hid a smile. Harry might well be the notional head of the family, but it seemed to her that, in practice, it was this spirited old lady who ruled the roost. Despite her astonishment at Bridget's callous greeting, Eveleen could not help have a sliver of admiration for her grandmother. Now she was turning back to Eveleen. 'And you, girl. What do you say your name is?'

'Eveleen.'

For the first time, real emotion flickered on Bridget's face as she looked back at Mary. 'So, you still thought enough about us to name her after my mother, eh?' Her mouth stretched into a wistful smile. 'Another Irish colleen, eh?'

'Irish?' Eveleen blurted out before she could stop her inquisitive tongue. 'You don't sound Irish.' Eveleen had only ever met an Irishman once; a travelling man who had passed through Bernby, pots and pans rattling on his carrier's cart. There was no hint of his rich brogue in Bridget's speech.

The old woman sniffed. 'You should have heard my father.' Suddenly she lapsed into such a perfect imitation of the Irish brogue that Eveleen laughed aloud. 'His name was Michael O'Hallaran, so it was, and a foiner man you never did see. He could drink anyone under the table, so he could. God love him.'

There was a mischievous sparkle in Bridget's eyes, but then, reverting to her normal speech she said, 'Now, go and fetch the boy back here. We'd best be seeing what we're taking on.'

Eveleen gave her mother's arm a squeeze. 'You'll be all right?'

'Of course, she'll be all right. What do you think I'm going to do to her? Eat her alive?'

Mirth unexpectedly bubbled up inside Eveleen. Her eyes sparkled and her laughter spilled over. Catching her merriment, the old woman cackled with laughter and the tension in the room eased.

'Oh sit down, Mary,' Bridget waved a bony hand towards a chair. 'You make the place look untidy.'

The room, though small and cluttered with a lifetime of belongings, was anything but untidy. Eveleen settled her mother into a chair opposite Bridget. 'I'll get Jimmy,' she said and hurried out of the door and along the path. As she did so, she saw a man emerge from one of the buildings. A big man with broad shoulders and strong limbs who, despite his size, seemed to spring along as he walked. Eveleen faltered a moment and paused to look at him. His gaze met hers and he frowned, his heavy eyebrows meeting across the bridge of his large nose. He had a bushy grey beard and moustache that completely hid his mouth, but his dark eyes were piercing. For a workman he was smartly dressed, Eveleen thought. A white shirt and tie and a dark suit that even had a waistcoat. On his head was a bowler hat. Irrationally at such a moment, Eveleen could not help wondering if he wore his hat when working at his machine. The picture in her mind made her want to laugh, but she kept her face straight as she returned his stare.

Behind the man, taking little running steps to keep up with his huge strides, was Rebecca.

This, thought Eveleen, must be her uncle, Harry Singleton. Now she gave an uncertain smile, but her tentative greeting was answered only by a deepening frown.

Eveleen pulled her shawl more closely about her and hurried away to find Jimmy.

Moments later they returned to the house and walked into a violent family quarrel between Harry and the old woman. Mary was still seated by the fire, saying nothing, and Rebecca was standing nervously behind her grandmother's chair, twisting her fingers together, her dark blue eyes huge in her pale face.

Eveleen looked swiftly towards her mother. Mary's face was ashen and the girl guessed that for her it must seem as if the intervening twenty or so years had never happened. Mary was back with her family, about to be cast out once again.

Eveleen hurried to her side leaving Jimmy standing awkwardly by the door. 'Come on, Mam, we're going. We're not staying here for you to be insulted like this.'

'Insulted, you say?' Harry's deep, booming voice was shouting so loudly that the ornaments on the mantelpiece seemed to dance. 'And didn't she insult the name of Singleton? Bringing disgrace on to this family?'

Eveleen whirled around and faced him, her fists clenched at her sides. 'Maybe in your eyes, she did. But she's suffered for whatever she's done and if my father could forgive her and' – she glanced meaningfully at Bridget – 'take her on, then I would have thought her own family could do as much.'

She dredged around in her memory for something her mother had told her about the man standing in front of her. Then she remembered. Slowly and deliberately she said, 'I understand you're a chapel-goer?' And now, latching on to the words her grandmother had used only minutes earlier, she added, 'Well, we don't expect a fatted calf, but I'd have thought you could have welcomed her back into the family fold.'

'Don't you dare preach to me, girl.' The man shook his fist in her face, but Eveleen stood her ground.

Behind them the old woman was cackling with laughter. 'You've met your match now, Harry. She reminds me of myself when I was young. She even looks like me. And she's got my hair.' The last words were said wistfully, for only wisps of white hair peeped from beneath Bridget's lace cap.

Eveleen was not finished yet. 'And isn't there another parable about the rejoicing in heaven over the sheep that was lost and is found?'

The man grunted. 'I'm pleased to hear you know your Bible but let me tell you, the lost sheep needs to show true repentance of her sins to earn forgiveness.'

Uncle and niece continued to glare at each other until Bridget said sharply, 'For goodness' sake sit down and let's talk this out calmly.' Catching sight of Jimmy skulking in the shadows near the door, the old woman raised her shrill voice and said, 'Come here, boy, let's be having a look at you.'

Jimmy came forward reluctantly and stood before her. Bridget glanced from one to the other of her new-found grandchildren. 'Are you twins? Now I see you properly, you look very alike.'

Jimmy stuffed his hands deep into his pockets and muttered, 'No, she's a year older 'n me.'

Bridget laughed. 'So she thinks she can boss you about, eh?' Then her laughter faded and she nodded thoughtfully, but her steady gaze was still on the youth's face. 'But you'll not be told what to do for much longer, though, will you, boy?'

Listening, Eveleen marvelled at the old woman's shrewdness. Jimmy had never been easy to control, even as a child, and Bridget had summed him up in seconds. For a brief moment, Eveleen wished they were staying here. She knew she would have a strong ally in her grandmother. Yet she could not allow her mother to be treated so shabbily by her family. 'Well, he'll have to do as he's told for a while longer.' She turned to her brother. 'Go and ask Bill to turn the dray round.'

'Now, now, girl, sit down, I said. You too, Harry. Rebecca, make these poor folks a cup of tea. It's the least we can do.'

Eveleen glanced at the girl, who was already scuttling away to do her grandmother's bidding. 'Please could you take some tea out to Bill? We've come a long way.'

Rebecca nodded and disappeared.

'Now then,' Bridget began when everyone was seated. She did not intend to mince her words as she said, 'You hurt us all badly, Mary, but we never wanted you to leave home.'

Eveleen saw her mother glance at Harry, but she lowered her gaze again without saying anything. Bridget too had seen the gesture, but went on, 'To run off without a word to any of us. That was almost worse than getting yourself pregnant with the likes of Brinsley Stokes. Your poor father went to his grave not knowing whether you were alive or dead. That was cruel, Mary. Cruel and thoughtless.'

Mary looked up at last. 'I thought you wanted me gone. You made my life hell on earth after you found out. All of you. Not one of you had a word of understanding for me. Telling me that he wanted nothing more to do with me. That he'd gone away. If only I could have seen him, talked to him, just one more time . . .' Her voice trailed away as Mary relived the misery.

Now Eveleen noticed a quick glance pass between Bridget and her son.

'You think you could have persuaded him to marry you, eh?' Bridget was leaning forward. 'The daughter of a humble stockinger. His sort don't marry the likes of us.'

Eveleen shuddered. The words echoed those her mother had used to her only a few short weeks ago.

'His father could have ruined all of us,' Bridget went on. 'Don't forget, he was the bag man.' The phrase mystified Eveleen, but now was not the time to ask questions.

Bridget went on. 'Your father went to see him.'

Now Mary's head shot up. 'I didn't know that.'

'Well, he did and was told in no uncertain terms that if the lad married you he'd be cut off from his family without a shilling. The Stokeses were well off by our standards even then and now they are partners in a factory in Nottingham.'

'So,' Mary said, not really taking in everything her mother was telling her. She was still lost in her own bitterness. 'Brinsley chose to cut me off instead?'

'He was only eighteen.'

'Nineteen,' Mary said softly.

'Nineteen, then. But he'd still have needed parental consent to marry you. And Herbert Stokes was never going to give that. Never in a million years. Herbert Stokes was determined to rise in the world. And he did, but he didn't want his son to make an unfortunate marriage and hinder his grand plans.' Bridget's voice dropped and she reached across to touch Mary's hand. 'Didn't you love Brinsley enough to want what was right and best for him? Never mind what it did to you? Did you really want to ruin his life, because that's what it would have done?'

Tears spilled over and ran down Mary's cheeks. 'I thought he loved me.'

'I'm sure he did . . .'

Mary finished the rest of Bridget's sentence. 'But not enough.'

Eveleen pursed her lips, forcing herself to remain silent. It was not her place, she knew, to say anything, but she felt revolted at what these people had done. They had obviously made life so unbearable for Mary that she had run away. She had given birth in the dark and the cold in a ditch and it had almost been the death of her. If it hadn't been for the kindly and, to Eveleen's mind, truly Christian Walter Hardcastle, Mary might well have died along with her child.

And yet – Eveleen had to be honest – perhaps they had been right. Perhaps the marriage between two young people of very different backgrounds would not have worked. And Mary had carried those instincts into the upbringing of her own daughter when she had vehemently opposed Eveleen's association with Stephen Dunsmore.

And she had been right. So heartlessly had Stephen – just like Brinsley Stokes before him – proved her mother right.

Seventeen

'So, are we going or staying?' Jimmy piped up. ''Cos Bill says he wants to get unloaded and find himself lodgings afore it gets dark.'

'You're staying,' Bridget said firmly, glancing at Harry as if daring him to defy her. 'And they can live with you, Harry. There's only you and Rebecca in that end house. Plenty of room for three more. And this feller, Bill, whoever he is, he can bed down for the night too.' She turned to Mary and Eveleen. 'I've got lodgers who work for us. This place is full, mi duck, else I'd have you here.'

Suddenly Mary smiled. 'Eh, I haven't been called that for twenty years. Mi duck.' And she actually laughed. 'Now I know I'm home.'

They moved into the end house with Harry Singleton and his daughter, Rebecca, and slipped into a routine remarkably quickly, although the phrase "settled in" hardly applied. Eveleen felt far from comfortable in the strict, dour atmosphere of her uncle's house and Jimmy grew more truculent and difficult with each day. As for Mary, she was a bundle of nerves, jumping every time Harry spoke. Her anxiety to please him was pathetic.

They had been given the attic bedroom. Eveleen and her mother would share the double bed while Jimmy had a straw-filled mattress on the floor under the steeply sloping ceiling.

'Huh,' Mary said as she hauled herself up the steep, narrow stairs. 'My old room back. I haven't even graduated to a proper bedroom.'

'I'll have to tidy it up a bit. We haven't had any lodgers recently,' Rebecca explained apologetically.

They pushed their tin trunks into one corner beside a box of Rebecca's old books and discarded toys. Eveleen picked up a small school slate and touched its cool, black surface, evoking poignant memories of her father. She smiled wistfully, remembering her own childhood as she glanced at the toys: a game of draughts, a set of quoits, the coloured rings piled on to the wooden peg, and a child's cricket bat.

'Don't bother on our account,' Mary said stiffly to Rebecca. 'We won't be staying long.' She went to the marble-topped washstand under the window and laid out her hairbrush and comb. There was a rose-patterned ewer and bowl and beside them, a linen towel edged with lace. Mary picked it up and fingered the lace, examining it closely.

'Fancy,' she murmured, 'this is one of mine.' She replaced the towel and turned to the bed, running her palm across the patchwork quilt. 'And Mother and I made this together when I was about twelve.' She glanced around the room, shaking her head in wonder. 'It's not changed in all this time.'

Secretly Eveleen was quite impressed with the house. It was much smaller than the farmhouse they had lived in, but the parlour of her uncle's house, overlooking the yard, seemed to her to be well furnished. The black-leaded range where all the cooking was done dominated the room. In front of it a pegged rug covered part of the brick floor and to one side was set the master's chair, a high-backed wooden Windsor. To the right of the range, set in the alcove, were cupboards and on the left-hand side, beneath the window, was a table covered with a plush gold-coloured tablecloth. Pictures adorned the walls and one, Eveleen noticed, was a portrait of a sweet-faced woman who looked very much like an older Rebecca. Eveleen presumed it to be her mother.

In the far corner of the room stood an organ and beside it a small table covered with a lace cloth. Standing in the centre was a blue and white bowl holding a fleshy-leafed aspidistra. Beside that was a brass-faced grandfather clock that ticked solemnly and struck loudly every hour.

Behind the parlour, with a window facing out on to the street, was the kitchen. A shallow stone sink drained to an outside gutter, although all the water had to be carried into the house from the pump in the yard and heated on the range. Beneath the stairs leading to the two upper floors was a small pantry.

As they had climbed the narrow stairs on their way to the attic room, Eveleen peeped into the two bedrooms on the first floor.

The largest – obviously her uncle's room – held a wrought-iron double bed. In the far corner was a dressing table and near the door was a washstand with pretty patterned brown and white tiles. At the foot of the bed was a wooden blanket chest. Everywhere there was evidence of the industry in which this family was engaged. The flounces on the bed and the counterpane were lace-edged and, though she could not see them, Eveleen suspected that the pillow cases, and maybe even the sheets too, would be edged with lace.

Rebecca's room was smaller, but furnished in much the same way as her father's, the main difference being that hers was a single bed. They had to pass through her room to reach the one above.

Jimmy winked at the girl and said, 'You'll have to watch out I don't catch you in your nightie.'

Rebecca blushed and dropped her gaze while Eveleen smacked the back of her brother's head.

'Hey, what's that for?'

'You know,' Eveleen warned darkly, but Jimmy only grinned cheekily at her. 'At least,' she went on, 'now we're all going to be in one room, you won't be able to stay out half the night without Mam finding out.'

She kept her voice so low that only he could hear. The look of dismay on Jimmy's face made her want to laugh, but then his mouth twisted as he said, 'Be in bed by ten o'clock every night? Not likely, Evie. Not me.'

'We'll see, won't we?'

'Yeah. We will.'

They glared at each other for a moment in a silent battle of wills, until Eveleen relented a little. This tragic change in their circumstances was just as hard on her young brother as on any of them. She smiled as she whispered, 'Just be thankful you aren't having to share the bed with Mam.'

And suddenly the brother and sister were laughing together.

It wasn't so much the fact of sleeping beside her mother that irritated Eveleen. In truth, in the cold attic, they were warmth for each other. It was not even the woman's snoring which kept the girl awake occasionally that tested Eveleen's patience but rather Mary's constant entreaty every night as they got into bed.

'Oh, Evie, when can we go back? I hate it here. When can we go home?'

Eveleen would say, 'One day, Mam, I promise you. One day I'll take you back home.'

Sometimes, they would lie together talking softly, going over the day's events.

'What happened to Uncle Harry's wife? Do you know?' Eveleen asked her mother on the second night of their residence.

'I asked Mother today. Rose died about six years ago when Rebecca was ten.'

There was silence then Eveleen asked, 'And Rebecca has kept house for him ever since?'

''Spect so.'

'You'd think she'd want to go out to work. Have a little independence of her own, wouldn't you?'

'Independence? With Harry for a father? Oh, Eveleen, you've a lot to learn about your uncle if you think he'd even dream of such a thing.'

'Talking of work, I must start in the morning to look for something. It's good of Uncle Harry to have taken Jimmy on as an apprentice.'

'Where is he? He should be in bed by now. Harry will be locking up in a minute and coming upstairs.'

'Serves him right if he's locked out,' said Eveleen, turning on her side with her back to her mother and preparing for sleep.

'Don't be so hard on Jimmy. He doesn't like it here. I know he doesn't.'

'Well, he doesn't have any choice in the matter. Like I say, he's lucky Uncle Harry's at least giving him a try.' She gave a wry laugh. 'He's only got to fall out of bed into work.'

'Mm.' Her mother's voice was growing sleepy, but just before she fell asleep she said, 'It's not the best job in the world. Those machines are heavy to operate and the work's hard on the eyesight. My poor little Jimmy.'

'It's better than a lot of jobs. He's warm and dry and—' But the only response from Mary was a gentle snore.

The following morning Eveleen made her way down the brick path to the workshops standing at right angles to the row of cottages.

The noise of the machinery deafened her even as she climbed the stairs to the workroom and beneath her feet it felt as if the whole building was shaking. She stood at the top of the stairs looking about her. The machines, closely spaced with the operators sitting back to back, were set in a row down the side of the room beneath the long window that she had noticed from the outside on the day of their arrival. Against the opposite wall, too, there were machines even though the light would not be so good there. On the wall above each machine hung a glass bowl filled with acid to reflect the light on to the knitter's work. No one looked up at her appearance at the top of the stairs; they had not heard her above the clatter, so for some time Eveleen stood watching, fascinated by the rhythmic operation the framework knitters carried out with a series of complicated hand and foot movements. She watched carefully and by the time she turned and went down the stairs again, she believed she could carry out all the movements in their proper sequence.

Maybe Uncle Harry would allow her to learn to operate one of the machines. She would speak to him later. She could see now for herself why it was important not to be disturbed during work. Perhaps, she thought, if the rhythm were interrupted at the wrong moment, the whole piece of knitting could be ruined. And while from a short distance away she had just now watched her uncle at work, he had not looked up once to acknowledge her presence. Perhaps he had not even been aware that she was standing there.

At the bottom of the stairs she almost bumped into a young man about to take the steps two at a time. It was the same one who had winked at her cheekily the previous day.

'Oh, sorry,' he mouthed, catching hold of her as she stumbled against the wall. Even down here conversation was impossible because of the noise from the machines above them and from the lower floor too. Although Eveleen twisted herself free of his grasp and said, 'S'all right,' they continued to stare at each other. She gave a quick nod and stepped to one side to pass by him and out into the yard once more. But the young man moved in front of her. 'Hey!' He had to shout to make himself heard. 'Not so fast.' He stepped outside and when she followed, he asked, 'Are you Eveleen? Old Harry's niece?'

Eveleen raised her eyebrow. My word, she thought. We've only been here a couple of days. News does travel fast. But, of course, it would in such a close, confined community. She nodded and the young man's grin widened.

'Pleased to meet you, miss.' He held out his hand. His grasp, when she put her hand into his, was warm and firm. He wore a shirt with the sleeves rolled up to his elbows, a tie, a waistcoat and trousers. Most of the men, Eveleen noticed, wore some kind of headgear, caps or bowlers, hanging them by their machines while they worked but putting them on immediately they stepped out of the workshop. This young man wore neither and she could see that his straight, light brown hair was cut very short. His hazel eyes were looking into hers and when he smiled the laughter lines around his eyes crinkled mischievously.

He was still holding her hand, so Eveleen pulled herself free of his grasp and again stepped to one side to walk past him, but he side-stepped once more to bar her way. 'My name's Andrew Burns and I work for your uncle, so' – he winked at her – 'we'll be seeing a lot of each other.'

'Unfortunately, Mr Burns,' Eveleen said primly. 'Unfortunately.'

His face fell. 'Aw, don't be like that. All uppity. And there I was thinking how nice yer looked.'

He looked so like a boisterous little puppy that had just been smacked that Eveleen could not stop the smile that twitched at the corner of her mouth. Seeing it, he said triumphantly, 'There! I knew I was right.' Then he leant towards her conspiratorially. 'I know, you don't want to let your uncle see you getting friendly wi' me. That it, eh?' He shook his head and added wisely, 'Well, you're quite right. He's a hard man. Keeps poor little Rebecca on a tight leash. She's hardly allowed out the door let alone allowed to speak to the likes o' me. He'll have trouble with her one day, if he's not careful. She'll break out.'

Eveleen stared at him. For a young man, he had a wise head on his shoulders, she thought.

Was that what had happened to her mother, she wondered, a generation earlier? Had she been kept on such a tight leash that, at last, she had broken loose and run wild and free?

'I must go,' she told Andrew and, lest he should try to stop her, added, firmly, 'Really.'

He stepped aside and gave a mock bow. 'We'll meet again.'

'No doubt we will,' she murmured.

As she walked towards the houses, her back straight, her head held high, she did not look back although she sensed that Andrew was standing watching her.

He did seem nice. Friendly and a bit of a rogue. She allowed him that. But, Eveleen told herself sternly, he's a man and I'm done with young men for good.

Eighteen

With three women in Harry Singleton's house, the chores were shared, but there was other work at which they each took turns. While the larger knitting frames in the workshops were operated by men, smaller stocking- and sock-making machines were part of the furniture in many of the houses in the locality.

'I expect I can still remember how to work a Griswold,' Mary murmured as she watched her niece working.

Rebecca looked up shyly. 'I'm sure you can, Aunt Mary. When I've finished this, would you like to have a go?' She glanced from Mary to Eveleen and back again. 'And you too, Eveleen. There's nothing to it really.'

'It looks easy enough,' Eveleen remarked as she watched her cousin turning the handle of the circular knitting machine, the needles sinking and rising again like a wave to form loop after loop and row upon row of knitting. 'It's very clever, though.'

'Father would be so pleased if all three of us could work the machine.' Rebecca pulled a wry face. 'I've often found it hard to keep up with the amount he wants, what with keeping house for him and the washing and seaming. I used to do the yarn winding, but there are two children in the street house' – she jerked her thumb over her shoulder towards the back-to-back house that faced the street – 'so they do that now. And their mother does a lot of the seaming up. And, of course, we sometimes have lodgers, young men who come to work here and then there's extra cooking and baking.'

Eveleen held up her hands in mock horror. 'Oh stop, stop, Rebecca. You're making me feel tired listening to you. And I thought farm work was hard.'

'It's lucky,' Rebecca went on with a glad smile, 'that the attic room was unoccupied when you arrived.'

'Or there might have been no room at the inn, eh?' Mary murmured and smiled a little sadly.

Rebecca laughed softly. 'I'm sure Gran would have made sure you stayed – somehow. I think she's very happy to see you again.'

Mary glanced at her shrewdly. 'But what about your father?'

Colour crept slowly up the girl's neck and face. Uncomfortably, she looked away. 'I'm sure he is pleased to see you.'

'But?' Mary persisted.

Rebecca shrugged and seemed to be struggling to find the right words. Eveleen, who had been listening to the conversation, came to her rescue. 'Don't ask her awkward questions, Mam,' she laughed, trying to make light of the matter. 'What can you expect him to feel? His home's been invaded by three homeless waifs and you're asking if he's pleased to see us? Come on, don't embarrass Rebecca.'

Her cousin cast Eveleen a grateful glance and, more confident now, said, 'I'm sure everything will be all right.' Then with a spark of mischief added, 'Especially if you can both knit socks on this machine.'

The three women laughed together and a bond between them was formed. From this moment, their lives would be as intertwined as the knitting they created.

With only a little practice, Mary was soon working the Griswold. Eveleen took a little longer to learn to cast on and off.

'It's easy once you get going, but it's very different to milking cows,' she laughed and then could have bitten off the end of her tongue as she saw the homesick look on her mother's face.

Later that same afternoon, Eveleen found Rebecca peering out of the parlour window overlooking the yard.

'Are you watching for your father coming in for his tea?'

The girl shook her head. 'No. He's working late tonight. He has a job to finish. The bag man comes in the morning.'

'Tell me, what is a bag man?'

'He's like a middle man. He brings the yarn from the warehouses in Nottingham and then sells the finished garments for us too.'

'Does your father own all those machines?' Eveleen asked innocently and was surprised when Rebecca burst out laughing.

'Oh no. He'd be a wealthy man if he did, wouldn't he?'

Eveleen was puzzled. 'But he owns all this, doesn't he? The workshops and the houses?'

Now Rebecca nodded. 'Yes. Gran's parents came to England at the time of the potato famine in Ireland. At first they were down south, London, I think, but then they came here. Gran married a local man. He was a framework knitter working in his parents' home. When they married they moved into this cottage and began to build the workshops in the yard and later more cottages. I think all this was once farm land.'

'Really?' Eveleen thought of the street outside and the houses all squashed together. She couldn't imagine it ever having been fields with cows grazing or chickens running about the yard.

'So who does own all the machines?'

Rebecca smiled. 'It's a bit complicated, perhaps, for an outsider to understand.'

But Eveleen was intrigued. It was such a different way of life to what she had been used to. Whilst part of her missed the open fields and the mist rising over the flat land, there was something about this place, this life, that excited her. She wanted to become part of it – at least for the time they were here. One day, she knew, she would have to fulfil her promise and take her family back to Bernby. But in the meantime she wanted to learn about the hosiery industry, to learn the trade that was in her maternal family's blood.

Rebecca glanced out of the window again, but there was no one in the yard so the two girls sat down together.

'Father owns four of the machines and the others are owned by all sorts of people. The knitters own some themselves, those who don't want to work in their own home or build their own workshops. Our bag man owns about half a dozen, I think, and some frames are owned by local people, like Mr Mills, the butcher.'

'The butcher?'

Rebecca laughed. 'He doesn't knit himself, but he owns the machine and rents it out to a framework knitter, see?'

Eveleen was doubtful. 'I think so. But you're right, it does sound complicated.'

Rebecca ticked off the points on her fingers. 'So the man who does the work, the framework knitter or the stockinger, whatever you like to call him, pays rent to the owner of the machine and the owner pays a rent to my father for having the machine in the workshops.'

Eveleen's quick mind was rapidly doing sums. 'So Uncle Harry collects rent from all the machines owned by other people?'

'That's it. Of course there are other expenses the knitters have to pay for.' Again she ticked them off one by one. 'Needles and oil, the seaming – unless their wives or children do it – candles, coal, and then if a machine needs a major repair they have to call in a framesmith—'

'Oh stop,' Eveleen said, 'I'm bankrupt already. However do they make a living?'

'We have a saying round here, "As poor as a stockinger". But we're lucky really. Most of our workers are fit and healthy and my father keeps the rent low deliberately. He says he'd sooner have the machines all working than lying idle because some poor feller can't make enough to pay his way.'

'Sounds reasonable.' Eveleen pondered a moment and then said, 'So the bag man brings the yarn, the local children wind it, the men knit it and then wives and daughters do the seaming up.'

'And the washing. Sometimes the garments get oil on them from the machines.'

Eveleen remembered seeing the girl coming out of the washhouse at the end of one of the workshops on the day of their arrival. So that had been the reason for washing being done at an odd time of the day, she thought.

'Then the bag man fetches the finished garments and takes them to the warehouses, or wherever, in Nottingham,' Eveleen concluded.

Rebecca nodded. 'That's about it, yes. Mind you, there are some ruthless men among the bag men, but my father knows what's what. He goes to Nottingham every so often just to be sure we're all being given a fair price for our work.' She laughed again. 'Even us for our socks on the Griswold.'

Eveleen was quiet for a moment. Her mother's sweetheart had been a bag man, or at least his father had, back then. Had he been a ruthless exploiter of the poor stockingers, she wondered, as well as a heartless deserter of a pregnant young woman?

'Oh, here they come.' Rebecca jumped up from her chair and went to the window again.

Eveleen went to stand beside her. 'Who?'

'The lads from the workshops. They're going to play cricket.'

'Cricket?'

Rebecca turned to look at her. 'I'm sorry, I forgot. I thought your mother might have told you.'

Eveleen shook her head. 'My mother told us nothing about her life here.'

'Because the knitters are sort of self-employed they can vary their hours of working to suit themselves. And sometimes work is slack anyway. So,' Rebecca ended simply, 'they play cricket.'

'And your father doesn't mind?'

'Mind?' Rebecca laughed. 'He's the first to pick up the bat and be shouting for someone to bowl to him.'

'Where do they play?'

'They have matches on the cricket ground down near the railway, but our lads practise here. Look—'

Eveleen peered through the window and saw Andrew Burns carrying a cricket bat and positioning himself in front of the pump.

'They use the pump as the wicket. Oh, Father must have finished work. He's joining in. Now, you watch him bowl. He played for the county a few years ago,' she added proudly.

'Did he really?' Eveleen could not keep the surprise from her voice.

Harry had appeared from the workshop. He had left his jacket behind and though dressed in just trousers, shirt and waistcoat, he still wore his bowler hat. Standing at the far end of the yard near the pigsties, he rubbed the ball down his leg and then ran a few paces along the brick path, brought his arm up behind him and over in an arc. He released the ball and it bounced once before Andrew took a swipe at it, knocking it into the patch of herbs.

Among the young men gathered as fielders, Eveleen saw Jimmy scrambling over the fence to retrieve the ball while Andrew was running the length of the brick path and back again, shouting out the number of runs he was making as he ran. 'Two.'

'Come on, Jimmy. Find that ball.'

'Four.'

'Here, here, throw it here.'

'Five.'

'Run him out.'

The yard was alive with shouting, laughing and the thud of the ball against the bat. The game went on until dusk when one or two lads drifted away to go home. Soon only Harry, Andrew and Jimmy were left playing in the yard.

'Do you think,' Eveleen said to Rebecca, 'they'd let us have a go?'

'Oh no!' Rebecca was shocked. 'Girls don't play cricket.'

'Well, it's high time we did. Come on.'

Eveleen was already at the door, lifting the latch and stepping into the yard, with Rebecca saying fearfully, 'Oh, Evie, I don't think we should—'

But Eveleen was already walking towards the pump and saying, 'Come on, Andrew, let's be having a go.'

The lad's mouth dropped open and he seemed too stunned to make any protest when Eveleen took the bat out of his hand and turned to face her uncle.

Harry hesitated for a moment but then bowled a gentle underarm ball towards Eveleen. She brought the bat back and swiped at the ball. She hit it fair and square in the middle of the bat and the ball skidded along the brick path to be blocked by Harry's boot.

'Right, mi lady,' Harry said, and though she could not see if his mouth was smiling beneath the bushy beard, she could hear the amusement in his voice.

Out here, Eveleen thought, he's like a different man, but then she had to concentrate for Harry had retreated as far back as he could and was beginning his run-up. Now he bowled overarm to her, the ball leaving his hand as fast as any of the balls she had seen him deliver to the boys. The ball came flying towards her, bounced and somehow met the flat of her bat. It flew into the air, sailed above Jimmy's outstretched hand and was heading straight for the windows of the upper storey of one of the workshops.

'Oh no,' Eveleen breathed. 'Now I'm in trouble.'

There was the sound of shattering glass and the dull thud of the ball dropping on to the floor. All eyes were turned up to look at the broken pane and then they saw Wilf Carter's face at the window, shaking his fist.

Eveleen swallowed fearfully as she glanced at her uncle. But to her surprise, and by the look on her face

Rebecca's too, Harry Singleton put his hands on his sides, threw back his head and roared with laughter.

'First team next week, lass,' he spluttered. 'First team next week.'

Nineteen

'Now who can that be when we're just about to sit down to dinner,' Eveleen muttered, exasperated by the knock at the door.

'I don't want to see anyone.' Mary's voice was high-pitched with fear.

Eveleen shot her a glance but said nothing as she opened the door to a middle-aged woman in a black skirt and white blouse with a lace shawl about her shoulders. Her brown hair, liberally streaked with grey, was drawn back into a bun. She was plump and stood with her arms folded beneath the shelf of her bosom. When she smiled, her eyes, full of curiosity, twinkled.

''Hello, mi duck,' she nodded as she greeted Eveleen, but craned her neck, trying to see past the girl and into the room behind her. 'Is she here?'

Eveleen's face cleared. 'Oh, you want Rebecca. I'll just—'

'No, no. It's Mary I've come to see. Mary Singleton. My George said he'd seen 'er riding through the village on a dray.' Her inquisitive eyes grew even brighter. 'Has she come home? Is she here?'

'Well . . .' Eveleen was uncertain. If the woman chose to peer through the window at the side of the door, she would be able to see Mary sitting by the range. Eveleen was still hesitating when her mother spoke resignedly.

'Let her in, Eveleen. I'd better get it over with.' Then

she raised her voice and said, belligerently, 'Come on in, Gracie Allenby – if you must.'

The woman almost pushed her way past Eveleen in her eagerness. 'Well, I never did,' she said as she stood before Mary looking down at her. 'Mary Singleton as I live and breathe.'

'It's Mary Hardcastle now, Gracie.'

'And I'm Gracie Turner.'

Mary looked up with a sudden spark of interest. 'You married George?'

Gracie nodded and added proudly, 'I did and we've 'ad six kids. Eldest is fifteen, youngest is four.' Her tone softened and her eyes were sympathetic as she asked, 'What about you, Mary?' Her glance flickered briefly over Eveleen and then back to Mary's face. 'This your lass, is it?'

Now the hostility in Mary's tone was undisguised. 'What if it is? What's it to you?'

Eveleen held her breath but Grace only laughed and, without being invited, sat down in Harry's chair on the opposite side of the hearth. 'Aw now, Mary, don't be like that. Don't bear grudges, mi duck. Not after all this time.'

Eveleen stood silently watching, ready to intervene if the visitor should distress her mother, but Mary was glowering at Gracie Turner and appeared to be quite able to defend herself. 'Forgive and forget, eh? Well, if you want me to do that, you'd better ask my dear brother to do the same.'

'Oh Harry!' Gracie laughed and dismissed him with a flap of her hand. 'That brother of yours should have been a preacher. In fact, it's always surprised me that he isn't. He'd have made a good one alongside that feller who gave you such a hard time. Jeremiah Tranter. "Tranter the Ranter" we called 'im. D'you remember?'

Eveleen felt the laughter bubbling up inside her, but she was still anxious for her mother.

'As if I could ever forget,' Mary said. 'I'll never set foot inside that chapel again.'

Gracie laughed, a loud infectious sound. 'Don't blame the chapel, mi duck. It was years ago. Times have changed a bit since then. We've got a lovely young feller as our minister on the circuit now.'

Mary eyed her suspiciously. 'Are you trying to tell me that none of the preachers stand up in that pulpit and harangue the congregation for their sinful ways?'

Gracie tried hard, but could not deny it.

'No, I thought not,' Mary said grimly, her mouth pursed. 'And you and all the rest followed suit, didn't you? Banned from teaching in the Sunday school, I was, and not allowed on any of the outings. And you, Gracie . . .' Mary leaned forward now, almost menacingly. 'I thought you was my best friend.'

Gracie looked ashamed. 'I was, Mary. But mi dad was as hard as yours. He forbade me to see you.' Now she leant forward and touched Mary's hand. 'I came round here one day though. Sneaked out, I did.'

'I don't remember that.'

'You'd gone,' Gracie said, and even after the intervening years there was still sadness in her tone. 'Run away, you had. I came to tell you that I was still your friend, no matter what. Me and Georgie and some of the other village young 'uns. But you'd run away without a word to any of us.' Now there was reproach in Gracie's voice.

'That's as maybe.' Mary sounded a little mollified, but still not wholly believing.

'My dad found out and I got a right thrashing for coming here, I can tell you,' Gracie went on, but now she was beaming. 'But here I am, large as life and twice as natural, to tell you what I came to tell you then. I'm still your friend. I always was and I always will be.'

Mary stared at her for a long time and then said, quietly, 'Eveleen, would you make us both a cup of tea, please love. Me and Gracie here have got a bit of catching up to do.'

Things might have continued in a fairly settled way for by the end of the first week a routine had been established. Jimmy was learning a trade in his uncle's workshops and the three women were already working well together.

But then came Sunday and with it the first confrontation between Mary and her brother.

'Eveleen,' Harry said at breakfast. 'You will go with Rebecca this morning. She teaches at the Sunday school. You can help her and, in time, you may be able to teach too.'

'Yes, Uncle,' Eveleen said. She liked children and knew she would enjoy helping her cousin.

Harry now included Mary and Jimmy too. 'You'll all be ready for this afternoon's service by two fifteen,' he decreed as he rose from the breakfast table. 'And you, young man,' he added, pointing a finger at Jimmy, 'don't think you can go out roaming the streets, making an exhibition of yourself. In this house we read the Good Book on a Sunday and Rebecca will play hymns on the organ for us later. Then there's Chapel again tonight at six.'

Eveleen saw Jimmy's horrified face and wanted to giggle, but knew she must not.

It was Mary who answered Harry. As she rose and

began to stack the breakfast dishes, she said, 'I'm well aware of the debt we owe you, Harry, and that because we are living in your house there are rules we must abide by. Jimmy will not disgrace you and both he and Eveleen will accompany you and Rebecca to the services in the chapel.' She faced him squarely. 'But I will not be attending any service in that chapel. And I think you know why.'

Eveleen heard Rebecca's little gasp of alarm and then it seemed as if everyone in the room was holding their breath.

The frown that seemed to be ever present on Harry's brow deepened and his voice was harsh as he said, 'You will attend each and every service, Mary. Everyone who lives in these four houses and in Chapel Row,' he waved his hand to encompass the neighbouring homes and even those in the rest of the street, 'indeed, all the people from the village who work in my workshops attend the services. Why should you be any different, might I ask?'

Mary's voice rose. 'You should know why. Or have you forgotten how that Christian congregation' – her tone bitter – 'treated me?'

'That was your own doing.'

'And are you still denouncing young people who "fornicate"?'

'Mary!' His admonishment was like a whiplash. Eveleen saw her mother flinch and knew that despite her valiant show of strength she would not defeat Harry. He ruled his small world and while Mary was a part of it, while they all were, they would obey him.

By two o'clock that afternoon Eveleen was proved right for when they all assembled in the living room Mary was dressed in her best black costume with its tight-fitting waist and leg o' mutton sleeves. She held a hymnbook in her hands, but her face looked as if she was about to be led to the scaffold.

'I'll go and help Gran,' Rebecca murmured and scurried out of the house.

Mary was startled out of her own problems enough to say, 'You don't drag poor Mother to Chapel surely, Harry?'

'It does her no harm,' he said pompously. 'The rest of the week she only moves from her bed to that chair and back again. It does her good to get out twice a week.'

'No doubt you consider it's good for her soul, too,' Mary said tartly before she could stop herself. She was rewarded by Harry's deepening frown.

As they trooped outside, Eveleen saw her grandmother, leaning heavily against Rebecca, coming along the path in front of the houses. Bridget winced with each step she took and their progress was so painfully slow that Eveleen hurried forward to take her other arm.

'There, Gran, lean on both of us. Is that easier?'

The old lady paused a moment, bringing them both to a standstill. She glanced from one to the other and smiled. 'My two granddaughters,' she murmured, pride in her tone. Then she looked towards Jimmy and her smile broadened. 'And that scallywag of a grandson.' Eveleen felt Bridget squeeze her arm. 'I'm glad to have you here, mi duck. All my grandchildren together. It's grand, isn't it, Rebecca?'

Rebecca smiled across at Eveleen and agreed. 'It is, Gran, it is.'

It took them ten minutes just to cross the narrow street to the chapel.

'You young 'uns shouldn't be bothering with the likes of me,' the old lady said. 'Mind you,' she added and gave her cackling laugh, 'I'd be hard put to even get there without you.'

Mary was pacing up and down outside the door.

'You going to stay there all day?' Bridget asked her. Then her tone softened. 'Come on in with us, lass. They can't bite you.'

Mary did not pause in her pacing. 'Can't they?' she said bitterly. 'They had a good try once.'

Eveleen and Rebecca helped their grandmother inside and down the aisle to the front pew where Harry was already seated, his head bent forward in prayer. Beside him, kicking his heels against the wooden seat, Jimmy sat gazing around him, turning every so often to gape at newcomers.

As Bridget sat down heavily, Eveleen turned to her brother. 'Stop that this minute,' she hissed at him. Then she put the flat of her hand at the back of his head and, none too gently, pushed his head forward. 'Say a prayer. And make it a good 'un, 'cos I reckon you need it.'

She was about to sit down next to him so that she could keep him in check during the service when she realised that her mother had still not followed them in. Giving a click of exasperation, Eveleen hurried out to find her.

'Come on, Mam. It'll be starting soon.'

'I don't want to come in, Evie. You don't know what they're like.'

Perplexed and anxious, Eveleen spoke more sharply than she intended. 'It'll mean trouble for all of us if you don't come in. Please, Mam,' she begged and took hold of her mother's arm. She was shocked to feel that Mary was shaking but she could not, dare not, give way. 'Come on,' she urged, more gently now. 'It'll be all right. Sit between me and Jimmy. You'll have too much to do to keep him in order to have time to worry about other folks.'

At that moment Gracie Turner came hurrying up the street, puffing and panting, afraid of being late. Summing up the situation swiftly, she linked her arm through Mary's. 'Come on, mi duck. You can sit with me, if you like.'

'Thanks, Gracie, but I'd better sit with my family.'

To Eveleen's relief Mary allowed Gracie to lead her inside and settle her in the family pew before taking her own place further back. But as Eveleen slipped in beside her, Mary clung to her arm as if she would never let it go.

'I want to go home, Evie. Take me home,' she whispered yet again.

Eveleen patted her hand, distraught that she could not respond to Mary's desperate plea, for she knew that her mother did not mean back to the house across the street, but back home to Lincolnshire.

Although their mother had never been religious, Walter had taken both his children to church regularly, but this service was like nothing Eveleen had ever attended before. Sitting in the front pew, they were directly beneath the preacher. He was a tall, heavily built man with white hair and a long, white beard. Thick curling eyebrows, white too, overshadowed deep-set eyes, and his face was set in stern lines. Not once did a smile even touch his mouth. He led the congregation through the service, through the prayers and the hymns, and while Eveleen did not know some of them, much of the form of the service was familiar.

But it was when it came to the sermon that the atmosphere changed completely. The preacher stood in the pulpit and harangued the congregation for their sinful ways. He shouted and stormed and could promise them only hell and damnation from a vengeful God unless they repented their sins this very moment and from this day forth led a blameless life.

At the first blast of his outrage, Eveleen had jumped physically. Her heart had thudded in trepidation and she had begun to understand her mother's fears. But as his diatribe continued with what seemed to the young girl mounting hysteria, Eveleen found her thoughts wandering, her mind shutting out his accusations.

This was not how she imagined the Lord. To her mind – and she recognized it might be a rather naïve and childish picture – God was a huge figure, about ten times the size of an ordinary man, who sat on a giant throne somewhere up in the clouds. He had a long, silky white beard and a wrinkled face that was wreathed in smiles. His eyes twinkled merrily at the mischief his creation caused. He would take his children on to his huge lap and pat their heads and pardon them their so-called sins when they sincerely begged his forgiveness. Even when faced with real wickedness, his eyes would be sorrowful rather than angry or vengeful.

On his right hand sat his son, resembling, Eveleen thought, the picture she had once seen of Jesus called "I am the Light of the World". He had a sweet, rather sad face. But then hadn't he suffered so terribly to save the whole world?

As the preacher shook his fist above the heads of his congregation and castigated them, Eveleen took her mother's trembling hand and put it through her own arm.

She patted it and, giving a disparaging nod of her head towards the preacher, whispered, 'It's all right, Mam. God understands, even if he doesn't.'

Whatever Mary had done in her life, she had already, to Eveleen's mind, been punished enough here on earth. With the confidence of youth, Eveleen had a firm trust and faith in a loving Father rather than a vengeful God. Her earthly father had been kind and loving and forgiving, so why should her Heavenly Father be any different?

'It's all right, Mam. Everything's going to be all right,' she murmured again, and was reassured to feel Mary's fingers squeeze her arm.

Twenty

'Gran, what happened to Mam at the chapel all those years ago?'

Later that day, Eveleen had entered her grandmother's house and sat down opposite the old woman. Wearied by the painful walk to the day's two services, Bridget leant back in her chair. She was lost in thought for a few moments, perhaps deciding how much to confide in her granddaughter, before she went on, 'When your mother got herself into trouble, we had a minister here at that time called Tranter.'

It was the name Eveleen had already heard but she said nothing and allowed her grandmother to continue.

'He was very – very . . .' Bridget sought for the right words. 'Hell-fire and brimstone.'

'I thought the one today was a bit like that.'

'Old Tranter was ten times worse than him – or better, according to your point of view. Years ago, it was the practice in our chapel to denounce wrongdoers before the congregation and Tranter believed in carrying on the old tradition. That's what he did to poor Mary. She was made to stand up in front of the whole congregation and confess her sins.'

'You mean – you mean, the minister shamed her in front of the whole village?'

'Oh aye,' Bridget said in a matter-of-fact way. 'Usually, the two concerned are brought before the chapel elders, but of course, they couldn't get hold of Brinsley Stokes. His family considered themselves a cut above the rest of us poor stockingers and they were church-goers anyway. I suppose they thought of themselves as gentry.'

'The man who was the father of Mam's baby was gentry?'

'Not what we'd think of as gentry. Middle class, maybe.' Bridget gave a cackling laugh as she added, 'It's what the *real* gentry would call "new money", earned from being in trade.' As she said the final word, she pulled the corners of her mouth down, imitating the condescending attitude of the upper classes towards a man who, by the dint of his own efforts, raised himself to a higher standard of living.

'How did my mother meet him?' It was important to Eveleen to fill in the gaps in the picture she was already building up.

The old woman sighed. 'His father was the bag hosier then. Brinsley was a nice young man, but that was the trouble, he was so young. They both were. But that didn't stop them falling in love and, of course, her father and Harry didn't approve. Neither did his parents when they found out.'

'And you, Gran? What about you?'

'Me? Oh, I just did as I was told.'

'I don't believe that for a minute.'

Bridget's bright eyes twinkled. 'Oh, lass, you're so like me, you know me already, don't you?' Her expression sobered. 'But be careful, love. Curb that wilful streak just a little, because it's still a man's world out there. You can kick against it now and again, and sometimes you can get your own way. But only for a while, because they'll win in the end. They always do.' She sighed. 'Aye, it's still a man's world all right.'

There was silence between them for a few moments before Eveleen prompted gently, 'So, what happened when everyone found out, apart from the scene in the chapel, I mean?'

'In a way, I could understand your mam running away, though I was so hurt and angry at her for not letting me know where she was and that she was all right. Oh yes, I'd've tanned her backside for her and no mistake if I could have got me hands on her.'

With the intervening years having lessened the anger, Eveleen now felt able to say with a saucy smile, 'Perhaps that's why she didn't keep in touch.'

Bridget laughed too and Eveleen thought, She *is* like me. Just like me. We even have the same sense of humour. Though they'd only known each other a few days, already a strong bond was growing between Eveleen and her grandmother.

Now Eveleen said soberly, 'But I have to agree with you, she should at least have let you know she was all right. It was cruel not to. Mind you, from the bits she has said, and even yet I can't quite piece it all together, I think the truth is that for some time after she ran away from here, she was anything but all right.'

Bridget sat up straight. 'Tell me.'

Eveleen spoke slowly, trying to tie all the threads of her mother's story together. 'I think she found work on the land and I suppose, being with child, it was very hard for her. She – she said her child was born in a field while she was working. In the cold and in a ditch, she said, and that's how it died.'

Bridget closed her eyes and sank back against the chair. Concerned that she had said too much, Eveleen leant forward and took her hand.

'Gran, I'm sorry. I shouldn't have told you.'

'Of course you should, child. I need to know. Even after all this time, I still need to be able to understand why.'

There was silence in the small room until Bridget asked, 'So when and how did she meet your father?'

'I think he was living alone at the time. His parents had died and he took her in. She was very ill and he looked after her, I think, but when she got better the wife of the man he worked for' – for a moment her own memories of the Dunsmore family threatened to overwhelm her, but she went on bravely – 'didn't approve of them living in the same house and not being married. She went to work at the big house for a while until' – an impish note came into her tone – 'Dad "took her on" and married her.'

Her grandmother did not respond to her humour. Instead she looked straight into Eveleen's eyes and said, 'Your father must have been an extraordinary man to do that.'

'He was,' Eveleen said simply. 'He was kind and gentle and – and *good*.' She met her grandmother's gaze steadily and said, 'He was what *I* would call a true Christian.'

Now Bridget did smile and said softly, 'Aye, I know what you mean, lass.'

After another pause, Bridget asked gently, 'If it doesn't hurt too much to talk about it, tell me about your life, about your father and what happened to him.'

So, sitting in the tranquillity of that first Sunday afternoon in Flawford, in the tiny parlour of a stockinger's cottage, Eveleen told her grandmother about her family's life in the farmhouse on the Dunsmores' estate.

'He was gathman—'

'A what?'

'He was responsible for all the livestock, even the herd

of milkers and the beasts kept for beef. Both Jimmy and I worked on the farm, me in the dairy mostly, but I'd have to help out wherever there was work to do. Sometimes, in the middle of the night, I'd have to help Dad deliver a calf. Oh I loved that,' Eveleen's eyes shone as she relived her former life. 'Snug and warm in the cowhouse, even on the darkest, coldest night with the wind whistling through the rafters. Just me and Dad helping a new life into the world. And then at harvest-time, all the workers on the estate had to help get the crops in. That was fun too when our dinners would be brought out to the fields and we'd sit in the shade under the trees . . .'

On and on she talked but not once did she mention Stephen Dunsmore. Her memories of him were locked firmly away. The happy times when she had truly believed he loved her were buried deep, so deep that they could not surface above the final hurt and insult he had inflicted upon her.

'You make it sound an idyllic life,' Bridget said.

Eveleen shrugged. 'It was hard work for all of us and we weren't well off. But we were never hungry or without boots on our feet.' Softly, she added, 'Mam misses it dreadfully. All she wants is to go back and I've promised her that, one day, I'll take her home. One day we'll go back to Lincolnshire where she was happy.'

'Aye, aye, I can understand that too,' Bridget said, a note of sadness in her tone. 'But you must realize, Eveleen, she will never be able to recapture her former happiness.'

'Why?' Eveleen asked defensively. 'Do you think I can't, or won't, keep my promise to her?'

Bridget leaned forward and said seriously, 'I think you'll do everything you possibly can to keep your promise, even to the extent of sacrificing your own happiness.

What I mean is that she can never know that same happiness, because *he* won't be there. Even you can't bring back the dead, lass, and her Walter won't be there, now will he?'

'No,' Eveleen whispered. 'But I have to try, Gran. I have to try. It's the only thing that will keep her going.'

Before she left her grandmother's cottage, Bridget asked, 'Has your mother taught you how to make bobbin lace then?'

Eveleen shook her head.

'Right then,' the old woman said firmly. 'Every Sunday afternoon after Chapel, you come here to see me and I'll teach you. I may not be able to see well enough to do it myself any more, but I can still teach you. I've already taught Rebecca and I'd like to think that both my granddaughters were carrying on the family tradition.' She wagged her forefinger playfully at Eveleen. 'But not a word to your uncle, mind. He's very strict about no work being done on the Sabbath and we wouldn't want to upset him, now would we?'

Although a smile twitched at the corner of her mouth, Eveleen managed to say seriously, 'Oh no, Gran, we wouldn't.'

Twenty-One

It was on a Sunday afternoon, a few weeks after their arrival in Flawford, that Eveleen was obliged to change her opinion of her uncle just a little. The impromptu cricket match had already shown her, very briefly, another side to the stern, dour man who forced his own rigid principles and beliefs on all his family and even on all those who worked with him.

She arrived outside her grandmother's cottage as usual and was about to enter, had even lifted her hand to push open the door that was already ajar, when she heard voices from inside. The shrill voice of her grandmother and her uncle's deep rumbling tones. She was about to move away again to return later but then the sound of her own name being spoken caught her attention and held her there. She knew it was wrong, knew she should have gone away, but the temptation to eavesdrop was too strong.

'I'm not one given to handing out praise,' Harry was saying.

'Don't we know it.'

He went on, ignoring Bridget's sarcasm: 'Eveleen has mastered the Griswold very well. Between the three of them, they've more than doubled what Rebecca could manage on her own. And she's a neat worker with her needle at seaming.'

'Earning their keep, are they?'

'Ah well now, I wouldn't go as far as that,' Harry said

cautiously. 'But Eveleen's a worker, I'll say that for her. She carries on long after the others of an evening. I've watched her. She examines her own work with a critical eye and tries to improve all the time.'

Bridget gave her cackling laugh. 'Well, if she's a worker, then she might even earn your approval, Harry Singleton. Eventually.' Harry gave a grunt and Bridget went on. 'What about the lad? How's he shaping up?'

Now Harry had not even the faintest praise for his nephew. 'He's less than useless. He'll find any excuse to leave his frame, and when he is sitting at it his work is not fit to sell.'

'Oh dear,' Bridget said, but Eveleen could still hear the sarcastic amusement in her grandmother's tone. Then, more seriously, Bridget urged, 'He's not the stuff the girl's made of, I grant you. They might be alike in looks, but that's where the likeness ends. They're totally different in character. But those youngsters've been through a lot just recently. Give the lad a bit of time, Harry.'

He gave another grunt of disapproval. 'I'll give him a bit longer. He's operating an old frame that's not needed for anything else at the moment, but he's heading for trouble, you mark my words. Eveleen tries her best to keep him in line, but she's not going to manage it for much longer.'

'It's a great pity,' Bridget mused, 'that Eveleen wasn't born the boy. She's strong and determined to do the best for her mother and brother. But whether she'll get any thanks for it is another matter. Strikes me . . .' The old lady was musing now and her voice dropped a little so that Eveleen could scarcely hear. 'Mary's soft with the lad, but too hard on the girl. Now, I wonder why?'

After a moment's pause, while Eveleen stood on her

toes ready to flee at the sound of her uncle preparing to leave, she heard him speak again. 'You're right, Mother. Eveleen's twice the character of the lad. She'd've made a fine framework knitter.'

'And,' Bridget put in slyly, 'you'd've had someone to carry on the family business then, wouldn't you?'

'Maybe. Aye, maybe so.' There was the scrape of a wooden chair on the brick floor and Eveleen moved away but not before she had heard her uncle's final words. 'And don't think I don't know about your Sunday afternoons teaching the lass your bobbin lace. But this time I'll turn a blind eye. At least it's keeping the Devil from finding work for her idle hands. She's better here with you than consorting with the village lads on a Sunday afternoon like her brother.'

Bridget's shrill laugh followed Eveleen as she scurried away down the path. 'Oho, you can turn a blind eye, Harry Singleton, when it suits you. When you can see a few more shillings being earned . . .'

As Eveleen hurried away towards the coal store on the pretext of collecting coal for her grandmother's fire, she could not help feeling the warm glow of her uncle's approval, even though she knew he would never say it to her face.

Perhaps, after all, things weren't going to be so bad for them here. If only, she thought, I can make Jimmy toe the line.

'Ugh, what's this? It's like eating a jellyfish.'

Jimmy prodded the thick white fleshy substance on his plate, while Eveleen stifled her laughter and kept her own eyes downcast. She knew what Jimmy meant. On their only trip to the seaside years earlier – a Sunday school outing from Bernby to the east coast – they had found a jellyfish on the beach and prodded it with a stick. Digging her fork into whatever it was on her plate, Eveleen thought, felt much the same.

'It's tripe and onions,' Rebecca said in a small voice. 'If you don't like it, Jimmy, I can get you something else.'

'You'll do no such thing, Rebecca. Sit down and eat your tea,' Harry boomed. 'Jimmy will eat what's given him or he'll go without.'

Jimmy pushed his plate away and muttered, 'Then I'll go without.'

'They're not used to it, Harry,' Mary put in tentatively, then turning to Jimmy, pleaded, 'Please, love, just try a little more.'

But Jimmy was already standing up. 'Sorry. I'm off out.' He glanced round the table and grinned. 'I'll go and see Jane.' Jane lived near the village green with her parents. Her father and brother were both framework knitters in Harry's workshops.

Jimmy pushed his chair under the table and moved to the door. Taking down his scarf from the peg behind the door he turned back and, as a parting shot, he added, 'Her mam makes a lovely stew.'

Eveleen risked a glance at her uncle's face. It was purple with rage. Instead of shouting after Jimmy, he seemed bereft of speech. Mary was nervous, her knife and fork trembling in her grasp. But it was the expression on Rebecca's face that shocked Eveleen the most.

Her dark eyes were huge in her pale face and she was staring at the closed door through which Jimmy had just left. She looked hurt and, yes, Eveleen thought, rejected.

Jimmy had done far more than insult the meal she had prepared. He had wounded the girl herself.

The rest of the meal continued in a stony silence, but Rebecca ate nothing.

The tension between uncle and nephew grew worse over the days that followed.

'You'll serve that up to him, Rebecca, each and every meal until he does eat it,' Harry boomed after Jimmy had left, his bushy eyebrows almost meeting above the bridge of his nose as he frowned. 'Do you hear me?'

Rebecca, pale and tearful, said, 'Yes, Father.'

Eveleen said nothing, but she knew her brother. There was going to be trouble.

The horrified look on Jimmy's face when the tripe and onions were placed before him the following morning at breakfast would have made Eveleen laugh if the atmosphere in the room had not been so fraught. Mary glanced from Jimmy to Harry and back again. With trembling fingers, she touched Jimmy's hand.

'Please eat it, love. You'll get used to the taste.'

Jimmy stood up, pushing back his chair in such a swift movement that it toppled backwards and crashed to the floor. 'I won't. It's horrible. I'd sooner starve.'

'Then as far as I'm concerned,' Harry boomed, 'you can.'

The two men glared at each other, while the women looked on helplessly.

Jimmy turned and left the house, slamming the door behind him. Mary began to wail. 'Eveleen, let's go home.'

Eveleen put down her spoon and got up from the

table. She left the house, but more quietly than her brother, and went in search of him.

He was leaning moodily against the pump and, as she neared him, he repeated his mother's plea, 'Let's get out of here, Evie. Let's go back home.'

Eveleen stood with her hands on her hips. 'Look, Jimmy,' she said firmly. 'It's high time you started acting like a man instead of a boy. Start taking a bit of responsibility, for Heaven's sake. You're the man of the family. Why do you leave it all to me?'

'Because you're so much better at it than me, Evie.'

'You mean I'm the bossy one.'

'No, no, I don't mean that. I'm being serious. You're the only one who can look after Mam. I can't.'

'But you're her blue-eyed boy. You can't do any wrong in her eyes. We both know what's going to happen now, don't we? With this tripe and onion nonsense.'

He glanced at her questioningly.

'You're going to stick it out and so's Uncle Harry. Neither of you is going to give way. That meal is going to be served up to you until there's green mould growing on it. And then what's going to happen?'

Jimmy grinned. 'I'll die of food poisoning and all the girls will weep at my funeral.'

'No. Mam is going to be caught in the middle and will be smuggling food to you. Rebecca, too, I shouldn't wonder.'

Jimmy's grin widened. 'She's all right, is Rebecca.' Then he appeared to be calculating. 'How long do you reckon it'll keep?'

Eveleen shrugged. 'A day maybe.'

'Right then. I'll stick it out today and I'll eat it tomorrow morning. I'll make my point and then I'll let the old bugger think he's won.'

'It's not quite the way I meant, but I suppose it'll do.'

'It'll have to. 'Cos it's all you're getting.'

The cricket season was over, but that did not stop the young men and boys employed in Harry's workshops from practising in the yard on fine evenings until the deepening dusk made seeing the ball quite impossible. Then, much to Eveleen's dismay, she would hear them clattering out of the yard, not to go home, but to the pub the Brown Cow, at the end of Chapel Row. If they could no longer play cricket, then they could talk about it, and where better than over a pint?

'You wouldn't think they'd have a pub at the end of the street where there's a chapel,' Eveleen said, ranting herself for once.

'It was probably there first,' Mary put in. 'Besides, there are two chapels further along the road on the opposite side. Don't you worry about Jimmy. He'll not go into a pub. And he'll be home by ten, just like he's always been.'

Eveleen wondered if her mother was really as blinkered about her son as she made out. But Mary was sitting placidly by the fire, her bobbin lace on her knee, her head bent over her work. Eveleen felt a lump in her throat. At any moment Mary might glance up and expect to see Walter sitting on the opposite side of the hearth. The tranquillity would be spoilt. But Mary did not look up. Eveleen wondered if her mother were deliberately inhabiting an imaginary world of her own, pretending that she was back home beside her own fireside with her husband. Anxious not to break the spell, if it gave her mother comfort, Eveleen tiptoed out of the house and across the road to the chapel where she had promised to help her cousin with the Wednesday night evening classes for the Sunday school children.

Later that night when they all went up the stairs to their rooms, Jimmy was still not home.

'Don't lock the door, Harry. He'll be home any minute,' Mary pleaded, but Harry, frowning and silent, made a great performance of turning the heavy key in the door. For once, Eveleen was in sympathy with her uncle. If Jimmy couldn't come home at a decent hour, she thought, then he can sleep in the pigsties.

It was half past one in the morning when she heard the gate into the yard bang and two drunken voices be raised in song and then collapse into silly giggling.

'Oh no,' she breathed and quietly slipped out of bed without disturbing Mary. She descended to Rebecca's room, opening the door as quietly as she could, but the click of the latch woke the girl.

'What is it? What's the matter?' Rebecca's fearful voice came out of the darkness.

'It's Jimmy. He's shouting and carrying on outside. If he wakes your dad—'

She didn't need to say more, for already Rebecca was throwing back the covers and getting out of bed. 'Oh dear. I'd better come down. I know where Father puts the key. I'll let him in.'

'You stay there. You'll only be in trouble.'

'I don't mind. Not – not if it's for Jimmy.'

There was silence between them as Eveleen strained through the darkness to see Rebecca's face. She would have said more, but at that moment there was such a banging and rattling on the door that both girls scuttled down the stairs as fast as they could.

'Quick, Rebecca, you find the key while I light a candle. He'll wake everyone in the row at this rate.'

Rebecca was shivering with cold and fright but laughing nervously at the same time. She could hardly get the key into the lock. 'Thank goodness Father's a heavy sleeper.'

'Even he won't sleep through this if it goes on,' Eveleen muttered. 'Hurry up, do.'

At last the key turned and Rebecca pulled open the door. Jimmy fell against her, almost knocking her over.

'Oh there you are, pretty Rebecca. See Andrew, Rebecca's come to let me in. Andrew?' He raised his voice, but, sensibly, Andrew had gone into his own house next door.

'Shush,' Eveleen hissed and grabbed hold of Jimmy by the scruff of his jacket. 'Come in and just keep the noise down.'

Jimmy swayed and put his finger to his lips, imitating Eveleen. 'Sh-shush. Quiet as little mi – hic – mice. Sh-shush.'

Between them, the two girls hauled Jimmy into Harry's chair.

'You go back to bed, Rebecca. I'll see to him.'

'No, no, you go. If your mother wakes up and finds neither of you there, she'll likely start a commotion that will wake Father.'

'That's true, but—'

'Go on,' Rebecca urged. 'I'll stay with him. No one will miss me and I'm always up first anyway.'

Eveleen glanced doubtfully at the frail girl and then at her brother, his head lolling to one side, a glazed look in his eyes and a stupid grin on his face. 'Well, if you're sure . . .'

'Of course I am. Go on, before you're missed.'

Reluctantly Eveleen saw the wisdom of the girl's suggestion and went back upstairs to bed. Though she slept fitfully, she did not hear Jimmy come to his bed under the eaves nor Rebecca return to her room.

When Eveleen came down the next morning, there was no sign of Jimmy. Rebecca was bustling between pantry, scullery and kitchen preparing breakfast.

'Where is he?' Eveleen asked. 'I'll knock their heads together, him and Andrew, when I catch up with them.'

Rebecca smiled, a pink tinge to her cheeks. 'He's all right. He – he slept it off on the hearthrug. He's outside having a wash under the pump.' Her smile widened. 'Waking himself up.'

Eveleen glanced out of the window and saw Jimmy with his head under the spout, while a green-faced Andrew Burns pumped the icy-cold water.

'Serves 'em both right,' she muttered and then turned to ask, 'What about you? Did you manage to get some sleep?'

Rebecca, the pink tinge in her face deepening, avoided meeting Eveleen's frank gaze. 'Me?' she said airily. 'Oh don't worry about me. I'm fine.'

Twenty-Two

Eveleen was chafing at what she thought of as idleness.

After a few weeks of living in Flawford, she had learnt to make socks on the Griswold machine in the house. She helped Rebecca with the seaming of the garments knitted in the workshops and, of course, shared all the household chores. And her grandmother had told her that already she had surpassed her own mother's skill in making bobbin lace.

'Mary never got her work as neat and even as that,' Bridget confided. 'But don't you let on.'

Daily now, Eveleen listened to their uncle ranting that Jimmy was hopeless and that he was taking up a knitting frame that could be put to better use. Jimmy had passed his seventeenth birthday and she, her eighteenth, yet her brother seemed to have gained nothing in the way of common sense or a willingness to apply himself.

'I'll run away to sea if you keep on at me, Evie,' he said morosely when she tried to reason with him.

'Look, Jimmy, we're lucky that Mam's family took us in. And even luckier that Uncle Harry is prepared to teach you a trade. And a good trade at that.'

'Huh. I don't see him making a fortune even for all the hours he works. And the other fellers who work here take home a pittance.'

'And you think you'll make your fortune at sea, do

you?' she answered sharply. 'What are you going to be? A pirate?'

Jimmy grinned. 'Now, there's an idea.'

She had to laugh in spite of her exasperation with him. 'Oh you!' She punched his shoulder playfully, then asked seriously, 'You wouldn't really run away and leave us, would you? We ought to stick together. At least until we can go back home.'

'And how do you think we're going to do that when we only make a few miserable pence a week between us?'

'You've got to try harder, Jimmy. Uncle's fast losing patience with you.'

'Well, if you think you can do any better on one of those frames, why don't you have a go. It's hard work, let me tell you—'

'Me?' Eveleen said and then again, suddenly thoughtful, she repeated, 'Me?' As Jimmy's derisory challenge took root, she murmured, 'Why not me?'

Now Jimmy was scoffing. 'He'd never let you. He won't have women working in there, I can tell you. Andrew told me.'

But Jimmy had not overheard the conversation between their uncle and grandmother. There was a determined glint in Eveleen's eyes as she said, 'We'll see about that.'

'Huh,' Jimmy said again, shoving his hands deep into his pockets and turning away, 'Pigs might fly.'

Over the following few days, Eveleen gave a lot of thought to the idea. She made several excuses to visit the workshops and lingered as long as she dared to watch the men at work. She was careful not to catch her uncle's eye, for he would certainly have gestured that she should be about her own work. No doubt he would have misconstrued her reasons for being there, thinking that she was flirting with the young lads. She kept her distance from Andrew Burns, for he never lost an opportunity to talk to her and would wink cheekily at her.

She was confident that she could learn how to operate a frame and the only thing that worried her was the physical strength that was obviously required. But she had worked on a farm, she reminded herself. She had lifted churns of milk and sacks of corn. She had stood on the top of a stack at threshing time and wielded forkful after forkful of straw. Her muscles flexed involuntarily at the memory.

Eveleen left the workshop and walked back down the brick path towards the cottages, returning to her own work. On Sunday, she decided, she would talk to her grandmother. Bridget and she had drawn even closer and she knew the old woman would be her ally.

If anyone could help her persuade Harry to give her a trial at one of the frames, then it was her grandmother.

'Gran,' Eveleen began the following Sunday, as she sat working the pillow lace under her Bridget's guidance. 'Do women ever operate the frames?'

The question obviously startled the old lady.

Eveleen paused in twisting the bobbins one over the other to form the spidery web of lace and repeated her question.

'I don't know about anywhere else, but they never have here.' Bridget's shrunken mouth widened into a smile. 'Your uncle would think it a distraction to the fellers to have a woman working alongside them.' She put her head on one side and eyed Eveleen thoughtfully.

As shrewd as ever she said bluntly, 'Are you thinking of taking Jimmy's place?'

Eveleen met her grandmother's gaze squarely. 'I'd like Uncle to teach me how to operate a frame.' Then she added deviously, 'Perhaps with me there, Jimmy would work harder. He'd not like to be outshone by his sister.'

Bridget laughed. 'You crafty little monkey.' Then, thinking aloud, she murmured, 'Well, your uncle doesn't like to have frames standing idle, and by what he said yesterday there'll be another from tomorrow morning. One of the older fellers was taken ill on Friday.' She shook her head and sighed. 'Poor old Alfie. He worked for your grandfather ever since he started this place.' The old lady's mind was wandering off into her own memories but far from being irritated, Eveleen was fascinated.

'When we first got married we came to live here in an old tumbledown cottage.' She pointed down to the ground. 'That stood where these houses are now. Your granddad started with just one frame at home and I worked the stocking-machine and made pillow lace. We worked from dawn to dusk and then some. He had this dream, you see, that he'd build workshops, run his own little factory. He bought this place because it had a good-sized garden to it and he could see the possibilities. Then he started to build the workshops, brick by brick with his own hands. It took years.'

She fell silent and gazed out of the window as if her old eyes, which could not see clearly around her now, could see perfectly back into the past.

'If Uncle would only teach me,' Eveleen said, trying to keep her growing excitement in check, 'there might be other people who would employ me.'

Bridget was dragged back to the present by Eveleen's remark.

'There might be,' she said guardedly, not sounding too hopeful. 'But I'm not sure any of them would employ a woman, let alone a young girl.'

Eveleen's smile broadened and her eyes twinkled as she said, 'We'll see.'

'No, no, it's impossible.' Harry shook his head. 'It's unheard of.'

'Why, Uncle Harry?' Eveleen said evenly, keeping her tone respectful and deferential.

'Well, because it is.' She could sense he was wavering. Whatever her uncle was, strict and uncompromising, he was also honest and truthful.

'But is there any good reason why I shouldn't learn, Uncle Harry? Other than that it isn't usual?'

Now he looked her up and down, appraising her.

'I worked on a farm, Uncle,' she reminded him gently. 'I'm used to hard work. Physical hard work. I'm not afraid of it. Oh, I'm not saying I could operate a frame at once. I can see how difficult it is—'

'So that's why you've been hanging around the workshops is it? I thought you were eyeing young Burns.'

'You needn't be afraid of anything like that with me, Uncle Harry.'

The man put his head on one side and regarded her thoughtfully. 'You're a pretty young lass and one day—'

Eveleen shook her head firmly. 'No, Uncle. I'm not interested.' There was no need to tell him of the unhappy experience that had destroyed her trust in men. Instead, she used the weapon that she knew would be most effective with this forbidding man. 'I only want to work and work hard. You and Grandmother have been very kind to us, taking us in, especially after what happened years ago. I know that. But we don't want to be beholden to you for ever. I have to get this family back on its feet.'

Harry nodded. 'Well, lass, you've got spirit, I'll give you that. Pity your brother isn't out of the same mould.' His expression lightened and Harry came as near to smiling as he ever would. 'You know your grandmother has been pleading your cause?'

Eveleen smiled up at him. 'I hoped she might. And she did say' – Eveleen's heart was in her mouth as she played her final card – 'that there's a frame not working now, because of Alfie.'

The frown was back and yet Eveleen could see the calculating look in his eyes. Anything – even this slip of a lass – was better than having a frame standing idle. 'Aye. It's his frame, mind you. I'd have to ask him. In fact, I'd have to ask the other fellers. Can't risk having a riot on my hands.'

Eveleen waited in a fever of excitement, pressing her lips together to stop more words tumbling out.

'Tell you what. After work at night, I'll give you a trial. If you shape up, lass, then we'll see. Can't promise more than that.'

'No, Uncle, you can't. But I won't let you down. I promise you.'

'You'd better not, lass.'

'Now, I'll show you first and then you can have a go. We'll only do one strip although this is a wide frame and would usually produce three strips at once.'

Harry hoisted himself on to the leather straps that formed the seat in front of the frame. First he pointed out all the different names of the parts: needles, jacks, sinkers, presser bar and treadles.

'You've got this metal frame and inside this you've got these plates. These are called the sinkers and they push the yarn around the needles to create loops. The needles are spring-bearded needles.'

He picked up a loose needle from a box of parts at the side of the machine and held it out towards Eveleen. 'The pointed end is bent into a hook which is closed by the presser bar.'

'Do the needles move in and out like the Griswold's move down and up?' she asked.

'No, no. On the Griswold they're latch needles but on this machine the needles don't move at all. Now, watch carefully, Eveleen. It's all a case of operating your feet and hands in a series of movements. At the base, look' – he pointed down to his feet – 'there are three pieces of wood called treadles. The two outer treadles are attached to that large wheel.'

Eveleen bent and peered through the workings to see a large, solid wooden wheel at the back of the frame. Harry went on explaining while Eveleen tried to take it all in, her quick mind racing to keep pace with his demonstration.

'And also attached to that wheel by these cords is the yarn carrier taking yarn from the bobbins at the top. Now, this treadle in the middle is attached to this bar called the presser bar and that's brought down to close the needles. So, Eveleen, my hands work these handles on either side of the machine with my thumbs on these two metal plates. My left foot is always on this sinking pedal and my right moves between the two treadles and the presser bar in the middle.'

Eveleen nodded, her eyes bright with excitement as Harry began to operate the machine. 'First, I bring the sinker bar forward . . .'

Fascinated, Eveleen watched the various parts of the machine begin to move under Harry's experienced hands and feet. There was a sudden noise as the yarn fled across the needles and the jack sinkers fell between the needles creating a loop across every two needles.

'You can't make a loop round every needle at once,' Harry explained. 'The yarn would snap. So, now we bring down a second series of sinkers by pressing on these thumb plates and these form a loop over every needle. See?'

'Yes, yes, I see,' Eveleen could hardly contain her eagerness and her fingers itched to try for herself. 'The first set of sinkers went up a bit,' she said.

Harry glanced over his shoulder. His beard hid his mouth but there was a smile in his eyes. 'That's right.' There was a hint of pleasure in his tone at her quick understanding. 'That's so that all the loops are equal. Now.' Harry pulled the carriage forwards and the new loops were pushed into the hooks. The carriage was lifted, the presser bar brought down to close the hooks and then the carriage was pulled forward again to bring the old loops over the closed hooks. A new row of knitting was formed.

'And then we start again,' Harry said as he carried on working several rows, but at a much slower rate than the knitters normally worked. 'The best knitters can work forty-two rows a minute,' he told her.

At last he stopped and swung his legs over the seat. 'Right, now you have a go.'

Her palms were clammy as she wriggled on to the seat.

'If you can't reach the pedals, we'll have to get you your own seat made.' He gave a short bark of laughter. 'That's if you shape up, lass.'

Licking her lips, Eveleen put her hands and feet where she had seen her uncle place his on the machine.

'Take it steady and I'll tell you what to do.'

She followed his instructions carefully and when the first row of loops fell to form a new row, she felt a thrill of achievement.

'And again,' Harry said, and repeated his instructions.

Again and again, row upon row, until cramp seized the back of her calves and her thumbs ached from pressing on the metal plates, but Eveleen kept on.

There were no words of praise from Harry, but there was no criticism either. And that, for Harry Singleton, was praise enough.

Gradually, he stopped repeating every single move, just giving a reminder now and again, until finally he fell silent and watched her steady, rhythmic flow of movements and the rows of neat, perfect knitting.

Eveleen went on until the yarn ran out on the bobbin. Then she turned to the man still standing at her side. He gave a brief nod and said, 'Tomorrow night I'll show you how to take off the finished strip and thread it all up from scratch. Leave it for tonight. No one will touch this machine tomorrow. Come along, now, Rebecca will have our supper ready.'

Eveleen swung herself off the seat. She staggered a little as she stood up and found her legs were trembling. Her neck and shoulders burned with pain and, as she stumbled after her uncle, she rubbed her aching thumbs and wrists.

But her physical discomfort was nothing to her for she was filled with exhilaration and hope.

Harry paused at the top of the stairs. 'You've got the hang of it now and all you need is practice. Come up here every night and in a week I'll see how you're shaping. You can use that old yarn there.' He pointed to a basket of hanks lying in the corner. 'It's below standard, but it'll do for you to practise on.'

'Thanks, Uncle Harry,' Eveleen said, sounding a little breathless after the exertion it had taken to operate the heavy machine.

He nodded and, as he turned away and clumped down the stairs ahead of her, she heard him mutter again, 'Pity the lad's not like you.'

Twenty-Three

'What did they say, Uncle Harry?'

Eveleen had not been able to keep still but had paced up and down outside the row of cottages. It was a week since Eveleen had sat in front of the frame for the first time and her uncle was asking the workers now, this very minute, if they had any objection to his niece working alongside them. Eveleen felt as if her future – the whole future of her family – depended upon their answer. She pictured each of the men in turn, trying to guess whether they would be for her or against her. The younger ones, Andrew Burns among them, would be on her side. They would laugh and tease her, she knew, but she couldn't for one moment imagine them objecting. It was the older workers who worried her. They didn't like change. They didn't like going against tradition. A woman's place was in the home, not in the workplace. A young lass like Eveleen should be occupied within the home or sent into service. That was their thinking, she knew.

As she paced, she wrapped her arms around her, the pit of her stomach churning with nerves. She wished she dared to creep up the stairs and listen to what was happening, but she did not want to risk being caught eavesdropping.

As she reached the end house and turned to walk back again, she heard a sharp tap on the window and turned to see her grandmother beckoning her inside. She opened the door and stepped into the warm living room.

'For Heaven's sake, child, stop pacing up and down like a caged lion,' the old lady grumbled, easing herself back into her chair beside the fire. 'You're getting me all of a dither just watching you.'

'But, Gran, it's so important to me. I've tried so hard.'

'I know you have. Harry's been telling me.'

'He has?' Eveleen still could not sit down, but moved restlessly about the room.

'Oh aye. Singing your praises, he was.'

'He was? Really?'

'Yes, really. And that's rare. Harry's not one to hand out praise, not even when it's due, I can tell you.'

Eveleen bit her lip to stop herself blurting out what she had overheard previously. She sat down opposite Bridget and leaned forward. 'What did he say? Tell me.'

'Said you'd surprised him by the way you'd stuck at it. He knows how tough it is and he didn't think you'd even manage to operate the machine, but you're stronger than you look, he says. And you've got a will of iron.' Bridget laughed. 'He said it was a pity the boy isn't the same as you.'

Eveleen pulled a wry face but said nothing even though, silently, she was forced to agree. She didn't want to be disloyal to her brother but Jimmy was giving her increasing cause for concern. He'd taken to going out every spare moment, hanging about with the other village lads, especially Andrew Burns. Eveleen wasn't sure that Andrew was a very good influence on Jimmy. But then she sighed. She had no illusions about her brother at all and if she were to be absolutely honest, she had to admit that Jimmy was more than likely the bad influence on Andrew.

At that moment the door opened and Harry came in,

his huge frame filling the small room. Eveleen, her gaze on his face, rose slowly to her feet, her heart thudding painfully.

She could tell nothing from his expression. It was as stern and unreadable as ever.

'Well?' Bridget said sharply. 'Don't keep this poor lass in suspense any longer.'

Harry nodded. 'They've agreed to give you a try. Mind you, some of 'em weren't keen.'

Eveleen gave a cry of delight and flung herself against Harry, throwing her arms about him. 'Oh thank you, thank you, Uncle Harry.'

Harry pushed her away. 'Now, now, there's no need for such unseemly behaviour. If you're going to act like that . . .'

At once, Eveleen stood back. 'I'm sorry, Uncle. It was – it was just that I'm so relieved, so thrilled.'

He nodded and said gruffly, 'Well, all right, then. But remember, you must keep yourself to yourself in the workshops. I don't want any goings-on with those lads. Especially that Andrew Burns. He'll chase anything in skirts. Why, he's even dared to cast his eyes at Rebecca.'

Eveleen didn't know whether to laugh or cry. Poor Rebecca, she thought, not allowed even to speak to boys. Kept at home as a drudge, her only outing on Sundays to the chapel just across the road. Though she must respect her uncle's wishes, at least for the time being, there was no way Eveleen was going to allow herself to be treated in the same way.

She could guess who the objectors in the workshops had been without them being named and her mouth tightened with determination. I'll show them, she thought. I'll just show them. But she did not voice this, knowing that her uncle would not take kindly to such bravado. Instead, with pretended meekness, she said once more, 'I won't let you down, Uncle.'

'Well, lass, time will tell,' was all he said this time. Eveleen's heart sank. She could see in his eyes that he was still doubtful about her.

As he left the cottage and she made to follow him, Bridget hissed, 'You'll show 'em, lass. You'll show 'em.'

Heartened, she bent and kissed the old lady's cheek. 'Oh, go on with you,' Bridget flapped her away but not before Eveleen had seen the pink tinge of pleasure that suffused the wrinkled cheeks.

Andrew Burns was there to greet her early the following morning when Eveleen presented herself for her first day. Wearing her plainest, most shapeless dress and with her wayward hair tied firmly back beneath a headscarf, Eveleen considered she was hardly likely to inflame the senses of even the most flirtatious male in the workshops.

But there he was, waiting for her at the bottom of the steps, grinning widely. 'I'll look after you, Eveleen,' he said, bounding up the stairs ahead of her. 'Any trouble and you just let me know about it.'

'Thank you, Andrew, but—'

Before she could say any more, he stopped suddenly, turned and bent down towards her to whisper, 'I've made you your own seat. Come on, I'll show you. It's just for you and you take it with you wherever you go.'

Eveleen stared at him blankly. 'How do you mean?'

Patiently, he explained. 'You know the seats made with leather straps stretched across pieces of wood?'

She nodded.

'Well, everybody has their own, made to measure, if you like, and if he moves frames, he takes his seat with him so that it's just the right size and shape for 'im to be comfortable. You need to be comfortable, Eveleen, if you're going to sit all day long at a frame.'

Now she understood. She had only operated the machine for a few hours each evening when all the men had gone home. Even then, she had found her arms and legs aching when she stumbled down the stairs.

'Only,' Andrew was saying, 'yer've got to help me in return.'

Standing on the step below him, Eveleen gaped up at him. 'Me help you? How?'

'You can help me to get to see Rebecca wi'out her dad knowing.'

'Rebecca!'

'Shh.' He glanced fearfully up the stairs, but already the clatter of machinery was drowning their conversation from eavesdroppers. 'Her dad mustn't know. If he finds out, he'll sack me.' He grinned. 'Or worse.'

Eveleen shook her head, 'Oh, Andrew, I'm sorry. I'd love to help you, but I can't. My uncle's been very good to me – to all my family. And now he's giving me this chance, I can't do anything behind his back.'

The young man's face fell but then he shrugged philosophically. 'Oh well then. But you won't tell 'im, will you? You won't give us away?'

Eveleen shook her head. 'No, I won't do that. But I'd rather not know anything about it.'

'Fair enough.' He started back up the stairs, but then hesitated once more. 'There is something you could do for me though.'

'What?'

'Keep that brother of yours away from Rebecca. She's mine.' Then he turned and hurried up the rest of the stairs, leaving Eveleen staring after him in astonishment.

Jimmy interested in Rebecca? Oh no, surely not. He was only a boy.

No, he wasn't, Eveleen reminded herself. He was seventeen now and he'd been working since the age of twelve.

Already her little brother would think himself very much a man.

Eveleen's first day in the workshop did not go well.

She was nervous of the other men's reactions towards her and consequently overanxious. And now she had another worry on her mind. A worry put there that very morning by Andrew. She would have to watch Jimmy and Rebecca for herself. She could not allow a liaison between them. Her uncle would be appalled and she didn't think even her grandmother would condone it.

The work she produced that day was a mess with uneven stitches and broken threads that she would have to darn by hand.

Harry stood over her. 'You'll have to do better than that. And you've a needle broken there. It's missing a stitch.' He pointed to the ladder-like line of missed stitches. 'Didn't you notice?'

Mortified, Eveleen shook her head.

Harry gave a grunt and turned away, sounding every bit as if he now thought he'd made a grave mistake in giving her a trial.

Andrew was at her side. Close to her ear, he whispered, 'Don't worry. Stay behind tonight and I'll show you how to put a new needle in. We have to do minor repairs to the frames ourselves.' He jerked his thumb over his shoulder. 'He won't employ a framesmith unless it's something really serious.' He winked and grinned. 'That'd cost too much for that old skinflint.'

When she left the workshop that night every muscle in her body seemed to be aching. It was the longest period of time she had worked at the machine. As she stepped into the cottage, more trouble awaited her. Mary had lapsed into one of her moods of depression and was sitting by the fire, a shawl drawn around her shoulders, while Rebecca scurried between the kitchen and the parlour, hurriedly laying the table. It was a job that Mary normally did.

Eveleen sighed and closed her eyes, thinking to herself, This is all I need. Then she went to lay her hand on her mother's shoulder and shake it gently. 'Come on, Mam, it's suppertime.'

Mary shook her head. 'I don't want any. I'm not hungry.' She raised a tearful face, reached up and clung to Eveleen's hand. 'I want to go home, Eveleen. Take me home. I hate it here.'

'Mam, hush . . .' Eveleen began, but too late, Harry had heard his sister's words as he came in from the scullery after washing his hands.

'If that's how you feel, Mary, then you'd better leave. We've put ourselves out for you and that's how you repay us. The ingratitude, Mary. And don't forget . . .' He wagged his forefinger at her. 'Don't forget, we could be letting the room you and your children are occupying to proper rent-paying lodgers. And they'd be better workers than either your son,' and he added with pointed emphasis to remind Eveleen that she had not fared well that day, 'or your daughter.'

'She doesn't mean it, Uncle Harry,' Eveleen said

swiftly. 'We are grateful to you. You know we are. But she's missing Dad.'

'She's not the only one to lose someone. Don't you think I still miss my Rose every single day? But my faith carries me through.' He nodded towards Mary. 'You'd do better to pray to the good Lord for His help, Mary, than sitting there wringing your hands, wallowing in self-pity and being ungrateful to those who've taken you in.' Then he added with the bitterness that even now he could not quell, 'Even against their better judgement.'

Mary dropped her head into her hands and wailed aloud. 'Oh, you're cruel, Harry. Cruel and heartless. You were twenty years ago and you haven't changed.'

'I am what I am, Mary, and I've no intention of changing.'

Eveleen looked at her uncle, torn between sticking up for her mother against his unforgiving attitude and trying to keep the peace between them to safeguard their future. Common sense prevailed. With a supreme effort to hold her temper in check, she said, 'I'm sorry, Uncle Harry.' Then turning to her mother she said, 'Come along, Mam. If you're sure you don't want anything to eat, let me take you to bed.'

She eased her mother up and helped her climb the narrow stairs, Mary moaning and complaining every step of the way. 'I want to go home, Eveleen,' was all she would say, over and over again.

An hour later, when Eveleen wearily descended the stairs to eat her cold supper, it was to find Jimmy and Rebecca in the scullery, whispering and giggling with their heads close together, while Harry snored in his chair by the fire in the parlour.

*

The following day, Eveleen determined to put all her other worries out of her mind and concentrate on her work. If she didn't make a good showing today, then her uncle would change his mind – and quickly – about allowing her to work for him. Her future was hanging by a very tenuous thread anyway. He had only agreed to train her because he didn't like to see a machine lying idle and, at present, he could find no one better to operate it. Should a man, or even an inexperienced boy, come along, Eveleen knew she would be replaced at once.

She had to be twice as good as any man to hold on to her place at the machine.

So, as she strode down the brick path to the workshops, she was annoyed to see Andrew Burns hanging about in the doorway, watching for her.

''Morning,' she said briefly and made to pass him to climb the stairs. Andrew caught hold of her arm.

'Tell 'im to stay away from her,' he hissed. 'I know they're cousins, but he's not acting like a cousin towards her.'

Their faces only inches apart, Eveleen stared at him. 'Whatever do you mean?' she asked, trying to sound as if she couldn't begin to guess, even though she had more than an inkling now about what was going on between her brother and Rebecca.

'They were out here in the yard last night. In the dark. And he was kissing her.'

Eveleen gasped. Now her surprise was genuine. Things had gone even further than she had thought. She glanced fearfully up the stairwell, hoping no one had overheard Andrew. 'I'll speak to him,' she muttered and pulled herself free.

'You'd better.' His threat followed her as she ran up the stairs. 'Else I will.'

At least there was one good thing about it, Eveleen thought as she slid on to the leather straps forming the seat in front of the frame. It's not me that Andrew Burns is interested in.

She was unprepared for the sudden shaft of jealousy that ran through her. It wasn't that she was attracted to Andrew Burns or that she wanted him to court her. It was just the thought that her life stretched before her, empty and lonely.

But that is the way it has to be, she told herself firmly. I'm never going to let another man hurt me the way Stephen Dunsmore did. Besides, I've a promise to keep, she reminded herself.

But the thought brought her no joy and the burden of the vow she had made settled even more heavily on her young shoulders.

Twenty-Four

'Jimmy, it's got to stop.'

Jimmy scowled and looked mutinous. 'What?'

'You know very well "what". Your carryings on with Rebecca, that's what,' Eveleen muttered as they walked down the path towards the cottages at the end of the day.

'Huh, chance'd be a fine thing. If the old man's not watching us like a hawk, then Burns is making sheep's eyes at her and looking daggers at me.' He laughed. 'Good job duelling is out of fashion. Reckon I'd be called out.'

Eveleen grasped her brother by the shoulder. She was as tall as he was and now, almost as strong. 'Just you listen to me. If you upset Uncle Harry, we'll be out on our ears.'

'So? Why should I care? I'll go to sea.'

'If you don't care about yourself, then spare a thought for poor Mam. And me.'

Their faces were close together in the gathering dusk. 'Please, Jimmy,' she pleaded.

'Look, Evie, I don't want to rock the boat any more than you do. At least,' he said mysteriously, 'not yet.'

'What do you mean – not yet?' Eveleen asked sharply.

Slyly he glanced at her and then looked away. 'I don't want to stay here for ever, any more than our mam does.'

Eveleen kept her voice low so that none of the workers passing by them on the path to go home would overhear.

'So why don't you work a bit harder? The sooner we get some money together, the sooner we can go home.'

'Do you think of Bernby as home too, then?'

'Of course I do. Whatever made you think I didn't?'

He scuffed the toe of his boot on the ground. 'I didn't think you'd want to go back there. Because of . . .' He cast her a sideways glance. 'Because of *him*.'

Eveleen felt her mouth tighten. 'He's nothing to me. Not any more.'

Jimmy arched his eyebrows as if he didn't believe her for a moment, but he said no more about it. Instead, he said, 'Besides, you seem to be getting well in with the old woman. I thought you was feathering your nest, like.'

Eveleen was appalled. 'Oh, Jimmy, how can you think that of me?'

'S'what I'd do. Given half a chance.'

Her grip on his shoulder tightened. 'Is that what you're doing with little Rebecca? Trying to wheedle your way into the family by the back door? Because that's not the best way to get into her father's good books.'

''Course not,' Jimmy said defensively. 'I – I really like her. Honest, Evie.' He grinned suddenly. ''Sides, I couldn't get into his Good Book unless I grew wings and polished me halo.'

'All right then,' Eveleen said, but for once she was not laughing with him. She was still not wholly convinced of the purity of his motives. 'Because I'll tell you something, Brother dear. Whatever your reasons for chasing after Rebecca are, genuine or otherwise, Uncle Harry's not going to like them one bit.'

Through the gloom she saw his grinning white teeth. 'Mebbe not. But that doesn't bother me. Just so long as Rebecca does.'

With that he twisted himself free and, stuffing his

hands into his pockets, walked towards the house, whistling jauntily.

'Oh, Jimmy,' Eveleen murmured. 'Just what trouble are you getting us all into now?'

Eveleen decided to tackle the problem from the other angle. She decided to speak to Rebecca. Her opportunity came when Harry asked her to give Rebecca a hand with the washing one morning instead of going to the workshop.

'There are several long johns and men's vests got oil on them. And Mr Buxton will be here for them at the end of the week.'

'Who's Mr Buxton?'

'He's the bag man or bag hosier.'

'What does the bag man do exactly?'

'He gets the orders for us. He supplies the yarn and then collects the finished garments and takes them back to the warehouse in the city. And he won't be happy if they're less than perfect. Here,' she pushed a bundle into Eveleen's arms. 'These all need washing. Then they need stretching and laying out to dry in the sun.'

'Where?'

There seemed little room here. Not like at home, she thought, where there had been the yard and the fields and . . . She closed her mind against her memories.

'On those boards there.' Rebecca pointed to four or five wooden boards leaning against the wall in the washhouse. 'Line them up as many as you can along the pathway. The rest can hang over the washing line.'

As they worked together, plunging the knitted garments into the warm water, squeezing them and then laying them on the boards, stretching them into the finished shape, Eveleen said, 'I've been wanting to talk to you.'

The girl glanced up swiftly and then bent her head over the tub as if she guessed what her cousin was about to say.

Eveleen came straight to the point. 'Look, Rebecca, you can tell me to mind my own business if you like, but be careful of our Jimmy. He's – he's . . .' She bit her lip. She didn't want to be disloyal to her own flesh and blood, yet she had to be truthful. She tried to phrase it casually. 'He's only young and all young fellers want a bit of fun before they settle down. Just don't take him too serious, will you?'

Rebecca kept her face hidden as she worked the dolly peg in the rinsing water, swirling the garments round and round. As the silence between them lengthened, Eveleen went on again, feeling almost as if she were plunging herself into hot water.

'And what about Andrew? Isn't there some sort of understanding between you two? Don't let Jimmy—'

She could not finish her sentence before the girl's head shot up and she almost shouted, 'No, there isn't anything between me and Andrew Burns. He likes to think there is. But there isn't and there never will be.' She thumped the dolly peg into the water, causing it to splash even over the high sides of the tub as she added, 'Not now.'

Not now, Eveleen thought with a sinking heart. That could only mean one thing: not now that Jimmy has come on to the scene. Eveleen plunged another garment beneath the soapy water, wishing that it was her brother's head she was dunking.

*

The weeks flew by for Eveleen in a haze of weariness. She worked long hours at the frame as well as still doing her share of household chores and even took a turn at the Griswold in the winter evenings when it was too cold to continue in the workshops.

'Do you know,' Jimmy grumbled, 'there's ice on the *inside* of them long windows and sitting next to them to work is worse than living in an igloo.'

'You'll have to work a bit harder.' Eveleen didn't dish out any sympathy. Nor did she tell him that her own fingers were often blue with cold and her feet felt like blocks of solid ice in the morning. By the time all the workers arrived and the machines were clattering busily, it didn't seem so bad to her.

'Only one fire to heat the whole room.' Jimmy was determined to find fault.

'It'd be colder still out at sea.'

But he was not to be cajoled out of his gloom. 'Well, I'd rather be out there than stuck in this place. And one day, I just might be.'

Eveleen laughed. She'd heard his threats so many times before, she no longer believed them.

Christmas came and Eveleen was surprised to find that the small community celebrated in style. On Christmas Eve Harry planted a Christmas tree in one of the vegetable patches in the yard and decorated it with lighted tapers and bright, shining trinkets fastened to the branches. There were presents for everyone; shawls and scarves, socks and ties. While, quite naturally, their revels were firmly rooted in the traditions of the chapel, nevertheless, they ate heartily on Christmas Day – goose, plum pudding and fruit cake. Mellowed by good food, everyone attended the service at the chapel, including, to Eveleen's surprise, Jimmy, sitting between her and Rebecca. Even Mary, greeted at the chapel door with open arms by a red-cheeked Gracie Turner, needed no persuading to attend.

The Christmas spirit seemed to last into the New Year, but then, towards the end of January, the whole nation was cast into mourning by the death of the queen.

'There's not many folk left alive who can remember us having a king,' Bridget remarked. 'Why even I wasn't born until a year after she came to the throne and I'm as old as Methuselah's mother!' She gave a cackle of laughter and earned herself a reproving glance from a solemn-faced Harry.

'We'll close the workshops on the day of her funeral as a mark of respect,' he said.

Bridget, sharp as ever, remarked, 'According to the paper it's not going to be 'til a week on Saturday.' She eyed him speculatively. 'So you won't be losing a full day's work anyway.'

But Harry, as ever, had the last word. 'There'll be a special service in the chapel,' he said. 'And everyone will attend. Including you, Mother.'

As he left the cottage, Bridget grumbled, 'Why do I always have to open my mouth and let it say what it likes.'

Eveleen stifled her laughter. It was what she often said of herself.

Winter gave way to spring at last and cricket bats were brought out from the back of cupboards and practice at the pump in the yard began in earnest. There was great rivalry between Andrew and Jimmy as to who would be picked to play for the village team that year. But it was on the Sunday school outing when the trouble Eveleen had feared really came to a head.

When the weather improved and may blossom dappled the hedgerows, Harry announced, 'There's to be a picnic for the Sunday school children a week on Saturday.' The men and the youngsters, he decreed, would go on bicycles, the ladies and very young children would ride in horse-drawn wagons with forms from the chapel to provide seating.

'We only go just outside the village to a meadow near the brook,' he told Eveleen.

Her heart missed a beat. 'I – I don't think we'll come, Uncle,' she began and, seeing his perpetual frown deepen, rushed on. 'It might upset Mam. Going into the countryside and especially beside the brook might remind her too much of home. There was a beck that ran behind our house. That – that was where I found my father.'

'I see.' Harry pondered for a long moment before saying, slowly, 'Mary can stay at home, then, with Mother. But you and that brother of yours will come.'

'Father will find you both a bicycle,' Rebecca said, her eyes sparkling with an unaccustomed excitement.

'A bicycle!' Eveleen was horrified. 'But I've never ridden one.'

Rebecca's eyes widened in surprise. 'Then it's high time you did. You've ten days to learn. You can borrow mine and I'll teach you.'

For the next few days for an hour after tea, when the men went off to the cricket field to play now that the evenings were lighter, Rebecca wheeled her bicycle out of the washhouse and into the street. While Eveleen stood watching, Rebecca mounted the cycle and rode solemnly up and down.

'Now, your turn.'

Eveleen eyed the contraption warily. 'I'll fall off,' she muttered.

'Of course you won't. Come on. Hitch yourself on to the saddle. I'll hold you.'

With Rebecca almost supporting her bodily at first, Eveleen took her first tentative lesson. After the first week she could ride up and down Ranters' Row with Rebecca running alongside and only holding on to the back of the saddle.

'You're still steering too much,' Rebecca panted. 'You're sort of – doing it too deliberately. Just pedal and move the front wheel only as much as you feel you need to keep your balance. It just becomes – well – a sort of instinct really, I suppose.'

Three days before the picnic, Rebecca said, 'You're getting too good for me.' She put her hand to her breast, pretending to be breathless. 'I can't keep up with you.' So saying, she let go of the saddle.

'Oh no,' Eveleen cried. 'Don't let go.'

For a moment the bicycle wobbled dangerously, but then suddenly she was riding completely unaided. As she rode to the end of the street, turned in a wide arc and rode back towards her, Rebecca clapped her hands. As Eveleen slowed the bicycle by putting her feet to the ground and came to a standstill near Rebecca, the girl said, 'And now all you need is an outfit.'

Eveleen stared at her.

'We can't have you going on the Sunday school outing dressed like a milkmaid.'

'Thanks,' Eveleen said tartly, sounding offended.

At once, Rebecca's eyes filled with contrition. 'I'm sorry. I didn't mean it . . .'

But Eveleen laughed aloud. 'I'm teasing you, Rebecca. I know my clothes are old-fashioned and countrified. But what can I do? I can't afford to buy any smart new clothes.'

Rebecca regarded her thoughtfully. 'You've got a long black skirt, haven't you?'

Eveleen nodded.

'Well then, all we need to do is to shorten it a little to just above your ankles. And I've got a pretty white lace blouse you can have. And Gran's got a piece of black silk. I'm sure she'd let us make you a tie and a band to match to go around your straw boater.'

'I haven't got a boater.'

'Ah, but I've got two.' Rebecca's eyes twinkled triumphantly. 'So you can have one.'

'But I can't— ' Eveleen began.

'Yes, you can.' Rebecca contradicted her with far more asperity in her tone than Eveleen had ever witnessed from the shy girl. Linking her arm through Eveleen's, Rebecca went on, 'Please take it. I absolutely love having you here. You and Jimmy.' Her cheeks were faintly pink and then she added hurriedly, 'And Aunt Mary, too, of course.'

'Of course,' Eveleen said demurely. The two girls glanced at each other and burst out laughing.

The day of the outing began well enough. Picnic hampers and baskets of all shapes and sizes were loaded on to the wagons and then at nine o'clock everyone met on the village green.

'Are you sure you don't feel like coming, Gran?' Eveleen had asked Bridget.

'My Sunday school outing days are long gone.' She squinted up at Eveleen. 'Is your mother going?'

Eveleen shook her head. 'No. I – I haven't told her exactly where we're going so, please, don't tell her, will you?'

The old lady looked surprised. 'Why ever not? You're only going just outside the village, aren't you?'

Eveleen explained the reason for her concern. 'Luckily,' she went on, 'Mam doesn't want to come anyway. Says she'd rather stay here on her own and have a bit of peace and quiet. So she hasn't asked too many awkward questions.'

'She won't be on her own. I'm here. Tell her I expect her to come for her dinner.' Bridget frowned. 'And I won't take no for an answer.'

'All right, Gran.' Eveleen stooped and kissed Bridget's cheek. 'I'll tell her.'

As Eveleen rode her borrowed bicycle to the green, she saw that Rebecca was already there with Andrew on one side of her and Jimmy on the other. Bright spots of colour burned in the girl's cheeks. As Eveleen watched, Rebecca deliberately turned away from Andrew and began an animated conversation with Jimmy.

'Isn't it a lovely day? We're always lucky with the weather.'

Eveleen pursed her lips as she dismounted and wheeled her bicycle near to Andrew. She raised her voice and said pointedly, 'I didn't know you could ride a bicycle, Jimmy.'

''Course I can. I learnt on Ted's.'

Eveleen glared at him. Yet another skill that Jimmy had learned under Ted Morton's guidance. She wished everything that Ted had taught him could have been as useful.

Andrew confided in a whisper, 'And I was daft enough to lend 'im a bicycle an' all. Now he's going to be riding alongside Rebecca all day. I don't know which would be worse. Ridin' beside her but knowin' he's on her other side or not being able to be with her at all.'

'Oh dear, you have got it bad.' Eveleen tried to tease him out of his despondency, but the only reward for her pains was a baleful glare from the lovesick young man. 'Don't worry,' she tried to reassure him. 'When my uncle gets here, I expect Rebecca and I will have to ride alongside him.'

But when Harry arrived riding his own bicycle, sitting very upright so that his bowler hat did not fall off, he solemnly led off the procession from the green and did not appear to have noticed that his daughter was riding between two very attentive young admirers.

Twenty-Five

It was, as Rebecca had remarked, a beautiful day. The sun was high in a cloudless sky as the cyclists forged ahead, shouting and laughing with the horsedrawn wagons plodding along behind them. They passed through the village and came to the place where the brook, bordered by trees and bushes, meandered through the fields.

Already she could hear the shouts and squeals as the youngsters took off their boots and stockings and paddled in the cold water. When the wagons arrived with the rest of the party, the younger children ran about the meadow, shrieking and laughing, like caged wild birds suddenly set free. Eveleen smiled. She could remember herself and Jimmy on their one and only outing to the sea, running across the sand to the sea to dance like mad things at the water's edge, playing catch-us-if-you-can with the waves rolling on to the shore. Now she watched indulgently as the youngsters pranced about at the edge of the brook, daring each other to put a toe into the water.

She turned to see Andrew offering his hand to Rebecca to help prop her cycle against a tree while Jimmy fetched the wicker basket that she had packed for their picnic from one of the wagons. Andrew offered her his arm and, when Rebecca put her hand through it, Eveleen saw the look of triumph that the young man threw at his rival, who was struggling with the heavy basket.

If it had not been for her niggling worry about her brother and Rebecca and the trouble it might cause, Eveleen would have been amused by the antics of the two young men.

Andrew spread a rug on the grass for Rebecca to sit on, while Jimmy placed a cushion behind her. Andrew handed her the parasol he had been carrying for her. Jimmy opened the basket and offered her a cooling drink.

Eveleen had never seen her brother playing the courteous suitor and soon her concerns were pushed aside by the comedy being played out. She saw Rebecca glance around her, but her father was taking a walk along the banks of the brook, one of the local preachers at his side. They were deep in conversation, no doubt on chapel business, Eveleen thought, so engrossing, it seemed, that for once he had completely forgotten about his daughter.

Rebecca, seeing her father at a safe distance, lay back against the cushions. The two young men glared at each other and then sat down, one on either side of her. They lay down too.

Andrew snuggled his shoulder close to hers. Boldly Jimmy took hold of her hand. Rebecca closed her eyes and Andrew's eyelids began to droop.

Only Jimmy lay staring up at the bright sky above them.

Eveleen sighed and leant back against a tree, resting her head against its gnarled trunk. She felt comfortably, blissfully drowsy in the warm sun with only the sound in the distance of the children's laughter as they played among the trees and splashed in the brook. A light breeze rustled the leaves above her and bumble bees buzzed close by . . .

*

'There's a fight in the woods. Come and see.'

At the sound of a voice close by, Eveleen awoke with a start.

The young lad who had made the announcement was already running back towards the trees on the far side of the meadow. All the youngsters, the children and youths and girls, rose with one accord and began to run too.

Eveleen glanced round. The rug where she had last seen Rebecca and her two admirers was unoccupied. Feeling as if her heart was rising into her mouth, Eveleen scrambled up. Instinctively she knew that the fight would be between Jimmy and Andrew.

Eveleen began to run.

'Come on. Through here.' The lad leading the way was already crashing through the undergrowth, brushing aside branches in his excitement. 'This way.' He panted out an explanation to those nearest to him as he ran. 'Burns started it. He found Hardcastle in the woods with his girl. Kissing and carrying on, they were. There's going to be fireworks when her father finds out.' For the sake of those who had not already guessed, he added triumphantly, 'It's Rebecca Singleton.'

When they arrived at a small clearing and ranged themselves around its edges, the fight was still going on. Already, Jimmy's nose was bleeding and Andrew had a cut above his left eye. But neither seemed to feel, or even be aware of, their injuries. They stalked around each other like fighting cocks. A sudden flurry of punches was exchanged, bringing exclamations from the watchers.

'Go on, Andrew, smash his face in.'

'My money's on you, Jimmy. Go on.'

Several of the lads watching were already inching forwards, punching the air themselves as if they were already involved.

Jimmy stepped forward and landed a punch directly on Andrew's nose. He fell to the ground while Jimmy stood over him, victorious. The shouts around them grew louder but Andrew was already struggling to regain his feet. Jimmy stood back and allowed his opponent to get up, but the lad, though upright, was unsteady, swaying backwards and forwards. One more punch and . . .

Eveleen pushed her way through the crowd and ran towards them. 'Stop it. Stop it, this minute.'

She ran between them, turning towards Jimmy, trying to protect Andrew from any further punishment. With his blood up and intent on his adversary, Jimmy did not see her and the punch intended for Andrew's chin landed instead on Eveleen.

She fell, face downwards, and lay quite still.

At once their fight was forgotten as both youths bent over her prostrate form.

As if through a thick blanket of fog, Eveleen heard Jimmy shouting at her and felt him shaking her shoulder. 'You stupid thing, Evie. What did you do that for?'

Then everything seemed to go very dark.

Eveleen could not understand why her bed felt so hard and cold and why, as she slowly opened her eyes, she could see sunlight filtering through the trees and hear the rustling of leaves. Then she became aware of voices around her and of someone stroking her head. She opened her eyes, saw faces peering down at her and heard Rebecca say, 'Oh, Evie, please wake up. Please be all right.'

Then she heard another voice, louder and angrier.

'What's going on? Make way.'

Harry was standing over her, a towering giant of disapproval.

'They was fighting, mister.' A village lad, too young to be at work yet and therefore ignorant of Harry Singleton and his harsh rules, piped up. 'It was that Jimmy Hardcastle and Andrew Burns.' The boy's grin widened. 'They was fighting over your Rebecca, mister.'

'What?' Harry grabbed the informer, as if it was his fault. 'What's that you say? Fighting over my daughter? What do you mean? Speak up.'

The boy squirmed in his grasp. 'Le' go, I'll get my dad on to you.'

There were sniggers around them. The boy's father was a stockinger at the workshops and would not get involved in an argument with Harry Singleton if he valued his livelihood. Harry released the boy, pushing him away from him so that the youngster fell to the ground. The boy scrambled up and shoved his way through the crowd, realizing, too late, his mistake in opening his mouth. It would earn him a hiding from his father.

Harry reached down and hauled Eveleen to her feet. Already the side of her jaw was swelling. 'What's all this about, Eveleen? I demand to know.' He glanced at his daughter. 'Rebecca?'

'Nothing, Father. It was just Jimmy and Andrew being silly. They – they were just messing about and then it – sort of – got out of hand.' Her voice faltered and faded away and she hung her head to hide her face, now no longer flushed with excitement but fiery with shame and embarrassment.

Eveleen put her hand to her head. The earth still felt as if it were swimming around her. All she wanted was to lie down somewhere and go to sleep. She felt sick too.

Harry released her and she swayed, threatening to fall again, but Rebecca put her arm about Eveleen's waist to support her. 'Please,' the girl whispered, close to Eveleen's ear. 'Please don't tell him, Evie.'

Tell him what? Eveleen thought stupidly, her thoughts still reeling.

Then, as her senses began to return, she asked, 'Where – where are they?'

'Gone. They fled when they saw Father coming.'

Eveleen closed her eyes and shook her head a little, trying to clear it. 'Just as well,' she said tartly. 'But wait till I catch up with the pair of them, never mind your dad.'

'Whatever were you thinking of?'

When they arrived home, Eveleen grabbed her brother and hauled him into a corner of the yard, anger giving her strength.

'I'm sorry, Evie, I didn't mean for you to get hurt. You shouldn't have stepped between us like that.'

'I'm not bothered about that.' Eveleen brushed aside her own discomfort and the swelling bruise on her jaw. 'Are you stupid? Uncle Harry knows now, doesn't he?'

'It was him. Burns. He started it,' Jimmy muttered morosely.

'I don't care who started it. What I want to know is, what's going on between you and Rebecca? I've warned you before. You'll get us thrown out of here.'

'So what?'

'So what? You ask me "so what"? Are you stupid, Jimmy Hardcastle?'

'Oh leave off, Evie. You're getting as bad as him. Preaching. You'll be standing in that pulpit alongside the minister soon.' He pulled away from her. 'I'm going out.'

'You'll do no such thing.' She lunged at him, trying to

catch hold of him again, but he stepped smartly away. 'You'll come to Chapel tonight, Jimmy. At least that might—'

'Oh no, I won't. 'Bye, Sis. I'll be late home. I'm keeping out of his way till he's calmed down a bit.' Safely out of her reach now, he grinned cheekily and added, 'Say one for me.'

'It's more than one you'll be needing, Jimmy Hardcastle.' Eveleen shouted after him. 'I'd wear me knees out before I'd said enough to save you.' But he was gone, banging the gate behind him.

Shaking her head in exasperation, she opened the door into the cottage to be met by the full force of her uncle's wrath.

'I want him out of here.' He shook his fist in her face as if she were to blame for all the trouble. Eveleen faced him bravely, though her heart was thudding painfully. Out of the corner of her eye, she could see her mother sitting in the chair by the fire, her head in her hands. 'He's not to go near Rebecca again. As for Burns, well, I'll deal with him.'

Eveleen licked her lips. 'Uncle Harry,' she said, with far more calmness than she felt. 'I'm sure Jimmy and Rebecca are only friends. Just—'

'Oh aye. And do "just friends" lie on the ground, deep in a wood, kissing and—'

Eveleen felt the flush creep up her neck and face. 'Who told you that?'

'Rebecca, of course. I got it out of her. She's in her room. I've warned her, I'll take me belt to her if I catch her even speaking to either of them again.'

'It was wrong of them. But . . .' Before Eveleen realized what she was saying, her rash tongue was asking, 'But are you going to keep Rebecca locked away from young fellers all her life? She's seventeen. Surely . . . ?'

Harry's face was contorted with rage. 'You dare to question me, girl,' he thundered and began to raise his hand. For a moment Eveleen thought he was going to strike her, but then he seemed to be aware of what he had been about to do and, with a supreme effort, the big man controlled himself. Instead, he shook his fist close to her face. 'While you live under my roof, you'll do as I say. You hear me?'

'I hear you, Uncle,' Eveleen said, her quiet tones a deliberate contrast to his wrath.

'I want him out of this house,' Harry said again. 'I'll not sack him this time, but if he dares to try anything again, he's out. In fact, you're all out.' He glanced around at Mary, but she made no move, gave no sign that she had even heard his threats. 'Now.' Eveleen could see that he was making an effort to control his temper. 'I'm going to the chapel. I'll expect you to be there for the special service in half an hour. All of you.' He jerked his thumb upwards indicating his wayward daughter sent to her room in disgrace. 'And mind she comes, Eveleen. I'm counting on you.'

As the door slammed behind him Eveleen looked helplessly at her mother. It was gong to be a hard enough job to get Mary and, possibly, Rebecca too to the chapel in time for the service Harry evidently always insisted should be held after every Chapel outing. As for Jimmy, she had no chance.

Andrew Burns was already seated with his mother in their usual pew when Eveleen entered, pushing a reluctant

Mary in front of her. Rebecca, her head down, followed dutifully. She, more than any of them, knew what her father would be like if she dared to disobey him again. Eveleen glanced at Andrew and saw that his left eye was swollen and closed. It looked raw and painful and his mother kept darting anxious glances at him. But the young man stared sullenly ahead and did not even acknowledge the presence of the girl over whom he had been fighting. Eveleen hoped that perhaps he had learned his lesson and would leave Rebecca alone. Moments later she was on her knees praying fervently that this was so.

As for Jimmy, well, she would think of a way to deal with him.

Twenty-Six

'You're to go and lodge at Gran's,' Eveleen told Jimmy later that same night.

She had waited up for him and now, gone midnight, he was creeping into the darkened house expecting that everyone would be safely in bed.

'Heck, Evie, you made me jump. I thought it was him waiting for me with a big stick.'

'You can joke, Jimmy. You'll be laughing on the other side of your face soon if you don't watch out. He's given you a final warning. Any more trouble and you're out. We all are.'

Jimmy pulled a face at her and Eveleen felt the urge to slap him. But she kept her hands clenched and firmly by her sides. 'So,' she went on, trying to keep her voice low so that no one would hear. 'You can sleep here tonight, but tomorrow you move your things to her house.'

'There's no room,' Jimmy argued. 'She's got lodgers.'

'One of them's going to Mrs Burns. It's all arranged.'

'I see. Trying to put as much distance between us as he can, is he?'

'He'll put a lot more distance between you, if you don't watch it. And keep your voice down. We don't want him down here.'

'I'm not frightened of him,' Jimmy said boldly, but Eveleen, even in the dim lamplight, had seen the flicker of fear in his eyes.

'Of course you're not,' she tried to appease him. 'But you ought to respect him more, Jimmy. He is giving us a home at the moment and employment, don't forget.'

'I'm hardly likely to,' Jimmy muttered, glowering. 'Since you keep pushing it down me throat every five minutes. I'm off to bed.'

As he made to pass her towards the stairs, she caught hold of his arm. 'Jimmy, please, for my sake, and Mam's, please do what you're asked.'

'What I'm told, you mean.'

Their faces close together for a moment, the brother and sister looked into each other's eyes, seeing themselves mirrored in each other's face. At last Jimmy smiled. 'All right, Evie. I'll be a good boy.' But then he added ominously, 'For now, at any rate.'

Eveleen had been wrong about Andrew Burns. She had thought he would be frightened off by Harry's threats, but the following morning as she went down the path towards the workshops, he was waiting for her.

He grabbed her arm. 'Eveleen, I've got to see Rebecca. I've got to talk to her.'

'Andrew, don't. The poor girl's in enough trouble as it is.'

His eyes widened. 'Trouble? What sort of trouble? You don't mean she's – that he's . . .' His grip tightened on her arm. 'If she is, I'll kill 'im.'

'What are you talking about?'

'She's not in the family way, is she?'

Eveleen gasped and said swiftly, 'No, of course she isn't.'

Andrew looked into her face. 'She might well be, from

what I saw yesterday. Half undressed, the pair of them were.'

Eveleen stared at him in dismay and she began to tremble. 'You – you're not serious. You're making it up to make trouble for our Jimmy.'

Andrew's face twisted. 'I'd like to make trouble for 'im all right and no mistake. But no, I wouldn't make trouble for Rebecca. I love her, Eveleen. I have done for a long time. And until your blasted brother came on the scene, I thought I had a chance. I thought she liked me. And we were doing it all proper. Not behind her dad's back. But now, all because of Jimmy, 'er dad'll tar me with the same brush. I won't stand a chance either now.'

'Andrew, I'm sorry. Truly I am, if Jimmy's come between you. Look, I've got to get to my work now. And you'd better too. Let's talk later. Maybe we can help each other.'

Andrew's face lightened. 'You'll help me? I thought you'd be on Jimmy's side.'

'Not this time,' Eveleen said grimly. If what Andrew said was true about what he had seen the previous day in the woods, then even Rebecca had not admitted the whole truth to her father. 'This time,' she went on, 'he's really gone too far.'

Preoccupied with her family's problems, Eveleen had a bad day at her frame, but her uncle, no doubt just as worried, did not notice. Eveleen slipped out of work early that evening to make sure that Jimmy was gone from the house before their uncle arrived home.

'I'll go altogether,' Jimmy grumbled, hoisting a pillowcase of his few belongings on to his back. 'At least, I would if it wasn't for Rebecca.' He grinned archly. 'I've got a good reason to stay now.'

'Oh no, you haven't. Uncle Harry would never let her marry you.'

'Who said anything about marriage?' Jimmy said airily. 'I'm not the marrying kind.'

'And what if she gets pregnant?' Eveleen asked baldly.

'That's her problem.'

'Jimmy! How can you be so callous?'

She remembered he had said something very similar before and, unbidden, into her mind came the image of Stephen Dunsmore. His fair hair and handsome features. And those brilliant blue eyes that could shine with love and then, so suddenly and ruthlessly, turn cold.

'Typical,' Eveleen said bitterly. 'Just like a man.'

'Thanks for the compliment,' Jimmy said, as he slammed the door of the cottage and walked along the path in front of the row of houses towards their grandmother's home.

Eveleen breathed a sigh of relief and vowed to keep the two cousins apart. She turned and went into the scullery to find Rebecca peeling potatoes. She was sobbing, her tears falling into the water in the bowl. Her hands were shaking so much that Eveleen expected the knife to slip at any moment.

'Here, let me do that,' Eveleen said gently, taking the potato and the sharp knife out of the girl's hands.

Rebecca made no protest.

'Now, dry your tears and set the table,' Eveleen went on, briskly but not unkindly. 'Where's me mam?'

'Taken to her bed. She – she says all the trouble's upset her.'

'It would,' Eveleen said shortly and then rebuked herself for her impatience. No doubt this particular bit of family trouble was bringing back some very unhappy memories for Mary.

As the girl moved between kitchen and parlour, setting the table for supper, Eveleen pondered on the best way to help ease the situation. If only she could persuade Rebecca to focus her affections on Andrew Burns rather than Jimmy, then all might be well. She sighed. But even then, it sounded as if her uncle had no intention of letting his daughter walk out with any young man. As she dropped another potato in the saucepan of water, she wondered if the best way might be to talk to Harry himself first. Then she shook her head. No. That was not the way. She had tried already and he was so angry at the moment he would not listen to reason.

Perhaps her grandmother might help. Bridget had admitted that she regretted not standing up for her own daughter at the time of her troubles. Maybe, now, she would stand up to her son and persuade him to let Rebecca walk out with a young man.

A young man of whom Harry could approve.

'The table's ready,' Rebecca interrupted Eveleen's thoughts. 'I'll shell the peas.'

Eveleen nodded and took the heavy pan of potatoes through to the parlour to put on the hob to boil. Straightening up she went to the window overlooking the yard. There was still a light in the workshop window near where her uncle's frame stood.

Going back into the kitchen, she said carefully, 'Rebecca, Andrew was asking after you today. He wants to talk to you.'

The girl looked up. 'Well, I don't want to talk to him.'

'Why not?'

The girl shrugged. 'I don't like him.'

'He's very fond of you.'

Rebecca hung her head and said nothing, but Eveleen

was not about to let the matter rest. 'From what he said, I thought that you were friends.'

Rebecca's head came up quickly. 'What did he say?'

Eveleen decided that the time had come for complete honesty, if she was to prise Rebecca away from Jimmy. 'He said that he loves you and that before Jimmy came on the scene he thought he had a chance with you.' Eveleen bent towards her. 'Did he?'

'Maybe,' Rebecca was defensive now. 'But not any more. It's Jimmy I – I love now. And he loves me. I know he does.'

'Have you – have you . . . ?' Eveleen was at a loss as to how to ask the question delicately.

'That's none of your business,' Rebecca almost snapped, showing the most spirit that Eveleen had ever seen.

But her defensive answer told Eveleen what she most feared to hear.

'Gran, will you help me sort Jimmy and Rebecca out? We've got to put a stop to it. Right now.'

The old lady leant back in her chair and closed her eyes. 'Oh, Eveleen, I'm too old for all this trouble. Maybe if I was a few years younger—'

Before Eveleen could hold back the words they were out of her mouth. 'But you didn't do anything when you *were* younger, did you? You didn't stick up for my mother against her father. You let them make her life so awful that she ran away.' Instantly the words were said, Eveleen regretted them. 'Oh I'm sorry, Gran. I shouldn't have said that.'

Bridget sighed wearily and tears watered in her old

eyes. 'Tell the truth and shame the Devil, eh, Eveleen?' she murmured and smiled sadly. 'But you're right. I'm all talk and no do. That's me.' She lifted her head and looked straight into Eveleen's eyes. 'You're like me, but you've more spirit than I ever had. Mind you never lose it, love. Don't let anyone rule you, Eveleen. Not anyone. Not even if you fall in love. Don't fall so hard that you lose your own personality. You're someone in your own right, Eveleen. Never forget that.'

Softly Eveleen said, 'I won't, Gran. But what are we going to do about Jimmy and Rebecca?'

The old woman rested again. 'It'll sort itself out,' she said tiredly.

Eveleen watched as Bridget's eyes closed and she dozed. But would it? the girl asked herself and found no answer.

Over the following days, Eveleen watched the pair like a hawk. As far as she could see, Jimmy seemed to be obeying Harry's orders. He never came to their cottage. He didn't even linger to talk to Rebecca when he passed through the yard to work and she just happened to be going to and fro between the house and the washhouse, her arms full of laundry. If either of them looked about to disobey, Eveleen had to admit that it was Rebecca who looked the most likely.

Often she would find the girl standing at the parlour window overlooking the yard. She was watching for someone. That much was obvious. In the evenings when the young lads played cricket in the yard, Jimmy was no longer among them. Andrew always positioned himself behind the pump, playing wicket keeper so that he could be close to the window of the cottage. Eveleen saw him casting anxious, pleading glances towards it, but Rebecca would turn away, deliberately ignoring him.

'Rebecca,' Eveleen said at last, exasperated. 'Forget Jimmy. He's not worth it. Believe me.'

'I don't know why you're so against us.' Rebecca turned tearful eyes upon Eveleen. 'I'd have thought you'd have been happy for us. Don't you like me, Eveleen?'

'Oh, Rebecca. It's because I like you – I love you – that I'm so afraid for you. For both of you.' Eveleen ran her tongue over her lips before saying carefully, 'I know he's my brother, Rebecca, but even I have to admit that he's not – not reliable. And your father can see that. He'll never allow you to marry Jimmy, even if . . .' She faltered, unwilling to hurt the girl further by telling her of Jimmy's own views on marriage.

'My father will never allow me to marry anyone,' Rebecca said bitterly. 'He wants to keep me here an old maid. Just to look after him.'

'Oh no, surely not.'

'Oh yes, surely yes,' Rebecca mimicked bitterly. 'If I want to get married, the only way I'll ever be able to do it is to run away. Just like your mother did.'

'That was different. That was because she was in disgrace and – and she was . . .' Eveleen faltered, staring at Rebecca. She noticed now the girl's white face, the blue smudges beneath her eyes.

'So,' Rebecca whispered. 'Where's the difference?'

'Oh no,' Eveleen breathed, feeling as if she had been punched hard in the stomach. 'Oh, Rebecca, no!'

They stood for several moments just staring at each other, Eveleen with a look of horror on her face, while Rebecca was pale and silent and yet with a strange expression of relief. Eveleen guessed that the girl had carried her secret for some time and now, sharing it with someone, eased the fear, even if only a little.

But Eveleen felt as if she had been handed yet another burden to carry; a weight that threatened to crush them all.

She put out her arms and enfolded the girl to her. At the show of kindness, Rebecca's resolve crumbled and she wept against Eveleen's shoulder. Awkwardly Eveleen patted her back. 'There, there, don't cry. We'll sort it out.'

But Eveleen's brave words held far more confidence than she was feeling inside.

Now there was going to be real trouble.

Eveleen still fretted over Rebecca and fumed over Jimmy. How could he have been so thoughtless, so stupid? The only respite she got was when she was at her work. For a few hours she determined to put aside all thoughts of the impending cataclysm and to do her work well. Ruefully she admitted that she had every need to. Soon, she thought, they would be leaving here. When the news broke, as break it must, they would be out on the streets once more.

And where to this time? Back home? But to what? They were no better off now than when they had left Bernby. She sighed. Perhaps they should never have left. Perhaps they should have tried harder, she and Jimmy, to find work locally in or near Grantham and to rent a small cottage somewhere.

But we did try, she reminded herself. We tried very hard. At the time, coming to her mother's family had seemed the best solution, but she had not known exactly what they were coming to. She had pictured her mother's family as being like her own, with a kindly, understanding father at its head. Harry Singleton was no Walter Hardcastle. And that had been Eveleen's mistake.

'Here, I want a word with you.' One evening after work she grabbed hold of Jimmy's arm and, anger giving her strength, hauled him into the empty washhouse, slammed the door behind her and leant against it.

'What's got into you, Evie?' For a moment he looked angry. Then he grinned. 'Oh, I get it. You've arranged for Rebecca to meet me here, have you? I knew it. I knew you'd be on our side eventually.'

'Nothing of the sort,' Eveleen snapped.

His face fell. 'Well, in that case, I'm off. I've got a date in the village.'

'Oh aye,' Eveleen's voice hardened. She had suspected as much for she had heard Jimmy's whistling as he came back into the yard and towards Bridget's cottage late at night. He was either out with a group of youths in the village or seeing a girl. 'Oh aye,' she said again. 'Going to get another one pregnant an' all, are you?'

In the dim light, she could see that Jimmy's jaw dropped. It gave her a second's devious pleasure to see that he actually looked shocked.

She nodded and folded her arms, still leaning against the door. 'That's wiped the smile off your face, hasn't it?'

'You – you don't mean it.' He tried to laugh, but the sound was brittle. 'You're having me on.'

She bent towards him, her gaze holding his. 'Do you think I'd really joke about a thing like that? Rebecca's having your child and the poor girl's frightened out of her wits. So, Jimmy Hardcastle, what are you going to do about it?'

He stared at her and then his lip curled. 'Nothing.'

'Nothing? What do you mean, nothing?'

He stuffed his hands into his pockets and cocked his head on one side as he returned her gaze boldly now. 'How do I know it's mine?'

Eveleen lifted her right hand and slapped his face hard.

Twenty-Seven

Eveleen never told Rebecca the full conversation that had taken place between her and Jimmy in the wash-house, merely that Jimmy now knew about her condition.

'Oh, you shouldn't have told him,' Rebecca wailed.

'He's got to know. You can't keep it secret for ever, Rebecca.'

A look of sheer terror crossed the girl's face. 'Don't tell my father. Please, Eveleen.' She clung to Eveleen's hand in desperation.

'He'll have to know,' Eveleen said quietly. 'Sooner or later.'

'Then – then let it be later. As late as possible.' She cast about her, seeking escape. 'I'll go away. Yes, that's what I'll do. I'll have to. I can't stay here. Jimmy will take me, won't he?'

'I think,' Eveleen said slowly, 'that once the truth comes out, we'll all have to leave. Your father won't want us here any longer.'

'It's not your fault. Or your mother's.'

'Maybe not. But I doubt your father will see it that way.' She thought a moment and then added, 'Rebecca, maybe we're misjudging your father. Maybe he will stand by you. You're his only daughter. You're all he's got. Surely he won't turn his back on you.' She hesitated and there was doubt in her own voice as she added, 'Will he?'

'If you think there's the slightest chance of that, then you really don't know my father,' Rebecca said bitterly.

'Then I really think we should tell Gran.'

Rebecca shrugged her thin shoulders. 'She'll not do anything.'

To that Eveleen had no answer. She was very much afraid that Rebecca was right.

They were singing Eveleen's favourite hymn. Sitting close together in the pew, they looked like any other happy, close-knit family. But Eveleen could feel the tension in the air so tangibly she could almost reach out and grasp it. Jimmy was sitting at the far end of the pew, squashed against the wall, while Rebecca had been placed almost at the opposite end with her father sitting on her right-hand side near the aisle.

After the service, Eveleen planned to take Rebecca with her on her usual afternoon visit to their grandmother. But today there would be no lace-making done.

Today they had something to tell Bridget. And the good Lord alone knew what would happen after that. Eveleen closed her eyes and offered up a fervent prayer.

If ever she had needed to pray in her life, she needed to do so now.

'This is nice. Both my granddaughters paying me a visit.'

Unaware of the bombshell about to explode, Bridget welcomed them. 'Sit down, sit down. Don't make the place look untidy,' she joked.

They obeyed her, but both of the girls sat on the edge of their chairs, glancing at one other, each waiting for the other to begin.

Seeing how white and frail Rebecca looked – far from gaining weight because of her pregnancy, the girl looked to have lost it – Eveleen licked her dry lips and said, 'Gran, we need to talk to you. We've . . .' She glanced across at Rebecca, but the girl was now sitting with her eyes downcast, her fingers laced tightly together in her lap. 'We've got a bit of a problem.' Even as she said the words she almost laughed hysterically at the understatement.

Bridget leant forward in her chair, looking from one to the other.

'There's no easy way to tell you this, Gran. Rebecca is expecting a baby.'

The old lady closed her eyes, groaned and flopped back in her chair. Eveleen half rose but then Bridget opened her eyes. Looking at Rebecca she said harshly, 'You little fool!'

'Gran—' Eveleen began.

'You keep out of this, miss. This is family business.'

'But we're family. We're—'

'Aye, you are. But I wish you weren't. If it hadn't been for you coming here, this would never have happened.'

Eveleen felt the colour drain from her face as she stared at the woman in front of her. The woman she had believed loved her, loved all her grandchildren. She had thought that Bridget would help them. But already the old woman's mood had turned against them. She was ready to side with the person who she knew would be the victor in any family quarrel. Her son, Harry.

And then Bridget said the words that Eveleen had expected to hear from her uncle, but never from her grandmother.

'You've brought trouble back to our door, Eveleen. Your mother's a bad lot and she's tainted this girl with her wickedness.' She leant back in her chair. 'You'd better pack your things. You'll be out of here before nightfall, I can guarantee you that. And you'll be taking her with you.'

'Oh Gran, I thought you'd help us. I thought you would understand. When we've talked you've sounded as if you regretted what happened twenty years ago. As if you wish you'd acted differently. Now's your chance to—'

The sharp eyes in the wrinkled face opened wide. Now there was a look of vindictiveness in them that Eveleen had never seen before. 'Don't you tell me what I can or can't do, girl. When Harry finds out about this, you'll be out on your ears. The lot of you. And there's nothing I can do to stop it.' Her head dropped and though she muttered the last few words, Eveleen heard them. 'Even if I wanted to.'

Shocked, Eveleen rose. Rebecca was now in tears. Sobs shook her thin shoulders and she sat hunched in her chair. As Eveleen looked down on her, she knew that from this moment on she had another being for whom she was responsible. Two, if it came to that. For there was the unborn child to consider too.

'You'd better get your things packed. We'll likely be homeless by tonight. We've told Gran so I don't expect it'll be long before Uncle Harry hears.'

'What did you want to go and do a daft thing like that for?'

Eveleen clicked her tongue against her teeth in exasperation. 'You're as naïve as Rebecca. She thought that as long as no one knew, the problem would go away. Well, it won't.'

'You're the one that's naïve, our Evie, if you thought

any of them here would help. Why didn't you let me find us somewhere else to go first before you went opening your big mouth?'

'Oh thanks. So it's my fault we're in this mess, is it? I rather think it's your fault, not mine.'

'Mebbe. Mebbe not.'

'Don't start that again.'

'How do you know it's not Andrew Burns' kid? He's always sniffing round her.'

'I do know,' Eveleen said shortly. 'And if you cared about Rebecca at all, you wouldn't even think such a thing of her.'

'If she let me, how do I know she didn't let others.'

Eveleen shuddered. Her brother had just confirmed what she had believed. He was no better, but probably no worse either, than most men. They wheedled and begged and promised the earth and then, afterwards, they believed the worst. Thank goodness, she thought yet again, she had held out against Stephen Dunsmore.

Sadness washed over her. Was there no man in the world who would really love and cherish her?

Twenty-Eight

Eveleen had been wrong about one thing. Bridget did not tell her son and so Eveleen had a few days' grace to think and to plan.

Nottingham, she decided. There would be work there. Now that both she and Jimmy could operate frames, she was sure that there would be work in the hosiery industry for them. Somehow she would have to take a day off from work to go to the city. But it was going to be difficult to explain her absence to her uncle.

The solution came from an unexpected quarter.

'She is, isn't she?'

The very next morning, Andrew was waiting for her as she went to work, barring her way up the staircase until she answered him.

Eveleen nodded, miserably.

'I could break 'is neck,' the lad muttered, and Eveleen believed that if her brother had been there at that moment, Andrew would have done just that. 'What are you going to do, 'cos he'll throw you out, once he knows.'

'I know,' Eveleen whispered hoarsely, aware that Andrew was now referring to her uncle. 'I want to get to Nottingham to see if I can find us work and a place to live, but,' she spread her hands helplessly, 'I don't know what excuse to make to Uncle Harry.'

Andrew looked thoughtful. 'Pity you haven't got some lace to take to the city.'

Eveleen gripped his arm. 'But I have. My grandmother's been teaching me pillow lace. I've got balls of it in my bedroom.' She didn't tell the young man that the work had been done every Sabbath afternoon.

'There's your answer then. Tell your uncle you're going to sell your lace in Nottingham.'

Eveleen blinked. 'Can I do that?'

He shrugged. 'There's something called the Lace Market there. I 'spect it's where folks sell their lace.'

Eveleen's face brightened. 'You've been?'

'No, but I've heard talk about it.'

'Do you think I might find work there?'

'Dunno, but if you don't there are big factories. They employ a lot of folks to work their machines. You could try them.'

'Where are they?'

'Dunno. You'd have to ask.'

Now that she had two possibilities, however vague, Eveleen said, 'Right then. I'll go. In fact,' she added with a calculating gleam in her eyes, 'I'll ask Uncle Harry if I can go with him on Saturday.'

Once a month on a Saturday, Harry went to Nottingham to sell the stockings and socks knitted on the Griswold and assorted garments that had been made in the workshops other than those the bag man disposed of.

'By heck!' For a brief moment the two young people forgot their trouble and smiled at each other. Andrew shook his head and glanced at her admiringly. 'You've got some nerve, I'll say that for you. Doing it right under his nose.'

Eveleen's smile faded and her mouth was grim. 'Serves

him right. He should be the sort of father poor Rebecca could turn to.' Tears prickled at the back of her eyes as she thought about her own father and how, if she had found herself in such trouble, she could have gone to him immediately. Oh, he would have been saddened, disappointed in her, but he would have stood by her and helped her.

Hadn't he done just that years ago with Mary when Harry Singleton had helped to turn out his own sister?

Harry grumbled and groused when Eveleen asked if she could go to the city with him the following Saturday. Usually, anxious to please and to earn a few extra pennies, Eveleen worked all day on Saturday, when the young lads and even her uncle occasionally took time off to play cricket matches.

'I know you're not very fast yet on the frame, but your work is very neat and saleable.' It was all that mattered to Harry Singleton.

'I thought I could learn how things are done. I know you go yourself once a month, just to make sure the bag man isn't cheating you . . .'

'Oh now, hold on a minute.' Harry held up his hand, palm towards her. 'That is man's business, Eveleen. I won't have you interfering in trading.'

'But I wanted to take my lace to sell at the Lace Market,' she said, facing him. Eveleen Hardcastle, her conscience smote her, you are becoming an adept little liar.

A look passed between them, she with a wide-eyed and innocent expression, he with the knowledge deep in his eyes of what exactly did go on in Bridget's cottage on a Sunday afternoon. 'It's not the kind of market you're thinking of. But I can sell that for you. I can get a better price than ever you would get. I know the right people.'

Eveleen thought quickly. She needed to take the lace to show prospective employers her skills. She could cut small pieces off each pattern she had made and hide them in her reticule. He would never know. She smiled at him. 'Thank you, Uncle, I'd be very grateful.' She cocked her head on one side and added, coyly, 'But I really would like to see the city.'

'Well, I suppose you can go. But don't start making a habit of wanting to go gallivanting off to the city, will you?'

'No, Uncle Harry. I won't.' She turned away before he could change his mind.

The omnibus from Flawford set them down in Broad Marsh. Eveleen looked about her. This was her first visit to a big city and she felt a tremor of excitement.

'Come along. Don't dawdle. We haven't got all day.'

Pretending obedience, Eveleen followed. Harry had said they would be returning home in the early afternoon, but Eveleen had ascertained when the very last omnibus left for Flawford. That was the one she would be catching, she promised herself.

Harry set off, his long legs striding out so that Eveleen had to take little running steps every so often to keep up with him. They turned to the left and walked a distance, then to the right and walked again. Eveleen found herself craning to look up at the grand buildings as she passed by. One street was lined with elegant houses.

'This is where a lot of the lace manufacturers and warehouse owners live,' Harry said. 'They make a better living than we do.' He sounded bitter, but Eveleen couldn't help thinking that the Singleton family had done quite well for themselves. Finally they turned to the left again and Harry said, 'This is Stoney Street.'

They walked a distance and came to stand in front of a magnificent building shaped like a huge E. It was four storeys high.

'This is the warehouse where I do my business.'

'Where do we go in?' Eveleen asked. 'Up those steps and through that arched doorway?'

'I do, yes. But you can't come with me.'

Eveleen's heart skipped a beat. Unwittingly her uncle was playing right into her hands. She had wondered how she was going to be able to slip away from him and now here he was giving her that very opportunity.

'Now, give me your lace. I'll show it to the buyer I deal with. But I can't make any promises, mind.' Eveleen handed her uncle the bag containing the rolls of pillow lace. It represented hours and hours of fine work, but all Harry said curtly, was, 'Now don't go wandering off.'

Absently, her gaze on the finely dressed men climbing the steps in long coats and bowler hats with stiff wide collars and ties, she nodded. Further along the street, she noticed men and women, dressed more like she was, hurrying in through a much lowlier entrance. They must work here, she thought.

As her uncle disappeared through the huge, ornate door, Eveleen walked towards the other entrance.

'Excuse me,' she stopped a woman about to hurry in through the door. 'Do you work here.'

'Er – yes, mi duck.'

'What do you do?'

The woman looked wary for a moment and she glanced Eveleen up and down. Then, appearing to like what she saw, she smiled and said, 'Well, I don't exactly work *here* but mi daughter does. She works on the third floor trimmin' and scallopin' lace. But sometimes I do work at home for 'em.'

'So they don't make anything here then?'

The woman shook her head. 'Not really. The lace is made in the factories and then brought here to the warehouses to be finished. And, like I say, they have a lot of homeworkers an' all.'

'Do – do you think they have any vacancies? I'm a quick learner and I don't mind what I do.' She fished in her reticule and brought out the small samples of her lace work that she had kept back from uncle. 'This is my work. Is it any good?'

'I don't reckon they've any jobs going at the moment, but you could ask.' Then the woman examined Eveleen's lace closely. 'That's very good.' Eveleen felt the woman's keen gaze on her. 'But you'd not make enough for a livin' just working at home, mi duck. The miserable beggars don't pay much, even for the finest work. You'd be better off trying to get work in a factory or a warehouse and doing this on the side at home to make a bit extra.' She gave a wry laugh. 'Aye, and you need to, I can tell you. Even the men's wages are a pittance. Anyway, don't get me going on that subject, else we'll be here all day. If you're lookin' for work,' she went on. 'The best way is to go to the factories.'

'Do you know where they are?'

'I should do. My old man works at one. Reckitt's on Canal Street. I do work at home for them an' all.'

'Do you? Do you really?' Eveleen's heart leapt hopefully. 'How do I get there?'

The woman rattled off directions, naming so many streets that Eveleen was mesmerized. Seeing her helpless look, the woman said, 'You don't know Nottingham, do you?'

Eveleen shook her head. 'No, this is my first visit. I got off the omnibus in Broad Marsh.'

'Ah well, that helps a bit. Canal Street isn't far from there. Go back and ask directions from there. It'll be easier for you.'

Eveleen smiled, instinctively liking the first person in the city she had met. 'Thank you,' she said as they parted. 'You've been very kind. I hope we meet again.'

The woman chuckled. 'Nottingham's a big place. But I wish you luck. And you never know, if you get a job at Reckitt's then you might meet up with my old man. Tarr-ra, mi duck.'

Twenty-Nine

Eveleen had a good sense of direction and found her way back to the corner turning into Broad Marsh without difficulty. Then she asked a man for directions again.

'Keep straight on this road and you'll come to a junction with Canal Street to the right and Leen Side to the left. Where are you looking for?'

'Reckitt's.'

'Oh aye, well, you can't miss it. It's got big green gates with the name painted in white lettering.'

'Thank you,' Eveleen said and set off once more. She was wishing now that she had had the sense to stop and buy something to eat and drink. She had seen a tiny shop selling teas, sweets and ice cream – a rare treat that would be – but she was so anxious to find work that she had ignored the messages from her rumbling stomach and her dry mouth. She walked on, pausing only to flatten herself against a wall as a fire engine, drawn by two black horses, their smooth coats shining in the sunshine, came rattling past her at full gallop. On the four-wheeled carriage sat eight firemen dressed in dark tunics with shiny brass buttons and helmets. The pedestrians in the narrow street parted quickly to let the vehicle through, but as soon as it had passed they continued going about their business.

Startled by the clanging bell and the thundering horses, Eveleen stared after the engine as it disappeared round a corner. She glanced about her. No one else appeared unduly concerned. For them, she thought, this must be an everyday occurrence. Recovering her composure, she walked on. She was coming now to a poorer part of the city. No longer were there grand houses, but tall, terraced houses with doors stepping straight out on to the cobbled street. Grubby-faced children played in the road while careworn mothers scrubbed the step outside their homes, trying to keep the city dirt at bay.

And yet, even here, Eveleen still felt that prickle of excitement. The place seethed with life. Here, Eveleen thought with fresh hope, her family could lose themselves, away from Harry and his strict regime.

She saw the green double wooden gates. One stood open, but the left one was still closed and bore the single name "Reckitt". Already she could hear the clatter of machinery. She glanced up and saw the now familiar sight of the long line of windows on the top storey.

'I can't escape him even here,' she murmured, thinking of her uncle's workshops.

Taking a deep breath, she stepped through the door and went towards the factory entrance.

'You need to see Mr Carpenter. He sets folk on. He's about somewhere.'

Eveleen was tired now and hardly looked her best for an interview for a job. She smoothed down her hair and adjusted the shawl about her shoulders. She lifted her head and straightened her back, trying to ignore her aching feet and weary limbs.

'What does he look like?'

The girl grinned. 'He's big and fat and ugly. And watch yourself, 'cos he's a devil for the girls. But he's not so bad. He's fair, I'll give him that. Look, wait here a minute, I'll see if I can find him for you.'

The girl's kindness brought tears of gratitude to Eveleen's eyes, but she blinked them away and smiled. 'Thanks.'

Eveleen stood in the cold and waited. Already the light was beginning to fade and lamps were being lit in the factory so that the workers could continue late into the evening. Unbidden, the picture of her uncle's round globe above his frame came into her mind. She sighed. If only Jimmy hadn't been such an idiot, they could have settled in very happily there. In time, Eveleen might have been able to buy her own frame and, with a lot of hard work, she could have made enough money to take them all back home.

Back to Lincolnshire where her mother wanted to be.

But Jimmy had ruined everything and now they were in a worse situation than before. There were times, Eveleen thought, when she could quite cheerfully wring her brother's scrawny neck.

'I've found him.' The girl was back and beckoning to her. 'This way.' She winked at Eveleen. 'I've told him there's a pretty girl wants to see him. He won't refuse to see you now. Come on.'

The girl led the way round a corner and along twisting, narrow passages. Arriving at a door leading into a tiny office, she gestured to Eveleen to go inside. 'Good luck,' then she smiled and whispered. 'And mind you stay this side of his desk.'

With a laugh she was gone, running along the passageway towards the stairs to the upper floors.

Eveleen stepped into the room. The bulk of the man sitting behind the desk seemed to fill the small office and she marvelled that he could even fit into the chair he was sitting on. As he looked up, his jowls wobbled and Eveleen had to stifle her laughter. The girl's saucy description of him had been most apt. His face was round and florid, his fat cheeks marked with tiny red veins. His bulbous nose fought for prominence over his thick, wet lips and he had dark folds of skin beneath his eyes. And yet, when she looked into those eyes, Eveleen could see the man inside the mound of flesh. There was humour and kindness and, yes, like the girl had said, a spark of devilment.

'Mr Carpenter?'

'That's me, young lady, and what can I do for you?' His bold glance appraised her and yet Eveleen did not find it offensive. She did not fear this man as she might have done a more handsome one. In a strange way, she felt sorry for him. He had feelings, just like everyone else, even though he presented a ridiculous figure.

'I'm looking for a job, Mr Carpenter.'

'Ah well, now.' Josh Carpenter leant back in the chair, which creaked in protest. Eveleen found herself holding her breath in case it should give way beneath him. 'Then we'd better have a nice little talk, hadn't we? Pull up that chair, mi duck. Sit down and tell me all about yourself.'

So Eveleen sat and found herself telling him about herself, *all* about herself. The words tumbled out and it seemed as if, once the floodgates were opened, she could not stop the deluge. She told him about her father's death and how she now felt responsible for her mother and younger brother. She told him about her uncle, his workshops and his devotion to the chapel. She even told him how Harry Singleton inflicted the rigid way of life he led himself upon all those around him.

'There's nothing wrong with that,' she said hastily. 'He's a good man and I'm sure his way of life is right, but—'

The big man finished for her. 'But it takes a lot of living up to, mi duck, doesn't it?'

Eveleen nodded.

'Aye, there's a few manufacturers and warehouse owners round here who worship at a particular church and expect all their workers to attend regularly too.'

Perhaps she had told him too much, perhaps she had sounded disloyal to her own family. He seemed so understanding, but he was still a man, Eveleen reminded herself sharply.

'And now,' he was asking. 'You feel it's time to move on? To get away?'

'There's more to it than that, I'm afraid.' She had come this far, she thought, he might as well know the full story.

'My uncle has a daughter. He keeps her very . . .' She strove to find the right words to be fair to her uncle. 'Well, she's all he has and—'

'Keeps her well and truly under his thumb, does he?'

Eveleen nodded, startled by this man's astuteness. There was a lot more to Mr Carpenter than being big, fat and ugly. She'd only just met him and yet there was something so comforting about him.

'My brother and Rebecca have become – have been . . .' She faltered, but again the big man let out a long, sympathetic 'Ahhhh.'

'Rebecca is expecting my brother's child. And when my uncle finds out—' There was no need to say more for Josh Carpenter nodded, understanding at once.

'You've taken a lot on for one so young.'

Eveleen sighed. 'We'll all have to leave. Rebecca too.

We'll have to look after her now. And the child, when it comes.'

'So the girl's father really won't stand by her?'

Eveleen shook her head vehemently, cutting in, 'No, he won't.'

Josh Carpenter rubbed his hand on his face and murmured, 'Well, now, let's see. You say you can make pillow lace?'

Eveleen bent down and picked up the bag she had dropped beside her chair. She pulled out the pieces of lace she had made and passed them to him.

Josh examined it keenly. 'This is well done. Very well done.'

'And I can work one of my uncle's knitting frames.'

Josh pulled a wry face. 'Sorry, mi duck, but we don't have women working the machines.'

Eveleen felt a swift stab of disappointment. It must have shown on her face, for Josh said quickly, 'But you say your brother can operate a machine? They're not knitting frames we have here of course. They're twist lace machines, but I'm sure your brother would soon pick it up.'

She nodded and bit her lip, stopping herself telling him that Jimmy was neither as good a worker as she was nor as reliable. She would just have to make sure that her brother changed his ways. Instead, she asked, 'But do you have any jobs for women in the factory?'

'Oh yes. This is a factory-cum-warehouse, see. So the goods that are made on the machines go straight to the warehouse building next door and we have different workshops and a lot of the workers there are women. So, young lady, when you get settled in Nottingham, bring your brother to see me and we'll see what we can do for both of you.' He held out his hand to her and Eveleen stood up. She smiled at him and shook his hand. 'Thank you, Mr Carpenter. Thank you very much.'

As she walked out of the gates of the factory, Eveleen gave a little skip of sheer joy. Their luck was turning, she could feel it. The sky above the tall buildings was darkening now and she could feel a few spots of rain on her face. She would have to hurry to catch the last omnibus to Flawford. If she missed it, she faced a walk of five miles or more.

She had no time left now to seek lodgings for the family, but she had achieved a great deal that day and, though she felt tired and very hungry now, she was also elated. She had the promise of work for Jimmy and herself and she had seen the trading area known as the Lace Market. It was not quite the kind of market she had expected, with open stalls and traders standing behind them shouting their wares. It was a much more refined way of trading, but at least she now understood how it all worked, or at least she thought she did.

'We'll have to stay a night or two at a small hotel at first,' she murmured to herself. Not for long though, she vowed, for it would be expensive. Maybe a temperance hotel would be the answer. She smiled a little at the thought that her uncle would approve of her thinking, then pulled a wry expression as she remembered that he would have very little else to approve of. She still had to face his anger for disappearing and losing herself in the city, and missing the omnibus home.

The two solid green doors were now both closed, but Eveleen pulled one open, passed through and pulled it to behind her. She paused a moment to take one last glance back at the name painted in big letters on the doors. Now that they were both closed she could see the name of the factory and warehouse in full.

Reckitt and Stokes.

She felt a strange tremor run through her. Oh, it couldn't be. Could it? Stokes was the surname of the man who had been her mother's sweetheart. The man who had, so heartlessly, run away from his responsibilities and left poor Mary to face the shame and humiliation alone.

It couldn't be him. It was too much of a coincidence. And yet she remembered that her grandmother had said that Brinsley Stokes was in partnership in a factory in Nottingham now.

Eveleen, her mouth a tight line, stared at the name, almost as if it might come alive and materialize into the person himself.

'Well, whoever you are, Mr Stokes, I'll work for you,' she murmured. 'I'll work as hard as I know how. But perhaps you'd better keep out of my way or I might not be responsible for what I do.'

As she turned to hurry back to Broad Marsh, she realized that she would have to be very careful not to mention the name to her mother. And she would have to swear Jimmy to secrecy too.

Thirty

When Eveleen returned to Flawford, no mention was made of where she had been and why she was so late home. A far worse storm had broken and her mother had been the cause of it.

Mary, hearing Rebecca retching over the chamber pot in her bedroom, had remarked on it at breakfast.

'I only asked,' Mary wailed, spreading her hands in supplication to Eveleen as soon as she stepped into the cottage. 'Was she ill? Was it something she'd eaten? Then I laughed and said it sounded just like morning sickness. I was only joking, Eveleen, I never thought for one moment that she – of all people . . . But she turned as white as a sheet and burst into tears. Then, of course, Harry—'

'Don't tell me,' Eveleen said wearily. 'He got it out of her.'

Mary nodded.

'Where is he now?'

Mary plucked at her apron. 'He's – he's gone to the chapel.'

Eveleen's face was grim as she put down her bag, pulled her shawl about her shoulders and said firmly, 'I'll go and find him.'

'Do be careful, Eveleen, I've never seen him in such a temper. Not ever – not even . . .' Her voice faltered and she dabbed at her eyes with the corner of her apron. 'Not even twenty years ago.'

Eveleen walked across the road and opened the door leading into the chapel. Closing it quietly behind her she stood a moment watching her uncle kneeling alone on the cushioned step in front of the rostrum, his arms resting on the communion rail. His forehead was resting on his hands clasped tightly in prayer. Even from here she could hear his low murmuring. In front of him a vase of flowers rested on the small communion table and towering above him were the dark polished panels of the pulpit with steps on either side. Resting on the top rail of the pulpit was the lectern with the heavy Bible, still open at the page where the preacher had left it the previous Sunday.

As she watched her uncle, Eveleen felt a stab of pity for him. Rebecca was his only child, his beloved daughter. She was all he had left in the world and now, in his eyes, she was despoiled, shamed and full of sin.

Eveleen crept forward and sat down in the family pew to wait until Harry had finished. She pulled one of the embroidered hassocks forward and knelt, bowing her head in a prayer of her own. At once her vision of God came into her mind. He was stretching out his hand towards her and his face, though sad, was full of compassion. She prayed to him to give her strength, to give her the courage to do the right thing and the common sense to know what that was.

She heard a movement and opened her eyes to see her uncle easing himself stiffly to his feet. He turned to look at her. For a long time they stared at each other. The sadness had etched another ten years into his face in the space of a day, Eveleen thought, her heart going out to him. But there was no compassion in her uncle's face, no understanding or forgiveness.

She began, 'Uncle—' but he raised his hand to stop her.

'Don't say a word, Eveleen, because there's nothing you can say that can alter anything. Your mother has brought shame to my door again.'

'My mother is not to blame for this. It's Jimmy's fault and – and Rebecca's.'

He shook his head. 'Not Rebecca. She was a sweet, innocent flower who would never willingly have allowed him to – to–'

'Are you accusing Jimmy of – of . . .' The word was too ugly, too appalling for Eveleen to utter, especially in this holy place.

'He must have forced her. It must have been against her will.'

Eveleen stared. Then she realized that her uncle was twisting the truth to fit what he wanted to believe. He could not bear to think that his precious daughter could have committed such a sin and the only way around that was to accuse her lover of rape. This was worse than even she had feared. Jimmy was in danger. Harry Singleton could have him arrested. Her heart began to thud painfully. Perhaps he had done so already. Then she took hold of her wild thoughts. No, no, her mother would have told her at once if anything like that had happened. She would have been hysterical.

Trying to speak calmly, Eveleen said, 'We'll leave at once.'

'It would be for the best, Eveleen.'

She stood up and turned to leave but not before she had lingered a moment to say huskily, 'I'm sorry, Uncle Harry. Truly I am.'

For a moment, his head was bowed. When he raised it she saw tears in his eyes. 'Take Rebecca with you, Eveleen. I do not want to look on her face again.'

The lump that rose in Eveleen's throat threatened to

choke her. At that moment she did not know for whom she felt the sorrier, Harry Singleton or his daughter. He looked a lost, lonely and desolate man.

'It's late now but we'll be gone by Monday,' she promised him.

He seemed about to say more but then, looking away, he nodded. As she moved out of the family pew, he took her place and she left him sitting there, alone in the chapel. As far as she knew, that was where he stayed for the remainder of the night.

He could not bear to be under the same roof as the rest of his family.

Eveleen slept very little. She lay beside her mother in the attic room, staring into the darkness listening to every creak of the house settling itself for the night. Her mother, too, was restless, tossing and turning and muttering in her fitful sleep. Below them, Eveleen could hear Rebecca moving about her bedroom. No doubt she was collecting her bits and pieces together to leave. Every so often, she caught the muffled sound of the girl sobbing.

Throughout the following day, Harry did not return to the house and none of the family attended the Sunday services at the chapel.

Very early on the Monday morning, Eveleen knocked on the door of her grandmother's cottage. She opened the door and called softly. 'Jimmy, are you up?'

'You can come in,' Bridget called. Eveleen stepped into the room and was surprised to see her grandmother fully dressed and sitting in her chair by the fire. Then she realized that Bridget had probably not been to bed the previous night either.

'So, he's found out then,' Bridget said without preamble.

Eveleen sighed and sat down opposite her, feeling a pang of regret that this would be the last time she would be able to sit and talk to her grandmother. Despite her moods, Eveleen had become very fond of Bridget. She didn't even blame her – not any more – for not having the strength to stand up to her son and champion Rebecca. She was old now and frail. Though her spirit was still there, Bridget was not as resilient as she might once have been.

What Eveleen could not forgive her for was that she had not stood by her own daughter all those years before.

'He's like his father,' Bridget said suddenly. 'Unforgiving.' As if reading Eveleen's thoughts, she went on. 'I know you think I should have done more to help Mary, but you didn't know her father. John was a hard, God-fearing man. A good man, mind you, like Harry. No one can say he wasn't. But he was unforgiving of anyone's weaknesses. To his mind, Mary had committed almost the worst sin possible that a woman can commit. If I'd stood up for her against him, I'd've had to leave with her.' The old eyes were looking straight into Eveleen's now. 'I had to make a choice.'

Eveleen nodded but could find no words to say except the same as those she had said to her uncle. 'I'm sorry, Gran. So very sorry.'

'It's not your fault, love. I know that and so does Harry at the bottom of him, but he can't admit it. It's that no good brother of yours that's to blame. Him and Rebecca. She's not so innocent as Harry would have us believe. Oh, I know what he thinks, but I have told him I don't agree with him on that. She's weak and imagines herself in love with your Jimmy and she was daft enough to give way to his pestering.' She nodded wisely towards Eveleen. 'But you'll have to make him toe the line now, girl, and face up to his responsibilities, else he'll bring yet more trouble your way.'

Eveleen nodded. 'I know.'

'I'm sorry to see you go. I was proud to have all my grandchildren around me.' The old lady lapsed into silence and Eveleen knew that that pride had been cruelly snatched away.

She sprang to her feet. 'Jimmy,' she called out harshly. 'Get down here this minute. We're leaving.' She bent and kissed her grandmother's papery cheek. 'I'll miss you, Gran,' she said with a catch in her throat.

'Aye, and I'll miss you.' For a moment Bridget clutched at Eveleen's hand. 'What's to become of us, eh? What's to become of us all?'

For the first time, Eveleen spared a thought for the old lady. There would be no one left here to care for her now. No doubt Harry would employ some girl from the village to cook and clean and wash for him and his mother.

But it could never be the same for Bridget as having her own family around her. She had drawn strength from their youth and vigour and, despite the sharpness of her tongue, Eveleen truly believed she had rejoiced in her daughter's return.

They took the carrier's cart to Nottingham rather than the omnibus. Between them they carried their personal belongings. At the last moment, Eveleen had hurried to the workshop and snatched up the seat that Andrew had made for her.

'I don't know what you want to lug that thing about with you for,' Jimmy muttered morosely.

Eveleen said nothing. She was so angry with her

brother that she only spoke to him when it was absolutely necessary.

Their journey was a nightmare. Rebecca did nothing but sob and cling to Jimmy's arm and Mary complained bitterly. 'I don't want to go to the city, Eveleen. I want to go home. Back to Bernby. We were happy there. Take me home, Eveleen.'

The words seemed to echo round and round in Eveleen's mind. The promise she had made to her mother was going to be harder to achieve than ever.

Thirty-One

As they alighted from the cart, once again in Broad Marsh, Eveleen asked the driver, 'Do you know of any cheap hotels where we could stay? Only for a couple of nights,' she added hastily.

'Not that'd be suitable for ladies, mi duck.' The man pondered a moment and then added, 'You'd do better to go to one of the working girls' homes. There's one or two of them.' He glanced at Jimmy. 'Don't know if they'd take him, though. He might have to try the Young Men's Christian Association.'

'Not bloody likely,' Jimmy muttered and Eveleen gave him a sharp nudge.

'Wash your mouth out and shut up. You'll do as you're told for once.'

Jimmy glowered and, though he said no more, Eveleen noticed that he pulled his arm free of Rebecca's limpet hand causing the girl's sobs to grow louder.

The carrier cast a strange look at Jimmy but turned back to Eveleen. 'I reckon they have a house of refuge on Chaucer Street. He could try there, but it's a fair step. Right the other side of Market Place.'

Eveleen did not even know where Market Place was, but she was sure they could find it.

'Where is there a working girls' home? We'll try there first.'

'That's easier. There's one in Castle Gate. Go along

here to the end of Broad Marsh.' He pointed in the opposite direction to that which Eveleen had walked with her uncle. 'Turn right and then left and that's Castle Gate. I'm not sure where the house is exactly, but you can ask then.'

'Thanks,' Eveleen said. 'Thanks very much.'

The man glanced round at them and, seeming to catch something of the atmosphere of misery and desperation, he murmured, 'Good luck, mi duck.'

'Thanks,' Eveleen said again and added, under her breath, 'I'm going to need it.'

As Eveleen hitched up the baggage she was carrying and began to lead the way along the street, Jimmy said, 'I aren't staying in no Christian place. I've had enough of ranters to last me a lifetime.'

Eveleen dropped her belongings to the ground, whirled round on him and gripped his shoulders. She shook him hard, 'It's your fault we're in this mess. You'd do better to try to help—'

'It's not Jimmy's fault,' Mary said rousing from her apathy. 'Don't blame him. I won't have you blaming him.' Her glance went to Rebecca and then came back to rest on Eveleen. 'It's your fault, Eveleen, bringing us here in the first place.' And, unspoken, other words lay between them. And it was you who caused your father's death.

Mary linked her arm through Jimmy's. 'Never mind her. You'll look after me, Jimmy, won't you?'

'I don't know where to go.' Jimmy glanced resentfully at Eveleen. 'We'll have to do what she says.'

Eveleen picked up her bundles, tucking the seat under her arm. 'It's only for a night or two until I find us a house to rent or something. I'll ask at the factory. Mr Carpenter might help.'

'Who's he?' Jimmy asked as they began to walk again, this time with his mother hanging on to his arm.

'The man who's going to give you a job, that's who. And you'd better be nice and polite to him. No making fun of him. You hear me?'

'Why? What's the matter with him? Got two heads, has he?'

'No.' Eveleen tried to explain. 'He's a rather – rather large gentleman, and – and – he's not exactly handsome. But you just remember, our livelihood might well depend on that man.'

'You mean he's a big, fat, ugly bugger,' Jimmy said and then dodged smartly out of the way as Eveleen dropped one of her bags again and her hand came up to swipe good-naturedly at him. 'He'll be just right for you, our Evie, 'cos you can't seem to keep the good-looking ones, can you? If you'd raised your skirts for Master Stephen, then maybe we'd all be living in clover by now.'

Laughing unkindly, he marched ahead along the street, dragging Mary with him and leaving Eveleen to help Rebecca.

They found the Home for Working Girls and the woman in charge was happy to take the three women but shook her head at Jimmy.

'We can't take men in here.'

'Oh please,' Eveleen cajoled. 'It's only for a couple of nights. Just until I can find us a place to rent.' Eveleen swallowed hard before she offered, 'I'll pay you a little extra.'

The woman eyed Jimmy dubiously, even though he was trying to adopt the most innocent expression he could muster. But then her eyes began to gleam at the thought of some extra money in her pocket. 'He'll have to behave himself else I could lose mi job.'

'He will,' Eveleen said firmly.

'All right then, just so long as it is only for a couple of nights or so.'

The following morning as they stood together side by side in front of Mr Carpenter, Eveleen could feel Jimmy shaking with suppressed mirth. Unseen by the man on the other side of the desk, she put out her foot and trod heavily on Jimmy's, and she held it there until he put his hand behind her back and pinched her arm. They glanced at each other, each of them testing the other out. Then Jimmy grinned in capitulation and turned towards Mr Carpenter.

'Good morning, sir. I think my sister has told you we're both looking for work. I'm a good worker, sir, and I'll give you no trouble.'

The shrewd man eyed him suspiciously. Eveleen bit her lip, wondering if Mr Carpenter was going to let slip all that she had told him about her family. But all he said was, 'Aye well, lad, we'll see, won't we? Now, you go down this passage here. Turn left at the bottom and you'll see a little office on your left just before the door into the machine shop. Ask for Bob Porter. Tell him I've taken you on as an apprentice on a Levers machine.' Josh's round face broke into a smile. 'Tell Bob to put you with Luke Manning. He'll keep you in line.'

Politely Jimmy touched his forelock and said, 'Thank you, sir.' Then he stepped out of the tiny room and out of sight of the big man, he winked at his sister, jerked his thumb towards Mr Carpenter and mimed lifting his skirt, had he been wearing one.

Eveleen almost took a step towards him, but Jimmy laughed, winked again and, thrusting his hands into his pockets, set off down the passageway, whistling merrily.

She turned back to meet Mr Carpenter's eyes and before she could stop herself, she said, 'I don't know what he's got to be so cheerful about. It's all his fault we're in this mess.'

The man nodded sympathetically. 'I can see he's got a bit of the devil in him. But he's not the only one. We've a lot of apprentices here, lass, and I have to keep me eye on 'em all.' He tapped the side of his huge nose. 'Don't you worry, love. He's just one more I'll be watching.'

Her smile was genuine as she said with relief, 'Thank you, Mr Carpenter.'

'Now, mi duck. Let's see what we can find for you to do, eh?'

'Thank you, sir. There's just one more thing. Do you know of anywhere where we could take lodgings? There's four of us.'

'Soon to be five, eh?'

Eveleen nodded.

He rubbed a handkerchief across his forehead wiping away beads of sweat. 'Now I'll have to think about that. Where are you staying at the moment?'

When Eveleen told him, he pulled a face. 'That'll be costing you.' He smiled, his jowls wobbling, 'And the rules'll be a bit rigid, I bet.'

Eveleen smiled. 'We're used to worse than that, Mr Carpenter.'

'Can't promise anything, mind, but I'll see what I can do. I'll ask around the factory.'

Eveleen thanked him again and then waited while he heaved himself up from the chair and lumbered his way around the desk and out into the passage. 'But for now, we'd better set you to work, lass.'

He led her to the adjacent building. They climbed five flights of stairs with Josh pausing on every landing to regain his breath. 'I don't – come up here – very often,' he puffed and smiled. 'You can see why.'

Eveleen smiled kindly at him but could not think of a suitable response. When they reached the top floor Josh led her into a large, airy room with large windows on all sides. The noise greeted them as they opened the door, but this time it was not the clatter of machinery but the chattering of the forty women at work in the room. They were all seated, except for one woman who appeared to Eveleen to be some kind of supervisor.

The sound of their voices died away as they became aware that Josh Carpenter had entered the room. One or two glanced up, stared for a moment at Eveleen and then bent their heads again over their work. The woman and young girls were all neatly dressed in high-necked blouses and long dark skirts and everyone seemed to have their hair smoothly coiled or plaited into the nape of their neck. In stark contrast Eveleen felt suddenly wild and unkempt and her dress and shawl shabby.

'This is the inspection and mending room,' Josh explained. Each worker had a bale of lace fabric spread over their knees and spilling on to the floor and Eveleen could see that they were examining the material carefully and mending any faults.

Josh raised his voice. 'Miss Brownlow, could you spare me a moment please?'

The supervisor left the table where she had been inspecting a length of dress lace and came towards them.

'This is Miss Eveleen Hardcastle. She has shown me some of the pillow lace she has made and it is very fine.'

He glanced at Eveleen and smiled, 'Very fine work indeed.' He turned back to Miss Brownlow. 'So I am sure she would be suitable for the work here.'

It was a statement not a request and the woman, thin-faced and with a hooked nose that dominated her features, could only purse her small mouth and nod in reluctant acquiescence.

Josh turned to Eveleen. 'Miss Brownlow will look after you and I'll not forget what you asked me. I'll see what I can find out. Come and see me after work.'

As the door closed behind him, Eveleen felt the curious eyes of all the women in the room upon her. She heard the soft laughter that rippled through the room like a breeze. Close by she heard a young girl murmur, 'Another one for Josh's harem, eh?' And Eveleen felt an embarrassed flush creep up her face.

Thirty-Two

'Miss Binkley,' the sour-faced supervisor called forward one of the young women. 'Look after her and show her what to do.' Miss Brownlow's scathing glance raked Eveleen from head to foot. 'I don't expect she'll be much use, but we'll have to take her if he's taken a fancy to her.' She gave a loud sniff. 'And perhaps a little responsibility will do you no harm.' With her back ramrod-stiff, the woman went back to her table. Unseen, the girl pulled a face. Miss Binkley, about the same age as Eveleen, was fair-haired with blue, mischievous eyes, a small nose and a laughing mouth. She touched Eveleen's arm in a friendly gesture and whispered. 'Don't worry, she's only jealous. I don't reckon she's ever had a man in her life, not even one like old Carpenter. Come on,' she led the way carefully through the mounds of delicate fabric on the floor. 'My name's Helen, by the way. Sit near me and I'll show you what to do.'

One or two of the other women sitting nearest to Helen looked up and smiled, but soon, resuming their chatter as they worked, they had forgotten all about the new girl.

At the end of that first working day, Eveleen found her way back to Josh Carpenter's office.

'I'm sorry, but I've been so busy this afternoon. One

of the machines went wrong.' He pulled a face and Eveleen held her breath, praying that it had nothing to do with Jimmy. But as Josh continued, she let out her breath in relief. 'I haven't had the time to ask around. But I'll see what I can do tomorrow.'

She smiled her thanks and went outside. Jimmy was already halfway along the street with two or three other youths of his own age. Eveleen had the uncomfortable feeling that her dear brother would not arrive back at their lodgings until much later that night and then probably he would be rolling drunk and likely get them thrown out.

For once, however, Eveleen held her impetuous tongue in check. If she called out to him, belittled him in front of his newfound friends, Jimmy would then do it deliberately.

Eveleen sighed. Either way, she couldn't prevent the inevitable.

'Please, just one more day.' Eveleen was obliged to plead with the woman running the home the following morning, after Jimmy had woken half the house – maybe even half the street – sitting on the steps outside in the early hours and singing at the top of his voice. Eveleen had scuttled down and dragged him in but not before the warden, or whatever she was called, had heard him too.

'I am sorry,' she added.

The woman mellowed enough to say, 'It's not your fault, Miss Hardcastle. I can see that. But I stretched the rules to let him stay here at all and see what he does?'

'I know,' Eveleen said helplessly. 'And we'll move out as soon as I find somewhere, I promise.'

'All right then, but if he comes back in that state tonight, I won't have him in the house. He'll have to sleep in the street.'

Eveleen nodded and went upstairs to drag her leaden-headed brother from his bed. 'Come on, you,' she said roughly. 'You've cost us our place here. I'm not going to let you lose your job an' all.'

Nearing the lunch break, a man came into the inspection room. He stood in the doorway and looked about him. He spoke to one of the women nearest the door and she gestured towards Eveleen.

Helen nudged Eveleen. 'Looks like you've got yourself an admirer already.'

'That's Fred Martin,' Sarah, who sat near Helen and now Eveleen too, remarked. 'He's married to Win and they've got six kids. Their eldest daughter works at the Adams' place on Stoney Street.'

Helen pulled a face at Eveleen and grinned. 'He can still come looking, though, can't he?'

'Not if Win catches him, he can't,' someone else close by said.

That was the thing about factory life, Eveleen was swiftly learning. Whatever was said to the person sitting next to you was overheard and usually taken up by half a dozen others.

The laughter rippled around them as the man stepped carefully among the workers towards Eveleen.

'Hello,' he said, nodding at her in greeting. 'My missis has sent me. Said to watch out if any new girls turned up here and I was to be sure to ask you if you was getting on all right.'

Eveleen dropped her work, stood up and held out her

hand, smiling as she did so. 'Oh you must be the husband of the kind lady I met in Stoney Street when I came the other day looking for work. It was her suggested I came to Reckitt's. She said you worked here.'

The man's smile broadened. 'That's my Win. She collects lame ducks. No offence, love.'

'None taken,' Eveleen said at once. 'I was certainly a lame duck that day by the time I'd finished tramping the streets.' The man laughed and those listening around them joined in.

'So,' he went on. 'Are you all right, 'cos I'll have to report back now I've found you.'

'Yes, thanks. I'm fine. And it's thanks to your wife I am.'

'Good,' he nodded, raised his hand and made to turn away. 'I'll tell her that. She'll be pleased to have helped you, love.'

'There is just one thing,' Eveleen said hastily. 'You don't happen to know of anywhere to rent do you?'

'Just for you?'

Eveleen shook her head. 'No. There's four of us.' Eveleen bit her lip. She had been about to say more but there were too many listeners for her to want to confide more. All around them the women had fallen silent and were listening intently.

Fred wrinkled his forehead and said, 'I don't know of anywhere but I'll ask the wife. She might. I'll let you know tomorrow.'

'Thanks. I'd be ever so grateful.'

As he left, she sat down again and resumed her work. The buzz of conversation rose again and soon Eveleen and her problems were forgotten. Only Helen said, 'I'll ask around too for you.'

Eveleen opened her mouth to express her thanks when

she noticed that once again the workers had fallen silent. Then a whisper rippled through the room like a breeze.

'It's him. It's Mr Stokes himself. By the door, look. He's just come in.'

'I hope that handsome son of his is with him.'

'Shut up, Lucy. You're too old for him. The lad's not even twenty.'

'Mebbe he'd like an older woman. I'd like the chance to teach him a thing or two.'

Eveleen looked up to see that two men had entered the room. The first was a man in his mid-forties. Tall and slim with dark hair that was greying at the temples, he had clear-cut features, a long straight nose and a firm jaw. The second man was much younger and, quite obviously, the son of the older man, for he resembled him in looks and build. The first man looked about him, his expression stern, but the young one smiled and nodded to the women nearby.

'Oh, isn't he the most handsome man you've ever seen in your life?' Helen sighed ecstatically.

Eveleen stared at the young man until, as if feeling her eyes upon him, he turned to look at her. Boldly she held his gaze for a long moment, then dutifully she bent her head over her work again.

'No, he isn't, actually. But then I have no liking at all for handsome men,' Eveleen said, unable to keep the bitterness from her tone as Stephen's fair, chiselled features were suddenly in her mind's eye. 'I'd sooner have an ugly one who was kind and reliable.'

'In that case,' Lucy piped up. 'Look no further. Old man Carpenter's going free.' The ripple of laughter around her made the older man look across towards where Eveleen was sitting and frown.

Eveleen concentrated on her work and took no more

part in the whispered conversation among the other women. She didn't want to incur the wrath of one of the owners of the factory on only her second day there.

Not until the two men had gone did she say, 'Who did you say they were?'

'That's your employer, Eveleen. That was Mr Brinsley Stokes and his son, Richard.'

So, she had been right. The older of the two men had been her mother's lover more than twenty years earlier. And now it was too late. She had the promise of work for both her and Jimmy. Work she dare not give up just because one of the owners had once treated her mother so shamefully.

Eveleen frowned over her work and, for a moment, her fingers trembled as she thought of the shock it would give her mother if she ever found out.

She would have to make sure that never happened.

'You're quiet,' Helen said. The muted buzz of conversation had begun again once Mr Stokes and his son were out of earshot.

Eveleen looked up and forced herself to smile. 'Sorry.'

Helen leaned closer. 'You're taken with him, aren't you? Master Richard.'

'Of course not,' Eveleen snapped. 'I've told you, I'm not interested in handsome men. You can't trust them any further than you can throw them.'

Instead of taking offence at her sharpness, Helen said quietly, 'You've been hurt, haven't you? Someone's hurt you very badly.'

At the kindness in her new friend's voice, Eveleen felt a lump in her throat and tears prickle behind her eyelids. She bent her head and tried to hide them, but Helen touched her arm. 'I'm sorry. I didn't mean to upset you. Forget him, whoever he is. He's not worth it.'

Eveleen gave a watery smile and looked up. 'You're right there. He wasn't.'

'But they're not all like that, you know,' Helen said gently. 'Don't tar 'em all with the same brush, just 'cos one's been a right bastard.'

Eveleen said nothing. She couldn't expect Helen to understand.

She had fallen in love with Stephen Dunsmore. She had given him her heart completely and he had crushed it. She was never, she vowed, going to give herself to any man like that again. She was not going to give anyone the chance to hurt her again.

The meeting – although it could hardly be called that – with Brinsley Stokes and his son had disturbed her. She couldn't confide in Helen, nice though the girl seemed, and by lunchtime she was in such a state of agitation that she went in search of Jimmy.

She slipped into the machine room, even though she knew she should not be there. She walked down the aisles of machines until she came to where her brother was working. She stood watching him, taking in his every movement.

Luke Manning, the skilled twisthand deputed to train Jimmy, shouted orders above the clatter of the machinery. He was a thin man in his late forties or early fifties, with thinning grey hair and a slight stoop to his shoulders. His face was pale and gaunt, but his mouth was pursed in a cheery whistle, even though his tune could not be heard above the racket. Catching sight of Eveleen, he winked at her, pointed to Jimmy and then raised his eyes to the ceiling and shook his head in mock despair.

Then she saw Luke gesture with his hands, explaining yet again an operation that even Eveleen had just witnessed him showing her brother. A few minutes later,

Luke pointed to her and signed that Jimmy could take a short break to speak to her.

Shouting above the noise she said, 'Can't you try a bit harder? I saw him having to show you the same thing twice and I've only been here a minute or two.'

'Reckon you could do better, do you?' Jimmy snapped.

'I could make a darn sight better job of it than you're doing.' She moved closer and dropped her voice, although above the clanking machinery all around them it was doubtful they would be overheard anyway. 'Look, Jimmy. You need this job. Try and make a go of it.'

Jimmy glared at her resentfully. 'Don't boss me about, Evie, else you'll be sorry. I've enough of 'em round here shouting orders at me all day long. And the feller who takes over from us' – the twisthands, as the machine operators were called, worked in shifts so that the machines were kept running for twenty hours out of every day – 'he's been tittle-tattling to the foreman already. I'm sick of it, I tell you. For two pins, I'd be off to sea.'

Eveleen's patience snapped. 'This is only your second day.' She stopped and sighed. She didn't want to fall out with her brother. 'Look, I'm sorry. At least give it a go, eh?'

'Well,' he said slowly and then grinned at her. 'Just for you then.'

They smiled at each other, then Eveleen said, 'I didn't come here to find fault with your work'

'There's plenty doing that already,' Jimmy grimaced but his good humour had been restored. 'What did you come here for then?' He grinned cheekily at her. 'Just wanted to walk past all the fellers, eh? Let 'em all see what a fine figure of a woman you are.'

Eveleen laughed at his absurdity. Nothing had been

further from her mind. Then her expression sobered. 'I shouldn't really be here anyway, but I had to see you. I have to talk to someone.'

'What's up?'

'Do you realize who we're working for?'

He blinked. 'What d'you mean? I'm working for Luke Manning and over him is this bugger of a foreman called Porter. And above him, it's Carpenter—'

'Watch your language, Jimmy.'

Jimmy laughed. 'Oh, I aren't working for Holy Joe now, Evie. There's worse language than that flying round here, I can tell you. I reckon that's why they keep the "ladies" from coming in here.'

'Is that what they used to call Uncle Harry behind his back? Holy Joe?'

'Oh aye. And worse.'

Eveleen still had such mixed feelings about her uncle. Part of her admired him for the way he tried to live his life and yet . . . She pulled herself back to the problem of the moment. 'Never mind about that now. No, I mean do you know who the boss is? The man whose name is painted on the factory gates. Stokes. It's Brinsley Stokes.'

Jimmy still looked puzzled. 'So? What about it?'

'That's the man who caused our mam all that trouble. Years ago.'

Jimmy stared at her. 'You're not serious?'

Eveleen nodded. 'I am. Gran told me his name. And how many other Brinsley Stokes do you think there are round here?"

'What on earth did you want to get us a job here for then? I'm likely to kill him if I get near him.'

Eveleen spread her hands. 'I thought it was a coincidence. That it couldn't be him. It wasn't until I heard his first name this morning – Brinsley – that I knew for definite. It's such an unusual name, it's got to be him.' She leant closer, speaking urgently, 'Look, just don't tell Mam, that's all. She needn't know.'

Jimmy opened his mouth but before he could speak, a loud voice spoke close behind Eveleen making her jump. 'What the bleedin' hell are you doing in here, girl? Get yourself out of here. Right now.'

Eveleen turned to find herself facing the irate face of a stocky, balding man.

'Sorry, Mr Porter,' Jimmy was saying at once. 'It's me sister. Spot of family bother. Off you go, Evie. I'll see you later.'

'And don't let me catch you in here ever again. Women aren't allowed in here.' He looked her up and down with a leering glance. 'Takes their minds off their work, see.'

'Sorry, Mr Porter,' she mumbled and hurried away, her face burning, as, behind her, she could hear catcalls and whistles from the men working the machinery.

It was certainly a very different place to her uncle's workshops.

Thirty-Three

Jimmy finished his shift at six in the evening, the same time that Eveleen left the warehouse.

'I should be working 'til seven,' she told him, 'but I told Miss Brownlow I was feeling unwell. She let me go but I don't reckon she believed me. 'Eight until seven are my hours and until twelve on a Saturday.' She smiled. 'Bit different to life on a farm, eh? When we had to work the clock round at lambing time or when one of the beasts was calving.'

'Give me that any day, though, even if we did have to work the clock round. These shifts are getting to me, Evie. I don't know if I'm coming or going.'

'You'll get used to it,' was all she said. 'You'll have to.'

They fell into step together.

'So,' he began, continuing their earlier conversation that had been interrupted. 'You're not going to tell her?'

'What'd be the point? It'd only upset her. He's hardly going to come riding up on a white charger and carry her off into the sunset to live happily ever after. Life's not like that,' Eveleen said, her thoughts drifting back once more to Bernby and the fair-haired, blue-eyed man who had promised her heaven.

Jimmy grinned. 'She might want to see him. Get to know him again. You never know, they might—'

'He's married,' Eveleen said impatiently, surprised by

Jimmy's romantic nonsense. 'His son was with him when they came into the inspection room today.'

'Oh well, I don't care what you do. I shan't tell her.' He cast Eveleen a sly look. 'There's a lot I don't tell me mam.'

'Now why doesn't that surprise me,' Eveleen said, but Jimmy's grin only widened. Then he went on. 'They came into our place an' all this afternoon. Handsome chap, ain't he, the son? Just your type, Evie. That'd be a turn-up, wouldn't it, if you married the son.'

'Don't talk daft.' Eveleen was angry now. 'His sort don't interest me.'

'They did once,' Jimmy said, watching her closely.

'Well, they don't any more,' she snapped back and marched up the steps and into the home. I've far more pressing things on my mind, she thought. Getting us out of this place, for one.

The following morning when she arrived at work, the first thing Eveleen did was to ask Helen if she had heard of anywhere for them to rent.

The girl shook her head. 'Sorry, Eveleen, I haven't.'

Eveleen managed to smile and say, 'Thanks for trying.'

'I'll keep asking,' the girl promised.

About halfway through the morning, Fred appeared again at the doorway of the workroom to be greeted by calls and saucy remarks from the women. Eveleen could not stop herself from smiling. They're almost as bad as the men, she thought.

But Fred was only grinning good-naturedly and making his way towards her. 'You're in luck, lass. The missis has heard of a house in our yard, would you believe? If you like to come home with me after work, she'll take you to see it. She's going to get a key from the owner today.'

Eveleen leapt to her feet and threw her arms around him. 'That's wonderful. Oh thank you, thank you.'

She became aware of the laughter around her and she stepped back, embarrassed by her own behaviour.

'Miss Hardcastle!' came Miss Brownlow's voice. 'I think you forget yourself.'

'I'm sorry,' she said at once to Fred. 'But you don't know what this means to me.'

The man nodded kindly, quite unperturbed by her impetuosity. 'That's all right, love.' He laughed. 'I enjoyed it, but don't tell the missis.' He winked at her and said, 'See you outside the gate at knocking-off time, eh?' Fred worked in the warehouse carrying the heavy bales of cloth up and down the stairs to the different levels for sorting, dying, scalloping and trimming as well as to the very top for final inspection. He was lithe and muscular, no doubt from all the exercise he got each day.

She nodded, 'Thanks, Fred. I'll be there.'

'Hello, mi duck. It's nice to see you again.'

'Oh Mrs Martin, I'm so pleased to see *you* again. I wanted to thank you for all you've done to help me. You were so kind that day and you're still helping me now.'

The woman flapped her hand in embarrassment. 'Do call me Win and think nothing of it. Glad to help.' She turned to her husband. 'Your supper's in the oven, Fred, I'll just take this lass down to look at the house, though whether we'll see much in the dark, I don't know.'

'Take some candles,' Fred suggested. 'Or better still, I'll light a lamp for you.'

While they waited, Win said, 'I don't even know your name.'

Eveleen told her and then went on to explain why she needed a house so desperately.

'There are four of us, me mam, me brother and our cousin.' She bit her lip and said no more about Rebecca. Time enough for Win to find out about that later.

'Well, it won't be much of a place, love. This whole area's called Narrow Marsh and this is Foundry Yard. It's overcrowded and you have to share privies, but if you keep your own place clean, it's not so bad. Me and Fred have lived here ever since we got married and I wouldn't move if you gave me a palace. Folks is friendly round here and we all help each other.'

Eveleen smiled. Win Martin was certainly friendly and if all her neighbours were the same, then Eveleen could put up with harsh conditions.

'Ah, here's Fred with the lamp. Let's go and have a look.'

Only minutes later, they were walking into one of the back-to-back houses.

'There'll be three floors,' Win explained as they stepped into the room on the ground floor. 'There's the range . . .'

It was smaller than the one back home in Bernby, but Eveleen said nothing. She looked down at the cold, damp brick floor and thought, The sooner we get a fire going in here the better.

The furnishings were sparse: a table and three wooden chairs. They had left more than this behind in the farmhouse.

'There's a cupboard under the stairs for food and that.' Win opened it to show the empty shelves.

'It's all been left very clean,' Eveleen remarked, feeling she should say something as Win led the way up to the next floor.

'There's only one bedroom,' she said flinging open the door, 'but it's a good size.'

'I thought you said three floors.'

'Oh aye, of course, you could maybe use the room above here as another room for your brother.'

They climbed the ladder to the attic room under the eaves. It had the long window down one side.

'These houses are often occupied by stockingers,' Win said. 'And this is where they'd work. I use our top room for drawing lace. The younger girls help me too with the jennying.'

'Tell me, what is jennying?'

'The twist machines make the dress lace in breadths, each one separated by a draw thread.'

Eveleen nodded.

'When it comes off the machine all in one piece, it goes to you in the inspection and mending room. There are various other processes – bleaching, dyeing, dressing an' all that – and then it's sent out to homeworkers who separate all the breadths by "drawing". They wind the lengths of lace on to cards and that's what's called jennying.'

'So now I know,' Eveleen laughed and turned her attention back to their new home.

Jimmy could sleep to one side of this room, she was thinking, and leave space for her mother and Rebecca to work up here in the day.

'There's a tap in the yard we all share. It's all right until it gets cold in the winter and freezes up.' Win pulled a wry face. 'The privies are at the end of the yard and they're all right until it gets too hot in the summer and they pong to high heaven.'

She cast her eyes to the ceiling, but she was laughing.

'It's great, Win. Thank you so much.'

'It's in good order,' Win said, holding the lamp high. 'There's no damp patches on the ceilings or walls. When we moved into our place, you should have seen what Fred had to do to make it weatherproof.'

'It wonderful, really,' Eveleen said, clasping her hands. 'And it's so near to work too. Only just round the corner. How can I ever thank you?'

The woman looked at her and said gently, 'The look on your face is thanks enough, mi duck. Leave everything to me. I'll see the rent man tomorrow and get you a rent book sorted out. Now, come back home with me and have a bite to eat before you set off back to that home. You've a fair walk back and it's starting to rain.'

By the time she arrived back at the home, Eveleen was soaked to the skin, but she didn't care. She and Jimmy had work and now she had found them a house with friendly neighbours.

The relief was enormous and the move, which they were able to do the following Sunday, was far less traumatic that either of their two previous, hasty departures.

Of course all her worries and responsibilities were not going to disappear overnight, but at least now her family were housed, fed and clothed. There was just enough money coming in from both her and Jimmy to keep them. There would be none to spare for luxuries, but at least they had enough for the moment.

'And you can both earn a little extra here at home

lace-making,' she said to her mother and to Rebecca once they were settled into their new home. 'Or drawing and jennying.'

Rebecca said hesitantly, 'Eveleen, I'm sorry, but I'm not very good at pillow lace.'

'What? Didn't Gran teach you?'

Rebecca shook her head. 'Yes, but I've never done much. Father always wanted me to work the stocking-machine at home. He – he said there was more money to be made.' She hung her head. 'I'm sorry.'

Eveleen sighed and murmured, 'It's not your fault.'

This was a double blow. If her mother was refusing to help and Rebecca was not able, how were they ever going to earn that little bit extra that they needed so desperately?

'Mam, will you at least teach Rebecca pillow lace?'

Mary shook her head. 'Oh, I can't think about that just now. Leave me alone, Eveleen.'

Eveleen turned away. There was no getting through to her mother when she was in this mood. She'd leave it a few days and then see.

But Mary's mood did not dispel. She seemed permanently sunk in depression and despair and all she would say again and again was a pitiful, 'I want to go home, Eveleen.'

Thirty-Four

'I just hope this isn't tripe and onions again.' Jimmy pulled a face as he sat down at the table and looked down with suspicion at the plate Rebecca placed before him.

'No – no, Jimmy. I know you don't like it. I wouldn't do that.' She smiled uncertainly, her eyes never leaving his face.

Watching, Eveleen sighed inwardly. Rebecca's adoration of her rogue of a brother was plainly written on her face.

Jimmy stabbed at the food experimentally. 'What is it?'

'Pig's fry. We call it "Poor Man's Goose". Silly name really.' She tried to laugh light-heartedly, but the sound was forced. 'There's nothing of a goose in it. It's pig's liver, heart and kidney.'

'It's like Mam makes,' Eveleen said.

Jimmy brightened visibly. 'Is it?' He twisted round to look at Mary huddled in her chair by the fire. 'Did you make it Mam?'

Mary shook her head. 'I'm too ill, Jimmy. I have a dreadful headache. It's the smell of this place and having to share the privy with all these awful people.' She gave a dramatic shudder. 'I can't stand it.'

Eveleen was tempted to defend their neighbours. She liked the inhabitants of the yard; they were friendly and had welcomed the Hardcastle family into their midst. But she bit back the words while Jimmy pulled an unsympathetic face, rolled his eyes, and turned away. He took a mouthful, chewing it round and round, considering.

'Not bad,' he said. 'Not bad at all.' He cast a sideways glance at Mary before adding, 'Not as good as yours, of course, Mam, but not bad.'

Rebecca was pink with pleasure and emboldened to ask, 'After supper, shall we go out for a little walk, Jimmy?'

Jimmy stared at her as if she had taken leave of her senses. 'A walk? Where to, for Heaven's sake?'

'Well,' the girl stammered, her colour deepening but now through embarrassment. 'I – I'd just like to get some fresh air, that's all. I don't mind where we go.' The remainder – 'as long as I'm with you' – went unsaid.

'Fresh air,' Jimmy scoffed. 'Here? You must be mad. All you'll get is a lungful of smoke or the smell from the sewers.'

'The air at home was fresh and sweet and clean and . . .' Mary dissolved into tears. 'You see, Eveleen, Jimmy misses it as much as I do. Don't you, Jimmy?'

Eveleen could not let this pass. 'I seem to remember when we were living in the country, all he could do was talk about going to sea.'

'And I still might,' Jimmy said and, as Mary's sobs grew louder, silent tears ran down Rebecca's face.

The brother and sister glared at each other, but all Jimmy said was, 'What's for pudding?'

'I don't think Jimmy loves me any more, Eveleen.'

'Oh Rebecca, I'm sure that's not true. He's so young.

You both are. Only just seventeen. You were both very foolish, you know.'

'But I thought he loved me.' The girl's eyes filled with easy tears. 'He said he loved me and wanted us to get married.'

'That's what they all say.' Eveleen could not stop the bitter remark.

Her eyes brimming, Rebecca said, 'Did he just want to marry me because of my inheritance? That's what Father said.'

'Did he indeed?' Eveleen murmured, her mind calculating swiftly. Her uncle was sitting on a little gold mine. Perhaps if Jimmy and Rebecca had not been so hasty, all that might one day have become theirs. Why hadn't she thought about that before? She wondered what consideration Jimmy had given to it.

Rebecca was speaking again, 'Father said that if anyone ever did want to marry me, it'd only be to get their hands on his business.'

'What a cruel thing to say.'

'It looks like he was right, though, doesn't it?'

Eveleen took the girl's hands. They were cold. She chafed them, trying to warm the girl physically and raise her spirits. 'Look, I know my brother's not perfect. He's thoughtless and irresponsible but he's not cruel and calculating.' Hoping she sounded convincing, for she knew it was not quite true, Eveleen added, 'Besides, he's not clever enough to have thought all that out.'

She could see that Rebecca was still not reassured, so she went on, 'And he would hardly have got you into this state if that had been his reasoning. It wasn't quite the best way to worm his way into your dad's good books, was it?'

Rebecca smiled tremulously and shook her head. 'It was what he always said though, if anyone showed an interest in me. Any young man, I mean. He said it about Andrew.'

'Well, that's plain daft,' Eveleen said at once. 'Andrew truly loves you. Even I could see that and I'm certainly not the best judge when it comes to men.'

Rebecca's eyes were wide. 'Why?'

'Oh never mind just now. Maybe I'll tell you one day. But not now. I can't talk about it now.'

Rebecca nodded. She didn't understand, yet she sensed that it was a painful subject for Eveleen.

'Now then,' Eveleen said briskly, changing the subject. 'I've got a surprise for you. Since I can't persuade my mother to teach you to make lace I've been keeping my eyes and ears open. I asked Josh Carpenter if he knew of any way I could get hold of a Griswold. Like the one you had at home?'

Rebecca nodded.

'And guess what?' Eveleen went on triumphantly. 'He's found me an old one lying in one of the outbuildings at the factory.'

She smiled as she remembered the pleasure on the big man's face when he had presented her with the rusting machine. 'Needs a bit of cleaning up, but if you smile nicely at Fred Martin, I bet he'd do it up for you. Good with machinery, is Fred.'

Eveleen had been ecstatic in her thanks and had even reached up and planted a kiss on the man's fat cheek. He put his arm around her waist and squeezed her against his belly.

'You're a nice lass,' he said gruffly. 'Not like most of the girls here. They only know how to poke fun at a feller.'

Eveleen had felt a moment's fear. Had her rash gesture of gratitude given him the wrong idea? But in the next moment he had released her, patted her shoulder and said kindly, 'Run along, mi duck, before I forget myself.'

Now she told Rebecca, 'Fred's cleaning it up. He said it'll take him a week or so. All the needles are rusty.'

Rebecca looked the happiest she had looked for weeks. 'That's wonderful. Now I'll be able to earn some money to help out. You've been so good to me, Eveleen. I do so want to help.'

Good to her, Eveleen thought. We've been anything but good to her. It's all our fault that she's in this predicament and she's saying we've been good to her. But Eveleen kept her thoughts to herself and hugged her cousin.

Alone, Eveleen began to think more rationally about what Rebecca had told her. Rebecca was Harry's only daughter, his only child and consequently his only heir.

Maybe . . . Eveleen's eyes narrowed thoughtfully, calculating objectively. If Jimmy could be persuaded to do the decent thing and marry Rebecca, then maybe one day, Uncle Harry would relent. Jimmy would be set for life and she could take their mother back home to Lincolnshire.

For once, Eveleen vowed, her rebellious young brother must be made to toe the line.

'Jimmy, I want a word with you.'

Eveleen grasped his shoulder with a strength that was surprising for a girl. But her days on the farm were still not forgotten and, with walking to and from work each day and housework when she got home each evening, she was as physically fit as she had ever been. Instead of being defeated by the sheer hard work of it all, Eveleen seemed to thrive on it.

'Now what?' he said, trying to shake her off, but Eveleen kept tight hold of him.

'Walk home with me tonight and I'll tell you. It's the only time we get to talk alone. You never seem to want to stay at home in the evenings now.'

'What, with that miserable pair? Mam just sits in her chair all day long and Rebecca keeps bursting into tears. She won't even let me near her any more. Y'know, for a bit of you-know-what.'

'Wash your mouth out, you,' Eveleen said angrily. 'Don't talk about your future wife like that.'

'My what?'

If it hadn't been such a serious matter, Eveleen would have laughed out loud at the look of horror on his face. Instead she forced herself to say primly, 'Well, I hope you're going to do the decent thing by her. Surely you're not going to let the baby be born a – a . . .'

'If you think I'm going to tie mesen to that miserable cow, you can think again.'

'Jimmy, please. Don't talk about her like that. You've caused her misery.'

He twisted himself free of her grasp. 'Leggo. I've got to get back to work.'

Eveleen released him, but she realized that her devious brother had said the one thing that would make her let him go.

Her eyes narrowing, her gaze followed him as he walked into the factory.

This time, there was no swaggering walk and cheerful whistle.

She was waiting for him outside the gates when she knew his shift ended. It had meant her leaving her work an hour early but it was the only time she could snatch a few moments alone with him to try to talk some sense into him. She had pretended to be suffering stomach cramps to persuade the supervisor to allow her to leave.

'I meant what I said, Jimmy. It's your child she's having. You know very well it is. I don't want you trying to wriggle out of it by putting the blame on someone else. Rebecca's a good girl and if you hadn't filled her head with your lies just to get your way, she wouldn't be in that condition. And you know it, don't you?'

'Do I?' Jimmy was determined to be defiant to the last.

'Yes, you do,' Eveleen flared.

They walked in silence until he said, 'We're too young to be tied up, Eveleen.'

'You should have thought about that before. She's well and truly tied up now, isn't she?'

'She should have said no.'

'Oh yes, here we go. The old, old story. It's all the girl's fault. Jimmy, you took advantage of a young lass who's hardly been allowed out the door except to go across the road to the chapel. For all I know she might not have been told the facts of life properly. Maybe she didn't even know what you were up to.' She glanced sideways at him. 'Did she?'

'*I* don't know,' he muttered. 'It's not my problem.'

'Of course it's your problem. It's your bairn she's having.'

Again there was silence until he said suddenly and triumphantly, 'We can't get married. We're both under age. Even if I was willing – and I'm not – her father would never give his consent.'

'I intend to go to see him and ask him.'

Jimmy stopped walking and stared at her, causing her to pause too. 'Go back there? To him? You wouldn't?'

'Of course I would. I'm going on Sunday.'

For a moment the young man looked frightened. Then his face cleared. 'You can't. I bet there's no carrier's cart on a Sunday.'

'Yes, there is. I've checked.' Quietly, but with her tone full of steely determination, Eveleen added, 'And even if there wasn't, it's only about six miles. I'd walk.'

Thirty-Five

'You've got a nerve, girl, I'll say that for you. Showing your face here again.'

'I had to come, Gran. I have to speak to Uncle Harry.'

'I don't expect he'll want to speak to you.' Bridget looked up sharply, suddenly anxious. 'Is something wrong? Is it Rebecca?'

'No, no. She's fine. At least, as fine as she can be. She's very unhappy.'

'She's brought it all on herself,' the old woman said stiffly. 'I haven't got a scrap of sympathy for her.'

'So I see,' Eveleen said grimly.

Bridget glared at her and then looked away. 'What do you want to see her father about?'

'I need his permission for them to get married.'

'He won't give it.'

'Why ever not? Why won't he help us to make the best out of the situation? What's done, is done. At least we can make sure that his grandchild – and your great-grandchild – is born in wedlock.'

'Go and ask him yourself. He's in the chapel. Spends half his time there now. He'll tell you.'

'I will,' Eveleen said determinedly and marched out of the cottage and along the brick path, but before she reached the gate, she heard someone calling her name.

'Eveleen. Eveleen. Wait.'

She turned to see Andrew Burns coming towards her.

'How is she? Is she all right?' he was asking before he even reached her.

'She's fine.'

The look of relief on his face left Eveleen in no doubt, if indeed there had ever been any in her mind, of this young man's feelings for Rebecca.

'I thought something must have happened with you coming back here.'

Eveleen shook her head, reluctant to tell Andrew the reason for her visit. It could only bring him more pain. But Andrew was far more astute than she had given him credit for.

'You've come to see about them being married, haven't you? You've come to get his permission?'

There was nothing Eveleen could do but nod assent.

'Well, if he does marry her, he'd better treat her right. Else he'll have me to deal with. And I'll make a proper job of it next time. I'll mind you're not there to break us up.'

'Andrew, I'm so sorry.' She was reaching out to touch him, but he turned away. Sadly she watched him go.

A few minutes later she pushed open the door of the chapel, her heart thudding with nervousness. Her uncle was standing high up in the pulpit at the lectern reading silently from the huge Bible that always lay there.

She walked down the aisle knowing he must have heard her come in, yet he did not look up. She stood right beneath him near the communion rail and even when she spoke his name softly he did not look at her.

'Uncle Harry, please hear what I've come to say.'

He closed the old leatherbound book with loving care and, at last, he met her gaze.

Eveleen licked her dry lips. 'Uncle, please will you give

your permission for them to be marr
the child can be born in wedlock.'

She could see that he was strugglin
science. His inner turmoil showed plain
Then he stepped down from the pulpit and
He took hold of her shoulder and pushed h
family pew.

'We'll pray together, Eveleen. We'll ask for guidance.'

Willingly Eveleen knelt beside him, put her hands together in prayer and closed her eyes.

Half an hour later when her knees were sore and her legs cramped, her back aching and her hands cold, she was still in the same position. She opened her eyes and stole a look at the man beside her. He was still muttering quietly in prayer as he had done throughout the time they had both been kneeling there. Eveleen eased her aching limbs and shifted her position but her uncle droned on. Then she began to heave herself up to sit on the seat, but his hand shot out, pressing her firmly on the shoulder to keep her kneeling position.

Another ten minutes passed before he allowed her to rise and sit back on the pew. Stiffly he did the same and they sat in silence while she tried to rub life back into her limbs.

She felt his gaze on her and turned to look into his eyes. The sadness she saw there turned her heart over with pity for him.

'Have you an answer?' he asked her quietly.

She nodded. 'Whatever they've done wrong – and I know it was wrong, Uncle – it's not the unborn child's fault. Why should it be born without a proper name? Why should it have to go through life with the stigma of being called a . . .' She hesitated over the word. She had blaspheme in the chapel. '. . . dreadful name,' nished instead. Softly, she added, 'Can't you forgive hem, Uncle, because He will?'

He looked away from her then, his gaze roaming around the chapel and coming to rest once again on the Bible. Slowly, he nodded. 'Very well, Eveleen. I will agree to their marriage, but I – I can't bring myself to attend the ceremony.'

For a moment his stern face threatened to crumple, but he rubbed his hand across his eyes and with a supreme effort controlled his emotion. 'It's every father's wish to walk his daughter down the aisle on her wedding day. But now I have no wish to do so. I cannot bring myself to see her ever again.'

There was no more she could say or do to persuade him and while she had got what she came for – his written permission for his young daughter to marry – the victory was a hollow one.

She decided to walk back to Nottingham rather than wait for the last omnibus late in the evening. By the time she reached the yard where they now lived it was dark.

She pushed open the door thankful to be home and looking forward to a cup of tea and warming her toes by the range. She was met by the sound of Mary's wailing. When she heard the door, Mary rose from her chair by the fire and rushed towards Eveleen, her arms flailing.

She hit out at her, striking her on the shoulder and then about the head, 'He's gone. You've driven him away. He's left us. Jimmy's run away to sea. My Jimmy. My baby. He's gone.' More blows rained about her head and shoulders before Eveleen was able to catch hold of her mother's wrists and hold them firmly.

'Calm down,' she shouted above Mary's hysterical

unti[illegible]
glanced round [illegible] her into a chair and [illegible] hiccuping sobs. [illegible]here
arms folded over her sto[illegible]into [illegible]cowering in a corner, her
child. [illegible] protect her unborn

'Did she go for you, an' all?'

The girl nodded.

'Has she hurt you?'

'Not – not really.'

Beneath her grasp, she felt her mother go limp and Eveleen loosened her hold. Once she was sure that the onslaught was not going to begin again she let go completely and stood up. 'Now then. Will one of you tell me what's been going on?'

Rebecca only huddled further into the corner, sobbing quietly. Eveleen looked down at her mother. 'Well?'

'After you'd gone this morning, he was in a right temper. Shouting and carrying on. "Eveleen'll get that old bugger to agree to it," he said. "Everything always has to be her way. She always gets what she wants. And she will this time."'

Eveleen gasped and felt the colour drain from her face. How could Jimmy say such things about her? All she'd ever tried to do was take care of the family after their beloved father had died. Her knees gave way as the spirit drained out of her. Though she continued to stare at Mary as she ranted on, Eveleen sank into the chair opposite.

'"She's done it now," he said. "I'm really going to do it this time. I'm off to sea." And with that, he packed his things and went.'

Mary raised resentful eyes to Eveleen. 'If you hadn't pushed him to marry the girl, he'd have stayed with us. It's all your fault, Eveleen. All of it.'

pressed heavily upon Eveleen, ... Her
night. All their troubles had started back
shire when she, Eveleen, had beli...
a handsome young man.

Thirty-Six

Though her body ached with weariness, Eveleen slept little that night. Her mind was in turmoil. Her first thought, after the initial shock had worn off, had been to go in search of her brother. He could hardly join up on a Sunday, but she knew it was pointless. He could be anywhere by now in the vast city of Nottingham, and early the following morning he would no doubt be on his way to London or to a seaport to sign on.

She felt a stab of envy that he had broken free and then, despite his callous act, admiration for his daring. But there would be no such escape for her and he had left her with even greater problems than before.

Now she had to earn enough money to keep all of them.

The following morning Mr Porter stormed into the women's workroom.

'Where is he? Where is that idle blighter? You, girl, where's that blasted brother of yours?'

For some reason, Eveleen's instinct told her to hold back the truth, at least for a day or two. Knowing Jimmy, he could well be home by nightfall.

'Isn't he here?' she looked up with wide, innocent eyes. 'I'm so sorry, Mr Porter. I'll wring his neck when I catch up with him.'

The man grunted and seemed a little mollified by her willingness to condemn her brother. 'Well, see you do, lass. Meantime, get him back to that machine. He's not much use at his job yet, but Luke is a good teacher and if anyone can lick him into shape, Luke can.' Then he wagged his finger at her. 'And you can tell him, if he doesn't buck his ideas up and work harder, he'll be out on his ear anyway. I don't mind telling you, if I could find a youngster who was a quicker learner than him, he'd be out. Luke says he has to keep showing him what to do every morning. He can't seem to remember anything from one day to the next.' Perceptively, the man added, 'Or he doesn't want to.' Bob Porter turned away, grumbling and muttering to himself.

Eveleen stared after him as a daring and devious plan began to form in her mind. Her heart began to thud with excitement. Could she pull it off? If she was found out, she'd be sacked at once. But it was worth a try. They could hardly be worse off than they were at this moment. Her wages were a pittance – the family could not survive on those alone.

But if she could earn Jimmy's wage, then . . .

Eveleen bent her head over her work, trying to still her trembling fingers, trying to do her own work properly, at least for the rest of the day.

For tomorrow she would take her brother's place in the machine shop. They hadn't been here long enough for people to get to know him that well. And yet Jimmy had worked alongside Luke Manning for a few days. Would he guess? Could she really pull off such a daring deception?

Eveleen pressed her lips together determinedly. She had to.

There was only one thing she was going to regret. Tonight she must cut off all her glorious hair.

'Oh Jimmy, Jimmy. You've come back.' Mary rose from her chair and held out her arms to the figure that stood in the doorway. It didn't seem to register with her that the person had come from upstairs and not in from the yard. 'I knew you wouldn't desert us. Didn't I tell you, Eveleen?' She looked around her and then raised her voice. 'Eveleen? Where are you? Come here. Jimmy's come home.'

Rebecca came running from the scullery, her face alight with joy.

From her position by the door, it broke Eveleen's heart to have to say quietly, 'No, he hasn't, Mam. It's me.'

Mary turned startled eyes back to stare at her and Rebecca's mouth dropped open. Then tears of disappointment welled in her eyes.

'I'm sorry,' Eveleen said swiftly.

Mary, too, dissolved into tears, holding the corner of her apron to her mouth. 'How could you be so cruel, Eveleen? To dress up and pretend to be him. How could you do it?'

'It's not a game, Mam. I mean to take his place at the factory.'

Surprise caused Mary's tears to cease. 'You're not serious. You'll never get away with it.'

'I deceived you, didn't I? His own mother.'

'The light's poor in here,' Mary persisted. 'Besides, you don't know how to do his work.'

Eveleen moved forward and sat down. Mary sank into her chair and Rebecca, drying her tears as she became intrigued by Eveleen's bold plan, sat down too.

'I've watched him work, only the once I grant you, but when Mr Porter came looking for him yesterday, he said that Jimmy was not much of a worker anyway and Luke Manning – that's the twisthand who's training Jimmy – had to keep showing him what to do. I saw it with me own eyes an' all. Now, if I can only get him to do that for another day or two, I can soon pick it up.'

'Oh, Miss Clever,' Mary said sarcastically. 'You think you can do a man's job better than Jimmy, do you?'

'Jimmy could have done it if he'd really wanted to.' Eveleen sighed. 'But let's face it, Mam. All he's ever wanted was to go to sea. Maybe now he's going to be happy.'

'He was happy on the farm,' Mary insisted defensively. 'He was happy back home.'

'No, he wasn't, Mam. If you're honest, you know he wasn't.'

'What will happen if you're found out?' Rebecca asked softly.

'I'll be sacked on the spot. I know that, but it's a risk worth taking.'

'But if you're fired, we – we'll have nothing.'

'There are other factories. Other places to work. I'd soon get work again.' She pulled a face. 'Even if I have to go back to women's work.'

'What about Fred and Win? She's always popping in here. What are we going to tell them?'

Eveleen had been concerned only about the people at work: Mr Carpenter, who had been so kind to her and Helen, who was fast becoming a firm friend. And then, of course, there was Luke Manning. He was her greatest fear. Even Bob Porter was another threat, but the man she really had to convince was Jimmy's teacher at the lace machine.

Now she stared at her mother in horror. She had completely forgotten about Win and her husband.

She thought quickly. 'We could say that I've had to go back to Uncle Harry's to look after Gran. That she's not well.'

'Wouldn't it be me who would go back?' Rebecca asked in a small voice. 'I would want to if it was true.'

Eveleen bit her lip. She did not know how to answer the girl without sounding heartless. Rebecca saved her the need for she answered her own question sorrowfully. 'But they wouldn't want me there, would they? You're right, Eveleen. If anyone had to go back, it would be you.'

The following morning, Eveleen dressed in clothes that, fortunately for her, Jimmy had left behind. Striped shirt, braces and trousers and a black waistcoat and jacket. She stood looking at herself in the mirror. She did indeed look just like her brother except that her features were softer and there was no downy growth on her chin. She frowned at her reflection. She hadn't stopped to think about that. But then, Jimmy hadn't started shaving yet, so perhaps no one would notice. At least her hair, cut short now, curled just as Jimmy's had done, and beneath the shapeless man's clothing all sign of her womanly shape was well hidden.

She slipped out of the house into the darkness of early morning to arrive at the factory for Jimmy's early-morning shift. Four o'clock in the morning until nine and then again from one o'clock until six in the evening, with another worker taking the hours in between and afterwards until midnight. At least, she thought, I can get some work done at home between nine and one.

As Eveleen walked up to the gate, her heart was pounding and her mouth was dry with nervousness. Any moment she expected a raucous voice to shout, 'Hello, Eveleen. What are you doing dressed up in your brother's clothes?'

But as they all hurried, hunched with the cold, into their work, the other men did not even glance at her.

Feeling as if her heart was rising into her mouth, Eveleen took a deep breath and walked in through the factory gates.

Thirty-Seven

'Again? You're asking me to show you again?'

Eveleen nodded. 'Just once more, Mr Manning. I'm sure I'll get the hang of it soon.' She tried the sort of joke she was sure Jimmy would have used. The sort of quip he always made to get himself out of trouble. 'It's a lot different to milking cows.'

'Well, we'll try for a bit longer but you know, it doesn't rest with me. And Bob Porter's got his eye on you. If you don't buck your ideas up, lad, you're going to be out on your ear. And where were you yesterday? Bob doesn't like anyone taking the odd day off here and there.'

Eveleen had her answer ready. It would make her sound more laddish. She hung her head as if in shame. 'I had a drop too much to drink the night before.' It had been a Sunday night, so she added, 'One of the lads had a party at his house. It won't happen again, though, I promise.'

Luke pulled a wry face. 'It had better not. I'll say no more this time, but watch it. And don't you ever turn up the worse for wear after a night out, lad, else you'll be sacked on the spot. That's one thing Porter's a stickler on. And rightly so.' Luke nodded. 'Oh yes, rightly so. You've got to have your wits about you operating these machines.'

Now Eveleen could answer him far more truthfully

than ever her brother would have been able to do. 'I won't, Mr Manning.'

'Right then, lad. Let's show you all this once more.'

As she watched Luke, Eveleen felt a growing excitement. She could do this. She knew she could. Until this moment, she had worried that she might not be able to carry out all the tasks of an apprentice twisthand. The machines were heavy to operate. But Eveleen was strong and now she knew she could do it.

Luke stood back. 'Now then, let's see you have a go.'

As she stepped forward and laid her hands on the levers, Eveleen felt a thrill run through her such as she had never felt in her life before. At her fingertips she had a new skill, a skill that could earn her good money.

A few minutes later, Luke said, 'Well, you're shaping up better this morning. Mind you keep it up.'

Eveleen did not turn round, did not even answer him. Her whole concentration was on this wonderful machine; she was fascinated to see how the threads twisted into a pattern as delicate as a spider's web.

As she walked out of the factory gates again that night, Eveleen wanted to skip with joy. She had loved every minute of the day and the final cherry on the cake had come only a few moments ago when Luke had said, 'You've done much better today. Why you couldn't work like that before beats me.' And he had gone away shaking his head at the callowness of youth.

Eveleen had hidden her smile. The following morning and every morning after that, she knew she would not need to ask for his help any more. Already she knew exactly what was expected of her. Except perhaps when new work was given to them, but then he would expect Jimmy to have asked to be shown how to do it too.

As she walked along, she pushed her hands into the pockets of the trousers that had once been Jimmy's and tried to adopt his swaggering walk. She even tried to whistle, but that was going to need more practice.

'Jimmy!' She heard the familiar voice calling behind her and stopped. It had been bound to happen. There she was, she thought, congratulating herself that she'd pulled it off. She had been jubilant, but her celebrations had been premature. Now she was going to be found out. This was one of the people she had most feared meeting.

With a sigh of resignation she turned to see Josh Carpenter hurrying towards her as fast as he was able. His size made him walk with a rolling gait like a sailor on board a ship. Wheezing with the effort, he reached her and panted, 'Jimmy. Glad I've caught you. Where's your sister today? Not ill, is she?'

Eveleen felt a stab of guilt for her deceit when she saw the genuine concern in the man's eyes. Just in time she remembered not to lick her dry lips. It was not a habit of Jimmy's. She dropped her voice a tone lower and tried to speak in the offhand way that he would have done.

'Aw sorry, I was supposed to come and tell you. I forgot.' It was so alien to her nature to act as if she were unfeeling but it was the way Jimmy would have behaved. 'She's had to go back to Flawford. The old woman's ill.'

Josh's face fell. 'I'm sorry to hear that. But she will be coming back? I'll keep her job open for her. Tell her that. Tell her I'll keep her job open for her.'

A lump rose in Eveleen's throat at the man's kindness. But his eagerness was pathetic and she knew that Jimmy would have sneered at Josh Carpenter at this moment.

Eveleen could not bring herself to do that. The new Jimmy would have to retain some of the real Jimmy's character traits, but by degrees Eveleen would act more like herself. Now, she said, 'I'll tell her, Mr Carpenter. But I think it might be a while before she's back.'

The way was cleared now for whatever might happen. If Jimmy stayed away, their grandmother could remain in her make-believe sickbed. If he came back, then Eveleen too could be said to have returned home.

As Mr Carpenter looked even more dejected, Eveleen turned away, unable to bear the look on the big, kind man's face.

'I really liked your sister,' she heard him murmur as she moved away. Eveleen swallowed. Jimmy would have laughed out loud, jeered at the man, even if it had jeopardized his job.

That was one thing that Eveleen would never do. As she walked out of the gates and turned for home, she smiled to herself. They say leopards never change their spots, she thought. Well, Jimmy Hardcastle, you certainly are doing now.

When she arrived home it was to find Fred Martin standing proudly in front of the Griswold stocking-machine sitting on the table. The once rusty piece of machinery now positively gleamed.

Eveleen opened her mouth and began to say, 'Oh Fred,' in the tone of voice that the delighted Eveleen would have used. Just in time she caught herself.

'You've made a good job of that, Fred.' Jimmy was cheeky enough to have dispensed with the polite 'Mr Martin' by now.

'Rebecca's just been telling me that your sister has had to return to Flawford. I'm sorry to hear that.'

Eveleen and Rebecca exchanged a glance. In her chair by the fire Mary glowered, but to Eveleen's relief she said nothing.

With a forced brightness, Rebecca said, 'But it's me who's going to be using this, Mr Martin. I don't know how to thank you. It means I can work at home and help out a bit now that we've lost one of the wages.'

Eveleen let out her breath. Rebecca was prepared to play along with her scheme and she suspected that Mary would too, especially if it meant that she could continue to sit idly by the fire all day long.

Well, that was going to have to change too, Eveleen promised herself as she gave a brief nod towards Fred Martin, turned and headed for the stairs, leaving Rebecca to express the effusive thanks that once Eveleen would have done.

After a hurried supper, which Rebecca was anxious to have cleared away, the girl sat down at the table with the restored machine in front of her.

'Mr Martin's even brought me some yarn to get me started. Isn't he kind?'

'A lot of people have been very kind to us since we arrived in Nottingham,' Eveleen murmured and Rebecca looked up.

'Kinder than we were to you when you came to us, eh?'

'Oh I didn't mean that,' Eveleen said at once.

Rebecca sighed. 'But it's true, Evie. I know it is and I'm ashamed that I didn't do more to make you welcome.'

Eveleen sat down at the table opposite her and looked

at Rebecca. The girl had been sunk in misery since Jimmy's departure and Eveleen had despaired that she was ever going to raise her or Mary from their depression. But now, watching Rebecca as she ran her hands knowledgeably over the machine and threaded up the yarn in readiness to begin work, even at this late hour in the day, Eveleen could see that her young cousin now had a new purpose. The Griswold had restored her pride. It was something she could do and do well and she could contribute to the family's income.

'Don't tire yourself, though, will you?' Eveleen said gently to her, but forbore to add, You must think of the baby. At this moment she did not want to spoil the girl's pleasure by reminding her of her problems. She was only too happy to see a tentative smile returning to Rebecca's wan face.

Eveleen stood up and moved to the hearth to stand over her mother. It was time Mary Hardcastle started to pull herself together too.

'Now, Mam,' Eveleen began, firmly, but not unkindly. 'Rebecca's going to be busy earning a bit extra for us, so you're going to have to look after the house. And it's high time.' She reached up to the shelf at the side of the fireplace and brought down Mary's workbox holding all the bobbins for making pillow lace. She opened it and carefully lifted everything out. She moved one of the wooden chairs usually placed at the table in front of her and rested the pillow on its seat. Then she began to sort out the bobbins to try to pick up the threads of the piece of lace that her mother had started just before the tragedy of Walter's death had happened. She had worked on it spasmodically during their time at Flawford, but since their arrival in Nottingham it had lain untouched in her workbox.

She heard a gurgling sound and both she and Rebecca looked swiftly at Mary. Startled, they saw that she was leaning back in her chair, tears running down her face. But to their amazement, her tears were of laughter.

'Oh,' Mary gasped, holding her midriff as if the laughter actually hurt her. 'You don't know how funny you look sitting there, dressed as Jimmy but doing a woman's work. If he could see you now. If Jimmy could see you now.'

Eveleen and Rebecca glanced at each other and then back at Mary. And then they, too, began to laugh until their sides ached.

Thirty-Eight

After that evening when their laughter had broken the tension, everyone seemed in better spirits. Rebecca was the happiest she had been since the awful moment she had realized she was pregnant and even Mary roused herself enough to attempt a little lace-making during the day. She and Rebecca shared most of the household chores in the morning and then sat down to their stocking-making and lace-making in the afternoons.

If there was no supper on the table when Eveleen arrived home after a long day's work, she forbore to complain. She was only thankful that the atmosphere was a great deal pleasanter in the house and also that they were making productive use of their time. For the first time since her father's death, Eveleen had caught a brief glimpse of the woman her mother used to be when she had been loved and cherished by the gentle Walter Hardcastle. It gave her a glimmer of hope.

'I don't know how long you're going to be able to keep up the pretence,' Mary said. 'I'm surprised no one's twigged on to you yet.'

Eveleen had been playing the part of her brother for more than a week, and while there had been one or two moments when she thought her deception might be discovered, she had still carried it off. The hardest part was not letting her façade slip, not even for a moment, and always remembering to act as Jimmy would have done.

Already she had become a willing apprentice to Luke and had earned praise from him. 'Well, you've turned out better than I expected, lad. See what you can do when you put your mind to it?'

Eveleen had hidden her smile.

Now, she answered her mother. 'I don't think Jimmy'd been there long enough for anyone to really get to know him.'

'If you get caught, you'll be out.'

'Yes, Mam. I know that, but for the moment, it's a risk worth taking.'

'But you can't be a boy for ever, Eveleen,' Rebecca said softly. 'I mean you might meet someone nice and want to get married.' Her voice trailed away. Her future hopes and dreams were in tatters, but it didn't stop the young girl having romantic notions for someone else.

'That's the least of my worries,' Eveleen said with feeling.

Josh Carpenter rarely came to the machine room. Although he was in overall charge of the factory and answerable only to Mr Stokes, the day-to-day running of the machine shop was Mr Porter's domain. Eveleen had thought herself safe from having to speak to Josh and the only times when she feared she might encounter him were when she arrived and left each day.

So it was a surprise one morning to glance up and see him standing near by. She gave him a brief nod – as Jimmy would have done – and concentrated on her work, but her fingers were trembling. Had she been discovered? Had Josh realized just who she really was?

Josh watched her working for a few moments, then leaned towards her and shouted above the clatter. 'I don't want to stop you working, but come to my office when you knock off, will you?'

Eveleen nodded. Her heart sank and she sighed inwardly. Only just over a week in the job and she had been found out. She doubted she would be even allowed to go back to her job in the workroom with the other women. No one in the management or workforce would take kindly to her deception.

Later that day, as she stepped nervously into his office and stood facing him, she remembered to keep up the act. She stood facing him with her hands in her pockets, a resentful expression on her face. It was how Jimmy would have acted at being delayed from escaping from the place.

'Have you heard from your sister? Is she all right? When is she coming back?' Josh, far from being the imposing figure Eveleen had once thought him, now looked rather vulnerable.

'She's fine,' Eveleen said truthfully, but then the lies had to start and did not come so easily to her lips. 'But Gran's still ill. We don't know when she's coming back.'

Disappointment etched lines into the florid face. 'Oh.' He gave a great sigh that seemed to come from deep inside his huge frame. 'Do you go to see her on a Sunday?'

Jimmy would certainly not have made any such effort, so Eveleen shrugged and said evasively, 'I might.'

'If you do, give her my regards. Her job's still here for her.'

'Righto,' Eveleen said and left the office whistling through her teeth. She had been practising on the way home each night and now had Jimmy's whistle almost perfect. But once outside the factory gates, she ceased her merry tune. She didn't feel in the least merry tonight, even though she was relieved that the reason Josh had wanted to see her had not been what she had feared.

She had mixed feelings about Josh's obvious interest in her as Eveleen. She wasn't sure whether she was completely comfortable about it. Surely a man of his age – he was old enough to be her father – could not be interested in her romantically? Surely he couldn't imagine . . . In a world where his position isolated him anyway and where his size made him a figure of fun for cruel, unthinking people, she had been nice to him, polite to him. Like a flower thirsting for water, he had soaked up her kindness.

I could write to him, she thought. I could write and thank him for getting us the Griswold and for his kind messages. Then 'Jimmy' could bring it into him next Monday morning as if he had seen me on the Sunday.

She felt so sorry for the man. Surely that couldn't do any harm. Besides, Eveleen wasn't even here, at least, not that he knew.

So, after chapel on the Sunday evening, Eveleen sat down to compose her letter. It had been at Rebecca's surprising insistence that they still attended Chapel.

'It's so much a part of my life,' she had said simply. 'I have to go. I *need* to go.' So Eveleen had gone along with her and had found some solace for herself in the services conducted by a young preacher who was far less fiery than the minister in Ranters' Row.

Now, as she sat down to write, Eveleen thought, At least I don't have to pretend for a few moments. At least I am writing this as myself.

Dear Mr Carpenter, she wrote. *Jimmy tells me that you have been asking most kindly after me, for which I thank you.* She hesitated to write anything about her

Gran. Suddenly, she felt overcome with a strong sense of superstition. What if by acting out her grandmother's illness, she made it become a reality? Was she tempting Fate? Then Eveleen shook herself and put such fanciful notions out of her head. *I can't say when I'll be back so if you have to let my job go, I shall understand.* As the days passed, Eveleen was increasingly sure that Jimmy would not come home. And she wanted to try to be as fair as she could to Mr Carpenter. She was deceiving him enough already, her guilty conscience reminded her.

I also want to thank you so much, she went on, *for getting us the stocking-machine. I hear that Mr Martin has finished repairing it and Rebecca is thrilled. She is making stockings faster than we can find people to buy them. With many thanks, yours sincerely, Eveleen Hardcastle.*

She read the letter through three times before she was satisfied that she had not made any glaring mistakes.

She folded the paper into four and wrote on the outside *Mr Carpenter – Personal* and then laid it on the table for 'Jimmy' to deliver the following morning.

Thirty-Nine

It was not Josh Carpenter who caused Eveleen any awkward moments the following day, but Richard Stokes.

Brinsley Stokes and his son, making their daily rounds through the factory, passed close to where Eveleen was working. Glancing up she saw them approaching and, fascinated to see the man who had once been her mother's lover close to, she stared at Mr Stokes senior. He did not appear to notice her scrutiny, but the son paused by her machine, a slight frown of puzzlement creasing his forehead. So intent had been her concentration upon the father that when Richard spoke to her she jumped.

'You're new here, aren't you? How long have you been here?'

'Couple of weeks, mister,' she said in the offhand way her brother would have answered.

The young man was still frowning. Close to, he was even handsomer than she had thought him the day she had seen him in the women's workroom. His hair was like jet, smooth and shining. His skin was dark, his jawline was strong and clearly defined. His thick black eyebrows were a gentle arch, but it was his dark brown eyes, so like her own, that caught and held her attention. He smiled at her now and the tanned skin around his eyes wrinkled endearingly with laughter lines.

'You seem familiar,' he murmured. 'Have I seen you before?'

Eveleen's heart was in her mouth. He knew her. He recognized her from the workroom and now she was about to be unmasked.

She manufactured a shrug. 'Dunno,' she muttered. 'You might have.' Then, a little belligerently, she added, 'I've been stood here for the past two weeks at this machine and you come every day.'

'Mm,' he said, seeming to accept her reasoning, but his thoughtful gaze was still upon her. 'Possibly.' His frown deepened. 'But there's something about you. You look . . .' Then he appeared to shake himself and laughed. 'I must be imagining it. For a moment, I thought . . .' He laughed again and added, 'Oh well, never mind what I thought.'

As he moved away, Eveleen's heart was hammering so loudly inside her chest she thought that he must hear it even above the noise of the machinery around them. She could easily guess what had been in his mind. He thought that the young lad standing at the lace-making machine was remarkably like a girl he had seen in the women's workroom.

Well, I am, Eveleen reminded herself. I mean, I am even if it really was Jimmy standing here. But somehow she had the uncomfortable feeling that Richard Stokes had seen something more than just the likeness that had always been between the brother and sister. He had looked so deeply into her eyes that the depths of her soul had trembled.

He was very good-looking. *Nice* looking, she thought, not just handsome. He's got kind eyes – warm brown eyes, not cold blue ones. Then she reminded herself sharply that she had better concentrate on her work. She didn't want to slip back into Jimmy's ways and lose Luke's respect. It had been hard enough to earn after

Jimmy's careless start. One more mistake and she could be out of a job.

Besides, she reminded herself fiercely, she wanted nothing to do with handsome young men. But the girl inside the boy's outward appearance was startled by the sudden stab of disappointment she felt that Richard Stokes could no longer see her as a woman.

He came again the following day and the day after that. And always he paused beside her workplace, allowing his father to move ahead out of earshot while he spoke to her.

On the third day, he was smiling broadly as he approached her.

'Now I know why I thought you seemed familiar,' he said at once. 'Mr Carpenter has just been telling me about your sister in the workroom. I saw her in there a week or two back.' He winked conspiratorially and leaned closer. 'Such a pretty girl. Marvellous hair.'

Eveleen tried to adopt the expression that she knew would have been on Jimmy's face. A slightly sneering, disbelieving look. Never in a million years would Jimmy have acknowledged that his sister was remotely nice-looking, never mind pretty!

Eveleen shrugged and said gruffly, 'She's all right, I suppose. Got a temper on her, though.'

'Mm.' Richard was looking keenly at her. Even now Eveleen had the uncomfortable feeling that somehow he was disbelieving the evidence in front of his eyes. 'Well, perhaps she has reason,' he said in softer tones, so that, above the noise, Eveleen did not hear his words. Working in the machine shop, however, she was fast becoming adept at lip-reading and so guessed what he had said. In reply, she gave the nonchalant laugh of her brother.

Richard was leaning closer again. 'When you see her, give her my best wishes and tell her I hope your grandmother will soon be well enough for her to return to us.' He nodded, stepped back and then moved away, walking down the aisle between the rows of machines with an easy grace.

Despite her vow to have nothing to do with handsome young men and the impulsive and dramatic change in her persona, Eveleen began to look forward to Richard's visits to the factory each day. He would smile and nod to her though he would not always stop to speak. Often Eveleen was too busy to pause in her work, but she was always very aware of his nearness.

Against her will, she began to watch the doorway for his arrival, and more than once was reprimanded by Luke for inattention.

'You're slipping back into your bad ways,' he grumbled. 'I'll have to tell Bob Porter about you if you don't buck your ideas up. I've my own job to think about, y'know.'

'I'm sorry,' Eveleen said, uncharacteristically as Jimmy. Luke cast a sideways glance at her and Eveleen could have kicked herself, not only for her inattention at her work but for allowing herself to think about Richard Stokes.

For the remainder of that week she refused to glance at him when he paused at the end of the long machine.

But always, even without looking up, she was acutely conscious of his presence.

*

A week later it was Richard who caused her to make her most disastrous mistake yet – even by Jimmy's standards. It was ironic that she had been so intent upon her work that she had not seen him enter the machine shop and was unaware of him until she felt him touch her shoulder.

She jumped physically and, to her chagrin, gave a girlish gasp. But Richard was smiling and mouthing the words, 'How's your sister? Any news?'

Eveleen shook her head and Richard shrugged, raised his hand in acknowledgement and moved away.

Her gaze followed him.

Suddenly she felt a clout across the back of her head that sent her reeling and she fell to her knees in the aisle between the rows of machines.

Luke was standing over her, his face purple with rage and roaring at the top of his voice above the noise.

'Look what you've done.'

Eveleen scrambled up. To her horror a thread had broken and she had failed to notice it. Now a flaw was running the length of the fabric.

'That's it, I've had enough of you. I'm telling Bob Porter to fire you. I thought you'd mended your ways, but the first few days you were here I had my doubts about you. Seems I was right all along.'

Eveleen felt her face grow crimson as Luke's tirade continued. There was nothing she could do to prevent the girlish blush.

'You've had enough chances now,' the man went on waving his fist in her face. 'You're out.'

'Hold on a minute,' a voice spoke behind them and they both turned to see Josh Carpenter standing there, a letter in his hand. 'What's going on?'

'It's this young lad. He's useless.'

'But you told me only last Friday that he was shaping

up much better.' Josh glanced worriedly from one to the other. 'My office when your shift ends – both of you.'

He turned away, still carrying the letter, which, Eveleen was sure, had been another addressed to her.

She turned to Luke unable to stop tears glimmering in her eyes. 'I'll put it right, I promise.'

'Pigs might fly,' he grunted. 'Well, I'm not letting my work go to the inspection room like that. They'll likely try to get my pay docked.'

'I'll mend it. I—'

Luke shot her a strange glance. 'That's women's work. Know someone who'll do it for you, do you?'

Eveleen bit her lip but did not answer. Even if she risked revealing her identity she intended to repair the long mend, as they called the flaw.

When the length of lace came off the machine, Eveleen bundled it up and, at the end of her shift, carried it with her as she and Luke Manning walked side by side to Josh Carpenter's office.

'So, what's all the trouble?' Josh was frowning, his face even redder than usual as he mopped at his brow with a large, greyish handkerchief.

'No trouble, sir,' Luke said smoothly. 'Not now.'

'Well, what was the trouble then? Come on, I want to know. I saw you clout this young lad. You're not the sort to do that, Luke, without good reason. I know that.'

Although she kept her voice gruff and resentful, Eveleen could no longer stay totally in Jimmy's character. She liked Luke and it had been her foolishness that had caused the problem.

Damn and blast all handsome young men, she thought, including Richard Stokes.

'It was my fault, Mr Carpenter. A thread broke and I

didn't notice it.' She indicated the fabric she was carrying. 'But I'll get it mended.'

For a moment, Josh's jowls sagged sorrowfully. 'If your sister were here, lad, she'd mend it.' He glanced up at Luke. 'Lovely worker, she is.'

'Aye, well, we all mek mistakes. And if he can get it mended . . .' Luke, his anger gone, was now prepared to champion his young apprentice.

Josh leant back in his chair and linked his podgy fingers across his belly. 'So you're prepared to give him another chance.' Josh's tone seemed to Eveleen to be more of a statement than a question. Luke must have noticed it too, for he said deferentially, 'If you think I should, sir.'

Josh looked sternly at Eveleen. 'As long as you'll be more careful in future and keep your mind on your work, lad.'

'Yes, sir,' Eveleen whispered. 'Thank you, sir.'

Josh leant forward again. 'That'll be all, Luke, thank you.'

As Eveleen turned to leave too, Josh said, 'A moment, lad, if you please.'

When Luke had left the office, Josh handed the letter across his desk. 'Take this to your sister when you see her again, will you?'

Eveleen merely nodded as she took the envelope. She could not, at this moment, trust herself to speak. So guilty did she feel that she was on the verge of breaking down and confessing her deception.

As she escaped into the passage outside, she found Luke was waiting for her. 'Looks like you've got a champion, boy.' His tone was friendly again, his earlier anger forgotten, but as he put his hand on Eveleen's shoulder and walked alongside her out of the factory, he said, 'Or is it your sister that old bugger's interested in, eh?' When Eveleen did not reply – she did not know what to say – Luke dropped his hand and added, 'Well, just you tell that lass of yours to mind herself with him. See you tomorrow, bright and early.'

Eveleen nodded. 'Thanks, Mr Manning.'

Again, just briefly, there was a strange look in his eyes as he said, with a veiled warning, 'And no more chatting when we have – er – visitors round the factory, eh?'

Eveleen's heart skipped a beat. It was obvious that Richard's attentions had not gone unnoticed. At once Eveleen said, 'Mr Richard was asking me about me sister an' all.' Feigning resentment, she added, 'Can't think why.'

Now Luke laughed and there was a look of relief in his eyes. 'From what I've heard, your sister's a very pretty girl. Can't say I've seen her but it sounds as if I've missed something if even Mr Richard's asking after her welfare. She must be summat special.'

They had reached the gates and Luke turned in the opposite direction to the way Eveleen went.

Still chuckling, Luke shouted, 'Tarr-ra,' leaving Eveleen standing very still, staring after him.

His remarks had left her with a warm glow and, despite her resolve, the image of Richard Stokes's handsome face was in her mind's eye.

Forty

There was little privacy in the house in Foundry Yard so Eveleen waited until her mother and Rebecca had gone upstairs before she pulled the letter from her pocket and opened it.

Dear Eveleen, Josh had written in forward sloping script. *I am sorry that your grandmother's illness keeps you from us. We miss your lovely smile*. Eveleen drew in a sharp breath. The word '*We*' had obviously been altered from '*I* ' and all that the single letter implied.

'Oh no,' she groaned aloud to the dying embers in the grate and the soft lamplight. 'Don't say they're right and he really has got a thing for me?'

She sighed. Was there no man who would be a true friend? Young or old, handsome or ugly? Were they all just after the one thing? Perhaps she was being naïve. Perhaps there was no such thing as a true friendship between the sexes.

She read on. *Don't worry about your job. There'll always be room for a good worker like you in our workroom. Your brother is shaping up very nicely now, Luke tells me. Maybe with you being away, a bit of responsibility is good for him. Although I hope that part of it doesn't last for too long. I am so glad the Griswold is proving useful. I might be able to help with the selling of the socks. Tell your brother to bring some to show me and I'll see what I can do. Take care of yourself and hurry back. With kind regards, Josh.*

The letter was innocent enough, she supposed, but then she gave an involuntary shudder. If it had fallen into the wrong hands, there was enough in the words to hint at something more. What factory manager, Eveleen asked herself candidly, writes to a lowly girl worker from the inspection room?

They don't, was her honest answer.

She sat there until the embers had grown cold. By the time she rose from the chair and went up the stairs she had decided that she would not reply to Josh's letter, but then she caught sight of the pile of socks that Rebecca had made waiting for a buyer. Eveleen bit her lip. Just one more letter to thank him, she promised herself, and, as Jimmy, she would take some samples for Josh to see. After that, no more letters. As Jimmy, she might have to fend off his enquiries about Eveleen, but surely when she did not reply to any future correspondence from him and did not return to work, Josh would eventually forget about her.

As she slid quietly into the bed she shared with her mother, Eveleen could not prevent a stab of disappointment as she realized the full extent of the charade she had undertaken.

Never again could she talk to a man, any man, as a pretty, lively young girl.

The pattern went on much the same for the next two weeks. Even though Josh answered her second letter immediately, this time Eveleen did not write back. She was managing to concentrate on her work, although she was intensely aware of his nearness whenever Richard

Stokes was standing in the aisle close by her. And almost daily Josh would waylay her on her way into or out of the factory.

'I've found an outlet for your cousin's socks and stockings. Bring 'em all in tomorrow.'

'Right,' Eveleen said. 'Ta.'

And then, as he always did, Josh asked, 'How is your sister? Any news?'

Towards the end of the second week, as the shift ended, Josh handed her another letter as she was leaving.

'Take this to your sister. You'll be seeing her on Sunday?'

'I dunno,' she answered gruffly and shrugged.

'Then tell me the address and I'll post it,' Josh said, his fingers closing again on the letter as if to retrieve it from her grasp.

'No,' Eveleen said swiftly, suddenly afraid. If letters started arriving in Ranters' Row addressed to her from a strange man, her uncle's view that she and all her family were destined for hell and damnation would be justified in his eyes.

'I'll take it to her,' she said brusquely, snatching it back from his reaching fingers. She pushed it into the depths of her pocket, crumpling the offending letter carelessly.

Why, oh why, she asked silently, did he have to go on writing to her? It's your own fault, a small voice inside her head answered. You shouldn't have encouraged him. You should never have replied to his letter in the first place. You should have killed this before it even started.

Several men passing by had witnessed Josh handing the letter to her but Eveleen walked out boldly with the rest of the workers. To try to avoid them, to linger behind until they'd all left, would look even more suspicious. So, pushing her hands into her pockets, she walked jauntily out of the gates and set off for home.

They were waiting for her round the corner at the end of the street. A gang of lads and one or two of the older men from the machine shop.

'Here he comes. Carpenter's little darling.'

'We knew the old bugger liked the lasses, didn't know he had a liking for lads,' one of the older men leered, pretending to give a shudder as if the mere thought offended him. 'What's he put in the letter, eh? Asking you to meet him down a dark alley, is he?'

Eveleen glanced at him out of the corner of her eyes. 'The letter is for me sister . . .' She couldn't stop herself hesitating pointedly before she added with heavy sarcasm, 'sir.'

'Oh aye, I'll believe you. Thousands wouldn't.' His eyes narrowed as he added, 'But who do you like, boy? Carpenter or young Stokes?' He prodded his finger at her. 'I saw you eyeing the boss's son. Well, you're barking up the wrong tree there, son. He'll be earmarked for some society girl, you can bet your last 'apenny on that.'

Forgetting for a moment just who she was supposed to be, Eveleen felt the tears prickle at the back of her eyelids. She bit hard down on her lower lip. Her deception was bringing more ridicule to Josh. Was that the way to repay the man's kindness?

They encircled Eveleen, calling her filthy names and punching her so that she was pushed from one side of the circle to the other, then to and fro until she fell to the ground on her hands and knees.

She was sick with fear, terrified of what they meant to do to her. But she was trapped. They were all around her. There was no escape and no friendly face. They stood over her, leering down at her, jeering at her.

One of the young men straddled her back, as if to ride her like a horse. Holding her, he pushed his hand into her pocket and pulled out the letter. 'Let's see old Carpenter's love letter.'

Still, sitting astride her, his weight crushing her, he ripped open the letter and held it aloft.

'*Dear Eveleen.*'

All around there were whistles and ribald remarks. 'Oho, is that your name, ducky, when you're not at work?'

'No, it is his sister's name,' another spoke up, for the first time with a word in her defence.

'I bet there ain't no sister,' the young man still sitting on her back sneered.

'No, no, there is. She used to work in the warehouse.'

But the lad on Eveleen's back was not listening. '*Dear Eveleen*,' he went on. '*I was disappointed not to hear from you again.*' There were loud jeers around her and, straining not to give way beneath the lad's weight, Eveleen caught the sob that rose in her throat. '*Please write back and let me know how you are faring. Your friend, Josh.*'

'Oho, *your friend*.' He caught hold of Eveleen's short hair and jerked her head upwards. He stood up and hauled her to her feet. 'Well, let's have a look at just what it is that old Carpenter likes.'

'I tell you, it's not him, it's his sister Carpenter's after.' But the lone voice of protest was shouted down.

They crowded closer with willing, eager hands to grab her and wrench off her jacket.

Eveleen began to scream but they only laughed.

'He screams like a girl,' someone said, still unaware that he spoke the truth.

They pulled the braces from her shoulders and while

one man holding her lifted her off her feet, others yanked at her trousers. Eveleen kicked out and caught one of them in the face with her boot. He cried out and stepped back, holding his cheek. Then, swearing at her, he lunged at her and tore off her shirt.

'Come on, let's finish the job. Let's make him walk home naked through the streets. That'll teach him.'

Though she struggled she was powerless against their number. They ripped off the man's vest and long johns she was wearing and then there was a sudden silence. They stood back and the man holding her set her on the ground.

'My God. He's – she's a girl.'

Eveleen stood, her head bowed, tears coursing down her face, trying to cover herself with her arms. Then a sudden spurt of anger made her lift her head to face them all. She dropped her arms and, shamelessly, stood naked before them.

'Aye, come on, take a good look, 'cos that's all you're going to get.'

They were shuffling uneasily now. One or two picked up the items of clothing and handed them back to her, sheepish and embarrassed. They were trying not to look at her and yet, being healthy, lusty men, they could not stop themselves looking upon the young, firm and shapely body of the girl.

Eveleen, her anger driving out her embarrassment, pulled on her clothes. 'There, seen enough, have you?'

They parted the circle and allowed her to walk out of it, but then one of the younger men said, 'Hey, wait a minute. Do you mean to say you've been posing as a lad to get work in our machine shop?'

Eveleen turned to face him. Now her secret was out, there was nothing more to lose. The following morning even Josh Carpenter would not stand up for her. Not this time.

She held up her head proudly. 'Yes. My brother, Jimmy, did start work on that machine but then ran away to sea. I was working with the women, but the pay's rubbish. So I took his place. I needed the money.'

'We've all got families to support,' someone muttered. 'You're taking a man's place. A man who needs a job.'

'I needed the job.' She glared round at them. 'I've my mother and the girl my dear brother's left pregnant to support.'

There was grumbling among them until one of the older men spoke up. 'We don't mean to be hard on you, love. In a way, I admire you for what you've done. Those machines aren't easy to operate and from what Luke was saying, you're coming on a treat now even though you weren't much good to start with.' He glanced round at the others and grinned suddenly. 'That explains it. She must be a better worker than ever her brother was.' Then his face sobered. 'But it's not fair on the rest of us. If we let you carry on, there's no telling where it'll lead.'

'Aye, we'll have women taking over. Taking all our jobs.'

The first man, who seemed to have appointed himself as spokesman, spread his hands apologetically. 'So you see, we can't let you stay, even if we wanted to.'

A lump in her throat, Eveleen nodded. 'I know,' she said huskily and turned away before they should see the tears in her eyes.

'We'll put in a good word for you, love,' one of the older men shouted after her. 'See if Carpenter will give you your old job back.'

'Or mebbe you could work as a winder,' someone else suggested.

'We'll ask Carpenter not to sack you, love.'

Not trusting herself to speak, Eveleen glanced back over her shoulder and raised her hand in acknowledgement.

Not until she arrived home did she allow the tears to fall.

Forty-One

'I told you it wouldn't work. I said you'd get caught.'

Mary was triumphant that her pessimism had been proved right.

Rebecca put her arm about Eveleen's shoulders. 'Don't cry, Evie. You'll get work somewhere else. There's plenty of other factories round here. Or you can work at home with us.'

Eveleen did not answer. She didn't want to hurt the girl's feelings by saying that while their money was very useful, even necessary, the bit that homeworkers brought in, even three of them, would not be enough to support the household. And very soon Rebecca would have a baby to care for and even less time to work.

'If you hadn't driven my Jimmy away,' Mary said resentfully. 'None of this would have happened. In fact, if you—'

Eveleen's patience gave way and she snapped, 'Yes, yes, I know. It's all my fault. Everything that's happened is my fault.'

Mary wagged her finger at her, seeming for a brief moment more like the mother Eveleen remembered. 'Don't you back answer me, miss.'

'I'm sorry, Mam,' Eveleen said, as the fight drained out of her. She took a deep breath and tried to concentrate on their current problem. 'Maybe if I can get a job like I had before in the women's workshop and then work at home at night too, it wouldn't be far short of the pay I was getting at the machine.'

'You can't work the clock round, Evie,' Rebecca said gently. 'You'll make yourself ill. Why don't you go and see that nice man you mentioned. What's his name?'

'Mr Carpenter.'

'Yes. Him. Maybe he will help you.'

Eveleen shook her head. 'Not this time,' she said sadly and then, thinking aloud, added, 'It's a pity, though. I really don't want to leave Reckitt and Stokes. They're one of the best places to work around here.'

'What name did you say?' Mary's voice was shrill.

In an unguarded moment, Eveleen had let slip the name she had meant to keep from her mother.

'What name did you say?' Mary repeated. She was not going to let the matter drop.

'Reckitt's,' Eveleen murmured, desperately trying to divert her mother's attention.

'No, no. You said another name.'

Reluctantly Eveleen said, 'Stokes. The firm's called Reckitt and Stokes.'

She was quite unprepared for the light that shone in her mother's eyes. Eyes that had been doleful, almost lifeless, for so long. 'It's him, isn't it? It's Brinsley Stokes.'

Eveleen nodded.

Mary reached out and touched her daughter's hand. 'Have you seen him? How does he look? Tell me, Eveleen. Please.'

'He looks fine. He – he . . .' She hesitated to cause her mother further pain, yet it was better that she knew the truth. 'He visits the factory most days and he – he brings his son with him. Richard Stokes.'

'His son? He has a son?'

Eveleen nodded.

Mary sat a moment, digesting this new information. 'Of course,' she murmured, lost in her own thoughts. 'He's moved on. Got married. I should have expected that.' She sighed, accepting the fact, coming to terms with it though the knowledge brought her no pleasure. She rallied again and asked, 'You say he looked well?'

'Yes. He's very handsome. He's still got dark hair but it's grey here.' Eveleen touched her own hair just above her temples. 'It makes him look distinguished.'

A smile played around Mary's mouth and her eyes had a faraway expression. 'Oh yes, he always looked very distinguished. Tall and slim. Is he still slim? He's not run to fat, has he?' Her tone was scathing as if the very idea appalled her.

Eveleen hid her amusement and shook her head. 'No, and his son is very like him. The same looks, build, everything.'

By looking at the son, she could see the man that her mother had fallen in love with so desperately all those years ago. Now she could understand. To believe oneself loved by such a man would have been heady wine indeed.

'Mm.' Once again Mary was lost in her own thoughts, years away from the kitchen in the little back-to-back house. But to Eveleen's surprise her mother did not seem distressed. In fact the conversation seemed to have brought comfort to her.

Eveleen shook her head. Her mother was a mystery to her. She doubted she would ever understand Mary's strange mood swings if she lived to be a hundred.

'I should like to see him again,' Mary murmured. 'Just once more.'

*

The following morning Eveleen dressed in her own clothes and tied a scarf over her cropped hair. She was fearful of the interview ahead, but it had to be done. She had to face Josh Carpenter.

'How could you do it, Eveleen?' he said the moment she stepped into his office. 'How could you deceive me so?' He was red with anger and hurt pride. 'You've made a laughing stock of me.' Bitterly, had added, 'Or I should say, more of a laughing stock, because I'm that already.'

His anger was dying even now and all that was left was the hurt and sorrow. 'I really thought you liked me. Oh, I don't mean any romantic nonsense. I'm not that blind or stupid. I'm a big fat bugger and old enough to be your father. But I thought you liked me as a person. I thought you could see beyond this mound of blubber to the person underneath.'

Now that any lingering doubts were swept away by his admission of the nature of his interest in her, Eveleen was able to say genuinely, 'But I do like you, Mr Carpenter. And I'm truly sorry I deceived you. But when Jimmy went off, I was desperate. I couldn't keep the family on what I could earn in the workroom.'

'Why didn't you come and talk to me? I could have helped you.'

'Could you?' There was a challenge in her tone. 'Could you really? Could you have paid me more than you paid the other women? Could you really have employed me anywhere in this factory on better pay? As a woman?'

Josh stared at her for a moment and then dropped his gaze. 'No. You're right. I couldn't.'

'No,' Eveleen said softly, 'you couldn't. So – I had no choice.'

'But you must have realized you'd be found out eventually.'

'I had to do something.'

'Eveleen, was it all lies?'

She frowned. 'I don't understand what you mean.'

'Was it all part of the cunning plan?' The bitterness and anger were back in his tone. 'Did you write to me just to make it more plausible that Eveleen was away from home?'

Her surprise at his suggestion was so genuine that he could not fail to see it.

'I wanted to thank you for giving us the stocking-machine. Really I did. I was so very grateful. I still am. And then, when you replied, well, I didn't know what to do. Part of me wanted to keep on writing to you, but I . . .' It was her turn to be embarrassed to admit that she had feared his interest in her was more than that of a friend. She leaned towards him. 'I meant every word of what I said in those letters.'

'Right then,' he said and hastily cleared his throat. 'Well, we'll forget all about it, shall we? Only thing is,' he looked at her and smiled, 'I can't let you go back into the machine shop.'

Eveleen managed to smile. 'I didn't for one moment think you could.'

He heaved himself up from behind his desk. 'I'll take you back to the workroom. Set you to work in there again.'

'You're – you're not going to fire me?'

Josh smiled. 'You deserve it, you little minx, but no, I don't want to do that. I can understand why you did it. Besides, you're a good worker.' He winked at her. 'And I'm not in the habit of cutting off my nose to spite my face. There's just one thing though. They'll all know in there what you've been up to. You might get a bit of trouble.'

'I can stand that,' Eveleen said, determined that she would. If Josh Carpenter was on her side, she didn't care about anyone else.

He took her to the workroom and informed the woman in charge in a loud voice so that most of the other women could hear too that Eveleen Hardcastle had returned home from looking after her grandmother.

The thin woman pursed her mouth in disapproval and glared at Eveleen, but she dared to say no more than, 'Yes, Mr Carpenter.'

As she took her former place, Helen looked up. 'You've got a nerve,' she hissed. 'Expect us to welcome you back here with open arms after what you've done, do you? Well, we're not going to speak to you. Not any of us.'

Eveleen looked around her. It seemed as if everyone was looking at her. Then, one by one, they averted their eyes and carried on with their work.

There was total silence throughout the workroom.

'I've got me old job back,' Eveleen told Mary and Rebecca when she returned home that evening.

'We've been thinking about you all day,' Rebecca said, placing a hot meat and potato pie in front of her. 'We didn't know whether you were still working there or were tramping the streets looking for other work.'

Eveleen pulled a face as she sat down and picked up her knife and fork. After all the tribulations of the day, she was ravenous now. 'I would be, if the other women had their way. None of them are speaking to me.'

Rebecca gasped. 'Not even Helen? I thought she was your friend.'

Eveleen shook her head and said sadly, 'Not now, she isn't.'

It was hard to brave the hostility every day. The silence continued for three days until the women began to talk among themselves, a little at first, and before long the buzz of the workroom was back to normal. But still they excluded Eveleen.

The supervisor, never particularly friendly with anyone, now seemed to pick purposely on Eveleen. She found fault with her work and gave her the most difficult tasks to do. But the worst to bear was the averted eyes, being passed on the stairs with heads turned away. It was as if she wasn't there, as if she didn't exist.

Eveleen kept her head down and worked steadily. She didn't even look up when Brinsley Stokes and his son made their daily rounds.

It was Richard Stokes who unwittingly made matters even worse. As soon as he saw her, he wove his way between the workers and came to stand in front of her. 'I'm pleased to see you back.' His deep voice was soft and gentle and there seemed, even to Eveleen's cynical heart, to be genuine concern in his tone.

She glanced up at him briefly and murmured huskily, 'Thank you, sir.'

She swallowed painfully. He didn't know about her deception, she thought. He's acting as if he thinks I've just returned from caring for my sick grandmother. She could feel the tension around her. The disapproval of the other women seemed to come at her with the physical force of waves pounding the seashore. She bent her head over her work wishing he would go away and leave her alone.

He was bending over her now, speaking softly to her. 'I must leave you to your work, but I'll see you again.' As he moved away, she breathed a sigh of relief but once he had left the room, the taunts began.

'Oho, what's she got that the rest of us haven't, eh?'

'Lifting your skirts for him an' all, are you?'

'Dropping her trousers, more like.'

Eveleen said nothing, but her fingers trembled. She had experienced the cruelty of men, but she had never thought that women could be so spiteful.

Eveleen put up with the situation for two weeks but then, even she had had enough. One evening as their working day ended, she rose to her feet and addressed the whole room.

'I want to apologize to you all for what I did. It was nothing personal against you. A lot of you' – her glance took in Helen and one or two others sitting closest to her – 'were very kind to me when I first came here and I was very grateful.'

'You've got a funny way of showing it,' someone muttered.

'I'm not going to stand here and give you a sob story to try to win your sympathy—'

'You'll have a job,' someone else said scathingly.

Eveleen carried on. 'But I did have my reasons for what I did. And they were good reasons.'

'Aye, you wanted more money. Don't we all? You didn't stop to think of that, did you?'

Eveleen licked her lips. 'It's true, I did want more money, but not just for myself.'

Beside her, Helen slowly rose to her feet. 'She won't tell you herself, but I will.'

'No, Helen, please—' Eveleen began, but Helen held up her hand to silence her. 'They ought to know. Then they can make up their minds whether they're going to carry on treating you this way – or not.' Without even waiting for Eveleen's agreement, Helen climbed on to her chair. Now she had the undivided attention of everyone in the room. It was time to go home, but no one made a move to leave. Someone opened the door and stepped into the room, but no one looked around. No one took any notice. Even the supervisor was listening.

'A few months ago Eveleen was living on a farm in Lincolnshire. Then her father died suddenly. He was found face down in a ditch.' There was a ripple among the listeners. 'It was Eveleen who found him.' The ripple grew louder and now there was a tentative feeling of sympathy. 'They lived in a tied farmhouse and so the family were turned out of their home. They came to Flawford, to Eveleen's uncle. Jimmy, Eveleen's brother' – Helen smiled a little now – 'was a bit of a lad. He got friendly with their cousin – their *girl* cousin . . .'

Already some of the listeners were ahead of her. 'That's right,' Helen nodded. 'He got her pregnant. Her father turned them out and so they came to this district bringing their cousin with them. So now there's four people to support.' Helen ticked them off one by one on her fingers. 'Eveleen, her mother, Jimmy and Rebecca, the cousin. And there's a baby on the way. Eveleen got both her and Jimmy a job here. She worked here with us and Jimmy was in the machine shop.'

Now there was puzzlement among some of the listeners. Someone shouted from the back, 'So how come she ended up dressing up as her brother and working in there?'

'I don't know,' Helen said, looking down now at

Eveleen. 'That's the story as far as I know it. Will you tell us the rest yourself, Eveleen?'

'I don't want your pity,' Eveleen said, tight-lipped.

'Don't worry. You won't get it,' someone snapped. 'Just get on with it and tell us. I've got a home to go to, even if the rest of you haven't.'

'All right.' Eveleen was reluctant to tell her family's secrets to these women who had treated her so harshly, yet she knew this would be her only chance to explain. She ran her tongue over her dry lips and went on. 'I tried to persuade Jimmy to marry Rebecca. I even went back to Flawford to get my uncle's permission. She's under age. They both are. But – but then he ran away. He's gone to sea and we haven't heard a word from him since.'

The women stood quietly absorbing this information. She didn't need to say any more. They could work the rest out for themselves. With her brother's wage – the only man's wage – gone, there would not be enough to support three women and a baby.

Now they could understand, but whether they could sympathize and forgive was another matter. They shuffled their feet and murmured to each other, moving now towards the door. They would sleep on it and only by morning would they decide.

As the room emptied, Eveleen glanced at Helen as she climbed down from the chair. 'I don't know whether to smack you or hug you,' she said.

The girl grinned. 'As far as I'm concerned we'll carry on as we did before all this happened. All right?'

Eveleen nodded and said a heartfelt, 'Thanks.'

'See you tomorrow,' Helen said and moved towards the door.

Only as her gaze followed Helen across the room did

Eveleen become aware of the person who had entered the room earlier.

Richard Stokes, leaning against the wall near the door, with his arms folded and looking directly at her, must have heard every word.

Forty-Two

'Well, well, well.'

He pushed himself off the wall and came towards her, his gaze never leaving her face. He stood in front of her and looked down at her. A small, amused smile played at the corners of his mouth and then widened so that his eyes sparkled and the laughter lines deepened. 'I can't tell you,' he said very softly so that she had to strain to hear the words, 'how glad I am to discover that you are – and have been all along – Eveleen.'

'I am sorry for the trouble I've caused. Mr Josh has given me another chance and I promise it won't happen again.' She spoke stiffly, already on her guard against this handsome man standing so close to her and looking at her so intently.

Richard Stokes shrugged. 'I wouldn't mind if it did. Just,' he added impishly, 'so long as I know that underneath those dreadful boy's clothes you really are Eveleen.' His gaze was roaming over her now. 'The only thing that's a real shame,' he murmured, 'is that you've cut off that glorious hair.'

Eveleen stiffened. Why did he have to start to get personal, almost flirtatious? Why couldn't a young man just be friendly without . . . ? Eveleen sighed inwardly but her guard against his flattery went a little higher.

'I must go,' she said, just short of sounding curt.

She side-stepped to go around him towards the door,

but he put out his hand to touch her arm. He did not take hold of her but his gesture was meant to delay her. He was still looking at her earnestly, his dark brown eyes now filled with concern. 'It's a sad story. If there's anything I can do . . .'

'I don't want your pity,' she snapped and he withdrew his hand swiftly, as if the touch of her burned him.

He gave a stiff, almost mocking, bow. 'I'm sorry. I did not mean to offend you, Miss Hardcastle.'

'I just want the chance to work hard and earn a living. If you really want to help, you could think about the pitiful wages you pay your women workers.'

With that she turned away and marched out of the room leaving him staring after her.

Her anger carried her out of the factory gates and halfway home before she sighed and groaned aloud. 'Now you've really done it. You won't even have a job to go to by the morning.'

Like her mother had always warned her, sometimes she was far too outspoken for her own good.

But the following morning she was not summoned to Josh's office and she took her place in the workroom as usual. Only this morning there was a subtle difference in the atmosphere. Helen greeted her cheerfully.

'I don't know about anybody else,' the girl said in a loud voice so that most of the other women could hear her. 'But I've decided to forgive and forget. What you did was wrong, Eveleen, but I reckon you had good reasons.'

No one else said a word, but throughout that day and the days that followed, there was a noticeable shift in the general attitude towards Eveleen. Some of the other women followed Helen's example and gradually began to include Eveleen in their conversations once more. Only a few continued to ignore her completely and refuse to speak to her. She didn't let this bother her but what did sadden her was that Josh Carpenter now seemed very careful in his treatment of her. She had little reason to go to his office so there were no chances for private conversations. Though he would nod to her when they happened to meet accidentally, there was wariness in his eyes.

Eveleen sighed inwardly. She hadn't meant to hurt the big man who had shown her such kindness. Despite the jibes from others, she had never really felt threatened by his interest in her.

But if Josh's interest in her was waning, there was one whose attentions were becoming more noticeable.

It wasn't long before Helen remarked, 'Mr Richard's coming to the workroom a lot more these days. I reckon he's sweet on you, Eveleen.'

Eveleen shuddered. Uncannily, the girl had used the very same phrase that Jimmy had used about Master Stephen Dunsmore.

The very words that had started all the trouble.

Life continued in much the same manner for the following weeks and months. Eveleen brought home her pay from the factory while Rebecca worked hard, often late into the night, at the stocking-machine. Mary helped in fits and starts. Some days she would be reasonably cheerful and would willingly contribute to what she regarded as their 'going home' fund. On other days she would be sunk in depression once more and would sit by the fire all day, lost in self-pity and sobbing because there was no word from Jimmy.

'I don't even know if he's alive or dead,' she wailed. 'Oh my baby boy.' Then she would say harshly to

Eveleen, 'It's all your fault. If you hadn't caused your poor father so much worry in the first place. And now you've driven Jimmy away. Now I've lost two sons.' On and on the tirade would continue and always ending with the same wailing plea, 'Take me home, Eveleen.'

'Get to bed, Rebecca,' Eveleen said gently late one night when the girl looked pale and wan in the lamplight. 'You look worn out and, besides, you can hardly reach the machine now for the bump.'

She was trying to make light of the situation but she was becoming increasingly concerned about Rebecca's welfare. While the girl never complained, there were dark shadows under her eyes and her cheeks were hollowed. Although her pregnancy was obviously far advanced, the rest of her body looked thin.

Rebecca heaved herself up. 'I will if you don't mind. I've got the most dreadful backache—'

'What?' Mary spoke suddenly from her chair by the fire, making both girls start. They turned to look at her. 'Backache, you say?'

'Yes, I've had it all day.'

'Hardly surprising,' Eveleen remarked. 'You're having to sit at such an unnatural position now to reach the machine.'

'It's not that,' Mary snapped. 'It's the baby. Lots of women start their labour with back pains. I did.' For a moment both girls stared at her. 'Get her upstairs, Eveleen. I'll go for Win.'

The most animated they had seen her for weeks, Mary was already reaching for her shawl hanging on a hook behind the door. 'Go on. Don't stand there all night. Get the girl upstairs else she'll be giving birth here on the hearthrug.'

Eveleen was to look back on the hours that followed as a nightmare. Win arrived only minutes after Mary's first pronouncement that Rebecca must be in labour and followed the two girls upstairs to the back bedroom.

'Plenty of hot water, Eveleen, and towels.'

Eveleen hurried downstairs at once to carry out Win's instructions, leaving the older woman to say comfortingly to the frightened young girl, 'You'll be fine, love. It's going to hurt a bit, but just think in a few hours you'll have a lovely baby in your arms.'

'I don't want it . . .' were the last words Eveleen heard Rebecca say as she left the bedroom. 'I want my father. Please – I want Father.'

As she hurried down the stairs, Eveleen made herself another impossible promise. I'll get him for you, Rebecca. I'll bring him here if it's the last thing I do.

Forty-Three

By five o'clock in the morning, Win said, 'You'll have to get a doctor, Eveleen. The poor girl's exhausted. She's so tiny. I – I can't cope with it.'

'Is there something wrong?'

Win looked helpless. 'I don't know. I'm fine at births if everything's straightforward, but . . .' She said no more but the unspoken words frightened Eveleen.

Eveleen pushed aside the thought that they could not afford the expense of a doctor and said, 'Where's the nearest?'

'Go and knock my Fred up. Tell him I said we need a doctor. He'll know then that it's urgent. He'll get one.'

It was two hours before a doctor arrived at the house. The moment he entered the bedroom, he took one look at the girl on the bed and opened his bag.

'You'd better go downstairs,' he said to Eveleen. 'Mrs Martin can assist me.' The middle-aged man with kindly, well-worn features, smiled briefly at Win. It was a face that had seen all of life's tragedies. 'We're old team-mates, aren't we? As soon as I get a message from Mrs Martin, I know I'm really needed.'

When he drew out huge forceps, Eveleen hurried away feeling sick and closing her ears to the girl's screams. She was glad of the excuse to escape, yet she would have braved it out and stayed if the doctor had needed her.

'Will she be all right?' was Mary's first, anxious question as Eveleen sat down in front of the fire beside her mother. She was shivering, but from anxiety, not the cold.

'Oh I hope so. I do hope so.' Eveleen's fervent whisper was like a prayer.

As if sensing the girl's feelings, Mary held out her hands. 'Come, kneel with me on the rug,' she said gently. 'Let's pray together.'

Eveleen gave her mother a startled glance, but then she sank to her knees. It was strange, she was thinking. While her mother flatly refused now to attend services, there must still be a deep-rooted faith in her. A faith that had been planted in her childhood and, though it might have withered, refused to die completely.

Eveleen closed her eyes and put her hands together and pictured the huge figure dressed in white sitting on his throne in the sky. His face, in her imagination, was etched with deep lines of sadness and his eyes were fathomless depths of compassion. She pictured him reaching out with a huge hand, the hand that held the world in its palm. She imagined she felt him touching her head. So vivid was the scene that she fancied she could feel his power flowing into her and seemed to hear him say, in deep comforting tones, 'Be strong, child. Be brave and strong. I am here to guide you.'

But however hard she willed herself to hear the words, the voice in her head gave her no promise that everything would be all right.

Later Eveleen made hot drinks as she and Mary sat together straining to hear sounds from upstairs.

'It's gone awfully quiet,' Eveleen said worriedly.

'At least she's not lying in a stinking ditch with only an old gypsy woman to hold her hand,' Mary murmured.

'Oh, Mam.' Eveleen reached out and took her mother's hand.

Mary said no more. Now was not the time to be dwelling on that time and its tragic outcome. 'Just so long as they both come through it this time,' she whispered.

The baby girl came into the world at eight o'clock in the morning but in the same moment the mother's life ebbed away.

When they had first heard the child's cries, Eveleen and Mary had leapt up from their chairs and clutched each other in excitement. 'It's over. Oh thank God.' But when the doctor came down the stairs, his face was grave. At once, they guessed the worst.

'I'm so very sorry.' He stood before them, weary and dishevelled. 'There was nothing I could do.' The concern, the disappointment at his failure was written in the man's eyes and in every line of his face. He glanced from Mary to Eveleen and back again. 'She – she was asking for her father. Is he not here?' He glanced around him as if looking for the man.

Not knowing the circumstances the doctor had perhaps presumed that Rebecca was Mary's daughter and Eveleen her sister.

Stunned by the news, Eveleen could only shake her head, while Mary let out a wail and covered her face with her apron. She rocked to and fro in the chair.

'The baby's strong and appears quite healthy, though I'll call back to examine her properly later today.'

'A girl,' Eveleen murmured. 'She's had a baby girl?'

The doctor nodded. 'Have you a name for her?'

Eveleen realized that they had never even discussed a

name for Rebecca's baby. She glanced down at her mother but Mary was lost in her own misery. The years fell away and she was mourning that other loss too.

Eveleen's mind was in turmoil. She couldn't think properly and yet the doctor was waiting for an answer. He seemed to want the child to have an identity before he left the house.

'Bridget,' Eveleen murmured, thinking of the old woman in the cottage – only a few miles away but separated by a deep chasm of bitterness. 'After her great-grandmother.'

The doctor nodded, satisfied. 'And the surname,' he asked gently, aware that not only was the young girl's father missing, but there had been no sign, no mention even, of the baby's father.

Eveleen had to say, 'I don't know.' Then she was obliged to say, haltingly, 'The child is my brother's, but – but they weren't married. Rebecca is . . .' Tears blinded her for a moment as she was forced to say hoarsely, '. . . was our cousin.'

'In such circumstances,' the doctor's voice was infinitely kind, 'the child takes the mother's surname. 'Unless the father is here.'

'He isn't,' Eveleen said shortly, unable to hide the resentment in her tone.

The doctor nodded understandingly but probed no further. 'In that case then, I'm afraid that the father's name cannot appear on the birth certificate.'

Eveleen flinched. The child would be registered as illegitimate and the stigma would follow her all her life.

'Shall you put her into an orphanage?' The doctor's tone was gentle but his question appalled Eveleen. Her head snapped up and she looked directly into the man's eyes. 'Oh no,' she said, determinedly. 'Never. I'll look after her. She's my responsibility now.'

Eveleen stood beside the bed and looked down at Rebecca's still and silent form. Her face was pale, but two bright spots of colour still burned in her cheeks. Eveleen picked up the girl's limp hand and held it to her cheek. It was still warm and Eveleen, though she knew it was hopeless, for a moment fancied that Rebecca was only asleep.

'Poor darling,' she whispered. She closed her eyes and held Rebecca's hand to her lips. Against the slim fingers, she promised, 'I'll look after your little one. I promise.'

Another promise made. Another burden to carry. And yet, she thought as she whispered 'goodbye' to her cousin, what else can I do?

She left the bedroom, closing the door softly behind her and stood a moment at the top of the stairs to wipe away the tears that filled her eyes. Then she took a deep breath, squared her shoulders and went downstairs.

Entering the kitchen, she found Win sitting in Mary's chair, feeding the baby.

'Where's my mother? She could be doing that.'

Win's eyes softened as she looked down at the tiny mite in her arms. 'I don't mind.' Then she cast her eyes to the ceiling. 'Your mam's gone upstairs. To the top floor, I reckon. She says she's going to sleep in the room your Jimmy had.'

Eveleen nodded but her heart sank. She had a feeling that her mother was slipping into one of her moods.

'Win, could you look after the baby for a day? I'll have to go to Flawford to see my uncle. He has to know.

Besides . . .' She bit her lip. 'I don't know what he wants to do about the funeral.' It was already late to be setting off to travel to Flawford, but Eveleen could delay no longer.

'Of course I can, mi duck. But what about your mother? Doesn't she want to look after her?'

Eveleen shook her head and her mouth tightened. 'I suspect my mother has taken to her bed for a while.' She glanced at Win, unwilling to confide all her family secrets, yet the woman had been so kind. So she told part of the truth but not all of it. 'Years ago she lost a baby and this has brought it all back.'

Win nodded sympathetically. 'I'll look after them both, love. And I'll see to poor Rebecca too.' The woman sighed and said sadly, 'I help 'em into the world and I help 'em go out of it.'

Touched by her thoughtfulness, Eveleen hugged her.

'There, there,' Win murmured, patting Eveleen's back, trying to give her some crumbs of comfort. 'Off you go. You go and do what you have to. You haven't got an easy job either, love.'

Eveleen was lucky. A carter gave her a lift part of the way and soon she was turning into the narrow street in Flawford. Her heart was beating fast as she stepped into the yard. The noise of machinery came from the workshops. That was where he would be.

As she walked towards the door leading up to the stairs to where her uncle sat at his frame, Andrew Burns was coming down.

He stopped on the bottom step and stood looking down at her. His face was in shadow, but she could feel the tension in him. 'What is it? What's happened?'

Eveleen opened her mouth to say that she must speak to her uncle first, but no sound would come. Sorrow choked her and tears filled her eyes and spilled down her cheeks.

He stepped down and came to her, holding out his arms. Sobbing, Eveleen clung to him, burying her face against his shoulder. 'Did she lose the baby?' he asked gently.

Against him Eveleen, still unable to speak, shook her head.

She felt his whole body tremble as he breathed against her ear. 'Oh no. Dear Father in Heaven, no!'

Eveleen raised her tear-stained face and drew herself gently out of his arms. 'Will you – will you go and fetch my uncle down, please?'

The young man nodded as if now he too were unable to speak. He turned and dragged himself back up the stairs.

Eveleen leant against the whitewashed wall and closed her eyes. When she opened them again, her uncle was standing at the turn in the stairs looking down on her. He came slowly down to her, his gaze fastened on her face as if he was trying to read there what the dreadful news was before she even spoke.

As she stood before him, Eveleen thought these were the hardest words she had ever had to say in her life, harder even than breaking the news to her mother about her father's death. Then there had been other people with her. Jimmy had been there and their neighbours.

Now, Eveleen faced her forbidding uncle alone.

'Uncle Harry. I'm so sorry. Rebecca, she – she's gone.'

Harry frowned and asked harshly, 'Gone? What do you mean gone? Run away?'

'No, no.' She was handling this very badly. Giving him

false hope when there was none. Then the words came out in a rush. 'No, she had the baby. A girl, but – but she had such a bad time. There was nothing the doctor could do. She – she died, Uncle Harry. This morning. Rebecca died this morning.'

The man's big frame was immobile and his expression did not alter, except perhaps that the frown deepened. He was motionless for several minutes before he said steadily, 'Thank you for telling me, Eveleen.'

Then, to Eveleen's amazement, he turned and began to climb back up the stairs to his work.

She caught hold of his arm. 'Uncle Harry. What am I to do? What do you want me to do?'

'Me?' His voice was hard, as unforgiving as ever, and his words chilled her. 'Why should it be anything to do with me?'

'She's your daughter. I thought—'

'Then you thought wrong.'

He pulled free of her grasp and clumped up the stairs. Eveleen stared after him unable to believe what she had heard. Then she blurted out, 'She was calling for you. The last words I heard her say were, "I want my father".'

He paused. He stood still for a long moment but he did not look round. Then slowly he continued his way up the stairs.

Forty-Four

Eveleen stumbled her way to her grandmother's cottage, opened the door and went in without waiting for an invitation.

Bridget was sitting in her usual chair before the fire. She glanced up at the sound and, unlike her son, read the dreadful news in Eveleen's face before she spoke. 'So one of 'em's gone then? Which? Or is it both?'

Eveleen sank down into the chair opposite and stared at her grandmother. 'He – he doesn't seem to care,' she said, still in shock at her uncle's response.

The old woman's face worked before she said, 'He cares, but he can't show it. He hides behind this unforgiving front. But underneath . . .'

Eveleen, regaining some of her senses though her uncle's attitude had left her reeling, said, 'You could have fooled me.'

'So,' Bridget was looking at her granddaughter. 'Tell me what's happened.'

Eveleen related the dreadful events of the past day and night, ending with, 'The baby's strong and healthy. We're going to baptize her Bridget.'

The old lady smiled wistfully. 'Another little Bridie,' she murmured. She lapsed once more into a perfect Irish brogue. 'Ah me dada would have been that proud, so he would.'

'Is that what they called you, Gran?'

Bridget nodded. 'Me dada always called me Bridie.' She smiled gently as she remembered but her eyes were sad and watered as she gazed into the flickering flames in the grate. 'Michael O'Hallaran,' she murmured, slipping into the Irish brogue once more, the speech of her childhood. 'The foinest Irishman that ever drew breath, so he was.' There was silence between them before she murmured, 'We should never have left Ireland.'

'Why did you?' Eveleen prompted gently, though she knew something of the story already.

Bridget sighed deeply. 'The potato failure in 'forty-five. Not one year, but four years in a row. A lot of families left then. Some went to America. We came to England. I was about nine. To London first and then, because my father got work as a hosier, we moved to this area. Later, of course, I married Alfred and I've been here ever since.'

'Your husband must have been a very clever man to have built all this from nothing.' Eveleen waved her hand briefly to encompass the cottages, the yard and the workshops.

'I don't know about "clever". He worked hard, I know that. All the hours God sent, as they say.'

There was another long silence before Eveleen, rolling the name around in her mind, then spoke it aloud. 'Bridie. I like it. That's what we'll call Rebecca's little one. Bridie.'

As she was leaving, with still nothing resolved about Rebecca's funeral, Eveleen found Andrew waiting for her by the gate.

'Did she suffer?' he asked bluntly.

Eveleen could not meet his eyes and her hesitation told him the answer. He groaned and said bitterly, 'Tell that brother of yours if I ever set eyes on him again I'll kill him.'

Eveleen pulled her shawl closely around her shoulders. 'You'll have to stand in line then, because if I ever catch up with him, I'll kill him an' all.'

'What do you mean?'

Of course, she reminded herself. Andrew didn't know. None of them here knew about Jimmy. The last time she had visited Flawford, it had been to ask for her uncle's permission for them to be married.

Gently she said, 'He ran away. The day I was here last time, when I got back, he'd gone.'

'You – you mean, he never married her?'

Eveleen shook her head.

Andrew punched his fist into the palm of his hand. 'I wish I'd known. I wish you'd told me, Eveleen. I'd have married her, if she'd've had me. I'd have given her baby my name.'

Eveleen reached out and touched his arm. The lump that seemed to have been constantly in her throat since the previous day grew. This man's love for the dead girl overwhelmed her. After her own disastrous romance, she had never thought that such an unselfish love existed in any young man.

But before her stood a young man who would have done anything for the girl he loved.

'I'm sorry, Andrew,' she said.

They stood together in silence until he said, 'What's – what's going to happen to her? Are you bringing her back here?'

Eveleen shrugged helplessly and told him of her uncle's attitude. 'I don't understand him. He won't even tell me what he wants me to do.'

'Bring her back here,' Andrew said firmly. 'Have a service in the chapel for her' – he nodded across the road – 'and have her buried in the cemetery. I'll look after her grave.'

'Are you sure? Won't my uncle . . . ?'

'Never mind about him. Do it, Eveleen. It's what Rebecca would have wanted.'

Eveleen nodded. 'She was calling for him. For her father. Her last words were of him.'

'Did she – did she ever ask about me?' The young man's decisiveness deserted him.

'Of course,' Eveleen answered quickly. Too quickly. 'When I got back last time, she wanted to know how you were.'

Andrew smiled sadly. 'Good try, Eveleen. But you don't fool me. But thanks for the lie.'

He turned away before she should see the tears that brimmed in his eyes begin to fall.

'What on earth are you spending all our savings on her funeral for?' Aroused from her lethargy, Mary now screamed at Eveleen. 'We'll never get home at this rate if you go squandering every penny we've earned.'

'Just remember who it was who earned us that little bit extra that we could put away,' Eveleen shot back. Mother and daughter glared at each other, then Mary's glance fell away.

'It should be Harry paying for it all, not us,' she muttered.

'I'd agree with you there, Mam, but since Uncle Harry wants nothing more to do with his daughter, not even her funeral, I don't have much choice.'

'Why are you taking her all the way back to Flawford? You don't need to do that.'

'Maybe not.' Eveleen was trying very hard to hold on to her patience. 'But Andrew says it's what Rebecca would have wanted. It's the least we can do.'

Mary shot another resentful glance at her daughter, but said no more. It was not the least they could do and they both knew it. But in their hearts both women knew it was what should be done.

'Oh have it your way then,' Mary muttered, and climbed the stairs to the top-floor room where she slammed the door as if she meant never to open it again.

Two black horses, groomed to shine in the pale sunlight, pulled the enclosed box-like hearse in which the coffin rested. High on the driving seat a man in a black coat and silk top hat held the reins and the long whip in black gloved hands. The sad little funeral party set off from the back street in the city and into the country, Eveleen driving the pony and trap she had hired behind the hearse.

'I 'spect we'll be the only ones there,' Mary grumbled. 'That lot' – she referred with scathing bitterness to the villagers of Flawford – 'won't come to a sinner's funeral.'

Mary had taken a lot of persuading to come, but Eveleen had managed it. Now she sat in the trap clutching Rebecca's tiny baby, who was warmly wrapped in a lace shawl that Win had given them.

'Andrew will be there.' Of that, Eveleen was confident. 'And what about Gran? Won't she come?'

Mary sniffed. 'Shouldn't think so. Not if Harry's not going. She wouldn't dare. She's all talk and no do, is your grandmother.'

'She might surprise you,' Eveleen said, but even she was not hopeful.

As the ponderous procession reached the village, Eveleen said, 'The place seems deserted. There's nobody about.'

'They're all staying indoors out the way so they don't have to take their hats off or bow to the coffin.' Mary's bitterness went deep, very deep, Eveleen realized sadly.

But as they turned into Ranters' Row, Eveleen gasped. The narrow street was full of people, so crowded in fact that the driver had to halt the vehicle to allow the throng to part to let them through.

Several of the women wore black bonnets and shawls and all of the men wore something black as a mark of respect. Whatever they could unearth among their own belongings, or beg or borrow from neighbours, Eveleen suspected. One or two, perhaps unable to find anything else, wore black armbands on their sleeves.

As the horses' hooves clattered on the cobbles the gathering fell silent.

'Nosy beggars,' Mary muttered as Eveleen helped her down from the trap. 'Coming to gawp and revel in some poor girl's downfall.'

Eveleen glanced about her. There didn't seem to be much revelry. One or two women held handkerchiefs to their faces and all the men had removed their hats and caps and stood, solemn-faced, with their eyes lowered. To the forefront, stood Gracie Turner, tears running down her cheeks.

As they stepped through the door of the chapel, even Mary's eyes widened in surprise. Not another villager could squeeze inside. Only the Singletons' family pew had been left empty for the chief mourners. As Eveleen, carrying the child now, and her mother moved down the aisle they could see that only one person was sitting there already. Bridget.

Men, women and even children were squashed into every pew and those who could not find a seat lined the aisle so that the bearers, Andrew among them, had difficulty in carrying the coffin to the rostrum. The door was left open so that the people who were still in the street could hear the service. It seemed that out of the whole village there was only one person missing.

Harry Singleton was not present at his daughter's funeral.

Eveleen was quite unprepared for the warmth, the sympathy and the compassion that enfolded the family. The minister was a young man whom Eveleen had not heard preach before. She was struck at once by his humanity, by the caring and forgiving attitude that was so evident in the way he conducted the funeral. As the service continued she was overwhelmed by his solicitude, and when it came to his address and he spoke with such love and concern for the dead girl that Eveleen broke down and sobbed, burying her face in the shawl wrapped around the motherless baby in her arms.

The service over, the four young men hoisted the coffin on to their shoulders and walked slowly out of the chapel and down the street. They made no move to slide the coffin back into the hearse. They would carry their sad burden on their shoulders all the way to the cemetery. With one accord the whole of the congregation fell into step behind them. As they passed by the windows of the cottages that looked out on to the street, Eveleen glanced up, straining to see beyond the glass and into the scullery of her uncle's home.

Standing well back from the window, hoping not to be seen in the shadows but caught by Eveleen's sharp eyes, Harry was watching.

Later, back in Eveleen's grandmother's house, Andrew tenderly took the baby from her arms. Holding her, he looked down into the tiny face, searching, Eveleen was sure, for a likeness to the girl he had loved so much.

'She's a pretty little thing,' he said and even managed a tremulous smile. 'I thought she'd be all red and wrinkly, being so little.'

Eveleen shook her head. 'No, she was even pretty when she was born. She's been good this morning, thank goodness, but you should hear her when she's hungry and starts to yell. She's a real little fighter.'

'Good job,' Andrew said soberly. 'She's going to need to be.'

'And there's something else she's going to need too.' Eveleen's tone was a mixture of sadness at the mother's death and bitterness at the father's desertion.

Andrew looked at her, a question in his eyes.

'We're going to have her baptized. I'm going to see the minister before we leave today. And I feel . . .' Eveleen ran her tongue over her lips. 'I think she ought to have godparents. Andrew, would you be her godfather?'

Despite the sadness of the day, Andrew's smile lit up his face. 'I'd be honoured, Eveleen. Thank you.' They seemed to Eveleen to be only the dregs of comfort yet as he looked down at the sleeping infant in his arms Andrew said again, 'Oh thank you,' as if she had given him the moon.

Forty-Five

Eveleen had not been to work since Rebecca's death. On the morning following the funeral, there was a knock at the door of their home.

'Who can that be at this hour?' she grumbled, picking up the baby who was whining. Any moment now Bridie would open her mouth wide and start to yell lustily.

Carrying the infant in her left arm, Eveleen opened the door to find herself staring into Josh Carpenter's face.

'Oh!'

Eveleen had been so preoccupied for the past few days that she had not given a thought to letting her workplace know what had happened.

'Please, come in, Mr Carpenter.' She led him into the kitchen. 'Do sit down,' she invited. 'You'll excuse me if I get on with her feed. She'll start to raise the roof any minute now.'

Josh eased his large frame into the chair at the side of the range and watched, fascinated, as Eveleen deftly juggled with the feeding bottle and tube. In a few moments the infant was sucking noisily.

Sitting opposite him, Eveleen said, 'I am so sorry. I never thought to send word. Fred Martin would have told you for me if I'd thought to ask him.'

His gaze still upon the child, Josh nodded. 'He did come to tell me that he thought you would be off work for a few days. But he was very evasive. Wouldn't tell me exactly what was the matter.' He glanced up briefly at Eveleen but then his gaze went back to the child. 'I thought you were ill, Eveleen. Of course, I should have guessed, but you never told me when the baby was expected.' He dragged his gaze away from the infant and glanced at Eveleen. 'How is the mother?' He gestured towards the child as if to say, Shouldn't she be doing that?

Eveleen was touched by his concern. He had taken the trouble to leave work and walk all the way to her home. She sighed, and when she had finished telling him the sad events of the past few days, Josh shook his head in sympathy. 'I wish I'd known what was happening, Eveleen. Maybe there is something I could have done to help.'

Eveleen hesitated and then took the plunge. 'There is something I would like your advice about.'

Josh spread his hands. 'Anything.'

She looked down at the baby. 'I just want to do everything right by her. I want to know that I'm doing everything legally. That I can be her – what do they call it – her guardian?'

'You want to adopt her?'

'I suppose so. You see, my brother is her father but his name can't be on her birth certificate because they weren't married. She's had to be registered in her mother's name. Singleton.'

'Leave it with me. I'll find out about it for you.' He frowned. 'There is just one thing. I think you're too young to adopt her yourself. It would have to be an older person. Your mother, for instance.'

Eveleen nodded.

'What's her name? Just so I've got all the facts.'

'Mary Hardcastle, now, but she was a Singleton before

she was married. Rebecca's father and my mother are brother and sister.'

Josh nodded and heaved himself up out of the chair. 'Leave it with me,' he said again. He stood a moment uncertainly, looking as if he wanted to ask something else but did not know quite how to phrase it delicately.

'I'm – er – afraid they will have stopped your pay at the factory for the time you've had off.'

'Oh yes, I understand that.' She smiled up at him. 'Just so long as I haven't lost my job altogether.'

'No, no,' he reassured her swiftly. 'Mr Richard said I was to be sure to keep it for you.'

'Mr Richard?' Eveleen was so startled she let the feeding tube slip and Bridie yelled in protest. When Eveleen had popped the teat back into the little mouth and there was a contented silence once more, Josh said, 'Oh yes. That's why I'm here this morning. Mr Richard sent me.'

'Oh,' was all a very surprised Eveleen could say.

Later that day, while the baby was sleeping, Eveleen climbed the stairs to the top floor where her mother was still sleeping in the makeshift bed that Jimmy had used.

Apart from the day of the funeral, Mary had not got out of her bed since the day after Rebecca had died.

'Why don't you come back down to our room? Win washed all the sheets yesterday. Everything . . .' Eveleen felt the familiar lump in her throat swell. It seemed to have been constantly in her throat for the past few days. She swallowed it determinedly. 'Everything's clean and . . .' She hesitated to say bluntly that all trace of the poor girl, who had given birth to her child there and then died, had been washed away.

'I'm all right here.' Her head buried beneath the covers, Mary's voice was muffled. 'Leave me alone.'

Eveleen let out an exasperated sigh and tried a different tack. 'Mam, I need to go back to work as soon as possible. You'll have to look after the baby.'

Mary burrowed even further beneath the covers so that Eveleen could hardly hear the smothered, 'I can't.'

For half an hour Eveleen begged, pleaded and finally got angry, shouting so loudly at her mother that even down two flights of stairs the baby began to wail. All to no avail. Mary flatly refused to get out of her bed.

'I don't know what to do to get her up,' Eveleen said helplessly to Win, who had arrived by the time she came back downstairs.

Picking up the baby, Win said, 'You might try setting fire to the bed.'

'Eh?' For a moment Eveleen stared at her and then she began to laugh. After the sorrow of the last week, it was good to have an excuse to laugh. Eveleen held her side and spluttered. 'Oh don't, Win. It hurts.'

The older woman chuckled. 'You go to the shops, Eveleen. I'll stay with this little treasure.'

'Would you?' Eveleen said gratefully. 'I do need a few things.' She pulled a face. 'Though how I'm to pay for them, goodness knows.'

'I can lend you—' the kindly woman began, but Eveleen held up her hand. 'Thanks, Win, but I'll manage.' She frowned and murmured, 'If only I could get back to work next week.'

She saw Win glance at her, a thoughtful expression on her face.

*

Two hours later when Eveleen stepped back through the door with her shopping, she stopped in surprise. Mary was sitting in her chair by the fire, fully dressed with her hair neatly pinned into a bun, and she was nursing the baby.

Win stood behind her chair and, unseen by Mary, winked at Eveleen above her head. 'We've got it all arranged between us. You can go back to work on Monday morning, mi duck. I'm going to bring my lace across here and between us, we'll look after the house, the baby and each other.'

Eveleen stared at her in disbelief, glanced at her mother and then looked back at Win. Later as she put her shopping away, she whispered, 'I don't know how you did it, Win, but you're a miracle worker.'

Win grimaced. 'I thought I'd gone a bit far at one point. I told her a few home truths and I don't think she liked it.' The older woman glanced shrewdly at Eveleen. 'Seems your brother was her favourite. That right?'

Eveleen nodded.

Win gave an unladylike snort. 'I thought as much. Well, I told her in no uncertain terms that you was worth ten of 'im and she was a very lucky woman that you hadn't washed yer 'ands of her a long time ago 'cos it's what she deserved.'

Eveleen gasped, startled by Win's frankness. Yet it seemed to have worked. 'I can't tell you how grateful I am,' she said.

The older woman chuckled. 'Tell you the truth, it gets very lonely some days working at home when the young 'uns are at school. I'll be glad of the company. Besides,' she added, a little sheepishly, 'I love little babies. I just can't stay away from 'em.'

'Well, thanks anyway. I do need to get back.' Eveleen held up her purse and shook it, adding, 'I've exactly one farthing left to me name.'

She didn't say any more to their neighbour but privately Eveleen thought, Hardly a sum of money that's going to get us back home to Lincolnshire.

Forty-Six

When Eveleen returned to work the following week, Helen was eager for news. 'She's had it then? Well, come on. What did she get and are they both all right? And when can I come and see the babby?'

Soberly Eveleen said, 'I thought you might have heard, with me being away from work so long.'

Now that she really looked at her, Helen saw Eveleen's sorrow. 'What's happened? Nobody's said anything.'

'She had a baby girl. She's a lovely little thing, but Rebecca died.'

'Oh no!' Helen whispered. 'I'm so sorry.'

There was a murmur of sympathy around her from the women sitting nearby. In that moment, the last vestige of resentment against Eveleen, at least among those working closest to her, died away.

'What's going to happen to the baby?'

'We're taking care of her. My mother, me . . .' She couldn't miss out the wonderful Win. 'And Win, who's been a very kind neighbour to us.'

At the look on Helen's face and her earnest, 'Oh, Eveleen, I am sorry. Me an' my big mouth.'

But Eveleen found it a relief to be able to talk to someone about the baby and now the women with whom she worked were friendly again, she chattered about the child, what she looked like and what they intended to call her.

The supervisor was standing over her. 'They want you in the office,' she said, sharply. 'I don't know who runs this place. You've been away over a week and now they're calling you out. If I had my way . . .' The woman turned away muttering and grumbling beneath her breath.

'Take no notice of the old sourpuss,' Helen whispered. 'But just you watch yourself with old man Carpenter. I reckon he's got his eye on you.'

For once the remark didn't bother Eveleen. She just grinned and said, 'Better to be an old man's darling than a young man's slave, eh?'

Helen pretended to wince as if being Josh Carpenter's darling was the worst fate she could imagine. Eveleen chuckled as she left the workroom to make her way to Josh's office. Halfway along the corridor, she was surprised to see Josh lumbering towards her.

'Eveleen, I wanted to catch you before you get to the office to explain.' He mopped his brow with his handkerchief and, breathless from hurrying, said, 'You know you asked me to find out for you about you caring for the child?'

Eveleen nodded.

'I didn't quite know how to set about it so I thought Mr Richard would be the best person to ask.' He paused a moment but when Eveleen remained silent, waiting for him to go on, he continued. 'I thought he'd know about the law, you see, or he'd certainly know someone who did. He's got friends among solicitors and people like that.'

Get on with it, Josh, Eveleen wanted to say, but steeled herself to stay silent and wait patiently.

'I gave him all the details, but he says he'd like to talk

about it to you himself. They're waiting in my office for you now.'

As she hurried away all Eveleen was thinking, her heart in her mouth, was, I hope he's not going to say I can't keep her. Oh dear Lord, please don't let him say that, she prayed to the huge figure in white sitting up there in Heaven. In her anxiety, it hadn't registered in her mind that Josh had said 'they are waiting for you', so when she reached the office, she was surprised to see not only Mr Richard sitting there, but also his father, Mr Brinsley Stokes.

The two men half rose from their seats as she stepped through the door. How polite they are, she thought, irrationally at such a moment, to get up out of their chairs for the likes of me.

'Sit down, my dear,' Mr Brinsley said. His voice was deep and his eyes were filled with concern. 'Mr Carpenter has told us something of the recent tragic events in your life.'

This was the first time Eveleen had been really close to the man who had been her mother's sweetheart and lover. This was the man who had caused her mother so much pain, who had deserted her when she had needed him the most. And, although he couldn't possibly know it, his show of kindness towards Mary's daughter now felt like a further act of betrayal to the girl.

He was more than twenty years too late.

'I'm sorry you've been troubled, sir. I thought Mr Carpenter might be able to help me. That's all. I didn't intend him to worry you with my problems.' Her hostile glance included Richard. 'Either of you.'

Father and son glanced at each other and then Mr Brinsley cleared his throat and leant towards her, resting his arms on the desk. 'But we would both like to help you, my dear. Please believe me. Now, I've asked my solicitor to find out what all the legalities are so that you can keep the child and bring her up as your own.'

'I can't afford fancy solicitor's fees.' Eveleen knew she was being unfair. The man sitting before her couldn't know who she was or even begin to guess at the reason for her rudeness.

'Don't concern yourself about the cost,' he said gently. 'We'll see to all that.'

Eveleen's chin defiantly went a little higher and there was no hint of the gratitude that should have been there in her tone. 'Thank you, sir, but I'll manage.' As long as it doesn't cost more than a farthing, she thought dryly.

Her antagonism was fuelled by Richard saying, 'I told you she'd be prickly, Father.'

Eveleen glanced at him and felt her mouth tighten. If you only knew, she thought. I could wipe that smile off your face in five seconds flat.

Brinsley cleared his throat. He shuffled some papers on Josh's desk unnecessarily and was obviously ill at ease. 'There's something I would like to ask you, my dear. I hope you don't mind?'

Eveleen knew she was in no position to refuse, so she sat there, her face like a thundercloud, while he struggled to find the right words. 'Er – the names Mr Carpenter gave us. Well, I just wanted to ask you. Er . . .' Still he did not seem able to phrase the question.

With blinding clarity, Eveleen suddenly realized what he was trying to say, but she kept silent. She took pleasure in seeing the man struggle.

'Your mother, Mary?' His dark eyes were looking directly into Eveleen's. 'Was her name really Singleton before she married?'

Eveleen nodded, watching him closely. 'Yes,' she said with deliberate emphasis on every word. 'She used to live in Flawford in Singleton's Yard in what they call Ranters' Row.'

She was quite unprepared for the effect her words had. There was such a look of longing and of loss deep in Brinsley Stokes's eyes. The colour drained from his face, leaving it ashen. His hands, still lying on the desk, trembled and he seemed, suddenly, to find difficulty in breathing.

'Father? Father, are you all right?' Richard was bending over him, his hand already on the older man's shoulder.

Brinsley waved one hand and said huskily, 'Yes, yes, I'm fine.'

He pulled in a painful deep breath and looked straight into Eveleen's wide-eyed gaze. Now it was Eveleen's turn to pull in a sharp breath. She was shocked to see unshed tears brimming in the man's eyes.

Brinsley closed his eyes and sighed. 'It must be,' he murmured more to himself than to anyone else. 'It can't be a coincidence. It must be her.'

'Oh it is, Mr Stokes.' She could not stop the words spilling out of her mouth, could not hide the years of resentment against him. 'It is the girl you deserted and left pregnant more than twenty years ago.' Bitterly, thinking of Jimmy, she added, 'It seems as if history repeats itself in our family.'

Richard's hand was still resting on his father's shoulder and she saw it tighten, but at this moment she dare not meet the younger man's eyes. She kept her hostile gaze directed solely at Brinsley Stokes.

He was staring back at her, his colourless lips slightly parted in a gasp. 'Deserted? And – pregnant? Mary was – pregnant?' His face worked, threatened to crumple as he whispered, 'You say she was expecting a child? *My* child?' Even Eveleen, determined to detest this man, to make him suffer as much as it was in her power to do so, could not fail to hear the incredulity in his tone.

All the anger and the hurt against him, and now Jimmy too, seemed to boil up inside her. 'Don't try to tell me you didn't know.' Remembering the more recent denial by her brother, she added, 'Don't you dare to say it wasn't yours.'

He was shaking his head in bewilderment. 'I didn't know about the child. I swear I didn't. But no,' he added hoarsely. 'I'm not going to deny that it's mine.'

'Oh!' That, more than anything, surprised her.

He leant on the desk and buried his face in his hands and groaned aloud.

'Father,' Richard was anxious now. He turned angry eyes towards Eveleen. 'I think you'd better leave.'

Brinsley looked up. 'No, no. I'm fine.' He patted his son's hand that still rested on his shoulder. 'Really.' Then, suddenly brighter and with renewed spirit, Brinsley began to flash questions at Eveleen. 'How is she? Is she well? And the child? Was that – is that you?'

Eveleen shook her head. 'No, she had a baby boy.' Still needing to twist the knife that she had already plunged in deep, she said, 'She gave birth to him in a ditch with only a gypsy woman to hold her hand.' Her voice flat, she added, 'The child died and my mother nearly died too.'

He was shaking his head again. 'And I never knew.' He was gazing at Eveleen as if trying to find a likeness in her features to his lost love. 'I must see her. Do you think she will see me?' The yearning in his tone was evident and against her will Eveleen found her resolve to hate him begin to crumble.

He sounded sincere. If she let herself, she could almost believe that what he said was true. That he had not known about her mother's pregnancy. But even yet she was not prepared to forgive. 'I was told you went away. That you left her.'

'I – did. My parents arranged for me to go away to London to learn other aspects of our trade. But I explained all that to Mary in a letter. I wrote to her time and again . . .' His voice faded away as realization came to them all. 'She never got the letters, did she?'

'I don't know,' Eveleen said truthfully, 'but it sounds very unlikely.'

'But what happened? Why – why did she – have to give birth in such dreadful circumstances? I don't understand.'

'Her family treated her very harshly and she ran away from home. She found work on the land, but after she lost the baby she was very ill. Then she met my father. He—' Her voice broke now in the telling. 'He was a wonderful man, who loved her dearly. She was happy with him, I think, through the years.' She stopped and there was an unspoken 'but' lying between them.

Brinsley cleared his throat and tried to speak, though she could see that he was deeply affected. 'Do you think,' he asked again, 'she would see me?'

'I don't know,' was all Eveleen could answer him. 'But I'll ask her.'

Forty-Seven

'No, no,' Mary's voice began to rise hysterically. 'No, I don't want to meet him. I – I can't.'

Eveleen stood looking down at her. Despite the protest, she thought that there was a tiny part of her mother that still longed to see Brinsley Stokes again. She had been too quick to refuse, too vehement.

'You said the other day that you wanted to see him.'

'*See* him, yes, but not to meet him. Not to have to talk to him.'

'He says, Mam, that he knew nothing about you being pregnant.'

Mary's head snapped up. 'He's lying then.' There was a pause and Eveleen saw the doubt creep into her mother's eyes. 'Isn't he?'

Eveleen sat down. 'I'm loath to admit it, but he – he seemed genuinely shocked when I told him. But you know me, Mam,' she added, 'I can't trust a man further than I can throw him.' She smiled, trying to lighten the tension with a little humour. 'And most of 'em I can't even pick up!'

A small smile flickered on Mary's mouth but it did not reach her eyes, clouded with doubt.

Eveleen leant back in the chair and gave herself a few moments' respite. The baby was quiet and she and Mary had had their supper. A few minutes' respite before she began her evening work at the stocking-machine wouldn't hurt. 'Maybe I'm wrong, Mam. Maybe there are some men you can trust.'

'You could trust your dad,' Mary murmured, gazing into the glowing coals in the range.

Eveleen closed her eyes and thought about her father. She could see his face so clearly she almost believed that if she opened her eyes he would be standing there in the room with them. He was smiling that slow smile and his eyes were twinkling with mischief, just like they had when she was being particularly stubborn.

Then the vision of him faded and a picture of Stephen Dunsmore's face thrust its way into her mind's eye. Fair hair and blue eyes that had once been bright with passion and desire had turned, overnight it seemed, so cold. The mouth that had kissed her so tenderly and whispered such promises had, in the end, uttered only lies. When his father had handed him the reins of running the estate, the power had gone to the young man's head and she was no longer 'suitable'.

Then that final insult when he had ridden by on the day of their departure. He had deliberately ignored her. She could never forgive him for that.

She dragged her thoughts resolutely away from Stephen and stood up. 'This isn't getting the work done.'

But Mary was still daydreaming. 'What does he look like now?' The wistful note in her tone made Eveleen pause and force herself to say quite truthfully, 'He's – he's a very handsome man.'

'He always was.' The longing that she had heard in Brinsley Stokes's voice was echoed now in her mother's.

'I wonder,' Mary murmured, 'if he really didn't know.'

Eveleen sighed inwardly and sat down again. This was not the time to be worrying about work. Tonight her mother's need was greater than Eveleen earning a few more coppers, precious though those pennies might be.

'I made myself believe he'd deserted me,' Mary went on. 'I clung to that thought.'

It was an odd thing to cling to, Eveleen thought. It would have seemed more natural to hold on to the belief that he had not known. Her mother's next words explained it. 'The anger kept me going, you see,' she said simply. 'If I could blame him more than I blamed myself, then I could survive.' She shook her head. 'Only my poor little baby didn't.'

It was all tangled up with her harsh upbringing, Eveleen thought. Mary had needed someone to blame. She had not been able to forgive herself for bringing supposed shame on her family nor for the death of her child. Blaming Brinsley for what she had believed had been his desertion of her had given her a focus and had eased her own conscience.

Softly Eveleen asked, 'Mam, what do you really want? Do you want to see him?'

'I . . .' Mary began. Slowly she nodded and whispered, 'But I'm so afraid.'

For a few days they let the matter rest, but Brinsley Stokes was impatient. Once more Eveleen was called to Josh Carpenter's office, much to her supervisor's annoyance, to find Brinsley pacing up and down the tiny space in front of the desk.

'Sit down, sit down,' he said his tone testy with impatience. 'Have you told her? What did she say? Will she see me?'

Eveleen remained standing and faced him squarely.

'She's like me,' she said, her tone betraying nothing. 'She doesn't quite know what to believe.'

The man continued his pacing and ran his hand distractedly through his neatly combed hair, leaving it ruffled and sticking up in all directions.

Relenting, though only a little, Eveleen said, 'Give her a little more time. Part of her wants to see you, yet she's so afraid.'

'Afraid? Of me?' The idea appalled and saddened him. 'But we loved each other. Oh I know we've married other people since and it reassures me to think that she knew happiness with your father.' He shrugged his broad shoulders. 'I've been happy with my wife. She's a lovely woman, a good woman, but . . .' He hesitated and for a moment seemed uncertain. Eveleen caught a glimpse of the young man he had once been. A little shy perhaps and diffident. So obedient to his parents that he had never questioned, had never dreamed that they would deceive him. As she stared at him struggling to find the right words, Eveleen felt some of the ice around her heart beginning to melt.

Huskily he said, 'You never quite forget your first love, Eveleen.'

'Don't you?' the ice hardened once again. 'Oh I think you can if you make yourself.'

She was close to him now, looking into his dark eyes that were so like his son's and those eyes were looking straight into hers, plumbing the depths of her soul. He shook his head slightly. 'It makes me very sad, my dear, to see such bitterness in one so young. Tell me, is it on your mother's behalf or on your own that you bear such a grudge against men? Or is it against just one man in particular?'

With a bluntness that was bordering on rudeness, Eveleen said, 'That's none of your business.' Belatedly she added a more polite, 'sir.'

But Brinsley only smiled, though his smile was sad and did not reach his eyes. 'If you ever want to talk about it,' he said quietly, 'I'm a good listener.'

'Are you? Are you really?' Eveleen burst out, all the worry and tension and bitterness flooding out of her. Before she could stop her rash tongue, she had said, 'Then it's a great pity you weren't listening twenty years ago.'

She turned and ran from the office, tears of frustration and rage blinding her. Just who did he think he was, trying to worm his way back into her mother's life after all this time?

Oh, he had a nerve. And so did his son. No doubt, she thought bitterly, he'll be just the same.

Forty-Eight

A week later Josh was waiting for her near the workers' entrance of the warehouse as Eveleen finished her shift.

He mopped his brow. 'I couldn't face the stairs, mi duck, but could I have a word?'

Eveleen smiled and said, 'Of course, Mr Carpenter.' She was aware of the whispering and tittering among the other women leaving work. With impetuous mischief, Eveleen's eyes glinted wickedly as she said to Josh, 'Come on, let's give the old biddies something to talk about.'

Boldly she stepped forward and linked her arm through his.

'Eh?' For one startled moment Josh's face was a picture, but then, realizing what she was about, he chuckled and said, 'You little minx.'

'Well,' she said as they walked side by side laughing softly. 'It'll give 'em summat to gossip about for a week. It'll make their day.'

'And mine,' Josh said gallantly, clearly enjoying the fun.

When they reached his office, he gave her hand a little pat and ushered her into the chair on the visitor's side of the desk. Then he took his own behind it, easing himself into it with a sigh of relief. 'I just wanted to tell you that Mr Richard asked me to let you know that all the legalities seem to be proceeding satisfactorily about your adoption of the little one.' He pulled a comical face and added. 'I rather think those are the solicitor's words, not Master Richard's and certainly not mine.' He laughed and his jowls wobbled.

Eveleen smiled, relieved at his words. But then she was surprised by a sudden shaft of disappointment that Richard had not sought her out to tell her the news himself. In fact, now she thought about it, neither Richard nor his father had visited the inspection room recently.

Not since the day she had run from this very office after her rash remark to Brinsley.

Haltingly, she asked now, 'Did – did Mr Richard say anything else?'

Josh wrinkled his brow thoughtfully. 'No, I don't think so.' He looked at her keenly. 'Was there something else?'

'No – no,' Eveleen said hurriedly, unwilling to confide further. The secrets of more than twenty years ago were not hers to divulge. She stood up. 'I'd better get home. Thank you for telling me.'

'Eveleen . . .' Now it was Josh who seemed a little uncertain. 'I was wondering – I mean – would you mind if I came to see the little one?'

Eveleen stared at him for a moment, but seeing genuine concern on his face, she nodded. There was something more. Deep in those kind eyes there was a haunting sadness. 'Of course you can.'

The Sunday of Bridie's christening dawned bright and clear.

'It's going to be a lovely day,' Win said as she came into the house almost before it was light. 'Fred's organized his mate to bring his pony and trap for us at eight o'clock. What time's the service?'

'After the usual service in the chapel this afternoon.'

Win tried, unsuccessfully, to hide her smile. 'How's Mr Carpenter getting there? You have asked him, I suppose?'

Josh Carpenter was now a frequent visitor to Foundry Yard. The first time he had settled himself in a chair beside the range and held out his arms to take the baby, Eveleen had stared at him open-mouthed. But she had placed Bridie in the crook of his arm and then stood back to watch him. The tiny child nestled against his soft body and gazed up into his face as if drinking in the man's features.

Josh smiled down at her. 'She's not frightened of my ugly mug, is she?'

Eveleen said nothing but watched Josh's gentleness with the tiny mite.

As he looked down at the infant in his arms, Josh said slowly, 'You might not believe it, but I was married once.' He paused and then added sadly, 'My wife died having our first child. A boy. He died too.'

Eveleen glanced at her mother who was staring, wide-eyed, at Josh, her fingers trembling against her mouth. Eveleen turned away and went into the scullery, leaving them together. If her mother wanted to confide in the big man, then that was her business.

Mary never said what had passed between them and Eveleen did not ask, but after that day, Josh came to the house once or twice a week, always bringing a little gift for the baby and sometimes a posy of flowers for Mary.

'He's making his own way there,' Eveleen said now in answer to Win's question.'

Win glanced about her and whispered. 'Is your mam all right? Is she going to go?'

Eveleen held up two crossed fingers. 'So far, yes. But you never know with my mam. This morning she might have changed her mind yet again.'

'Do you think the rest of your family will attend?'

'That's what's worrying her, I think. Part of her wants them to be there, the other part is dreading it.'

Win nodded, though she could not quite understand all that went on in this family. All she knew was that this spirited young lass, now busily feeding and dressing a tiny baby that was not even her own, had a lot on her plate.

Fred and his mate arrived promptly and everyone, including Mary, climbed up into the trap. They set off at a spanking pace in good time to travel the few miles to Flawford, a basket holding the baby's feeding paraphernalia at their feet.

'You'll need to go somewhere to feed and change her before the service, won't you?' Win said softly to Eveleen and glanced anxiously at Mary, hoping that above the noise of the wheels, she would not hear. 'Is there anyone's house you can go to?'

'When we went to the funeral, we went to my grandmother's. But today' – Eveleen looked up smiling – 'I think the godfather will oblige. He lives in one of the other cottages.'

'So,' Win said slowly, 'you're going close to your uncle's home? Right next door to Bridie's grandfather?'

Eveleen nodded 'And her great-grandmother's house.'

Win shook her head. 'I don't understand it. How anyone can hold it against a tiny mite like this, I don't know.'

With great feeling, Eveleen said, 'You don't know my Uncle Harry.'

'Maybe, after today,' Win said, determination in her tone, 'I will.'

Andrew must have been watching out for them for only seconds after the trap had drawn up outside the gates, and before they had had a chance to climb down, he was pulling open the gate and holding out his arms to take Bridie.

Eveleen saw the smile on Win's face and knew that even before he had been properly introduced, Bridie's prospective godfather had endeared himself to her.

'Come along in. Everything's ready.' He led the way to his cottage, which was between Harry's at one end and Bridget Singleton's at the other.

'Oh, Andrew!' Eveleen exclaimed as she stepped into his front parlour. Before her spread on the table in the centre of the small, cramped room were plates and plates piled high with food: sandwiches, scones and buns, dark brown squares of ginger parkin, and lacemaker's cake cut into slices and spread thickly with butter. 'You shouldn't have gone to all this trouble.'

Andrew, still carrying the baby, only grinned. 'Not every day do I get an excuse to have a party.'

'It's a grand spread, young man,' Win said and moved forward to greet him. 'I'm Win, one of Bridie's godmothers. Eveleen's the other, of course. I'm pleased to meet you.'

Andrew nodded, but keeping tight hold of the baby, did not put out his hand to take Win's. He smiled and echoed, 'Pleased to meet you. Make yourselves at home. Mrs Hardcastle, come and sit near the fire.'

The room was full of chatter and bustle as the party

all squeezed in to Andrew's front room. Now that he had welcomed everyone, Andrew sat down and gently eased open the folds of the shawl. 'Oh, but she's bonny,' he said. 'She's altered even since I last saw her.'

'They alter every day when they're little,' Win said, leaning forward to join in the admiration. 'You'll have to come over and see us as often as you can.'

'I will,' Andrew said promptly. 'I'll come on Sunday afternoons.' He glanced up at Eveleen and added, 'If that's all right with you.'

'Of course it is,' she said quietly, marvelling again at his devotion. He would come all that way every week, walking the six miles or so if necessary, just so that he could see Rebecca's baby.

There was a knock at the door and Eveleen, being the nearest, opened it.

'Mr Carpenter. You made it then? Do come in.'

The big man squeezed himself into the already crowded room. He mopped his forehead and said, 'Reckon I'll just stand by the door, Eveleen. And please, do call me Josh when we're not at work.'

Eveleen smiled and introduced him to Andrew, the only person in the room whom Josh had not met before.

Josh nodded and then craned to see the baby. 'How's the little one? Been all right on the journey, has she?'

'Good as gold,' Win said.

'Eveleen,' Andrew said. 'Do you want to make everyone a cup of tea? Everything's ready in the scullery and the kettle's boiling there on the hob. And please, everyone, help yourselves to something to eat.'

Eveleen smiled. Obviously Andrew had no intention of letting go of the baby. She pulled off her gloves and went through to the scullery.

While the adults drank tea, Eveleen prepared Bridie's bottle.

'I'll give it to her,' Andrew said. 'Just show me what to do.'

The women in the room exchanged a glance that said silently, what a wonderful husband for Rebecca and father this young man would have made. If only she had lived, there would have been some happiness for her if she had been prepared to take it.

Josh eased himself down on to a spindly-legged chair next to Mary and began a conversation. 'How are you, Mrs Hardcastle? Lovely day for a ride out into the country, isn't it?'

Eveleen, hearing his words, held her breath for a moment. That was not the best topic of conversation he could have chosen. Even though he had seen her often over the past few weeks, he probably still did not know of Mary's hankering to return to the open fields and the huge skies of Lincolnshire.

But, strangely, Mary was smiling at him. 'Oh, Mr Carpenter—'

'Josh,' he prompted gently.

Her smile widened. 'Josh, then. I wish you could see the place where we used to live. It's beautiful. My husband was head cowman for the Dunsmores and we lived in a tied farmhouse on the estate. That's why we had to leave when he died, you see.'

Josh nodded, understandingly.

'But we shall go back one day. Eveleen's promised to take me home again as soon as she can.'

Though his attention was on the child, Andrew had heard the conversation and looked up at once. 'You're leaving? You're going back to Bernby?' The disappointment was written plainly on his face and even Josh looked crestfallen too.

Eveleen pulled a comical face, trying to make light of it. 'It'll be a while yet on the wages I get.'

'Eveleen, you promised,' Mary's voice rose a little.

'Yes, Mam,' Eveleen said quietly, trying to calm her at once. 'And I'll keep that promise. One day we will go home, but it won't be for a little while yet.'

Now she was torn among those in the room. Her mother, to whom she had made a solemn vow, and the new people in their lives, who so obviously cared about them now: Andrew, Win and Fred, and even Josh Carpenter. Their feelings mattered too.

Into the silence, Eveleen said briskly, 'Time I was getting madam here ready for her big moment. Now, Andrew, unless you want to learn how to change her nappy . . .'

Andrew laughed and handed Bridie over. 'I think I'll give that a miss, if you don't mind.'

The laughter that followed lightened the tension and even Mary was smiling once more.

Just before it was time to leave for the service, Eveleen slipped out of the house and knocked on the door of her grandmother's cottage.

'Come in, come in,' came her imperious voice and Eveleen knew before she even stepped into the room what kind of welcome awaited her.

'So you've brought her bastard back to be christened, have you?'

'It's not the bairn's fault, is it, Gran?' said Eveleen quietly.

The old woman merely grunted and said, 'Well, I hope you're not expecting us to come.'

'I didn't expect Uncle Harry to, no. But I thought you might. You came to Rebecca's funeral.'

'Aye, and much good it did me. He wouldn't speak to me for a fortnight afterwards.'

'Then that's his problem.'

Bridget squinted up at her. 'Very forthright for a slip of a girl, aren't you?'

Eveleen smiled. 'Yes, I'm like you. Haven't you always said what you thought?'

'And a lot of good that's done me an' all. I'm still doing what other folks tell me to do. First, my parents, then my husband. Now I have to obey my son.'

'Why?' Eveleen countered. 'Why do you have to obey him?'

For a moment the old lady floundered. 'Because he – because he's the man. The head of the family.'

Craftily Eveleen said, 'I would have said you were the head. You're the oldest. What do they call it?' She sought in her mind for the right word. 'The matriarch of the family.' With a note of gentle pleading, she added, 'Won't you come, Gran? Please. She's your great-granddaughter.'

The old woman's face worked as she fought the inward battle, but years of obedience still remained strong. She shook her head. 'No, I can't. I'm sorry.'

From the tone of her voice, Eveleen believed her, but she returned to Andrew's cottage disappointed.

A little later as they trooped out of the house and across the road to the chapel, Eveleen glanced back to see her grandmother standing at her kitchen window, her face almost pressed to the glass. This time, however, there was no sign of her uncle skulking in the shadows watching his granddaughter being taken to her baptism.

Forty-Nine

Eveleen was amused to see that as they went to and from the chapel, Josh offered his arm to Mary, sat by her when they returned to Andrew's cottage and fetched and carried food from the table for her.

In the tiny kitchen, Win nudged Eveleen. 'I reckon your mam's found herself an admirer.'

Eveleen chuckled. 'Well, his excuse at first was that he came to see the baby, but now I wonder.' For once she was feeling relaxed, almost happy. The service had gone well, apart from the moment when the minister doused the baby with water and Bridie set up a squealing that echoed out of the chapel and into the street. Everyone had laughed and assured a flustered Eveleen that it was a good sign.

'Driving out the Devil, she is.'

Now, back at the house and surrounded by such loving, caring people, Eveleen was able, if only for a few brief hours, to lay aside her worries and enjoy the moment.

If only this day could last for ever, she found herself wishing.

'Why won't you let my father see your mother?'

The feeling of contentment had been all too brief. The following day, Eveleen found Richard waiting for her during her dinner break.

'I have asked her, and the idea upsets her.'

Richard's gentle eyes flashed with an unusual fire. 'I have my doubts that you've even told her.'

'I am not in the habit of lying,' Eveleen said loftily.

Richard's left eyebrow arched. 'Really?' he drawled. 'And you don't call impersonating your brother and deceiving us all a form of lying?'

Eveleen felt the colour suffuse her face. 'That was different. I was desperate.'

He leaned closer. 'And my father's desperate to see her again. He wants to help. He can't bear to think he caused her such misery and yet he never even knew about it.'

Now it was Eveleen's turn to doubt. 'Really?' she echoed. 'Do you honestly expect me to believe that he knew absolutely nothing about it at the time? Or did he "conveniently" not know? Surely, he must have known he might have left her pregnant?'

Richard was really angry now. 'I tell you he knew nothing. He was only nineteen, for God's sake. At that age, you still believe everything your parents tell you. You believe they know what's best.'

'Oh yes, they knew what was best for him all right. But they didn't care what happened to a slut of a girl who was daft enough to believe the sweet nothings of a young feller out for a bit of fun.'

Appalled, Richard stared at her. 'You believe that? You really believe that she meant so little to him?'

'You're all the same. You so-called gentry.' Her verbal attack was scathing. 'You'll take your fun wherever you can get it, but you'll always marry your own class.'

Now the conversation was more about the two of them than about his father and her mother.

'And you think my interest in you is just as – shallow?'

'What interest?' she snapped.

He blinked and, for a moment, was disconcerted. 'Well, I don't visit the workroom to see the other women, I can assure you, or to check up on the supervisor. Miss Brownlow does a good job.'

'You haven't been near the workroom for over two weeks.'

There was a hint of sarcasm in his tone as he said, 'So you noticed?' Eveleen felt her cheeks glow pink, but even she could not tell whether it was from embarrassment or anger. His tone was gentler as he went on. 'I've only kept away because of this business between your mother and my father. Don't you know how difficult it's been for me to stay away? How hard it's been not to see you?'

Eveleen echoed the words that her own mother had once used to her. 'What could the likes of you possibly want with the likes of me?'

He shook his head wonderingly, but his gaze never left her face. 'Eveleen Hardcastle, don't you know I'm falling in love with you? That all I want is your happiness? That I'd do anything to help you, to look after you. Yes, you and all your family. Even that reprobate of a brother of yours, wherever he is. If I could find him, I'd do my damnedest to bring him back to face his responsibilities.'

His declaration, so unexpected, shook her, but her indignant anger was so high now that she did not stop to think what she was saying. 'If you thought so much about me, you'd pay me more so I can keep my promise to my mother.'

'Promise? What promise?'

'To take her back home. Back to Bernby. That's the only place where she's ever going to be happy again. She doesn't want to be here, not with all the reminders of the past. And she doesn't like the city life. She wants to go home.'

As she turned and flung herself away from him, Richard stared after her thoughtfully.

'He's been. He's been here to see me.'

By the time Eveleen arrived home late that evening, Mary was hysterical and Bridie was shrieking. Hurrying to the makeshift cradle – the bottom drawer from a chest of drawers – she lifted the child out. The baby was soaking and red with anger.

Eveleen turned on her mother. 'Have you fed her?'

'I tell you Brinsley Stokes has been here.' Mary was wringing her hands agitatedly. 'This afternoon. How could you, Eveleen? I told you I was afraid to see him.'

Eveleen was enraged by the arrogance of the Stokes family. 'How dare he?' she muttered. For some reason she could not have explained herself her anger was directed not at the father but at the son.

As she busied herself preparing a bottle for the screaming child, Eveleen said, 'It's not my fault, Mam.'

'Of course it's your fault. It's all your fault. If you hadn't been carrying on with young Dunsmore, your father would still be alive. And if you hadn't brought us here, none of this' – she flung out her hand towards the innocent child – 'would have happened either. And I've lost my Jimmy too. My baby boy. Oh you've got a lot to answer for, Eveleen Hardcastle. I wouldn't like to be in your shoes on Judgement Day.'

Harassed and worried, Eveleen snapped, 'And I wouldn't be in your shoes in the next few minutes if you don't let me get this poor child fed and changed. Sit down, Mam, and for goodness' sake, just shut up!'

Mary sat down suddenly, so shocked she could only gasp, 'Eveleen!' As she recovered a little, she began to wail. 'You've no respect for your mother. You don't care how I've suffered. How I'm still suffering. And seeing him today brought it all back. I can't bear to stay here any longer. Eveleen,' her plea was pitiful as she said, yet again, 'take me home. Please take me home.'

Eveleen never knew what made her wake up in the middle of the night with a start. There was no sound from the cradle nor could she hear her mother's snoring from the room directly above her. Eveleen turned on her side as sleep threatened to claim her once more. Then her eyes flew open again. Suddenly she realized what had disturbed her peaceful sleep.

The house was too quiet. There was no sound of the baby's snuffling breathing or from Mary as she turned and murmured in her sleep or snored loudly, as she did when she lay on her back with her mouth wide open.

In one swift movement Eveleen had thrown back the bedclothes and put her feet to the floor. The cradle was empty, the blankets that wrapped the child gone too.

On bare feet, Eveleen rushed upstairs to the top floor. Her mother's bed was neatly made, looking as if it had not even been slept in that night.

Frantic now, Eveleen hurried down the two flights of stairs to the kitchen. The grate was cold, the room silent and empty.

Her mother and the child were nowhere in the house.

She went to the door and looked around the dark, wet yard. Rain was falling steadily and the night was black with not a glimmer of light from the moon or the stars.

'They'll be soaked through,' she muttered. 'Oh, Mam, how could you?'

Of course, she knew where they had gone. Seeing

Brinsley Stokes again had brought back all her unhappy memories. His visit must have disturbed Mary's mind so much that she had set off in the night to go home, taking the child with her. In her confused state, Rebecca's baby had become that other baby that she had lost. But Mary wasn't going to lose this one. No one was going to take this baby away from her.

'Poor Mam,' Eveleen murmured to herself as she dressed hurriedly, pulling on her warmest clothes. She was beside herself with anxiety, but she was no longer angry with her mother. The poor woman needed help and pity, not censure.

Once more, Eveleen felt the weight of guilt. She had been impatient and sharp with Mary's wailing last night when she should have been more understanding. She should have listened to her mother and comforted her and reassured her that everything would be all right. Promised her yet again that, one day, they would go back home.

But Mary had not been able to wait for that. She had set off in the dark, in the cold and the wet, with the child in her arms, to walk back home to Bernby.

Fifty

Eveleen's banging on Win's door threatened to wake the whole yard.

A sash window above her was pushed up and Fred stuck his head out. 'Who is it?' he asked quite calmly, and then, at his next words, Eveleen understood why someone knocking on his door in the middle of the night was not an unusual occurrence for him. 'Want the missis, do you? Which is it?' he asked in a matter-of-fact manner. 'Birth or a death?'

'Fred, it's me. It's Eveleen.'

'Eveleen?' Now there was surprise in his tone. His head disappeared at once and she heard muffled voices. Only a minute later she heard the door being unlocked and opened.

'Whatever's wrong, mi duck?' said Fred, barefooted, his thin legs like sticks beneath his nightshirt. 'Is it the babby?'

'Sort of.' Breathless from running, Eveleen put her hand to her chest and leant against the wall. 'It's me mam. She's gone.'

'Eh?' the man was startled. 'What d'you mean? Died?'

'No, no,' Eveleen said swiftly, and pushed the dreadful thought aside that in this weather that eventuality was a strong possibility. And the child. Poor little Bridie out in the cold, crying with hunger.

'She's gone out and taken the baby with her. I – I think she's trying to walk home.'

'Right,' Fred said, and seemed to be thinking quickly. 'Right. Come inside, lass, and sit down while me and Win get dressed. Then I'll knock Joe up. He'll lend us his pony and trap again.'

'In the middle of the night?'

''Course he will. He's a good sort is Joe.'

The next half an hour was a flurry of activity. As they waited for Fred to return, Win asked, 'What brought this on, d'you reckon?'

'She – she's always wanted to go back home. Back to Bernby.'

'Oh I know that,' Win nodded. 'But why now? What happened to set her off in the middle of the night?'

Eveleen bit her lip. If these good people were going to help her they deserved to know the truth. The whole truth.

'It was Brinsley Stokes.'

Win's eyes widened. 'Mr Stokes? How on earth—'

Haltingly at first and then in a rush, Eveleen told Win her mother's pathetic story from the beginning right until the moment when Brinsley had found out who Mary Hardcastle really was.

'I never thought for a moment when I asked Mr Carpenter to help over my adopting Bridie that it would lead to all this. Mr Stokes came to the house yesterday to see her. When I got home she was hysterical. The baby was screaming at the top of her voice. Mam hadn't fed or changed her.'

'Oh, mi duck, I am sorry. I should have been there, but our Elsie was poorly and—'

'It's not your fault,' Eveleen said swiftly. 'If it's anybody's, it's mine. I shouldn't have snapped at her last night. I should have understood and . . .' Tears spilled down her cheeks and she covered her face with her hands. 'She's right. It is all my fault.'

'Of course, it isn't,' Win tried to reassure her, but her words brought no comfort to the wretched girl.

Fred returned with the disappointing news that Joe's pony and trap was already out on hire for the next three days. 'It's out of town an' all,' Fred reported dolefully. 'No way of getting it back quickly.'

'Who else has got a trap? Think, Fred,' Win said.

'I am, love. I am doing.'

Suddenly Eveleen sprang to her feet. Her tears dried as sudden hope spread through her. 'Josh – I mean, Mr Carpenter. He had a pony and trap the day he came out to the christening. He must have got that from somewhere.'

Fred's yes lit up. 'That's right, lass.'

'Do you know where he lives?'

Fred nodded. 'Round the corner from the factory.'

Eveleen clutched his arm. 'Oh please go and wake him up, Fred. He won't mind. I know he won't. I'll come with you.'

They hurried through the wet streets while Win stayed behind to pack food and drink into a basket and gather together warm blankets. 'Poor things'll be frozen when you find them,' she said as they left.

Eveleen bit back the words, If we find them.

It seemed an age before Josh lumbered down the stairs to answer their urgent knocking.

'What's up?' he asked before he had seen who was standing there. 'Factory on fire, is it?'

'Worse than that, Mr Carpenter,' Fred said. 'Eveleen's mother's gone off in the night.'

'Mary? Whatever for?'

'She's taken the baby with her.' Eveleen's voice rose frantically. 'Please, Josh, we need a pony and trap. Where did you get that one you came to the christening in?'

'Eh? Oh,' Josh, woken from a deep sleep, was having a hard time taking it all in quickly. 'It's Mr Stokes's. Mr Richard lent me it.'

'Oh no,' Eveleen breathed and sagged against the doorframe in disappointment. 'That's it then. There's nothing more we can do. At least till morning.'

Now Josh was fully awake and worried. 'Of course we mustn't wait until morning. If she's gone out in this lot' – he nodded at the weather – 'and with the baby. Oh poor little thing.' Then he pulled his mind back to the emergency. 'Mr Richard won't mind. He'll organize it. Even in the middle of the night. 'Specially when he knows who it is who's asking.'

The veiled reference to Richard's interest in her was not lost on Eveleen even in this moment. Grimly she said, 'It's all his fault that it's happened.'

'Why?' As Josh asked the question he was gesturing them inside and leading the way into his kitchen.

'Mr Brinsley visited my mother yesterday and I think his visit upset her so much that – that she's gone out of her mind a little.'

Josh stopped and turned to look at her. 'Mr Brinsley? Whatever would he go and see your mother for?'

So, Eveleen thought, whatever my mother had told Josh on his frequent visits to their house, she had not confided everything. She sighed. 'It's a long story, Josh. She knew Mr Brinsley years ago.'

The big man blinked and he and Fred exchanged a glance. Although Win now knew the whole story, there had been no time to enlighten Fred. 'Oh,' Josh said and then, with a kind of understanding, 'oh, I see.'

She knew he didn't. Not really. How could he? But perhaps he guessed at least a little of the truth.

Looking worried, Fred ran his hands through his hair and Josh mopped at his brow.

'We can't leave things till morning, lass,' Josh said. 'Something's got to be done. Leave it to me.'

'But—' Eveleen began to protest, but he was already lumbering towards the stairs.

'Just let me get dressed,' he said.

Fred laid a hand on her arm. 'Leave it, lass. Don't argue. He's the man to help you. Just accept it and be grateful.'

Eveleen bit her lip but said no more. She didn't mind Josh Carpenter helping, but she certainly did not want the Stokes involved. At this moment, she did not know which 'he' Fred meant.

It was only minutes before they heard Josh's heavy tread on the stairs again yet the wait had seemed like hours. Josh was wheezing as he came through the door, but he was smiling. 'Good job for us that Mr Brinsley likes to live in town. If he was the sort of man who wanted a fancy house on the outskirts of town, we'd be the rest of the night getting to his place. Now, Fred, you go and get the pony and trap from the stable at the factory and bring it up to the house.'

'Didn't we ought to ask first?' Fred asked.

Josh dismissed the necessity with a wave of his hand. 'He'll say yes, of course he will. But me and Eveleen will go to the house and tell him, just in case . . .' He did not complete the sentence but added authoritatively, 'Let's get going. The sooner we get that pony and trap the sooner we can get after them.'

While Fred hurried away towards the factory, Eveleen fell into step alongside Josh. He was in charge now and, for once, Eveleen was prepared to leave it to him.

She did not want to ask favours of the Stokes family, but she had no alternative.

Fifty-One

'How far do you think they could have got?'

They were driving through the streets. Richard, sitting on one side with Fred and Eveleen squashed on the seat beside him, held the reins, while Josh sat on the opposite side. The trap was scarcely big enough to hold the four of them, but the pony, despite the weight, was managing a good pace.

'I don't know,' Eveleen muttered. She was resentful because Richard had insisted on coming with them. 'I don't know what time she left. Her bed looked as if it hadn't been slept in. If she left soon after I went to bed, they could have been gone five hours.'

'Mm.' Richard seemed to be calculating. 'I would estimate that she would walk at about two miles an hour. It wouldn't be much quicker than that if she was carrying the child.'

'Wouldn't she stop to rest?' Josh put in, sounding as if he didn't think he would be able to walk one mile in an hour.

'Probably,' Richard said. 'Would she know the way, Eveleen?'

'I don't know. When we left home, we went to Flawford and from there, we came here.'

'Might she go back there? To Flawford?'

'No,' Eveleen snapped. 'Not in a million years.'

The three men were silent but not one of them could have failed to notice the bitterness in her tone.

More calmly Eveleen added, 'She'll be trying to get home. Back to Bernby. That's where she thinks of as home.'

'We'll take the main road out of the city towards Grantham, so let's just pray that that's what your mother has done.'

Silently, Eveleen began to pray to the kindly, white-robed figure in Heaven.

It seemed to the anxious girl as if the streets of houses were neverending but at last the buildings thinned out and they were passing through countryside.

'Now,' Richard said, 'keep a sharp look-out for any sort of place where she might have taken shelter. This rain's getting worse.'

It was driving against them now, stinging their faces, but the pony was trotting on valiantly at Richard's gentle words of encouragement.

'She'd shelter in a barn,' Eveleen said and couldn't resist adding, 'It's what she did last time.'

No one answered her, but squinted through the rain and the darkness, straining to catch sight of the woman and child.

Ahead of them the sky began to lighten and with the dawn the rain began to ease a little. Richard drew the trap to a halt.

'We must have come ten miles or more. She can't have got this far, surely?'

Josh looked anxiously about him. 'You wouldn't have thought so.'

'Do you think she might have got a lift with a carrier or on a cart of some sort?' Fred put in.

'That's a good point,' Richard said. 'What do you think, Eveleen?'

She shrugged. 'I doubt it. She doesn't like asking strangers for help.'

Richard turned away and muttered something beneath his breath but Eveleen, sitting furthest away from him, did not catch the words. Fred and Josh must have heard for she saw them exchange a look. Then Richard turned. 'So what do you all suggest we do now? Press on?'

'Yes,' Eveleen said firmly. 'But watch out for farmhouses and barns now. Bridie will be hungry . . .' There was a catch in her voice and tears welled in her eyes. Her anger and resentment against Richard Stokes died. She felt cold and wet and there was a knot of anxiety in the pit of her stomach. She covered her face with her hands and turned her head away so that they should not see her tears.

She felt Fred's arm around her shoulders. 'Hold up, lass. Hold up. We'll find them.'

Eveleen felt the trap jolt as she took a deep breath, lifted her head and said, with far more confidence than she was feeling inside, 'Of course we will. We've got to.'

They were passing the gateway into a farmyard, the house and outbuildings dark shapes against the grey sky.

'Stop a minute,' Eveleen said suddenly, and as Richard brought the vehicle to a standstill Eveleen forced her stiff limbs to climb down.

'What is it?' Josh asked, anxiety and hope in equal measure in his voice. 'Have you seen something?'

'No, but it's milking time.' If the moment had not been so serious she would have laughed at the puzzled looks the three men exchanged. She couldn't resist the temptation to say, 'Farm workers rise early. They're up and about and at work while factory workers are only thinking about it.' She gestured towards the farm. 'There'll have been someone about the yard for an hour or more. They might have seen something.'

The three men looked towards the farm and now, as they listened, they could all hear the sounds of life coming from the cowhouse.

'D'you want me to come with you?' Fred asked uncertainly. 'I will, but I don't like cows much.'

'I'll go,' Josh said and pushed himself up, rocking the trap as he climbed down. 'I've always fancied living in the country and working on the land.'

Eveleen glanced at him in surprise. 'Have you really?'

'Oh aye,' he went on as they walked towards the five-barred gate into the yard. 'When I was a little lad I came on holiday to a farm. Best holiday I ever had.' Then, despite the gravity of their mission, he laughed. 'Mind you, it was the *only* holiday I ever had.'

They reached the cowhouse and Eveleen opened the door to be met by the familiar smells of her childhood, the warm, comforting smell of the beasts and the straw that littered the floor. For a moment she stood breathing in the heady atmosphere and swayed momentarily as poignant memories of her father flooded through her.

No wonder, she thought, that her mother was so desperate to come back home. It was the only place Mary had known true love and security.

A man was walking towards them. 'What do you want? You're unsettling my beasts.' His tone was wary and held a note of warning as the cow nearest to the door where Eveleen and Josh were standing moved restlessly. It turned its head and looked at them with wide, nervous eyes.

Without thinking what she was doing Eveleen out of a long, inbred habit moved towards the cow and began to rub its hindquarters and croon softly in her throat. The farmer began to smile. 'Oh, so you know about cows, lass, do you? After a job, are you?'

She smiled at him, but the worry did not leave her eyes. 'Yes, mister, I do know about cows, but it's not a job I'm after at the moment. We want to ask you if you've seen anyone this morning. A woman carrying a baby.'

The man shook his head. 'No, can't say I have.' He looked at them and must have read the anxiety on their faces, for he murmured, 'Not the sort of morning to be out walking. And with a babby.'

Disappointed, but hardly surprised, Eveleen sighed heavily. She gave the cow's rump a final pat and turned towards the door. 'Thanks, anyway.'

'Wait a bit. Have you come far?'

'From Nottingham,' Josh said.

The farmer smiled. 'Then I reckon you could do with a bite. My missis'll be getting my breakfast. You're welcome to come in.'

'Well,' Josh looked towards Eveleen, guessing that she'd rather press on.

'We did bring a basket of food with us.'

'Aye, but it'll not be bacon, eggs and fried bread, will it?'

Eveleen could almost see Josh salivating and suddenly, despite the anxiety, she felt hungry too. 'That's very kind of you,' she said, trying to keep the surprise out of her voice. 'Are you sure your wife won't mind? There's two more waiting in the trap in the lane.'

The man threw back his head and roared with laughter. 'There's nowt my missis likes better than having a houseful of folks to cook for. Bring 'em in. Bring 'em in and I'll go and tell her we've got visitors for breakfast.'

It was just what the four of them needed, though Eveleen fretted at the delay and felt guilty as she tucked into the food.

'You'll feel all the better. Dan, go and feed that pony, an' all. Poor animal looks that bedraggled and miserable. Now, Mr Carpenter, more fried bread?' The farmer's wife, who was almost as round as Josh and with a red face, beamed at him. She liked a man who enjoyed his food. 'Another sausage?'

Fed and warmed, though not quite dry, they took their leave of the kindly farmer and his wife. 'We'll keep a look-out,' the farmer promised. 'And if we see them we'll take them in and look after them.'

Eveleen smiled her thanks, knowing, for once, that their promise was genuine.

Richard shook the farmer's hand. 'If you do see them,' he said, 'send word to the Reckitt and Stokes factory in Nottingham.'

'Right you are, sir.' The farmer touched his cap respectfully, recognizing the voice of authority when he heard it.

Fifty-Two

They drove on for miles until Eveleen said hopelessly, 'She can't possibly have walked this far. We must have missed her.'

'Unless she got a ride on a cart with someone,' Fred reminded her.

'But we're almost at Bernby. We're almost home.'

She felt the three men glance at her, but her gaze was straight ahead now, searching for familiar buildings.

Was it really only just over a year ago that she had travelled this road taking her away? It seemed an age away, another life.

'Take the next turn to the right, Mr Richard, please.' A little later Eveleen murmured, 'And now left.'

Richard nodded and guided the pony and trap down the rough cart track that led to the farmhouse where the Hardcastle family had once lived. Without pausing to consider whether it was what she wanted, he drew into the yard and halted. Then he turned to her. His tone was gentle as he said, 'Is this where you used to live?'

Unable to speak, Eveleen could only nod. She was looking at the house, drinking in the sight of it, reliving the memories, good and bad.

Richard said softly, 'It doesn't look inhabited.'

Startled, Eveleen looked closer. She had been seeing the house as she had always known it, had almost expected her mother to step out of the back door in her white apron, calling, 'Walter, Walter, your supper's ready.'

Now she saw that although the same curtains still hung at the windows, the glass was dull and dirty. The door was shut and no hens scratched about the yard grumbling to each other. No sounds came from the cowhouse.

There was a deserted feeling about the whole place.

White-hot anger flooded through Eveleen. 'Nobody's living here. They drove us out and yet nobody's even living here.'

'There's one thing though, mi duck,' Josh said. 'Your mam might well be here. That is, if she could get in.'

Eveleen clambered down from the trap and with a sudden spurt of renewed hope ran to the back door. She bent and scrabbled under a loose brick near the wall. Triumphantly she stood up and turned back towards them holding a key in her hands. 'It's still here. They haven't moved it.'

The men were climbing down now to join her and Richard was the first to reach her. Then the hope in her face died. 'She can't be in the house, can she, if the key is still under the brick?'

'No, probably not,' Richard said gently, 'but we'd better take a look anyway now we're here. It is the most likely place she would come. Could she have found another way in?'

Eveleen shook her head. 'I don't think so.' But she turned the key in the lock, stiff now with disuse, pushed open the door and stepped inside. She wrinkled her nose. The house was damp and unlived in. The furniture they had been obliged to leave was still there. Eveleen glanced around her. The pots and pans they had used every day, now dull with dust and lack of care, still lined the dresser.

Walter's wooden rocking chair still stood in its place near the hearth. Even the scraps of paper they had burnt just before leaving were still in the cold grate.

'I can't believe it. It – it's just as we left it.' Tears prickled her eyes at the injustice of it. 'No one's even lived here since we left.'

Richard touched her arm. 'Do you want me to look upstairs?'

Eveleen shook herself out of her reverie. 'No, no, I'll go.'

Only moments later she returned downstairs to say sadly, 'No, she's not here.'

'We've looked in the parlour,' Richard said. 'But now I think we should search all the outbuildings, thoroughly.'

As they moved outside it was raining again and the pony stood looking woeful and, despite the kindly farmer's attentions, still hungry. Eveleen, reared to think of the welfare of the animals even before herself, said at once, 'I'll see to the pony. If they've not even bothered to clear the house out, then maybe there's feedstuff still here.'

There was and soon she had fed and watered the animal and had drawn him into the shelter of the barn while the men searched the cowhouse, the large barn and its hayloft and even the henhouse.

'I'm so sorry, Eveleen,' Richard said, and there was no doubting his sincerity. 'I really thought, like Josh, when we saw the place empty, that she might be here.'

They were standing just inside the house, sheltering from the rain but with the door open, while they decided what to do next. The sound of hoofbeats in the distance came nearer and slowed near the gate.

Eveleen, recognizing the rider, drew in a startled breath and felt the three men with her glance at her. But she was staring at the rider as he trotted into the yard and dismounted.

He was as handsome as ever. He hadn't changed in the months since she had seen him, of course. But she had. Oh how she had changed. The scales had tipped and her love had now become hatred. Her face coloured as she stepped towards him.

'So.' His languid voice now held no appeal for her. 'We've become squatters now, have we?'

'Don't worry,' Eveleen said tightly. 'We're going. I wouldn't want to live in a house owned by you if you paid me.'

He threw back his head and laughed. 'There's no fear of that. I can get what I want without having to pay for it.'

His glance took in the three men with her and his left eyebrow rose in the way she remembered so well. Yet now there was a cruel, sardonic slant to it. Perhaps it had always been there, Eveleen thought, but she had been too blind to see it. Stephen's gaze had come to rest upon Richard and now there was a sarcastic twist to his smile.

'I see you still aim high, Eveleen.' He gave a brief nod and said directly to Richard, 'I hope she gives you as much pleasure as she once gave me.'

Eveleen's face went red with rage. His words implied far more than had ever passed between them. He meant to humiliate her in their eyes, especially in Richard's.

'How dare you?' Before she had stopped to think what she was doing, she had flown at him, clawing at his face. She was crying with rage. 'How dare you say such a thing when it isn't true?'

He caught hold of her wrists and held her easily.

'I hate you!' she spat at him. 'Hate you.'

He was laughing in her face. 'No you don't. You still love me. You only held out because you thought I'd marry you.' His lips curled again. 'You really had the temerity to think that I'd marry the likes of you. The daughter of our gathman.'

She kicked out at him and caught him on the shin, noticing with satisfaction his wince of pain. He released her and she would have flown at him again if Richard's strong arms had not come around her waist from behind and held her firm, while Fred stepped between them.

'I don't know who you are, young feller, but I think you'd better leave.'

'Had I really?' Stephen's voice drawled, but his blue eyes glittered dangerously. 'You're the ones who had better leave. You're trespassing. On *my* property.'

'We're going.' Now Josh moved forwards and brushed passed Stephen, deliberately using his bulk to knock the young man off his balance.

Richard, still keeping tight hold of her, whispered, 'Come, Eveleen. Your mother's not here. We ought to press on anyway and we're serving no purpose here.'

Suddenly her defiance deserted her and her spirit drained out of her. The worry over her mother and poor little Bridie, the return to her former home to find it empty and just as they had left it and to realize there had been no good reason for them to be turned out, then to come face to face with the man she had thought she loved – it was all too much. She hung her head in shame and defeat and began to sob.

Gently Richard turned her in his arms towards him. She buried her face against his chest and he held her tightly against him.

'We're going,' he said above her head to Stephen. His voice was controlled, but Eveleen could feel the barely suppressed anger in him. 'But you haven't heard the last of this.'

'Oh, I think we have. This is my land and you have no right to be here.' Stephen's lip curled again as he added scathingly, 'Whoever you are.'

As he helped Eveleen climb into the trap which Fred had brought out from the barn, Richard said, 'You drive, Fred.' And he sat beside Eveleen and held her close as they drove away.

Fifty-Three

They had not gone far before Richard signalled to Fred to halt.

'Now,' he said to Eveleen, offering her a white, neatly folded handkerchief, 'dry those tears and let's try to think what we should do next.'

Eveleen drew in a shuddering breath, raised her head and took the handkerchief. She blew her nose and felt better though she knew the humiliation would stay with her for ever.

Richard, however, was sensibly concentrating on the task in hand and she must do the same. The longer her mother and Bridie were out in this terrible weather, the more danger they were in.

'Is there anywhere else in Bernby where your mother might go?' Richard asked.

'I – I suppose she might go to Bill and Dorothy's.'

'Where's that?'

'If we go a little further on down this road it's on the right. But it's still on *his* land.'

'Never mind about him. I haven't time to deal with him today,' Richard muttered, 'else I would.'

Eveleen noticed that the other men exchanged a glance, but nothing more was said apart from Richard deciding, 'Right, we'll go and find Bill and Dorothy.'

As they rocked their way down the muddy cart track towards Bill Morton's cottage, Eveleen saw their old friend emerge from the lean-to at the side of the house. As soon as they were close enough for him to recognize her, he hurried forward, reaching up his arms towards her, his face one big grin. 'Eveleen, lass. By, but it's good to see you. How are you?' His voice faltered as, closer now, he could see her distress. 'Oh, lass, whatever's wrong?'

As they all climbed down from the cart Richard swiftly explained, his manner towards Bill at once entirely different from his attitude towards Stephen a few moments ago.

'Eveleen's mother is missing. She left home last night and we thought she might have come back home.'

'It's all she's ever wanted,' Eveleen hiccuped miserably as Bill hugged her. 'I promised that one day I would bring her back, but . . .'

'I know, love, and I know you did. But it all takes time. Poor Mary. She never was the most patient of women, was she? Now,' he said briskly. 'Come inside. All of you and have a hot drink and a bite to eat. You look starved to death, lass.'

As he ushered his unexpected guests inside the tiny cottage, he was calling to his wife, 'Dorothy, Dorothy, look who's here. Get that kettle singing, lass. We've guests for dinner.'

When Dorothy appeared she gave a squeal of delight and hugged Eveleen. At once she was making everyone welcome and fussing round them.

'What a good job I've made a huge pan of stew this morning. I must have known.'

'We don't want to impose—' Richard began, but his protestations were waved aside.

While they ate, Eveleen found herself bombarded with questions from Dorothy and Bill. The whole, sad story of their life since leaving Bernby was told and Dorothy reached out and touched Eveleen's hand. 'You poor lass. What a time you've had. And all that on top of finding your poor father dead in the beck.' She glanced around at the strangers who had come into her home, but who she could see at once were trying to help the girl. 'Life can be very cruel at times, can't it?' she remarked.

Back among people who had known her family well, Eveleen felt able to say, 'Mam always blamed me for Dad's death. She – she said my wilful ways had brought on his heart attack.'

'That's nonsense,' Bill said at once. 'You must never think that, love. Your dad must have had a weak heart. It ran in his family. His father died in just the same way.' He glanced around, telling the three other men whom he presumed would not know. 'Found in a field, he was, just like poor Walter. Besides,' he went on, looking directly at Eveleen, 'I remember your dad having funny turns now and then. When we were haymaking or harvesting. He often had to stop for a rest.' He shook his head. 'That wasn't normal. Not for a feller of his age.'

Eveleen felt some of the guilt she carried for that event slide away, but now there was an even more pressing need for self-reproach.

'I seem to bring trouble on everyone,' she whispered. 'On poor Rebecca, on my uncle and grandmother . . .'

'That was Jimmy's doing, lass, not yours. You can't be held responsible for what he did. He always was a little rascal even as a young lad. It doesn't surprise me one bit.'

'But I am responsible for my mother being so unhappy that she walked out in the middle of the night.'

To this, no one around the table could think of a comforting answer.

*

'We'll organize a search all around this neighbourhood,' Bill said a little later when the decision had been made that Eveleen and the three men should try a different route back towards Nottingham.

'I'm sure that kindly farmer we met will keep a watch out for her,' Richard said. 'So we needn't retrace ground we've already covered.'

Once more, arrangements were made for messages to be sent should there be any news.

Bill and Dorothy hugged Eveleen and told her not to worry. Then they shook hands with the three men and received their thanks with nods and smiles. Although the smiles were genuine, they were tempered by the anxiety that everyone was feeling.

Just where were Mary and the tiny baby?

Fred took the reins this time without being asked and Richard sat close to Eveleen. She leant against him, allowing herself to give in, just this once, she told herself, and enjoy the feel of his arm around her shoulders, the strength of him and the confidence and common sense he exuded. It was a relief to hand over, even if only for a short time, the heavy burden she had carried for so long.

She was weary, worn out with the responsibility that had been thrust on her young shoulders. She closed her eyes and her head drooped. As the trap rocked, Eveleen slept against his shoulder.

She woke with a start as the trap halted. 'Mam?' she began, for she had been dreaming about her mother and the child.

'I'm sorry,' Richard said at once. 'We're almost back at Nottingham and we've seen no sign of her. We've asked along the way, but nothing.'

Anguished, Eveleen said, 'What do we do now? Call the police?'

'Unless she's been found, that will already have been done by now. I left word with my father.'

Eveleen felt a flicker of anger and opened her mouth to protest. She didn't want Brinsley Stokes involved. If anyone was to blame for this, then it was him. He was to blame for all the unhappiness in her mother's life.

But the retort died on her lips. At this moment, she should take any help she could get – wherever it came from. She looked about her. They were indeed nearing the city, but she recognized that they were even nearer the village of Flawford.

'We're not far from my uncle's,' she said glancing at Richard. 'I don't think for a minute that she would go there, but—'

He took the words from her. 'You think we ought to make sure?'

She nodded and, as Fred turned the trap in the right direction, Eveleen instinctively drew closer to Richard.

Fifty-Four

'Gone? Gone where?' Andrew's face was white with fear. 'And taken Bridie? My little Bridie? Oh, Eveleen, how could you let that happen?'

Eveleen's shoulders sagged. Although she had not held out much hope that they would be in Flawford – she believed it was the last place her mother would come – she was still disappointed. And once more she was shouldering the blame.

Gently, because he could see the young man's distress was genuine, Richard said, 'It wasn't Eveleen's fault. Mary left in the night while Eveleen was asleep.'

Andrew glanced at her and then looked away. 'I'm sorry,' he muttered. 'Of course it's not your fault. I'm sorry, Eveleen.'

Eveleen nodded, but could not speak. Bridie was all Andrew had left of his beloved Rebecca. He was beside himself with anxiety. Now he was firing questions at them. Where had they searched? Had they called in the police? What were they going to do next and how could he help?

Richard answered him calmly, adding, 'We should go now but we'll let you know.'

'Can I come with you?'

'Of course you can. But what about your work?'

'Sod that!' Andrew said. He jerked his thumb over his

shoulder towards the workshops. 'He can go hang, for all I care. There's other jobs.'

Eveleen glanced up at Richard. As an employer, it was not the sort of reaction he would like, but she could see the sympathy for Andrew's sentiments written in his features.

'Come along then,' Richard said briskly.

As they came out into the street and he saw Fred and the cumbersome figure of Josh already sitting in the trap, Andrew faltered. 'Oh, I'm sorry, I didn't realize there were more of you.' He thought quickly and then added, 'Look, I'll borrow my mate's pony and trap. I'll follow you. I know the way.'

Richard nodded. 'Right, because I don't think we should wait for you.'

'No, no,' Andrew urged. 'You go.' He gave Eveleen a quick hug and said, 'I'll be right behind you. I'll come straight to your house.'

Eveleen nodded and climbed back into the trap. It was only as they moved away that she realized she hadn't even asked after her grandmother and her uncle.

Although the police had been informed earlier in the day, Mary and the child had not been found nor had word come to the factory from those looking out for them in the countryside.

'You'd better both go home and change into dry clothes,' Richard said to Josh and Fred, but the two men glanced at each other. It was Josh who answered their employer but Fred nodded in agreement. 'We'd sooner stay here, Mr Richard, thank you. There might be news. And if there is, this is where it'll come.'

When Richard finally took Eveleen home, a pony and trap were standing outside the door. Eveleen felt a brief surge of hope and then she saw Andrew pacing up and down the yard. Behind him, Win was hurrying towards them.

'Any news?' she called out as Richard drew the trap to a halt and Andrew held out his hand to help Eveleen climb down.

Eveleen shook her head sadly and led the way into the house. She ran from room to room, leaving them to follow her inside.

'Mam? Mam?' But the house was still and silent.

She returned downstairs and sank into the chair at the side of the range. Win busied herself reviving the fire and setting the kettle to boil.

'Now what do we do?' Andrew, fresher than the others, who had been looking all day and half the previous night, was eager to carry on the search.

'First,' Richard said firmly, 'Eveleen must rest. She's exhausted.' She felt them looking at her and knew her face was white, her eyes dark-rimmed with fatigue and worry. 'And I'm going home for something to eat, a wash, a change of clothes and then, if there's still no news, we'll begin again.'

'It'll be dark by then,' Andrew persisted. 'We won't find them in the dark.'

'Well, we—' Richard began but whatever he had been going to say was left unsaid. Someone was thumping urgently on the door and shouting.

'Eveleen? Eveleen, they've found her.'

A rush of adrenaline brought Eveleen to her feet and running to the door. She flung it wide to see Fred standing there, leaning against the wall, his hand to his chest.

'I ran – all the way – from the factory,' Fred panted in staccato bursts. 'Word's just come – from that farmer. He's found her.'

'Who? Bill?'

'No. That other one. Joe Elgin. That was his name, wasn't it? The one that gave us breakfast. She was walking past his farm.'

'Are they all right? Is Bridie all right?' Andrew, having followed Eveleen to the door, asked urgently. Richard and Win were close behind him, craning to hear the news.

'I must go to them,' Eveleen said. 'I've got to see for myself. The baby could have taken a chill. Anything.'

Without waiting for an answer, Andrew was already climbing into the pony and trap he had brought. 'Come on, Eveleen.'

Richard moved forward. 'Eveleen, you ought to rest.'

'No, no,' she argued. 'I'm fine now. Honestly.' Before anyone could stop her, she had climbed in beside Andrew.

'Can't you just have something to eat?' Win called. 'And you ought to change out of those wet clothes.'

'Eveleen, wait—' Fred was reaching out towards them, trying to delay them, but Andrew flicked the reins.

'I'm fine,' Eveleen insisted and, as they moved off, she called out, 'Thank you. Thank you for everything.'

Turning the corner of the yard, they passed Josh, puffing and panting, on his way in. It took a moment for him to recognize them and then he began to wave his arms. Eveleen could see his lips moving, but above the rattling wheels she could not make out his words. He was shouting something and gesticulating that they should stop, but Andrew only drove the pony faster.

Eveleen smiled and waved and nodded, hoping that

Josh would understand that they had already heard the good news.

As the trap was headed out of the city, Eveleen linked her arm through Andrew's and hugged it to her. 'Oh thank goodness they're safe.'

Already she had forgotten her weariness and the wet clothes that clung to her and made her shiver from time to time. All she could think of was holding Bridie in her arms. She couldn't reach her fast enough.

'I just hope the babby's all right,' Andrew said. Eveleen smiled to herself. Andrew's only thought was for the child. And then, guiltily, she realized that Bridie had been uppermost in her own thoughts too.

The journey seemed interminable but at last Eveleen was directing Andrew through the gates and into the Elgins' farmyard. It seemed an age since she had been there and yet it had only been that morning.

The farmer was coming towards them. 'She's in the house with the missis,' he said at once, without any greeting. 'But we can't get any sense out of her.'

'She'll be upset,' Eveleen murmured as the farmer led the way to the house. 'Is the baby all right?'

Joe Elgin stopped and put his hand on her arm. 'I'm sorry, lass, but she had no baby with her.'

It was as if someone had knocked the breath from her. Eveleen's whole body began to shake.

'Oh dear God, no!' Andrew ran his hand through his hair and his eyes were dark with fear.

Eveleen grasped the jamb of the open door for a moment's support. Maybe that was what Fred, and then Josh, had been trying to tell them. She dragged in a deep, steadying breath and then forced her legs to move into the kitchen.

Mary was sitting in front of the range wrapped in a blanket. Mrs Elgin was bending over her, coaxing her to drink a steaming cup of tea.

'Mam, oh Mam!' Eveleen put her arm around her mother's shoulders and hugged her. 'Thank goodness you're safe.'

Andrew, following her in, asked harshly, 'Where's the baby? Where is my Bridie?'

Eveleen knelt on the hearthrug and took her mother's hands into her own. 'Mam,' she began, trying desperately to keep her voice calm as she looked into Mary's vacant eyes. She knew from bitter experience that anger would only drive her mother deeper into the trance-like state she was in, or worse still, it might induce one of her bouts of near-hysteria. 'Mam, where is Bridie?'

The vacant eyes focused on Eveleen's face and yet the girl felt a shudder run through her. It was as if Mary did not even recognize her own daughter. 'In a ditch,' the poor woman murmured. 'Born in a ditch. In the dark and the cold.'

Eveleen gripped her mother's hands tighter. 'Mam, that was a long time ago. Bridie's fine. She – she—' The lump in her throat threatened to choke her. Oh let her still be fine. Let her be safe, she prayed silently. 'Bridie is Rebecca's little girl. Mam, where is she? Where have you left her?'

Mary's eyes were vacant again, seeing only into the past.

Joe Elgin filled the doorway. 'I've got a search party out.'

Eveleen stood up slowly. It was no use. Mary was so

sunk into her own little world that they would get nothing from her. But Andrew was not going to give up so easily. He bent over Mary, grasped her shoulders and shook her so hard that her head snapped backwards and forwards. 'Where is she, you stupid, stupid woman? What have you done to my Bridie?'

'No, Andrew, no,' Eveleen cried, pulling at him, but it took the burly farmer to step forward and drag the distraught young man away.

'That'll do no good, lad,' he said firmly, but with a gruff kindness in his tone. 'Can't you see, she's in a bad way herself.' He glanced at his wife. 'I've sent word for the doctor. She needs help.'

Mrs Elgin nodded in agreement and fussed over Mary who began to wail. 'Jimmy. I want Jimmy. Eveleen, take me home to Jimmy.'

Eveleen glanced quickly around at the others and then looked down at her mother. She was still not thinking quite rationally, but at least she seemed to be coming back into the present.

Again Eveleen knelt in front of her and though her own instincts were exactly the same as Andrew's – she too felt the urge to shake the truth out of Mary – she managed to say calmly, 'I'll take you home, Mam, I promise you. But first, tell us where Bridie is.'

The wailing subsided to a quieter sob.

'Bridie?' Mary shook her head. 'Poor motherless little mite. Cast out, just like me. How can Harry turn his back on his own grandchild, Eveleen? How can he do it?'

Gently Eveleen said, 'Is that where you took her? Back to Uncle Harry?'

'She didn't—' Andrew began but was hushed by both Joe Elgin and his wife.

Mary was shaking her head and now there was spirit in her action. 'No, no. I wouldn't take her there. Not back to *him*,' she said bitterly.

'So, where were you going?'

'Back home,' Mary said simply. 'Back to Bernby where she'd be safe.'

'Is that where she is? Back at Pear Tree Farm?' Could they have missed finding the child earlier that day? Eveleen agonized. Had Bridie been there all the time and they'd not seen her or heard her cries?

Mary was shaking her head. 'No. No, she got so heavy to carry and it was raining. She was hungry too. Crying and crying. She wouldn't stop.' She covered her face with her hands and rocked to and fro.

Cold terror seeped into Eveleen's being. What had her mother done? Had the child's crying driven her over the edge? Oh, what had she done? Eveleen swallowed the fear but now even she could not keep the tremble from her voice. 'Where is she, Mam? What have you done with her?'

'If you've hurt her—' Andrew began and struggled to break free of Joe's grasp, but the farmer still held him firmly.

'Now, now, lad. Hold on. She'll tell us in a minute.'

'I left her in a barn,' Mary began and added quickly, 'She's all right. She's warm and cosy in the hay loft. I went to find some milk for her and I thought I'd be quicker if I went on my own . . .' The faraway look was back on her face. 'I started to walk, but I couldn't find a farm and – and I got so tired.' Her voice trailed away. 'I can't remember any more.'

Joe took up the story. 'She did look sort of lost when we found her and she didn't speak to us at all until you got here, but she let us bring her in here and look after her.'

'Where's the barn? Where have you left her?' Andrew demanded.

'It can't be far away. We'll find her,' Joe said with more determination than either Eveleen or Andrew could feel.

Eveleen was the first to reach the door. She flung it wide and rushed out into the yard, straight into Richard's arms.

Fifty-Five

The local police and all the men from the neighbouring farms joined in the search and, after four hours, the child was found in an isolated barn in the corner of a field.

'I heard her crying,' the searcher placed the child tenderly into Eveleen's arms. 'She's hungry, poor little thing. But she was cosy and warm.'

Andrew hovered close by, peering over Eveleen's shoulders, itching to hold Bridie himself. 'Is she all right? Has she hurt her?'

'Of course she hasn't hurt her,' Eveleen snapped, but even she was thankful to feel the baby wriggling in her arms.

Richard put his arm around Eveleen's shoulders and gently led her to the trap. 'Let's get her back to the Elgins' farm.'

When they arrived back, the doctor was with Mary. He examined Bridie too and pronounced her fit and well, but ravenous. Drawing Eveleen to one side he said, 'I'm concerned about your mother. Physically she's taken no harm, but I'm not happy about her state of mind. I've arranged with Mrs Elgin for her to stay here and I'll call each day. Good food, fresh air and plenty of rest should work wonders, but I want to be sure.'

Eveleen bit her lip but nodded agreement. She would worry about how to pay the doctor's bills later.

'And you, young lady,' he said with pretended severity, 'should take the same prescription.'

Eveleen felt as if her legs would give way any moment, but she managed to say, 'I'll be fine, Doctor, thank you.'

It was not Bridie, or even Mary, who took a chill and developed pneumonia, but Eveleen.

After a few days' rest and being cosseted by the farmer's wife, whose name they learned was Sarah, Mary and the child were fine, as the doctor had predicted.

'I just wanted to go home,' Mary said tearfully, when Eveleen sat beside the bed in the big room at the rambling farmhouse and took her mother's hand.

'It's all right, Mam,' she said gently. 'You're both safe now. That's all that matters.'

'Yes, but I shouldn't have taken the bairn with me. I – I might have lost her, like – like . . .' Her voice petered away and Eveleen knew she was thinking of that other tiny baby so long ago.

'It's over now,' Eveleen patted her hand. 'We'll say no more about it.' But as her mother drifted into sleep, Eveleen began to worry again.

I must get her back to the country. Somehow I must or else this could happen again.

When she could see that her mother was sleeping peacefully, Eveleen slipped out of the room and went downstairs. As she entered the warm kitchen, she felt suddenly dizzy. She clutched at a chair for support, but there were wavy lines in front of her eyes. The room began to swim around her and then she felt herself falling.

She awoke to find herself lying in a huge bed. The room and the bed were warm, for beside her in the bed were four heated bricks wrapped in scraps of blanket, and a cracking fire burned in the grate, the flames leaping and casting dancing shadows on the walls and ceiling. Yet Eveleen was shivering with chills that felt as if someone was pouring cold water down her back.

A shadow rose out of a deep armchair near the window and came towards the bed.

'Eveleen?' a deep voice said and a cool hand rested on her forehead.

'Andrew?' she said and heard the name spoken in a croak. Was that really her voice?

'No,' the voice came again. 'It's Richard.'

'I'm so sorry . . .' she began, but it was difficult to speak. She felt as if she were breathing through cotton wool. 'I didn't – thank you properly.'

'Don't try to talk. You must rest. But first, if you can sit up a little, you must drink this. The doctor said—'

'Oh,' she gasped. 'A doctor. I can't—'

'Now listen,' his tone was still gentle, but firm now. 'You're not to worry about a thing. Your mother and the child are fine. They haven't taken any harm for their adventure. But you must take care and get yourself well again.'

'Where am I?'

'At the Elgins' farm. You remember, the kind farmer who gave us breakfast that day and who later found your mother?'

'Mm.' Talking made her breathless and there was a pain in her chest when she tried to breathe deeply. 'But I can't lie – here,' she said in staccato gasps. 'I must—'

'You *can* lie here, Eveleen. And there is nothing you have to do except rest and get well again. Everything is taken care of.'

Her mind was playing funny tricks on her. Why was Richard Stokes, her employer, sitting on the bed beside her and holding her hand? Now he was slipping his arm beneath her shoulders and easing her up and holding a cup of warm liquid to her mouth.

She began to cough and the pain in her chest was worse. She shivered again, yet her head felt as if it was burning.

'Don't lift my feet up,' she murmured. 'It feels funny.'

'I'm not touching your feet,' the voice said, but it sounded faint now. Eveleen closed her eyes. 'I must get up,' she murmured, but her limbs felt like lead. 'I must go to work.'

Her mind was playing funny tricks with her. She seemed to hear her father's voice calling her from a distance. 'Eveleen. Eveleen.'

There was a bright light and she tried to run towards it. 'I'm coming, Dad. Wait for me. I'm coming . . .'

But the light disappeared as suddenly as it had come and she was tossing and turning in the bed again. She felt something cool bathing her forehead and a voice that said soothingly, 'Try to sleep, my love. I'm here and I'm not going to go away. Don't worry about a thing.'

The voice lulled her. She felt secure and cared for. It was a wonderful feeling, she thought, as she drifted away, to have someone looking after *her* for a change.

Her sleep was fitful and disturbed by dreams. She felt as if someone was lifting her up in strong arms and then there was a woman's voice and capable hands were taking off her nightdress and pulling on a warm, dry one.

'She's wringing wet, poor lass,' the woman's voice said. 'We ought to get the doctor to take another look at her.'

'No, no,' Eveleen tried to say. 'I can't afford a doctor.'

Then there were other voices in the rooms. A man's voice and he was pressing something round and cold against her chest and bending over her as if listening intently. She tried to speak but her throat was dry and her lips cracked and sore. And her head ached dreadfully. The man had moved away from the bed and was talking softly to someone else in the room.

Eveleen tried to speak, but all she could hear was this strange mumbling, a jumble of words that made no sense. Her mind was drifting, not thinking clearly.

In the end she gave up trying. She closed her eyes and slept.

The next time she woke up, she felt better. She didn't feel as if her whole body was burning and yet shivery at the same time. At least she was not having nightmares any more. Strange, muddled dreams where she was running and running but her legs would not seem to move because she was dragging a heavy weight behind her. But now her head did not hurt so much and her thoughts were clearer.

She pulled herself up in the bed and saw that although sunlight streamed in through the window, a fire still burned brightly in the grate. At her movement, Richard rose from the chair by the window and came to stand beside the bed.

She tried to smile at him. 'Whatever are you doing here?'

There were dark lines of tiredness beneath his eyes and a day's growth of stubble shadowed his face.

'Looking after you.' He smiled and some of his anxiety lifted. 'Mind you,' his smile broadened. 'I don't seem to be making a very good job of it. You look awful.'

'Thanks,' Eveleen said and heard for herself that her voice was stronger. 'I feel it.'

The bed creaked as he sat down beside her. To her surprise he reached over and laid his hand on her forehead.

'Thank God,' he murmured more to himself than to her. 'The fever's broken.'

'I'm still hot.'

'Yes, but you're sweating it out now. Not burning up. That's a good sign.'

'Is it?' she managed to say with a tremulous smile. 'I'll believe you.'

'I wish you would,' he murmured, and she had the feeling that he was not just referring to the state of her health.

'Are they all right? My mother and Bridie.'

He sat quietly, watching her for a few moments before he said softly, 'They're fine.'

'How long have I been here?'

'Five days.'

'Five days!'

If her weakened body had let her she would have leapt up there and then in horror. As it was, she tried to pull herself up but found she was as weak as a new-born kitten.

She groaned as she fell back against the soft pillows. Before she had thought to whom she was speaking, for her mind was still a little slow to work properly, she said, 'Oh, I'll lose me job.'

She heard his soft chuckle. 'I don't think so. But if you do, I'll have something to say to the boss.'

She realized then and could laugh at herself. 'I'm sorry. I'm not thinking straight.'

She felt him pat her hand and then he got up. 'Now that you're on the mend, I must get back home.'

She looked up at him, standing so tall over her. 'You mean – you've been here all the time?'

He nodded but then, before she could say more, he said briskly, 'But now I must go. I'll come and see you again and if' – he wagged his finger at her now with mock severity – 'I hear any bad reports that you are not behaving yourself, I'll bring a big stick.'

Before she could say any more he had left the room and she heard his footsteps running lightly down the stairs.

And I still haven't thanked him, she thought.

Fifty-Six

Eveleen slept for a while and awoke to find Sarah Elgin bending over her.

'You're feeling better.' It was as much a statement as a question.

Eveleen nodded but immediately wanted to know, 'Mam and Bridie?'

'They're fine and thriving. Your mother's churning butter in the dairy and singing at the top of her voice.'

'Churning?' Eveleen began and then, amazed, added, 'And singing?'

'Yes, singing. And little Bridie's outside in the sunshine. I got my Joe to fetch the old perambulator down from the loft in the barn. We've cleaned it up and even painted it. And she loves it. Just lies there gurgling and crowing all day long.'

'I seem to have missed an awful lot,' Eveleen murmured and glanced towards the window, longing to be outside in the sunshine herself.

'You'll soon be back downstairs with us now you're on the mend. You'll feel weak for a day or two, but once you start eating properly, my good food and this lovely weather will help you. I can't believe the change in the weather after all that awful rain we had.' She crossed to the window and pushed up the sash. Warm air flowed into the room and Eveleen breathed in deeply, revelling in its fresh country air smell.

Then she was overcome by a fit of coughing, but Sarah only laughed. 'Cough it up, lass,' she teased, thankful to see the girl was so much better. 'It might be a gold watch.'

Sarah had thought for a day or two that they were going to lose her. Privately the farmer's wife believed that it was only the young man's own determination and constant care that had pulled the girl through. Richard refused to let her go and his will power had somehow reached her even through the depths of her fever.

'Now, let me help you out of that bed and into a chair. I'll give you a blanket bath and then change the sheets. You'll feel much better.'

'A what?'

'A blanket bath. You've been having them every day for the last five days. Didn't you know?'

Eveleen shook her head. 'I don't seem to know much at all about the last five days.'

She soon found out what a blanket bath was and when the woman had washed her with warm water as she lay on the bed, Eveleen did indeed feel refreshed.

'Now, let's have you out of bed and I'll change the sheets,' Sarah said.

As she sat up, swung her legs to the floor and tried to stand, Eveleen was appalled at how weak and wobbly she was. She groaned aloud. 'Oh, it's going to take me weeks to get back to work.'

'Don't you be worritting about that, love.'

'But we can't impose on your goodness any longer,' Eveleen began.

'I'm loving having you all here. And your mother's making herself useful. She's a big help. And as for the baby, well, you can leave her here with me for good if you want.' Then seeing Eveleen's expression, she added hastily, 'Only teasing, love. Of course you couldn't bear to part with her. She's a little darling.'

'But you must have had so much work looking after me.'

Sarah shrugged her plump shoulders. 'Not really. That young feller did most of it.'

Startled, Eveleen stared at her. 'He didn't give me the blanket baths, did he?'

Sarah chuckled at the idea. 'Oh no. I wouldn't let him do that.'

While Sarah stripped the rumpled sheets and spread crisp, clean ones on the bed, Eveleen asked, 'Where's Andrew?'

'He had to go back home, but he said he'd be back at the weekend.' She wrinkled her forehead and added, 'That's tomorrow. He'll be so pleased to see you looking better.' Sarah chattered on. 'And Josh is coming on Sunday.'

'Josh? Really?'

'Oh yes,' Sarah looked up and winked at Eveleen. 'He's been here a time or two. Mind you, I think he's coming to see your mother as much as anyone. I reckon he's sweet on her.'

Time took a sudden tilt and for a moment Eveleen's senses reeled. She was back in the kitchen at home – at the farm – and once again she could hear Jimmy's voice saying, 'I reckon Master Stephen is sweet on our Eveleen.'

'Jimmy.'

'What, love? What did you say?'

Not until Sarah asked the question did Eveleen realize that she had spoken his name aloud. 'Nothing,' she said, as her gaze went out across the flat fields. 'I was only thinking aloud.'

As Sarah bustled about the bedroom, Eveleen sat lost

in her own thoughts. For the first time for many months, she had a chance to sit and think.

Where was her brother and why had they never heard from him? He might have sent word, even if only to their mother. He knew how much Mary had always doted on him. Surely he could have spared a thought for her? Eveleen prepared herself for the shaft of impatience that usually accompanied thoughts of her rascal of a brother. But nothing came, and thinking about him she even found an amused smile twitching involuntarily at her mouth as she remembered their childhood. The scrapes he got into and how he had expected his older sister to cover for him, never to tell tales of him to their mother. It was Eveleen who always had to take the blame. He always had such a winning smile for Mary. He could wind his mother round his little finger and she would believe any story he told her.

Oh, Jimmy, Eveleen sighed inwardly, but now the words were not spoken aloud. Why did you have to do it? Why did you have to stir up trouble for me and then bring such tragedy on poor Rebecca?

And still I'm left carrying all the blame.

Andrew arrived the following day and was invited to stay the night, and on the Sunday Josh arrived, driving Mr Richard's pony and trap.

Eveleen was still not strong enough to leave her bedroom, but each day she sat out of bed for longer periods of time.

Josh lowered himself into a chair near her as she sat beside a window, flung open to let in the warm day.

'How can I ever thank you, Josh?' she began but he waved her gratitude aside.

'I'm just so glad to see you getting well again and that we found your mother and the babby safe.' He was thoughtful for a moment before he remarked, 'She's a different woman out here, isn't she?'

Eveleen nodded and her gaze went to the scene outside the window. She heard all the usual farmyard noises she had known for most of her life. The clatter of buckets. The lowing of cattle. The grumbling and scratching of hens about the yard. The occasional squeal of a pig. The sound of horses' hooves and the rattle of cartwheels.

It was home, especially for her mother. It was the only place Mary had ever known real happiness.

Eveleen gave a deep sigh. 'I've got to get her back here. Somehow I've got to find a place for us to live back home.'

Her gaze was intent upon the idyllic country scene below her, so that she did not see the gleam in Josh Carpenter's eyes.

The following Sunday, Josh was late arriving at the farm.

'I wonder why he hasn't come,' Mary said, her glance going to the farmyard gate for the fiftieth time that morning.

'Mary, how many more layers are you going to take off that potato. You've peeled the same one three times now,' Sarah said, laughing.

'Oh!' Startled, Mary dropped the potato into the bowl, the earthy water splashing her white apron.

'Come on, Mam, you go and sit outside with Bridie and watch the lane.' Gently Eveleen took the knife from her mother's fingers. 'I'll do these.'

'Are you sure, love? Are you sure you're strong enough?'

Eveleen felt tears prickle her eyes. It was the first time in an age that her mother had voiced real concern for her. She put her arms around Mary's slim waist and hugged her.

To her surprise, she felt her mother's arms creep around her and hug her in return.

As they drew apart they smiled at each other, a little embarrassed, and Eveleen's voice was unsteady as she said, 'I'm fine, Mam, honest. Off you go.'

'Well, I don't think he's going to come now,' Mary said as they all sat down around the dinner table. Her voice was flat with disappointment. 'He wouldn't be late for one of Sarah's Sunday dinners, I know.'

'Maybe he's just got delayed,' Sarah said comfortingly as she placed a joint of beef in front of her husband for him to carve. Then she moved between the range and the table placing tureens of steaming vegetables before them. 'Help yourselves.'

There was silence around the table except for the clatter of cutlery and crockery. When they were all served and began to eat, Mary picked at the food on her plate. 'I'm sure he isn't coming.' She put a piece of meat into her mouth and chewed it round and round, but all the time her gaze was on the yard beyond the window.

It was as Sarah stood up to clear away the plates that they all heard the sound of wheels.

Mary sprang up with more energy than Eveleen had seen in her for a long time. Sarah beamed, 'There you are, you see.'

But Mary was gone, flying out through the back door.

Joe Elgin and his wife exchanged a glance and then Sarah winked at Eveleen. 'I told you, didn't I?' But now the girl was sure that her words held more meaning than that she had been right about Josh's late arrival.

They squeezed in through the door, with Mary clinging to his arm. 'Why are you late? We thought you weren't coming.'

'I've kept a plate warm for you, Josh. Come and sit down,' Sarah called.

Josh beamed all round and eased himself into a chair at the table while Joe carved slices of beef and Sarah piled his plate with vegetables. Mary pulled her chair close to him and, as he began to eat, picked up her knife and fork and finished her own meal too.

Eveleen and Sarah glanced at each other in amusement. She's right, Eveleen thought, there is something going on between Mam and Josh. The thought pleased her. She liked Josh, and if he brought a sparkle to her mother's eyes again, Eveleen would be the very last person to complain.

They all waited until Josh and Mary had finished their first course and then Sarah served the pudding. When at last Josh pushed away his empty plate and leaned back in his chair with a satisfied sigh, he glanced around and said, 'I've got some wonderful news for you. Mary – Eveleen – you're going home.'

Eveleen, though she was feeling stronger with each day, could not stop the stab of disappointment. But she had known the day would come and knew, too, that she and her family could no longer impose upon the Elgins' goodness.

'Sarah says I can stop the night so that I can take you in the morning.' He went on, rubbing his hands together.

'Tomorrow,' Eveleen murmured. 'So soon?'

'Yes.' Josh could not keep the gleeful note from his voice. 'Yes, by tomorrow, we'll have you all back home.'

Fifty-Seven

'Now, are you sure you're going to be all right,' Sarah said, wrapping warm blankets around Eveleen as she sat in the trap early the following morning.

'We'll be fine.' Eveleen tried to reassure herself as well as Sarah, but she could not help thinking of the cold, unwelcoming house that awaited them in Foundry Yard.

'Now, Mary, you sit beside me,' Josh was saying and added to Sarah, 'You can put the cradle on the floor, between our feet.'

Sarah had found a wicker cradle in the loft too and had lined it and made little blankets for it. Now she was looking as if she didn't want to part with either the cradle or the child lying in it.

Eveleen reached out her arms. 'Please, come and see us whenever you can. You know our address in the city. We'd love to see you.'

Sarah looked up and smiled, but it was at Josh that she directed her glance. 'Yes,' she said softly. 'Oh yes, I'll come and see you all right.'

There was a flurry of goodbyes and then they were moving off. As they turned out of the gate, Eveleen said, 'You're going the wrong way, Josh.'

'No, no, I'm not. I thought your mother might like a little ride in the country before we go home. All right, Mary?'

Eveleen watched as her mother slipped her arm

through the big man's and said with a coy smile, 'Whatever you say, Josh.'

They were going in the wrong direction all together. They were heading towards Bernby and even further away from Nottingham.

Eveleen bit her lip and glanced at her mother. She was anxious that if her mother saw their former home empty and deserted and falling into disrepair it would upset her.

It had upset her, Eveleen thought, never mind her mother whose emotions were very unstable. But Mary seemed to be enjoying the drive and when they neared familiar landmarks, she cried out excitedly, 'There's Bernby church on top of the hill. Poor Walter's buried there you know. We ought to take flowers there before we leave, didn't we, Eveleen?'

'Yes, Mam,' Eveleen agreed reluctantly and glanced at her worriedly. She would love to visit her father's resting place, but to take Mary might bring all the memories, good and bad, flooding back. But Mary was still smiling and looking about her. Then before Eveleen could protest, Mary was pleading, 'Oh, do take us to the farmhouse where we used to live. I'd love to see it, just one more time. Please, Josh.'

Josh's eyes positively twinkled. 'If you're sure you'd like to see it, Mary?'

'I would. Oh, I would,' she breathed and then directed him happily, not realizing that Josh already knew the way.

Eveleen pulled the blanket closely around her and hunched her shoulders miserably. She didn't want to cause an argument, but she was sure that seeing their old home would swiftly dispel Mary's new-found happiness. It might even topple her over the edge into a bout of confused depression once more. At the Elgins' farm and under Sarah's placid care, Mary had been like her old self. Now, Eveleen was sure, all that was going to disappear in an instant.

As they pulled into the yard, Eveleen saw at once the change in the place since their last, brief, visit.

Hens wandered about the yard and from the pigsties came the sounds of noisy occupants. In the field close by, half a dozen cows grazed contentedly. She looked at the house. Windows were flung wide and curtains – still the ones they had left but now freshly laundered – blew in the breeze. The back door stood open to the warm, sunny day.

'Josh, we mustn't stay,' Eveleen said at once. 'Someone's moved in. Someone's living here now.'

'That's right,' Josh said as he looped the reins and stood up to alight, his weight wobbling the trap dangerously. He stepped down and held out his hand to Mary.

'Come on, Mary. I'm sure they won't mind us taking a look. You too, Eveleen.'

'I'll stay with Bridie,' Eveleen said at once, not wanting to see some other woman in her mother's kitchen, another man sitting in her father's chair. She was surprised and worried too that her mother could even contemplate the idea.

'No, no, you must come,' Josh insisted. 'Here, push the cradle to me. I'll carry her.'

So the three of them, with Josh carrying the wicker cradle, walked towards the back door. As they neared it a figure appeared in the doorway.

'Dorothy!' Mary cried in delight and rushed forward with her arms outstretched to embrace her friend. 'This is wonderful. Oh I'm so glad it's you and Bill living here.'

Dorothy returned the hug, but above Mary's head, her

glance went to Josh. Eveleen saw him wink. Then he put his finger to his lips and gave a little shake of his head.

'Come in, come in,' Dorothy said. 'Bill's here too.'

'Shouldn't he be at work?' Mary teased. 'He'll be getting the sack.'

'No, he's got the morning off to be here to see you.'

Mary glanced at her and frowned slightly. 'You knew we were coming?'

Again, Eveleen saw Dorothy glance helplessly at Josh, almost as if she realized she had said too much.

They've planned it, Eveleen thought. They planned it that we should call round this way. She didn't know whether to be grateful or angry.

'In you go, Mary,' Josh said blandly, ushering her into her former home.

Mary stood in the kitchen and slowly turned round, drinking in the sight. 'Oh, Dorothy, you've got everything just the way we left it. I could almost think . . .' Her voice broke a little and there were tears in her eyes, yet she was still smiling as she went towards the man sitting in Walter's chair by the bright fire in the range. 'Bill. How lovely to see you again.'

'Mary, love.' He rose from the chair and kissed her cheek. 'It's good to have you back.'

Mary sank down into the chair that had once been hers and looked about her again. Dorothy bustled between the kitchen and the scullery carrying a tray with cups from Mary's best china tea service on it.

Seeing it, Mary pointed. 'Do you know, that's the only thing I really minded leaving behind. It was a wedding present.' She laughed wryly. 'The only one we got.'

'Well, here it is, all ready for you,' Dorothy said and began to pour the tea. As she handed round the cups,

Dorothy asked, 'Is the little one all right, Eveleen? Does she need a feed?'

Eveleen nodded. 'She will soon. If you wouldn't mind, I should like to give her a bottle before we leave.'

Dorothy smiled and nodded, but dropped her gaze.

Bill had not sat down again in the chair by the fire and now he gestured towards it with a broad grin on his face. 'Here, Josh, you'd better get used to sitting in it.'

Josh laughed and went towards the chair. With great ceremony he lowered himself into it. 'Bit of a tight squeeze,' he said.

Bill chuckled again and said, 'We'll soon work that off you.'

Eveleen exchanged a mystified glance with her mother and then they both looked at Josh. He cleared his throat and looked embarrassed. 'I suppose I had better explain.'

Quietly Bill and Dorothy stood to one side, though they did not leave the room.

'You see,' Josh began, 'I've bought this place and a little bit of the land around it too. I've always wanted to live in the country.'

Mary stared at him. 'You're going to come and live here?'

Josh nodded. 'And I was rather hoping you might come and live here too. As my – my housekeeper.' He reached across and took her hands in his. 'Mary, please say you will?'

Tears were running down her face, but now they were tears of happiness. 'Oh, Josh, of course I will, but what about . . .' She glanced at Eveleen and then at the cradle.

'I mean, all of you. Eveleen and the baby too, of course. You're a family.'

'You want all of us to come and live with you?' Eveleen asked.

Josh nodded. 'I'd like nothing better.'

Eveleen wasn't sure about all this. It had been thrown upon them so suddenly. She needed time to digest the idea. She glanced at her mother, but there was no mistaking the joy and happiness on Mary's face.

She was back home where she had always wanted to be. Mary Hardcastle was back where she really belonged.

Tears sprang into Eveleen's eyes and she turned away and walked from the room and out into the yard. She went as far as the gate and leant on it, looking out across the well-known view.

She couldn't tear her mother away from this, not again. Couldn't take her back to the terraced house in Nottingham. She had to agree to Josh's proposal for Mary's sake.

But Eveleen was troubled. There was something about this whole thing that didn't quite ring true. She felt as if she had been manipulated, as if the decision had been made for her and that she had been put in the position of not being able to refuse.

Fifty-Eight

'I don't know how you managed it all and so quickly,' Mary marvelled for the umpteenth time during their first week. 'And however did you get the Dunsmores to sell it to you?'

Josh smiled. 'They were persuaded. Everyone has their price,' he added with an unusual smugness.

Eveleen glanced at him across the dinner table. That was exactly what was troubling her. At first she had not been able to understand what it was about the whole story that mystified her. Josh wanting to live in the countryside, seeing the place where Mary and Eveleen used to live, falling in love with it and buying the house and a parcel of land from the Dunsmores all in under a fortnight just did not seem plausible.

'There are still some legal documents to be drawn up and signed and all that' – Josh waved his hand – 'but because the place was still empty, they could hardly refuse to let us move in.'

Eveleen looked down at her plate. It was not quite what she would have believed of the Dunsmores, especially not of Stephen. She could sooner believe that he would have tried to block the sale completely, if he had known who was moving back into the cottage.

She licked her lips. 'Did – did the Dunsmores know exactly who was going to be living here? I mean, did they know we were moving back?'

Josh appeared to be trying to remember. Vaguely, he said, 'I'm not really sure if it was ever mentioned. But that's none of their business.' He smiled broadly. 'They don't own it any more, do they? Or at least, they soon won't, once the papers have been signed and sealed.'

'You mean, the sale's not yet complete? They could still change their minds?'

'Of course they won't.' Josh winked at her. 'Like I said, everyone's got his price. It seems as if that young feller we met has been spending money a bit too freely. Gambling, I shouldn't wonder. Anyway, it was lucky for us – for me – that he was only too pleased to sell off a bit of the estate to get some quick cash.'

So, Eveleen thought, yet another flaw in the character of the man she had once thought she loved. But the knowledge brought her no satisfaction, only a feeling of foolishness, remembering how besotted and blind to his faults she had been.

Eveleen glanced at her mother, who was serenely ladling out the hot vegetable soup she had made that morning. The smile never seemed to leave her face now. Mary was happy and contented. She was back home and she had a kind man to fuss over once more and to care for her. With a start of surprise, Eveleen realized that her mother had not mentioned Jimmy once during the past few days. Perhaps even Mary had now accepted the fact that he was doing what he wanted to do and would not come back to them.

It was still thoughtless of him to leave them without even a word, however, to disappear so completely. But that was her brother, Eveleen thought. Selfish to the last. But even she wished that they could just know that he was all right. She believed he owed them that much.

Eveleen sighed and tried to dispel her anxieties. But there was one thought that would not leave her.

Just how had a man like Josh Carpenter managed to find the money to buy a smallholding?

A week later, after he had disappeared for a day back to Nottingham, Josh returned to tell them both gleefully, 'It's all signed, sealed and delivered. This place is really ours now.'

Eveleen glanced at him and said quietly, 'Yours, Josh.'

'No, no,' he insisted. 'I've had your names put on the deeds as well. It belongs to all of us.'

Eveleen's eyes narrowed as she regarded him shrewdly. 'In that case, isn't there something that we have to sign?'

For a moment Josh looked startled. 'Oh no, I don't think so. I've signed. Er – um – sort of proxy, or whatever they call it.'

He seemed to be avoiding meeting her direct gaze now. Eveleen glanced at her mother's ecstatic face and decided to say no more – for the present.

Later, in the yard, she cornered Josh.

'Now, Josh Carpenter, I want the truth and I want it now.'

'What do you mean, Eveleen?'

'Josh, don't take me for a fool. With the greatest respect, there's no way someone like you could save enough money to buy a place like this. Oh I know you had a good job at the factory, but you'd never earn enough there if you worked till you were a hundred.'

'I – I've never had anyone to spend my money on, Eveleen. I – I've saved.'

'So why spend it all on giving comparative strangers their old home back?'

Now she could see that she was hurting him, but she drove on relentlessly. She had to know the truth, and she was sure that the story that Josh Carpenter had bought the property, land and animals was not the truth.

'You're not strangers, Eveleen. Please don't say that. I'm very fond of you both, and little Bridie, too. I wanted to see your mother happy again.' His eyes had a haunted look for an instant, then he said hesitantly, 'Don't laugh at me, Eveleen, but I was rather hoping that one day your mother might consent to become my wife.'

Eveleen felt ashamed. The sincerity in the man's statement was apparent. She could see it in his eyes. But she saw also that he had craftily turned her attention away from the financial side to the more personal and emotional side, of which there could be no doubt in her mind.

She sighed and shook her head. 'I'm not laughing. I'm sure you'd make her very happy.'

'I know she'd make me the happiest man alive,' he said, smiling now, some of the loneliness chased from his eyes.

Softly Eveleen said, 'But you're still not telling me the truth about how you bought this place, are you? I know *why* now and I believe you. But I don't believe that you've bought it.'

Josh fidgeted and shifted uncomfortably. He ran his hand over his forehead and Eveleen could see that there were beads of sweat standing on his brow.

'All right, all right, I'll tell you the truth. But you've to promise me one thing first. That you won't do anything about it. You won't cause trouble. And especially that you'll never, ever, tell your mother.'

Slowly, she nodded, but the truth was becoming clear to her, even as Josh began to explain.

I was right. It's not Josh who's bought our home for us at all. It's him. He's behind all this.

She heard the words coming out of Josh's mouth, but now she could scarcely take it in. Her mind was reeling, the world spinning around her. She felt dizzy and sick.

How could she live with this, knowing that he, of all people, owned the house they lived in?

Fifty-Nine

'You're being very selfish.'

Richard Stokes was now sitting behind the desk that had once been Josh Carpenter's.

Eveleen, her eyes blazing and her mouth tight, leant across the wide expanse and shook her fist in his face. 'Don't you dare to tell me what I am. Aren't I giving up my whole life to taking care of my mother and Rebecca's child? I made a promise to her and I meant to keep it. I'll be the one to take her back to Bernby, not you.'

'Of course you would have kept your promise and taken her back home,' he said smoothly, but he added pointedly, 'one day.'

'Oh you know how to dig the knife in, don't you? Well, if you and your condescending father paid better wages, I might have managed it a bit quicker.'

He rose and came round the desk to stand close to her. In so doing, he placed himself between Eveleen and the door so that she could not flounce off before he had said what he intended to say.

'I didn't want you to know about any of this and I'll give Josh Carpenter a piece of my mind when I see him.' The twinkle in his eyes belied the threat. 'But since you know part of it, you'd better know the rest.'

'The rest? What do you mean, the rest?'

'Won't you sit down?'

'I'd rather stand, thank you.'

'Very well.'

There was tension between them and a spark that had nothing to do with Eveleen's anger, yet she held on to that indignation. That was why her pulse was racing and her legs felt weak. It had nothing to do with the fact that he was standing so close to her she could have reached out and touched his face, traced the line of his strong jaw, smoothed back the unruly lock of black hair that fell on to his forehead, drowned in those dark eyes . . .

'We did it for your mother as much as for you. More so, really.'

'We?'

'My father and I.'

Eveleen was stunned to silence.

'My father feels very guilty about what happened years ago.'

Eveleen found her voice. 'So he should,' she muttered.

'Even though,' Richard went on firmly, ignoring her remark, 'he knew nothing about your mother's pregnancy and the tragedy that followed at the time. Now he wants to try to make amends as much as he can.'

'And what would your mother say to all that?' Eveleen asked sarcastically. 'If she knew.'

'She does know. My mother is a wonderful lady and very understanding.' His words were like a rebuke to Eveleen. 'My father told her everything. About how much he had loved your mother, had wanted to marry her, but because they were so young he had bided his time, hoping that when he reached his majority, he could go his own way.'

'But he went away. He left her,' Eveleen argued, still unwilling to believe that Brinsley Stokes had been entirely ignorant and therefore also completely innocent.

'He was only nineteen and thought it politic to obey

his family's wishes until he was twenty-one. But when he came back home, your mother had disappeared. He searched for her, but never found her. He waited for more than a year, hoping she would come back, but then he came to the conclusion that she had gone away – just like her family said she had – because she no longer loved him.'

Eveleen was struggling with her conscience. For so long she had believed that Brinsley had deliberately and callously deserted her mother when she had needed him the most, and yet . . .

'You don't believe me, do you?'

'I . . . I want to. Really I do, but . . .'

With great understanding, he said softly, 'But you've lived all your life with your version of the story and you cannot change.'

She shook her head. 'Not that long, I knew nothing about it at all until we went to Flawford. My father must have known.' Vividly she recalled his evasive answers to her probing questions. 'But we – Jimmy and me – we didn't.'

'It's hardly the sort of thing a mother would like to tell her children, is it?'

Eveleen met his gaze. For a young man, not much older than she was, he was very kind and understanding. Or was it only a façade? Would this kind, generous face dissolve into twisted disdain if he didn't get his own way?

'Don't you trust me?' he asked gently.

She jumped at how accurately he had gauged her thoughts. Trust? How could she trust any man after what had happened to her? She had trusted Stephen Dunsmore. She had even trusted her own brother and so had poor, naïve Rebecca and look where that had got her.

'I know you've been hurt,' he was saying and his tone

hardened as he added, 'and I think I've now met the man who hurt you so, but haven't there been others in your life who haven't hurt you? People who have loved you and cared for you and about you? What about your father and those nice people at Bernby? Bill and Dorothy. Their affection for you was plain to see.'

It was as if a door opened in her mind. His gentle prompting caused her to think about the other men she had known in her young life.

Her father. But that was different. Of course her father had loved and cared for her and had never let her down. But Rebecca's father hadn't, a little voice reminded her. When Rebecca had needed him the most, he had turned his face from her.

And then the others queued up in her mind's eye, demanding to be remembered.

Bill Morton, who had stood by the Hardcastle family, perhaps even jeopardizing his own job by doing so. Then Andrew Burns. How could she ever doubt his selfless devotion to Rebecca and, now, to Bridie? And Josh. Josh Carpenter, whom everyone ridiculed, had a heart of gold. He wasn't a lecherous figure of fun. He was wonderfully kind and caring. And a very lonely man.

And yet he had readily been party to deception. He had deceived her into thinking he had brought about their good fortune.

Richard was watching her. Perhaps he was even reading on her face the signs of her inner struggle. He moved closer.

'Won't you forgive us? You must see that if we had told you the truth, you would never have agreed to it.'

That was true, Eveleen was forced to admit.

'What about Josh?' she burst out. 'Was that all a lie too?'

Richard frowned, obviously puzzled. 'I don't understand.'

'Once he's got my mother installed in the country, is he going to leave her?'

The puzzled expression was replaced by one of understanding and then of gentle sadness. 'One day, I'll make the man who's hurt you so much pay for what he's done.' Richard's mouth tightened. 'Believe me, I'll make him pay. But as for Josh,' he shook his head. 'No, he's not going to abandon your mother. He's a happy man. A very happy man. You'll see. Over the next few weeks and months, he'll have shed several pounds and be as fit as a fiddle.' He moved closer and said softly, 'Oh Eveleen. Won't you believe us? Won't you trust me? Won't you at least give me a chance to prove how very much I love you?'

She looked into the depths of his brown eyes and she could see nothing but love and concern for her.

He took her hand and raised it to his lips. Gently, almost with a reverence, he kissed each one of her fingers. Then she felt his sigh as he looked up and met her gaze. She could not doubt the look in his eyes. Desire was there, yes. She recognized that. She had seen it before in another's eyes, but in Richard's deep eyes there was something more. So much more.

He gave a little shake of his head, a sad, almost defeated gesture. 'You're still in love with him, aren't you, Eveleen?'

'No, no,' she cried vehemently. 'I hate him. Hate him.'

Richard closed his eyes and sighed so deeply now that it seemed to come from the depths of his soul.

'Oh my love. My dearest love. Love and hate are blood brothers. Only indifference is truly the opposite of love.' He opened his eyes and, reaching out, tenderly touched her cheek. 'You can never truly love again until you can look at him and feel nothing. Absolutely nothing.'

She opened her mouth to protest but gently he laid his forefinger against her lips. 'But when that day comes, I'll be here waiting for you, Eveleen. I'll wait for you for ever, if I have to.'

Sixty

Eveleen was restless but did not know why.

She was back home in the country. The cows in the field nearest the house belonged to them now and were providing enough milk for the family with plenty to spare. She made butter and cheese and sold it in Grantham market. Another field was to be ploughed up and set with vegetables which would also be sold at market. With eggs from the chickens and a recent litter of pigs, Pear Tree Farm was becoming a thriving smallholding.

Josh looked to her to lead the way, but he worked alongside her in the fields, in the cowhouse, in the barn – anywhere where there was work to be done. The outdoor life had tanned Josh's skin to a healthy bronze and the happiness was written on his face.

As for Mary, she was back to her old self, happier, if that were possible, than she had ever been. She cosseted and fussed over the new man in her life and there was no denying that she was besotted with the baby. Mary had even, much to Eveleen's silent amusement, mellowed towards her. Gone were the sharp retorts and remarks that had always been the tone of the early relationship between mother and daughter.

There was only one cloud in her mother's sunny sky, as far as Eveleen knew. Still no word had come from Jimmy.

Everything should have been perfect in Eveleen's life,

so why did she feel restless? It was as if there was something missing. Why did she so often find her mind empty of rational thought and her dreamy gaze on the westward horizon?

She was happy here. Win and Fred had visited and Andrew came often, though she knew his main purpose was to see Bridie. She was back home, Eveleen told herself, where she had longed to be.

And yet . . .

'I don't know what's the matter with me,' Eveleen confided in Dorothy one day when she had pushed the perambulator down the track to Furze Farm to sit in the warm kitchen over a cup of tea.

'I s'pect you're missing the bright city lights.'

Eveleen laughed. 'I didn't get the chance to see any "bright lights",' she said. Then her smile faded. 'But do you know, I do miss it. The noise and the bustle.'

'And the people?' Dorothy prompted gently.

'Well, maybe one or two,' Eveleen said carefully.

There was silence between them, the only sound in the kitchen the settling of the fire in the range and the kettle singing on the hob, until Dorothy, changing the subject, said, 'I don't expect you've heard.' She was beaming. 'Our Ted and Alice Parks have got engaged.'

'Oh, that's wonderful news,' Eveleen said sincerely.

'Alice is so happy. Planning her trousseau and collecting bits and pieces for her bottom drawer.' Dorothy cleared her throat and glanced at Eveleen. 'They're getting married next month.'

Eveleen spoke without thinking, unable to keep the surprise out of her voice. 'Next month?'

Dorothy nodded. 'Yes, it's a bit sudden, but then

Alice's dad is holding a shotgun to our Ted's head.' To Eveleen's surprise Dorothy was laughing as she added, 'If you know what I mean.'

Eveleen's eyes widened and then she said tartly, 'Well, I hope Ted doesn't run off like our Jimmy.'

'He won't,' Dorothy said firmly. 'He's really looking forward to being a dad, even though they are both a bit young.'

'He's changed then,' Eveleen murmured.

'Why do you say that?'

'Oh nothing,' Eveleen said evasively. She could hardly tell Dorothy of the advice that Ted had once handed out to Jimmy. Obviously he was no longer following his own counsel.

'You – you don't seem to mind,' Eveleen said hesitantly.

'There's not a lot me and Bill could say. Our Ted was born only six months after we were wed. And he was a full-term baby.'

'Oh,' was all Eveleen could say but the comical look of confusion on her face made Dorothy burst out laughing.

There was someone coming down the track that led to Pear Tree Farm: a slim young woman, holding up her skirt to pick her way daintily around the puddles. Eveleen, emerging from the cowhouse, a bucket of milk in each hand, paused to watch her. The girl reached the gate, lifted her head and looked about her.

A wide smile spread across Eveleen's face and she almost dropped the buckets to the ground in her haste to reach her visitor. Her arms flung wide, she ran towards the gate calling out a greeting.

'Helen! Oh, Helen.'

'Eveleen!'

Their shrieks of joy, their laughter and the tumult of questions they fired at each other brought Josh and Mary out of the house. Linking her arm through her friend's, Eveleen drew her towards the house. 'Mam, Josh, look who's here.'

Josh came forward, smiling and holding out his callous-hardened hand. As Helen's eyes widened and her mouth dropped open, Josh chuckled, 'Yes, mi duck, it's really me.'

As she put her small hand into his, the girl said candidly, 'You look marvellous. So – so . . .'

'Much thinner,' Josh beamed and they all laughed.

'Come in, come in, love,' Mary said. 'We haven't met before, have we? But I've heard a lot about you.'

'This is my mam,' Eveleen made the introductions. 'And the little madam who's making all the noise is Bridie.'

They went into the house and Mary picked up the baby. 'You're hungry, my little precious, aren't you? There, there,' she crooned.

'You sit down, love. I'll make her feed,' Josh said, heading for the scullery.

Eveleen could not hide her laughter at the astonished look on Helen's face. 'Well,' the girl whispered, anxious not to cause offence. 'Who'd have thought it?'

Close to her ear, Eveleen murmured, 'Who indeed?'

For a moment the two girls watched the happy, domestic scene, then Eveleen said, 'I'll show you round.' She pretended to grimace as she said laughingly, 'We won't get our dinner until mi lady there has got hers. I'll take the milk into the dairy and then we'll go for a walk.' She hesitated and then added, 'Unless you're tired.'

Josh came back into the room as Helen answered, 'No, no, I'd love to see everything. I don't get into the country-side very often.'

'Dinner in half an hour then. If your mam hasn't finished feeding Bridie, I'll get it ready.'

The two girls exchanged another glance and hid their smiles.

'Oh, I nearly forgot.' Helen fished in the bag she carried and pulled out a dog-eared postcard. 'I've some-thing for you. Win said this came to the house you had in Foundry Yard.'

Eveleen took the card in her hand and turned it over. She drew in a breath sharply, making a little startled sound of surprise so that Mary and Josh looked up.

Eveleen raised her gaze to meet her mother's eyes. 'Oh, Mam, it's from Jimmy.'

'Jimmy!'

Eveleen nodded.

In Mary's arms the baby squirmed and protested. She could see the bottle but it wasn't coming to her mouth quickly enough.

'There, there, my pet,' Mary soothed and in a moment Bridie was sucking noisily. Then, quite calmly, Mary said, 'Well, read it out then.'

'It doesn't say much,' Eveleen looked down at the untidy scrawl. Schoolwork and her brother had never really been good companions. 'Just "*Dear Mam and Evie, I am well. Hope you are. I'm seeing the world. Love, Jimmy*".'

'Not a word of apology, I suppose?' Mary asked.

Eveleen shook her head and smiled. 'I can't ever remember Jimmy saying he was sorry for anything. Can you?'

'No,' Mary said tartly. 'But it wouldn't have hurt

him. Just once. He owes you that much, Evie, at the very least.'

For a long moment mother and daughter stared at each other. Then to Eveleen's surprise, tears filled Mary's eyes and ran down her cheeks. 'Oh, Evie, I'm so sorry. So very sorry. I don't know how you've put up with me.'

Eveleen hurried to her side and put her arms about her mother. Quietly Josh took the baby from Mary, who now clung to Evie and sobbed against her shoulder. 'I've treated you so badly, even when your poor father was alive.'

Stroking her hair, Eveleen soothed, 'It's all over, Mam. All forgotten.'

Mary pulled back a little and smiled through her tears. She patted Eveleen's shoulder. 'You're a good lass, Evie. And I do love you – very much.'

Now it was Eveleen's turn to feel the tears spilling down her face. Then suddenly they were laughing and crying and hugging each other, until at last Mary said, 'Go on, love. You go for a walk with Helen.' Her smile widened and her words included Josh and the baby. 'We're fine here.'

As Eveleen propped the card on the dresser, she murmured, 'I am glad we've heard from him. At least we know he's well.'

Again she and her mother exchanged a look. Eveleen knew that the arrival of news from Jimmy had completed Mary's contented world.

'It's like something out of a picture book.' Helen was ecstatic in her praise. 'Blue sky, green fields, even a stream and trees. Oh I've never seen so many trees.'

They were walking alongside the beck towards the

bridge, where they sat on the parapet and watched the water bubbling over the pebbles.

'Just look at the colours in that water,' Helen marvelled. 'Brown against the rocks but there's blue and green. Even purple.'

Fascinated, she sat watching the rushing water.

'You make it sound idyllic,' Eveleen teased. 'It's not so lovely in winter, when there's snow and ice and—'

Helen clapped her hands, 'Oh, I bet it is. Everywhere covered in white. How pretty it must look.'

'Pretty pictures, maybe, but not when you have to milk the cows with fingers you can't feel and trudge through two foot of snow to feed the pigs and—'

'Stop, stop. You'll have me crying in a minute.' They laughed, leaning against each other.

'Oh it's good to see you.' For Eveleen the sight of her friend had brought the touch of the city again: the pavements seething with life, the lighted shops, the bustle and the noise. She felt a sudden surge of excitement. 'Tell me,' she demanded eagerly, 'what's been happening?'

'Well,' Helen began slowly, with a coy glance. 'All the women in the workrooms have had a rise in their wages and we've been promised a little extra at Christmas. Oh, he's so good to us. Any suggestions we want to make for improving our working conditions, he said, we're to go straight to him.'

Eveleen swallowed and her voice was husky as she asked, 'Who? Who is this "he" who's doing such wonderful things?'

Before Helen spoke, Eveleen already knew the answer.

'Why, Mr Richard, of course. He's taken on the management of the warehouse now, while his father manages the factory side of things. But even he's making improvements, they say.'

So, Eveleen thought, another young man who had been given power over other people's lives. And yet, from what Helen was telling her . . .

There was the sound of hoofbeats in the lane coming closer and, intrigued, Helen twisted round to watch the horseman approach.

Eveleen kept her gaze fixed steadfastly on the beck, her back turned towards the lane. The rider reined in and Eveleen heard him speak.

'Good afternoon, ladies. I trust I find you well.'

She heard Helen's soft chuckle at her side and almost laughed aloud as in a very haughty tone Helen said, 'You do indeed, sir.'

'And you, Miss Hardcastle?'

She felt Helen's sharp elbow in her ribs and her whispered, 'Evie?'

Slowly Eveleen turned round and looked up into the face of the man on horseback. With a grand gesture she inclined her head and said quietly, 'I am very well, sir. Thank you.'

Stephen Dunsmore raised his hat and bowed his head towards them. He smiled his most charming smile and said, 'I bid you good-day, ladies.' Replacing his hat, he urged his horse forward. They watched him canter along the lane and turn in at the gates of Fairfield House.

'What a pompous, stuck-up little prig!' Helen said.

Eveleen gasped and stared at her friend until Helen laughed and said, 'Oh I know I've only just met him, but I'm pretty good at summing folks up. 'Specially fellers. I wouldn't want anything to do with him if he was the last man on earth.' Her merry laughter echoed across the fields as she spluttered, 'Mind you, whenever I say that me mam always says, "Don't worry, you'd be killed in the rush".'

Eveleen, her gaze still on the empty lane where Stephen had disappeared, said tentatively, 'How – how can you tell?'

'Tell what? What he's like, you mean?'

'Mm.'

'He's got cold eyes and a weak chin. I bet he can be a right charmer when he wants to be, but turn nasty if he didn't get his own way.'

Suddenly Eveleen was laughing and crying all at the same time. She put her arms around Helen and hugged her close. 'Oh, Helen, you're wonderful. I do love you so.'

'What did I say?' asked the mystified girl in astonishment.

But Eveleen couldn't tell her that when she had looked up into Stephen Dunsmore's face she had felt neither love nor hatred. No swift beating of the heart or trembling at the knees. No wanting to rush into his embrace or feeling the urge to scratch her nails down his petulant face.

At last she had been able to look at Stephen Dunsmore and feel absolutely nothing.

'So, when are you going back to Nottingham for good?' Mary, sitting contentedly by the fire with her pillow lace on her lap, her fingers deftly twisting and weaving the threads, asked her daughter.

'Trying to get rid of me, are you?' Eveleen smiled fondly at her mother and winked at Josh sitting in Walter's chair reading the newspaper. It didn't hurt her to see him in her father's place. He was a good, kind man – just as Walter had been – and she felt sure that her father would approve of Josh.

'Of course we are,' Mary said, laughing. 'What do I

want with a nineteen-year-old daughter around when I'm about to become a blushing bride myself?'

Eveleen gasped and looked from one to the other and back again. Then she leapt to her feet and flung her arms wide, trying to embrace them both at once.

'Oh when? Have you fixed a date?'

'We thought next Easter.'

The conversation turned to their plans; plans, Eveleen noticed with a pang, which did not seem to include her.

Her own thoughts drifted. She thought about the city that she had grown to love and the friendly people there. Win and Fred and Helen in particular, but there were others too. She loved Lincolnshire, the place of her birth, she always would, but she had seen something else now. She had witnessed another kind of life and it had twisted its way into her heart.

Her mother was home where she belonged and she had a good man to care for her once more. What did it matter how that had been achieved? That it had been accomplished was what mattered.

'Of course if you do decide to go back, we . . .' Mary hesitated and looked towards Josh who took up her words, 'We want you to leave Bridie with us, love.'

In that instant Eveleen felt the burden slip from her shoulders. She was free. Free to live her own life.

And, now, she was free to love again.

'Yes,' Eveleen murmured and began to smile. 'You're right, Mam. My life is back in Nottingham.'

'Right, that's settled then,' Josh said and added, mildly, 'Give my regards to Mr Richard when you see him.'

From behind his newspaper, he winked across the hearth at his bride-to-be.

Twisted Strands

With great affection and deep admiration
this book is dedicated to my uncle, Brian Copley,
who enlisted in 1914 at the age of sixteen in
the 8th Battalion Sherwood Foresters,
(Nottinghamshire and Derbyshire Regiment)
and served throughout the war.

Thankfully, he survived the trenches to live a long
and happy life and it has been a privilege to
share his memories and experiences through his
personal diaries of the time.

Acknowledgements

The area to the west of Grantham around Barrowby and Casthorpe, the village of Ruddington and, of course, Nottingham are once more the places of inspiration for the settings in this novel, although the story and all the characters are entirely fictitious. The siting of a factory and warehouse on Canal Street in Nottingham and the homes of all the characters within the city are also my own invention.

I am deeply grateful to Jack Smirfitt and all his colleagues at the Ruddington Framework Knitters' Museum for valuable information and advice. I also wish to thank Peter Mee, a former twisthand in the lace industry, who so kindly and generously shared his knowledge and experience with me.

My grateful thanks to all the staff of Skegness Library for their interest, encouragement and wonderful help with all my bizarre questions!

My love and thanks as always to my family and friends for their unfailing support.

One

Spring 1914

'I'll run away.'

The young girl, at that fledgling stage between child and young woman – gawky and awkward – stood in the middle of the yard watching her grandmother calmly peg out the washing on the line. The older woman was taking no notice of her and Bridie believed she didn't even care.

The girl promised not classic beauty, but an appeal that would be captivating rather than enslaving. Her lively spirit would attract friendship, loyalty, even love, but perhaps not idolatry or blind worship. But at this moment the twelve-year-old showed little of the adult she would become. Her face was an ominous cloud, her mouth a sultry pout. Her deep blue eyes, fringed with black lashes, flashed with bitterness and resentment and she flicked back her long, thick black plait in a gesture of impatience. Involuntarily her hands tightened into fists at her sides. She moved nearer to her grandmother. Thrusting her head forwards, she muttered through clenched teeth, 'I mean it. I will run away.'

'Oh aye,' Mary Carpenter was still hardly listening. She didn't even glance towards the girl, but bent and picked up the end of a wet sheet. 'And where would you run to?'

The reply came promptly. 'To me auntie Eveleen's.'

'Your auntie's too busy to be looking after a troublesome child like you.'

'I am not a child. I'm twelve. I've been working for seven months.' Her mouth twisted in distaste. 'And I hate it.'

Now Bridie felt her grandmother's glance. 'You're just like your father,' Mary said, but the words were an accusation not a compliment.

The girl bit down hard on her lower lip to stop it trembling, angry at herself that, not for the first time, the mere mention of her father could bring her close to tears; did, in the privacy of her room. It was strange that reference to her mother, who had died at her birth, did not have such a deep effect upon her. Maybe it was because her mother had not been able to help leaving her, whereas her father had done so out of choice. He had disappeared before her birth, refusing to marry her mother and deserting her even before their child had been born. As far as Bridie knew, he didn't know to this day whether he had a son or a daughter. Perhaps he did not even know of Rebecca's death. And worse still, to the child's vulnerable mind, he quite obviously did not care. Not once had he come back from the sea to meet her. Though he had sent home brief letters and cards spasmodically over the years, he had never even asked about her. As far as her father, Jimmy Hardcastle, was concerned, Bridie might as well not exist.

Now her chin rose defiantly. 'All right, I am like him. 'Cos he ran away didn't he? Well, I'm going to do the same, so there.'

Mockingly Mary asked, 'What? Are you going to run away to sea then?'

'I might.'

Pointing to the empty washing basket, Mary said, 'Now stop all this nonsense, child. Take that back to the wash-house, then come in and have your breakfast.'

The girl did not move. Mary sighed. 'It's high time you were about your work. Josh'll be needing your help. And besides,' she added, and now there was a gleam in her eyes as if she knew she was playing her trump card, 'who would look after your injured creatures? What do you think would happen to them if you weren't here? Josh hasn't time to be fussing with wild birds and rabbits. He's enough to do with our own livestock.'

Mary turned and marched back into the farmhouse, disapproval in the set of her shoulders. At fifty-four Mary Carpenter still had the slim figure of a woman half her age, though her hair, drawn back from her face into a neat bun at the nape of her neck, was now more grey than the rich brown it had once been. She wore a white apron over her long black skirt and a crisp, white cotton blouse.

Resentfully Bridie watched her go. It was the only thing that Mary could have said that would touch her; the only thing that could keep her here. The best part of her work on the farm – the part she really enjoyed – was caring for sick or injured animals. Bridie compressed her mouth and frowned. She took a step and then another and picked up the basket. She could not bring herself to leave the blackbird with an injured wing nestling in the hayloft or the wild rabbit with a broken hind leg in a hutch in the yard. She would let the little things go once they were well again, but for now they needed her. Her frown deepened; her grandmother knew that too.

Josh might look after them if she pleaded with him, but Bridie knew, even at her tender age, that once she was gone Mary would have her way. Bridie believed that Josh was fond of her, even though he was only her step-grandfather and therefore no blood relation to her. But in any confrontation between herself and her grandmother, Josh, although he tried to keep the peace, would always take Mary's part in the end.

Bridie was not so sure of her grandmother's affection. She had lived with Mary and Josh since babyhood and knew no other home, but as she had grown older she had begun to feel that she was here on sufferance rather than because she was truly wanted.

Suddenly her heart lightened. There was one person who loved her.

Andrew. Andrew loved her. If her grandmother didn't want her and her aunt Eveleen had no time for her, then she would go to Andrew. She would even take her menagerie with her. Andrew lived in a little cottage and, though she had never seen it, she was sure he must have a garden. Surely there would be room enough for her wounded creatures.

Her mind made up, she picked up the basket and skipped towards the wash-house.

He would be here as usual on Sunday and she would make him take her home with him. Back to the little village of Flawford, near Nottingham, where he lived. There would be plenty of room in his little cottage, for she knew he lived alone.

Yes, Andrew would take her home with him. Bridie could get Andrew Burns to do anything she wanted.

Two

For the rest of the day Bridie skipped through her work about the farm. She milked the cows in the cowhouse, singing at the top of her voice. In the dairy she churned the butter and she was still scurrying to and fro as she laid the table for their supper, whilst Mary and Josh sat on opposite sides of the hearth in front of the kitchen range. Josh warmed his feet on the fender and sighed contentedly. His huge frame filled the Windsor chair and the firelight glowed on his fat, red cheeks. His large nose dominated his face, but his kind eyes shone with love every time they glanced across the hearth towards his wife.

'Well, I'm pleased to see you've changed your tune, miss,' Mary remarked. 'Your mood changes with the wind.'

From behind his newspaper, Josh winked at Bridie and the girl hid her smile. Even though he adored her, Josh was not blind to Mary's little foibles. And if Bridie resembled anyone in her family, she knew it was her grandmother. Mary's own mood swings were like a weathervane. And then the words were springing from Bridie's lips before she could stop them, 'I must take after you then, Gran.'

Mary's head snapped up and her eyes widened. She half rose from her chair. 'You saucy little madam . . .'

Josh crumpled his newspaper and now even he was

frowning. 'Now, Bridie, don't cheek your gran. There's a good girl.'

'Sorry, Gran,' Bridie said airily, with no real note of apology and as she hurried back into the scullery, she was smiling. Soon, she was thinking, I won't be here to be cheeky to anyone. Soon I'll be living with Andrew in his little cottage.

It was an idyllic picture, but one that was purely in her mind's eye for she had never visited Flawford. She imagined that he lived in a tiny cottage, similar to the one down the lane where her friend, Micky Morton, lived with his parents. Micky was lucky, Bridie thought, and her mouth pouted involuntarily. He had been born only a few months after her, but his parents were married and he had grandparents, too, who lived nearby.

A cosy, whitewashed cottage, Bridie dreamed. That was where Andrew would live. With ivy climbing up the wall and a path leading up to a front door framed with roses. Tiny leaded-paned windows would sparkle in the sunshine from her polishing and a tantalizing smell of her baking would greet him as he came home each evening from his work as a framework knitter in the nearby workshop. Oh, how she longed to be grown up so that she could be Mrs Andrew Burns.

It was all she had ever wanted; to be married to Andrew. For as long as she could remember, whenever he had visited, she had rushed to meet him, her arms wide. He would catch her and swing her round and round, their shared laughter echoing around the farmyard. Then, setting her on the ground, he would kiss her forehead and press whatever little gift he had brought for her this time into her hands.

And his gifts were not always little. On her twelfth birthday he had presented her with an exquisite shawl he had knitted on his machine especially for her.

'I had to be careful the old man didn't catch me,' Andrew had laughed. 'But I did it in me own time, so there's not a lot he could say.'

Remembering, the smile faded from Bridie's mouth.

The 'old man' Andrew had referred to was Bridie's maternal grandfather. Someone else whom she had never met. Josh had explained it to her, so carefully, so gently. Perhaps that was why she loved Josh, for he, not her grandmother, nor her aunt Eveleen, nor even Andrew, had taken the trouble to explain the past to her. For that reason, Josh was the only one she would regret leaving.

'It's all a long time ago now, love,' Josh had said as they walked alongside the beck together, taking the cows back to the field after milking, her small hand tucked into his large one. 'And although it's not your fault, none of it – I'm afraid it does affect you. Quite unfairly,' Josh said firmly as he glanced down at her. He took a deep breath and seemed to brace his shoulders. 'Before your gran married me, she was married to the man who was your grandfather, Walter Hardcastle. But you knew that, didn't you?'

Bridie nodded. As they walked, she glanced down at the bubbling water. It was somewhere along here that her grandfather, Walter, had been found, face down in the water having suffered a heart attack. That much she knew, for she saw his grave every Sunday when her gran laid fresh flowers on it. Her gaze lifted to Bernby church standing on the hill in the distance beyond the beck. That was where he was buried.

'After he died so suddenly, the family had to leave Pear Tree Farm,' Josh went on in his kindly, rumbling tones. 'They went to Flawford, to your gran's family.'

'Where is Flawford?'

'It's a village just south of Nottingham,' Josh continued. 'They went to live with your gran's brother, Harry Singleton and . . .'

Bridie remembered interrupting him again at this point in her piping voice. 'Singleton? But that's my name. Why's he got the same name as me?'

The big man at her side had mopped his brow. 'Because your mother, Rebecca, was his daughter and – and . . .' He faltered over the delicate matter. 'You see, mi duck, your mam and dad weren't married, so you've got her surname.'

Bridie had been silent then, digesting the information, trying to work it out in her young mind. Then she said slowly, 'But my dad was Gran's son. I did know that much. So – so were him and my mam cousins?'

'Yes,' Josh said. 'First cousins.'

Again, she was silent. Then, in a voice so quiet that the man at her side had to strain to hear her words, she said, 'And he left her, didn't he? He left us both. He ran away to sea.'

'He was only young, love. No more than a boy, really.'

'Did you know him?'

'Briefly, when he worked in the factory in Nottingham for a short time. It was where I worked then.'

'I thought you said they went to Flawford?'

Josh smiled down at her. 'Oh dear, I'm not very good at this sort of thing. I'm not explaining it very well, am I, mi duck?'

In answer, Bridie smiled up at him, her cheeks dimpling prettily. She gave a little skip, her long black plait swinging. 'Go on,' she encouraged. 'Tell me what happened. Tell me why I've never met me grandfather Singleton.' For a moment there was hurt in her eyes. 'Doesn't he want to meet me?' Then she put her head on one side and eyed Josh speculatively. With a maturity far beyond her years, she asked shrewdly, 'Or is it me gran who won't let *me* see *him*?'

'I don't think so, love, though I have to admit she never sees him herself either.' He licked his thick lips. 'Harry's a hard man. An unforgiving man and he threw your poor mam out of his house when he found out she was expecting a child. In fact, he threw the whole family out, young Jimmy – your dad – and even your gran and Auntie Eveleen too. They all went to Nottingham to find work and that's how I met them.'

'My dad was with them then?'

Josh nodded. 'He didn't stay long, though. He wasn't much of a worker. Couldn't – or wouldn't – get the hang of operating a lace machine.' Suddenly Josh let out a loud guffaw of laughter that startled Bridie. 'Your aunt Evie would have made a better twisthand than him – if she'd had the physical strength, of course. Mind you,' he added reflectively, 'she was a strong lass in those days, having worked on the farm here.'

'Auntie Evie? Did she work in your factory too?'

Josh was still chuckling. 'It wasn't my factory, love. I only worked there. The factory belonged – still does – to Mr Brinsley Stokes and his son, Richard.'

'Uncle Richard?'

Josh nodded. 'Yes, he met your auntie Evie and fell in love with her.' He looked down at her as he added, his voice almost reverent, 'And I met your gran and fell in love with her. So some good came out of it all, didn't it?'

Bridie nodded, unable to speak. Perhaps it had. For them. But what about her? Her father had deserted them, her mother had died and, although she had her gran and Josh, Auntie Evie and Uncle Richard, her grandfather Singleton hated her so much that he never wanted even to meet her.

She drew in a deep, shuddering breath, trying to shut out the hurt and humiliation. There was really only one thing that mattered to her. Or rather, one person.

'What about Andrew?' she asked, trying to still the tremble in her voice.

'Andrew? What do you mean, "What about Andrew"? Sorry, I don't follow. He works for your grandfather and lives in one of his cottages. I thought you knew that. I reckon he was probably born there. I think his dad and mam worked for Harry an' all. He grew up alongside Rebecca, see? And he was very good to all the family when they were in trouble. And, of course, he's your godfather.'

'But he's – he's not related to me, is he?' She held her breath, willing him to make the reply she wanted to hear.

'No, he's not. He's not a blood relative, if that's what you mean. Though . . .' Josh had seemed about to say more, but stopped abruptly.

They had continued to walk along the bank, in silence now. She asked no more questions and only when they approached the gate into the farmyard did she say with a quaint, adult courtesy, 'Thank you for telling me, Grandpa Josh.'

On Sunday, dressed in the shawl he had given her, Bridie waited by the farmyard gate for Andrew to appear at the end of the rough cart track leading to Pear

Tree Farm. Then she saw him, wobbling dangerously on his bicycle as he negotiated the deep, muddy ruts. Picking up her skirts, she ran to meet him.

'Andrew, Andrew.'

The man's smile seemed to stretch from ear to ear when he saw her and he put his feet on the ground to bring the bicycle to a halt. Jumping off, he laid it on the ground and opened his arms to her. Laughing delightedly, Bridie ran into them and was lifted off her feet and swung round and round until she was dizzy.

As he set her down again, Andrew pretended to be out of breath. He put his hand on his chest and panted, 'You're getting far too big for such unladylike behaviour.' But the twinkle in his hazel eyes and the laughter lines that crinkled mischievously around them belied his words. He picked up his bicycle and, with one arm draped across her shoulders, they walked towards the farmyard.

'Aren't you going to ask me what I've brought you?'

Bridie smiled up at him as, her mouth twitching, she said with pretended primness, 'She that expecteth nothing shall surely receive.'

Andrew laughed loudly, startling the hens scratching in the yard, so that they squawked and ran mindlessly about in fright. 'You sound just like old Harry. Him and his preaching.'

'And Gran says you spoil me,' she smiled coyly up at him, knowing that he would never stop doing so.

'Well, if I can't spoil my favourite god-daughter, who can I, I'd like to know?'

Now she laughed aloud too, the sound bouncing on the breeze. 'You! I'm your *only* god-daughter.'

'There you are then. You're bound to be me favourite, aren't you?'

Bridie stopped suddenly and put her hand on his arm. 'Andrew, I want to ask you something. I was going to leave it till later, but . . .'

'Well, if you're going to ask me to marry you, the answer's "yes".'

'Good,' she said promptly, 'because when I'm older that's exactly what I'm going to do.'

'Eh?' For a moment, Andrew looked startled but, as Bridie rushed on, the look of surprise was replaced by one of genuine alarm as he heard her out.

'I want to come back to Flawford with you. I could be your housekeeper. I know you live alone and . . . and . . .'

'Hey, hey, steady on, love.' Andrew actually pulled away from her and held up his hand, palm outwards, as if to fend off her mad scheme. 'What's brought all this on?' He leant closer and said, trying to be stern though he always found it difficult where Bridie was concerned, 'Have you been falling out with your gran again?'

Bridie pouted. 'Not really, but I told her I'd run away and all she could say was that I was like me dad.' Passionately she cried, 'She doesn't care what I do or where I go. I said I'd go to Auntie Evie's, but she said she wouldn't want me either. But you do, don't you?'

He glanced away, unable to meet her eyes now and Bridie felt a chill run through her veins. She frowned and bit down on her lower lip to stop it trembling as she muttered, 'You don't either, do you?'

'It wouldn't be right, you living with me. A young girl with an old bachelor like me. Your gran wouldn't approve.'

Bridie began to protest. 'You're not old. You're . . .' Then she paused and frowned. Suddenly she realized that she had never really stopped to think what age

Andrew must be. He had always been just 'Andrew', whom she had idolized all her life.

'And then there's your grandfather,' Andrew was saying. 'Old Harry.'

Bridie pulled away from him. Pouting, she said, 'You're like all the rest. You don't care about me.'

Andrew grasped her arm so tightly that Bridie winced. 'Don't say that, Bridie. You know I care about you more than anyone else in the world. Don't *ever* say that about me.'

'Then why can't I come and live with you? And then, when I'm older, we can be married.'

She felt his grasp loosen and, as his hand fell away, he groaned deeply. 'Bridie, that's always been just a joke – a bit of fun – between us. I'm far too old for you. I'm almost twenty years older than you. You should marry someone of your own age, not an old feller like me.'

'You've never believed me, have you? Everyone's always laughed at me when I've said I'm going to marry you when I grow up.'

'Bridie, love, from what I'm told, all little girls say they're going to marry the man closest to them. Some even say their dad, or their brother—'

'No, no, that's not allowed.' Bridie was shaking her head vehemently.

'I know it isn't,' Andrew said quickly. 'What I mean is, they say that before they understand the – the . . . well, about life.'

She stared at him. 'I don't know what you mean.'

Andrew ran his hand through his brown hair. 'It's not for me to explain things to you, love. That's for your gran to do.'

'Oh, *that*! I know all about *that*.' Suddenly she seemed much older than her twelve years. 'You don't grow up on a farm without knowing what goes on. When the boar visits and—'

'Stop, stop!' Andrew put up his hands once more. 'You'll have me blushing.'

She grinned at him now and he put his arm about her shoulders again. Their easy friendship restored, they walked towards the house. 'When you're older you'll have an army of young suitors beating a path to your door and you'll forget all about wanting to marry me.'

She said nothing, but promised herself: Oh no, I won't. I won't ever stop loving you, Andrew Burns.

Three

Bridie led Andrew into the farmhouse by the back door, through the scullery and into the kitchen. Her grandmother was placing a huge piece of roast beef on the table in front of Josh, who wielded the carving knife against the steel with rhythmic movements to sharpen it.

'Hello, Andrew, come and sit down. Did you have a good journey?' Mary fussed around him, pulling out a chair for him at the table as she invited him to join their meal. Her tone sharpened noticeably as she turned to Bridie. 'Go and drain the vegetables in the scullery, girl. There are two tureens ready. Look sharp.'

Mary turned to the black-leaded range. A roaring fire heated the oven, where all their meals were cooked. On the opposite side was a tank for water, heated by the same fire and ladled out of the lid in the top. A kettle sat on the hob near the glowing coals, singing gently.

Bridie hurried between scullery and kitchen, carrying the tureens laden with steaming vegetables: potatoes, fresh spring cabbage and sliced runner beans preserved in salt from the previous growing season, washed thoroughly now and boiled, to enjoy through the winter.

Bridie loved Sunday dinner, especially when Andrew came. She would pull her chair close to his and listen as the grown-ups talked. Josh would tell him, in detail, all about the work that had been done about the small farm since his last visit. Today he had a piece of news.

'Stephen Dunsmore is selling off bits of the estate. Rumour ses it's to pay his gambling debts. Anyway,' he went on, beaming with pride at Mary, 'We've bought another field alongside the beck. We can increase our herd now.'

'More cows to milk,' Bridie said and cast her eyes to the ceiling.

'No, I – I mean, we . . .' He glanced at Mary in apology, but she only smiled fondly at him. Josh continued. 'We thought we'd buy beef cattle. Breed, you know?'

Bridie felt a thrill of excitement. 'We'd have baby calves?'

Josh nodded and Bridie clapped her hands.

'I thought you were set on leaving, miss,' Mary remarked drily and Bridie squirmed in her seat. For a moment the pull of more animals to care for was strong.

Puzzled, Josh glanced from one to the other. 'What's this?'

'Oh, nothing,' Mary said quickly, 'Only Bridie getting on her high horse and making idle threats when things don't suit her.'

Bridie opened her mouth to argue that her threats were anything but idle, but Andrew was shaking his head in wonderment. 'You're a marvel, Josh.' He smiled. 'How you've taken to the country life. If I didn't know you were a townie born and bred, I'd believe you'd never lived anywhere but here in the whole of your life.'

Josh chuckled and his jowls wobbled. 'There's a lot to be said for city life, but I always had a yen to be in the country.' He laughed again. 'Strange, isn't it? Eveleen and I seemed to have swapped places. She's taken to the city life.'

'That's because Richard's there,' Andrew said softly and there was an unmistakable note of longing in his tone. 'She's with the one she loves, isn't she?'

'True enough,' Josh said and touched Mary's hand across the table. 'And I'm with the woman I love.'

'Oh, Josh, you old softie.' Mary smiled and tapped his hand as if in gentle admonishment. But even the young girl could see from the pink tinge suffusing her grandmother's cheeks that age was no barrier to love. Bridie watched the interplay, feeling, as she always did at such moments, excluded. She leant against Andrew and smiled coyly up at him. 'Perhaps you'd like to come and live in the country too. Would you?'

'Oho, not me. There's not much I don't know about framework knitting. Trouble is – it's *all* I know. ' He pulled a comical face. 'And besides, I'm frightened of cows.'

Around the table, they joined in his laughter.

'So,' Bridie went on, 'tell us what's been happening to you this week.'

The guarded look that always seemed to come into his eyes when she asked about his home life was there again. 'Oh, just work as usual. You know.'

'No, I don't know,' Bridie burst out. 'I don't know because I've never been allowed to visit you. I don't know where you live and work and—'

'Bridie,' Josh spoke sternly. 'That's enough. I won't have you upsetting your grandmother.'

'But—'

'I said, that's enough!'

Colour suffused the girl's face and she bit her lip as

she flashed a defiant look at Josh, but she said no more. Beneath the table, Andrew squeezed her hand warningly.

For several moments, the meal continued in silence, the only sounds the singing kettle on the hob, the settling of coals in the range's grate and the clatter of cutlery against plates.

At last Mary laid her knife and fork carefully together and leant back in her chair and sighed. 'I suppose I ought to ask you how my mother is, Andrew. And – and my brother?'

Bridie gasped and glanced towards Josh. Even he hadn't told her that Mary's own mother was still alive. And this was a most unusual event. Mary never asked about her family in Flawford and now Bridie was very much afraid that Josh was going to blame her for having raised the subject.

Immediately Josh was reaching out again to take Mary's hand. 'Now, my dear,' he began, 'don't go upsetting yourself.'

Mary smiled at him. 'It's all right. I'm not upset. It's high time I at least enquired after them, even if I can't bring myself to go and see them ever again.'

Before Andrew could answer, Bridie, unable to restrain herself any longer, burst out. 'Your *mother*? You mean to say that I've got a *great*-grandmother and you never even told me? I thought there was only me grandfather.'

For a moment Mary looked shamefaced as her eyes met Bridie's accusing stare. The older woman's glance dropped away, but she nodded.

Andrew cleared his throat awkwardly and said, 'She's quite well. She doesn't get out much now, though. Her legs are bad.'

Mary smiled wryly. 'Not even across the road to the chapel on a Sunday? That won't please Harry.'

Andrew laughed. 'She still has to attend chapel. Both services on a Sunday. He sees to that. He pushes her across the road in a bath chair.'

The tension in the room eased a little as Mary smiled too. Then she murmured, 'I'm glad she's all right. It wasn't really her fault, though she could have supported poor Rebecca a little more. No . . .' Her voice hardened as she went on. 'No, it's Harry I blame.'

Andrew folded his arms, leant on the table and said quietly, 'It's him, if anyone, that's not so well these days. His eyesight is beginning to bother him, I think, although he will never admit it.'

'Huh!' Mary almost snorted. 'That's Harry.'

Again there was silence, until Mary, moving with a suddenness that made the others jump, got to her feet and began to stack the plates. 'Well, this won't get the table cleared and the pudding served. Look sharp, Bridie. Stir yourself.'

The subject was closed and even later, when Bridie tried to draw Andrew out some more, he was evasive. 'Look, love, it's up to your gran or Josh to talk to you about it all. It's really nothing to do with me.' And though she tried to wheedle more information out of him, Andrew pressed his lips together and refused to say anything.

'All right, then,' Bridie said, for once capitulating prettily. She tucked her arm through his. 'Let's go and look at the piglets. Bonnie has just had a litter of seven. And I'll show you the blackbird in the hayloft and the little rabbit in the hutch. I'll have to bring them with me when I come to live with you,' she informed him solemnly. But Andrew only smiled and said nothing.

The day ended happily with Bridie standing at the gate, waving goodbye as Andrew pedalled away on his bicycle.

Josh came to stand beside her. 'He's a good lad, that,' he murmured, watching the wobbling figure disappear into the gloom of evening. 'Goodness knows what time he'll get back to Flawford. To think he comes nearly every week just to see you.'

The thought gave Bridie a warm glow, but she said gallantly, 'He comes to see you and Gran as well.'

Josh chuckled and agreed. 'Of course, he does, love, but I don't think it'd be so often if you weren't here.' He put his arm about her shoulders. 'Come on, time you were in bed else you'll have your gran after you.'

'Just mind what you're doing, girl,' Mary snapped the following morning as Bridie turned the handle of the mangle. 'You'll have my fingers trapped if you're so erratic. For goodness sake, turn it steadily. Haven't I shown you often enough? Your mind's not on your job. That's your trouble. Daydreaming again, I'll be bound.' She clicked her tongue against her teeth in a gesture of impatience. 'I don't know what I'm going to do with you. You'll be the death of me, one of these days.'

'Oh, turn it yourself then,' Bridie let go of the handle and began to move away, but Mary lunged towards her and caught her arm in an iron grip.

'Oh no, you don't get away with it that easily. You'll stay here and do as you're told.'

Bridie twisted around to face her. 'No, I won't. I won't stay here another minute. You don't want me. You never have. I'm just some stupid girl's bastard who you've had to bring up.'

'Bridie!' Mary's grasp slackened in shock and Bridie pulled herself free.

'I'm going to live with Andrew. He wants me. He

loves me. Whatever you say, I know he loves me, even if no-one else does.'

'We all know that,' Mary gestured impatiently. 'Of course he does. You're the spitting image of your mother and she was the love of his life.'

Bridie felt as if the breath had been knocked from her body. The pain was physical. 'What – did – you – say?' she managed to gasp at last.

'I said, of course Andrew loves you because you remind him of Rebecca.'

There was a huge lump in her throat and tears prickled behind her eyelids, but Bridie was determined that her grandmother should not see her cry. She turned and staggered from the wash-house, her legs like jelly beneath her. In the fresh air, she pulled in deep, gulping breaths and strength flowed back into her. Though she heard her grandmother calling her name, Bridie picked up her skirts and ran out of the yard and into the field, down to the beck, splashing through it without even taking off her boots and stockings. Then, heart pounding, she ran up the slope towards the covert on the brow of the hill and disappeared into the shadowy coolness beneath the trees.

Breathless, she flung herself to the ground and sobbed. She'd stay here for ever, she vowed. She'd never go back home. She'd starve to death first and when they found her body they'd all be sorry.

Four

Pear Tree Farm lay amidst farmland to the west of Bernby, a small village on a hill just outside the Lincolnshire town of Grantham. Further west lay the Vale of Belvoir and in the distance, against the setting sun, were the ramparts of Belvoir Castle. Beyond that was the road to Flawford and the city of Nottingham.

Micky Morton found Bridie late in the day. She was asleep in the den they had built as children in the depths of the woodland known as Bernby Covert. The trees covered the hilltop behind the farm and overhung the lane leading up the slope past Fairfield House, the Dunsmores' mansion, and on towards the village.

'Your gran's on the rampage,' he said as he squeezed himself into the hide they had constructed of branches. 'And Mr Carpenter is tearing his hair out.' He paused and then tried to lighten his news by adding, 'What bit he's got left.'

Bridie sat with her arms wrapped around her knees drawn up to her chest. She had been here the whole day and now she was cold and hungry. At first she had cried and cried until she had fallen asleep, exhausted. Now her tears were all cried out and she was filled with a deep sadness that was an ache in the pit of her stomach.

'What's up, then?' Micky asked, blunt as ever and coming straight to the point.

'Nothing.'

'It dun't look like it,' he remarked drily. 'There's not a scrap of work been done about the place according to Mr C. They've been looking for you all day. Mind you, I could have saved 'em the trouble, but he didn't come down to me grandad's place until teatime.'

Micky Morton's grandparents, Bill and Dorothy, lived a short distance down the lane from Pear Tree Farm at Furze Farm. Just beyond that, in a small cottage, Micky lived with his parents, Ted and Alice. Micky paused and she saw him straining through the shadows to look at her. 'I knew where you'd be.'

'No, you didn't.'

'I've found you, ain't I?'

Bridie was silent.

'Your gran said you'd threatened to run away.'

Again, she said nothing, but tears that she thought were dried out prickled again as self-pity overwhelmed her. Now she had nowhere to run to. No-one wanted her. No-one loved her.

'Come on,' Micky said, standing up and grasping her arm. Though he was a few months younger than she was, Micky had been working on the farm ever since the age of seven during out-of-school hours. Now he had just passed his twelfth birthday, he was doing a man's work on the Dunsmore estate, where both his grandfather and his father worked. Indeed, Micky's whole family lived in dwellings tied to their employment. 'I'd better get you home before Mr Carpenter fetches PC Wilkins from Bernby.'

Reluctantly, knowing she faced even more trouble when she arrived home, Bridie allowed him to lead her from the den and out of the woods. They walked down the hill and paddled through the beck.

'There's Mr C now,' Micky said and Bridie looked up to see Josh hurrying towards them.

'Oh, Bridie love. Thank God you're safe.' He was reaching out to her, clasping her to his bulk in an awkward but genuinely fond embrace. 'Come on, let's get you home and into the warm. Have you been there all day? You must be starving.' He turned to Micky. 'Thanks, lad. I wish I'd asked you earlier. You could have saved us all a lot of worry.'

'S'all right, Mr Carpenter. See you, Bridie.' Pushing his hands into the pockets of his trousers, Micky sauntered away and was soon lost to their sight in the gathering dusk, though for some time afterwards they could still hear him whistling.

'She's a wilful little tyke who deserves a good hiding.'

Mary's tirade started the moment Josh opened the back door and ushered a reluctant Bridie into the kitchen.

'Now, now, Mary love. That would do no good. Bridie, be a good girl. Go upstairs and change your clothes. I'll get some hot soup ready for when you come down. Go on now,' he said, giving her a gentle push.

As she climbed the steep stairs, she heard their voices; her grandmother's raised in shrill anger, Josh's calm and rational.

'Fancy her saying no-one loves her. The very idea. Haven't we looked after her all these years? I didn't want another bairn to bring up, not at my age. And that's all the thanks I get. Well, if that's how she feels, she can go.'

'You don't mean that, Mary.'

'Oh, don't I? Isn't she the reason my Jimmy ran

away? And it's because of her he's never been back home in all these years.'

'I rather think it was Jimmy's fault that an innocent child who didn't ask to be born was brought into the world at all.'

'That's right.' Mary's voice was becoming hysterical now. 'That's right. Blame my Jimmy. You never liked him. It was always Eveleen with you, wasn't it? She couldn't do a thing wrong in your eyes, could she? And it's the same now with Bridie.'

In her bedroom, Bridie could still hear the sound of their quarrel but not what was being said. She groaned aloud, sorry now that she had catapulted her grandmother into one of her moods. But more than that she was sorry to have brought trouble upon the kindly Josh.

Still shivering from the cold of the woods, Bridie stripped off her clothes, washing herself all over with cold water from the ewer on her dressing table. Then she pulled on her warmest garments and crept downstairs. She listened a moment at the door at the bottom, which led back into the kitchen. Hearing no raised voices, indeed no sound of voices at all, she opened the door and stepped into the room.

Mary was seated in her chair by the range, her head bent over her pillow lace whilst Josh stirred the soup in a heavy black saucepan over the fire. It looked like an ordinary, calm and peaceful domestic scene, but Bridie could feel the tension in the air. Her grandmother had now retreated into a world of stony silence, her lips pressed together in disapproval whilst her nimble figures twisted the bobbins over and over to form the gossamer lace.

Josh glanced up and saw Bridie standing uncertainly in the doorway. 'There you are, love. Now come and sit down at the table, drink this and then away to bed with you for a good night's sleep.'

She did as he bade and whilst she sipped the soup he sat with her at the table. He leant towards her and spoke in a low tone. 'Now, Bridie, what you did today was wrong. You worried us both very much. But if you say you're sorry to your gran and promise never to do such a thing again, we'll say no more about it.'

Bridie looked up at him, looked into the ugly, but kindly face, and knew that his expression of concern was genuine. She held his gaze steadily and was able to say with far more truthfulness than she could do to her grandmother, 'I am sorry I worried you. Truly I am, but . . .' The next words were difficult to say, for as much as she had been hurt by Mary's thoughtless words, Bridie did not want to wound Josh, who had never once shown her anything but loving kindness. She took a deep breath and hurried on. 'I don't want to be a burden any longer to you and Gran. Maybe it would be better if I went away. Perhaps to – to Nottingham. Into service or . . . or something.' Her words faltered and faded as she saw the bleak look in Josh's eyes and, despite her desire not to hurt him, she saw at once that she had done so.

He dropped his gaze, looking down at his callused hand lying on the snowy tablecloth. His tone was heavy as he said, 'I presume you overheard what your Gran said?' He raised his eyes and caught Bridie's nod. 'She didn't mean it, love.' Then he half twisted in the chair and added, 'Tell her you didn't mean it, Mary.'

Her busy fingers suddenly idle, Mary raised her head slowly. For a long moment, grandmother and granddaughter stared at each other. The young girl's eyes pleaded for understanding, for a denial of the older woman's earlier words, but in Mary's eyes there was still anger and resentment. Mary's glance flickered briefly towards Josh as he said gently, 'Come now, Mary, love.'

Her grandmother sighed. 'Of course I didn't mean it, but . . .' she added, her tone still firm, 'she must learn not to be so wilful.'

Bridie saw the warning look still in her grandmother's eyes, but Josh seemed satisfied. The matter, for him at least, was at an end. 'There now.' He patted Bridie's hand and his round face shone. 'There now. We'll forget all about it. Off you go up to bed, love. Sleep tight.'

Normally Bridie retorted with 'And watch the bugs don't bite', but tonight she only smiled weakly and stood up. Josh rose too and held out his arms to her. She laid her cheek on his huge chest and he patted her fondly.

'There, there,' he murmured, close to her ear. 'It'll be all right.'

For a moment Bridie pressed herself against his comforting bulk, but in her heart she knew that nothing would ever be quite the same again. As she climbed the stairs once more to her bedroom, Bridie promised herself: I will go to Nottingham. I can get a job there. Maybe Auntie Eveleen will let me work at Uncle Richard's factory, even if she doesn't want me living with them. At the thought she felt another stab of anguish, but, defying the hurt, she vowed: I'll stand on my own two feet.

I'll show the lot of them.

Five

When she heard the front door open and Richard call out her name, Eveleen wiped the tears from her eyes, blew her nose and tried to plaster a smile on her face.

'I'm in here,' she called, praying that he would not see the telltale signs of her distress. That morning she had discovered yet again that she was not pregnant. She wasn't sure how many disappointments she could take and she knew that Richard felt each false hope as keenly as she did.

She smoothed unruly tendrils of her rich brown hair back into place and, as the door opened, she turned towards it and smiled bravely. 'You're home early. Lovely.' She went towards him, her arms outstretched. Her husband kissed her gently and then held her at arm's length.

'Oh, my darling. Again?'

She bit her lip, but could not stop tears welling. She nodded and was enfolded in his embrace. 'Don't worry, sweetheart,' Richard said, as he always did. 'One day, it'll happen. You're only young.'

'I'm thirty,' Eveleen said dolefully.

'What an old lady! Shall I buy you a walking stick or a bath chair.' His smile crinkled his eyes and lit up his handsome face. She smiled up at him, loving him more than ever, if that were possible, for the way he cajoled her out of her depression.

But today he was serious. He took her in his arms and held her close, murmuring against her ear, 'Evie, even if we are never to be blessed with children of our own, I'd still rather be married to you than anyone else in the whole world. Just remember that.'

'But your father wants an heir.' Her words were muffled against his shoulder. 'I know he does. And you do too, if you're honest.'

Carefully Richard said, 'It would be nice to have someone to pass on the Stokes's empire to. But it's not the end of the world. And there's always Bridie. She's your niece.'

'But she's no blood relation to your family. And – and she's a girl.'

Richard released her and laughed aloud, throwing back his dark head. 'I can't believe you said that. You of all people, who champion the cause of women better that anyone else I know by proving that you can run that huge warehouse single-handedly.' More seriously he added, 'Perhaps that's the trouble. Maybe you're doing too much.'

'Oh, Richard. I can't sit around doing nothing. We have servants galore to do the housework. What would I do with myself all day?'

'Sit on a cushion and sew a fine seam,' he teased.

Eveleen pulled a face. 'I'd sooner be sewing fine seams along with the girls in the inspection room. That's where I belong.'

'And chasing over half the city rounding up your homeworkers,' he admonished gently, tapping the tip of her nose with his forefinger.

She smiled wryly and was forced to acquiesce. But then her thoughts came back to her niece. 'Did you mean it about Bridie? I know you've always been fond of her, but to make her your heir. That's a huge step. And would your parents agree?'

Richard shrugged. 'She's still very young and she may not want it.'

Eveleen looked askance at him, as if she could not believe anyone could turn down such an opportunity. Richard spread his hands. 'She may not like city life, darling. She's happy in the country.'

Eveleen nodded. 'Yes, yes, she is. I don't think she'd ever want to leave the farm.'

'You don't really mean you're going to run away?'

Micky was appalled when Bridie confided her secret to him. 'Yes, I am, and don't you dare tell a soul, Micky Morton, else I'll cut out your tongue and feed it to the pigs.'

'You'd have to catch me first,' he grinned, but then his face sobered. 'Ya'll upset everybody if you do that, y'know.'

'And who's "everybody"?' Bridie asked scathingly. 'Me gran? I don't think so. I told you what she'd said, didn't I?'

'She didn't mean it. All parents say things they don't mean when they're angry.'

'She's not my "parent". That's the whole trouble. She felt obliged to bring me up just because her son got his cousin pregnant and then left her.'

'What about Josh, then?'

Bridie was silent, pulling at the grass on the bank of the beck where they were sitting, dangling their feet in the rushing water. 'He's the only one who might care a bit,' she agreed gruffly.

'I'd care, an' all,' Micky declared stoutly. 'You're my best mate. Even if you are a girl.'

Despite her unhappiness, Bridie gave him a playful shove. They were silent for a while until Micky asked, 'Where will you go?'

She glanced at him slyly. 'Shan't tell you. You might tell them.'

'I wouldn't.'

'You did last time.' Now she glared at him fully, accusingly.

He wriggled awkwardly. 'Well, yeah. I know I did, but that was different.'

'How?'

''Cos I didn't know what was going on. I mean, you could have fallen and been lying hurt somewhere.' He gestured towards the stream in front of them and needed to say no more. They were both remembering the story about her grandfather, Walter Hardcastle, being found dead, face down, in the water somewhere near this very spot.

'Well, I wasn't,' Bridie muttered.

'No,' Micky said carefully, 'but I didn't know that, did I? Not at the time. It'd be different if I knew you were safe but didn't *want* to be found.'

Bridie's eyes widened in surprise. 'Would it really? You mean you'd help me?'

Micky nodded, but added, 'I don't want you to go, but if it's what you really want, then, yes, I'd help you.'

Bridie gave him her most engaging smile. 'Right, then. Just be ready for whatever happens. As soon as I get the chance, I'm going, but I don't know how or when or even where I'll go. I just know that one of these days, I will go.'

'Well, afore you do,' Micky was grinning cheekily, 'there's one of our hens me dad'd like you to look after. The others have set on it.'

At once the image of a chicken with all its feathers pulled out around its tail, its skin red and sore from the vicious beaks of the other birds, came into her mind. Crudely Micky confirmed her fears. 'Its arse is pecked red-raw.'

She was silent a moment and then she saw his grin. 'You!' she flared and punched his shoulder. 'Your dad doesn't need me to look after his hen. He can do that for himself. You're just trying to keep me here.'

Micky's grin widened and he shrugged. 'It was worth a try.'

'Oh, you!' she said again, but she was laughing with him now.

Then, for a moment, Micky was very serious. 'You ought to go to someone, at least to start with,' he added hastily as she glared at him.

'I can look after mesen.'

'I know, I know,' he added hastily, 'but you are only twelve. I know you look older, being tall, but still . . . You ought to go to someone,' he ended firmly. 'What about Andrew?'

'No!' Her tone was harsh, causing the young boy to raise his eyebrows.

'You fallen out with him?' he asked bluntly.

'No,' she whispered. She knew he would hear the hurt in her voice, but thankfully he did not pursue it.

'Your auntie Evie and uncle Richard, then. He's a nice chap. He might be a bit posh, owning a lace factory an' all that. But he ain't a bit stuck up, is he?'

'No,' Bridie agreed, 'but they haven't any children of their own.'

'Why?'

'Dunno. Maybe . . .' She swallowed the lump in her throat, remembering what her grandmother had said. 'Maybe they don't want troublesome children.'

'Oh.' Micky looked puzzled. That was something he could not understand. To the country boy with three younger siblings, it seemed that married couples always had children. Nature was all around them and that was part of it. Confident that there must be some other reason, Micky said, 'Well, I'd give your auntie and uncle a try, if I was you.'

Six

As Eveleen walked towards the Reckitt and Stokes lace factory and warehouse, built side by side on Canal Street, she was aware of the admiring glances she attracted. Her luxurious curly brown hair was piled high in the fashion of the time and on top her wide-brimmed hat was perched at a jaunty angle. The tight-fitting jacket and the long straight skirt accentuated her slim, shapely figure. The costume was an emerald green with a white, frilled-neck blouse beneath it.

'Morning, ma'am,' one of the men greeted her as she climbed the stairs to the top floor of the warehouse. She smiled in acknowledgement, 'Morning, Joe.'

As she opened the door into the inspection and mending room she felt the familiar thrill of pride and she paused a moment to enjoy the scene. The large room, light and airy, was filled with the muted chatter of twenty women and girls, each with a bale of lace spread over their laps and spilling onto the floor as they meticulously mended any flaws and runs in the fabric. It was what Eveleen herself had done when she first arrived in Nottingham, desperate for work. She moved down the edge of the room, nodding and smiling at the girls, her eagle eye on their work as she passed. As she neared the end of the room, she raised her head to smile at the young woman who was the inspection room's supervisor.

'Morning, Helen.'

Helen Binkley rose from her seat and came towards her, stretching out her hands in greeting and bending forward to kiss Eveleen's cheek.

The two women had been firm friends since the day Eveleen had come to work here and it had given her enormous pleasure to promote Helen, quite justifiably for she was an excellent and trustworthy worker, to the post of supervisor when the previous woman had left.

Eveleen drew off her gloves and sat down at her own desk alongside Helen's. 'I've been thinking,' she said, coming to a sudden, impulsive decision, but keeping her voice low so that they would not be overheard. 'Would you be willing to take on more responsibility?'

Helen's bright eyes twinkled cheekily at her. 'Depends.'

Catching her meaning, Eveleen smiled and said playfully, 'Of course we would think of a fancy title to suit your new status.'

She paused, deliberately teasing Helen, who laughed merrily knowing full well she was being led on. 'A fancy title doesn't pay the rent, Evie.'

They laughed together. 'Of course, there would be a pay rise for you too.'

'Ah well, now you're talking. What exactly would all this extra work involve?'

Eveleen's eyes clouded. 'I think I might be overdoing it. If I'm honest, I do get very tired by the end of each week and perhaps . . .' The two friends stared at each other and Helen, understanding at once, said softly, 'You think it could be stopping you conceiving?'

Helen was one of the only two women in whom Eveleen had confided her great sorrow at not being able to give Richard the heir she knew he wanted. Despite his constant loving reassurance, Eveleen knew that, deep down, he longed for children. And his father, Brinsley Stokes, made no secret of the fact. 'When are you going to make me a grandfather?' he had asked regularly during the first years of their marriage. But now, after ten years, even he had stopped asking.

In answer to Helen's delicate question, Eveleen nodded and pressed her lips together to prevent them quivering. The latest disappointment, only this morning, was still fresh in her mind.

'Have you talked about this to your mother?'

Eveleen pulled a face. 'My mother's not the sort of person I can confide in. She's so wrapped up in her life with Josh.'

'What about Win, then?'

Win Martin, Eveleen's only other confidante, had been the very first person Eveleen had encountered on her arrival in the city. Win had not only advised her about obtaining employment, but had also found a house for Eveleen, her mother, brother and her pregnant cousin, Rebecca. Living in the same street for several months, Win had been a tower of strength to the young Eveleen, who, through the tragic circumstances of her father's sudden death, had found herself responsible for her family. Win was also the one to whom all the inhabitants of Foundry Yard turned in times of trouble. Birth or death or illness, Win Martin was ready to help.

'Not recently,' Eveleen answered Helen, 'but I'm seeing her later this morning. I might have a talk with her then.'

'I think you should,' Helen said, forthright as ever. 'What Win Martin doesn't know about babies isn't worth knowing.'

There was a silence between them until Helen prompted, 'So what would you want me to do?'

'Well, I wondered if you'd take over the management of all the middlewomen. It means a lot of walking, visiting them in their homes.'

Throughout the city women were employed as homeworkers for the lace industry. In each area a middlewoman collected the lace from the factory and distributed the work to the homeworkers living nearby. Eveleen had taken it upon herself to be the one to visit the middlewomen who worked for Reckitt and Stokes regularly and to help them with any problems they might have.

Helen beamed. 'I wouldn't mind that. It'd be a nice change from being cooped up in here all day.' Her eyes twinkled merrily. 'And all the walking'd keep me slim. But what about this place?'

'I'd still want you to be overall supervisor of the inspection room, but perhaps we could promote someone to be your deputy when you were out. Can you recommend anyone?'

Helen's thoughtful glance roamed over the heads of the women and girls in her charge. 'Well, there's one or two who might be all right. Do you mind if I think about it for a day or two?'

'Of course not. There's no immediate hurry. It's not as if,' she added sorrowfully, 'I am already pregnant and have been advised to rest.'

Helen reached out and touched her hand. 'Don't worry, Evie. There's plenty of time.'

But Eveleen, at thirty, felt the years were rushing by and though she smiled at her friend, the smile could not quite chase away the worry in her dark brown eyes.

*

Later that morning Eveleen walked to Foundry Yard and passed the door where she had lived when they first arrived in Nottingham, with a pregnant Rebecca fleeing from the wrath of her father, an unrepentant Jimmy and a depressed and difficult Mary. If it hadn't been for the help and friendship of the woman she was about to visit, Win Martin, Eveleen seriously doubted she would have survived that time. As she drew near Win's home she saw a cluster of women outside the door. She felt a moment's stab of fear. Was something wrong in the Martin household? Then she almost laughed aloud at her own foolishness as she realized what time it was. Win was a middlewoman for Reckitt and Stokes. She collected the lace from the factory and distributed it to all the women homeworkers in her area. And this was the time of day when all the homeworkers arrived on her doorstep to receive their day's allocation.

'Don't want her giving you more 'n me,' they would joke to each other.

They needn't have worried. Win was strict but fair, dealing out three dozen parts to each woman to take home and strip. The lace was manufactured in long strips joined by threads, which were then drawn out by the homeworkers to separate the lengths. The women then 'scalloped' the lace where it needed neatening and wound the finished lengths onto cards. This operation was known as 'jennying'. They would bring the lace back to Win's terraced house by eight o'clock the following morning, after they – and sometimes other members of their families too, even children – had often worked well into the night. Over the years Win had built up a group of women workers who were conscientious and meticulous.

There was a strange, friendly rivalry between the

homeworkers. Yet, if one of their number could not complete the required amount of finished yardage because of dirty or damaged work, the other women would contribute a few pennies each to make up her pay knowing that the favour would be returned.

Each morning Win returned the finished lace to the factory on her handcart and collected a new batch and the whole routine started again.

'Morning, Mrs Stokes.' The murmur ran amongst them as they parted to allow Eveleen to approach the door.

She smiled and nodded, recognizing familiar faces. 'Is Win home yet?'

'She's just sorting it out, then we'll be on our way.'

At that moment the door opened and Win Martin beckoned the first woman to step inside. Eveleen waited until the last one had hurried away down the street, a bundle of lace in her arms, before she stepped forward.

'Evie, I didn't see you standing there. Come in, come in. The kettle's singing. I always have a cuppa when they've all gone. Eh, fair wears me out, it does.'

'Oh dear.' Eveleen stepped into Win's kitchen. 'And I've come to ask you if you can take on more.' She pulled off her gloves and sat down without needing to be asked.

Win eyed her shrewdly. 'Summat wrong, love?' Then her face brightened. 'Don't tell me you're . . .?'

Quickly Eveleen shook her head. 'No, no. I'm not. But that is the reason I'm here. I've been thinking that perhaps I'm doing too much. I mean . . .' she faltered, blushing slightly. 'Do you think that could – could stop me conceiving?'

Win made the tea and set a cup in front of Eveleen before she sat down opposite. 'I've got to be honest with you, Evie, I've never heard of that being the case.' She gave a wry laugh. 'It's never stopped any of the women round here falling, yet they work as hard as any I know. Meaning no offence, love.'

'None taken, Win,' Eveleen murmured and sighed heavily. 'I suppose I'm just clutching at straws now.'

'But that doesn't mean to say it couldn't be true in your case. We're all different, love, and it's worth a try.'

'Anything's worth a try,' Eveleen said bitterly. 'I'll soon be too old. Oh, Win, I do so want to have a child. A son for Richard.'

'Aye, I know, I know. Life's unfair, in't it? There's me with six of 'em and though I love 'em all, I wouldn't say they was planned, if you know what I mean.'

The two women smiled at each other. Win reached across and patted Eveleen's hand. 'Don't give up hope yet awhile. One thing I have heard tell is that if you worry too much about it, get too desperate, like, then that can stop it happening.'

'Really?'

Win nodded. 'So just you put it out of your mind and enjoy yourself a bit more. And whatever it is you want me to do, the answer's "yes". I can manage it. Our Elsie'll help me.' Win was referring to one of her daughters.

'Elsie?' Eveleen asked in surprise. 'But I thought she'd just had a baby.' Everyone, it seemed to Eveleen, could have children but her.

'Oh, she has,' Win replied airily. 'But it's high time she was back on her feet and working again.'

'You're a hard woman, Win Martin.' The two women laughed together, both knowing that the exact opposite was in fact the truth.

Win's tone was gentle as she said, 'You take it a bit

easier, love. Get out and about with that handsome husband of yours and let nature take its course.'

'Darling? Darling, where are you?'

It was Richard's voice calling from the hallway. Eveleen hurried from the bedroom and leant over the banister.

Looking down, she asked, 'What is it? Is something wrong?'

He was smiling up at her and beckoning. 'Come down, I've a surprise for you. Come on, Evie.' He was as excited as a little boy.

Laughing, Eveleen ran lightly down the stairs. 'What is it?'

'You'll see.' He took her hand and led her into the morning room.

Eveleen gasped and her eyes widened. Lying across a chair was a warm coat with a fur collar and alongside it a hat with a long scarf.

'Put it on,' Richard said, picking up the coat and holding it out for her to slip her arms into.

'It isn't my birthday.'

Richard could not stop smiling. 'Ah, but there's a very good reason. That's the second part of my surprise.'

'You do spoil me,' she murmured, believing that he had arranged all this just to take her mind off her disappointment. 'It's lovely,' she said, running her hands down the soft fabric, whilst Richard fastened the buttons for her just as if she were a child.

'Now the hat.' Carefully he placed it on her head and then wrapped the long silk scarf across the crown of the hat and tied it under her chin. 'Wait there,' he instructed and hurried out of the room, returning moments later dressed in a long coat and a cap, with a warm scarf wrapped around his neck.

He took her arm and led her from the room, out of the front door and down the steep steps to the street. Directly outside their house stood a motor car.

'There!' Richard was triumphant. 'What do you think of that?'

For a moment, Eveleen was mystified and then realization dawned. 'You've bought a motor car!' Now, like a child herself, she clapped her hands. 'Oh, Richard, how wonderful!'

'It's a Model T Ford,' Richard said proudly. 'Come on, let's go for a ride.'

They giggled like two schoolchildren playing truant as he handed her up into the front seat.

'Are you sure you know how to drive it?'

'Oh yes, I've been taking lessons. And I've got my licence.' He reached up and kissed her on the mouth, not caring that they were in full view of the street. 'Do you think I'd risk endangering my lovely wife?'

It took several turns of the starting handle before the engine burst into life. Eveleen clutched at the side of the vehicle as the whole frame shuddered beneath her. But she was laughing, loving every minute.

Richard climbed in beside her. 'Hold on,' he shouted above the noise. 'Here we go.'

The sight of a motor car was not unusual in the streets of Nottingham, but once they left the built-up area and were bowling along the country lanes, they were amused by the stir they created.

Workers in the fields paused to watch their progress. Women came to the doors of the houses and cottages, wiping their hands on their aprons, to gawk at the noisy contraption. Children ran alongside the vehicle, shouting and laughing. 'Give us a ride, mester?'

It was a warm, spring day, the trees just sprouting into leaf. Bright dandelions scattered the grass verges and daffodils danced in cottage gardens.

Above the noisy engine, Richard shouted. 'Shall we go to Bernby and show your mother and Josh? And we'll take Bridie for a ride. She'd like that.'

Preoccupied, Eveleen nodded. Richard glanced at her, amused. 'Don't tell me. You want to have a try at driving?'

Eveleen grinned at him. 'How did you guess?'

Neither of them had any doubt about her ability to master the technique. Eveleen was a quick learner and she loved any kind of machinery. As a young girl she had learned to operate a framework-knitting machine under the tuition of her uncle, Harry Singleton. Later, in Nottingham, she had by devious means learned the basic skills of a twisthand on the huge lace machines in the Reckitt and Stokes's factory.

It had been at a time when Eveleen was desperate to earn enough money to keep her family together. Thanks to the kindly Win and Fred Martin they had a roof over their heads and work for both her and her brother, Jimmy as an apprentice twisthand in the factory and Eveleen in the inspection room. But then Eveleen had put pressure on her brother to do the decent thing and marry his cousin, Rebecca, who was carrying his child. Jimmy had no intention of being tied down and had even been cruel enough to suggest that the child was not his. He had run away to sea, leaving Eveleen as the sole breadwinner on a woman's meagre wage.

At that time Eveleen and her brother had been

remarkably alike, so much so that people often mistook them for twins. They had the same dark brown eyes, the same well-shaped nose, which on Eveleen was maybe just a fraction too large for real beauty. Their mouths were wide and generous and usually stretched in ready laughter. They even had the same rich brown hair colour, so when Jimmy had disappeared Eveleen had cut her own long tresses, dressed in his clothes and taken his place at the machine. She had been unlucky to be discovered, for she had the makings of a good worker; as good as any man it was said of her later. She could have been sacked for such a deception but Josh, as factory manager, had safeguarded her job in the inspection room.

Now she and Richard could laugh about the incident, which had gone down in the folklore of Reckitt and Stokes, but back then it had been one of the worst times in Eveleen's life.

Now she tucked her arm through Richard's and pleaded winningly, 'Go on. Let me have a go.'

'Maybe. When I've got a little more used to it myself.'

And with that, for the moment, Eveleen had to be content.

Seven

Hens scattered, squawking in alarm, even the curly coat pig shambled away, grunting noisily, as they drove into the yard at Pear Tree Farm. At once Bridie was beside them, jumping up and down in excitement. 'Take me for a ride. Please, *please*, Uncle Richard.'

Mary appeared in the back door of the farmhouse and came towards them. 'Richard, how lovely.' She went to him and held up her face for him to kiss her cheek. Bridie, hanging onto his arm, hopped from one foot to the other. 'We'll drive past the Dunsmores' big house. Even *they* haven't got a motor car.'

Laughing, Richard gently freed himself from Bridie's clinging hands and moved towards the side of the motor to help Eveleen alight. Close to her, Eveleen saw the look of concern cross his face at Bridie's innocent mention of the name Dunsmore. But as she put her hand into Richard's and stepped down, she said brightly, though with a hint of sarcasm not lost on her husband, '*What* a good idea, Bridie. Mam, how are you?'

She kissed Mary's cheek and then turned to see Josh lumbering towards them, his arms outstretched in welcome. 'Eh up, mi duck.'

Eveleen smiled warmly and put her arms as far round his girth as she could reach and kissed his weathered cheek. 'How are you, Josh?'

'Fine, fine,' he said as he always did but, drawing

back a little, Eveleen looked into his face. His answer had been a little too swift and there had been tension in his tone.

'You sure?' she asked softly, thinking that perhaps there was trouble between him and Mary. Her mother had always been a difficult person to live alongside with her temperamental mood swings. But it was unusual for Mary to quarrel with the man in her life. In Mary Carpenter's world, men were the superior beings and it was a woman's place to care for them, cosset them and pander to their every need. It had been so for as long as Eveleen could remember. Firstly with her own father and her brother, Jimmy, who could do no wrong in Mary's eyes. Now it was the same with Josh.

But today Eveleen could feel that something was wrong and as her mother's voice rose shrilly behind her, she knew the answer. 'Bridie, stop behaving like a child and leave Richard alone.'

Eveleen turned to see Mary grasping the girl's arm and physically dragging her away. 'Get back to the dairy and finish your work.'

For one awful moment, Eveleen thought Bridie was going to lash out at Mary. The girl's face was like thunder, her eyes glinting dangerously. Eveleen held her breath and only released it when she saw Bridie pull herself from Mary's grip, turn and march towards the dairy, her head held high in defiance.

Though the incident was not funny, Eveleen had a job to hide a wry smile. It was the way she would have acted at the same age.

Richard, too, had felt the atmosphere for he called after Bridie, 'When you've finished your work, love, we'll take you for a spin.'

'Don't encourage her, Richard. I don't know what's the matter with her these last few days,' Mary grumbled. 'Threatening to run away.'

'What?' Eveleen was startled.

'Oh yes,' Mary waved her hands airily. 'That's her answer to everything when she can't get her own way. She'd get a good hiding and told to be grateful she has a home if I had my way, but Josh is too soft with her. And as for Andrew when he comes, well, he treats her as if the sun shines out of her.' Then, suddenly, Mary smiled and she put her arm through Richard's and walked with him towards the house. 'But never mind that wilful little tyke. I've a batch of scones just out of the oven spread with jam and fresh cream.'

Richard glanced back over his shoulder and pulled a comical face of resignation. Eveleen nodded, but stayed where she was. As soon as they were out of earshot, she turned to Josh. 'Now, tell me. What has been going on?'

Josh ran his hand worriedly over his balding pate. His closed his eyes for a second, sighed and shook his head. 'Oh, Evie, I'm out of me depth, mi duck. They just seem to be clashing all the time. It's becoming a battle of wills.'

Eveleen put her hand through his arm and together they walked into the field and down towards the beck.

'I was like that at her age. Mam and me had some right old battles, I can tell you, with my poor dad in the middle of it all and Jimmy smirking on the sidelines and fuelling the fires whenever he could.'

'Aye. You were always a good lass and loyal to your brother, but he wasn't always the same to you, was he?'

'No,' Eveleen replied shortly and then deliberately brought the conversation back to Bridie, her immediate concern. She didn't want to think about Jimmy just now. 'Has something caused this bother between Mam and Bridie?'

Josh shook his head helplessly. 'Not that I know of, but then I'm not around them all the time. I don't know everything that passes between them, but I can feel something's not right.'

'Mm, so can I and I've only been here a few minutes.'

'She ran off the other day and hid in the woods. It wasn't until I went down to the Mortons and asked young Micky if he knew where she might be that she was found.'

'And you don't know why she did that?'

'It seemed to start from last Sunday when Andrew visited. They were talking about Flawford. Yer mam and Andrew, I mean. Mary asked after her own mother and Bridie got very indignant. It seems she hadn't realized that she had a great-grandmother still alive.'

'Ah,' Eveleen said, understanding at once. There was a pause and then she prompted, 'Was that all it was?'

Josh frowned. 'I think so and yet I can't see why that was enough to make her run off the next day, even if she was upset at not being told. Can you?'

They had reached the bank of the stream and stood watching the clear water babbling over rocks and boulders. They were silent for a few minutes, each thinking their own thoughts, then Eveleen said slowly, 'It's maybe only because she's growing up. She's almost thirteen and I can well remember thinking that because I was a working girl and earning a wage, I was a grown-up.' She sighed. 'It's a difficult age and Mam never was very good at understanding. Especially girls,' she added wryly.

'Your mother's a wonderful woman,' Josh declared stoutly.

'I know.' Eveleen squeezed his arm. 'And you make her so very happy. Nevertheless there's a "but" in there, isn't there, Josh?'

The big man sighed, but could not deny her words. 'I think Bridie could have overheard us talking.' He bit his lip, hesitant to be disloyal to his wife, yet Eveleen ought to know. 'Maybe she got the idea Mary has had her here on sufferance. But . . .' he added swiftly, leaping to Mary's defence, 'she didn't mean it that way. I know she didn't. Mary loves the child. We both do.'

Eveleen patted his hand. 'I know you do. I'm sure it's all a storm in a teacup. Bridie can be a bit wilful, I expect. Come on, let's go back and have some of those delicious scones of Mam's.'

Later Eveleen and Richard took Bridie for the promised jaunt in the new motor car, but above the noise of the engine talk was impossible and besides, Eveleen comforted herself, the child seemed happy enough now.

As they chugged along the lane, Bridie bounced up and down excitedly in the back seat, waving regally to anyone they passed and squealing with laughter when they passed an open-mouthed Micky Morton.

'Go up the hill, Uncle Richard. Past Fairfield House.'

Richard, with a brief glance at Eveleen, turned the motor to the left and up the lane towards where Fairfield House, the home of the Dunsmores, stood on the left-hand side.

Years ago all the land around had belonged to the Dunsmore estate. Eveleen's grandfather, Ben Hardcastle had worked for the Dunsmores and had lived in the tied dwelling of Pear Tree Farm. Walter, Ben's son and Eveleen's father, had worked for the estate all his life, yet only days after his death the family had been turned out of their home and had been obliged to find refuge with Mary's estranged family in Flawford.

It had been an unhappy time for the Hardcastle family. Eveleen, young and in love with Stephen Dunsmore and believing that he returned her love, was bitterly hurt by the young man's callous rejection of her and her family. It had been years before Richard's tender devotion had driven away the demons that haunted her because of it.

But Bridie knew none of this. Pear Tree Farm and the few acres surrounding it now belonged to Josh and Mary Carpenter. The young girl, innocent of the hurts of the past, had no cause to think any worse of the Dunsmore family than that they were the 'posh folks who lived at the big house'. All she knew was that her friend, Micky, and all the Morton family worked on the estate, their homes owned and their lives ruled by Stephen Dunsmore.

And so she was oblivious to Richard's anxious glances towards his wife, of Eveleen's hands, resting in her lap, clenching involuntarily. All Bridie wanted was to ride past the big, wrought-iron gates and show off Uncle Richard's fancy new motor car.

Richard took the car up the steep hill beneath the overhanging branches of Bernby Covert. At the top of the hill, he turned the car and they hurtled down again, Bridie shouting with delight. The tension left Eveleen's face and she clutched at her hat and laughed aloud too. But as they approached the gate to Fairfield House again, a horse cantered out, the rider unprepared for a horseless carriage rocketing down the hill towards him. Richard operated the brakes. The car slithered and shook and the horse whinnied and reared and then leapt over the hedge into the field opposite the driveway and galloped away, terrified by the noisy monstrosity. Halfway across the field, the rider was unseated and fell heavily to the ground where he lay motionless.

The car came to a shuddering halt and Richard cut the engine. At once Bridie was climbing out of the back seat. 'That was Mr Stephen. He might be hurt.'

'Bridie—' Eveleen began, but at once Richard put his hand on hers. Quietly he said, 'We must see if the fellow's hurt, my darling. But Bridie and I will go. You stay here.'

Already Bridie was running to the gate into the field a little further down the lane. Richard followed her, his long legs loping easily over the ground. Eveleen remained motionless in the car, her heart pounding, afraid to even look across the field towards where Stephen Dunsmore lay.

Eight

When Richard reached the prone figure, Bridie was already squatting beside him. 'Mr Stephen. It's me, Bridie. Are you hurt? Shall we fetch help from the house?'

To Richard's immense relief the man on the ground groaned loudly, rolled over and sat up slowly. He felt his head and then carefully all over his body. Richard stood watching. He had not even spoken to the man, leaving Bridie to play nursemaid.

'Can you stand up, Mr Stephen? Lean on me.'

The man looked up at Richard. 'What the hell do you think you were doing driving that monstrosity about the countryside like a maniac?'

'I'm sorry,' Richard said curtly, 'but you came out of that entrance without looking.'

'I don't expect to have to look on my own property.'

'I believe the lane is a public highway,' Richard said evenly.

Now the man was scrambling to his feet, hanging so heavily on Bridie's outstretched hand that he almost pulled the girl over. 'Is it, by God? We'll see about that.'

Once Stephen was on his feet, Bridie retrieved his riding hat and whip, lying a few feet away on the ground, and silently handed them to him.

Stephen, his fair hair blowing in the wind, took it

and glanced at her. His blue eyes sparked and his face was red with anger. 'Thanks,' he said curtly. 'Oh, it's you. The Carpenters' little bastard granddaughter, eh?' His lip curled and he turned towards Richard, staring at him. 'And I see who you are now.' His glance went beyond the two of them towards the motor standing in the lane.

He smiled maliciously. 'And the lovely Mrs Stokes, no less.' He pulled on his riding hat and slapped his whip against his leg. 'Well now, perhaps we'll say no more about it if you'll allow me to greet your delightful wife, whom I remember so *very* well.'

Puzzled, Bridie glanced between the two men. For a brief moment she thought Richard was going to punch Stephen in the face. She saw that his hands were clenched and he seemed to be having difficulty in keeping them firmly by his side.

'I don't think that would be a very good idea,' he said tightly. 'I'm relieved you're not hurt and I apologize that I was the cause of your horse being startled. But now we'll bid you good day.'

'Not so fast,' Stephen said through thin lips and he strode away towards Eveleen.

'Damnation take the fellow!' Richard muttered and hurried after him, Bridie running alongside to keep up.

As they reached the motor, Bridie saw Stephen doff his hat, bow in an exaggerated manner and say with heavy sarcasm, 'Well, well, well. Mrs Stokes. And how *are* you, my dear?'

Bridie glanced towards her aunt. Eveleen's cheeks were flaming, but her eyes were so cold and hard that Bridie gasped aloud. Eveleen's mouth was tight and she stared straight ahead, not even glancing at the man standing beside the vehicle. When she spoke, the tone of her voice matched her expression. 'I'm extremely well, thank you, Stephen.'

Richard lifted Bridie into the back seat and then moved to the front of the motor to swing the starting handle. As the engine burst into life and Richard climbed into the driving seat, Stephen moved back a pace and raised his hat once again, sarcasm in every movement.

As they drove home, no-one spoke, but even at her young age, Bridie could feel the tension between the two adults in the front seats.

'I'm just glad he wasn't injured,' Richard said. 'Or we might have been facing a lawsuit.'

Eveleen gave a very unladylike derisive snort and muttered, 'Knowing him of old, you still might be.'

'Oh, darling, please don't let him upset you. Not now.' They were standing alone together in the yard back at Pear Tree Farm. Richard put his arms around her. 'It's all a long time ago and . . .'

Eveleen was stiff, unyielding in his embrace. 'Richard, he . . .' Then suddenly the tension went out of her and she sagged against him. 'Oh, I suppose you're right.' She looked up at him and then, standing on tiptoe, kissed his cheek. 'What would I do without you?' she whispered.

Watching the tender scene from the scullery window, Bridie felt very envious and, suddenly, so very lonely.

'Where has the dratted child got to?' Mary was angry.

'Maybe she's gone to round up the cows for evening milking,' Josh said calmly.

'And when did she ever do anything useful of her own accord?' his wife snapped back.

Eveleen and Richard were ready to leave, but Bridie was missing. No-one had seen her since their return to the farm after their drive.

'She'll be hiding in the woods again. Well, she can stay there all night as far as I'm concerned.'

'Oh, Mam,' Eveleen said at once. 'You can't do that. It might be April, but the nights are still cold.'

'Your mam's only threatening,' Josh said. 'She wouldn't really want that.'

'Wouldn't I?' Mary muttered morosely.

Josh looked helplessly at Eveleen and Richard for a moment. A look that said: See what I mean?

'Do you want us to stay and help look for her?' Richard asked.

'No, no,' Josh tried to smile. 'We'll find her. If she doesn't turn up soon, I'll get young Micky to look for her.' His smile broadened. 'He seems to know all her hiding places.'

'It's ages since I saw the Morton family,' Eveleen said. 'We really must come and spend a day here and visit them. Anyway, we must get back now.' She kissed her mother and Josh and then the four of them went out into the yard. Mary and Josh stood watching as Richard started the car and, with everyone waving, drove out of the yard and up the rough cart track towards the lane.

Above the noise, he shouted, 'I don't like leaving whilst Bridie's missing. I hope she's all right.'

Eveleen tucked her arm through his. 'Josh will find her,' she said confidently and then, changing the subject, she smiled winningly at him. 'Now, before we reach the main Nottingham road, are you going to let me have a little drive?'

Richard gave an exaggerated sigh as if he were the epitome of a henpecked husband. 'Oh, very well then. I just hope the local bobby doesn't catch us. You're supposed to have a licence.'

He brought the vehicle to a halt and they changed seats. He gave clear and detailed instructions, yet the motor car still spluttered and bucked under Eveleen's efforts. But worse still, she could not immediately get the hang of steering and the vehicle veered wildly first to the right and then to the left, criss-crossing the narrow lane and bouncing over the deep, muddy ruts on the grass verge. Then they felt the vehicle begin to slide sideways into a shallow ditch. The motor car came to rest at a lurching angle, its nearside wheels firmly embedded in the water.

Richard hung onto the side to prevent himself being flung from the vehicle, whilst Eveleen could not help letting out a cry of alarm.

And from the back seat, under a rug, came an echoing squeal of fright.

Nine

As the engine noise petered out, Richard and Eveleen stared at each other and then slowly they turned together to look at the figure now sitting bolt upright on the back seat, startled and dishevelled but otherwise, like them, mercifully unhurt.

Their faces were a picture of surprise as they both said together. 'Bridie!' whilst the girl stared back belligerently.

'What on earth are you doing?' Eveleen asked.

'Running away,' the girl said promptly. 'To Nottingham.'

'You mean you want to come and live with us?' Richard asked.

The girl's chin rose defiantly. 'No, 'cos I don't suppose you want me either.'

Richard and Eveleen exchanged a swift glance then Eveleen asked, 'Whatever do you mean?'

Bridie bit hard on her lower lip, but not before the two adults had seen its sudden tremble. Richard reached over the back of the seat and touched her hand. 'What is it, love? You can tell us.'

Now tears filled the girl's eyes as she blurted out, 'I'm just some girl's bastard that nobody wants. Even Mr Stephen called me that, didn't he?'

'He *what*?' Eveleen cried and Richard's mouth tightened angrily.

'Yes, he did. Forgive me, Bridie, but in the heat of the moment I didn't really think about what he was saying. I wish now I *had* punched him on the nose.'

Even amidst her tears Bridie gave a hiccuping laugh. 'I wish you had too, Uncle Richard.' Then she sighed and said, 'But he's not the only one. It's what they called me at school.'

Eveleen gasped. 'Oh, how cruel!'

'Well, no-one's going to call you it ever again, if I can help it,' Richard said firmly. 'But now I want you to tell us exactly why you want to run away from your gran and Josh.'

Bridie plucked at the edge of the rug and avoided the concerned look on both their faces. 'It – it's not, Josh, so much as – as . . .' she mumbled, hesitant to speak ill of Mary to her daughter, but Eveleen was quick to understand and to end the sentence for the girl by saying wryly, 'My mother.'

Richard probed further, but gently. 'Is it something that's just happened?'

'Well – sort of.'

They waited, oblivious now of the time or even of their predicament, whilst the motor car's wheels settled even deeper into the ditch.

'She was telling me off. Nothing much, just that I hadn't fed the hens and that I was always running off to play with Micky and not doing my work.' She looked up at Eveleen. 'You know.'

Eveleen nodded and said softly, 'Yes, I know.'

'And then I said I'd run away and she said where to and I said I'd go to you.' Again there was silence, until Bridie blurted out, 'And she said you were too busy to be looking after a troublesome child like me.'

'Oh, darling.' Eveleen laughed, trying to make the

sensitive girl understand. 'That's just your gran's way. She's always been a bit – well – sharp.'

Richard was watching Bridie's face and said softly, 'There's more than that, isn't there, love?'

Bridie blinked but then nodded. 'It – it was about Andrew. You see, I thought if you and Uncle Richard didn't want me, then Andrew would. I was sure Andrew loved me . . .' Her voice, thick with disappointment, faded away.

'He does love you, Bridie. We all know that. *You* know that.'

'Yes.' The girl was leaning towards them now, almost shouting at them in her anguish. 'But *why* does he love me?'

The two adults stared at her, completely mystified. Then Richard gave an awkward laugh. 'You're getting a bit deep for me now, Bridie. You might well ask why anyone loves another.'

The girl shook her head vehemently. 'No, no. You don't understand. *He only loves me because I'm the daughter of the love of his life.* He doesn't love me for *me.*' She jabbed her forefinger into her chest with such ferocity that it hurt.

'Who on earth told you a thing like that?' Eveleen said, angry and disgusted at the person who could have been so unfeeling.

Bridie hung her head and plucked at the edge of the rug again, shredding the fabric between her restless fingers. 'Gran,' she muttered.

Eveleen groaned and closed her eyes for a moment. 'I might have known,' she murmured.

'Look,' Richard said, thinking quickly and leaning over the back seat to take Bridie's cold hand in his, 'we can't sort all this out sitting here and we've got to get help from someone to pull this contraption out of the ditch or we're never going to get home tonight. But I want you to promise me something, Bridie.'

The girl looked up at him trustingly. 'What?'

'If you will go back home now and be a good girl, Eveleen and I will say nothing about this to anyone.' As Bridie opened her mouth to protest, Richard went on firmly, 'And we'll let a week or two elapse and then we'll ask your gran to let you come and have a holiday with us in Nottingham. We'll have time to talk about this and to reassure you,' he squeezed her hand comfortingly, 'that we all love you because you're *you* and not because of whose daughter you are.'

Bridie smiled tremulously, but was still not convinced.

'And now,' Eveleen said brightly, 'because your auntie Eveleen has been so very naughty, we really must get help. It'll be getting dark soon.'

Richard laughed aloud and said, 'No-one's hurt, that's all that matters. Including our stowaway. Now,' he went on, 'who do you know with a big, strong carthorse?'

Bridie stood up and began to scramble out of the motor. 'Micky's dad. I'll run and fetch him.' And before either of them could stop her, she was running up the lane. 'Wait there,' she called back. 'I'll fetch Mr Ted.'

'As if we're going anywhere,' Richard remarked ruefully, as he climbed out and stood in the lane looking at his beautiful new motor car, tilted forlornly in the ditch. 'Really I ought to put you across my knee.' He arched his black eyebrows wickedly at his wife. 'If I didn't think you might enjoy it.'

'Really, Richard,' Eveleen admonished, but she was

smiling playfully. 'Fancy saying such a thing.' She stood up and held out her arms to him. 'Darling, I am sorry.'

'You're forgiven,' he said, lifting her out and setting her down on the road. Then he slid down the grass slope and tried to examine the motor.

'Do you think it's damaged?' Eveleen asked anxiously.

'As far as I can see, no.' Richard climbed back up towards her. 'Luckily the ditch is only very shallow and so the workings beneath the car haven't touched the bank. It's still actually resting on its wheels as far as I can make out. So, hopefully, not a lot of harm done.'

Eveleen gave a sigh of relief. 'Thank goodness.'

At that moment they heard the sound of clopping hooves coming down the lane and turned to see Bridie running ahead of a man leading a huge shire horse towards them. Walking beside him was a young boy about Bridie's age.

'It's Ted.' Eveleen clapped her hands. 'And that must be his son, Micky. Oh, it's ages since I last saw them.'

Richard smiled at his wife indulgently and, as she hurried towards them, her hands outstretched, he murmured wryly, 'Ah well, it's an ill wind that blows nobody any good.'

The motor had been pulled easily back onto the road and Richard, after a better inspection, declared that he thought no serious damage had been done. 'Mind you, if a wheel falls off between here and Nottingham, I'll know who to blame.'

He held out his hand to Ted Morton. 'Thank you so much for your help.'

'Glad to be of service, Mr Richard,' Ted said. Then he glanced at Eveleen and winked. 'But you don't have to cause an accident to get to see me, Evie. Come and visit me and Alice soon, won't you? And me mam and dad are always asking after you.'

Ted and Eveleen had grown up together and their fathers, living and working on the same farm estate, had been good friends. As a youth, Ted had flirted with her, but Eveleen had always managed to answer his saucy comments with good-humoured banter.

She laughed now. 'I see you haven't changed, Ted Morton. But we will come and see you all. I promise.'

As they lay together in bed that night, their arms about each other, Eveleen said, 'I don't know whatever possessed my mother to say such a thing to poor Bridie. Mind you,' she added bitterly, 'I ought to know.'

'I can hardly believe she would say such a thing.'

'Oh, she would. Believe me.'

'I've never seen that side of your mother.'

'You wouldn't. You're a man.'

'I don't understand.'

'My mother dotes on men of all ages. She's no time for girls.' Eveleen's sigh came from deep inside. 'If we had been lucky enough to have a son, she would have been besotted with him. But a girl? No.'

Richard's arms tightened about her. 'Don't say that in the past tense, my darling. There's plenty of time.'

'Is there? I'm the wrong side of thirty now.'

In the darkness, he kissed her forehead. 'Remind me to order you that bath chair.'

Eveleen dug him in the ribs.

'Ouch!'

'Serves you right.' She paused and then added seriously, 'But I did take to heart what you said the other day. I've made plans to cut down my workload a little. I'm giving Helen more responsibility.'

'I'm glad. It might help her too.'

They were silent, each thinking about Eveleen's friend. Shortly after their own marriage, Helen had begun walking out with a young man who worked in the factory. She had been ecstatically happy and they had been planning to be married, when the young man had been taken ill. Consumption had been diagnosed and the last sight Helen had had of him had been waving to him through the window of the hospital, where no visitors were allowed.

He had died during the week they had planned to be married.

'She went through a dreadful time,' Eveleen murmured, 'but just lately she's begun to look a little happier. I think she might have met someone else. She's not saying much, not even to me, but I can't blame her for that. She must feel rather afraid to love again.'

'Like someone else I know, though for a very different reason.'

Now Richard was kissing her mouth and all talk was stopped, except his murmured words of love.

Ten

'Mam, we've been thinking. We'd like Bridie to come and stay with us for a holiday.'

They were visiting one Sunday and Eveleen broached the subject as she helped her mother to wash up after dinner.

Mary crashed a plate down on the draining board and glanced over her shoulder. 'So that's what the little madam's been up to, is it?'

Eveleen kept her expression as innocent looking as she could manage. 'I don't know what you mean.'

'Oh, I think you do. She's been telling you how badly I treat her, no doubt making it far worse than it is. She needs a firm hand, Eveleen. She's a wild, disobedient little tyke and Josh won't discipline her, so I have to.'

Mary dried her hands on a towel and turned to face Eveleen. 'He treats her very much like your father, my poor Walter, used to treat you. You girls wrap these men round your little fingers and they can't see any wrong in you. Look at all that business with Stephen Dunsmore. If you had only listened to me, you'd have saved yourself and all of us a lot of heartache. And maybe,' she wagged her forefinger in Eveleen's face, 'just maybe your father would still be alive to this day.'

Eveleen had fought hard through the years to come to terms with her mother's accusation, but even now the words were like a knife in her heart.

'It was all your fault we were turned out of our home and had to go to Flawford and look where that led. Rebecca setting her cap at Jimmy and getting herself pregnant just to trap him. I don't blame him for running away to sea. I would have done the same if I'd been in his shoes, but it doesn't stop me missing him every day of my life. And I've you to thank for that.'

'Mam,' Eveleen said, trying hard to hold onto her patience, 'do you have to rake up the past and throw it at me every time we come home?'

'Only because, if Bridie comes to live with you, she'll copy some of your bad ways. She's better staying here with me where I can keep her in line.'

'I didn't say anything about her coming to live with us. I just said for a holiday.'

'Oh aye. But once she's there, she'll wheedle her way round you. And Richard, because he's every bit as soft with her as Josh is. She's desperate to get away from me. She even suggested going to Andrew's. I soon put a stop to that.'

Yes, I know you did, Eveleen thought resentfully, and in a very cruel way. But she held her tongue. Old as she was now, answering her mother back would still serve no purpose. She finished drying the dishes and pulled down the sleeves of her blouse. She wished that she had left it to Richard to speak to her mother. She was sure that he would have won Mary over.

By the time Josh, Richard and Bridie returned from their walk around the farm, Eveleen and her mother were barely speaking to each other. The two women were sitting in silence on either side of the fire in Mary's best parlour, a room only used on Sundays and special occasions. Richard came to the hearth and stood between them, rubbing his hands and holding them out towards the blaze, for the May day was unusually cold, a blustery wind blowing and rain threatening.

'All settled, then?' he asked, glancing from one to the other.

Eveleen shook her head. 'My mother doesn't trust me to look after her.'

Mary turned to Bridie standing near the table. 'Go upstairs, child. This is not for your ears.'

'But, Gran—' the girl began.

'Do as I say,' Mary snapped. The girl glowered and clamped her jaws together to silence any protest. She turned and wrenched open the door leading into the small hallway. No-one in the room spoke as they listened to her stamping her way up the stairs and slamming the door of her bedroom.

Josh ran his hand across his forehead and Eveleen and Richard exchanged a glance.

Frowning slightly, Richard pulled out a chair from beneath the table and placed it carefully next to Mary.

'And you needn't start your wheedling, either,' Mary said, but now her tone was playful and the look she cast up at him, coy.

Richard smiled at her. 'Just tell me,' he asked in his soft, deep tones, 'why you think we can't look after her properly.'

'I didn't say you.' Mary sniffed. 'I said her.' She nodded across the hearth at her daughter.

Behind them, Josh gave a sigh and lowered his bulk into a chair near the table, as if resigning himself to a long, wrangling argument. Then all at once, he stood up again. 'Evie, you come with me, mi duck. We'll leave your mam and Richard to talk.' When Eveleen seemed to hesitate, he added firmly, 'Come on.'

He took her coat down from the peg behind the back door and held it for her, whilst she slipped her arms in.

As Josh held open the back door for her, Eveleen overheard her mother, with a different, much gentler tone, say, 'I realize you must think I'm too harsh with Bridie, but I'm responsible for her. I know what can happen to young girls. Believe me. And sometimes, Richard, I am so afraid for her . . .'

'The rain's still holding off,' Josh said, interrupting Eveleen's eavesdropping. 'We'll walk to the beck.'

They walked in silence through the farmyard, hens scattering at their approach, through the gate and into the neighbouring field, which led down to the stream. It wasn't until they were standing on the bank, Eveleen's arm tucked through Josh's, and watching the rushing water that Eveleen said quietly, 'It was about here I found him.'

Josh nodded. 'Aye, I know, lass, I know.'

'She still blames me for his death, you know. She says that the worry over my involvement with Stephen Dunsmore caused his death.'

'That's nonsense.'

'I know. His family had some sort of weakness of the heart. His own father had died in much the same way. But you won't convince my mother of that.'

'When I first got to know you and your family,' Josh said. 'I knew things were – well – difficult between you and your mother, but at the time Mary and I married I thought it would get easier.'

'It did. Much easier.'

'Is it my fault do you think? Is she not happy with me now?'

'Oh, Josh, she's wonderfully happy with you. Don't

ever think that. This has absolutely nothing to do with you. What I mean is, it's not your fault in any way.' She sighed. 'It's me. Or rather, it's because Bridie is growing up and Mam has the same concerns about her as she once had about me.'

Josh digested her words and then nodded. 'I see what you mean.' He pulled a comical face and added, 'I think.'

Eveleen glanced at him. Carefully she said, 'And then there's her own unhappiness she suffered as a young girl.'

She was treading very tentatively, anxious not to divulge secrets that her mother had not shared with Josh. But he nodded and said quietly, 'Yes, she told me all about that, even before we were married.' He turned his head and smiled at Eveleen now. 'She was so afraid it would make a difference to me.'

Eveleen squeezed his arm. He was such a good, kind man and he loved Mary unconditionally. Eveleen believed that, whatever Mary might have done in her youth, it would have made no difference to the man standing beside her, just as it never had to her own father.

'Her family treated her so cruelly,' Eveleen said with compassion. 'There's no wonder the scars are still there.'

'It's a shame, though,' Josh reflected sadly, 'that the past is still blighting the present.'

Now he patted her hand as it rested on his arm. 'Mind you don't let that happen. Don't let Stephen Dunsmore's cruel desertion of you spoil your happiness with Richard.'

Eveleen's eyes clouded. 'I thought I was completely over the hurt, but when I saw him again the other week – you know, when our motor frightened his horse – I have to admit, though only to you, Josh, that it opened the wound again.'

Josh was firm as he said, 'Well, you really shouldn't let it. Richard adores you. He'll never hurt you.'

They walked back to the house and found Richard ready to leave, but it wasn't until they were in the car and heading home that he admitted, 'I didn't get any further with her than you did, darling. But we won't give up. It's time that poor child saw another side to life.'

From an upstairs window, Bridie, biting hard on her lower lip to stem tears that threatened, watched them leave.

Both Richard and Eveleen had come to her bedroom to say goodbye to her. They had hugged her and promised that somehow they would persuade her gran to change her mind.

But, as she watched them go, Bridie did not believe their promises. She felt betrayed and deserted by everyone around her.

Eleven

It took Richard three more visits to Pear Tree Farm and until almost the end of June to persuade Mary to allow Bridie to visit Nottingham.

'And only a week, mind. I want her back here next Sunday without fail. There'll be our haymaking soon. She'll be needed and Ted Morton says there'll be work for her on the estate. I don't want her getting used to a life of idleness.'

'Oh, she won't be idle,' Richard promised, winking at Bridie. 'We've got such a lot of things planned. She'll not have a minute to call her own.'

Mollified a little, Mary sniffed. 'I'm pleased to hear it.' Then she glanced at him shrewdly. 'But I don't expect it's honest hard work you've got planned for her, is it? Just a lot of gallivanting.'

What intrigued Bridie more than anything was the way her aunt and Richard lived.

'Who's the man who opened the door?' she whispered when she first stepped into the house.

'That's Smithers,' Eveleen said, leading the way into the morning room and crossing to the fireplace to pull on a bell cord.

Only moments later a young girl, not much older

than Bridie but dressed in the smart afternoon uniform of a parlourmaid, entered the room.

'Emily, would you bring tea for us, please?'

The girl bobbed a curtsy and left, but not before the two young girls had eyed each other.

'You've got a maid too?'

Eveleen laughed, 'Yes, darling. And a cook and a kitchenmaid, but that's all.'

'All!' Bridie exclaimed.

'A lot of people would have about twice as many. Smithers doubles as a butler and as Uncle Richard's valet, and Emily is a housemaid in the mornings and parlourmaid in the afternoon. And she acts as my personal maid too.'

Bridie pulled a face. 'And I thought I worked hard on the farm.'

'Richard is very fair to his employees both at home and at the factory,' her aunt explained as they sat down together to wait for the tea to arrive. 'And I would say your work is harder. You have to be out in all weathers and work even longer hours than our servants do.'

Bridie giggled. 'I can't get used to it. You having servants.'

Eveleen smiled and leant forward conspiratorially. 'It took me a long time to get used to it, too. In fact, I don't think I am even now. I'm always doing things for myself that Emily says should be her job.' She straightened up as the door opened. 'Ah, here she is with the tea.'

Fascinated, Bridie watched as the young girl set the tray on the low table near Eveleen.

'Thank you, Emily. I'll pour.'

The girl bobbed again. 'Very good, ma'am.'

'And would you take some tea to Mr Stokes? I think he's gone to his study.'

As the door closed behind her, Bridie said, 'Won't Uncle Richard have tea with us?'

'No, love. He's got some paperwork to do, but he'll join us for dinner naturally.'

Naturally, Bridie thought. None of this was 'natural' to her. She glanced at the clock on the mantelpiece. If she'd been at home now, she'd be setting the table for tea and then going outside into the yard to help Josh milk their six cows instead of sitting here in this elegant room, sipping tea out of delicate bone-china cups and nibbling at dainty fancy cakes.

'Won't I see him till tomorrow dinnertime, then?' she asked.

For a moment, Eveleen looked puzzled and then smiled. 'Oh, I'm sorry. I was forgetting. We have dinner in the evening. Lunch is our midday meal.'

'Oh,' Bridie said, realizing that she had a lot to learn about life in the city.

'Your bath's ready, miss.' Emily had woken her on her first morning at eight o'clock.

Bright light streamed through the curtains, which the girl had opened and, startled, Bridie jumped out of bed. 'Oh, whatever time is it? I'm late.' Then realizing where she was, she laughed. 'I forgot.'

'Your bath's ready, miss,' the maid repeated and added, 'And breakfast is served in the dining room at nine o'clock.'

'Bath?'

'Yes, miss. The bathroom's just outside your door, to the left.'

'Oh. Thank you.'

Bath night to Bridie was on a Friday in a tin bath on the pegged hearthrug in front of the kitchen fire, her gran pouring in hot water from the range whilst Josh was banished to the front room until she had finished. Now, it seemed, she was expected to bathe each morning.

When the maid had gone, Bridie tiptoed a little nervously into the bathroom and gasped. Shiny, patterned wallpaper covered the walls and on the floor was black-and-white chequered linoleum. A huge cast-iron bath with clawed feet, half full of steaming water, was against one wall and near the opposite wall was a marble-topped, tile-backed washstand with a bowl and water jug. This too was full of hot water. Soap and sponge lay in matching dishes and a brand-new hog's hair toothbrush had been laid out for Bridie's use. White, lace-edged towels hung on a rail and soaps and perfumes lined a shelf. Bridie had never seen anything like this in her life, but sinking into the gloriously hot water, she thought: I could get used to this.

Her aunt's home was so very different from the farm where both she and Bridie had been brought up. This was a town house in an elegant street of tall, terraced houses. It had an entrance hall with rooms on either side. What did Auntie Evie call them? Bridie wrinkled her nose, trying to recall. The morning room, the drawing room, and then there was the dining room and Uncle Richard's study too. And somewhere, at the back, there must be the kitchen and scullery and maybe a servants' sitting room. Upstairs there were four bedrooms, the bathroom she was in at this moment and then up another flight of stairs, were the servants' bedrooms.

What would her gran think to all this? Bridie

thought, as she began to soap herself all over, relishing the luxury.

How lucky Aunt Eveleen was to be married to a man like Uncle Richard. But then, the girl thought: I'd be quite happy to live in a tiny cottage with a tin bath on the hearth once a week, if only Andrew really loved me.

They did indeed do a lot of gallivanting. Eveleen took her round the city shops, buying her niece a dark blue dress with a white, lace-trimmed smock to wear over it, a coat and beret-type hat.

'Now, you really look a grown-up young lady,' Richard said as the girl paraded before him that evening. She didn't really, Bridie thought, for the style was still childish, but she had not liked to seem ungrateful for her aunt's generosity.

'Tomorrow,' Richard was saying, 'I'll take you on the river. And the following day I'll take you on a tour of the factory, that's if you'd like to see it. Then on your last night here, we'll take you out to dine in a smart restaurant and then to the theatre.'

Bridie clapped her hands. 'Oh, I'd love to see where you work.' Hurriedly, she added, 'Where you both work. Then when I'm back home I can picture you at home and at work too. I can imagine what you're doing.'

Eveleen and Richard exchanged a glance. Her words had a sad and lonely ring to them.

Twelve

'Do you know, Richard, it's a joy to see her delight in everything,' Eveleen told him as they sat across the breakfast table before Bridie appeared on her last morning with them. 'I've just heard her singing in the bath.'

'Mmm,' Richard said absently, not looking up from his newspaper.

'Darling, did you hear what I said?'

He lowered his paper and smiled at her, but she was quick to see that a worried frown did not quite leave his face.

'What is it, dear? You haven't minded having her here, have you?'

Now he laughed and, for a moment, the anxiety fled his face. 'Oh, my darling, of course not. She's an enchanting child. I've loved having her here,' he assured her, but now the apprehensive look came back as he prodded the newspaper with his forefinger. 'No, no, it's something here in the paper. It's looking increasingly as if we're going to be plunged into trouble in Europe. It might even lead to war.'

Eveleen blinked. 'War!' Wrapped up in her own little world of life with Richard, her work at the warehouse and overseeing all the homeworkers, Eveleen took little interest in news, politics and world affairs. Richard's prophecy was a profound shock to her. 'Who with, for goodness sake?'

'It's a bit complicated . . .'

'Too difficult for my little woman's mind to understand?' Eveleen bridled.

'No, no, darling. I can't understand why we need to be involved myself, but it sounds as if we might be. Archduke Franz Ferdinand, the heir to the Austro-Hungarian throne, has been assassinated in Sarajevo. He was shot by a Bosnian nationalist – a nineteen-year-old student.'

'Nineteen!' Eveleen was appalled. 'What on earth does a nineteen-year-old know about politics?'

Richard sighed. 'I'm very much afraid, my love, that at that age they think they know it all. It says here the archduke's wife flung herself across her husband and was killed too. She died instantly, he a little while later. You know,' Richard continued grimly, 'it reads as if it was a carefully planned plot. Earlier, they'd had a bomb thrown at their car, but had escaped injury then.'

'But why? What's he done? Why should someone want to kill him?'

'It seems,' Richard said slowly, scanning the printed page, 'it's something to do with the oppression of the Serbian people.'

Eveleen waved her hand, 'You're right, I admit it. It is too complicated for me to understand. Why should that involve Britain in a war? It's nothing to do with us.' When Richard did not answer, she pressed, 'Is it?'

'I suppose, put simply, if there's trouble in Europe we'll be involved, firstly in trying to keep the peace, but if that fails . . .'

'Oh, Richard, no,' Eveleen's eyes were wide with fear and she covered her mouth with trembling fingers.

At that moment they heard Bridie's footsteps outside the door.

'Don't say anything in front of Bridie. We don't want to spoil her first visit to us,' Richard said hurriedly.

With a supreme effort, they both turned to greet the girl with wide smiles.

'You've spoilt everything.' Bridie, in floods of tears, stamped her foot.

'Don't you take that tone with me, my girl, or I won't let you go again,' Mary snapped. 'Anyone would think you're not pleased to be home.'

'I'm not.' The rash words were out of her mouth before she could stop them. Horrorstruck, she stared at her grandmother.

'Well!' For a moment even Mary was lost for words.

'Gran, I didn't mean it.' Bridie rushed to her, trying to put her arms about the older woman's waist, but Mary pushed her away. 'I'm sorry. Truly, I am. I didn't mean it. It's just that I've had such a lovely time and – now you're finding fault with the clothes Aunt Eveleen's bought me and – and everything we've done.' She hung her head and muttered, 'And it just spoils it all.'

'You're the only thing that's been spoilt, my girl. Well, whether you like it or not, you are back home and here you're going to stay. Now, if you want to show me you're really sorry, you'd better get some work done.'

Gone in an instant were all the cosseting, the being waited on by Emily, having her bed made, her clothes laid out and her bath made ready. No more luxuriating in scented water and lying between fresh smelling sheets.

Bridie was home and back to reality with a bump.

*

The troubles in Europe dominated the conversation over the next few weeks.

'It's all a lot of nonsense,' Mary declared emphatically. 'Why do we have to get involved in trouble that's happened thousands of miles away?'

Josh, with a greater understanding of political matters, sighed. 'Well, as I see it – of course, I might be wrong—'

'Oh, I'm sure you're not,' Mary patted his shoulder as she passed by his chair. 'You men are so clever over such matters, but I still don't see why Britain has to become involved.'

She sat down at the table and leant her chin on her hand, smiling at him coyly, 'Explain it to me.'

Watching, Bridie smothered her amusement. Her gran was openly flirting with Josh, playing up to his vanity.

'We'll get involved because if we don't and a full-scale war breaks out, we could soon be next in line. We'll try to keep the peace.'

Mary smiled and said smoothly, 'I see.'

Josh eyed her over the top of his newspaper. 'Mary Carpenter,' he said, feigning severity, 'I do believe you're teasing me.'

She laughed, stood up and planted a kiss on the bald patch on the top of his head. 'Of course, I'm teasing you, Josh. What do any of us poor mortals know about politics and foreign parts? Why, I've never been further than a day trip to the seaside and I don't intend to either.'

'To the seaside? You've been to the seaside, Gran?' Bridie's face brightened. 'How did you get there?'

'On the train from Grantham.'

Bridie clapped her hands. 'On a train! I've never been

on a train. Oh, can we go? I've never seen the sea. Can we?'

'We could go on August bank holiday Monday,' Josh said. 'There'll be day trips on, I dare say.'

'Oh no.' Mary put up her hands. 'This child's done enough gallivanting for the time being. High time she settled down now.'

'But we could all go. The three of us,' Bridie said eagerly and even Josh looked at Mary hopefully.

'Oh aye,' her grandmother rounded on the girl. 'And who would do the milking and feed the livestock, might I ask?'

Bridie's face fell. Even though she had no personal experience, she realized that a day trip would take just that, the full day from early morning to late evening and the animals needed looking after during that time.

Crestfallen, she sighed. 'Yes, Gran,' she said, feigning meekness. She rose from the breakfast table and began to clear away the dirty dishes into the scullery, biting her lip to stop the tears of disappointment. She was not even heartened by Josh's helpless shrug, as if he too would have enjoyed a day at the sea.

As she went about her daily chores with an outward show of obedience, Bridie's heart hardened and her resolve to escape this life of drudgery grew stronger.

Thirteen

'You there, Bridie?' It was Micky's voice in the yard.

'In here,' she called from the dairy. She stopped churning as he appeared in the doorway. Wiping her sweating forehead, she went towards him. 'Isn't it hot? Too hot for the butter to come. It's taking me hours.'

'Here, I'll give it a go for you.' Micky grinned, showing white, even teeth against his tanned skin. His fair, straight hair flopped across his forehead and his blue eyes sparkled with merriment.

Out of breath from her labours, Bridie leant against the doorframe. 'I won't say no, 'cos I'm out on me feet.'

Micky took the handle and turned it steadily, whilst Bridie mopped her face, the back of her neck and her hands with a piece of old towelling. Above the rattling of the churn, Micky shouted, 'There's a day trip from the village to the seaside on Monday. You know, the bank holiday?'

Bridie nodded without looking at him. Instead she concentrated on carefully wiping each finger.

'Me mam and dad and us kids are going on it. Even me grandma's coming. Grandad's staying to feed the livestock, but we're all off. Why don't you come with us? We're going on the train from Grantham.'

'Gran won't let me.'

Micky stopped churning briefly. 'What?'

'I said, Gran won't let me.'

'How do you know?'

'Because I've asked her. She's says I've had enough holidays at me auntie Evie's.'

'Oh.' Micky's disappointment was obvious. 'That's a pity. I reckon we could've had a good time at the seaside. You an' me.'

'Yes,' Bridie said, her tone flat. 'We could.' She sighed and moved towards him. 'I'd better get on with this.'

'I'll do it,' Micky said, and began to turn the handle again, muttering, 'What an owd beezum your gran can be at times.'

Bridie managed a thin smile, but the misery in her heart deepened.

She tried once again at breakfast time the next morning, relating to Josh and her grandmother what Micky had told her.

'Why not let the lass go with the Mortons, Mary love?' Even Josh was pleading her case now. 'They'll look after her.'

'Huh! You think so? You don't know what Ted was like as a youngster. His son'll be just the same. After anything in skirts.'

'Mary, they're twelve years old, not seventeen. What on earth do you think they're going to get up to on a day trip to the sea with half the village with them?'

'She's not going and that's final,' Mary said firmly and added as a wily excuse, 'besides, Andrew's coming. You won't want to miss seeing Andrew, will you?'

On the Monday morning of the bank holiday, Bridie was up before dawn. As the rising sun cast its first fingers of light across the misty landscape and the sky to the east was streaked with pink and a glorious apricot colour, Bridie climbed the five-barred gate at the end of the yard and sat on top of it. Straight down the rough cart track and then the lane beyond was Furze Farm, where Bill and Dorothy Morton, Micky's grandparents, lived. Beyond that, about half a mile further down the lane, was the cottage where Micky lived.

There were sounds reaching her ears now, through the silence of the early morning; voices raised in excited anticipation of the day ahead. She saw the shadowy figures of Micky and his family walking up the lane towards Furze Farm, where they disappeared into the yard. A few moments later she heard the rattling of cartwheels and saw the farm cart come out of the gate and turn into the lane, coming towards her. When it reached the place where the cart track to her own home came straight ahead and the lane turned to their right on its way towards Bernby village and then on to Grantham, Bridie saw Ted pull the cart to a halt. He raised his hand and waved. 'You coming with us, love?'

'No, Mr Morton,' she shouted, her voice echoing eerily in the still morning. 'Have a good time, all of you.'

The two younger children were already squabbling in the back of the cart, with their mother trying vainly to calm their excitement. Bridie forced herself to smile and to wave. 'Bring me back a shell from the beach,' she called as Ted slapped the reins and the cart set off once more.

She watched them until they turned another corner and were out of sight. Straining her ears she could still just hear their voices as the cart went up the hill past Fairfield House and on to Bernby.

Bridie sat there staring into the distance as the sun rose behind her, feeling as if everyone had deserted her.

Andrew arrived mid-morning and Bridie went to meet him, but this time she did not run towards him, flinging herself at him so that he lifted her up and swung her round.

He put his arm round her shoulders and kissed her cheek, then stood back from her a little and looked down at her. 'What have I done?'

She could see the concern in his face, his eyes anxious. Suddenly she felt guilty. He knew nothing of what her grandmother had said. He had not changed. All right, his love for her wasn't what she had thought it to be – hoped it to be. But, if she was fair, that was hardly his fault. She decided to tell the truth, but not the whole truth.

She smiled at him. 'Gran says I'm too big now to be lifted up like a little girl. I should start acting more like a young lady. She's going to let me put my hair up when I'm thirteen in September.' She demonstrated, picking up her long, thick black plait and winding it in a circle around her crown.

All at once there was a haunted look in Andrew's hazel eyes and when he spoke, his voice was cracked with emotion. He reached out and touched her cheek tenderly. 'Oh, Bridie. That was how your mam used to wear her hair sometimes. You look so like her.'

He couldn't possibly know how his words hurt her.

Fourteen

'Oh no!'

On the Tuesday morning Richard was standing in the hallway, the morning paper open in his hands, as Eveleen came down the stairs.

'What is it?'

Slowly he raised his eyes and his voice was hoarse as he said, 'We've declared war on Germany.'

'Germany? Why Germany?' Eveleen asked.

'Mm?' Richard was only half listening, his concentration once more on the newspaper.

'I said, why Germany? I thought all the trouble started in Sarajevo when the Archduke was assassinated at the end of June.'

'It did,' Richard said grimly, turning a page of the newspaper. 'But it reads here as if that was just the spark that ignited a conflagration that was waiting to happen. Austria was bound to retaliate and they declared war on Serbia last week.' He sighed. 'The delicate balance of power that existed between all the nations trying to keep the peace has just gone horribly wrong.'

'But what's that got to do with Germany and us?'

'Germany's allied itself with Austria.'

'But – but our royal family's related to the Kaiser.'

Richard sighed. 'So's the Tsar. He's his cousin, but it hasn't stopped the Kaiser declaring war on Russia.

Family ties don't seem to matter when it comes to political issues. And now it seems as if the Kaiser has taken offence at Britain's attempts to mediate. Germany declared war on France a couple of days ago and now, because they've marched into Belgium, we've declared war on Germany.'

Eveleen's eyes widened in alarm as the dreadful truth began to sink in. 'All those countries involved already?'

Richard nodded.

'So what will it mean for us?' She put her hand on his sleeve. 'You won't have to go, will you?'

Richard's tone was sober as he said carefully, 'I won't be *made* to go, not at first, no. Lord Kitchener has been appointed Secretary for War and he's calling for volunteers.'

Eveleen gasped and her hand fluttered to cover her mouth. She knew him so well, knew what his words meant. 'You mean – you mean you *want* to go? You want to volunteer?'

His dark eyes regarded her soberly. Quietly he said, 'I shall think about it very seriously, my love. But I promise I won't do anything without talking it over with you first.'

She put her arms around him and laid her cheek against his chest and heard the steady beat of his heart. 'I won't let you go,' she murmured. 'I swear I won't let you go.'

Richard stroked her hair, but he made no answer.

'Well, thank the good Lord you're too old to go.' Mary slammed a tureen down on the table. 'What on earth is our government thinking of? Getting us involved in a stupid war that's none of our making.'

Josh was sitting by the range, devouring the newspaper.

'Oh, put that paper down, Josh, and come and get your dinner.'

Bridie was moving silently between the scullery and the kitchen table. She was anxious. She had listened to all the talk of war and she was suddenly very afraid. Micky had come to the farm that morning full, not of the trip to the seaside and bearing her a gift – he'd even forgotten to bring her a shell – but of the impending war.

'By heck!' Micky had said, thumping his fist against the palm of his other hand. 'I wish I was a bit older. I'd be off.' His eyes were shining. 'Me dad's talking about going. Lots of the young fellers from round here are going already. They're off to Grantham or Nottingham today to volunteer.'

'What do you want to go and get yourself killed for?' Bridie had asked him bluntly.

'Killed?' he scoffed. 'Who said anything about getting killed? I'd just like to go and fight for me country.'

'And isn't that what happens in a war?' Bridie asked quietly. 'Don't people kill each other?'

'Well, I suppose a few get killed,' the young boy admitted, but then he added proudly, 'but mostly you get mentioned in dispatches and the King pins a medal on your chest. Besides,' he added saucily, 'if I get wounded, you could be a nurse and look after me.' His grin widened. 'I'd like that.'

Bridie had said no more, but now, seated across the dinner table from her grandmother and Josh, she felt the fear rise in her throat.

'Who will have to go? Will Micky?'

'No, no, love,' Josh smiled at her, though the anxiety

did not quite leave his eyes. 'He's far too young. I don't expect it will last very long. A few weeks at the most.'

In a small voice she said, 'Micky said his dad's talking of going.'

'Ted?' Mary, in the act of spooning vegetables onto a plate, stared at Bridie. 'Well, now I've heard everything. Mind you, I suppose I shouldn't be surprised. He was a right tearaway when he was young. It's just the sort of thing he would do.'

'It's a very courageous thing to do,' Josh said, pouring gravy over his food. 'To volunteer to fight for one's country. If I was a few years younger—'

'Thank God you're not, then,' Mary said tartly. Glancing at Bridie, she said, 'Eat your dinner, child, and let's have no more talk of war.'

But Bridie was staring at Josh, her eyes large with fear now as she calculated quickly. Her voice trembled as she said, 'If Micky's dad's the right age to go, then – then so is Andrew.'

Now the three of them stared at each other. Josh nodded soberly, 'She's right, y'know. And Richard too. He's from the sort of family that would be one of the first to volunteer. See it as their duty to defend their country.' He reached out and covered Mary's hand with his large one. 'And you do realize, love, who might very well be caught up in this, don't you?'

She frowned thoughtfully, 'Well, any of the young fellers. Even Stephen Dunsmore, I suppose.'

'I was thinking more of someone who is already in the services.'

'I don't know who you—' she began and then she dropped her knife and fork onto her plate with a clatter. Her hands flew to her face as she stared, wide eyed, at Josh. 'Oh no! No!'

Slowly Josh nodded.

'Who?' Bridie asked urgently, her frightened glance darting from one to the other. 'Who do you mean?'

Now both of them turned to look at her.

'My Jimmy,' Mary whispered hoarsely. 'He's at sea. In the Royal Navy.'

Bridie gasped. 'My dad? You mean my dad?'

Sadly Mary nodded, whilst she gripped Josh's hand so fiercely that her knuckles showed white.

When Richard drove the motor car into the factory, the yard was crowded with workmen. Even some of the women were there instead of in the warehouse at their work.

'What on earth's going on?' Richard exclaimed.

'We'll soon find out,' Eveleen said grimly. 'There's Mr Porter pushing his way through to reach us.'

They climbed out of the motor and waited until Bob Porter, the general manager of the factory – the position that had once belonged to Josh Carpenter – reached them.

'Thank goodness you've come, Mr Richard. I can't get 'em to start work. It's all this talk of war. It's got the young fellers that excited. I reckon half of 'em are off to volunteer this minute.'

Richard nodded. 'I'll speak to them,' he said and pushed his way through the throng to reach some steps where he could stand above the crowd. Eveleen and Bob Porter followed in his wake.

It was a few minutes before he could make himself heard above the hubbub and gain their attention. 'I know that all of you will be anxious to answer the call of your country, but I would ask you to continue your work until we hear more news—'

'Oh aye, thinking it'll hit your pocket, Mr Richard? That all you can think about?'

Richard regarded the man steadily. 'It'll hit us all, Jake, and not only our pockets. All I can say to you now is that, when the right time comes, those of you who wish to volunteer will go with my blessing. And whilst none of us knows what the uncertain future holds for us, if the company of Reckitt and Stokes still exists at the end of it all, your job will be here for you when you come back.'

There were mutterings amongst the crowd. 'He can't say fairer than that, Jake,' one voice, raised above the rest, said. 'Yer've got to admit that.'

Jake Morrison, one of the younger twisthands, had the grace to look ashamed.

'And in the meantime,' Richard was still speaking, 'while you are away, the company will do its best to look after the welfare of your families.'

The comments grew louder at their employer's generous offer. Only Bob Porter, standing beside Eveleen, muttered, 'I 'ope he knows just what he's offering.'

But Eveleen was smiling, her eyes bright with tears of pride as she gazed at the tall, handsome and authoritative man who was her husband.

As the men filed into the factory, Richard stepped down and came towards her. 'Evie, go and talk to the women in the warehouse, will you? Try to reassure them that if their menfolk are bent on enlisting, we will continue to employ them. The women, I mean.' He smiled wryly. 'But just warn them that they might have to do other jobs to keep the factory going.'

Even in this dark moment of uncertainty, Eveleen laughed, relieved even for a brief moment to be able to say with light-hearted teasing, 'You don't mean you'd have women helping to work the machines?'

Richard smiled and touched her cheek and said softly, 'It's been done before, hasn't it?' He sighed and now he was very serious. 'And it might very well come to it, Evie, before we're through with this.'

Fifteen

Eveleen's task proved far harder than Richard's. She was faced with a clamour of fear, even tears from some of the women.

'My dad was killed in the Boer War. I know what war really means. If they go to war, we'll never see any of them again.'

'That's right. My uncle was killed in that lot, an' all. I don't want my young man to go.'

But there were several voices raised in patriotism. 'Well, I don't want to be married to a coward. I'd be right proud to see my Bert in uniform. If he goes, I'll wave him off with a flag just to show him how much I love him and how proud me and the kids are of him.'

The hubbub grew louder and the arguments flew back and forth. Rather than try to stop it, Eveleen let the women have their say.

Joining Helen at the end of the room, she said, 'Let them get it off their chests, then they might settle down to work.' She glanced at her friend. 'Are you all right, Helen? You look very white.'

The young woman nodded but her voice quavered as she said, 'I – I just don't want Leslie to do anything daft like volunteering, that's all.'

Eveleen smiled. 'Leslie? And who,' she asked pointedly, 'is Leslie, might I ask?'

Helen's cheeks turned a faint pink. 'Leslie Holmes. He works in one of the machine shops with Luke Manning.'

Eveleen nodded. She knew Luke Manning well and now she remembered having seen a tall, serious-looking young man working alongside him.

Helen continued hesitantly, her blush deepening. 'We – we've been walking out together. About two months.'

'And you never told me?' Eveleen pretended mock indignation.

Helen shrugged. 'After what happened before, I suppose I was a bit frightened to say much about it. In case, well, you know?'

Eveleen nodded and put her arm about Helen's waist. 'I know, love, I know,' she said huskily.

In the last few weeks she had observed the change in her friend. Helen was a pretty young woman with fair hair, a small nose and, usually, a laughing mouth. She had always been Eveleen's staunch ally, but since the untimely death of her fiancé, the once bright, vivacious Helen had been subdued, the grief haunting her. Lately, however, the mischievous sparkle had come back into her blue eyes and Eveleen had secretly crossed her fingers that the cause of it was some nice young man.

But now the bleak fear was back as Helen said softly, 'It's just the sort of thing Leslie'll do. I just know he will.'

As Eveleen hugged her friend, trying to offer what comfort she could, she was nevertheless thinking: Yes, and it's what Richard will do too.

*

Andrew arrived at the farm the following Sunday.

'I'm volunteering,' he told them proudly. 'I'm off to fight for my country.'

The colour drained from Bridie's face as she flung herself against him and wrapped her arms around him as if she would physically hold him there. 'No, no. I don't want you to go. You don't have to. I know you don't. Josh said you wouldn't have to go.'

Andrew was startled by her passionate outcry and even more surprised when her grandmother made no effort to restrain her. Instead Mary said, 'The child's right, Andrew. What on earth do you want to go for?' She glanced at Bridie. 'She's not got many of us in the way of family, poor kid. You're family to her. As good as.'

Bridie lifted her head and stared at her. They were the kindest words she'd heard spoken about herself by her grandmother for a long time, indeed if not ever.

'I feel I have to,' Andrew said. 'I want to. I want to get away from Flawford. I've lived and worked in that same little yard all me life. I want to see something of the world.'

'And you think going to war is a good way to see the world, do you?' Mary countered.

'I want to do something with my life. Something worthwhile.'

'Oh aye.' Mary was not going to give in. 'Throw it away, more like.'

'Well, wouldn't it be a worthwhile cause? In the defence of one's homeland?'

'No, no, *no*!' Bridie shouted and clung to him all the tighter. 'I won't let you go. I won't. I won't!'

'Now, now, love . . .' It was Josh who prised her clinging arms from Andrew. 'Let's sit down and talk about this quite calmly. You've got to respect a fellow's wishes. If Andrew feels it's his duty to go—'

'Duty! Pah!' Mary was vehement. 'It'll be our Jimmy's duty, I'd agree with you there. Though I wish it wasn't so. But he joined up, signed on or whatever they call it, into the Royal Navy and I daresay when you do that part of your pledge is to answer your country's call if need be. But why you?' She flung out her hand towards Andrew. 'Why civilians?'

'They're asking for volunteers,' Andrew said. 'There's several of us going from the yard.'

'What's going to happen to my brother's workshops then, if you young fellers all go rushing off to the war? Have you stopped to think of that, eh?'

'Well.' Andrew shrugged evasively. It was obvious that he had not. 'There'll be enough older men left. I expect the work'll drop off anyway.'

'That's just where you're wrong. What's wanted might alter a bit, but you all make knitted garments, don't you? Don't you think there's going to be a heck of a lot of garments needed to clothe an army?'

Andrew blinked. 'I hadn't looked at it that way.'

'No,' Mary said shortly. 'You wouldn't. You'd be better off staying put and helping the war by making the clothing that's bound to be needed.'

'There you are, you see,' Bridie said triumphantly. 'You don't need to go. You can be much more useful here.' She put her arm through his and gazed up at him imploringly. 'Do say you won't go. Please, Andrew.'

'I don't suppose,' Josh said thoughtfully, 'there'll be much call for lace if the war lasts for long. I wonder how it will affect Reckitt and Stokes?'

'Aye,' Mary said. 'I can't see soldiers wanting lace trimmings on their long johns.'

No-one even smiled at her effort to lighten the talk and there was silence as everyone's thoughts turned to Richard and Eveleen.

At that very moment a family conference was also being held in the Stokes's household. Richard and Eveleen were at the home of Richard's parents for Sunday lunch.

Brinsley Stokes sat at the head of the table. At fifty-five he was an older edition of his son, Richard. Looking at her father-in-law, Eveleen could almost see what her husband would look like in twenty years' time. He was tall and still slim, though his once black hair was now liberally peppered with white. His features were still remarkably clear-cut; a long, straight nose and a firm jaw. There were wrinkles around his eyes, but they were laughter lines rather than the signs of ageing. He was capable of looking quite stern, as he was doing at this moment, but his dark brown eyes were always kindly and full of concern.

His voice was deep and, when he spoke now, not quite steady. 'You must do what you feel is right, my boy, but like Eveleen I wish you'd give the matter a lot more thought before rushing in headlong on a wave of patriotism, praiseworthy though it no doubt is.'

Eveleen's glance went from her father-in-law to her husband, her eyes wide with fear, but for once she bit back the words on the tip of her tongue. Now that she knew Brinsley was on her side, she was sure Richard would listen to his parents, for whilst his mother had not yet voiced an opinion, Eveleen was sure she would discourage Richard's madcap proposal. What mother would gladly wave her only son off to war?

Sophia sat at the opposite end of the table, a serene,

sophisticated woman in her early fifties. Her hair was dressed in an immaculate, smooth chignon and her flawless face showed few signs of ageing. Her figure was slim, kept so by a rigid diet. She ran her household with the same discipline. She was the perfect hostess and the perfect wife and mother of successful businessmen, although she took no part in the life of the factory and, indeed, displayed little interest in the workings of the place that gave her a very comfortable lifestyle. But although Richard's mother was always friendly and kindly disposed towards her, Eveleen felt she was somehow distant, a little aloof perhaps. But surely, Eveleen thought, this time Sophia would intervene. This time she would have some feelings on the matter.

Sophia did, but to Eveleen's amazement they were not what she had imagined or what she had hoped for.

'My dear, Richard must be allowed to decide for himself without influence from any of us.' Her calm glance included Eveleen. 'As he says, the factory can manage very well without him. You are there to oversee everything and Eveleen,' her smile was warm as she included her daughter-in-law, 'if I understand it, has the warehouse running like clockwork.'

Richard smiled and, for a moment, his brown eyes twinkled with their usual mischief. 'What you mean, Mother, is that I am not really needed here at all.'

'I didn't quite say that, dear,' Sophia inclined her head towards him. 'What I should have said, perhaps, is that I admire your courage. It is laudable and I would be so proud to see you in an officer's uniform.'

Unable to hold back any longer, Eveleen sprang to her feet, pushing back her chair with a violent movement so that for a moment it tottered, threatening to crash to the floor.

'Proud to read his name in the lists of casualties? Proud to tend his grave?'

Richard, on the opposite side of the table, rose too. 'Evie, darling, please—'

Now she rounded on him. 'Don't "Evie darling" me. You don't care about me, about any of us, if you insist on this crazy notion.' Her voice softened a little as she turned to look down the table towards Brinsley. 'I know I've disappointed you not being able to present you with a grandson, an heir for you, but—'

'Eveleen . . .' Suddenly Richard's tone was firm. 'This is hardly the time or the place.'

'But,' Eveleen continued, disregarding his rebuke. 'I'm hardly going to have the chance now, if he gets himself killed, am I?'

Brinsley looked up at her, his dark eyes filled with the same sadness and hopelessness that she knew were mirrored in her own. They stared at each other for a long moment, so much of what had happened between their families surfacing in both their minds. They shared secrets from the past, in which, though fully aware of them, neither Richard nor his mother were involved. For a brief moment, it was as if Brinsley and Eveleen were alone together in the room, the other two forgotten.

Poignantly, Eveleen said softly, 'I won't have any more chances.'

Brinsley knew all about lost chances.

But now Sophia spoke, dragging them back to the present drama and pushing their unhappy memories into the background. The present was every bit as bleak as the distant past had been.

'My dears, Richard will be an officer. He won't be where the danger is. You'll see,' Sophia said, standing up and bringing the conversation, as far as she wished to be concerned in it, to a close. 'He'll make us all so proud of him, I know he will.' She moved down the table and kissed Richard's cheek fondly, before turning and making her way to the door out of the dining room. 'Besides,' she added, waving her hand airily, 'they say it's not going to last for long. He'll be home by Christmas.'

As the door closed behind her, the three people left in the room regarded each other gravely.

Sixteen

The four people at Pear Tree Farm looked at each other with equally solemn faces.

'So you're really set on it, then?' Mary broke the silence at last.

'I'm sorry, but yes, I am,' Andrew said quietly. There was apology in his eyes, but a steadfast determination in his tone. Nothing and no-one could change his mind.

'You don't love me,' Bridie cried passionately and now the tears were coursing down her face. 'Gran said you didn't and she was right.'

'I never said any such thing!'

'What?'

'Bridie, mi duck . . .'

The three of them spoke at once, Mary with indignation, Andrew with confusion and Josh with concern, trying to pour oil on what he could see would be very troubled waters any minute now.

Casting resentful glances at all three of them, Bridie muttered, 'You wouldn't go if you did.'

Andrew reached out and took her hand and even when she tried to pull free he held it firmly. 'You are the most important person in the world to me, you know that.'

She wanted to tell him, wanted to blurt out what her grandmother had said, that he only loved her because she reminded him of the great love of his life, but the words would not come. If he was going away, she could not let them part in anger, with misunderstanding between them. And, even at her tender age, she was mature enough to know that if she told him he would deny it. He would say he loved her for herself. But she realized now that she was no more than a child in his eyes. A dear, beloved child, of that she had no doubt, for whatever reason – but only a child.

Bridie swallowed the bitterness and knew suddenly it was time to behave more like an adult than a silly little girl. She would be thirteen next month.

Time to grow up, Bridie Singleton, she told herself, echoing the very words that her grandmother had said to her so often. And if this war lasted any time at all, things were going to be very different for everyone.

Andrew visited again on the last Sunday in August.

'Now just you be ready next Saturday.'

Impishly Bridie said, 'Next Saturday? Why? What's happening?'

Andrew tweaked her nose. 'Don't tell me you've forgotten it's your thirteenth birthday?'

Bridie could keep up the pretence no longer. She grinned. 'I can't wait,' she confided. 'Gran's shown me how to put my hair up and I've been practising all week.'

Andrew's face softened. 'We'll go into Grantham to have your birthday photograph taken.'

Every year on the Saturday nearest to her birthday Andrew had insisted that she should have her photograph taken in a proper photographer's studio. This year her birthday actually fell on the Saturday. 'And I should like to buy you something really special, especially as . . .' He stopped, cleared his throat and changed the subject, but Bridie guessed that he had been going to say, 'Especially as I shall be going away soon.' Instead, he continued, 'Do you think your gran would let me buy you a smart hat to go with your new hairstyle?'

'You can ask her.' She laughed. 'She's more likely to say "yes" if it's you doing the asking.'

'I will,' Andrew promised.

About mid-afternoon, they heard the sound of Richard's motor car pulling into the yard.

'Andrew.' Eveleen crossed the yard to greet him affectionately. 'It's far too long since we've seen you.' She drew back and studied him. 'You look well . . .' she began and then she saw the look in his eyes, the look that was on the faces of so many men these days. A cross between excited anticipation and dread of the unknown. 'Oh no,' she breathed. 'You're going too, aren't you?'

Mary, hearing her words, said, 'You don't mean to tell me Richard's been daft enough to volunteer an' all?'

Eveleen grimaced. 'Not yet, but he seems set on doing so.'

'But what about the business – the factory?'

Eveleen shrugged. 'He's leaving his father and me to manage everything.'

'Brinsley.' Mary spoke the name softly and, in spite of herself, she smiled. A look of understanding passed between her and Eveleen as Mary moved to her side and asked in a low voice, 'Is he well? How does he look? Have you seen him lately?'

Eveleen took her mother's arm and drew her a little apart from the rest. 'We had lunch at their house last week. He's fine.' She smiled impishly at her mother. 'As handsome as ever. Almost as good looking as his son.'

They bent their heads together, laughing softly. But their laughter soon died as they turned back to the others.

All afternoon the talk was of the war and how it would affect them, so directly now that their menfolk were to be involved.

'Mam, I was wondering. Would you allow Bridie to come to live with me for a while?' Eveleen asked her mother when they were alone in the scullery washing up the tea things. Bridie and Josh were doing the evening milking and Richard and Andrew were sitting by the fire which burned winter and summer, planning their uncertain future. 'I would love to have her. She could be a big help to me if Richard does go.'

Mary looked at her sharply. 'Is this suggestion because you think she's not happy here? Because you think her and me don't get on?'

'No, Mam, it isn't,' Eveleen said, pushing away the thought that deep down there was some truth in Mary's surmise. 'To be honest, I'm dreading Richard going away. I shall miss him so and I'd really be glad of the child's company.'

Mary was silent, plunging her hands deep into the washing-up suds as she pondered. 'Just so long as you remember, Eveleen, that she won't be a child for much longer. She's at that awkward age and it'll get worse before it gets better. I well remember your own "awkward age",' she added pointedly and Eveleen smiled wryly.

'I will look after her, Mam, but I thought she could work in the inspection room. She's a neat little needlewoman.'

'She's good at bobbin lace,' Mary remarked and added pensively, 'it's in the blood, isn't it, from both sides.'

There was silence for a moment until Eveleen asked tentatively, 'Does Andrew ever mention your mam and Uncle Harry?'

Mary emptied the washing-up bowl and dried her hands before she answered. 'I asked him not long ago. I think they're reasonably well in health, but lonely.'

'Do they still live in their own separate cottages?'

'I think so, but I think they both have lodgers who are employed in Harry's workshops, so they're not exactly alone.'

'Just lonely,' Eveleen murmured. Then as an afterthought she asked, 'How old is your mother now, Mam?'

Mary wrinkled her forehead. 'About seventy-five or six, I think. Andrew did say,' she went on, 'that Harry's having trouble with his eyesight.'

'Really? But he can't be that old, surely?'

'He's a couple of years older than me. He'll be fifty-six this year. But that job, sitting squinting at rows and rows of fine knitting all day. It's bad for the eyesight.'

They put away the plates and dishes and when the scullery was tidy Eveleen said, 'Well, what do you think about Bridie, then?'

Mary nodded. 'I'll talk to Josh, but yes, I think we'll have to let her go.' She smiled. 'I'll miss the naughty little tyke, but don't tell her I said so.'

Eveleen said nothing, but she was thinking: If only my mam would do exactly that, would tell the child how much they'll miss her, maybe poor Bridie would not feel so unloved and unwanted. She had no doubt that Josh would voice it, but, coming from her gran, it would mean so much more to Bridie.

*

'Now, which is it to be? The photograph first or lunch in the best place we can find?'

'The photograph,' Bridie decided. 'Can I have it taken in my new hat?'

'Of course you can.' Andrew smiled at her fondly and then added with regret, 'I wish you'd let me buy the whole outfit for you.'

Having gained Mary's permission to buy Bridie a new hat, Andrew had tried to go further. A smart costume, the sort worn by girls of sixteen or so, had caught his eye in the shop. 'Try that on, Bridie.'

Bridie pulled a face. 'I don't think Gran would let me wear that. It's a bit old for me.' In her determination to act in a more grown-up manner, Bridie had decided that the best way to start was by acquiescing to her grandmother's wishes. Perhaps she would even be able to persuade Mary to trust her a little more.

'The young lady's quite right,' the thin-faced, middle-aged shop assistant agreed. She smiled, showing large teeth that dominated her face. She turned to Bridie. 'You have a very generous father, miss, but—'

Bridie frowned. 'He's not my father,' she said swiftly.

The woman tried to purse her lips, though the action was difficult for her over the large teeth. She glanced disapprovingly from one to the other and they could guess the thoughts spinning around her mind.

Andrew looked uncomfortable. 'I'm her godfather,' he said gruffly.

'I see,' the woman said stiffly. She sniffed and went on, 'Well, it's still most unsuitable for a young girl. How old are you, miss?'

'Thirteen today.'

'Quite. I'm sure your mother wouldn't allow you to

wear that sort of costume until you were at least sixteen. Besides, you would need to wear,' she coughed discreetly and added, 'a certain undergarment to show the apparel to its best advantage.'

Bridie grinned mischievously, seizing her chance to embarrass the woman. 'Oh, a corset, you mean.' Then she capitulated with charm. Beside her, she heard Andrew trying to stifle his laughter. 'I'm sure you're right. Perhaps in a year or so's time. But I could, don't you think,' she went on, eager to have the woman on her side now, 'have a nice straw boater?'

The woman nodded, her disapproval melting a little at the prospect of a sale. 'I have just the thing, miss.' She hurried away, returning a moment later with a straw boater decorated with a ribbon. 'If the gentleman agrees, we can supply you with different coloured ribbons so that you can change them to match the colour of your coat or dress or whatever you are wearing. It will still be a most appropriate hat when you are a little older, miss.'

'What a good idea.' Bridie smiled, perching the boater on the top of her head.

'If you'll permit me . . .?' the woman murmured. Gently she moved the hat forwards a little so that it rested against the roll of plaited hair at the back of the girl's head and tilted, almost provocatively, over her forehead. Bridie peeped out mischievously from beneath its brim to see Andrew smiling down at her.

He cleared his throat and his voice was not quite steady as he said, 'You look adorable, Bridie.'

Neither of them noticed the look of disapproval return to the shop assistant's face.

*

Andrew insisted on having several photographs of Bridie, but she could not persuade him to have his taken.

'But I'd like one of you,' she pleaded. 'Won't you have one taken with me? Please?'

But Andrew was adamant. 'No. It wouldn't – look right.'

Bridie pursed her lips, knowing that the woman in the shop had caused this. 'Then what about one on your own? If you really are going to join up, I would so like a photograph.'

'One in your uniform would be nice for the young lady,' the photographer suggested. He was far more tactful than the woman in the shop had been. He smiled understandingly. 'I'm going myself. I got my papers yesterday. I've to report next week. These,' he indicated the camera and the plates he was taking of Bridie, 'will be the last photographs I take.'

Bridie stared at him and then swallowed hard at the poignancy of his words. Huskily she said, 'Until it's all over and you come back.'

The young man looked at her gratefully, but then shrugged. 'I hope you're right, miss, but who knows, eh?' He cleared his throat and added more briskly, 'There'll be a chance for you to get your photograph taken, sir, when you've got your uniform.' He grinned now. 'My mam won't let me go unless I promise to send her one.'

Bridie held Andrew's gaze. 'Will you promise to get one done and send it to me?'

Slowly Andrew nodded.

Seventeen

Shortly after her birthday, Bridie came to live with Eveleen in Nottingham. They all knew that very soon both Richard and Andrew would volunteer. They could not be dissuaded by anyone.

The Prime Minister, Herbert Asquith, had called for another half million men to sign up for the army. Recruiting posters, with Lord Kitchener pointing his finger outwards and exhorting Britons to 'Join Your Country's Army!', were appearing everywhere. And now, the papers said, almost as many men were joining the army in a day as were normally recruited in a year.

For the moment, the news from across the Channel was hopeful. In the first decisive battle on the Western Front, the Allies had driven the enemy back and removed the threat to Paris. British losses had been heavy, but one of the generals had remarked that they had not been 'excessive in view of the magnitude of the great fight'.

Eveleen almost ripped the newspaper to shreds when she read it. To her mind, even one casualty was one too many. As she was about to throw down the paper in disgust another item caught her attention and she picked it up again.

'First Shots Are Fired in War at Sea' the headlines screamed at her. Her hand flew to her mouth and she found she was holding her breath as she read on. Enemy submarines had sunk three British cruisers off the Netherlands. Hundreds had survived and had been picked up by another cruiser, only to be torpedoed again and cast back into the sea.

'Oh, Jimmy,' Eveleen whispered. 'I hope you're safe. God keep you safe too.' She closed her eyes and sent up a silent entreaty that her mother had not seen the newspaper. Even if they rarely heard from him, and despite what had happened in the past, Eveleen still cared about her brother and she knew that he was never far from her mother's thoughts. But she realized that the odds were stacked heavily against every one of the menfolk in her life coming safely home and the thought was like the cold hand of death clutching her heart.

Bridie said her goodbyes to Micky and his family, to her gran and to Josh, who had hugged her tightly.

'Don't forget, mi duck, we're always here for you. This is your home and always will be.'

Mary gave her a list of commandments, almost like Moses with his tablets of stone, Bridie thought impishly, trying to keep a straight face.

'Now don't you be getting into bad company. And don't go getting involved with soldiers. They'll be all over the city. You look a lot older than you are and you'll be attractive to the wrong sort of feller. Specially when they're going to war and not knowing if they're going to come back. They'll say all sorts of things to make you – well – do things you shouldn't.'

Bridie resisted the temptation to ask innocently: What things, Gran? She knew that Mary would see through her. Bridie hadn't grown up on a farm without understanding the facts of life from an early age. Instead she said meekly, 'Yes, Gran.'

The blackbird in the loft was long gone and the

injured rabbit had been released back into the wild some weeks earlier. Now there was nothing to keep her at Pear Tree Farm and, despite her gnawing fear over Andrew – and Richard and all the others who were planning to go – she was thrilled that her aunt wanted her.

Over the next few weeks Eveleen and Bridie found themselves so busy that they scarcely had time to mope. Eveleen was becoming more involved with the running of the factory, as well as overseeing the warehouse. Each morning she and her father-in-law met to discuss the immediate future of Reckitt and Stokes, but Richard refused to join them.

'Won't you help us, Richard?' Eveleen begged. 'We need to know what you want us to do.'

'I don't know what's going to happen over the next few months, years even. I'm not going to be here . . .'

Eveleen gasped in alarm. 'Oh, don't say that.'

Richard shrugged. 'My darling, none of us know how long this war is going to last. We have to face facts. Besides, I have things to see to before I enlist. I have to see our solicitor . . .' His voice trailed away and he said no more, but Eveleen shuddered inwardly. She guessed he intended to make a will. To her, it felt as if he was tempting fate.

'You know,' Brinsley Stokes said at their first meeting, 'we're going to have to train women to take the place of some of the men in the factory.' He glanced sideways at her, his smile teasing her gently.

Eveleen laughed, knowing he was remembering the time she had dressed up as a boy to take her brother's place alongside Luke Manning.

'Well,' she said coyly, feeling suddenly more light-hearted. Plunging herself into work and all its present problems gave her less time to think and consequently less time to worry herself sick. 'I think it's been proved that it's possible for a woman to work in the machine shop.'

They laughed together, remembering.

'They won't be able to become fully fledged twist-hands. You do know that, don't you? Some of the work required would be far too demanding physically. It's very heavy. But women could certainly do all sorts of jobs that assist the twisthands. Winding bobbins, threading and stripping.'

'What's stripping?'

'It's the last twenty yards on a bobbin that can't be used. It has to be stripped off by hand.'

'Oh, I remember now. Yes, Luke used to have me doing that.'

'We'll need to talk to the men who are left first. What I suggest is that we put a young woman with each of the old hands – the ones who aren't likely to volunteer or even to be conscripted, if it should come to that.'

Already, Eveleen thought with an inward sigh, another reminder. The war could never be far away from any of their thoughts.

Brinsley was continuing. 'I say "young women" because I think they'll be quicker to learn than the older ones, although, of course,' he wrinkled his brow, 'younger women may have more in the way of family commitments. What do you think, Eveleen?'

She thought a moment before saying carefully, 'If we pick single women first, then the young married women who have no children. If their husbands have gone to the Front, they're – they're not likely to have children now, are they?' There was a catch in her voice. Her statement so poignantly applied to herself.

Brinsley glanced at her and then his gaze dropped away. 'No, my dear,' he said softly and she knew he understood her feelings.

Eveleen continued determinedly. 'There are one or two I could recommend to you immediately from the inspection room and we could recruit young girls just out of school to take their place. I'll go and see Win Martin. She'll probably know of some.'

Brinsley nodded. 'How's young Bridie shaping up?'

Eveleen smiled. 'She loves it. She's the youngest there and of course all the women are making a huge fuss of her.'

'Good, good.' Brinsley stood up. 'Now we'll take a walk through the machine shop and see what gaps all this volunteering is going to leave us. There are several all planning to enlist along with Richard. By doing so they all hope to stay together. Did you know?'

Eveleen, unable to speak for the lump in her throat, merely nodded.

'We need to talk to Bob Porter about our plans to bring women into the factory,' Brinsley shouted above the noise as they were walking together down the aisles between the rows of machines. Every so often a machine stood idle, its operator already gone to war. As they moved into the office overlooking the machine shop, Eveleen said, 'He'll not like it. He's one of the old school. He'll say it'll cause more trouble than it's worth.' She smiled wryly. 'I could wish it was Josh still in charge at this moment. Bob Porter's not an easy man at the best of times.'

Brinsley helped himself to Bob Porter's chair and sighed as he sat down. 'I know. But we've got to try at least. Go and find him, my dear, would you?'

Eveleen half-turned and then glanced back at her father-in-law. 'Are you all right? You look very tired.'

Brinsley passed a weary hand across his forehead. He looked suddenly much older than his fifty-five years. 'I'm not sleeping too well,' he admitted. 'I'd begun to take it easy, to hand over the reins, as it were, to Richard, but now . . .'

He left the sentence unfinished, but Eveleen understood. He was going to have to work far harder than he had done in recent years and, coupled with the worry over his son and indeed his concern for all the young men he had employed who were now volunteering, the extra burden would take its toll.

Eveleen knew just how he felt. Already she was experiencing sleepless nights and extra responsibility was being thrust upon her too. But she was young and fit and determined to cope. Besides, by throwing herself into work she could put aside, even if only for a few hours, her anxiety over Richard.

A rush of affection for Brinsley, who had been involved with her family even before she was born, made her move to his side and offer, 'Will you let me take some of the weight off your shoulders? I mean, if women are coming into the factory, then maybe it would be better if Bob Porter and I worked together more.'

Brinsley shook his head and sighed. 'You're a sweet girl to offer, but you're doing enough already. It wouldn't be fair to expect you to do any more. You still have to cope with overseeing the warehouse and all the homeworkers.'

Eveleen sat down opposite him and leant on the desk. 'But I have Helen at the warehouse. She's more than capable of taking on more responsibility there. And I've already asked Win Martin to do the same. You see . . .'

She hesitated to reveal what was a very private matter between Richard and herself, but now she would have to do so. She took a deep breath and went on. 'You see, before this war started I'd been planning to do a lot less myself.' She looked him straight in the eyes now as she said softly, 'You must know how desperately I want to give Richard a son.'

Brinsley nodded.

'Well, we wondered if I was doing too much and that was – well . . .' she stammered to a halt. It was not the sort of thing that was talked about in polite circles and certainly not between a young woman and her father-in-law. But Brinsley came to her rescue. He smiled sadly and said, 'And you were planning to take life a little easier and see what happened, eh?'

Eveleen nodded and sudden tears filled her eyes. 'But now he's going away.' Then she brushed such a show of weakness aside impatiently and added firmly, 'I shall *need* to work. Harder than ever.'

Brinsley nodded slowly and said heavily, 'Maybe I do too. It gives you too much time to think if you're not busy, doesn't it.'

Eveleen nodded, then added, 'But you mustn't do so much that you become ill.'

'Nor you, my dear.'

She smiled again and said, accentuating the Lincolnshire dialect she had never quite lost, said, 'Oh, I'm tough as owd boots, mester.'

They regarded each other across the table, understanding one another's feelings implicitly.

'We'll work at it together then, Eveleen. It's what I'd like more than anything.'

'That's settled then,' Eveleen said as she rose. 'Now

I'll go and find Bob Porter.' She pulled a wry expression. 'I think he's going to take more persuading than anyone.'

'I ain't 'aving troublesome women in my machine shop and that's final.' Bob Porter was adamant. 'It's not that I've anything against women. They're all right. In their place. But that's not in a factory.'

'But, Bob, we've lost several men already and more are going each day.' Brinsley spread his hands with a gesture of inevitability. 'How do you think we're going to run the factory without using women?'

'There's young lads we can get and older men. Women's all right in the warehouse, I grant you. And working at home.' Bob jabbed his forefinger at the floor. 'But not here.'

Brinsley and Eveleen exchanged a look before he got to his feet. Drawing himself to his full height, he said with authority, 'Well, I'm sorry, Bob, but that's the way it's going to have to be. Now, Mrs Stokes will work with you. In fact, she will be responsible for the women workers, if that's how you feel.'

Bob Porter's face was like thunder and Eveleen sighed inwardly. Tight-lipped, Bob said, 'Whatever you say, sir.' He turned on his heel and marched out of the office.

'Oh dear,' Brinsley said with a thin smile. 'I think we've upset him.'

Despite her qualms, Eveleen forced herself to say brightly, 'Don't worry. I'll handle him.'

With a chuckle that chased away some of the anxiety from his face, Brinsley said, 'I don't doubt it for a minute, my dear.'

*

When Brinsley had left for the day, Eveleen faced Bob Porter in his office. 'Now, Bob, let's sit down and talk this matter out calmly.'

His head thrust forward belligerently and malevolence sparked in his eyes. 'Ain't nothing to talk about, missis. The boss has given me 'is orders and that's it.'

'No, Bob, it isn't. You're a very important part of the running of this factory. You know that. We're not trying to antagonize you or usurp your authority. It's just . . .' she sighed and for a moment her shoulders sagged. 'Oh, Bob, it's all sorts of things.'

The man stared at her. 'I don't understand.'

'Sit down, Bob, and let's talk. Please.'

The man made to sit in the visitor's chair in his office, but Eveleen gestured to the chair behind his desk where Brinsley had sat, the chair that was rightly Bob Porter's. 'No, no. This is your office, Bob. Not mine.'

The man gave an ungracious grunt, though he sat down in the chair. 'I thought you was tekin' over.'

Eveleen stood in front of the desk, looking down on him. She had invited him to sit down deliberately, but she remained standing. It gave her a feeling of advantage. 'We seem to have got off to a bad start.'

'Ain't no good start as far as I'm concerned, if you're bringing women in here.' He nodded through the glass partition separating his small office from the machine shop, a mournful look on his face as if all that he held most dear was about to be swept away.

'What is it you have against women, Bob?'

'Nowt. Just that to me a woman's place is in the home, looking after her family. Mebbe doing a bit of drawing at home. And it's all right young unmarried lasses working in the warehouse, I suppose, but . . .'

Eveleen's patience was being severely tested and

before she could prevent herself, she had snapped, 'Oh, very magnanimous of you.'

Bob, a stocky, balding man, leapt to his feet with surprising agility. 'Don't you play the high 'n mighty with me, missis. I remember where you came from. Off the streets.' His tone implied much more than that Eveleen and her family had once been homeless. 'And if it hadn't been for Mr Richard marrying you,' he wagged a grimy forefinger in her face, 'you'd still 'ave been there.'

Eveleen, her eyes flashing with anger, glared at him, their faces only inches apart, so close that she could feel the waft of his stale breath. 'But he did marry me,' she said pointedly. 'And right now it's me who could have you put out on the street.'

She drew back and willed herself to calmness, but her tone was icy as she said, 'Now, Bob, you have two choices. You can either work with me on this or you can leave right now.'

'Oh aye, reckon you could run this factory single-handed, do you?'

'No,' she said levelly, knowing that for the moment she had the upper hand. 'But there are plenty of men out there,' she waved her hand through the office window, 'who've worked here long enough and could take over your job tomorrow without batting an eyelid.'

A look of doubt crossed the man's face. 'Think so? It's not as easy as it looks.' His words were defiant, but she could see that his confidence was shaken. One word from Eveleen to her father-in-law and the factory manager knew he could be out on his ear. And without the words needing to be spoken, Bob knew that the man who had once held his position was now Eveleen's stepfather. No doubt Bob would think that Eveleen only had to ask and Josh Carpenter would come to her aid.

He was not a man to cave in too quickly, but she knew she had rattled his confidence. Defiant to the last, Bob said, 'Mebbe it's time I picked up mi scissors and hook and walked down the road, eh?'

'And where exactly would you walk to, Bob? You know as well as I do that all the factories are facing the same difficulties as we are.'

'Mebbe, but they aren't bringing women in,' he said scathingly.

'I think you'll find,' Eveleen said quietly, 'that, in time, they'll do just that. They'll have to if they want to survive.'

There was a long silence between them until at last Bob sat down in his chair again, leant back and linked his fingers across the paunch that drinking five pints every night in the pub on the corner of his street had caused. 'So,' he said sarcastically, 'what's this grand plan then?'

Eighteen

Bridie didn't think she had ever been so happy in her life. At least that would have been the case but for the ever-present worry over the war and all its consequences.

On her first morning Eveleen had taken her up to the inspection room on the top floor of the warehouse building and left her in Helen's care.

'You must remember to call her Miss Binkley when you're at work,' Eveleen had warned her. 'Not Auntie Helen.'

Bridie had nodded, speechless with excitement. Her hair was plaited, as always, but now it was wound around her crown and pinned in position. Her aunt had also bought a plain white blouse and a long black skirt for her to wear for work. Gone, now, was the frilled white smock of childhood. As they entered the workroom, Bridie could see that all the girls and women were similarly dressed. Only Helen, as the supervisor, wore a smart, close-fitting plum-coloured costume with a white, ruffle-necked silk blouse beneath it.

When Eveleen left, Helen said, 'Now, I'll put you with Mrs Hyde. She looks after all the newcomers.'

The woman was large and rotund, her grey hair scraped into a bun at the nape of her neck. But her round, florid face beamed a welcome. 'Come and sit by me. We'll soon show yer what's what.'

In spite of her nervousness at facing a roomful of chattering women, all of whom were eyeing her curiously, Bridie smiled. Mrs Hyde's way of talking was just like Josh's and immediately Bridie warmed to her.

It was not long before she had heard Mrs Hyde's life history. 'I've got seven kids and they're all terrors, the lot of 'em. But I wouldn't be without 'em for the world.'

'How old are they?' Bridie was wide-eyed and envious of a large family with brothers and sisters.

'Mi eldest daughter, Janie, she's eighteen. That's 'er over there. And next to her is Kathleen. She's seventeen. Then there's Bertie, sixteen. Joyce is fourteen. She's over there.' The woman twisted slightly in her seat and jabbed her sewing needle in the air towards a thin, mousy-haired girl stooping over her work. Mrs Hyde leant towards Bridie and lowered her voice. 'She's not ever so strong, bless her. Had scarlet fever as a bairn and 'as never been right since. Still, she's a good little worker and Mrs Stokes and Miss Binkley are very understanding if she has to 'ave a day off now and then. Then Christopher's nearly twelve, Lillian's ten and Connie's eight. They're still at school, o' course, but Christopher's going to start in the factory when he leaves.'

'How lucky they all are, to be part of such a lovely, big family.'

'You got brothers and sisters?' the kindly woman asked.

Bridie shook her head. 'No, there's only me. Me mam died having me.'

'Aw, that's a shame, luvvie.'

About her father, Bridie volunteered nothing.

*

At the end of September Richard and Andrew volunteered together with three more young men from Singleton's Yard in Flawford and seven volunteers from the Reckitt and Stokes's factory, one of whom was Leslie Holmes, Helen's young man.

'We've all enlisted in the Sherwood Foresters and we have to report to Newark next Friday,' Richard told Eveleen when he returned home. 'We'll be in the same regiment, even the same company, I think. Don't worry, I'll look after them all.'

'But who's going to look after you?'

'We'll watch out for each other,' he tried to reassure her, but she was not so easily convinced. 'We won't be going to France for ages yet. We'll have all sorts of training – a lot of drill, I expect – and all sorts of courses to go on.' He tickled her chin with his forefinger. 'Let's make the most of this last week. We'll all have a lovely day at the Goose Fair on Thursday, the day before we leave.'

Eveleen smiled thinly. Only a week and he would be gone.

On the Wednesday evening Richard, Eveleen and even Bridie and Andrew were invited to dinner at the home of Richard's parents. The atmosphere was strained. Andrew was uncomfortable in his best suit and starched collar and Bridie was nervous at being in such grand surroundings as the Stokes's elegant home. She dropped her knife on the floor and, when she bent to pick it up, her head collided with the manservant's, who had also bent down to retrieve it for her. Bridie was scarlet with embarrassment, even though Richard smiled at her understandingly.

'I don't know why you have to join the ranks, Richard,' Sophia was saying, angry and disappointed that she would not be able to boast to her elegant friends. 'You'd be so much safer as an officer too apart from, well . . .' She paused, realizing that her comments were a little out of place in the present company. Bridie, forgetting her own discomfort, glanced across the table at Andrew. But he sat silently, his eyes downcast, and she knew he was feeling every bit as awkward and out of place as she was. The thought comforted her. She glanced to the end of the table towards their hostess, admiring the elegant, sophisticated Sophia Stokes. She is very beautiful but she's cold, the girl thought with an astuteness beyond her years. Mr Brinsley's nice – he's like Uncle Richard – but she's only bothered about whether or not her son is going to be an officer.

In answer to his mother's remark, Richard only smiled. 'I'd much rather be with friends, Mother.'

At the end of the meal, as they moved from the dining room to the drawing room, the gentlemen accompanying the ladies instead of staying at the table to smoke and drink port, Andrew drew Eveleen to one side. 'I have something to ask you,' he said quietly.

'Of course I'll look after Bridie,' Eveleen said at once. 'You don't need to ask.'

He smiled, though his eyes were troubled with a hint of the apprehension that all those who had volunteered must be feeling. 'I know you will. It wasn't that. Eveleen, when I filled in the papers, I put you as my next of kin. I hope you don't mind?'

'Of course, I don't mind, but isn't there anyone else?'

Andrew shook his head. 'I have no family and I didn't want to put Mr Singleton's name. I – I'm not sure he would let you know – let Bridie know – if anything happened to me.'

Eveleen clutched at his arm. 'Nothing's going to

happen to you. To any of you.' She sounded so determined that Andrew could almost believe that the very strength of her will would make it so. 'It'll all be over in a few weeks and you'll be home again.'

There was a silence between them for a moment before he went on, 'And I've arranged for part of my pay – and that . . .' She wasn't sure what the 'and that' meant, but she said nothing. 'To come to you. Will you see that Bridie gets it? Put it in a bank account or something for when she comes of age.'

'Oh, Andrew,' Eveleen said unsteadily. He seemed to have thought of everything. But, even yet, he hadn't finished. And again he was thinking of others before himself. 'One thing more – and this is the most difficult to ask.' He bit his lip, as if still uncertain whether to make this particular request.

'Go on,' Eveleen prompted gently.

'Could you – will you – go to Flawford now and then to see that they're all right there?' He squeezed her hand tightly, emphasizing the need for his request – a request he knew would cause Eveleen a great deal of soul-searching and courage. He rushed on. 'I don't know what's going to happen there once I've gone.'

She forbore, at this final moment, to say in harsh accusation: Then why are you going? Instead she said huskily, 'Of course I will. I'll make sure they're all right.'

As the evening ended, much to the relief of both Bridie and Andrew, Richard said, 'So, are we all going to the Goose Fair tomorrow?'

'Oh, my dear,' Sophia said languidly, 'count me out. I can't bear all those crowds. Your father has promised to take me to Derby to see an old friend. Her son left for the Front last week. He's been in the army for several years. He's a regular.' She paused and added pointedly, 'Of course, he's an officer.'

Richard turned to Andrew. 'So, it's just the four of us, is it? You'll come, won't you, Andrew?'

Andrew shook his head apologetically, but before he could speak Bridie burst out, 'Oh Andrew, I've never been to the Goose Fair. You must come.'

'Bridie, love, I'd like nothing better. Believe me. But I must go home to see how things are. There's so many of us gone from what is only a small workshop anyway that . . .'

'You care more about them and your work than you do about me,' Bridie burst out petulantly. She was suddenly the little girl again.

Andrew regarded her helplessly. 'That's not true, but I just have to go home.'

'Can't you go the day after?'

Andrew shook his head sorrowfully. 'We leave at midday on Friday. There wouldn't be time. I'm sorry, Bridie.'

'What about you, Evie? You'll come with us, won't you?' Richard asked.

Eveleen glanced helplessly between her husband and her father-in-law. 'I – I don't think I can. I shall have to stay at the factory. One of us ought to be there. There'll be so many leaving the next day and so much to see to. I'm sorry, Richard.'

The first three girls brought in as auxiliary workers to help the twisthands had started that morning and Eveleen dared not leave them to the tender mercies of a very disgruntled Bob Porter. The reaction of the other male workers had been mixed.

'Mek a nice change, I reckon, seeing pretty lasses

about the place instead of your ugly mug,' Jake Morrison chafed a workmate. But when the girls had arrived dressed in long overalls and their hair tucked out of sight beneath a frilled cap, his face had fallen.

'Well, they do look a sight,' he had sniffed and turned back to his own machine.

'They've got to be sensibly dressed,' Luke Manning had pointed out. 'We can't have their hair or part of their dress getting caught in the machinery, can we?' He had walked over to where the three young women were standing with Eveleen. 'I'll tek one of 'em, Eveleen.'

Years before, Luke had been the one to try to train Jimmy and, unknowingly at the time, also Eveleen. He had never seen the need to change his attitude towards her just because she had married Richard Stokes.

Eveleen smiled at him. 'Thank you, Luke. What about the other two?' she asked. 'Who do you suggest for them?'

Luke glanced about him. 'Arthur for one, and Jake for the other.'

Eveleen frowned. 'Arthur, I agree, but I'm not sure about Jake.' It had been Jake who had raised a protest at the start of the war, suggesting that Richard's motives were less than altruistic.

Luke laughed. 'He's a bit of a loudmouth, but he's all right. And I'll keep me eye on the lasses.'

'Thanks, Luke,' Eveleen said, thankful to have at least one of the old hands on her side. Luke would be like a father to them, but even so Eveleen had wanted to be on hand whilst the new arrivals settled in.

'I'm really sorry, Richard,' she said again.

Richard regarded her gravely, 'So am I, Eveleen. So am I.'

Nineteen

'So, Bridie, it's just you and me, is it?'

Bridie nodded. 'Andrew can't come. He – he has to go home to see how things are at Flawford.'

Richard raised his left eyebrow sardonically. 'Seems they're smitten with the same bug.'

'Pardon?' Bridie was puzzled.

'Work's more important to them. Never mind, my dear. We'll have a lovely day. Just the two of us. How about it?' Bridie nodded and giggled as he crooked his arm with a gesture of gallantry. 'Your escort awaits, m'lady.'

They walked along, Richard shortening his long stride to match Bridie's steps. He was wearing, not his uniform as she had hoped, but a grey worsted suit, gloves and a trilby hat with a black band. He wore grey spats over black leather shoes and he carried a cane.

'You look awfully smart, Uncle Richard.'

He glanced down at her, his eyes wrinkling as he smiled. 'So do you. I like the boater.' Bridie was wearing the straw hat that Andrew had bought her, today trimmed with red, white and blue ribbons to show her patriotism.

'Why's it called the Goose Fair?' she asked.

As they walked, joining the throng all heading towards Market Place, Richard explained. 'Nottingham

Goose Fair has been famous for centuries. There's not much you can't buy there – even a wife!'

'A wife?' Bridie looked up at him.

'Not now, of course,' Richard chuckled. 'But they say that in the old days men used to auction their wives. I always thought it a bit dubious anyway. I mean, if a man had a good wife, why would he want to sell her?'

'I read a book about a man selling his wife to a sailor. He was drunk at the time, I think.'

'I expect most of them were. Farmers from neighbouring counties and even beyond used to walk here, driving their geese and covering about ten miles a day.'

'You mean the geese had to walk?' Bridie, tender-hearted as ever, asked. When Richard nodded, she murmured, 'Poor things.'

'They used to fatten them up in the cornfields after harvest.'

Bridie nodded. Even now, back home on the Dunsmore estate, geese were allowed on the stubble left in the fields after harvest. She laughed. 'They're like gleaners.'

'That's right,' Richard agreed and went on, 'but to prepare them for their long walk, the farmers would drive them over alternate patches of wet tar and sand to give them a sort of sole for their webbed feet.'

'How clever. So that's how the fair got its name?'

'Something like that. And, of course, it's very famous for cheese too, but there's a livestock market and a horse fair. They come from miles away. Some of the horses are wild and unbroken. And there's every kind of thing you can think of on sale.' He glanced down at her. 'I hope you've brought your purse.'

Bridie shook her head and grinned. 'It wasn't worth bringing, Uncle Richard. There's not much in it.'

'Don't tell me your aunt isn't paying you much?' he said, pretending to be scandalized.

Bridie laughed. 'I get what the other workers of my age get, but before I came here I didn't get much from Gran. I had to work for me keep, she said.'

'Did she indeed?' she heard Richard murmur, but then her attention was taken by the scene unfolding before her eyes.

They were nearing Market Place and already they could hear the sound of music from fairground organs. All around them, people seemed to quicken their pace, eager to be caught up in the excitement.

Forgetting, for a brief moment, her intention to be more grown-up and ladylike, Bridie gave a little skip and pulled on Richard's arm. 'Come on,' she urged. Together they were caught up in the flow of humanity moving towards the fun.

Bridie could not remember ever in her life enjoying herself quite so much. For a few hours they both forgot about the war. All around them, it seemed as if everyone was determined to do the same. Laughter and chatter filled the air, squeals of delicious fear from girls on the roundabouts and swings and the raucous shouts from young men who, already, had imbibed a little too freely.

'Now, what do you want to see next?' Richard asked.

'Everything!' Bridie flung her arms wide as if trying to embrace it all.

Richard smiled indulgently. 'Right then. We'll start with the menagerie. I know how you love animals.'

They made their way to the area always reserved for the largest menagerie. There were rows of large wagons. One side of each wagon was enclosed with iron bars, over which shutters were fastened when travelling. Now they were open for the public to view the animals. Lions and tigers, sea lions and seals and a very clever chimpanzee that kept the crowd enthralled with his antics.

On a patch of grass an elephant and two camels were giving rides to small children, but Bridie shook her head when Richard offered to pay for her. 'No, I'd sooner watch.' But when a man invited her to nurse a tiny, baby monkey, Bridie held out her hands eagerly. The little creature clung to her and when she tried to give it back it grabbed at the ribbons on her hat, threatening to pull it from her head. Laughing, she gently disentangled herself.

'You'm got a way with 'im, missy,' the man said. 'Like to keep 'im, would you?'

'I'd love to,' she said, 'but it's not possible. Besides . . .' She looked at the man shrewdly. 'Isn't he too young to leave his mother?'

'Ain't got no muvver,' the man said. 'Reared by hand, this little 'un.'

'Well,' Bridie said firmly, handing back the baby monkey. 'I think he needs a little more rearing before you sell him.'

They had not moved more than a few paces before Bridie saw the man offering the tiny creature to another couple with a young boy.

Bridie turned and, dodging through the throng, hurried back towards the man, ignoring Richard's warning. 'Bridie, leave it, love . . .'

'You can't sell him yet.' Bridie faced the man hotly. 'He's too young. It's cruel.'

'Now look 'ere, miss . . .' The man's weather-beaten face was suddenly fearsome. 'Don't meddle in matters you know nowt about.'

'But I do know. I live on a farm. I know when an animal is big enough to be weaned.'

'Clever little bugger, ain't yer?' the man sneered.

'That's enough.' Richard's quiet but authoritative voice spoke behind her. 'The girl's right. You shouldn't be trying to sell it yet.'

'He's older 'n he looks. Small breed, they are.' The man was trying to bluster his way out of trouble now.

'I'll pay you not to sell him . . .' Bridie began, but Richard touched her arm and bent to whisper in her ear. 'It wouldn't do any good, love. He'd only sell him again once our backs are turned.'

Looking at the rough clothes and the greedy eyes of the owner, Bridie could believe it.

'Can I have him, Dad?' The young boy beside them now had the monkey on his shoulder and was stroking it gently, the monkey clutching his finger, its bright, beady eyes round and large in its tiny face.

'Well, I don't know, son. What do you reckon, Martha?' The man turned to his wife, who, much to Bridie's surprised relief, smiled. 'If the man tells us how to look after him. Like this lass 'ere ses, he does look ever so little.' She turned to Bridie, 'But we'd look after him. I can promise you that. I had a monkey when I was a bairn, so I know a bit about them.'

Bridie smiled and nodded, but would not leave until she had witnessed the transaction taking place and the monkey borne away by the delighted boy.

Richard put his arm about her shoulders. 'Come, I think I'd better get you away from these animals before you want to buy them all.' But he was laughing as he said it.

Bridie slipped her hand through his arm again. 'Sorry, Uncle Richard. I know I get carried away when I think an animal's not being treated properly.'

Richard squeezed her hand to his side. 'Don't apologize,

Bridie love. If there were more people with your caring ways, the world would be a better place.'

His words brought a flush to her cheeks and a warm glow to her heart.

'Now,' Richard went on. 'First of all, I'll buy you a toffee apple. I used to love those when I was your age.'

To Bridie's amazement, Richard bought two and they walked around, licking and biting the toffee until they came to the tang of the apple beneath the sweet coating.

'You look so funny,' she laughed. 'Eating a toffee apple dressed in your posh clothes.'

Richard grinned down at her. 'Today, Bridie, I don't care. My mother's not here to scold.'

Bridie smiled impishly. 'Nor's my gran.'

'Come on . . .' He grabbed her hand and almost pulled her along in his eagerness. 'Let's go on the gallopers.'

They rode side by side on the brightly painted horses. Up and down and round and round until Bridie felt dizzy. But she loved it, laughing out loud as she held onto her hat.

'Now we'll go on the gondolas,' Richard said as they climbed down unsteadily from the roundabout. 'You'll think you're in Venice.'

After that, they stood for a moment, looking about them. They heard the raucous shouts of a showman outside a boxing booth.

'I think we'll give that a miss, if you don't mind, Bridie. I don't particularly want to see two men fighting. Not today.'

Bridie shuddered inwardly, understanding at once. Very soon Richard would be fighting in earnest. This day was for enjoyment, for revisiting childhood. Today he didn't want to be reminded of the battles to come.

Instead, Richard tried to win a coconut for her but,

despite three attempts, he could not knock one from its stand. 'I never was very good at it,' he apologized. 'It seems I'm still not.'

'Never mind, Uncle Richard.' Bridie tucked her hand in his arm and led him towards the ornate frontage of the bioscope with its gold-painted pillars and archways. 'Can we go in here? I've never seen moving pictures.'

They stepped into the darkness of the huge tent and took their places in the rows of seating facing the white screen. When the show began there were gasps of surprise from the audience. Bridie was enthralled by the flickering images, her gaze fixed on the screen, but she was aware that from time to time Richard glanced at her as if he was enjoying watching her pleasure as much as the show itself.

At the end, they emerged from the darkness and blinked as they looked about them. The light was already fading as the day drew towards night. Market Place was still busy, but now the majority of the people were youngsters, out to enjoy the evening. Young men waved tickling sticks, targeting the pretty girls. Bolder ones stole kisses, vying with their friends to be the one to kiss the most girls. And the girls, giggling together, threw confetti at each other and then at the boys to capture their attention.

Bridie watched them, wishing she were older and able to join in the fun.

'I think it's time we went home,' Richard said, though she could hear the reluctance in his tone too. 'Your aunt will be waiting dinner for us.'

Only one incident marred a perfect day.

As they were leaving, a woman was walking amongst the crowd handing out white feathers to any young man not dressed in uniform.

She approached Richard and, standing before him, her glance raked him up and down. Her lip curled disdainfully and she held out a white feather. 'You may be a little older than some of them here.' She spoke in modulated tones and Bridie noticed she was well dressed. 'But you're young enough.'

Richard's only answer was to raise his hat politely and give a little bow. Then he turned and walked away, leaving the woman staring after him, the feather still in her gloved hand. Bridie scurried to catch up with him.

'What was all that about? What is she doing handing out feathers?'

'A white feather, Bridie,' Richard said tightly, 'is a symbol presented to a man deemed a coward. She is suggesting that any man who has not taken the King's shilling is such a person.'

He was walking so quickly now, marching along angrily, that Bridie had to run to keep up with him. 'I don't understand. How can she possibly think . . .?'

Richard stopped abruptly and turned to face her. 'It wouldn't have happened if I'd been in uniform. Women like her are taking it upon themselves to present white feathers to anyone they think is young enough to volunteer.'

'But you have.'

'She doesn't know that.'

'Then I'll make sure she does,' Bridie said promptly and turned at once to hurry back to the woman.

Richard caught her arm, the anger gone from his tone now. 'No, leave it, love. It doesn't matter.'

'Of course it matters,' Bridie retorted hotly. 'I won't have anyone thinking you a coward, Uncle Richard, because you're not.'

'Oh, my lovely Bridie.' He laughed. 'I think I should

take you with me to the Front. You'd have the enemy routed in no time.' Then, more seriously, he said, 'No, leave it, my dear. It really doesn't matter. She's not important. And one more thing, Bridie.'

She looked up at him.

'Please, don't tell anyone else about this. Promise.'

'All right then, but I wish you'd let me set her right.' Bridie cast a frown back through the crowd to where she could still see the woman handing out the insulting feathers, then, reluctantly, she followed her uncle.

Twenty

'Darling, I'm so sorry I couldn't get away to come with you today,' Eveleen apologized as the three of them sat down to a late dinner. She had not arrived home until gone seven that evening.

'It's quite all right,' Richard said tersely, but his tone told her that it was anything but all right. 'What was so important to keep you at work until this time?'

Briefly Eveleen explained about her problems with Bob Porter. 'And I'm worried about your father. I know he's not old, but suddenly he seems very weary.'

Richard glanced at her in concern, his earlier chagrin forgotten. 'Is he ill? Ought he to see a doctor?'

'I don't know. Surely your mother would persuade him to do that.'

Richard glanced at her out of the corner of his eyes. Drily he said, 'I doubt my mother would notice anything was wrong unless he collapsed in front of her and interrupted one of her social gatherings.'

Eveleen gasped. 'Richard! That's the first time I've ever heard you criticize your mother.'

Richard shrugged and then his tone softened. 'I've always admired my mother. I still do. There have been certain things in my father's life before he met her, as you well know, that she has been very understanding about. I thought, at the time, that understanding came from a loving nature. But since I've known you . . .' His disappointment forgotten for a moment, Richard's eyes caressed her, his glance roaming over her face as if he would commit her every feature to a memory that he could carry with him always. 'Since I've known you, known your warmth, your concern for others . . .' His smile became a little wry. 'Even when they don't really deserve it. I've begun to wonder if my mother really *cares* about anyone except herself and her place in the eyes of her fancy friends.'

'Oh, darling, I'm sure she does. It's just . . .' Eveleen hesitated and then smiled. 'It's just she's come from a different background to me. She's sophisticated and elegant and – and serene. I'm from working-class stock. I was nothing until you married me, as Bob Porter was quick to remind me.'

'What?'

Eveleen tried to shrug it off, realizing too late that she had said too much. 'I told you, we had a bit of a set-to.'

'I didn't realize he'd insulted you. What exactly did he say?'

'It was nothing, honestly.'

'Eveleen.' Richard's tone was sharp and adamant.

Sighing, she recounted the conversation, adding, 'But I can handle it.'

'I'll speak to him . . .'

'No!' Now Eveleen was firm. 'Leave it. Please. You'll only make matters worse. I've got to be able to handle things while – while you're away.'

They stared at each other, until Richard capitulated, saying slowly, 'Perhaps I've been wrong to get caught up in this war.'

Eveleen could not bring herself to contradict him. She could not lie, not even to save his feelings. Instead, all she could say was, 'It's done now and we have to make the best of it.'

There was an awkward silence before Richard said, 'Aren't you even going to ask if we had a nice day?'

'What? Oh, I'm sorry.' The worried frown scarcely left her face as she tried to smile. There was silence and then she added, 'Well, did you?'

'It was wonderful,' Bridie said in a small voice, joining in the conversation for the first time. Her tone belied her statement. She was sitting between them, halfway down the table, pushing the food around her plate, hardly taking a mouthful. She had listened to the interchange between her aunt and uncle and had felt the tension between them. Then what was really distressing her came tumbling out as she raised tormented eyes to Richard. 'But – but now it's over and you're going away tomorrow. You and Andrew and – and . . .' Her voice died and her head drooped.

Richard reached out and covered her hand with his. 'I know, love. I know. But we'll soon be back. I'm sure we'll get leave.'

'But you'll be going to France. How will you come back from there?'

He smiled. 'They'll have it all organized somehow, I expect.' He was trying to reassure her, to give her hope, yet even the young girl could see that he wasn't sure himself of what he was saying.

Eveleen sat silently. It should be me asking my husband these questions, she thought guiltily. And it should have been me with him today. On his last day. She smiled at Richard, promising herself that later, in their bedroom, she would make it up to him. But first there were matters that must be discussed. 'Darling, I must talk to you after dinner. The factory . . .'

Richard stood up, his own meal hardly touched. 'I'm sorry, Eveleen, but I must go to see Mother and Father to say goodbye. Don't wait up.' His voice was tight and it was only when he looked at Bridie that he smiled. 'Goodnight, my dear, and thank you for a lovely day. I shall treasure the memory of it.'

He turned and left the room whilst Eveleen stared after him in dismay.

Weary though she was with the day's dramas at the factory, she was determined to stay awake until Richard came home, but when he returned after midnight Eveleen was fast asleep.

Eveleen woke with a start. The half-light of dawn filtered through the curtains, but the city was already awake. From the street she could hear sounds: the clip-clop of horses' hooves, the rattle of cartwheels and carriages. Even the sound of a noisy motor car, which sometimes still brought people rushing to their windows. The house, which Richard had bought just after their marriage, was in a street of tall, terraced houses, fashionable yet still not too far from the city centre or the factory.

She turned her head cautiously, anxious not to disturb Richard, but found that he was lying next to her, wide awake, his hands behind his head, and staring up at the ceiling.

She cuddled close to him and put her arm across him. 'Darling, I am sorry about yesterday. Forgive me?'

She heard his sigh and then his arms were about her and there was a sweet desperation in his kiss. Their love-making was tender, yet tinged with the poignant sadness of finality.

Later, as they were dressing, she asked, 'What time does your train leave?'

'Noon.'

'I'll just have to go into the factory first thing, but I'll be back in good time.'

The disappointment showed clearly on his face. 'I thought we might spend the morning together.'

Eveleen felt torn in two. 'I'm sorry, but I must go in.'

'I realize there must be a lot of adjustments to make, with several leaving today, but surely Bob Porter is quite capable of doing that.'

'Well, yes,' she said carefully. 'But I know he doesn't like me being more involved with the running of the factory now . . .' her voice faltered. 'Now you're going.'

'I'll come with you, then. Maybe I should have a word with him.'

'No,' Eveleen said sharply. 'No. It'll undermine my authority. I've got to win it on my own.'

Richard shrugged and all he said was, 'Very well.'

'But I'll be at the station. I'll be there to see you off. I promise.'

'Miss Binkley, please may I have a little extra time at dinner? I'm going to the station to see Uncle Richard and Andrew off.'

'There's no need. Your aunt will be there and you had yesterday off to go to the fair.'

'But they might be going away soon. Right away. To France.'

Helen's face was bleak. 'I know that only too well, Bridie. My – friend will be on the same train. But I can't leave and neither can many of the girls and women in this room who have relatives leaving today.' She waved her hand to encompass the other workers. 'Don't you think we'd all like to go? I'm sorry, Bridie, but you cannot be treated any different from anyone else.'

Bridie bit her lip but, as she took her place beside Mrs Hyde and picked up her work, her mind was scheming. I will go, she promised silently. She's not going to stop me. Bridie knew she was courting trouble, but she didn't care. She had to see Andrew off. She just had to. And Uncle Richard too, of course.

All morning Bridie was in a fever of excitement, watching the crawling hands on the clock. It earned her a sharp reprimand from the usually even-tempered Helen.

'What's got into you, Bridie? That run you've mended looks as if you've used a knitting needle. You must do it again and I don't want to be able to see where the mend is when you've done it.'

'Yes, Auntie . . . Miss Binkley,' she said hastily. 'Sorry.'

Helen moved away down the room, weaving her way amongst the workers, glancing at their work, checking and rechecking that all was as it should be. Bridie bent her head over her work. Tears filled her eyes.

'Here, let me do it.' At her side, Mrs Hyde whispered, 'Come on, 'and it over. You do this 'un of mine. It's only a little run.'

By the time Helen turned round at the end of the room and began to walk back towards them, the kindly woman and the young girl had exchanged their pieces of work.

'What the eye doesn't see, the heart doesn't grieve over,' Mrs Hyde murmured softly and gave Bridie a huge wink.

*

The railway station platform was seething with soldiers, with volunteers still in civilian clothes and with all their wives and loved ones seeing them off. At one end of the platform a brass band played military music. Banners and flags were waving and children ran about excitedly, unchecked by the adults, who were far too caught up in the drama of the moment to bother.

Brinsley and Sophia Stokes stood with Richard, an awkward constraint between them, whilst Bridie clung to Andrew as if she would physically prevent him from climbing aboard the train. If her strength had been enough, she would have done so.

Above the sound of the brass band playing, the cheering and calls of farewell and the hiss of steam from the engine, she shouted, 'You will write to me, won't you? I'll write every week and send you parcels. Mrs Martin says we're allowed to. Auntie Evie says Mrs Martin's getting a ladies' committee together to organize knitting things for the soldiers. I'm going to join it. I'll send you some lovely warm socks.'

Andrew hugged her hard and tried to smile, but there was a catch in his voice as he said, 'I can't wait to wear them.' He drew back a little and held her away from him, looking down into her upturned face. 'Listen, Bridie, I want you to do something for me. Something very important.'

She nodded earnestly.

Andrew glanced about him. 'I'd hoped Eveleen would be here to see us off, but it doesn't look as if she's going to make it.'

A few feet away Richard's anxious glance scanned the seething mass, his hopes fading with every second that Eveleen did not appear.

'She'll be here. I know she will. She wouldn't

miss Uncle Richard going. Or you,' Bridie added hastily.

'Well, you're here,' Andrew said softly and hugged her again, murmuring in her ear, 'my little Bridie.'

Her heart swelled with love for him, blotting out for a brief moment her terrible fear for his safety. 'What is it you want me to do?'

'Remind Eveleen to go to Flawford to see her grandmother. I have asked her and she promised to see that they're all right. I'm not sure what's going to happen there once I've gone.' For a moment his face was bleak with regret. 'I almost wish I hadn't volunteered now. They need looking after. Her uncle – your grandfather – too, though . . .' A small smile played at the corner of his mouth. 'He'd be the last to admit it.'

'I'll tell her,' Bridie promised. 'But she'll get here in time for you to tell her yourself. I know she will.'

But when the whistle blew and there was a mad scramble to board the train Eveleen had still not appeared.

Bridie hugged Andrew and then Richard. 'Can't they wait? She'll be here. She must have got held up.'

'Oh yes, she's got held up all right. Eveleen's got far more important things to do now that she's running the factory single-handed.'

Young as she was, Richard's bitterness was not lost on Bridie. 'Oh, Uncle Richard, she . . .' The final whistle drowned her words of excuse.

Richard kissed his mother's cheek, shook his father's hand and then turned back to Bridie, giving her a bear hug that almost lifted her off her feet.

'Take care of yourself, my little Bridie,' he whispered in her ear. 'And don't eat too many toffee apples while I'm away.'

He set her down, turned and pushed his way through the crowd. And although she watched him until he disappeared into the carriage, he did not look back. The guard walked down the platform, slamming the doors. Soldiers hung from the windows, waving and shouting. Bridie pushed her way to the edge of the platform, reaching up to touch Andrew's hand one last time. 'Take care, oh, do take care. Both of you. Come back safely.'

All along the length of the train, the same words were being echoed.

'Come back safely.'

As the train drew slowly out of the station, Bridie heard a cry close behind her and turned to see Eveleen pushing her way through the crowd, her desperate gaze on the moving train.

'Oh no, no!' she gasped as the train gathered speed. Standing on tiptoe, she waved wildly.

'He'll not see you,' Bridie said harshly. 'He was looking for you until the very last moment.'

'I couldn't get away and then the streets are so busy . . .'

'Yes,' Bridie said, twisting the knife even more, 'that's what Uncle Richard said. He said you'd far more important things to do now.'

She turned and began to follow the throng moving out of the station, leaving a forlorn and guilty Eveleen on the edge of the platform staring after the disappearing train.

Twenty-One

Brinsley and Sophia were waiting near the station entrance. 'Bridie, my dear, over here.' She heard his deep voice calling her. 'Where's Eveleen?'

'Watching the train. She was too late to say goodbye.'

'Oh dear,' Brinsley said. 'Never mind, they'll soon be home on leave, I expect before . . .' He cleared his throat and gruffly changed the subject. 'Go and fetch your auntie and I'll take you both for a spot of lunch. I don't know about you, but I'm hungry.'

Bridie opened her mouth to protest. She would be in enough trouble already for having disobeyed Helen. Then she sighed. So what would another hour matter? She retraced her steps, to find Eveleen still standing on the edge of the platform watching the train receding into a tiny speck. She did not move, not even when the train was gone from her sight.

Bridie, her anger dissolved by the look of anguish on her aunt's face, touched her arm. 'Come on, Auntie Evie. Mr Stokes is going to take us for lunch.'

'I couldn't eat a thing,' Eveleen murmured.

'Nor me,' Bridie said. 'But Mr Stokes is right. We ought to try.'

Brinsley found a table in the restaurant of a local hotel. 'Now, we'll sit here in the window,' he said, holding the chair for his wife. 'We've a good view.'

But the scene outside the window was only a further

reminder. Would-be soldiers marched in ranks along the street, heading for the station to catch yet another train, whilst the pavements were lined with well-wishers cheering them on.

The food was wonderful, but Eveleen and Bridie only picked at it. Sophia seemed unperturbed at having just waved her only son off to war and Eveleen found herself thinking that her mother-in-law's serene exterior went much deeper than the schooled outward appearance of a well-bred lady. She remembered Richard's words at dinner the previous evening. Perhaps he was right. Perhaps Sophia Stokes didn't really care. But there was no mistaking Brinsley's feelings. Whilst he tried to be jovial, tried to keep their spirits buoyant, Eveleen could see the anxiety in his eyes.

'Now,' he said, when the meal was finished and the coffee served, 'we need to have a board meeting.'

Eveleen looked startled. 'A board meeting? But that's only you and Mrs Stokes now that – that Richard's gone.' Was every sentence, everything they planned going to remind her?

'That's true. Since the only Reckitt left in the business died five years ago, the company has belonged entirely to our family.' He glanced at Sophia and his smile broadened as he addressed Eveleen. 'That's why, my dear, we want you to join the board of directors.'

'Me?' Eveleen was startled. 'But – but I don't know a thing about – about being a director. I'm – I'm . . .' She smiled wryly. 'I'm a worker, not a boss.'

'You underestimate yourself, Eveleen. You have run that workroom and all the homeworkers most successfully. And you've already become involved with the factory side. So, what do you say, my dear?'

'Well . . .' she said doubtfully and glanced at her mother-in-law. It was important to her that she had Sophia's support.

'We've discussed it at length – the two of us. And we talked it over with Richard last evening,' Sophia said in her soft, modulated tones. She patted Eveleen's hand. 'He, of course, was all for it.'

'In that case, I can hardly refuse, but I haven't the faintest idea what happens at a board meeting or what will be expected of me.'

Brinsley chuckled. 'You'll soon find out.'

Helen Binkley was angry. Very angry.

'You had no right to disobey me,' she said in a voice loud enough for half the workroom to hear her. 'You deliberately took time off without my permission. In fact, I forbade it.'

Red in the face, Bridie stood before her.

'It was very unfair on everyone else. I suppose, because you are Mrs Stokes's niece, you thought you could get away with it. Well, you can't. I shall have to speak to her about this. I have every right to dismiss you.'

Bridie raised her chin defiantly, her hands clenched by her sides. 'It'd've made no difference. It had nothing to do with her being my aunt. I'd've gone anyway.'

'Well!' Helen was robbed of coherent speech. 'I've never heard the like.'

'Now, now.' Mrs Hyde had heaved herself up from her chair and was coming towards them. 'Don't be too hard on the lass, Helen.'

Few people now called Helen by her Christian name

since her promotion to supervisor in the inspection room, but Mrs Hyde had worked there far longer than Helen had.

'She's only young and she wanted to see her family off. You can't blame her for that, when all's done and said.' Then the woman added bluntly, 'None of us know who's going to come back.'

There was a ripple around the room and the colour drained from Helen's face. 'You don't need to remind us, Mrs Hyde,' she said stiffly, her voice breaking. 'But there are several here who would dearly have loved to have been on the station platform today. Including me,' she ended bitterly.

'Aye well,' Mrs Hyde's tone was gentler. 'You're right there.' She turned to look down at Bridie. 'You were wrong to disobey Miss Binkley. But me and the others,' she gestured with a nod of her head towards the other women in the room, 'aren't going to hold it against you.' Then she added firmly, 'Not this time. From now on, you be a good lass and do what Miss Binkley says, eh?'

Bridie nodded and looked at Helen, who seemed to be struggling inwardly. At last she said, 'You're a very lucky girl to have such kind friends to stick up for you. Now, go and sit down and we'll say no more about it.'

But Bridie was determined to have the last word. 'I'm sorry I disobeyed you, but I'm not sorry I went to the station to see them off. There was only Mr and Mrs Stokes to see Uncle Richard off. And Andrew had no-one else but me.'

Helen stared at her in amazement. 'Whatever do you mean? Surely Eveleen was there?'

Bridie shook her head. 'No. She came, but she got there just too late. The train had gone.'

She turned away, leaving a shocked Helen gazing after her.

Eveleen was beside herself with remorse. She even thought of taking the next train and trying to follow Richard. She knew they were going to Newark, but where after that she had no idea. With a stab of guilt, she realized that she had not listened. She might never see him again and she had not even said a last goodbye. Her heart beat rapidly with fear each time she thought about it – he might never come back. She had been so resentful against him for volunteering in the first place, and then wrapped up in the problems at the factory, that she had let him go without a loving word. Even the memory of their love-making on that last morning was now spoilt because she had not said a proper farewell.

On her way to see her confidante and friend Win Martin, Eveleen walked along the street, her head held high, her back straight, determined that no-one should see the ache in her heart. She was dressed in a navy costume with a long, hobble skirt, with three buttons hiding a discreet slit to allow easier walking. The tunic-style coat was knee length with a broad waistband and a velvet collar. The feather in the small matching hat rippled in the breeze as she walked. Beneath it Eveleen's wild, unruly hair had been tamed into fashionable curls and waves, swept up into a chignon at the back of her head. Her outward appearance was that of a confident, fashionable woman of the town, but beneath lay insecurity and a terrible dread.

As she turned into Foundry Yard, the sight of the terraced house where she and her family had once lived brought the memories flooding back and she was again reminded of her brother. Only days earlier she had seen in the newspaper that the enemy were now laying mines indiscriminately in the North Sea, so that not only British warships fell victim but innocent fishing vessels and neutral ships too. Jimmy was in as much danger as the soldiers at the Front.

As she passed down the street to knock on Win's door, she knew that many of the women scrubbing their doorsteps, shaking their mats or returning from the market with heavy shopping were hiding the same anxieties she harboured.

Win answered the door quickly, flinging it open. 'Oh, Evie, it's you.' For the first time that Eveleen could remember, there was no welcoming smile on Win's face, even though she gestured for Eveleen to step inside.

'What is it, Win? What's wrong?' she asked at once. 'Because I can see there's something.'

Win pulled a face. 'It's our Elsie's husband. He's only gone and volunteered. Leaving our Elsie just as she's had the bairn, an' all.'

Eveleen groaned. 'Oh no! When did that happen?'

'He went same day as your man. Silly bugger went to a recruiting rally somewhere a couple of weeks ago and lots of the young fellers got swept up in all the patriotic nonsense.' She sniffed and added wryly, 'And some of the not-so-young fellers, an' all. One of 'em being our Elsie's Sid.' The fact that Win had resorted to swearing bore testament to the depth of her feelings.

'Win, I'm so sorry. What about your own sons?' Eveleen had hoped to confide in Win about her own guilt at missing waving goodbye to Richard, but Win had far deeper worries of her own. Now was not the time. The woman lifted her shoulders in a helpless shrug. 'They haven't gone yet, but I reckon they will.

It's spreading like wildfire amongst the young fellers. If you don't go, you're thought to be a coward. And if conscription comes in . . .' She left the rest of the sentence hanging in the air.

Win and Fred Martin's family were all grown up now, but as Win always said, 'They never stop being your bairns, do they?' And now she had sons-in-law to worry about too.

'What's going to happen, Win?' Eveleen whispered fearfully. 'How will it all end?'

But for once the woman who had helped Eveleen so much, who had always seemed to the younger woman to be a rock of common sense and optimism, could offer no word of comfort.

Twenty-Two

'That girl you've put with Jake, he's tearing his hair out. She's useless,' Bob Porter greeted her one morning.

'What? Oh, yes, right. I'll go and see.'

She found the girl, Gladys, in tears and Jake shaking his fist at her.

'What on earth is going on?'

'Just get 'er out of here, missis,' Jake roared above the clatter. 'She's forever tekin' the day off and when she is here, she's bloody useless.'

'Jake, please come to the office at the end of your shift and we'll sort it out then. We can't talk here,' Eveleen suggested, trying to keep her voice calm and her temper in check. 'Gladys, you'd better come with me now. You're in no fit state to work anyway.'

'That's bloody women for you,' Jake said, casting a vitriolic glance at the weeping girl. 'Turn the water taps on to get 'emselves out of trouble.'

Eveleen glared at him but said no more – for the moment. She would have plenty to say later, she thought grimly, as she put her arm about the girl's waist and led her away.

'Now,' Eveleen said, in the relative quiet of a room along the passage, well away from the machine shop and from Bob Porter's office. Eveleen had turned this into her office at the factory. 'Tell me your side.'

'I've been trying me best, ma'am, but he's that impatient.'

'Would you rather be put on another job?'

The girl nodded tearfully. 'I thought I liked machines. Y'know, they've always fascinated me.'

Eveleen nodded. She shared the same enthusiasm for machinery. But there, it seemed, the similarity between herself and Gladys ended. Whilst Eveleen had been a quick and deft learner, Gladys was not. 'But I just can't get the hang of the bobbin winding, missis, and the minute he starts shouting an' swearing at me . . .' The girl dissolved into easy tears once more.

Eveleen was thoughtful, staring at the girl yet not seeing her. An idea was forming in her mind. Gladys's performance in the machine shop had done the cause of bringing women into the factory no service at all. Sadly the girl had just proved right the men who were against the idea.

Now, Eveleen was thinking, if a woman were able to prove herself capable as an auxiliary worker, then perhaps the men's attitude would change.

'Don't worry any more, Gladys,' Eveleen said, 'I'll find work for you in the inspection room. See me in the morning. I'll have worked something out by then.'

'Oh, thank you, ma'am. Thank you very much.' Gladys stood up. 'I – I am sorry I've failed you, ma'am. I did so want to help with the war effort . . .' Her voice trailed away.

Eveleen stood up, more energy in her movement than there had been since Richard had left. 'You will be, Gladys, so think no more about it. Whatever job anyone does in these difficult times is helping indirectly, even if it doesn't feel like it.'

The girl smiled thinly, obviously wanting to believe what Eveleen said.

'Run along home now.' She patted the girl on the shoulder and walked with her to the factory entrance. There they parted and Eveleen, a spring in her step, ran up the stairs leading to the top floor of the warehouse.

'Do you know, Helen,' she greeted her friend, 'I've just had the most marvellous idea. Now, can you keep a secret?'

Jake presented himself at her office a few minutes after the end of his shift. Bob Porter was with him.

'Come in and sit down.' Eveleen smiled, hardly able to keep her face straight. The more she thought about her plan, the better she liked it, but she had no intention of telling either of the two men sitting opposite her.

'Now, Jake, Gladys herself has admitted that she cannot do the work, so I have found a place for her in the inspection room and I have also got a replacement for her with you.'

Jake groaned. 'I don't want another like her, missis. I'm sorry I offered to take one now.'

'I'd have thought you'd have learnt your lesson, Mrs Stokes, if you don't mind my sayin' so,' Bob Porter said.

Eveleen smiled. Hugging her secret to her, she was able to answer them serenely. 'As it happens, Bob, I do mind. Not all the girls and women we try out in the machine shop are going to be satisfactory. I know that. But that doesn't mean to say that none of them can do the work. I am sure there are plenty of girls who are capable of becoming skilled workers. It's just a case of finding them.'

'Well, that's where we don't agree, ma'am. I don't

reckon there's a female that's capable. I know they're only going to do the sort of labouring jobs, but even so they have to be quick and handy at it. The twisthands will rely on them. But if you reckon you can find one, Mrs Stokes,' he hooked his thumbs through his braces and rocked on his heels, 'then you can prove me wrong.'

Eveleen merely smiled and said nothing, but inside she was thinking: Oh, I'll prove you wrong, Bob Porter. You just wait and see.

After dinner that evening Bridie followed her aunt to Richard's study and stood in the doorway. 'Auntie Evie, Andrew asked me to tell you something. When they were leaving, he sent you a message. He said he'd asked you to go to Flawford to see the old folks. He's worried how they're going to manage without him.'

Eveleen was rifling through papers on the desk and made no reply.

'Auntie Evie, did you hear what I said?'

'Yes, dear,' Eveleen said absently. 'We'll go soon. One Sunday, perhaps. Now.' She shuffled the papers together, turned from the desk and held out her hand. 'I want you to come upstairs with me. I have something to show you.'

'What is it?' Bridie was intrigued in spite of herself. Eveleen's eyes were gleaming.

'You'll see. And I can't wait to see Bob Porter's face in the morning.'

Twenty-Three

At the start of the early morning shift the following day, Eveleen walked down the aisle between the machines. She was dressed in a coat-like overall, buttoned at the front, with a wide belt. A frilled cap covered her hair and she wore no jewellery except her wedding ring.

She arrived by Jake's machine and waited for him to turn and see her. She did not step into the twisthand's alley, the space that ran along in front of his machine. This was his domain and even Brinsley Stokes himself would not dream of going into the area until he had a nod from the man in charge of the machine.

Eveleen stood a moment, fascinated as always by the rhythmic motion of wheels and cogs, levers and bars, all working in harmony to twist thousands of fine threads into intricate and delicate patterns. She marvelled again as the finished length of lace came clanking slowly out of the machine.

As Jake turned, she saw the smirk on his face. 'So you're the new . . .' he began and then she saw his jaw drop as he recognized her. 'Mrs Stokes? You?'

'Yes. Me. You, Jake, are going to teach me all there is to know about bobbin winding, changing the bobbins, stripping and how to look after the machine when you want a few minutes' break.' Her smile widened. 'And anything else I'm capable of doing to help you. I had an excellent teacher years ago, Jake, so mind you're as good as Luke Manning.'

'But – but . . .' the young man blustered, 'it ain't right. I mean, what will Mr Porter say?'

'You heard what he said last night, Jake. That if I prove to him a woman can do the job as well as a man, then he'll have to change his mind.' She smiled winningly at him. 'So, Jake, who better to prove him wrong than me?'

'I'll be a laughing stock amongst me mates, missis,' Jake grumbled.

Eveleen put her head on one side and said quietly, 'Would another penny a rack whilst you're training me, and others, help you to deal with your workmates' teasing?'

A rack was the measure of cloth by which the twisthands were paid. On average they received sixpence a rack and could produce four racks an hour.

'What about mi butty?' Jake was quick to ask, referring to the twisthand who operated this same machine on the alternate shift.

'If he agrees to train someone else on his shift, then yes, he'd be paid the same,' Eveleen agreed. 'I propose to pay any man who undertakes to train women workers – properly, mind – the same.'

Jake's face cleared and for the first time he smiled. 'Right you are then, missis. Now, we'd better get started else we'll have the foreman after us.'

'You can't do it, Mrs Stokes. We'll have a strike on our hands.'

At the end of her first shift Eveleen took off her overall and cap, smoothed her hair and put on her costume jacket as she faced Bob Porter's red and angry face across her desk. Immediately she became the employer, no longer the employee.

'Are you referring to me working as an auxiliary or to the extra money I mean to pay those who undertake to train women?' Eveleen found it difficult to hide her smile as she remembered again the look on Bob Porter's face as he had walked through the machine shop that morning and seen her at Jake's side. Like Jake, he had not recognized her immediately, but when he had, his face was a picture; one that Eveleen would never forget.

'Both. You'll have the rest of the men up in arms.'

'Who is the union man in the factory? I'll talk to him.'

'Charlie Allen, but he'll do as I say. He took over from me when I took Josh Carpenter's place.'

Her mouth tight, Eveleen said, 'I see.' It seemed that despite being promoted to a management position, Bob Porter had not left behind his strong union affiliation. 'Right then. Sit down, Bob, and we'll get this matter sorted out here and now.'

'There's nowt to sort out, missis. It won't work and that's all there is to it.'

'Why? Just tell me why.'

'Women can't work machines. They haven't got the right kind of brain. They're mothers. That's what nature intended.'

He couldn't know how much his words wounded her. Eveleen swallowed hard and managed not to let the hurt show in her expression.

'I'm not suggesting that they can become twisthands,' she snapped. 'Few women would be physically strong enough, I know that. But your remark about the inability to learn is insulting. Besides, single women, at least, surely ought to have the right to earn their own living.'

Bob's lip curled. 'Oh aye, until they catch a feller to provide for 'em.'

Pointedly she glared at him. 'Sadly there may not be many left for them to catch.' She regarded him steadily. Bob Porter was a very bitter man. She could hear it in his tone, but she had no idea what had caused his seeming resentment against all women.

'Are you married, Bob?' she asked suddenly.

His head jerked up. 'What's that got to do with it?'

'Nothing,' she said mildly. 'I just wondered.'

He gave a grunt and there was a silence between them before he said morosely, 'I was, but she upped and left. Ran off with another feller.'

'I'm sorry.' There was no doubting the sincerity in Eveleen's voice, even Bob Porter could hear it. 'Betrayal is very hurtful.'

Bob stared at her. 'I shouldn't think you can begin to know what it feels like, missis. I don't reckon Mr Richard would ever . . .'

Eveleen shook her head, 'Oh no.' Her voice broke a little at the mention of his name. 'No, Mr Richard is a wonderful husband, but before I knew him, when I was very young, there was someone who hurt me very badly. I was naive and foolish.' Suddenly the memory of warm summer days and the excitement of her clandestine meetings with Stephen Dunsmore in Bernby Covert was so strong that she could almost hear the rustle of the leaves above them and feel his arms about her . . .

She drew in a sharp breath, hating herself for even thinking about Stephen when her beloved husband might, at this very moment, be facing death.

'I'm very sorry, Bob, truly. But you shouldn't let it

colour your whole view of women. We – we're not all like that.'

Now he sat down heavily in the chair on the opposite side of the desk and for a moment the fight seemed to drain out of him. It was as if her genuine sympathy had actually touched him for a brief moment. 'Aye,' he said. 'Aye, well, mebbe you're right, but I still don't reckon women's place is in a factory. They should be at home looking after their husbands and bairns.'

'We're only going to employ single women or married women with no children whose husbands have gone to war.'

'Oh aye.' Bob was disbelieving. 'That's what you say now, but it'll be the thin end of the wedge. As time goes on, you'll say . . .' He mimicked a woman's voice, high-pitched and whining. 'There's Mrs So-an'-So. Her husband's been killed and she's three bairns to support. Can't we find her a job?'

Eveleen laughed and was honest enough to admit, 'You may well be right, Bob. I can't deny it.' Then her expression sobered and she sighed. 'Bob, if this war goes on for any length of time, there's going to be a real shortage of men. More and more are going to go. There's talk already of bringing in conscription.'

A look of fear crossed the man's face. 'What age?' he asked sharply.

'Men between nineteen and thirty-five. I think I read somewhere that was likely to be the age range.'

Bob Porter relaxed visibly. 'Thank God I'm forty, then,' he said with a tinge of humour though the sentiment was heartfelt.

Eveleen could not resist the opportunity to say, 'I depends how desperate they get, Bob.'

He grunted and then realized that she was teasing him and had the grace to smile. He heaved himself to his feet. 'Well, missis, I can't support you in this. I never will, but you're the boss and since Mr Brinsley is on your side an' all, there's not a lot I can do about it, is there?' He stood above her, looking down at her. 'But I wish you'd stop this nonsense with Jake. You're making me look a fool in front of the fellers.'

Eveleen pursed her mouth and shook her head. 'I'm sorry, Bob, but I mean to carry on. I've something to prove. And not just to you. Oh, I admit when I first thought about it, it was just to prove you wrong, but now I've actually started I can see that I'm proving it to everyone. You, the other men, and even the women themselves.' She stood up and faced him. 'The only person who's going to look a fool, Bob, if I can't do it, is me.'

A fleeting expression crossed his face that said: And I hope you can't. But it was masked in an instant and instead he growled, 'Well, I still reckon you're stacking up a lot of trouble for yourself. That's all.'

Then he turned and left the room.

'I do wish you'd discussed it with me first, Eveleen. You've been very impulsive, my dear. I know your motives are admirable, but it's not really the place for a director of the company, is it?'

To Eveleen's disappointment, Brinsley disapproved of her action. He was sitting behind the desk in her office, his brow creased in a worried frown.

'I'm sorry, but don't you see, if I can prove that a woman can do the work . . .' She broke off suddenly.

Brinsley had put his hand to his chest and his face was distorted with pain. Eveleen hurried round the desk to him.

'Oh, what is it? What's the matter?'

'It's nothing. Just – just a little indigestion. That's all.'

'I'll get Fred Martin to take you home. You must rest.'

Whilst Eveleen now drove Richard's motor car, Fred Martin, Win's husband, had learnt to drive too and often ran errands for Eveleen, using the motor for the company, including driving Brinsley to and from the factory.

'I can't. If you're set on this madcap scheme, then I shall have to take on the administrative work.'

'No.' Eveleen spoke harshly. She was suddenly very frightened that Brinsley could be suffering a heart attack. Was this how her own poor father had died in the beck? Had he been suddenly overcome with dreadful pain and there had been no-one there to help him?

'I'm getting Fred to drive you home and sending a message to the doctor to come at once.'

'Don't fuss, my dear. It's only indigestion . . .'

'Well, the doctor will tell us,' Eveleen argued. 'But you're not to worry any more about the factory. Leave it to me. I'll cope.'

She would not allow it to be said that her actions had caused Brinsley to be unwell. She refused to carry that guilt too.

'Come along, let's get you home,' she said firmly and it was indicative of how ill he must be feeling that Brinsley did not argue.

Twenty-Four

As the days turned into weeks and Christmas came and went, the nation realized that the war was not going to be over in a few months. In January a new threat came from the air. A Zeppelin, a huge, bulbous monstrosity making a terrifying burring sound, dropped bombs on the Norfolk towns of Great Yarmouth and King's Lynn, killing civilians.

By March even the government was making urgent appeals for the women of Britain to serve their country by doing vital jobs, so releasing men for fighting. Now Eveleen felt vindicated. Surely not even Bob Porter could argue with the government.

Leave for Richard and Andrew was promised and then cancelled as the war intensified, but letters came regularly from them.

We are still all together, Richard wrote. *And everyone is fine. Sid is with us too. That was a stroke of luck, wasn't it? The whole brigade had a big inspection the other day by a general, no less!*

Eveleen and Bridie wrote every week. Eveleen, after working all day at the factory, often sat writing far into the night, sometimes falling asleep in Richard's study, her arms spread across his desk.

Brinsley had had no reoccurrence of the chest pains and the doctor had merely suggested more rest. Now Brinsley only came to the factory two or three times a week and never stayed very long. He did not even offer to attend to the paperwork. Eveleen had the uncomfortable feeling that, because he had not fully approved of her action in working in the machine shop, her father-in-law was tacitly refusing to help her.

Eveleen said nothing in her letters to Richard about her problems at home. Grimly determined, she soldiered on alone, learning the hard way. She felt as if she had been thrown bodily into a fast-flowing river and had to learn how to swim in order to survive. Daily she was forced to bite back sharp retorts in answer to Bob's scathing remarks. She needed him. She needed to draw on his knowledge as factory manager.

Reluctantly Eveleen had to admit that she could not manage without Bob Porter. And because of that she would have to put up with whatever he said or did.

At least, for the time being.

In April the news came of a desperate battle being waged near the town of Ypres. At the same time a new and terrible weapon was being launched by the enemy on the Western Front. An insidious, silent, greenish-yellow vapour drifted across from the enemy lines and crept into the Allied trenches. Without proper masks, the soldiers, choking and half-blinded, could only hold wet cloths to their faces as an inadequate protection against the chlorine gas.

On one of the occasions, all too rare nowadays, when she visited Win Martin in Foundry Yard, Eveleen felt weariness overwhelm her. 'Where is it all going to end, Win?' she asked her old friend.

'I don't know.' Win's cheerful smile was missing these days and there were dark shadows of worry beneath her eyes. 'Our Elsie's bairn's sick. He's wheezy. You know?' She tapped her own chest. 'It's the damp in these houses.' Win glanced around her own cosy home. The back-to-back houses in the narrow streets and yards of Narrow Marsh had not all had the loving care spent on them that Fred Martin and his wife had lavished upon theirs.

'I like it here,' Win said. 'I wouldn't think of leaving. I like the folks, but not everyone's as lucky as us.'

'Not everyone's as hardworking as you and Fred.'

'Aye well, that's as maybe. Our Elsie's Sid was all set to do up their place, but then he went and got caught up in the war.'

'How is he? Richard told me in one of his letters that Sid's in their company too. Have you heard from him?'

Win shook her head. 'He's not much of a letter writer, our Sid.'

Eveleen was appalled. 'You mean – you mean that Elsie doesn't hear from him?'

'Just now and then. He fills in one of them cards. Y'know, puts a tick to show he's well and then just signs his name at the bottom.'

How awful, Eveleen was thinking. She couldn't bear to think of life without Richard's reassuring letters.

'Can we go to Flawford this Sunday?'

'What? Oh, I'll have to see. Don't worry me now. I have these orders to look through.'

It was late and Bridie had been about to go to bed when she put her head round the door of Richard's study to see her aunt sorting through a mound of paperwork on the desk.

'The number of orders coming in is dropping off

alarmingly. One after another of our outlets seems to be closing.' Eveleen sighed, as Bridie stepped into the room and stood beside her. 'I suppose it's to be expected. Our exports have virtually stopped. At this rate there won't be a factory for the men to come back to after it's all over.'

Bridie wrinkled her forehead. 'I had wondered why there seemed to be less work coming to the inspection room, though at the moment there seems to be enough to keep most of us busy.'

'If things don't pick up soon I shall have to lay workers off.' Eveleen gave a humourless laugh. 'Mind you, Bob Porter will no doubt be pleased if we find we don't need women workers after all.'

'You'll need them for a while,' Bridie said in a small voice. 'There are six more men leaving on Friday.'

Eveleen looked up sharply. 'How did you know that? I didn't know.'

'Mrs Hyde told us today. Her sixteen-year-old son is one of them. He only started in the machine shop a fortnight ago, yet now he's going.'

'Sixteen! They can't go at sixteen, can they?'

Bridie shrugged. 'Mrs Hyde said them recruiting people aren't asking too closely what their age is. They just tek 'em anyway.'

Eveleen looked sorrowful for a moment at the thought of the brave young man volunteering. 'Sixteen,' she murmured again and shook her head at the sheer waste of it all.

'Could I have a word with you, Mrs Stokes?'

As Eveleen walked out of the machine shop towards

her office at the end of another shift, Jane Morgan, the trainee with Luke Manning, caught up with her.

Eveleen closed her eyes for a moment and groaned inwardly. Surely not another problem? She was so desperately tired. All she wanted to do was to go home and sleep the clock round. But she couldn't. She had vowed to prove that women could be as good as the male twisthands, but no-one else had all the administrative work of running the factory to attend to out of shift hours.

'Of course,' she replied to Jane. 'Come into the office.'

Once the door was shut, Jane, smiling broadly, said, 'Mr Manning reckons I'm ready to work with another twisthand as his assistant while he trains another lass.'

'Oh, Jane, that's really good news.' She smiled back at the girl. 'You've just beaten me to it. Jake said only today that there's not a lot more he can teach me.'

The girl put her head on one side and regarded Eveleen steadily. 'Will you be carrying on work, missis?'

Eveleen laughed and shook her head. 'No, Jane. I've plenty of other work I need to catch up on. I only did it to prove a point, but it seems you have done it for me. Mind you, I shall stay the course, just for the satisfaction of showing Bob Porter that not one, but two women have done it. However, we'll be putting you with someone else very soon. There are several of the young fellers gone and it's left some of the skilled twisthands very short-handed. I'll sort out the details with Mr Porter.' Her heart sank a little at the prospect, but then her resolve hardened. She was still the boss and he would have to do as she instructed.

'Will I get more pay, missis?'

Eveleen wrinkled her brow. 'I haven't had time to give it much thought, Jane, to be honest. But I don't see why not.'

'But it'll be less than a man'd get doing the same job, won't it?' There was resentment in her tone.

Slowly Eveleen said, 'You have got a point there.' Then, a little too impulsively, she said, 'Yes, I agree. If you can cope on your own and do all the work that's expected of you, then, yes, you should be on the same wage as a man in the same position would be.'

Jane beamed. 'Thank you, missis. I knew you'd be fair.'

'You can't do that. Put a woman on the same wage as a man?' Bob Porter, when he heard of Eveleen's latest promise, was incensed. 'We'll have a riot, let alone 'em downing tools.'

'Whyever not? If she does exactly the same work as a man.'

Bob's lip curled. 'Oh aye. And what happens when there's something heavy to lift?' Once more he mimicked a weak female. 'Oh, can you help me? I can't lift that.'

'I said,' Eveleen repeated slowly, 'if she does the same work as a man would do. And that's *exactly* what I mean.'

Bob shook his head. 'It won't work. I tell you, it won't work.'

He turned on his heel and left the office. Eveleen stared after him with the uncomfortable feeling that Bob Porter intended to see that her proposal had no chance of working.

*

'Well, missis, I don't reckon there's much more I can teach yer. You could work alongside any twisthand now, like Miss Morgan.' Jake nodded across the aisle to where Jane was winding bobbins. The girl did not see them watching her, her gaze was intent upon her work.

Eveleen laughed and held out her hand. 'Thank you for everything, Jake. You've been an excellent teacher.'

The young man grinned. 'As good as Luke Manning?'

'Oh, every bit as good,' Eveleen said, her eyes twinkling mischievously. She had done it, her heart was singing. She had proved herself capable and, better still, so had Jane Morgan.

What argument could Bob Porter possibly have now?

Eveleen found out the following morning. When she arrived at the factory, a little later than usual now that she was no longer to work a shift at the machine, she found the factory strangely silent. Jane was the only one working, loading huge reels of yarn onto a barrow.

'What's happened?' Eveleen asked her. 'Where is everyone?'

Jane pointed. 'Out the back. In the yard. Mr Allen's called a union meeting.'

'Has he indeed?'

Tight-lipped, Eveleen marched out of the back entrance to the factory and paused to take in the scene.

But it was Bob Porter who was standing on a box addressing the men thronging around him.

'He's gone off to war without a thought for his employees leaving an old man and a woman in charge. And you all know where *she* came from,' he sneered. 'She was nowt but a worker in the inspection room.' His voice changed, became placating. Eveleen grudgingly admired his clever oratory. 'I've done me best for you all, but the place is falling apart. We aren't getting the orders in now. There'll be no work for anybody soon, if it carries on.'

Unobserved, Eveleen crept closer.

'And then she brings women in. I tell you, she'll be trying to train 'em as twisthands next. Trying to work our machines.'

'Well, the missis could do it, an' all . . .' To Eveleen's surprise, it was Jake who raised his voice in protest. 'If she was strong enough.' He laughed and those around him joined in. 'And it's not like me to admit that, but I've gotta be fair. Mrs Stokes is a worker.'

When the noise died down, Luke Manning, too, spoke up. 'Jane Morgan's done well an' all. She's a good lass.'

'But don't you realize?' Bob leant towards them to emphasize his point. 'They're tekin' men's jobs, men's livelihoods.'

There was whispering amongst his listeners until Luke asked, 'How come? No-one's been laid off, even though the amount of work has slackened off a bit. They've only taken on women to replace the young fellers who've volunteered.'

'I tell you, you – ' Bob jabbed his finger towards Luke and glanced at Jake too – 'are training women to take men's jobs.' He nodded sagely. 'Women are cheap labour. They don't get a man's wages.'

'That's not right.' Luke shook his head. 'Miss Morgan said that she's to be paid the same rate as a lad doing the same work.'

The grumbling grew louder.

'And is that fair?' Bob countered at once. 'To give a *woman* equal pay to a man?' He jabbed his finger towards them all now. 'It's taking away a man's pride.

The man's a breadwinner for his family. Always has been. Always will be.' Bob dropped his voice and the crowd fell silent. 'And another thing. Do you really think that these women are going to give up their places, earning their own money, when the war's over and all the men come home?'

The muttering rose once more in belligerent anger and, as Eveleen pushed her way to the front, fists were shaken at her and voices raised.

'Listen. Listen to me, please.'

'Let her speak,' Luke shouted above the rest. 'Let's at least hear what she's got to say.'

When the noise had abated, Bob Porter stepped off the box and, with a sarcastic gesture, invited her to step onto it. Eveleen found her knees were trembling. As she faced the hostile crowd, for a moment she could not speak. Then, taking a deep breath, she said, 'Mr Porter is quite right.' She paused as a murmur of surprise rippled amongst the men. 'Orders are falling off and, yes, if it continues there won't be enough work for everyone.'

Now they faced her silently with stony expressions.

Eveleen spoke quietly now, knowing she held their attention. 'But there are six more men leaving us on Friday and –' She glanced around at them all, at the faces before her she knew so well. Working amongst them over the past weeks, she knew each and every one of them personally. And, best of all, they knew her. Perhaps these workers knew more about her now than Bob Porter did.

She had worked with them, eaten with them, laughed with them. And she had mourned with them when the news from the Front was bad and a former workmate was reported killed. Gradually, without realizing it themselves, they had begun to treat her as one of their own.

Eveleen had proved herself one of them.

'– there will be more going each week until we are left with those too old to go and young boys, barely trained.' She paused again and, now, no-one spoke.

'You all heard what Mr Richard said before he left. When you come back, after it's all over, your jobs will be here waiting for you. And if – if Mr Richard does not come back, I swear to you now that I will honour his promise.' She lowered her voice and said quietly, but with sincerity. 'A woman will never, ever, take a man's job. Not in this factory. The women themselves know that. They have been employed on that basis. And, yes, I have agreed the same rate of pay for women as long as they do exactly the same work as you men.'

She paused for a few moments whilst the men talked amongst themselves, then she raised her voice. 'Now, it's up to you. If you decide to strike in protest,' she shrugged her shoulders, 'then I can't stop you, but I must warn you that there is less and less work coming in. Because of the war many of our overseas outlets are closed to us now. And if we cease to operate, what work there is will go to other factories in the city.' She paused significantly and then added, 'I'll leave it to you to decide.'

Further explanation was unnecessary. The men knew full well that if Reckitt and Stokes's trade went elsewhere, even for a short time, in these difficult circumstances the factory would never recover. They would never win back lost trade.

Eveleen stepped down from the box and without another glance at anyone she marched back into the building and went at once to her office, intending to work on orders and invoices. But she could not concentrate and paced the floor restlessly until, after half an hour, the door was thrown open and Bob Porter stood there.

For a moment they stared at each other, he, red in the face with anger, she, her eyes wide with the unspoken question.

'Well, missis, I hope you're satisfied.' His voice was tight with resentment. 'You've won. You've beaten me in front of me own workers and made a right fool out of me. They've believed you, the silly buggers.' He shook his head in wonderment. 'By heck, but I've got to hand it to you, missis. You're clever. But one day you'll come unstuck, and don't expect me to be there to pick up the pieces 'cos I'm giving you me notice here and now and—'

Eveleen shook her head. 'Oh no, you're not, Bob Porter. This factory needs you. The men need you. I need you. I might have proved a point over training to be a twisthand and I might have won, as you put it, today. But I can't run the factory. You know that very well.'

His face twisted into a sneer. 'Well, get your precious Josh Carpenter back then.'

Eveleen shook her head. 'No, Bob.' She drew in a deep breath and knew she had to lie deliberately. 'I don't want Josh back.'

What she wouldn't have given at this moment to have Josh walk through the door with his cheery, 'Eh up, mi duck,' and to know that the factory was once more in his safe hands.

Bob shook his head. 'Nobody makes a fool out of me, missis. I'm going and I'm going this minute. There's plenty of other jobs in this city and, even if there aren't, the army'll take me.'

He turned and pulled the door to behind him with a slam of finality.

With trembling fingers, Eveleen reached for the chair and sat down as her legs gave way beneath her, the full weight of responsibility pressing down upon her.

Twenty-Five

Bridie held out a letter to Eveleen.

'Andrew's still asking if we've been to Flawford. He's very worried about them. You promised we could go just after Christmas and I've kept asking you and asking you. And now it's April already and we still haven't been.'

'Does he really think I've time to go traipsing over there when I've everything to look after here, now that Mr Stokes isn't well and Bob Porter's walked out on me too?'

'It is your grandmother and your uncle.'

'I don't need reminding,' Eveleen snapped. 'But why should I concern myself with people who turned us out when we desperately needed help? A man who turned his back on his own daughter and has made no effort in over thirteen years to meet his granddaughter?'

Bridie looked down at the letter in her hand, at Andrew's sprawling writing. She folded it carefully to put it away in her treasure box, yet knowing it would be brought out time and again to be read and reread just like the others she had received from him. His letters kept him close to her, told her he was still alive, still surviving.

She looked up at her aunt. 'If you haven't time to go –' the accusation in her voice was ill-concealed – 'then I'll go.'

Eveleen stared at her for a moment and then gave a wry, humourless laugh. 'Good luck to you then. You'll certainly need it.' She relented a little to say, 'I'll get Fred to take you.'

Then she sighed. 'The people we really ought to visit are your gran and Josh. We haven't been for ages. I tell you what,' her face was suddenly brighter, 'we'll go on Sunday and we'll talk to your gran about Flawford.'

'She'll try to stop me going, if you do,' Bridie said morosely. 'I don't think we ought to tell her.'

'Oh no, you keep the child away from them. I won't have her going anywhere near them, not after the way they treated me. All of us, if it comes to that.'

Bridie had been right. Mary would not hear of the girl visiting their estranged family in Flawford.

'I only let Andrew visit us here because he knew the situation and respected it. He never spoke about them unless I asked and I trusted him not to go home tittle-tattling to them about what was going on here. Oh no, Eveleen, you're not to let her go.'

Bridie glowered at her aunt, as if to say, I told you so.

As ever, it was Josh who brought a calming influence to the discussion over the dinner table. 'Would you agree to her going if I went with her?'

Mary glanced at him. 'You? Why should you want to go?'

'Well, from what the lass says about his letters, Andrew seems very worried about them.'

'Then he shouldn't have gone off playing the hero, should he? He should have stayed and shouldered his responsibilities.'

'They aren't really Andrew's responsibility, though, are they?' Bridie said quietly. 'They're not his relatives.'

'Aye, an' he's the lucky one they're not,' Mary said sharply. 'And don't you start giving your opinions about things you know nothing about, miss. We'll decide whether you go or not and I say you don't.'

Across the table Eveleen smiled at her mother, 'Well, for once, Mam, you and I are in agreement.'

Bridie kept her gaze lowered so that no-one would see the spark of defiance leap into her eyes. The more they told her she should not visit her grandfather and great-grandmother, the more determined she was to do so. As the conversation around her turned to other matters, a plan began to form in Bridie's mind. She said nothing and listened with only half an ear as Eveleen said, 'Josh, I need your advice. The orders for dress lace are falling. We had another order cancelled last week and now I have several bales of finished lace stored in the warehouse and no buyers. Maybe I'll find a use for it somewhere, but it's the future I'm worried about.'

Josh was thoughtful for a moment. 'You say there's still a demand for curtaining?'

Eveleen nodded. 'Goodness knows why, but yes, there is.' She stared at him, puzzled. 'But we have Levers machines, not curtaining machines.'

Josh smiled. 'Then get some.'

Eveleen was surprised. 'But you don't have both sorts in one factory, do you?'

'Not usually, no, but these are unusual times. And, from what I hear . . .' He grinned sheepishly. 'Oh, I still know what's going on even if I do live out here in the countryside. From what I hear, there are lace factories closing every month because of the war. Now, there'll be machines going cheap. Talk to Mr Stokes, mi duck.

He'll see the sense of it. He's a clever businessman. He'll not want to see his factory go to the wall because of a war.'

'But where would we put them? You don't mean get rid of the Levers?''

'Lord, no. You'll want them again when all this lot's over. But I bet there's still plenty of unused space in the factory just being used as a dumping ground at present. There was when I was there and I don't expect it's changed. Get it cleared out and you'll be able to have a new machine shop.'

Eveleen thought of the clutter filling an area right next to the existing machine shop. She put her arms around him. 'Oh, Josh. Thank you. You're so clever.'

'Haven't I always said so,' Mary put in proudly. 'But don't start asking him to come back to Nottingham, 'cos I need him here.'

Eveleen and Josh exchanged a fond glance, as Eveleen said with feigned meekness, 'I wouldn't dream of asking, Mam,' even though that very idea had been her first thought the day that Bob Porter had walked out.

As she drove home, Eveleen said, 'I'll take you home, Bridie, but I must go and see Mr Stokes right away about this. It's such a good idea of Josh's, but I must talk to my father-in-law about it. I don't know why I didn't think of it myself. You'll be all right, won't you?'

'I'll be fine,' Bridie murmured, her mind busy with her own plans.

For a time, Brinsley was thoughtful when Eveleen told him of Josh's suggestion. Then, as she watched him, the spark of interest that seemed to have been missing for some time was rekindled in his eyes.

'That's a capital idea, Eveleen. I'll get on to it first thing in the morning.' His face sobered. 'One of my old friends has just been forced to close his small curtain-making factory. He may be only too pleased to sell his machines.'

Whilst she was delighted that Brinsley was once more becoming enthusiastically involved, she had a confession to make. Swiftly, the words tumbling out, she told him of the recent events, culminating in Bob Porter's resignation.

As she fell silent, Brinsley grunted, 'Stupid fellow!' He glanced at her and smiled. 'Don't blame yourself, my dear. He's always been a volatile type. To my knowledge that's the third time he's picked up his scissors and hook and walked out.' His smile widened. 'But he always walks back in sooner or later. Mind you, perhaps this time the factory will run better without his disruptive influence.' Brinsley cleared his throat and added, 'I have to admit, Eveleen, that you were right to have women trained. And by doing it yourself you blazed the way. I apologize for having doubted you.'

Swift to forgive, Eveleen hugged him impulsively. 'Oh, you don't know how happy that makes me. Thank you. I thought I'd made you angry with me.'

Brinsley chuckled and patted her shoulder. 'My dear, dear girl, I could never be angry with you for long. Let's just hope that there's enough demand for curtaining to justify the purchase of the new machinery.'

They both recognized that there was still a risk. Trade for curtaining might fall off too and then what?

As Eveleen drove home, she felt happier that her father-in-law was once more taking an active interest in the business. But even he could not take away the ever-present worry.

Could they keep the Reckitt and Stokes factory going until Richard came home? And what if . . .? Determinedly, Eveleen kept her mind from even dwelling on that awful possibility.

Somehow she must keep his factory working. It was a talisman. If Reckitt and Stokes survived then Richard would too.

Eveleen clung to that belief.

On the following Saturday, when Bridie should have gone into work for the morning, she feigned severe stomach cramps.

'Maybe I should call the doctor,' Eveleen said worriedly, standing by Bridie's bed whilst the girl writhed and moaned and clutched her stomach.

'No, no, I'll be all right.'

'But you've not had anything like this before. I've never known you be ill. Not so much as a cold.'

'Oh, I have. I often get these sort of cramps, you know, every month. But they've never been as bad as this.'

Eveleen nodded understandingly. 'I suppose it's your age,' she murmured. 'But if they go on, we'll have to see the doctor.'

'They'll soon go. They usually do,' Bridie said and then, taking a risk, she added, 'I'll try and come into work later.'

As she had hoped, Eveleen said at once, 'No, no, there's no need. I'll explain to Helen. After all, you'd be finishing at one o'clock anyway.'

As she left the bedroom, Eveleen turned at the door. 'I'll send Emily up with a tray.'

'Thank you, Auntie Evie, but I really don't feel like eating at the moment.'

'Well, ring for her if you change your mind. 'Bye now. I'll see you later.'

Bridie lay perfectly still, her heart beating rapidly, listening. When she heard the front door close and her aunt's footsteps tapping down the street, she flung back the bedcovers and leapt out. Dressing quickly, she crept down the stairs and let herself out of the front door, running swiftly to the place where she could catch the early omnibus to Flawford.

She was on her way to meet her grandfather and great-grandmother for the first time.

Bridie stepped down from the omnibus and looked about her. She had no idea where her family lived. All she knew was that their name was the same as hers: Singleton.

Children were playing cricket on a patch of land in the centre of the village. Bridie presumed it was the village green, though there was no grass. A woman, large and round and homely looking, stepped awkwardly off the omnibus behind Bridie, struggling to carry bulging shopping baskets.

'Let me help you,' Bridie offered.

'Aw thanks. A bit of help's worth a lot of pity, they say.'

'Where are you going? I'll help you carry them.'

'I don't want to take you out of your way,' the woman said. Now she was looking directly at Bridie, frowning slightly, her head on one side in contemplation.

Bridie grinned. 'Trouble is, I don't know which is my way. Maybe you can help me.'

Slowly the woman said, 'Aye, I reckon I can. You're poor Rebecca Singleton's lass, aren't you?'

Bridie's mouth fell open in a startled gasp. 'How – how do you know?'

''Cos, mi little lass, you're the spittin' image of her. I knew Rebecca all her life. She were a quiet, docile little thing.' Bridie felt the woman's scrutiny again as she added, 'You've a bit more of the devilment in your eyes than she had. 'Spect you get that from that rascal of a father of yours. It was the worst day's work Mary ever did, bringing her family back here.' The woman shook her head sadly. 'Poor Rebecca. If it hadn't been for him, she'd have been happily married to Andrew Burns with a brood of bairns around her now.' The woman smiled down at Bridie. 'I shouldn't be tellin' you all this. T'ain't your fault, though, what went on in the past, is it?'

Bridie grimaced, smiling ruefully as she did so. She had warmed immediately to this outspoken woman. 'I suppose not. But I seem to get the blame.'

They walked along side by side for a few moments, then Bridie picked up on something the woman had said. 'You must know my gran then.'

'I know 'em all. The whole family. I've lived in this village all me life. But you mean Mary?'

'Yes.'

'Me an' Mary were best pals when we was young. Cut me to the quick when she ran off without a word to anyone.'

Bridie stopped walking, staring at the woman in surprise. 'My gran? Ran off?'

The woman stopped too and turned back to face her. 'Oh aye. Didn't you know?'

Bridie shook her head.

'Ah.' The woman appeared to be struggling with her inner self. Whether to impart a juicy morsel of gossip or whether she should hold her counsel. Her better nature won and she shook her head. 'They ain't told you then. Well, t'aint my place. You'd best ask yer family. Talking of which,' she went on briskly, resuming her walking, 'I'd best take you to Singleton's Yard. I'm not sure what sort of a reception you'll get, mi little lass. Specially from *'im.*'

'Who's "him"?'

'Harry Singleton. Your grandfather. Heartless beggar. Turning 'is own daughter out just 'cos she made a mistake that a lot on us have. 'Im an' all his chapel ranting, yet he couldn't be forgiving to 'is own. Hard man, he is, as you'll find out. Yer mam were just a lass who fell in love, that's all.' The woman sniffed. 'Pity it was with a wrong 'un. But there you are, that's life. Here's my little place.' They had arrived outside a row of cottages and the woman pushed open a white-painted gate and walked up the path. 'I'll just put me shopping down . . .' She paused and then asked, 'Would you like a cuppa?'

'Yes, please,' Bridie said thankfully. Feigning illness, she had had nothing to eat or drink that morning. She followed the woman into a neat and homely kitchen.

'Sit yer down and I'll soon mek us a cup.'

'I don't know your name.'

The woman laughed. 'No more you do. My name's Gracie Turner. Sit down, love, mek yourself at home. Now, what's your name then? I know who you are. It's as plain as the nose on yer face, *who* you are. But what d'they call you?'

'Bridie. Bridie Singleton.'

'Bridie, eh?' Gracie smiled knowingly. 'After the old woman.'

Bridie sat down at the scrubbed kitchen table. 'Is that my great-grandmother?'

'Aye, that's her. Bridget Singleton. Poor thing, not much of a life she's 'ad.' As she bustled about her kitchen making tea, Gracie chattered.

'Why do you say that?' Bridie asked curiously, her mouth watering as Gracie put a plate of buttered scones on the table. Her fingers itched to take one, but she held back out of politeness.

'Go on, lass, tek one.' Gracie laughed. 'I can see you're hungry. You were on the early bus, weren't you? I stayed in town overnight. Me eldest daughter's married and lives there and I was minding the bairns for her last night. Did me shopping yesterday.' She gestured towards the baskets. 'But what my old man's going to say when he sees that little lot, I don't know.'

She laughed as she said it and Bridie knew that, whoever her husband was, he wasn't going to say very much.

'Come from Nottingham, have you?'

Bridie nodded. 'I'm staying with my auntie Eveleen.'

Gracie placed the teapot on the table and sat down opposite her with an exclamation of delight. 'Eveleen. Ah, now there was a lovely lass. She didn't 'alf go through it, poor love. What with Mary moaning and groaning all the time and that brother of hers . . .' She cast a shrewd glance at Bridie and added apologetically, 'But I shouldn't call him names. He is your dad, after all.'

'You can say what you like about him, Mrs Turner,' Bridie said tartly, reaching for another scone. 'I've yet to meet him.'

Now the woman's mouth dropped open as she stared at Bridie. 'Wha . . .? You mean to say, you've never . . .? He's never . . .?'

Bridie shook her head. 'I've not been told very much about my family, Mrs Turner. In fact,' she smiled warmly at the woman, 'you've told me more about them in the last ten minutes than I've known the whole of me life. But I did know that me dad ran away to sea before I was born *and* . . .' she added with a trace of resentment, 'before he married my mother. That's why I'm called Singleton and not Hardcastle.'

Gracie was contrite. 'I'm sorry, mi little lass, if I've opened my big mouth and let it run away with itself.'

'Please, don't apologize. It's high time I knew about my family, but it all seems to be such a big secret, especially with my gran. Mary, I mean,' she added to make it clear about whom she was talking.

'I'd best say no more, 'specially not on that subject.' Gracie clamped her lips together to stop them uttering any more gossip. 'Drink up and I'll show you the way to Singleton's Yard, but I'll not come in with yer, if yer don't mind. I'm not exactly Harry Singleton's favourite person.' She smiled ruefully. 'Bit too free with me tongue. I'm likely to give him a piece of me mind when I see him and I wouldn't want you to get off on the wrong foot with him because of me.' The woman dropped her voice, but Bridie's sharp ears picked up her words. 'That'll happen without any help from me.'

Twenty-Six

They were standing at the end of a narrow street.

'This is Ranters' Row,' Gracie said, smiling. 'That's what us locals call it, but its proper name is Chapel Row. It's a dead end as you can see and your grandad's place is up there on the left-hand side.' The woman placed her hand on Bridie's shoulder. 'Good luck.' She turned to go and then glanced back. 'If you need any 'elp, you know where I live.'

'Thank you, Mrs Turner.'

Bridie took a deep breath and walked up the street, coming to a halt in front of a solid green gate. To her left was a long brick wall with windows and a door in the centre. Bridie pushed open the gate and stepped inside.

She was standing in one corner of a rectangular-shaped enclosure. To her left was a line of cottages, the back wall of which was obviously the one facing the street. Now she could see the front doors of the three homes facing the yard. The street side of the building had looked austere, but on this side a huge tree climbed the walls, straddling the whole frontage. Curiously she looked about her. A brick path ran in front of the cottages and halfway along it was a pump. From this, another path ran the length of the yard, branching off to the buildings on each side and at the far end. There were patches of garden on either side of the path, but the ground was neglected, growing wild and any plants were choked with weeds.

There was no-one about, the place seemed deserted, but then she became aware of the noise of machinery. Bridie stared up at the two-storey buildings. These were obviously not homes. On each floor there was one window, with tiny square panes, running the full length of the wall. Bridie smiled, knowing at once what these were.

These buildings were her grandfather's workshops. The windows were just like the ones in the back streets of Nottingham, where lacemakers and framework knitters worked in their own homes.

This was where Andrew worked. She glanced back towards the cottages, wondering which one was his home. Suddenly she felt close to him and tears started in her eyes. She had longed to see his home and, although she was here at last, he was not. Impatiently she brushed away her sentimental thoughts and approached one of the buildings. Inside, she climbed the steep stone steps to the upper floor, the clatter of machinery coming closer and closer.

At the top, she was standing in a long room. The machines, twenty or so, were set close together with the operators sitting back to back, and in a row down the side of the room beneath the long window. Only three machines were in use, two operated by older men and one by a young boy about Bridie's age. Against the opposite wall, too, there were machines, even though the light would not be so good there. These stood idle.

No-one had noticed her arrival; they had not heard her above the clatter so, for some time, Bridie stood watching the rhythmic operation of the framework knitters, trying to work out which of the two men was her grandfather.

As if feeling her gaze, the young lad looked up and grinned cheekily at her. Bridie smiled back, but the boy did not get up and come over to her. Instead, he shrugged and gestured towards the man sitting directly behind him. Then he pulled a grimace and drew his hand across his throat, intimating to Bridie what he thought the man would do to him if he left his work.

Bridie nodded, understanding. For a moment, she stood unobserved, watching the man. He was a big man, but his broad shoulders were stooped with the long years spent at his machine. He had a bushy white beard and moustache, which completely hid his mouth, and his heavy eyebrows met across the bridge of his large nose. He wore thick spectacles, but even with their aid he leant forward, peering at the rows of knitting as if he had trouble seeing them. She moved forward into his line of vision, hoping he would see her, but his whole attention was on his work.

After a few moments the young lad slid off his seat, tapped the man on his shoulder and gestured towards Bridie. The man looked up, squinting towards her. Without even pausing in his operation of the machine, he gestured with a swift, angry movement of his head that she should leave. The boy lifted his shoulders in a shrug then stepped nearer to her, putting his mouth close to her ear to shout, 'He'll not stop till dinnertime. You'd better go.'

But now the man did leave his work. He stepped towards them, his arm raised, and dealt the young lad a blow across the side of the head that sent him reeling halfway across the room. 'Get back to your work, you idle beggar. And you,' he thundered, turning to

Bridie, 'be off with you. And don't come here to see him again.'

For a moment, she thought the man might hit her too, but she stood her ground and faced him squarely. Now two machines were stopped, only the one worked by the other older man still making a noise, and Bridie could make herself heard. 'It's not him I've come to see.' Taking a chance that this was the right man, for he seemed to be the one in authority, she added, 'It's you.'

'What d'you want?'

She was aware of the boy's curiosity and even the other man, though still working, kept glancing at her.

Well, they'd all know sooner or later, she thought, so she lifted her chin and said boldly, 'I reckon you're me grandad.'

She saw the man start and then he leant closer, squinting at her. Suddenly he gripped her shoulder and hustled her towards the top of the stairs, almost pushing her down them in front of him, but keeping hold of her shoulder with such a strong grip that his fingers dug into her.

Out in the yard, he spun her round to face him. 'Now, I don't know who you are or what you're after, but I don't want to see you round here again. That clear?'

Bridie stared at him. Then, quite calmly, she gripped his wrist, trying to release his grasp on her. 'Let go,' she said firmly. 'You're hurting me.'

'I'll hurt you, you little tyke.' It was the same name, the same tone that her grandmother, Mary, had used so often that Bridie almost laughed aloud. But the moment was far from funny.

'That's a nice way to greet your granddaughter, I must say.'

The man released her suddenly as if the touch of her was burning his hand. 'I haven't got a granddaughter.'

'Yes, you have.' For a brief moment, Bridie wondered if she had picked the wrong man in the workshop. Maybe the bent, wizened little old man on the other machine was Harry Singleton. But some instinct told her she had made the correct choice.

She lifted her chin higher, staring boldly up at him. 'You had a daughter, Rebecca, didn't you?'

He was about to deny it, even opened his mouth to refute it, but the words never came. Suddenly the huge shoulders sagged and he put out his hand to the nearby wall to steady himself.

'She's dead.'

'I know that,' Bridie said, her tone gentler, 'but I'm her daughter, Bridie. I've lived with me gran, Mary. She's your sister, isn't she?'

He nodded dully, but still he kept his gaze averted.

'She'd never let me come to see you.'

He gave a harsh, humourless laugh. 'Well, that doesn't surprise me.'

'She said you wouldn't want to see me.'

Now he was silent and to her, desperate to hear his denial, it was instead confirmation.

'Even Andrew wouldn't let me come.' There was a catch in her voice.

Now the man met her gaze, but he was still frowning. 'Andrew? Andrew Burns? What's he got to do with it?'

'He's my godfather. He used to come most Sundays to the farm to see me.'

'Well! Well, I never.' Harry – for now she was sure it was her grandfather – seemed genuinely surprised, but he was still not pleased. 'And how long has this been going on?'

Bridie shrugged. 'As long as I can remember.'

'He never said.' There was accusation in his tone.

'It was in his free time. You don't own him.'

'Mebbe not. But I employed him. I gave him his living. And I own the cottage he lives in.' He jerked his thumb over his shoulder. 'I could sack him and turn him out of his home, if I had a mind. Just like that.' He snapped his finger and thumb together. His voice dropped to a deep, aggrieved rumble. 'In fact, I might just do that. His place is standing empty now the silly young beggar's volunteered. Rushed off with all the rest of 'em into the Good Lord only knows what.'

'Which is his cottage?' Bridie asked, craning her neck to look beyond the huge frame of the man standing in front of her.

'What's it to you? Don't think you can go meddling in there.'

'Andrew wouldn't mind.'

'*I* don't know who you are. You could be anybody, for all I know.'

'Yes, you do,' Bridie insisted. 'I'm Rebecca's daughter. I even look like her. Andrew said.'

'I can't see the likeness myself.'

'That's because you can't see very well now, can you?'

'Who told you that?' he barked, his resentment surfacing again swiftly.

'I don't need anyone to tell me. I watched you at work. I was stood there for ages before you saw me.'

'Can't hear anything above the noise.'

'Mebbe not. But you were squinting at the knitting as it came off the machine. And there was a flaw in it you didn't notice.'

'Cheeky little baggage, aren't you? You're not like

my . . .' he began, almost tricked into acknowledging that at least it was a possibility that she was his granddaughter. As if to counter his moment of weakness, he made an angry gesture with his right arm. 'Be off with you. And don't come here again.'

Bridie regarded him steadily. Far from being frightened of him or fazed by his anger, she felt sorry for him. It was obvious his once thriving business was struggling. Only three to carry on the work; an old man, a young boy and a man who could hardly see now. It was obvious Harry Singleton needed help. But he was too stubborn to seek it.

She would go – for now – but first there was someone else Bridie wanted to see. With a quiet dignity that belied her tender years, she said, 'I'm going nowhere, Grandfather, until I've seen my great-grandmother.'

Twenty-Seven

Bridie let herself into the end cottage in the row. She stood a moment until her eyes became accustomed to the gloom. Then she glanced around the room, cluttered with possessions accumulated over the years. Everywhere was covered with a film of dust. There was no fire in the grate in the range, only ashes not yet cleaned out. The range itself was dull and neglected. She tiptoed through into the scullery to find unwashed post and bits of mouldering food. There was a stale smell about the place too. In the far corner of the scullery was the staircase and Bridie climbed it, calling out as she went.

'Are you there, Great-Gran?' She didn't know what else to call the old lady who lived here. The full title – great-grandmother – was such a mouthful, but she didn't want to appear in the old lady's bedroom unannounced and startle her.

A querulous voice came from the larger of the two bedrooms on the first landing. 'Who's that? Is that you, Lil?'

Bridie pushed open the door. The old lady was lying in the double, metal-framed bed against a mound of greyish-looking pillows. Her white hair stuck up in unkempt tufts and her thin face was a network of lines and wrinkles. Her bony, purple-veined hands plucked at the covers and her voice was frail as she quavered, 'Who are you?'

Bridie moved to the side of the bed and began to say, 'Don't be frightened, I'm . . .' but the old woman clutched at the covers until her knuckles were white and shrieked, 'Rebecca!'

Bridie stopped and gasped in surprise as they stared at each other. Both were startled but the old lady had a look of sheer terror in her eyes.

Bridie reached out towards her. 'I'm Rebecca's daughter, Bridie.'

'Bridie?' she quavered. Then she moaned and closed her eyes. 'Oh, dear Lord. She's come for me. It's my time. Rebecca's come for me.'

'Great-Gran,' Bridie said firmly. 'Please listen to me. I'm Bridie. I'm Rebecca's daughter. But I know I look a bit like Rebecca.'

The old lady seemed to be recovering her senses a little after the first shock. She opened her eyes and stared at her. 'Bridie? Your name's Bridie too?'

'My name is Bridie,' the girl said mystified. 'But what do you mean "too"?'

'That's my name, Bridget, but me da always called me Bridie.'

The young girl beamed. 'Then obviously I'm called after you.'

'After me? Why?'

The poor old thing confined to her bed was obviously confused. Patiently Bridie explained. 'Because I'm your great-granddaughter.'

The old lady blinked, trying to focus her watery eyes on the figure standing at the end of her bed. 'My . . .' She began and then lapsed into silence, lost in thought and trying to catch hold of vague, ephemeral memories. Then she let out a long sigh and fell back against the pillows.

'Bridie. Now I remember. Eveleen came with a little baby, Rebecca's baby, and said they were going to call her after me.'

'That's right,' Bridie said eagerly. Perhaps the old lady was not so senile after all. Perhaps all she needed was a little tender loving care.

'Brought the baby back here to be christened in the chapel across the road. But Harry didn't go. Harry wouldn't even go to the poor little mite's christening.'

That 'poor little mite' was me, Bridie was thinking. But she said nothing, allowing the frail old lady to come to the truth in her own time.

Bridie moved closer to the bed. 'I can't stay much longer today, but . . .'

Bridget's bony hands were reaching out. 'Don't go. Stay and talk to me. Nobody comes to talk to me now.' The voice was pitiful. 'Please, don't leave me.'

'Great-gran, I have to go.' Bridie gave a nervous laugh. 'My Aunt Eveleen's going to skin me alive as it is for coming. She doesn't know I'm here.'

'Eveleen.' The old lady said the name as if it had not been spoken aloud for years. 'Ah yes, Eveleen. I always liked Eveleen. Strong, she was. Braver than all the rest of us put together.'

Questions tumbled around Bridie's mind. There was so much she would like to ask, so much that her great-grandmother must know. Instead, anxious that the old lady should not be upset any more, she said, 'I'll make us both a cup of tea before I go.'

'Aye, I could do with one.' Her voice was stronger now, laced with resentment. 'That Lil should have been in this morning but she hasn't been near.'

'Who's Lil?' Bridie asked.

Bridget tossed her head. 'Lives in the cottage facing

the street. She's supposed to clean for us. Make our meals an' that, but half the time Harry has to do it when he's finished work.' She sniffed. 'Still, there's no-one else to do it, so I s'pect we'll have to put up with 'er doing it when she feels like it.'

Several minutes later, Bridie helped her great-grandmother to sit up in the bed, plumping the pillows behind her. 'Now, here's your tea. Don't spill it.'

'You'd make a good nurse,' Bridget said, slurping her tea thirstily.

'Does my grandfather live here with you?' Bridie asked as she perched on the end of the bed to drink hers.

'No. He lives in the cottage at the other end.'

Bridie ran her tongue over lips that were suddenly dry. 'So – so Andrew lives in the cottage next door? Between the two of you?'

The old woman squinted at her. 'That's right. But he's not here. He's gone to the war.'

Bridie nodded. 'I know.'

There was silence between them as they drank their tea until Bridie said, 'I can't stay much longer. I must get the omnibus back to Nottingham. Will my grandfather be finishing work soon?'

The old lady gave a wry laugh. 'What? Him? No. Works all day and 'alf the night now.'

'Really?' Bridie was surprised. From what her aunt had told her, work at the factory was falling off. So why . . .? Her great-grandmother's next words gave her the answer.

'He's pulled out the place with work, and no-one to do it now all the young fellers have gone off to the war.'

'I don't understand. Where's all the work coming from? Auntie Evie says the Reckitt and Stokes's factory is going through a bad time. No-one wants lace in wartime.'

'Well, no, they won't. But what your uncle makes is knitted garments. Fine underwear – long johns, vests, socks. And all the officers' families round here are climbing over themselves to have well-made garments for their boys. We're getting orders from Nottingham and even other places, now word's spreading. And when Queen Mary appealed to the Empire to knit three hundred thousand pairs of socks for the troops, well, Harry nearly had a heart attack.'

Bridie placed the empty cups on the tea tray and bent to kiss the old lady's wizened cheeks. 'I must go now, Great-Gran. I have to go back and face my aunt. But, whatever she says, I will come back.' She glanced around at the neglected room and thought of the state of the rooms downstairs. 'You need me far more than she does,' Bridie murmured.

As she passed Andrew's cottage on her way out, Bridie peered through the windows. She could see little of the dim interior, but she laid her hand against the door and whispered, 'I'll be back. I promise I'll be back.'

'Emily, how is Miss Bridie?' Eveleen asked as soon as she stepped over the threshold that evening at six o'clock. Although it was a Saturday and the workforce usually finished at lunchtime, nevertheless Eveleen had remained at the factory.

Brinsley had visited that morning and, feeling much better than he had of late, had involved Eveleen in lengthy discussions on the seriousness of the current state of the order book. He had insisted on touring the machine shops and talking to the men and women now working the lace machines. He had even climbed to the top floor of the warehouse to visit the inspection room and speak to Helen. Then he had stopped at each floor on the way down.

When their tour was over, he had insisted that Eveleen should go to lunch with him in the city. By the time they had finished, it was three o'clock and Eveleen still had paperwork to complete at the factory before going home.

'I haven't seen her all day, ma'am,' the girl replied now, taking Eveleen's coat and hat. 'Dinner will be ready in half an hour, Cook says.'

'Thank you,' Eveleen said absently, but her mind was still on her niece. 'Is she still in her room? Haven't you been to see if she wanted anything?'

'You said to leave her and she would ring, ma'am.'

Eveleen clicked her tongue against her teeth in agitation. 'I know I did, but – all day! Surely you thought to go and check that she was all right?' When the young girl looked crestfallen, Eveleen said, 'Oh, never mind. I'll see for myself.'

She ran lightly up the stairs and, opening the door quietly in case Bridie was asleep, tiptoed into the bedroom. The bed was unmade but empty and, further along the landing, the bathroom showed signs that Bridie had washed hurriedly. On closer inspection, Eveleen found that the girl's clothes, including her outdoor hat and coat, were also missing.

Downstairs she rang for the young maid. 'She seems to have gone out. Are you sure you heard nothing?'

'No, ma'am. Mind you, I've been down in the kitchen for a lot of the day, so I wouldn't have heard her going out of the front door.'

'And you haven't looked in her bedroom all day?'

The girl shook her head, easy tears starting in her eyes. 'I'm sorry, ma'am, if I should have . . .'

'No, no,' Eveleen held up her hands. 'It's not your fault, Emily.' More to herself now than to the maid, Eveleen murmured, 'But I wonder where she can have gone.'

'Maybe she felt a little better and went to work?' Emily tried to suggest helpfully.

Eveleen shook her head. 'No, I'd have seen her.'

'Maybe she's gone shopping.'

Eveleen wrinkled her brow. 'It's possible, I suppose. But she's never been into the city on her own before.'

'Would she go home, I mean back to the farm, to see her gran?'

Eveleen stared at Emily. 'No,' she said slowly. 'No, I don't think she'd go there. But now you've made me think, I know exactly where she has gone.'

Emily still looked puzzled. 'Where, ma'am?'

'Never mind,' Eveleen said, her mouth tight, 'but just wait until the little madam gets back home.'

Twenty-Eight

'You deliberately disobeyed me.'

An hour later, Bridie was facing an angry Eveleen. 'I'm sorry you're cross with me, Auntie Evie, but I'm not sorry I went.'

Eveleen gasped and her eyes widened in surprise at the audacity of her young niece. But as the girl went on, her anger died to be replaced by her own guilt.

'Andrew was right, Auntie. They do need help badly.' Swiftly she explained all that she had seen in Singleton's Yard. 'My grandfather doesn't want us there. Doesn't seem to want anyone, but poor Great-Gran, she needs looking after, Auntie Evie. She'll die, else.'

'Oh, I think that's being a bit melodramatic, Bridie.'

The girl shook her head vehemently. 'No, it isn't. I called at Mrs Turner's on the way back to catch the omnibus and . . .'

'Mrs Turner?' Eveleen searched her mind for the memory of the large, bustling woman who had been her mother's childhood friend. 'Gracie Turner,' she murmured.

'That's her,' Bridie went on. 'Well, when I told her that Great-Gran thought I was someone called Lil coming up the stairs, Mrs Turner said there was no wonder they were in a state. She said that this Lil is a right – she hesitated, trying to remember the unfamiliar word – 'a right slattern.'

Despite her growing anxiety, Eveleen had to smile, but it soon faded as Bridie stepped nearer her and put a hand on her arm. 'Auntie Evie, I am sorry I disobeyed you, but they do need help. Both of them. My grandad can hardly see, and the poor old lady, I don't think she can get out of bed without help. And,' she added pointedly, 'there's no one to help her.' Looking into the girl's dark blue eyes, Eveleen could read her genuine distress.

She patted Bridie's hand, 'It's all right. You're forgiven.' She pulled a comical face of contrition. 'It's me who should be saying sorry. It's me who should have gone.' She was ashamed to think that it had been a thirteen-year-old girl who had undertaken what should have been an older person's responsibility. 'But I didn't think we'd be welcome there.'

'Oh, we're not,' Bridie said airily. 'But that's not the point, is it? They need help, both of them, even if they won't admit it. And,' she grinned impishly at her aunt, 'whether they like it or not, they're going to get it.'

'Oh, Bridie.' Eveleen opened her arms to the girl. 'Give me a hug.'

They stood together holding each other close, drawing comfort from each other, united in their loneliness, in missing the menfolk they adored.

'Come,' Eveleen said at last, taking Bridie's hand. 'Let's go and have the dinner that's Cook's been holding back for an hour and discuss what we're going to do.'

'Do you think we should go to the farm and talk it over with your gran?' Eveleen said as they reached the pudding course.

'I've only ever heard her ask Andrew about them

once or twice.' Bridie's voice hardened. 'Do you really think she's bothered?'

Eveleen sighed. 'She harbours such a lot of bitterness about things that have happened in the past.'

'What things?'

Eveleen regarded her steadily. 'I can't really tell you. Not just now, anyway. Maybe one day.'

'About my mother and me, you mean?'

'That's part of it,' Eveleen said carefully.

Sharply inquisitive, Bridie said, 'But not all of it?'

Eveleen shook her head. 'Oh no. Not all of it. Not by a long way.'

For a moment they were both quiet, lost in their own thoughts, before Bridie dropped a bombshell into the silence. 'Why don't I go and live there and look after them?'

Eveleen's spoon clattered into her dish. 'I don't think that's a very good idea. Your gran wouldn't like it.'

'Gran's got nothing to do with it,' Bridie said, once more sounding very much older than her years. 'We've just decided that she's probably not that bothered.'

'I don't think we ought to say that . . .' Eveleen began, but Bridie interrupted impatiently, 'Well, you know what I mean.'

'But I need you here,' Eveleen protested.

Gently Bridie said, 'No, you don't, Auntie Evie. Not really. There's dozens of young girls in Nottingham who'd leap at the chance to work in Reckitt and Stokes's warehouse. You don't really need me.'

'But I want you here, Bridie,' Eveleen insisted. 'You said yourself your grandfather doesn't want you there. Doesn't want any of us.'

Bridie laughed, her blue eyes glinting with a sudden steely resolve. 'I know, but they need me, Auntie Evie.

There's a big difference, isn't there, between being wanted and needed. For a long time I didn't think anyone wanted or needed me.'

'That's not true, Bridie . . .' Eveleen began to protest.

'I know. I know that now.' The young girl, who was growing up so fast, almost before Eveleen's eyes, said gently, 'Gran and Josh must have wanted to keep me as a baby, because they needn't have. And Andrew . . .' Her voice wavered slightly as she thought about him soon to be in a foreign, dangerous land. 'I know he does love me. In his own way.'

'We all do, Bridie,' Eveleen said softly.

The girl nodded and then, with words that tore at Eveleen's heart, she said simply, 'But for the first time in my life someone really *needs* me.'

'If you're really sure, then . . .' Eveleen began.

'I am. There's no-one to look after Great-Gran. Grandfather is working all hours, even though his sight is bad. There's only him, one other old chap and a young lad in the workshops. They can't cope with all the work that's coming in.' She laughed as she repeated the old lady's words. 'They're pulled out the place.'

'What?' Eveleen was suddenly alert. 'What work?'

'It seems everyone's after their knitted undergarments to send to the men at the Front. You know?'

Eveleen stared at her and slowly shook her head. 'No, I don't know. Explain it to me slowly.'

Bridie repeated all that her great-grandmother had told her. 'Funny, isn't it?' she added. 'You've got too many workers and not enough work and he's got more . . .' Her voice faltered as she stared back at her aunt. Slowly her own mind began to realize what was going on in Eveleen's. 'He's got more work than he can cope with.'

'Exactly!' Eveleen sprang to her feet and held her arms wide. 'My darling Bridie. I think you've just brought home another answer to help save your Uncle Richard's factory.'

'But – but you can't make those things on lace machines, can you?'

'No, of course not. But we can send workers out to Flawford or bring the work into the city. There must be a lot of frames standing idle now since their operators have gone to war. Maybe we could even bring some into the factory. We're already making plans to turn over to curtain-making machines and with knitting machines too . . .' Eveleen clapped her hands in delight. 'Richard's factory will survive. Oh, Bridie, I know it will.'

The strain of the past few weeks was lifted and Eveleen, despite the ever-present worry over all the men at war, looked happier than she had done for months.

Bridie smiled and asked impishly, 'So I'm forgiven, then, for going to Flawford?'

Eveleen laughed. 'Oh yes, Bridie, you're forgiven.'

They hugged one another and danced around the room. They came to a breathless halt and leant against each other.

'There's just one thing,' Eveleen panted. 'We'll have to tell them at Pear Tree Farm. I need Josh's advice about all this now.'

Bridie pulled a face. 'Oh, all right then. But Gran'll be mad I've been to see them. And she'll try to stop me going back there. I know she will.'

'You'll do no such thing.'

Mary was adamant and she turned to Josh for his

support. 'You'll back me in this, won't you, Josh?' She whirled back to face Eveleen and Bridie and wagged her forefinger at them. 'I knew it would cause trouble, her coming to live with you. You haven't time nor, to my mind, the inclination,' she added, derisively, 'to be keeping your eye on her properly. I told you, she's a wilful little tyke who needs a firm hand. Well.' Now she turned her attention directly to Bridie. 'Well, you'll be feeling the back of mine, if you're not careful.'

Bridie glanced at Eveleen and saw her mouth tighten and saw too, Josh glancing helplessly from one to the other of them. He was caught up in a quarrel, rooted in the distant past, that was none of his making.

Bridie forced herself to keep calm. Reasoned argument might convince her grandmother as no childish pouting and stamping of feet ever would. 'Gran,' she said quietly, but with an adult firmness that Mary had not heard before, 'if you'd only seen them, you'd understand why I must go back and care for them. You wouldn't leave animals in that state.'

'Have you been?' Mary glared accusingly at Eveleen. 'Have you seen for yourself because I wouldn't believe a word she's saying? I think it's all—'

'No, Mam,' Eveleen cut in. 'But I mean to take her there anyway, when she goes, so I shall see for myself.' She glanced swiftly at Bridie, who, despite her resolution to keep calm, had opened her mouth to protest, 'Not that I don't believe you, Bridie, I promise you. But I want to know that you're going to be all right. That you'll be able to cope there on your own.'

Bridie closed her mouth, smiled and nodded, 'I'll cope, Auntie Eveleen. If I can't,' her smile widened to a mischievous grin. 'I'll call in reinforcements. I'll fetch Mrs Turner.'

'Gracie Turner?' Mary picked up the name. 'Oh, I might have known she'd be sticking her nose in where it's not wanted.' She glowered at them all, including Josh. 'But it seems as if it's all decided. I don't really know why you've come here to ask me.'

'Maybe we shouldn't have, but you're still Bridie's guardian and—'

'Then I say she's not to go,' Mary snapped.

Only just managing now to hold onto her temper, Bridie asked, 'Why, Gran? Just explain to me why you don't want me to go.'

There was an awkward silence in the room, a tension between the three adults that the girl could not understand.

'Because – because . . .' Mary was hesitant, her glance roving round the room as if unable to meet the steady gaze of her granddaughter and as if she was searching for a plausible excuse. Bridie had the distinct feeling that she was not hearing the whole truth. Not from any of them. Mary jumped up suddenly, galvanized into action. 'Do what you like then, but don't come running back to me when they treat you badly.' She nodded. 'You'll soon be back. You'll not stand it there five minutes.' And she added sagely, 'I know them. And you.' She turned to Eveleen again. 'You'd better go there every week while she's there to see what's going on.'

'It's probable I shall be going there quite a lot, Mam. That's the other thing I wanted to talk to you about. Well, to Josh really.'

Swiftly she explained all the circumstances, the lack of work in the city and the abundance of orders at Singleton's Yard. 'Do you think we can do it, Josh? Turn our workforce to making clothes for the troops?'

'I think, mi duck,' he said slowly, 'that it's the only

way you're going to survive the war. But will your uncle agree?'

Before Eveleen could answer, Mary butted in. 'Huh! You're asking if Harry will agree to making money? You might well ask if the sun will rise tomorrow morning.'

The tension between them eased and Eveleen and Bridie left soon afterwards, Josh giving Bridie a firm hug.

'Ne'er mind what yer gran says, mi duck. If you've got trouble, you come back here. You know yer gran. Her bark's worse than her bite.'

Bridie smiled up at him. 'I know,' she said softly to the big man alone. 'And I know *you*.'

There was no need for further words between them; their understanding was mutual.

As Eveleen drove the motor car back towards Nottingham, she breathed a sigh of relief. 'That went better than I expected.'

'Better!' Bridie exclaimed in surprise.

'Oh yes. Believe me, she could have stopped you going. She is your legal guardian and there's not a thing I could have done about it.'

'Oh.' Bridie was thoughtful for a moment before she asked, 'Then why didn't she?'

Eveleen frowned. 'I don't really know, Bridie. Maybe, deep down, she does want someone to look after them. But she won't go herself. Never in a million years.'

'Why? What happened to make her so bitter?'

'Don't ask me, love. It's not my place to tell you. Maybe when you're older . . .' was all her aunt would say and with that, for the moment, the girl had to be content.

Twenty-Nine

'Oh, it's you. I might have known you'd be behind sending her here.'

On the following Sunday morning, Eveleen and Bridie knocked on the door of the first cottage in the row in Singleton's Yard. Now they stood facing Harry Singleton as he squinted at them, peering into first one face and then the other.

'May we come in, Uncle?' Eveleen asked, stepping across the threshold before he had time to refuse.

'Seems like you're in,' he grunted, turned and shuffled back towards his chair by the range, feeling his way past the furniture.

Eveleen bit her lip as she watched him. He was a changed man from the last time she had seen him thirteen years before. She glanced around the room, which had once been so neat and shining. Now papers, clothes, bits and bobs cluttered every surface. The white tablecloth, looking as if it hadn't been removed between meals for a week, was stained with spills.

Eveleen sat down in the chair opposite him. 'Uncle Harry, Bridie has come to stay here a while to look after you and Gran.'

'We don't need anyone.'

Eveleen smiled, though a little sadly. Not quite all the fiery independence had gone.

'Gran needs some help, even if you don't.'

'She's got Lil Fairbrother . . .' He jerked his thumb over his shoulder, indicating the adjacent cottage, the one facing the street. 'She looks after her.'

'She's not doing a very good job of it,' Eveleen said bluntly and beside her Bridie felt a shaft of admiration for her aunt.

He grunted. 'It'll do for us.' Then he roused himself, seeming to summon up some of his old strength, some of the vigour that Eveleen remembered so well. 'I don't want you or her here. You brought trouble on this family. Aye, you and your mother before you.' He flung out his arm towards Bridie. 'Born in sin, she was, thanks to you and your precious family. And I lost my lovely Rebecca because of it. I don't forget, Eveleen, and I don't forgive.'

'I'm very sorry to hear you say that, Uncle. I thought perhaps by now, you could find it in your heart not to bear a grudge against an innocent girl. It was none of her doing, now was it?'

'It was your brother who took my girl down. Shamed her and – and . . .' For a brief moment the big man's voice trembled. 'And caused her death. But for him, she'd have still been here to care for me and her grandmother.'

Indeed she would, Eveleen thought bitterly. An unhappy spinster tied to a life of drudgery. But she gave nothing of her own thoughts away. Instead she said, with as much gentleness as she could muster, 'But now her daughter is here instead.'

'Well, we don't want her.' It was his last vestige of fight, for now he lay back in his chair and covered his eyes with his hand.

Eveleen leant across and touched his knee gently and,

using the very words that Bridie herself had used, said, 'Maybe not, but you do need her, Uncle Harry.'

'Now it's come to it, I don't like leaving you here.'

Later, standing beside the motor car in the narrow street, Eveleen looked down at the slight figure of the girl in front of her. She looked so young and yet, suddenly, there was an air of inner strength about her. A determination that now had nothing to do with wilfulness. There was a sense of purpose in her eyes and a firm resolution to the set of her jaw. Bridie was a girl with a mission.

At the thought, Eveleen smiled inwardly. How ironic, in view of Harry Singleton's devotion to the chapel, that that was the phrase that should spring to her mind.

As she hugged Bridie, she said, 'Are you sure the money I've given you will be enough? By the look of it, you'll need to restock the pantry.'

'It'll be fine till you come again.' She laughed. 'I shall enjoy playing at being a housewife.'

'There won't be much "play" about it, love. But don't forget, if you have any problems, let me know at once. Promise?'

'I will, Auntie Evie, and thank you for everything.'

Eveleen held her close. 'It's me who should be thanking you.'

As she drove home alone, Eveleen was already missing Bridie's lively company. When she opened the door and stepped into the house, even the knowledge that below stairs there were servants did not drive out the feeling of emptiness and loneliness. She dined alone in the immaculate, yet soulless, dining room and vowed that in future she would eat on a tray in her cosy sitting room, instead of placed at one end of the long polished table staring at the empty chairs. Richard's, and now Bridie's too.

Work, she promised herself as she got into the huge bed, work was her salvation. There was plenty to organize, much to do and tomorrow she would talk to Brinsley. She lay down and, as she always did, she put out her hand to touch the pillow where Richard's head should be and, like that, she fell asleep.

Bridie lay down on the rug in front of her great-grandmother's range and pulled a moth-eaten blanket from the spare bedroom over her. She had lit a fire in the range and now the downstairs front room was warm, even though the mustiness of neglect had not yet been driven out. She would sleep here for her first night, for the spare bed upstairs was damp. Tomorrow she would lug the mattress down to air before she would consider sleeping on it.

Upstairs the old lady now lay between fresh sheets, warmed earlier in the day in front of the fire. A fire now also burned in the grate in her bedroom and Bridie had spooned hot soup into the toothless mouth.

She had seen nothing of her grandfather since the moment Eveleen had left. Bridget, and the sorry state she was lying in, were the girl's first concern. At least her grandfather was mobile. He was capable of climbing the stairs to his bed and of getting himself some sort of a meal, meagre though it might be.

Tomorrow, Bridie promised silently as sleep claimed her, I'll sort him out too.

The following morning the girl was awake early, stoking up the fire in the range and preparing a breakfast tray for her great-grandmother. There was little food in the house and Bridie suspected the same would be true of her grandfather's home. When she had made the old lady comfortable and given her her breakfast, Bridie saw her uncle making his unsteady way to the workshop. Once she knew he was safely at his framework knitting machine, she felt she could investigate.

First she toured the small cottage where Bridget lived. The front door opened directly into the living room and beyond that was the scullery, out of which steep stairs led to the first-floor landing, where there were two bedrooms. From that floor there was a ladder to an attic bedroom, which bore signs of once having been occupied, no doubt by male lodgers who worked for her grandfather. Then, leaving her great-grandmother's home, Bridie walked along the path and, holding her breath, tried the door of the cottage at the opposite end of the row. This was her grandfather's house and the place where her own mother had once lived. The layout was much the same as Bridget's home, but the opposite way round. Bridie had been right about one thing: there was little food in the pantry. Her heart thumping, she climbed the stairs, peeping into the main bedroom and the smaller one on the first floor. She swallowed hard as she looked at the single bed, still neatly made. Had this been where Rebecca had slept? Then she climbed the ladder to the attic room. Here an iron bedstead with a mouldy mattress still stood in the room and the floor was littered with old toys and books and the junk of many years. Bridie picked up an old school slate and ran her fingers over it. There was even a tiny piece of white chalk. These must have belonged to her mother and the girl felt a strange affinity with the long-dead woman. She was touching something that Rebecca had once held. Her fingers were now resting in the same place that her mother's had once done. Somehow, here in the place where her mother had lived, Rebecca was almost a living, breathing presence. Suddenly, for the first time in the whole of her life, Bridie felt close to the woman who had borne her and she wanted, desperately, to know much more about her. Reverently she fingered the other toys. She must have been a very special person, Bridie thought, to have earned Andrew's undying devotion. He had never married, never, so far as Bridie knew, even looked at another woman.

If only, she thought, brushing away an unbidden tear, he would love me in the same way.

She stood up, promising herself that when time allowed she would clean this attic room and set Rebecca's belongings out as she would have liked. She would wash the lace-trimmed runner on the dressing table and the patchwork quilt folded at the end of the bed. She would clean and tidy this room and keep it as a lasting memorial to the child, the girl and the woman who had perhaps once slept here.

Downstairs again, Bridie stepped out into the yard and looked about her. Investigating the other buildings, she found that at the end of the building on the right-hand side there was a wash-house, with a copper, rinsing tub, dolly pegs, posser and a mangle.

'I'll soon have that going,' she murmured, closing the door for the moment. She walked between the two workshops on either side, hearing the clatter of the machinery coming from the upper floor of the one to her left. It seemed to be the only one now where any work was being done, for when she peeped into the other workshops she saw the lines of idle frames. Auntie Evie will soon have those busy, Bridie thought to herself, smiling, if I know her. The buildings across the end of the yard housed communal lavatories for the workers as well as for the residents of the cottages, a coal store and an empty pigsty, where the smell of the one-time occupants still lingered.

Bridie turned and walked back towards the cottages, coming to a stop in front of the door of the centre dwelling. Her hand trembled as she touched the doorknob and turned it. To her surprise, it opened and, holding her breath, Bridie stepped into Andrew's home.

Thirty

Bridie moved around the living room in Andrew's home.

Although a thin layer of dust lay everywhere, everything was painfully neat and tidy. Bridie sat in his chair by the range and let her eyes roam around the room, drinking in the sight of his belongings. Her glance came to the mantelpiece above the range and she rose to look closely at the photographs there. Her eyes widened and she gasped.

Each, in its own silver frame, was a photograph of her, one for every year of her life from babyhood to the age of twelve. Tears filled her eyes and the images before her blurred.

'Oh, Andrew, Andrew,' she whispered brokenly.

Then she moved to the roll-top desk in the corner and lifted the unlocked lid. Yet more photographs of her were laid out in neat bundles. There were a few envelopes or letters tied up with ribbon and, before she even touched them, she knew that they were what she had sent or given him. Christmas cards and birthday cards that she had made for him from the time he had given her a box of paints. Bridie wrinkled her brow, trying to recall how old she had been. Five was it, or six? There was even the letter she had sent to him when he had been ill and unable to visit the farm for a few weeks. Her childish scrawl evoked the memory of that time and how she had missed seeing him so dreadfully, yet again forbidden by her grandmother from visiting him at his home.

She wandered through to the scullery, where the pots and pans were neatly stacked, poignantly awaiting a need for their use. Then she climbed the stairs and stepped into the main bedroom. Here again everything was so heartbreakingly neat and tidy. On the small table beside his bed stood a larger copy of the last photograph on the mantelpiece downstairs, the one taken on her twelfth birthday.

'But there should be another one,' she said aloud. 'We had one taken in Grantham when I was thirteen, just before they left . . .' And then she understood.

That photograph was missing because he had taken it with him to war.

In May, the sinking of the *Lusitania* brought America down firmly on the side of Britain and her Allies. At the end of the month, Richard wrote that he had had an inoculation that day – *Not very pleasant*.

Because the months had passed and Richard, Andrew and the others had not been sent overseas, Eveleen – and Bridie too – had begun to hope that they would never go. But now it sounded as if they were being prepared. A month later his letter contained news that made Eveleen's heart leap in fear.

Three hundred and fifty men have been warned for draft, some from our company – Sid is one of them. Andrew and I did our best to get on the draft, but no go. So we have to kick our heels and wait! We are going to musketry school in Luton on a machine-gun course instead. I don't know if we'll get leave before we go overseas. We do get the odd thirty-six-hour pass, but it isn't long enough to get home.

'Can you believe it?' Eveleen exclaimed to Bridie on one of her weekend visits to Flawford. 'Richard talks as if they can't wait to get over there.'

Bridie was solemn-faced. 'I suppose they feel that's what they've volunteered for.'

Eveleen glanced at her. Bridie seemed to have grown taller during the last few weeks. She was still only thirteen, but now seemed so much older. The war had taken away her childhood, bringing her worries and possibly grief that no young girl ought to know. She was frowning now as she went on. 'I don't know if I ought to say this . . .'

'Go on,' Eveleen prompted gently.

'Well, I didn't want Andrew or Richard or any of them to go, but – but now they have, I do feel ever so proud of them. And yesterday I saw more volunteers marching along the village main street. Some of them didn't look much older than me. They looked so brave, all going off to war. I – I couldn't help joining in the cheering, even though part of me still wanted to run up to them and tell them not to go.'

There were tears in Eveleen's eyes as she held out her arms to the girl. 'Oh, Bridie, I know exactly what you mean. I feel just the same. All mixed up inside.'

'But they're still here in this country, aren't they? Andrew and Richard.' Bridie was determined to be optimistic. 'Maybe it will soon be over and they won't even have to go to the Front.'

'Maybe,' Eveleen murmured, but said no more. She read the papers each day and they gave not even a glimmer of such a hope.

Further Zeppelin raids on the east coast of Britain had killed twenty-four people.

'It's getting a bit too close for comfort,' Mary muttered and Josh, who seemed to have his head buried in a newspaper most of the time, said, 'The government are denying that they're going to bring in conscription, but they passed the National Registration Bill. I reckon that's the start of it.'

At the beginning of August Eveleen received the letter from Richard that she had been dreading. As she read the words, she gave a little gasp and, with trembling fingers, felt her way to a chair to sit down.

We've been warned for draft and will probably be leaving in a few days. Oh, and I've been appointed Lance Corporal, so Mother should be pleased . . .

Eveleen closed her eyes and groaned aloud, wishing in the same moment that Bridie was here with her and yet glad that she was not. Eveleen's mind raced. Perhaps they wouldn't go. Perhaps word would come that hostilities had ceased and they wouldn't be needed. But she knew it was a vain hope.

The letter slipped from her lap and fell to the floor as Eveleen covered her face with her hands and wept.

Richard's next letter came from France.

Reveille 4 a.m. We struck camp on the 10th August, marched twenty-one miles in full overseas kit to Watford – very hot day. Now we know what all that training was for! Pitched camp for a few days and then caught the train to Southampton, embarking on a paddle steamer at 5.30 p.m. on the 18th. Arrived Le Havre at midnight, where we stayed till noon the next day and then went up the Seine to Rouen. It was a good journey. You wouldn't believe that not that many miles away there's a war going on. We're in a rest camp near Rouen, so we've had a look at the cathedral and even went up the spire! We are to be on guard at the docks. Don't worry – most of us are still together. Andrew and Leslie are fine, but we've had no news of Sid . . .

It was only a week later that Eveleen had to write to Richard to tell him that Sid had been wounded very badly in the leg and had arrived back in England. She paused, her pen hovering above the paper. Elsie is lucky, she thought, at least Sid is still alive and she will have her husband back with her. But the words remained unwritten.

The following week there was no letter from Richard, nor one from Andrew to Bridie. Eveleen's anxiety grew, but she tried to suppress it by throwing herself into her work. She arrived at the factory earlier each morning and left later every evening. But even there the war and its tragedies were never very far away.

Luke Manning, who seemed to have stepped, unofficially at present, into Bob Porter's shoes met Eveleen at the entrance to the factory one morning. 'You'd best get to the warehouse, Eveleen. There's trouble in the inspection room.'

'Trouble?' Eveleen said, her brow puckering. 'Where's Helen?'

'Seems she's the cause of it.'

'Helen?' Now Eveleen was shocked. She turned and then looked back briefly and nodded towards the factory. 'Everything all right?'

Luke smiled. 'Don't you worry. We're right as ninepence now he's gone.'

Her eyes widened. 'You mean Bob?'

Luke nodded grimly. 'He was a troublemaker. He

should never have been promoted into Josh Carpenter's job. We're best without him. Only trouble is there's not going to be much work for any of us soon, is there?'

Eveleen smiled now. 'I want to talk to you later, Luke. I've got some ideas about what we can do. But now I'd better get to the inspection room.'

Eveleen smiled as she hurried towards the warehouse. It had come as a pleasant surprise that Luke, and perhaps the rest too, were pleased to see the back of Bob Porter. There was nothing to stop her recruiting more women if only she could find the work for them. But now, she hoped, she had the answer in her uncle's yard.

Every day more and more men were volunteering and the workforce at Reckitt and Stokes – indeed at all the workplaces throughout the city – was being rapidly depleted. And now Eveleen had official approval for employing women. The government had appealed for women to serve their country by signing on for war work. Perhaps the making of lace could not be classed in that category, but the manufacture of clothes for the troops certainly would.

Eveleen climbed the flights of stairs to the top floor, breathless when she arrived in the inspection room. The women were all crowded at the far end of the room and no work was being done. The lengths of fabric lay strewn about the floor, as if work had started that morning only to be cast aside.

As Eveleen approached the huddle of women, they became aware of her presence, nudging each other as they spotted her. They fell silent until the only noise left was the sound of uncontrollable weeping. Then they stepped back, parting to make way for Eveleen until she saw the cause of the women's concern and the reason they had deserted their work.

Helen was sitting on the floor rocking backwards and forwards, her arms wrapped around herself, her face wet with tears. Mrs Hyde knelt beside her, her arm about the young woman's shoulders. As Eveleen knelt down too, she and Mrs Hyde exchanged a helpless look.

'Her young man's parents have had a telegram, Mrs Stokes.'

There was no need for Mrs Hyde to say any more.

Eveleen took the distraught Helen home with her. Since the death of both her parents Helen had lived on her own, but this was no time for the young woman to be alone.

Eveleen tried to comfort her, but there was nothing she could say or do that would bring Leslie back. With the first death to touch their lives so closely, Eveleen's terror for Richard, and for Andrew too, increased.

For the first time, she was truly glad Bridie was safely in Flawford.

'He could still be alive,' Eveleen tried to give Helen a vestige of hope to cling to when at last she heard the exact words of the telegram. 'It only says, "missing, *presumed* killed".'

Helen raised her face, swollen and blotchy from the tears she had shed, yet at this moment there was an almost pitying look on her face. 'Evie, they can't find half the bodies. They're blown to bits by the shells. Sometimes they don't find anything, not even their tags.'

Eveleen shuddered and said nothing. There was nothing she could say.

Helen's weeping had stopped now, as if she had cried and cried until there were no more tears to shed.

'There'll be no grave even, just his name recorded somewhere. In a book, maybe, or on a monument. Along with thousands of others, he'll just be a name. Nothing more.'

'Helen, don't say that.' Eveleen squeezed her hand. 'He'll always be so much more to everyone who knew him, especially to you.'

'I seem to lose everyone I love, Evie, don't I? First Ronald, now Leslie. Even both my parents. They were only in their sixties. It's too soon, Evie. I lose everyone far too soon.'

Again, there was nothing Eveleen could say. She could only put her arms about the grieving young woman, hold her close and wonder how long it would be before she too would be mourning her loss.

And Bridie? What about Bridie? How would the poor child cope if word came that Andrew had been killed?

At that moment Bridie had more pressing matters on her mind. Although Andrew was never far from her thoughts, indeed living here in Flawford she felt closer to him than ever before, but her every waking moment was taken with caring for her great-grandmother. At least she was making headway with her. Now the old lady had regular and nourishing meals, her clothes were washed and the house was warm and comfortable.

But Bridie was getting nowhere with her grandfather. He refused resolutely to acknowledge her presence. Although he made no effort now to send her away from Bridget's house, he made it clear he wanted nothing to do with her. He closed and locked the door of his cottage whilst he worked. If he passed her in the yard, he turned his head away.

'Great-Gran, why doesn't he want me here?' Bridie settled herself on the end of the old lady's bed.

Now that she was well cared for Bridget's mind had improved and, whilst she still occasionally absent-mindedly called her great-granddaughter Rebecca, she was almost back to what must have been her normal self.

'It goes back a long way, lass,' Bridget said. 'None of it's your fault, yet you're taking the brunt of his bitterness.' She closed her eyes and sighed. 'And there's nothing I can do about it. Maybe once I could have stood up to him, but I'm too old and too tired now.'

Bridie reached out and patted the wrinkled hand. 'I don't expect you to fight my battles,' she said and smiled mischievously. 'I'll fight me own.'

Bridget smiled at her. 'You've a lot of your auntie Eveleen in you, love. She's a fighter.'

'Auntie Evie?' Bridie said in surprise. 'Really?'

'Oh aye. When her father died suddenly, she carried that family. And they caused her a lot of trouble. But I expect you know all that.'

'No, I don't.'

'Then mebbe I should keep my mouth shut.' The old lady gave a toothless grin.

Bridie laughed. 'I was rather hoping you wouldn't, Great-Gran.'

'Oh well, maybe I'll tell you all about it one day. When you're older.'

It was the same answer that her aunt Eveleen always gave her. What were all these family skeletons, the girl wondered, and would anyone ever tell her what they were?

She bit her lip, watching the old lady. 'Just tell me

one thing, Great-Gran. How can I get Grandfather to talk to me?'

Bridget lay with her eyes closed and Bridie thought she had fallen asleep, but then, without opening her eyes, the old lady said, 'You could try attending the chapel services on a Sunday.'

Thirty-One

On the following Sunday Bridie walked across the road to the chapel and stepped inside. She saw her grandfather sitting in the front pew, his head bowed in prayer. The congregation now consisted mainly of women, old men and young boys. There were only one or two younger men of volunteering age and they looked wary and ill at ease as if, at any moment, they expected to be challenged as to why they were not in uniform. Perhaps they're expecting to be handed a white feather, Bridie thought, remembering the look on Richard's face that day at the Goose Fair.

She slipped into the pew beside Harry Singleton, knelt on the hassock, put her hands together and closed her eyes. When she heard his movement beside her, she sat up on the seat but kept her gaze firmly on the lectern, where a huge bible lay open. When the minister came through from the room behind the rostrum, the congregation rose and the service began.

'Well, what did he say?' Bridget was impatient to know what had happened when Bridie returned to the cottage.

'Nothing. I sat next to him. I didn't even look at him. Not once. I didn't speak and nor did he.' Bridie grinned at her. 'Two can play at that game.'

Bridget chuckled. She was sitting up in bed now, a

lace shawl around her shoulders, looking much better and a good deal perkier than when Bridie had first visited three weeks earlier.

'Now . . .' The young girl began to bustle about the bedroom. 'Let's get you looking your best. Auntie Eveleen might come this afternoon.'

'Do you feel like a little drive into countryside, Helen? I ought to visit Flawford today to see how Bridie is coping.'

It's a lot for a young girl, she thought. She was surprised that Bridie hadn't packed her belongings and come back to Nottingham long before now.

'No, no. You go, though, Evie. I don't want to be a burden to you.' Helen's eyes filled yet again with ready tears.

'You're not that and you never could be.' Eveleen put her arm about her. 'But I think you should come with me. I'd be glad of your company. I don't quite know what I'm going to find when I get there.' Then she added persuasively, 'And besides, it's what Leslie would have wanted. He wouldn't have wanted you to shut yourself away from the world. It doesn't mean you're being disloyal or that you'll stop thinking about him.'

'I think about him every moment,' Helen whispered. 'I don't know how I'm going to carry on without him.'

Life certainly had dealt poor Helen a double bitter blow, Eveleen thought, but aloud she said, 'I know, love. But you're going to have to be every bit as brave as he was when he volunteered, when he went into battle . . .' Her voice faltered as she added softly, 'When he laid down his life.'

Helen was lost in thought for a moment. Then she

raised her head, scrubbed away the tears from her face and tried to smile. 'You're right. He was brave, wasn't he?'

Eveleen nodded.

'Then I must be too. Yes, I'll come with you.'

They set off after an early lunch, Eveleen driving the motor car along the city streets and out into the countryside. Helen sat beside her, well wrapped up, for the late summer day already had the smell of autumn in the air. At first, she sat huddled in rugs and shawls staring straight ahead, but as their journey progressed she began to look about her. She glanced up at trees that now and then formed a canopy above their heads as the road passed beneath them. Then she watched cows and sheep in the fields.

Eveleen breathed a sigh of relief. She had been right to persuade Helen to come. Already there was a pink glow in her cheeks, and she was taking an interest in the world around her for the first time since she had received the dreadful news.

As they reached the village, Eveleen slowed the vehicle and stopped outside a row of cottages.

'Is this it?' Helen asked as the noise of the engine died.

'No, but there's someone I want to speak to first, if she's at home. Come on, we'll go and see.'

'Are you sure you want me to come?'

'Of course.'

They climbed out and walked up the narrow garden path towards Gracie Turner's front door.

'Eveleen!' The large woman beamed with delight and flung her arms wide in welcome, as if to embrace them both at once.

Eveleen made the introductions as Gracie ushered

them into her warm, inviting kitchen, which smelled of fresh baking bread.

'That little lass of yours,' Gracie launched straight in without preamble and Eveleen held her breath at what she might be going to hear now, 'is a marvel.' Eveleen heaved a silent sigh of relief as Gracie continued. 'The old lady's looking grand. She's still bedridden, but she's perked up no end.'

'What about my uncle?'

'Oh, him!' Gracie snorted derisively. 'I don't think even Bridie will be able to win him over.' She laughed. 'But do you know what the little minx does?'

The two visitors shook their heads as Gracie's double chin wobbled with laughter. 'She goes to all the chapel services and sits beside him in the family pew. Never looks at him, never even speaks to him, just comes and goes. She's playing him at his own game and he can't say 'owt 'cos she's not doing 'owt wrong, is she?'

Eveleen shook her head wonderingly. This was a new Bridie she was hearing about.

The surprises continued for her when they arrived at Singleton's Yard. As she opened the door of her grandmother's cottage, the smell of roast beef met them.

'Auntie Evie – and Helen too. How lovely. Come in, come in,' Bridie greeted them as if welcoming them into her own home. 'Dinner'll be ready in a minute.'

'Oh, darling, we've eaten. I never thought.' For a moment Bridie's face was crestfallen, then she brightened and smiled impishly. 'Never mind, maybe me grandad would like a plateful. I'll take one along when I've taken Great-Gran's up.'

'I'll do that,' Eveleen said, pulling off her gloves. She turned to Helen, 'Make yourself at home, love. I'll just help Bridie in the scullery.'

Once in the back room, Eveleen hurriedly broke the sad news to the young girl of Helen's loss. Though she did not cry, Bridie's eyes filled with sympathy for Helen and sudden terror.

'Oh, Auntie Evie,' she whispered. 'What about Andrew and Uncle Richard?'

Eveleen squeezed her arm and nodded. 'I know, love, I know. But we must keep our spirits up. Now,' she said in a louder voice, 'which do you want me to do? Take Gran's up to her or beard the lion in his den?'

'You take Great-Gran's,' Bridie said. 'She's been reckoning on you coming. I'll take his lordship's, though I'll probably get it thrown in my face.'

Bridie walked along the path in front of the cottages, carefully carrying a plate heaped with meat, potatoes, carrots and cabbage and a well-risen, nicely browned Yorkshire pudding. She knocked on her grandfather's door, but when there was no answer she opened it and stepped inside. She blinked two or three times before her eyes became accustomed to the gloom. Then she could see her uncle sitting in a chair by the range.

The table in the centre of the small room was bare, showing no sign that he had eaten a Sunday dinner.

'Hello, Grandad,' Bridie greeted him brightly. 'I've brought you some dinner. Auntie Evie and her friend have come, but they've already eaten.'

'Well, you can take it away,' Harry said gruffly. 'And don't call me that.'

'Why not?' the girl said pertly, her head on one side. 'It's what you are.'

'Not by my choice.'

'We can't always have the things we want in life,' Bridie said, placing the plate on the table. 'Can we? Now, where do you keep your knives and forks?'

Harry roused himself, rising to tower over her. 'I thought I told you to take it away.'

Bridie stood still, undaunted, unafraid of his large figure looming above her. She put her hands on her hips and glared up at him. 'Are you going to waste good food? There's nowt wrong with my cooking. Me gran – your sister – taught me.'

'Oh aye? Did she tell you to put poison in anything you served to me?'

Bridie gasped. She was so shocked that for a moment she could think of nothing to say, then she blurted out, 'Are you wrong in the head? Don't talk so daft.'

'Don't you speak to me like that, you cheeky young wench.'

Suddenly Bridie giggled. She put her hand on his arm. 'Oh, Grandad, don't let's quarrel. I wish you'd let me get to know you. I'd love us to . . .'

He snatched his arm away from her as if her touch had burned him.

'I told you not to call me that,' he thundered. 'And get out of my house.' He thrust his face close to hers. 'You're not welcome here.'

Bridie was trembling, but was determined to show no fear, nor let him see how upset she felt. She managed to shrug her shoulders. 'Have it your way, then.' She turned away and pulled open the door, glancing back once to say, 'Eat your dinner afore it gets cold. I'll come back for the plate.'

Later in the afternoon, when she knew her uncle would be at the chapel, Bridie returned to the cottage to fetch the plate.

The untouched meal still lay on the table, where she had left it.

Thirty-Two

'You wouldn't think anyone could be so stubborn, would you?' Bridie said, showing her aunt the cold, congealed meal later.

Eveleen chuckled. 'You ought to keep heating it up and leaving it for him until he does eat it. It's what was done to us as kids if we didn't eat anything.'

'Me gran still does,' Bridie said, with feeling. She was thoughtful. 'No,' she murmured, 'I shan't do that. I'll just keep taking him nice meals. Every day from now on. Until he gives in.'

Eveleen sighed. 'It's up to you, love. But you'll be wasting your time and a lot of good food. He'll never give in.'

Bridie raised her gaze to meet her aunt's eyes, a glint of determination in her own. 'Neither will I, Auntie Evie. Neither will I.'

'Bridie seems to be managing very well,' Helen said, shouting above the noise of the motor as they drove homewards. Helen herself looked better for the outing, but Eveleen did not remark upon it. 'And your grandmother's a character, isn't she?'

Eveleen smiled, thinking of the hour she had spent that afternoon with the old lady, whom she had not seen for over thirteen years.

Bridget had held out her arms to Eveleen when she had entered the bedroom, tears coursing down her wrinkled cheeks. 'My dear girl. How I've missed you. Come and kiss me.'

Eveleen had bent and kissed her cheek and then had hugged her, alarmed to feel the bony thin body. She sat on the bed and took Bridget's hands in hers. 'You need looking after.'

The old lady chuckled with delight. 'Bridie's doing a fine job of that. She's a grand girl.' Bridget put her head on one side and met Eveleen's gaze with bright, beady eyes. 'Reminds me a lot of you.'

'Me?' Eveleen was startled. 'But I thought she was more like Rebecca.'

'Oh, to look at, yes. But she's more spirit than poor Rebecca ever had. She's – what's the word I want?' She thought for a moment and then said triumphantly, 'Feisty! That's it. She's bold as brass, but for all the right reasons. Just like you always were.' She sniffed. 'Pity you didn't get more support from that rascal of a brother of yours. If it hadn't been for him and Rebecca being so foolish, you'd all have still been here.'

'Maybe,' Eveleen said guardedly. 'But Mam would never have settled here for long. She always wanted to go back to Lincolnshire.' And, she was thinking, if we hadn't been forced to go to Nottingham, I wouldn't have met Richard and Mam wouldn't have met Josh. Aloud, she said, 'My only regret is that we haven't been able to see you in all these years.'

The old lady sighed. 'That's partly my own fault, isn't it? I should have been stronger. Stood up to my husband all those years ago over your mother, and then I should have supported Rebecca and you against

Harry.' She sighed and added regretfully, 'I'm all talk and no do, that's me.'

'Don't blame yourself. We live in a man's world, or at least,' Eveleen added, prophetically, 'we have until now. I think somehow this dreadful war is going to change all that. You'll never guess what . . .' Skilfully turning the subject away from the old lady's morbid and guilt-ridden reminiscences, Eveleen began to tell her how, because of the war, women were now being employed in the Nottingham factory.

'Who'd have thought it?' Bridget said shaking her head. 'It makes sense, of course, but I can't see Harry ever having women working his frames.'

'He nearly did once,' Eveleen reminded her. 'Remember? He taught me how to operate a framework knitting machine.'

'I do,' Bridget laughed, 'But for goodness sake don't tell Bridie, else she'll be down that path and into the workshops before you can say knife.'

'I'm afraid Grandfather won't even acknowledge her existence,' Eveleen said sorrowfully, 'let alone let her help him in any way.' And she told Bridget about the uneaten dinner.

Bridget gave a very unladylike snort. 'Then he's even more of a fool than I thought he was.'

Eveleen smiled as she stood up, 'Well, I need to talk to him and this time I just might have a proposition to put to him that he can't refuse.'

'Women? Women at my machines? In my workshops? Never. The men wouldn't stand for it.'

Eveleen faced her uncle across the hearth in his

cottage as she said quietly, 'What men, Uncle? From what Bridie tells me, you've hardly anyone left.'

He cast her a furious look, but could not deny the truth. She leant towards him. 'Uncle, it's sound business sense. You've lost nearly all your workforce. I've plenty of women anxious to work – needing to work – and yet little for them to do. If the single girls and young married women without children came out here . . .'

'I don't want a lot of flighty wenches bringing trouble to the village.'

Eveleen sighed. 'It's not very likely, with nearly all the young men gone.'

Harry grunted, but again he could not argue with fact.

'And I'm sure,' Eveleen went on, pressing her point, 'there are plenty of women in the village who wouldn't mind taking in lodgers. As for my end of things, I am hoping to buy some frames for the factory.'

'How do you know you'll have the outlets? Surely the government has got all that sorted.'

'Mr Stokes is handling that side of things. He has the contacts. Knows all the right people. We've already got one contract for five hundred pairs of long johns – just like the ones you've always made here. And socks! Well, it seems they can't get enough of them. I'm hunting out all the Griswold machines I can lay my hands on. The women can work those in their own homes, like they always have.'

A Griswold, a small, hand-operated machine that could be attached to a table, produced a knitted tube. It was ideal for making socks.

'What about my private orders?' Grudgingly, in spite of himself, Harry could not help showing interest. 'The ones the officers' families have ordered for them? I can't let folks down.'

'They'll all be honoured.'

He was silent for a long time until at last he nodded. 'I don't like to see the workshops empty and if it'd be helping the war effort . . .' Eveleen said nothing but knew that Harry was also thinking of lining his own pockets. 'But don't think,' he added gruffly, 'that you can worm your way in here because of this. You can take that girl home with you.'

Eveleen stood up. 'This has nothing to do with Bridie. This is purely business. But as for her leaving, no, Uncle Harry. Bridie is staying.'

The war was now more than a year old, yet, despite her constant worry, it was an exciting time for Eveleen. Plans for the changes at the factory and the involvement of her uncle's workshops were going well. Brinsley was enthusiastic and helpful. He also looked much better. He was enjoying business lunches with his contacts, who could assist with their scheme. There was only one point on which Brinsley disagreed with Eveleen.

'It's a pity you let Bob Porter go. He was a good man,' he said reproachfully. For once Eveleen held her tongue. She had not been sorry to see the man go and, better still, she now had the support of her workers at the factory. They were only too pleased that she had found alternative work for them, as the orders for lace were dwindling with each day. She found several frame-work knitting machines for sale, many of them owned by men who had worked in their own homes before volunteering. Now, sadly, they would never return to work them again.

'I can't bear to see it standing there,' one widow had told Eveleen. 'Just take it out my way, missis.'

Eveleen had paid the woman generously and, along with several others, had it transported to an unused room in the factory that became known as the knitting workshop.

'There's a couple of our chaps who've had experience on these machines,' Luke told her. 'They're willing to train the rest of us.'

Eveleen smiled. 'Men and women?'

Luke chuckled. 'Oh aye, women an' all. They'll play an important part.'

Each morning Eveleen hurried to the factory and returned late in the evening. But there was one day when a knock on her front door made her take the morning off.

Emily entered Eveleen's bedroom as she was dressing. 'There's a Mrs Martin at the door, ma'am.'

'Win? Here?'

Though they were good friends, Win had rarely visited Eveleen's home and then only at Eveleen's insistence.

'She – she looks ever so upset, ma'am. She's crying.'

'Oh no!' Eveleen breathed. 'I'll come down at once. Please show her into the morning room.'

Only minutes later Eveleen entered the room to find Win pacing the floor, a handkerchief pressed to her lips, her eyes red from weeping.

'It's our Elsie's Sid. He's been sent home from the hospital. He's with her now but, oh, Evie, he's a changed man. He's swearing and carrying on. He – he even hit her the other day when she was holding the babby.'

'Is there anything I can do?'

'I've got to get him away from her. He's not bad enough now to be kept in a military hospital and none of the local hospitals will take him either. I'm at me wit's end, Evie. Really I am.'

'What's Fred say?'

Win glanced at her nervously and then looked away. 'I – I daren't tell him everything that's going on, Evie. If he knew . . .'

She needed to say no more. Eveleen knew that Fred would leap to his daughter's defence.

'It's all he's been through. It's just not our Sid. He was a lovely feller before he went away. But now . . .' Win's voice trailed away in defeat.

'I'll try to think of something, Win,' was all Eveleen could promise. She stood up. 'In the meantime, I'll come with you to Elsie's and see for myself.'

Eveleen had not encountered Win's son-in-law before, but she could well imagine that the man she met that morning was a very different personality from the man Elsie had married.

'What d'you want, you interfering busybody?' was his greeting as Win stepped through the door. 'Leave me and mine alone.'

Elsie came into the room from upstairs and Eveleen almost gasped aloud to see her black eye and swollen lip.

'You're coming home with me, m'girl, right now,' Win said at once. 'Leave this brute to fend for 'imself. When your dad hears about this—'

'Oh aye,' Sid cut in nastily. 'Reckon I'm frightened of a feller who's too old to go to the Front.' He prodded his own chest. 'I've faced the Hun, I have. And she . . .'

he caught hold of his wife's arm and twisted it viciously, 'is going nowhere.'

'Ma, I'll be all right, but take the baby for a few days, will you?' Elsie pleaded.

'Aye, you can take that squealing brat and keep it, for all I care,' Sid said.

Half an hour later, Win and Eveleen left the tiny, terraced house, Win carrying her grandson clutched to her breast. The child was crying; a strange, gasping sound that bore no resemblance to the lusty bawling of a healthy infant.

'There, there, my pet. You'll be all right. Your daddy's just poorly. To think how tickled pink he was when the little mite was born. I can hardly believe what's happening now.'

'I'll send for the doctor. That child's ill, Win. Even I know that,' Eveleen added wryly.

'Oh, I can't afford—'

'Don't worry about it.' She put her hand on Win's arm. 'After all you've done for me over the years, it's the very least I can do.'

'Well, for once I'm not going to argue. I can swallow me pride when one of me own's in need. And this little chap is.'

'Yes,' Eveleen agreed. 'And so's his poor father.'

Thirty-Three

Eveleen once again asked Helen to go out with her on the Sunday. This time she intended to visit Pear Tree Farm. Helen took both Eveleen's hands in hers. 'Evie, you've been wonderful. You still are, but if it's all the same to you I think I should go home today. I've got to make the effort some time.'

'No, you haven't. You can stay here as long as you want.'

'I know and I can't thank you enough for having me here. But I'd like to go home, just for the day to start with, and then maybe stay a night or so. See how it goes.' Helen had returned to work very quickly after the dreadful news of Leslie's death, but Eveleen had insisted that her friend stay with her.

'If you're sure.' Eveleen had to agree. It was a sensible idea.

So Eveleen drove out to Bernby alone. The last few weeks had flown by and it was September already. It was a peaceful, warm, late summer day. Only the sound of Eveleen's motor car and birds, frightened into flight by her approach, disturbed the calm. It was hard to believe that only a few hundred miles away across the sea a savage war was being waged. At least, she thought, in this weather the trenches would be dry. Although perhaps the heat was just as uncomfortable with all the equipment and heavy packs the soldiers had to carry.

She passed through the village of Bernby, but as the vehicle emerged from beneath the trees of Bernby Covert overhanging the lane, the engine spluttered and died. The motor car free-wheeled down the hill, coming to rest by the ford across the beck. For a moment Eveleen sat there helplessly, wondering what to do. She had no idea about the internal workings of the car. She clambered down and tried to restart it by swinging the starting handle, but the engine only gave a brief stutter and refused to fire into life.

As she stood in the middle of the lane, biting her lip, she heard the sound of hoofbeats behind her and turned to see Stephen Dunsmore riding towards her.

'Oh no,' she breathed. 'Not him.'

There was nothing she could do, no means of escape. She was obliged to wait whilst Stephen dismounted. As he came towards her, she could not fail to notice his unsteady gait and when he came closer and took her hand, she could smell the alcohol on his breath.

'My dear Eveleen, how lovely you look.' His bold gaze ran appraisingly down the tight-fitting costume she wore. He raised her hand and brushed her fingers with his lips, his gaze holding hers. 'Are you, by any chance,' he asked softly, 'a damsel in distress?'

She pulled her hand away and replied, 'If you mean am I having trouble with the motor, then, yes, I'm afraid I am.' She arched her eyebrows and enquired sarcastically. 'Any good with engines, are you?'

'I'm afraid not,' Stephen drawled, 'But I know someone who is. If you'd care to come to the house . . .' He gestured towards the gateway to Fairfield House, which was only a few yards up the lane, 'Then I'll send for him whilst we – er – wait.'

There was an undercurrent in his tone that suggested so much more.

'I'd be glad of your help,' Eveleen unbent enough to say, 'but I'm quite happy to wait here.'

'Oh, but I insist,' Stephen said, his blue eyes glinting in the way she remembered so well when he was determined to get his own way. Then he turned on the boyish charm. 'Please say "yes", Evie . . .' And then he whispered softly, 'For old times' sake.'

She was in no position to refuse. She needed his help. Or rather, she needed the help of the mechanically minded man he knew. Forcing herself to smile, she put her hand on his arm and said, 'Thank you, Stephen. I'd be obliged for your help.'

They walked together towards the big house, Stephen leading his horse. The front door opened as if by magic at his appearance on the driveway and the sour-faced butler held it open for them to step inside. At once Stephen barked orders, for refreshments for them both and for the man to be sent for to attend to Eveleen's motor car. The manservant closed the front door, bowed in acquiescence and disappeared below stairs.

'Please,' Stephen said smoothly, 'come into the morning room.'

Eveleen felt as if she were a fly being invited into a spider's web.

The room surprised Eveleen. It had an unlived-in feel. It wasn't that it was neglected – far from it. Every surface gleamed. Not a speck of dust could be seen and a fire glowed in the grate. But there was nothing personal lying about that spoke of recent occupation. No book or newspaper being read and laid aside; no embroidery being worked by the lady of the house, Stephen's mother, or perhaps by now his wife.

'Please sit down.' Stephen gestured towards the sofa and went towards a drinks cabinet. 'Tea will be here in a moment. Or perhaps you would prefer something stronger?'

Eveleen shook her head and almost said: What, at eleven-thirty in the morning? But she held her tongue and watched in silence as Stephen splashed a generous measure of whisky into his glass, which was obviously not even his first of the day.

He put his glass on a small table and sat down beside her. 'Well, well, who'd have thought it?' His gaze roamed over her, taking in her appearance from head to toe; the blue tailored suit with an ankle-length skirt and a white lace blouse beneath. Eveleen removed her straw hat and smoothed back her hair into its neat pleat.

'My lovely Eveleen, all grown up,' he murmured and there was no mistaking the tinge of sadness in his tone. 'Are you happy, Evie, or do you still remember the times we had? They were good, weren't they?'

Eveleen returned his gaze steadily. 'I remember them very well, Stephen. But I was young and foolish and had no way of knowing that your intentions were far from honourable.'

Stephen ran his tongue round his lips in a lascivious gesture and made no attempt to deny her accusation. 'You can't blame me for trying. Pity your "honour" was stronger than your love for me.'

For a brief moment Eveleen's voice softened. 'I loved you very much, Stephen.'

He took her hand again and squeezed it gently. Before she could stop him, his lips were on her mouth, gently pleading. 'Oh, Evie,' he whispered against them.

Eveleen closed her eyes and the years fell away. She

was once more the naive young girl who had responded to his kiss and to his sweet words. She could almost hear the birdsong above them in the trees of Bernby Covert, where they had met in secret, and feel the soft grass beneath them. He had been her first love . . .

Her eyes flew open and she pulled away with a startled gasp. Ashamed and angry with herself, she sprang up. 'Don't.'

He too rose and tried to take her hands again, but she backed away from him, holding out her hands, palms outwards to fend him off. 'Don't,' she repeated. It seemed to be all she could say, but he took no notice and reached for her, pulling her roughly into his arms. She struggled, pushing against him, but his mouth found hers, urgent now, no longer gentle.

'You still love me. You know you do,' he muttered, between hard, demanding kisses. She twisted her face away, but he buried his head against her neck, his hand now gripping her breast.

With one almighty heave, she pushed him from her and they stood staring at each other, panting hard; he with longing, she with the sheer effort of resisting him.

'How dare you?' she spat, her eyes blazing. Gone in an instant were any tender memories of him. Now the recollection of his callousness, when she had needed him most, returned.

'You loved me. You've just said so.' His blue eyes were dark with desire.

'That was then,' Eveleen said harshly.

'And now?'

Her voice broke at the thought of Richard. How could she have allowed what had just occurred in this room? 'I'm very much in love with my husband.'

'But he's in a faraway land, isn't he, Evie? Fighting for hearth and home. Whilst I,' he came towards her again, holding out his hand in supplication, 'am here.'

'Don't touch me,' she began, but at that moment the door was opened by the butler bringing a tray laid with a silver teapot and bone china cups and saucers.

He set it on the low table in front of the sofa and began to pour. Helplessly Eveleen smoothed her dishevelled hair. Escape now was impossible. The manservant straightened up from his task. 'The boy has gone to fetch young Morton, sir. Will there be anything else?'

'No. Get out,' Stephen snapped. The interruption had come at precisely the wrong moment for him.

Eveleen looked at Stephen as the butler left the room. 'Morton? Is that Ted Morton?'

'No,' Stephen growled. 'His son – whatever they call him.'

'Micky,' Eveleen said. 'But he's younger than Bridie. What does he know about motors?'

Stephen shrugged. 'He works with motors somewhere in Grantham.' He glanced up at her and added testily, 'Oh, do sit down, Evie. I promise not to lunge at you again.'

Eveleen sat down, but this time she chose an armchair so that Stephen could not get close to her.

They drank tea in uncomfortable silence until Eveleen said, 'I thought Micky worked for you?'

'He did. I sacked him.'

'Why?'

For a moment, although Eveleen wondered if her eyes deceived her, Stephen looked ill at ease, almost embarrassed. Gruffly belligerent, he said, 'Can't employ all my workers' offspring. Not enough for them to do.'

Eveleen stared at him. The Dunsmore estate was huge. Then she remembered that a few years back Josh had said something about Stephen selling off parcels of land. Perhaps . . .

She glanced around the room, noticing again the absence of a woman's presence. 'How are your mother and father?'

Stephen shrugged indifferently. 'Hardly see them. They live in London. He's a big noise in the government now. And with this war . . .'

With characteristic bluntness – a trait she had never been able to correct – Eveleen asked, 'So, will you be volunteering?'

'Me?' Stephen laughed. 'What on earth would I do a daft thing like that for?'

Torn between her own anger at Richard leaving her when she had begged him not to and a sense of pride that he had the courage to do just that, she stared at the man before her, seeing him suddenly as he was now. His handsome face was puffy, probably from over-indulgence in drink. Tiny red veins mottled his cheeks and his body, once so trim and firm and lean, had given way to fat. The charm, which had once been boyish and attractive, was now more of a lecherous leer. For a moment she allowed herself to mourn the loss of his fair, Adonis-like, good looks and even had a fleeting regret for the idyllic time of her youth when she had believed herself in love with him and he with her.

Realizing at last what a self-centred man Stephen really was, Eveleen said slowly, 'No, I don't suppose you would.'

*

'Eveleen. How lovely.' Josh came towards her across the yard at Pear Tree Farm. 'We'd've waited dinner if we'd known you were coming today.'

Eveleen climbed down and kissed his plump cheeks in greeting. 'I should have been here in plenty of time, but my motor car broke down.'

Josh glanced at the vehicle and Eveleen laughed sheepishly. 'I ran out of petrol.'

Josh stared for a moment and then laughed too. 'Well, you're here now. Come along in. I'm sure your mother has some food left.'

Whilst she ate they sat at the table with her, plying her with questions about Richard and Andrew, Bridie, and what was happening at Flawford.

'The child has put me to shame,' Mary admitted. 'I really ought to visit, but Harry . . .' She gave a shudder and said no more. There was no need.

Eveleen put out her hand and touched her mother's. 'We understand, Mam. But I think Gran would like to see you.'

'We'll go, Mary. Soon. I'll be with you.'

'Yes, yes,' Mary agreed readily. 'I should go. If anything happens to my mother, I'd regret for the rest of my days that I hadn't gone.'

'I'll come to fetch you and take you in the motor car,' Eveleen offered.

Josh chuckled. 'I'll bring a spare can of petrol.'

'What? What's that?' Mary's sharp ears missed nothing.

'I ran out of petrol in the lane,' Eveleen admitted, her face turning pink. 'Micky Morton found out what the trouble was.' She omitted to tell them about her encounter with Stephen Dunsmore and skilfully turned the conversation away. 'He seems very clever with mechanical things. He tells me he has a job in Grantham.'

Josh nodded. 'Aye. Dunsmore sacked him – reckoned he hadn't enough work to support all the Morton family.'

'It's to be expected,' Mary put in. 'Since Stephen Dunsmore's selling up the estate bit by bit to finance his drinking. And gambling, so they say.'

'The lad's been working in the town the past couple of months,' Josh went on. 'Doing well, so Ted says.'

'He soon found out what was wrong,' Eveleen smiled ruefully. 'Says it's common with lady drivers.'

'I think you're very brave to drive it at all, Eveleen,' Mary said. 'I know I couldn't.'

Picking up on his wife's earlier remark, Josh said, 'We've bought a bit more land off him, Evie. The field on the other side of the beck, right up to where the trees of Bernby Covert start. So now we can get some more beast.'

'It'll make a lot more work for you, won't it, Josh?' Eveleen said worriedly. Although only in their fifties, the pair now no longer had Bridie's youthful vigour.

'I shall just get beef cattle, so's not to cause more dairy work.'

'I've got Micky's younger sister helping in the dairy now. She's a good little lass,' Mary said and murmured, 'But I still miss Bridie.'

'Then I'll take you to see her. How about next weekend?'

Later in the afternoon Eveleen took Mary to Bernby church to lay flowers on Walter Hardcastle's grave.

They stood side by side, looking down at the place where Eveleen's father lay.

'I've been a lucky woman, really,' Mary murmured. 'After – after my bit of trouble, running away from home and that, I was so lucky to meet your father. He was a wonderful man. And now I've got Josh. He's so thoughtful and kind, Evie.'

Eveleen squeezed her mother's arm, but said nothing.

As they turned away and walked back towards the motor car parked near the gate, Mary asked tentatively, 'How is Brinsley? Does he ever ask after me?'

Eveleen smiled. 'Often, Mam. And he's fine now. He wasn't too well a few months back, but now he's very much involved in our new plans.'

'What new plans?'

'I'll tell you more over tea because I want Josh to hear about them too.'

A little later as they sat down to cold ham and tomatoes, Eveleen said, 'You remember me asking your advice, Josh? Well, things are going very well. I've managed to buy several knitting machines and Griswolds. Four boys, too young to volunteer, and three women have already moved out to Flawford and now we have a knitting workshop within the factory.'

'I'm glad. Turning to war work should keep the factory going.' His face sobered. 'I wish there was more I could do to help the war.'

'You are,' Mary declared stoutly. 'You're supplying food.'

'I know, but . . .' Josh shrugged his huge shoulders and spread his hands. 'It doesn't feel like I'm doing much.'

'There is something you could do,' Eveleen said slowly, glancing from one to the other, 'but it would involve both of you and it wouldn't be easy.'

Swiftly she explained about Win's son-in-law.

'Bring him here, love,' Josh beamed delightedly. 'Good country air and Mary's cooking will soon have him right.'

Eveleen glanced at her mother, half expecting Mary to protest, but instead there were tears in her eyes as she reached out and touched her husband's hand. 'There you go again, always thinking of others.'

'You don't mind though, do you, Mary love?'

Mary pressed her lips together as if to trying to prevent more tears flowing. 'No,' she said huskily. 'No. I just hope that perhaps somewhere someone is treating my Jimmy with as much kindness.'

Thirty-Four

It was a merry little party that bowled along the country lanes from Bernby to Flawford the following weekend.

Josh and Mary sat in the back seat, whilst Helen, bravely trying to hide her own sadness, sat beside Eveleen. Mary held onto her hat, giving little squeals of alarm as Eveleen rounded the corners. 'Don't go so fast, Eveleen. You'll tip us over.'

By the time Eveleen turned the motor car into Ranters' Row, Mary was pink cheeked and breathless. 'Oh my!' she gasped, patting her chest. 'You'll give me a heart attack.'

Josh helped her down and Eveleen noticed that she clung to his arm as they went into Singleton's Yard. There was no-one about, but from the workshops came the gratifying noise of busy machinery.

'My goodness!' Eveleen exclaimed. 'Uncle Harry's even got them working on a Sunday.'

Then a joyful shriek made them all jump and Bridie was running towards them along the path in front of the cottages.

'Gran. Grandpa Josh. Oh, how lovely.' She flung herself against them, hugging them rapturously. Tucking her arm through Mary's, she almost dragged her along the path towards the end cottage, chattering delightedly. 'Auntie Evie let me know you were all coming. Dinner's ready and Great-Gran's managed to get downstairs for the first time.' Bridie beamed. 'Especially in your honour.'

Eveleen looked concerned. The last time she had seen Bridget, the old lady had looked too frail even to get out of her bed, let alone manage the steep staircase.

Catching the look, Bridie reassured her. 'Mrs Turner helped me, Auntie Eveleen. Great-Gran's all right.'

'Oh aye,' Mary remarked. 'Gracie Turner'd have to have her neb in.'

'She's been very good,' Bridie countered. She leant closer to her grandmother and dropped her voice to a whisper as they passed by the cottage in the middle of the row. 'Lil – she lives in the cottage behind Andrew's – she was supposed to be looking after Great-Gran, but she wasn't making a very good job of it. Only came in when she felt like it. Anyway, here we are, come on in.'

They clustered into the tiny front room to greet the old lady, who was sitting by the range as if she were holding court. At first the atmosphere was strained and awkward, but once dinner was served on the snowy cloth and they sat around the table the conversation became easier.

At the end of the meal even Mary was obliged to say, 'That was lovely, Bridie. You're a credit to me.'

Everyone laughed, but Bridie said quite seriously, 'Thank you, Gran.' Then she rose from her place and began to pile a plate high with meat and vegetables. She also spooned bread and butter pudding and custard into a bowl. 'I'll just take this along to me grandad.'

Eveleen smiled at her. 'Will he eat it?'

'Shouldn't think so for a minute,' the young girl replied cheerfully. 'He hasn't yet. But I live in hope.'

As the door closed behind her, Bridget shook her

head and said, 'He's a stubborn old fool. That girl takes him a dinner every Sunday, aye, and sometimes in the week. But will he eat it? He'd sooner starve than give in.'

When Bridie returned, Mary, Eveleen and Helen were already clearing away and washing up in the small scullery, whilst Josh sat across the hearth chatting to Bridget.

'Do you mind if I go to chapel?' Bridie said.

Mary turned to look at her in surprise. 'You go to chapel?'

Bridie nodded. 'It's all part of the plan to win me grandad round, but don't tell him I said so.'

'I've no intention of saying anything to him,' Mary replied drily and plunged a dirty plate into the bowl of soapsuds as if she wished it were her brother's head she was dunking.

Bridie grinned and exchanged a knowing glance with her aunt. Then she said, 'You won't go before I get back, will you? Only I don't want to give him the chance to say that I've missed a service,' she giggled, 'because of entertaining.'

'No, no, we'll still be here,' Eveleen assured her. 'Off you go.'

The preacher was one of the 'fire and brimstone' ministers who had given Ranters' Row its local name. He stood on the rostrum and harangued the congregation for their sinful ways. Bridie sat placidly watching his antics, whilst beside her Harry Singleton grew more and more excited, waving his arms and shouting 'Amen' at the end of each sentence the preacher delivered. At the end of the service, Bridie waited by the door whilst

Harry shook the man's hand, pumping it up and down vigorously.

'Grand sermon, Minister,' he said. 'We don't get enough like you these days. All simpering do-gooders, that's what the new breed is now.'

They talked for a few moments more before they both came down the aisle towards her.

She smiled and asked, 'Did you enjoy your dinner, Grandad?'

'I've told you not to call me that,' he growled and made to push past her. 'And you're doing nowt but waste good food.'

The minister paused in front of Bridie and smiled down at her from his great height, his bushy side-burns bristling. 'Is this your granddaughter, Harry?' he boomed, his voice as loud as if he were still addressing the full congregation. He held out his huge hand and gripped hers tightly, making the girl wince. 'I'm very pleased to meet you.'

'She's no granddaughter of mine,' Harry said abruptly. 'I disowned my daughter when she got herself into trouble.'

The minister glanced from one to the other, perplexed for a moment. Then, as realization dawned, a look of disapproval crossed his face. To Bridie's surprise, it was not directed at her but at her grandfather. 'Harry Single-ton – I'm ashamed of you!'

'Wha . . .?' For a brief moment, Harry was discon-certed, but then his mouth tightened and he actually had the temerity to shake his fist at the minister. 'You mind your business, Mr Simmonds, and I'll mind mine.' Leav-ing a shocked minister and an even more surprised Bridie, Harry turned and marched across the street towards his home.

'Well!' The man seemed lost for words and at once Bridie said, 'I am sorry, sir, but my grandad is very bitter about what happened in the past. I don't know everything except that I was born out of wedlock. I think that is the politest way to put it.' She smiled up at him ruefully, then added sadly, 'And my mother died at my birth.'

The big man put his hand on her shoulder. Suddenly all his bluster and fire was gone and his tone was gentle and understanding. 'My dear child, then you should be loved and treasured even more.'

At this stranger's unexpected kindness, tears sprang to her eyes more readily than if he had treated her harshly.

'Thank you,' she murmured, her voice breaking. She dropped her head as she added, 'I wish my grandfather felt the same.'

She felt the minister squeeze her shoulder. He said no more, but she saw him looking thoughtfully across the road in the direction of Harry's home.

'I must go,' Bridie said. 'It's been nice to meet you, sir.'

The man patted her back and his voice boomed with goodwill once again. 'Take heart, my child. I'll see what I can do to help.'

He walked across the road at her side and she left him with his hand raised to knock on her grandfather's door.

Thirty-Five

'Did you hear it?' Mary said as they climbed into the motor car to go home. 'Whatever was all that shouting as we passed Harry's cottage?'

Bridie, standing beside the vehicle, said, 'It's Grandad and the minister. I think they're arguing over me.'

'Over you?' At once Mary was suspicious. '*Now* what have you been up to, girl?'

'Being born, Gran,' Bridie said simply. 'That's all.'

'Eh?' Mary was mystified and even Eveleen looked at her questioningly.

Bridie sighed. 'I think the minister's telling him off for the way he treats me because – because I'm illegitimate.'

Mary sniffed. 'Not before time, but I shouldn't think it'll do any good. He doesn't know Harry like I do.'

There was a flurry of goodbyes and much waving and Eveleen turned the vehicle around and headed down the street. Conversation was difficult between the four of them above the noise of the engine, so it wasn't until they reached Pear Tree Farm and were sitting together having a cup of tea, before Eveleen and Helen made their way back to Nottingham, that the conversation turned again to Bridie.

'Well, I have to say it and you know I'm not given to praising folk . . .' Mary began and her daughter hid her smile, 'but that child is doing very well.'

'She is,' Helen agreed. 'She was a good little worker in the mending room, but even I can see that she's in her element caring for people.'

'You'd certainly think so, Mam, if you'd seen Gran when she first went there. If Bridie hadn't insisted on looking after her, I don't know what would have happened by now.'

'I managed to sneak a look in the workshops whilst Harry was at chapel,' Josh said. 'The new folks you've sent there, Evie, are doing very well by all accounts.' He chuckled as he added, 'Even the women. There was an oldish man teaching a young girl. "What's this?" I said, "Working on a Sunday?" The old feller laughed and said, "Old Harry can turn a blind eye when it suits him."'

'How was the girl shaping up?' Eveleen was anxious to know.

'All right, as far as I could see.'

'It's surprised me that Harry's ever agreed to your plans, especially having girls working there,' Mary said.

'I don't think he had much choice if he wanted his workshops to survive,' Josh said. 'Your mother said his eyesight is poor now, but he won't admit it.'

Mary sniffed. 'If I know my brother, it's more a matter of money. He'll do anything to make a bob or two.' She glanced at Eveleen. 'He let you have a go on a frame when we lived there, didn't he? But that was only because he couldn't bear to see even one frame standing idle.'

Eveleen nodded. 'Yes, and if it hadn't been for the trouble over Rebecca and Jimmy, I think he'd have let me carry on working one.'

'Aye.' Mary was pensive. 'But for them, I reckon we might still have been living there.'

'No, we wouldn't, Mam,' Eveleen countered. 'When we were forced to leave here, I promised I would bring you back one day.' She pulled a wry face. 'Though I have to admit it would have taken me a long time on the wages I earned in the inspection room.'

The four of them laughed together, then Mary said, 'Well, Master Stephen's high 'n' mighty ways haven't done him a lot of good. Josh heard the other day that he's put the estate up for sale – what's left of it. Even Fairfield House is on the market.'

Eveleen digested the news with mixed emotions. It saddened her to think that the once great estate that had supported several families, her father and even her grandfather before him, had been broken up and sold bit by bit because of one spoilt, self-centred and dissolute young man.

'What'll happen to the families who still work for him? What about the Mortons?'

Mary shrugged. 'He'll turn 'em out, I expect, just like he did us, when he's no more use for them.'

'Micky works in Grantham now,' Josh put in. 'And Ted's volunteered. He went the day before yesterday.'

'Oh no, not Ted too.' Eveleen was sorry to hear that her childhood friend had gone. She hadn't even had a chance to say goodbye. Another 'goodbye' unsaid.

'Well,' Mary said, her mouth tight as she rose to clear away the cups and saucers, 'I tell you one person who won't be going. Master Stephen. He's too much of a coward.'

Eveleen stared at her. 'You've changed your tune, Mam,' she said bluntly. 'I thought you didn't hold with the war.'

'No more I do, but if all the fine young men – Richard, Andrew . . .' Her tone softened. 'And somewhere I expect my Jimmy's caught up in it too – why should someone like Stephen Dunsmore escape?'

'I don't think he will for long, love,' Josh said solemnly. 'If it goes on much longer, they'll bring in conscription, then he'll probably have to go.'

Mary's eyes were suddenly fearful. 'You won't, will you?'

Josh smiled, but there was a hint of regret as if, deep down, he would have liked the chance to prove his love for his country. 'No, love. I'm far too old. But – ' his face brightened – 'we'll do our bit here at home.' He turned to Eveleen. 'You bring that poor young feller out here as soon as you like. We'll look after him. What do they call him?'

Eveleen touched his hand. 'Sid Robinson. Thank you, Josh. Win will be so grateful.'

'We've all got to do our bit where we can. Even little Bridie's doing hers, looking after the old lady and her grandfather too, if only he'd let her.'

'He'll never do that,' Mary remarked as she disappeared into the scullery. 'Not till the sun shines both sides the hedge at the same time.'

'We don't need you here. We don't want you here. And you had no right to go snivelling to the minister, telling him of our family's shame.'

Harry's huge, outraged figure seemed to fill Bridget's living room. She sat still and silent, hunched in her chair by the fire, whilst, standing in front of her great-grandmother as if to protect her from his onslaught, Bridie faced him boldly.

'Great-Gran needs me even if you don't.'

'Lil can look after her,' he boomed.

'No, she can't. She's a slattern. Did you even know what this place looked like when I arrived? Did you even care enough to visit your own mother?'

'Don't you dare answer me back, girl—'

'I'm not afraid of you. I can walk out of here whenever I like—'

'That's exactly what I want you to do.'

'But I'm staying. I'm staying to look after me Great-Gran and I'd look after you too, you stubborn old man, if only you'd let me. But no, you're too proud, too – too unforgiving.' She flung her arm out towards the old lady cowering in her chair. 'You'd sooner watch her die than unbend enough to let me help. Well, I'm not going anywhere, so you might as well get used to it.' She took a step closer to the man. 'If you want me gone, you'll have to carry me out bodily.' Suddenly she grinned so saucily, so cheekily, that only the hardest of hearts could have resisted. 'And even then I'll come back.'

But it seemed that Harry Singleton's heart was made of stone. He turned on his heel and left the cottage. Bridie heard a sob behind her and turned to kneel beside the old lady.

She put her arms around her. 'There, there, Great-Gran, don't cry. It'll be all right. This war's got to be over soon and then Andrew and all the others will come home. Everything will be all right then.'

Everything will be all right for all of us, Bridie promised herself silently, if only Andrew comes home safely.

Eveleen drew the motor car to a halt outside her home. As the engine noise died away, Helen said, 'Eveleen, I can't thank you enough. I don't know what I would have done without you these last few weeks. I would never have got through.'

Eveleen covered Helen's hand with her own. 'Nonsense, of course you would.' She smiled gently at her friend. 'Darling Helen, it's your own courage that's carried you through. Leslie would be so proud of you.'

Helen nodded, smiling bravely through unshed tears, but she could not speak. Eveleen patted her hand. 'Come on. Let's go in. It's getting dark.'

'I won't come in, if you don't mind. I'll go home.' She bit her lip as she glanced at Eveleen. 'I've got to face being on my own at night sooner or later.'

'You should have said. I could have dropped you at your home first.'

'It's not far. I'll walk.'

'Well, just come in and have—'

The front door of the house had opened and Emily, holding up her skirt, was running down the steps. She was holding out a yellow envelope and her face showed signs of tears. She was breathless and anxious as she reached them.

'Oh, ma'am. I didn't know what to do. This came this morning. I didn't know where to find you. Oh, ma'am. It's a telegram. From the War Office.'

For a moment, Eveleen was frozen, unable to move, then she reached out and took the thin paper into her hands. She felt Helen slip her arm around her shoulders as, with trembling fingers, Eveleen tore open the telegram.

'Oh no!' Her fingers fluttered to her lips. 'It's Andrew. "Missing in action", it says. Oh, Helen.' She turned to face her friend, her eyes already filling with tears. 'However am I going to tell Bridie?'

Thirty-Six

'I don't believe it, Auntie Eveleen. Andrew's not dead. I'd know it if he was.' She put her hand over her own heart. 'I'd feel it here.'

Eveleen had sent word to Pear Tree Farm of the dreadful news, but she had come again to Flawford the very next day to break the news to her niece herself.

'It only says "missing". They don't know for sure,' Bridie insisted, denying even the thought that she would never see him again.

Eveleen watched her helplessly. How could she tell this young girl that the conditions out there were so terrible that men died, blown to a thousand pieces, so that no recognizable trace was ever found. That soldiers were buried together hurriedly during a lull in the fighting, their identities unknown, their resting place unmarked. Wounded soldiers, sent home from the Front, were telling the truth now about what this war was really like. And talk of it was rife amongst the workers at Reckitt and Stokes.

'Well, yes, that's true,' Eveleen said haltingly, feeling guilty at confirming Bridie's hope. Perhaps it would be kinder, in the long run, to convince her of Andrew's death. The sooner the girl came to terms with it, the better. 'But, darling, I don't think they would send a telegram if there was the slightest chance that—'

Bridie was adamant. 'Yes, they would. Mrs Turner's

got a friend in the village. She was telling me. She got a telegram about her son. Just the same as that.' Bridie prodded her finger accusingly at the offending piece of paper. 'And then he turned up alive. He'd been wounded and taken to a field hospital. His identity tag was missing and because he was unconscious they didn't know who he was. So it *does* happen.'

'Yes, of course it does, but . . .' Eveleen bit her lip, coming to a sudden decision, right or wrong. Let the poor child have hope for a while longer. Maybe coming to the truth gradually was the best way for Bridie. Eveleen forced herself to smile, though her own heart was heavy. She could not believe, not for a minute, that Andrew was still alive. Aloud she said, 'Pray God you're right, Bridie.'

She held out her arms and they hugged each other fiercely. When they drew apart, Bridie said quietly, 'If you're not in a rush to get back, perhaps you could sit with Great-Gran for a while. I – I'm going across to the chapel.'

Eveleen nodded, unable to speak for the lump in her throat. She watched the girl leave the cottage, pass by the window, her shoulders hunched, her head down. 'She knows all right,' Eveleen whispered. 'She knows the truth, but she's just refusing to believe it.'

Sadly Eveleen turned and went upstairs to tell Bridget.

'Aw, that's bad news,' the old lady was saying moments later. 'That child worships him.'

'He's been very good to her. Visiting the farm almost every week since she was a baby.'

'I thought as much, though he never said.'

'I suppose he didn't want to cause trouble here. Uncle Harry might have sacked him if he'd known.'

Bridget gave a wry laugh. 'I don't think so. Harry's no fool when it comes to money and Andrew was a good worker.'

Eveleen glanced out of the window at the workshops. 'He hasn't many of his own workers left now, has he?' she asked quietly.

Bridget shook her head. 'No, they've all gone. All the good ones, that is.'

Eveleen looked out of the window towards the workshops. Behind one of the long windows she could see the shadowy shape of her uncle.

'I'd better go and tell him about Andrew,' she murmured.

Bridie knelt at the altar rail until her knees hurt, yet she was unaware of the pain. She prayed aloud, talking to God as if he were standing in front of her.

'Please, don't let him be dead. Please let him be alive and come home to me. I love him so much. I don't care if he doesn't love me in the same way, only please let him come home. And Uncle Richard too. He's such a nice, kind man. Please let him be safe.'

Behind her, the door opened and closed again softly. There were tiptoeing footsteps and the squeak of protesting woodwork as someone sat down in one of the pews, but Bridie scarcely noticed.

'Please, stop the war. All the maiming and killing, it can't be what you want. I know it can't. I'll take care of Andrew, even if he's injured. Only let him be alive and I'll look after him for the rest of my life.' Her fingers were so tightly laced together in supplication that they were white, the feeling in them almost gone.

Stiffly, she shifted and became aware of the discomfort

in her legs. She bowed her head and ended her prayers. 'God bless all my family. Gran and Josh and Eveleen. And please, God, spare my great-gran and help me to care for her properly and keep her safe. And God, bless my grandad and help him to know that I'm so sorry I'm a disgrace to his family, but I want to know him. I so want to love him.' Then she repeated the words she had heard the minister intone at the end of his prayers, ending with the customary 'Amen'.

She stood up, bending forward to rub the life back into her limbs before turning to walk down the aisle. She drew breath sharply as she became aware of the motionless figure of Harry Singleton sitting in a pew at the back. But she did not even glance at him. Holding her head proudly, she walked down the aisle and out of the chapel.

She didn't notice that he was watching her every step of the way or see the tears rolling silently down his cheeks.

'Great-Gran! Great-Gran!' Bridie was racing up the stairs, arriving breathless in Bridget's room. But her eyes were shining and the grin on her wide mouth seemed to stretch from ear to ear. 'You're not going to believe this. He's eaten it. I did his favourite, like you told me. Lamb's liver fry and he's eaten it. Every last bit. Look!'

She had even brought the empty dinner plate upstairs to show to the old lady.

Bridget smiled, eyeing the plate and then looking at the girl's face, flushed with triumph.

'Well, well. He was either starving hungry or you've won.'

Bridie nodded. 'We'll see what he does tomorrow.'

But the next day's plate was cleared too and whilst Harry still never came to his mother's cottage, still never spoke to Bridie as she passed him in the yard, he now ate the meals she prepared and left on his table each day.

It was a small, but significant victory.

Bridget improved with each day and, as the weeks passed, she grew stronger and now she was dressing and coming downstairs each day.

'You can wheel me across to the chapel on Sunday, Bridie.' She smiled widely at her great-granddaughter. 'Harry'd like that. It'd be another feather in your cap in his eyes if you got me to a service.'

Bridie put her arms around the old woman's shoulders, knowing that she was making the suggestion more to help her than because she hankered to attend chapel. 'Only if you're sure you're up to it.'

'I'm up to it, love. I haven't felt so well for years.' Her beady eyes, bright in the wizened face, twinkled with merriment. 'Must be having you around.'

They laughed together and Bridie hugged her. 'I'm so glad I came here,' she whispered. 'So glad I've found you.'

'Not half as glad as I am,' Bridget said with feeling. 'I'd have been a goner now if it hadn't been for you.'

'Oh no, Great-Gran, I'm sure—'

'Oh yes, I would,' Bridget said with asperity. 'Lil was happy enough to pocket the money Harry paid her to look after me, but she didn't give a damn. And I was too weak to do anything about it. I shan't have her back in here when you go.'

'Trying to get rid of me, are you?'

'No, love.' The old lady looked pensive. 'But you

don't want to be tied to this place with an old woman and a stubborn old fool of a man. Anyway, I bet Eveleen's missing you even though she never says anything. And your gran, if it comes to that.'

Bridie was thoughtful. Mary's attitude towards her on their visit here had surprised, yet pleased, the young girl. It was the first time her grandmother had shown anything approaching affection towards her.

'But while you are still here – ' Bridget's voice dragged her back to the present – 'you can get me to chapel this Sunday.'

There were plenty of willing helpers on the Sunday afternoon when Bridie manoeuvred the cumbersome borrowed bath chair across the road.

'We'll not get that through the door.' Georgie Turner, Gracie's husband, scratched his head thoughtfully. 'Tell you what. Leave it outside here and me and one of the other lads'll help her inside.'

Bridie stifled her giggles at Georgie Turner calling his cronies 'lads'. They were all over fifty if they were a day! But she kept her face straight and said, 'Thank you, Mr Turner.'

'Can you walk, Mrs Singleton?' Georgie now addressed Bridget.

''Course I can,' she began indignantly, but then was obliged to confide, 'but I do need help.'

The minister whom Bridie had met before took the service. At the end he stood by the door, shaking hands with everyone as they left.

'Ah, Harry Singleton's granddaughter, if I'm not mistaken,' he boomed so that those left could not fail to hear. He shook her hand vigorously and then Bridie saw him glance beyond her. 'You come to your senses yet, Harry?'

Harry pushed past them, his face like thunder. 'I told you before,' he muttered, 'you mind your business, Minister. And I'll mind mine.'

Ignoring the man's outstretched hand, Harry strode across the road towards Singleton's Yard. Bridie's heart felt as if it had dropped inside her and she almost groaned aloud. Oh no! She'd been making headway, she thought, even if it was only a very small step, and now the minister had unwittingly spoilt it all.

The next day and in the days that followed Harry did not eat the dinners that Bridie took him.

'Stubborn old fool,' Bridget muttered, whilst the young girl looked sadly at the wasted food and murmured, 'I just wish the minister hadn't said anything.'

September 1915 had brought news of an autumn offensive on the Western Front with combined attacks by the French and the British. The newspapers spoke of victories, but Richard's letter, received later in the month, gave a different picture.

> *We haven't been involved, but we hear that what could have been a successful attack overrunning a village as the enemy weren't expecting our lads, failed in the end because reserves were late arriving and the enemy had sealed off the breach.*

He ended, as always, by sending his love to Bridie. *I hope the poor child hasn't taken the news of Andrew too badly.*

Eveleen had folded his letter thoughtfully. The

trouble was that Bridie had not accepted the news at all. She stubbornly refused to believe it and Eveleen feared that eventually, when the girl was obliged to face facts, her grief would be all the more terrible.

Thirty-Seven

Bridie received a letter from Richard.

> *Today is the first of October and how I wish I was with you back home in dear old Nottingham and visiting the Goose Fair. I can still taste that toffee apple and hear the fairground music, but I expect the fair has been cancelled this year. Still, after the war, we'll go again. All of us.*

She was acutely aware that he did not add '. . . who are left.'

Bridie felt guilty not sharing this letter from Richard with her aunt. Eveleen always brought the letters she had received from him for Bridie to read. But the girl felt her uncle's reference to their day spent at the Goose Fair would revive unhappy and guilty feelings for Eveleen. The next letter she was able to show her.

> *I have had my first experience under shellfire. We had to go out on a digging party. We split up into small sections with twenty-yard intervals between us. Suddenly everyone else dived into the ditches on either side of the road. I heard an awful shriek and a terrific explosion and I soon made a dive for the ditch too. I was told these are five-point-nines and that I'll get to know the sound only too well! Now we're getting shelled every day on our way back. Perhaps it has*

something to do with the German 'sausage' overhead – that's an observation balloon.

'He's not told me any of that,' Eveleen remarked, folding Bridie's letter and handing it back to her.

'Perhaps he doesn't want you to worry too much,' Bridie soothed, wondering whether she should have shown Eveleen the letter at all. Trying to change the subject, she said, 'He hasn't mentioned Andrew. Do you think Uncle Richard thinks he's still alive somewhere too?'

Now it was Eveleen's turn to feel guilty that she had not shown her niece the letter in which Richard had intimated that he had accepted the news of Andrew's loss. Now Eveleen could think of nothing to say in answer.

In the following months Richard wrote often to Bridie and it seemed that he found it easier to write to her about the conditions at the Front than he did in his letters to Eveleen.

In November Richard wrote,

I have been in the trenches for the first time. We left our billets in platoons at dusk. It was very dark and strangely quiet. When we left the road we entered a long trench known as the communication trench. It was in a dreadful condition; knee deep in water and it was still raining! I didn't sleep much the first night. It takes a bit of getting used to when rats as big as cats snuggle under your armpits in the night to keep warm! We stayed there for eight days – four days in support and four days in the front line. The daytime was spent in trench repairing and the night in sentry duty – two hours on and four off. We all stand at battle positions one hour before dark and again an hour before dawn. After that we stand down and get our fires going to boil water and fry bacon, being careful not to make much smoke or this brings the shells! We were lucky on our sector – it was very quiet, though we had to be careful to keep below the parapet because of snipers. Now we have been relieved and have gone back to digging.

Eveleen and Bridie still continued to show each other the letters they received, but those to Eveleen gave news only of the times that he was away from the front line. His letter in December was cheerful.

We've been relieved by the 7th SF. We had a six-hour march and were all very tired, but at least we've seen the last of the trenches and the mud – for a while anyway! We seem to be moving about a lot just now. At one time we were billeted in a small château on the banks of the Lys.

To Bridie he wrote,

Feeling rather war torn and my feet are not too good. I've had a touch of flu and felt very wonky whilst on guard duty.

No letter came for over a month and both Eveleen and Bridie began to feel anxious. His next letter to Eveleen explained the long silence.

Haven't been able to write for a while. At the beginning of January A and C Companies (I'm in A) left for M . . . in the south.

The rest of the name had been heavily scored out, but from what followed, Eveleen guessed the place was Marseilles.

It took us three days by train to get there and where we were camped had a splendid view of the Château d'If. Don't know why we were taken all that way – maybe the officers know, but they're certainly not telling us. However, a few of us were lucky enough to get passes into the city and docks. Had tea at a restaurant and then went to the pictures. Visited Notre Dame de la Garde – superb view of the gulf and the islands and indeed the whole city. I had to be vaccinated so my arm's a bit painful, but it hasn't stopped me visiting the zoological gardens and the Palais de Longchamps. Then, suddenly, we were on the move again. We marched eight miles back to the station, where we were given a splendid send-off by the locals. Another three days on the train, but travelling through the valley of the Rhône was wonderful . . .

A letter to Bridie admitted,

The thirteen days in the south were great, but it makes coming back to the trenches all the harder. And now it's snowing . . .

'He must know we swap letters,' Bridie remarked, trying to make light of the marked difference between them. 'He's just telling us different news, that's all.'

Again, Eveleen said nothing.

At the beginning of 1916 the House of Commons voted overwhelmingly for military conscription and in February well-off families were urged to dispense with their servants. But Emily – the only one in Eveleen's household who was still young enough to do useful war work – left of her own accord.

'I'm going into munitions, ma'am,' she said as she handed Eveleen her written notice.

'After it's all over, Emily, come back and see me, won't you?'

'Oh yes, ma'am,' the girl smiled, but Eveleen had the distinct feeling that once her maid had tasted life outside domestic service, the girl was unlikely to want to return.

No letters came from Richard throughout February.

'You haven't had a letter, Bridie,' Eveleen asked anxiously, 'and not shown it to me?'

'No. Have you?'

Eveleen bit her lip and shook her head. Then she decided to confess. 'There's been only one letter I haven't shown you. After – after Andrew was posted missing.'

'Why? What did he say?'

'Just – just that he hoped you hadn't taken the news too badly.'

'Oh,' Bridie said quietly. So she had been wrong. Richard did believe that Andrew had been killed.

Eveleen was watching her. 'What about you?'

'What – what do you mean?'

'Are there any letters you haven't shown me?'

Bridie smiled apologetically. 'Only one. The very first he ever wrote to me. He – he talked about us going to the Goose Fair and – and I thought it would upset you.'

Eveleen smiled sadly. 'We've both been trying to protect the other, haven't we?'

Bridie nodded. 'But I promise I've shown you all of them since. And I will in future, whatever's in them.'

Eveleen held out her arms. 'So will I.'

Bridie hugged her aunt and against her shoulder she murmured, 'But I wonder why he hasn't written lately.'

*

At the beginning of March there was a knock on the cottage door in Singleton's Yard.

Bridie opened it to see a tall figure dressed in soldier's uniform standing there. His back was to the light and for a moment she could not see his features. She drew breath sharply and for an instant the name sprang at once to her lips. Andrew! But then she realized he was too tall. Her fleeting disappointment evaporated when she realized the visitor's identity. She gave a delighted squeal and flung herself against him.

'Uncle Richard!' She pulled him into the living room, firing questions at him without giving him a moment to answer. 'Oh, you're home! Is Auntie Eveleen with you? Are you home for good? Is the war over? Great-Gran, this is Uncle Richard. Sit down, sit down. I'll make a cup of tea. Oh, it's wonderful to see you.' And again, she hugged him. Richard put his arms around her and held her so tightly he almost squeezed the breath from her. At last he released her a little, but still stood with his arms about her.

It was Bridie who pulled away and said, 'Come and meet my great-grandmother.'

Richard bent and took the old lady's hand. 'I'm pleased to meet you, Mrs Singleton.' Then he sat down in the chair on the opposite side of the hearth. For a moment Bridie stood biting her lip and looking down at him. There was something different about him. He smiled at her in the gentle way he always had, but the smile did not reach his eyes.

'What is it?' she asked quietly. 'What's happened?'

He looked up at her, puzzled. 'Happened? Er – nothing, as far as I know. Why?'

'Oh, I just wondered. I mean . . .' her voice faltered and she turned, murmuring, 'I'll get the tea.' As she prepared the tray, she glanced through the open door from the scullery. He was talking to the old lady, his head bend slightly to one side in that kindly, solicitous manner he had always had and for a moment Bridie thought she had been mistaken. He was as he had always been, but when she carried the tray through, mashed the tea from the kettle on the hob, poured and handed him a cup, she could see again that there was something different about him.

It was in his eyes. As he talked, there was no change of expression in his eyes. Even when he smiled, it was a merely mechanical stretching of his mouth and not an emotion he was really feeling. His eyes were like those of a dead fish.

She sat down and, at a lull in the conversation, asked again, 'Are you home for good?'

Richard shook his head. 'No, I'm afraid not. Just on leave. I've been very lucky to get back to England. Oh, we get leave in France, but there's never enough time to get all the way home.'

Bridie watched as he sat gazing into the glowing coals in the grate. 'Is it very bad out there, Uncle Richard?'

As he turned his head slowly to look at her, Bridie could have bitten her tongue off for having asked the question. The look in his eyes that had replaced the vacant expression was far worse. Terror, horror, even loss of faith – all were there.

'Don't ask me, Bridie,' he said huskily. 'You don't want to know. Believe me, you really don't. If there is such a place as hell, it couldn't possibly be worse than the trenches in France.'

Thirty-Eight

She took him to the workshops, up the stone steps to meet her grandfather, and was gratified that Harry had the courtesy to shake his hand, although his manner was gruff and unwelcoming.

As they stepped into the yard again, Bridie blurted out, 'He doesn't want me here. He never speaks to me or comes to Great-Gran's cottage.'

Richard put his hand on her shoulder. 'You've done a grand job here, Bridie. Eveleen was telling me, but perhaps now that the old lady's better it's time for you to come back to Nottingham.'

Bridie glanced towards Andrew's home. 'I want to stay here. At least, a while longer. I – I'm waiting for Andrew to come home.'

His fingers tightened on her shoulder. 'Bridie, love, you must come to terms with the facts. Andrew isn't going to come back.'

'How do you know? Did you see him killed? Have you seen his body?'

'No, but he went out with a raiding party at night. When they do that they have to remove all identification marks and badges. Two men didn't come back. Andrew was one of them.'

'What happened?'

Richard shrugged. 'No-one knows. The two of them got separated from the rest and in the dark they just disappeared. Maybe they got taken prisoner, but – but shots were heard, so . . .'

'So,' Bridie took up his sentence, 'it was just presumed that he – and the other feller too – had been killed.'

'It's all we can do, Bridie. We can't go looking for them.'

The girl tried to imagine what a battlefield must be like as, haltingly, Richard tried to explain. There were lines of trenches, he said, on each side protected by barbed wire and a stretch of ground between them called 'no man's land'. Was that where Andrew had gone missing? she wondered. Perhaps he had been lying out there, still alive but needing help.

'Can't you look for them in the daytime?'

'If you so much as put your head above the trench parapet, a sniper will pick you off. We use a kind of makeshift periscope made with mirrors to look across to the enemy lines.'

Despite what they all said, despite even what Richard said, who knew better than anyone, Bridie refused to give up hope. She looked up at him, her eyes afire with determination. As if by the strength of her will, she could make it so, she said, 'He will come back, Uncle Richard. He's not dead. I know he's not.'

The following day Bridie went to see Gracie Turner.

'I've been thinking,' she said, once they were sat at the kitchen table, a cup of tea and freshly baked scones in front of them. 'Maybe I should go back to Nottingham. Auntie Eveleen is so busy at the factory. She works such long hours. Now Emily's left her and Uncle Richard told me that Cook's legs are bad now, maybe I should go back. I can always come back here when Andrew comes home.'

''Course you can, mi little lass. The old lady's a lot better and I can look after her now, if you want me to.'

Bridie beamed. 'That's why I've come to see you. I was hoping you would. I don't want that Lil back in her house.'

It was all settled between them, even that Gracie should cook meals for Harry.

'It needn't be every day,' Bridie said, 'maybe just two or three times a week. Just so's he gets a good meal now and again. You know? That's if he'll eat them!' she added wryly.

'Oh aye, I know all right. He's a fool to himself is Harry Singleton. Always has been. But if them at the chapel told him to jump in the river and drown himself, I reckon he would. He takes after his father. Hard-hearted old bugger, he was. No wonder your poor gran ran away like she did.'

Bridie's eyes widened. 'Me gran? Ran away from home?'

'Oh aye,' Gracie said, filling both cups for a second time and settling down to impart a piece of gossip, completely forgetting that she had once said it was not her place to divulge family secrets. 'She fell in love with a young feller and got herself pregnant. Denounced in front of the whole congregation, she was, by her own family. Well, by her father and her brother, Harry.'

Bridie gasped. 'What do you mean "denounced"?'

Gracie waved her hands vaguely. 'It's a very old custom. Gone long since in most places, but not here.' She nodded her head. 'Old man Singleton, that's your great-grandmother's husband, he believed in all that sort of thing. If anybody did anything wrong, 'specially adultery and what they call fornication . . .' Gracie grinned. 'Doing what comes naturally, that's what I call it. Anyway, they used to haul the culprits up in front of the whole congregation and make 'em confess their sins.'

'They did that to Gran and her – her young man?'

Gracie shook her head. 'They couldn't get hold of him, else they would have done. He was from a well-to-do family in Nottingham. His family sent him away, so poor Mary was left to face the shame alone. Then she ran away and we didn't hear from her again until she and her family – your auntie and your dad too, of course – arrived on Harry's doorstep.'

Bridie was thoughtful, piecing together the rest of the story. That was how her mother, Rebecca, had met Jimmy Hardcastle and had fallen in love with him and become pregnant. And then she too had been cast out by Harry Singleton.

'Who was me gran's young man?' she asked suddenly.

'Oh, well now, I'm not rightly sure.' Gracie was avoiding meeting her direct gaze and Bridie had the distinct impression that the older woman knew far more than she was telling now. Gracie stood up and began to clear away the cups and saucers, bustling about as if to avoid answering any awkward questions. 'I've said too much already,' Bridie heard her murmur. 'Me an' mi big mouth. It'll get me into hot water one of these days.' Raising her voice, Gracie changed the subject. 'Now, it's all settled then. I'll look after your gran and you go back to Nottingham and help your auntie Eveleen.'

'I'm so sorry, Evie. I – I can't.'

They lay in the big bed together, holding each other

close. Richard had not been able to make love to her, even though Eveleen's body yearned to offer him comfort.

'It's all right. It doesn't matter,' she tried to reassure him, yet she knew he would feel his failure as keenly as she did. She kissed him tenderly and whilst he returned her kiss, there was none of the passion, the sudden spark of fire, that had always been between them.

She mourned its loss, but understood. She had not questioned him about the conditions in the trenches, but she too had seen the dreadful look deep in his eyes.

'We'll go out tomorrow. We'll go to the farm.' She had been disappointed because Richard had made no effort to visit the factory, had displayed no interest in it at all or in everything that she was accomplishing. Apart from his trip to visit Bridie in Flawford, he had been nowhere. He had sat in the morning room all day, each day, just staring into the fire.

'A day in the country will do you good.' She kissed his cheek and then pulled out of his arms. 'Try to sleep now.'

She lay beside him staring into the darkness and slept only fitfully herself, disturbed by his restlessness and his mutterings. More than once he shouted out and she held him in her arms as he trembled and buried his face in her neck, his tears wet against her skin.

Eveleen drove the motor car the following morning. At first Richard sat morose and silent beside her, but gradually he began to look about him. The day was cold and sharp, but already there was a feeling of spring in the air. Lambs, without a care in the world, pranced in the fields and snowdrops dappled the grass verges.

As they drew into the yard, Josh came towards them,

his arms stretched wide in welcome. Behind him was Sid, limping towards them but smiling broadly. Wordlessly he shook Richard's hand and then turned to Eveleen as Josh drew Richard away towards the house.

'I can't thank you enough, missis, for bringing me out here. Your mam and dad – ' he was referring to Josh, not knowing that he was Eveleen's stepfather – 'have worked a miracle. It's the countryside. It's so calm and peaceful. It was the noise out there that got to me, missis. The shelling and the gunfire getting nearer and nearer and never knowing when it was going to be your turn. It was living with the constant fear. And we was all afraid, missis, every man jack of us. It didn't stop us doing what we had to do, but anyone who tells you he wasn't afraid is a bloody liar. Beggin' yer pardon, missis.' Eveleen smiled understandingly as Sid went on, 'But I'm fine now, honest. I was only saying yesterday, I'm ready to go back home now. I won't be like I was, missis, I promise. How I could have treated my Elsie like that . . .' He shook his head. 'I don't know. I'm that ashamed.'

Eveleen touched his arm. 'It wasn't your fault. You were ill. But if you really feel well enough, you can come back with us this evening. We'll take you home.'

Sid's face brightened. 'That'd be grand. Not that I'm not happy here, but I want to get back to Elsie.' He pulled an apologetic face. 'I've a lot of making up to do.' He glanced over his shoulder and nodded towards Richard. 'He doesn't look so good himself. Just got leave, has he?'

Eveleen nodded, but could not speak for the lump in her throat.

Mary fussed around Richard until Eveleen felt quite left out. But she smiled to herself – her mother had always been this way. The men in Mary's life were paramount and girls and women of little importance. And perhaps, Eveleen reminded herself, young men of Richard's age were a substitute for the son she never heard from.

After dinner Richard went outside to walk around the smallholding with Josh. Mary, watching them from the scullery window, shook her head sadly. 'Oh, Eveleen, he's a changed man.'

'I know,' Eveleen agreed, but tried to be positive. 'But when the war's over and he comes home then everything will be all right. I'm sure of it. It's just – well – knowing he's got to go back and face it all again. It can't be easy.'

'Has he got to go back? I mean, he volunteered. He's done his bit now. Can't he be – well, I don't know – be released or something?'

Eveleen bit her lip and shook her head. 'No. He joined up and he's there for the duration now.'

'Can't he just – not go back?'

Now Eveleen was vehement. 'No. He'd be shot as a deserter.'

Mary gasped. 'Do they really do that?'

Eveleen nodded. 'Oh yes.'

Soberly they both watched as the two men walked across the yard and into the field.

'Today's been marvellous for him, Mam. For the first time since he came home he's begun to relax.'

'Why not stay a few days then? Till he has to go back?'

'Oh, we can't. I have to get back. The factory . . .'

Mary cast a wry glance at her daughter. 'Surely your husband's welfare comes before the factory,' she said primly.

'Well, yes. But Richard agreed to me becoming a director whilst he's away. I don't want to fail him.'

'You'll be failing him if you drag him back to the city, where he's obviously not quite so at ease. But if you don't want to stay,' there was accusation in her tone, 'then let Richard stay with us for a few days. Bridie's bed is always made up and aired in case she arrives back suddenly.'

Eveleen said, 'If he wants to, of course he can.'

But when the two men returned to the house and the idea was put to them, Richard shook his head sadly. 'I would love to have stayed, but I have to report back the day after tomorrow. We – we sail for France in three days' time.'

'So soon?' Eveleen cried and put her arms about him, steeling herself not to beg him to stay, to desert, as moments ago her mother had suggested.

As the light began to fade, they said goodbye, Sid profuse in his thanks. 'I wish all my mates could have had what you've given me.'

As they were driving home up the hill towards Bernby, Richard glanced up the driveway of Fairfield House. 'Is he still there?'

Carefully Eveleen said, 'I believe so.'

'The place looks neglected.'

'The whole estate is up for sale. Even the house. It seems Stephen has drunk and gambled away the family fortune,' Eveleen explained.

'Oh, so that's it. I thought he might have joined up.'

Eveleen gave a wry laugh. 'I don't think Stephen Dunsmore will go to war willingly.'

His voice was lower now and above the engine noise Eveleen only just caught her husband's words. 'Perhaps he's the sensible one.'

Thirty-Nine

'Do you know,' Eveleen was telling her father-in-law three days later, as they walked around the factory together, 'Sid is so much better. We brought him back on Sunday evening. It was like a miracle to see the change in him. Even Richard managed to relax a little, although he was only there a few hours.'

'Yes, Richard did mention it when he came to say goodbye before he left. I expect it was the peace and quiet. They say that on the south coast you can hear the gunfire from France. Imagine what it must be like to be there.'

Brinsley and Eveleen exchanged a sober look.

'I suppose,' she said thoughtfully, 'that, even though Sid was back home, somehow it's never completely quiet in the city, is it? Not even at night. Perhaps that's why he couldn't recover here.'

'Not like in the country,' Brinsley agreed. He was silent for a moment and then asked, 'Have you seen the wounded around the city? Those that are so badly injured they'll never go back to the war?'

Eveleen nodded and bit her lip to stop it trembling. 'Yes,' she said at last. 'It – it's frightening, isn't it?'

'One of our former employees came to see me yesterday. He's lost an arm and can't find work. Of course, he can't go back to his previous job as a twisthand.

Even he knows that. But I'm trying to find something for him to do. Any suggestions?'

'There might be something in the warehouse. I'll see what I can do.'

Brinsley nodded his thanks. 'Of course, what would do him good is a spell in the countryside.'

They both spoke at once. 'What we ought to do—' 'Couldn't we—?'

They laughed and then Brinsley continued. 'What we ought to do is buy a property somewhere in the countryside for the soldiers to go when they're discharged on medical grounds. A place to convalesce where they can heal physically and mentally. Perhaps they could even learn new skills that would help them to find employment of some kind. I'm a wealthy man, Eveleen. I'd like to do something like that. I'd feel I was doing my bit to help with the war.' He glanced at her and then looked away, adding softly, 'It – it would help me to think I was keeping Richard safe.'

Impulsively Eveleen reached out for his hand and held it. 'Oh, I knew you'd understand. That's just how I feel about the factory. If I – if we – can keep it going, if it survives, then so will Richard. I – I thought I was being silly.'

Brinsley shook his head. 'No, my dear, we're just clinging on to any kind of belief that will give us hope.'

They smiled at each other and walked on, but now Eveleen had a faraway look in her eyes as a plan began to form in her mind. 'Would it have to be near Nottingham?'

'Well, not too far away. It's our own boys we want to help.'

'What about Bernby? Is it too far away?'

'Bernby?' The older man looked startled. 'Where –

where your mother lives?' There was an unmistakable look of longing in his face for a brief moment as he asked gently, 'How is she? How is Mary?'

Eveleen touched his hand in an understanding gesture. 'She's well – and happy.'

Brinsley nodded but seemed as if he could not speak for a moment. Then he cleared his throat, murmured, 'I'm glad,' and then turned back to their previous topic of conversation. 'Why do you suggest Bernby?'

'I just might know of a place that would be perfect.' Eveleen's heart beat a little faster. Fairfield House, Stephen Dunsmore's home. She could not prevent the tinge of vindictive pleasure it would give her to become the owner of that house.

'Leave it with me,' she said. 'I'll find out if it's still for sale.'

'Eveleen, my dear, what a lovely surprise.' Stephen Dunsmore staggered across the floor of the morning room at Fairfield House. Although it was only eleven in the morning, he was already obviously drunk.

'Stephen,' she said calmly, drawing off her gloves and moving to stand in front of the roaring fire. She held out her hands to its warmth before turning to face him.

He lurched towards her. 'To what do I owe the pleashure.' He grinned foolishly, standing in front of her, swaying slightly.

She regarded him steadily. The handsome young man she had once believed she loved with all her heart was now a bloated, dissolute wreck. Stephen had been her first love and he had spurned her, turned his back on her when she most needed his love and protection. When her father had died, he had been instrumental in having them turned out of their tied farmhouse, Pear Tree Farm. Now her mother, along with Josh, owned that farm. That had been a small, but sweet, vengeance. Richard had made that possible, but today Eveleen was here to wreak her own revenge in a much bigger way.

She moved to pull the bell rope to summon the butler.

'Shall we have some tea?' she said, smiling sweetly at Stephen. He looked startled for a moment, then he grinned.

'Make yourshelf at home, lovely Eveleen.'

'Oh, I will,' she said and sat, uninvited, on the sofa. Stephen dropped down heavily beside her and leant towards her, the fumes of alcohol on his breath wafting into her face. 'Thish ish very nice.'

She looked at him fully then. The once smooth face was now blotched with ugly red patches. The bright blue eyes were now bloodshot and his hands trembled.

The butler entered and Eveleen glanced coolly at him. 'Tea and scones, if you please, Tomkins.'

The man glanced at Stephen, who nodded his approval. Eveleen smiled inwardly. The manservant, who had always treated her with disdain, was shortly in for a shock. As, indeed, was the man seated beside her. Even when the butler had closed the door, Eveleen waited, not wanting to be the first to open the conversation that must begin.

'I'll be leaving here soon,' Stephen said. 'I've had to sell the estate. This blasted war . . . it's been the ruin of us.'

'The only thing that's ruined the Dunsmore estate, Stephen, is you.'

'Eh?' Her words penetrated his befuddled state and drove home deeply. He pulled himself away from her, tried to stand, but found he could not. He sagged back against the cushions and protested weakly, 'What right have you to say that?'

'I have every right because it's the truth. Your grandfather built up this estate virtually from nothing. Incidentally, with a great deal of help from my grandfather, who was granted the tenancy of Pear Tree Farm. Your father carried on the good work, again,' she added pointedly, 'with no little help from my father. It wasn't until you – the third generation – were put in charge of running the estate, when your father became involved in politics, that it began to go downhill. You've drunk and gambled away your inheritance.'

'How dare you?' He scrambled to his feet and stood over her, his fists clenched. Slowly Eveleen rose too and faced him squarely. 'Oh, I dare, Stephen. I dare because I am now the owner of Fairfield House and all the surrounding land. In fact, I own all the Dunsmore estate.' Then she added scathingly, 'What's left of it.'

'You vindictive bitch!' Veins bulged in his neck and throbbed at his temple. For a moment, Eveleen thought he might have a seizure. 'How the hell did you manage that?'

'Agents working for me spoke to your father. He was only too glad to sell up, to salvage what was left of the estate before every last penny went across the bar or the gambling tables. I now own every square of ground, every brick, every stick of furniture.' In truth, it was Brinsley's money that had bought it, but he had insisted that the names on the deeds should be Richard and Eveleen Stokes.

'When the war's over, my dear,' he had said, 'it will be a wonderful country home for you. A marvellous place to bring up my grandson.'

Eveleen turned away from Stephen and went to stand

once more in front of the fire. In clear ringing tones, she said, 'You will vacate these premises by the end of the week, *Mr Dunsmore*.'

Eveleen stood in front of the white marble fireplace watching the man who had once treated her so callously, waiting for the surge of triumph, for the sweet satisfaction of revenge.

But it did not come. Instead her victory over him was hollow and shameful. She had used the wealth of her husband's family to make the purchase. Her outward reason had been to give help and succour to wounded veteran soldiers, but Eveleen knew that, deep down, her motives had not been completely unselfish, as were her father-in-law's.

Stephen lurched across the space between them, tripped on the carpet and almost fell against her. Regaining his balance, he stood in front of her and shook his fist in her face.

'You scheming, heartless bitch,' he spluttered again.

She faced him, outwardly calm. 'And weren't you just as heartless sixteen years ago when you had Jackson throw us out of the only home we had? At least you have a home to go to. I presume that your parents have a house in London. You're not exactly out on the streets, are you, Stephen?'

'I might as well be,' he mumbled, turning away from her as the truth of his situation began to sink in. 'I can hardly face my father now I've lost the family estate.'

There was silence between them, whilst he shambled around the room, touching objects, gazing at pictures and portraits of his family. It was a pathetic gesture and if he had hoped to appeal to Eveleen's softer side he almost succeeded. The sight of this once-proud, handsome man – a man she had idolized – stripped of all his possessions and reduced almost to poverty shook her resolve. But then he reeled towards the drinks cabinet, picked up a decanter and splashed liquid into a glass. He drank it in one gulp and poured another, which quickly followed the first. The spark of sympathy Eveleen had begun to feel died in that moment.

'I shall enlisht,' he slurred the words, even though by his bold statement he was trying to salvage a vestige of dignity. Then he pointed a shaking finger at her. 'You will be sending me to my death.'

Eveleen trembled inwardly, but she lifted her chin and defended herself stoutly. 'No, I'm not. I'm buying your house, not sending you to the Front.'

But deep inside the feeling of guilt would not go away.

Forty

As a small compensation for her actions, Eveleen kept on all the staff at Fairfield House, even Tomkins, the sour-faced butler, who had always treated her with such contempt. He was too old to find other employment. Besides, having worked at Fairfield House all his adult life, he would be useful, Eveleen thought. She smiled to herself. It would be punishment enough for him to think that she, the once scruffy daughter of the estate's stockman, was now his employer.

'Life will be very different for you all here,' she told them as she explained the plans she had for the estate and the house in particular. 'The land will still be farmed and Bill Morton will be the estate bailiff. But the house is to become a convalescent home for soldiers.'

They took her news stoically enough, glad still to have employment and she heard later that the estate workers had accepted the changes with the same thankfulness.

At Pear Tree Farm Mary could hardly take in the news. 'What would your father have thought? To see you as the owner of all this.' She waved her arm to encompass all the land around them. Then she glanced ironically at her daughter. 'And all of it without having to marry Master Stephen.'

Eveleen stood in the middle of the farmyard as she had done so many times in her life. Behind the house, to the east, the fields sloped down to the beck and then rose again on the other side towards the trees of Bernby Covert lining the hilltop. The place where, as a young, wilful and oh-so-innocent girl, she had run to meet Stephen, flinging herself into his arms, her face upturned to receive his passionate kisses. But the sweetness of that time had been soured by his selfish, callous attitude.

To the left on the brow of the hill she could see the spire of Bernby church, where her beloved father was buried. What, indeed, would he think to all this? She shuddered inwardly, knowing instinctively that he would not be proud of the way she had helped to bring about Stephen Dunsmore's downfall. He would not condone spiteful revenge. She even doubted he would have approved of the greater issue of the war, which had all of them caught up in a national fervour of retaliation.

She turned and walked to the gate to lean upon it and look westwards towards the ramparts of Belvoir Castle, standing proudly on the distant hill. 'But you would approve of the role that Fairfield House is going to play in the future wouldn't you, Dad?'

So clearly, in her mind's eye, she saw his face, and he was smiling at her.

'Can I go and nurse the soldiers, Auntie Evie? Oh, can I?'

Bridie had been back home in Nottingham for a few weeks, working in the inspection room and keeping Eveleen company. But when she heard of her aunt's plans she begged to be involved.

'I like caring for people,' she said. 'I really enjoyed

looking after Great-Gran. I think I'd like to be a nurse when I'm older. Wouldn't that be a good place to start?'

Eveleen regarded the girl standing in front of her. In the last few months Bridie had grown in stature and matured in character. Before her stood no longer a child, but a girl on the threshold of womanhood. At almost fifteen she had filled out, her figure was now nicely rounded and her face was captivating. Her eyes were her best feature. Dark blue, they shone with enthusiasm and determination.

'Please say you'll let me go.'

Eveleen sighed, reluctant to lose Bridie's company again, and yet there was sense in what the girl said.

'It might mean you living back at Pear Tree Farm again. I don't think your gran will agree to you sleeping in at Fairfield House.' She smiled. 'Not with all those soldiers there.'

Bridie laughed, but saw the truth in Eveleen's statement. 'Maybe it would be best, anyway. I can help a bit at home, around the farm.' Her face sobered as she added quietly, 'And I might be glad to get away from time to time. There'll be some dreadful sights.'

They were both silent, each thinking about the wounded they had seen around the streets of the city, some even reduced to begging.

'There'll be no shortage of takers for the places,' Eveleen murmured. Briskly she went on, 'I tell you what, you can sit in with me on the interviews next week. I'm appointing a matron first and after that all the nurses we shall need. The doctor at Bernby has already agreed to help. We'll go on Sunday and stay at Pear Tree Farm.'

'Why don't we stay at Fairfield House?' Bridie asked innocently.

Turning away so that she did not have to meet the girl's questioning gaze, Eveleen said swiftly, 'No, no, I don't want to stay there.'

There was great excitement at Fairfield House. The legalities had all been completed in a surprisingly short time. The new staff had all been appointed and had been in residence for three weeks in their sleeping quarters on the second floor, where domestic staff traditionally slept. But now there were nurses to accommodate as well. Even the attics had been cleared out and made into bedrooms. Bridie, too, was to sleep in with the other nurses. The house had been cleaned from attic to cellar and had been transformed from a shabby and neglected house into a comfortable hospital cum convalescent home. Now, at the beginning of August, Fairfield House was ready to receive its first patients.

Dulcie Barton, who had been appointed matron, took Brinsley and Eveleen on a tour of inspection. 'The dining room and, of course, the kitchens will remain as such and the drawing room will be the patients' sitting room and recreation room,' she explained, throwing open the door to each one. In the corner of the newly styled recreation room stood a gramophone with a huge horn and nearby was a piano, complete with sheet music for the patriotic songs of the day.

'Do you think they'll want that sort of music?' Eveleen said doubtfully. 'I would have thought they'd want to forget all about the war.'

'You'd be surprised,' Dulcie said. 'Some of them will still want to cling on to their happier memories, the camaraderie. They'll want to remember their pals.' She turned to Brinsley. 'It was very thoughtful of you to provide the piano and especially the gramophone. It will be a blessing for those who can't make their own entertainment. So many will be confined to bath chairs or blinded.'

Brinsley nodded and cleared his throat. 'Don't mention it, my dear, and if there's anything else you can think of, let me know.'

'The library, too, will stay just as it is,' Dulcie continued with the tour. 'It will be a peaceful, quiet room for them.'

'We must make sure there are some more suitable books,' Eveleen remarked. 'I can't imagine these dusty tomes being of interest to the soldiers.'

'The morning room,' the matron went on, 'has been changed into a room for staff use, whilst the study is now my office. The small sitting room, which I expect the "lady of the house" used, has been changed into a treatment room and a surgery for when the doctors visit. No operations will be done here, but we may well receive quite severe cases. Now upstairs.' She led the way up the wide staircase. 'On the first floor the large rooms have been turned into small dormitories holding three or four beds and the smaller rooms hold two or sometimes only a single bed. We shall use these for very sick patients who need constant attention and may disturb the others.'

The whole place still reeked of fresh paint, but all the rooms seemed light and airy. The new single beds with clean white sheets, plump pillows and grey blankets awaited their patients.

'I'm very impressed,' Brinsley said. 'And the grounds are lovely. They'll find peace here, Eveleen, my dear. I'm really proud of you and so will Richard be when he hears.'

Eveleen quelled the feeling of guilt, but she suspected that her perceptive husband would see through her ulterior motive. She was regretting now, not what she had done in acquiring a beautiful rest home for soldiers, but the way she had done it.

'I've some news for you too,' Brinsley was saying, oblivious to Eveleen's guilty feelings. 'As you know, some of my contacts are connected with the War Office and various other government departments. It seems, my dear, that the authorities would be only too pleased to treat our little venture as additional accommodation for the military hospitals closest to us.' He shook his head sadly. 'It seems they are under a great deal of pressure.'

'But – but we wanted to take the wounded from the city streets. Those who are not bad enough to be hospitalized but who are not fit enough to find work.'

'I know, I know, my dear. And we will, we will. But the seriously injured must come first. Don't you agree?'

'I – suppose so, yes,'

'So,' Brinsley went on, 'the good thing is that we have already appointed properly qualified staff and the local doctor has agreed to visit daily, calling in colleagues when necessary. And now . . .' Brinsley put his hand on her arm and suddenly his tone was diffident and there was longing in his face. 'Do you think, I might be permitted to see you mother whilst I'm here?'

Bridie had found her vocation. There was only one cloud on her horizon, which was never far away from her thoughts: Andrew. She still believed fervently that he was alive somewhere and that one day he would come home to her. In the meantime she threw herself into her work at Fairfield House.

Dulcie Barton was a single woman in her forties. She had a pleasant face with calm, grey eyes, but when she smiled her whole face seemed to light up. Her wonderful smile had heartened many a desperately ill patient and given them hope. She had devoted her life to nursing and, whilst she was a strict disciplinarian and kept a necessary remoteness between herself and the nurses under her, she was nevertheless friendly and always approachable. She had taken a particular liking to Bridie, for she saw in the girl a genuine gift for caring for others and she took it upon herself to encourage her to look upon nursing as a career.

Dulcie was adept at handling the nurses with a firm yet understanding hand. So many of them were grieving privately for loved ones snatched from them by this dreadful war, but with her guidance these young women left their personal tragedies behind when they put on their nursing uniforms.

'You can wear a uniform just like the qualified nurses, Bridie,' Dulcie had explained to her. 'A long white apron with a bib, and a neat frilled cap, but your dress will have to be a different colour to show that you are a trainee. Now, I think red and white striped cotton would be most suitable. It will be different from the colours the others wear.' She smiled. 'At least here, in a private establishment, we've been able to choose our own colour scheme.'

The sisters, who had been appointed each wore a navy blue dress with a white triangular shaped head-dress, starched white collar and cuffs. The nurses wore dark grey dresses and both the sisters and the nurses wore long white aprons. Only Dulcie as matron wore the navy blue dress with no apron.

'Bridie won't accept Andrew's death,' Eveleen had explained to Miss Barton in confidence. 'I don't think she will until the war is over and – and he still doesn't come home.'

She felt the matron watching her. There was such a depth of understanding in Dulcie Barton's eyes, she experienced life's tragedies every day. Her voice was low and soothing, like soft velvet. 'It's very hard for a girl to come to terms with death and to accept that it can happen to someone she loves. What is the relationship between them?'

Eveleen explained. 'I think Andrew thought of her as his daughter, but as for Bridie . . .' She sighed and smiled sadly. 'She idolized him and *not* as a father.'

'I see.' Miss Barton was thoughtful and Eveleen felt she was watching her, almost calculating. 'Mrs Stokes, may I be frank with you?'

'Of course.'

'You already speak of Andrew in the past tense.'

Eveleen nodded.

Gently the matron went on. 'You have obviously accepted the War Office's assumption that he has been killed.'

Again Eveleen agreed silently.

'But Bridie has not.'

'She just refuses to. She's adamant he's alive. She – she says she would know, would feel it . . .'

Miss Barton nodded. 'You may think this strange, Mrs Stokes, but it might be best to allow her to think that, for the present. Oh, I don't mean to encourage it, to foster false hope, but just to let her come to the truth – if indeed it is the truth – in her own time and in her own way. At the moment – and this may sound a little callous to you – it may be in her best interests to allow her to believe he is still alive.'

All her life Eveleen had always faced up to the truth of a situation and been strong enough to deal with it. Even the things she had done wrong and regretted. Now she frowned, unable to comprehend that anything but the truth, however cruel, was best.

Dulcie went on. 'Bridie is going to be caring for young men, many not much older than herself. She will be called upon to carry out very – intimate tasks for them in the course of that nursing. Many men,' Dulcie smiled, 'whatever their age, imagine themselves in love with their nurses.'

Understanding began to dawn in Eveleen. She had wondered why most of the nurses that the matron had chosen were older rather than younger.

'So,' the matron continued, 'it might be safer – for all concerned – if Bridie's heart is engaged elsewhere. I know it might sound unfeeling, calculating perhaps,' Dulcie hurried on, 'but, believe me, I'm thinking of Bridie as much as my patients.'

Eveleen nodded. 'I do see your point.'

'This is just between you and me?' Dulcie asked once more.

'Of course.'

Forty-One

Richard's letters told of a quiet time in his corner of the war.

> *The days in the trenches are more 'restful' than the designated rest days when we do such a lot of digging. The weather is lovely at the moment – the trenches dry and it's very quiet. We have even had time to clean our boots and polish our buttons. I suppose this is because we are about six hundred yards away from the enemy front line here. We patrol our frontage at night and snatch sleep in the day.*

It was not so quiet on other war fronts. On 1 July a combined British and French offensive had begun near the Somme. By the end of the first day, nearly twenty thousand British soldiers had been massacred by enemy artillery and machine guns and twice as many had been wounded. The more serious casualties were patched up in field hospitals and then sent home to Blighty. By August, when Fairfield House opened, some of the wounded from the Somme had found their way to the Midlands and a few were brought to Bernby.

It was the first time Bridie had seen raw flesh wounds, men blinded by shrapnel, their eyes swathed in bandages. Some had terrible internal injuries, others missing limbs. And then there were those who suffered the effects of the terrible gas. But Bridie kept her feelings severely in check and, taking her cue from the older nurses, greeted them all with a welcoming smile and a cheery, bantering word. There was one lad – not much older than Bridie – who was crying out in pain as he was carried up the stairs and into one of the smaller rooms with only two beds.

'Put me in wi' 'im. I'll look after 'im,' an older man with both legs broken and a wound in his thigh said to an orderly.

'You'll 'ave to go where you'm put, soldier,' the orderly said cheerfully.

'But 'ee's me mate. We've bin together from since we joined up. I look out for 'im, see'

Bridie, walking behind the two stretchers being carried, said quietly. 'It'll be all right. Put them together . . .' She hurried ahead and opened the door. 'In here. Room Number Four. If Sister Jones wants them moved, we can do it later.'

'Ta, luv.' The older man grinned at her as he was carried in through the door and deposited on the nearest bed. He grimaced but made no sound of complaint and at once looked across to where his companion was still groaning and curling himself into a ball. Bridie stood beside the boy, biting her lip. She was anxious to help, but did not know how.

'Shot in the guts, he is,' the older man told her. 'Gets terrible pain, Nurse.'

Despite the awful sight, Bridie felt a thrill run through her. It was the first time a patient had called her 'Nurse'. It made her feel important and special.

Now she was really needed.

*

By nightfall all the patients were settled and the house relatively quiet, though from Room Number Four the sound of the young soldier's sobbing echoed along the landing.

'Sister says would you like to be moved out into another room?' Bridie whispered to the older man, whose name she learned from the board at the bottom of the bed was Jabez Field. 'I told her I didn't think you would, but she said I was to ask you.'

'No, no. I want to stay with 'im. Been in the trenches together, we 'ave. I ain't leavin' him now.'

Bridie smiled. 'No, I thought not.'

'What's your name, then?' he asked as Bridie handed him a cup of hot milk.

'Singleton.'

'Nurse Singleton. I'll remember that.'

Again, she felt the thrill at the title but said, 'I'm not a real nurse, only a trainee. You'd better just call me Singleton.'

The man slurped the hot milk, leaving a white line along his upper lip. He shook his head. 'No. If you're looking after us, in my eyes you're a nurse.'

Bridie beamed at him as she picked up the other cup of milk and went across to the other bed. The poor boy was writhing and moaning, his hands trembling.

'If you can't hold the cup, I'll help you to drink it.'

She held the cup to his lips, but even then he could not keep still enough to drink and almost knocked the cup from her hand, spilling some of the liquid.

'S-sorry,' he stammered.

'Doesn't matter,' Bridie said, mopping up the spill. 'Let's try something else.' She picked up the spoon from the saucer and gently spooned the milk, little by little, into his mouth. He spluttered a little at first, but then began to swallow and gradually he became a little calmer, though tears were still running down his face.

'I want me mam,' he whispered. 'I want to see me mam again. Just once, before . . .'

Bridie took hold of his hand. 'You'll see her very soon. We'll get you better and—'

'I ain't goin' to get better.'

Bridie opened her mouth to protest, but out of the corner of her eye she noticed a movement and turned to see Field shaking his head sadly and biting hard down on his lower lip. The girl swallowed. Gently she squeezed the boy's hand and murmured, 'I – I'll see what I can do.'

She settled him against his pillows and pulled the covers up to his chin. The boy was obviously exhausted, but the pain would not let him sleep. She moved to the end of the bed and looked at the name written on the board there.

Herbert Hyde. Bridie frowned. There was something familiar about the name and yet she just couldn't think what it was. 'Herbert Hyde,' she murmured aloud.

'We allus called 'im Bertie,' Field said, his voice husky with emotion.

And then she knew. This was Bertie, Mrs Hyde's son, who had volunteered aged only sixteen.

Bridie left the room and hurried down the stairs, going straight to the matron's office. Moments later she was standing in front of the desk, facing Dulcie.

'What is it, Singleton?'

'It's the young soldier in Room Four, Matron. I know him. At least, I know his mother. She works at Auntie Evie's factory. In the inspection room. He – he's asking for her. Says he wants to see her . . .' She gulped. 'One last time.'

Dulcie stared at Bridie, then asked sharply. 'Did he say that?'

Bridie nodded. 'I tried to tell him he would get better and would soon be going home, but – but he said he knew he wasn't going to get better.' She gazed at the matron with wide, solemn eyes. 'Isn't he, Matron?'

Dulcie sighed and glanced down at the papers on her desk, straightened them unnecessarily and then looked up to meet Bridie's gaze. Her voice was gentle as she said, 'No, my dear, he isn't. His internal wounds are so severe that the surgeons can do nothing. And now he has an infection.'

'Then – then can we get his mother out here to see him? Auntie Evie would bring her in the motor. I know she would. Please send word to her, Matron.'

Dulcie sighed and, in the privacy of her office, her tone softened. 'Bridie, my dear, your aunt can't transport the relatives of all the soldiers we have out here to see them.'

'But the Hyde family are special. They work for us. For the Reckitt and Stokes factory, I mean. Mrs Hyde and her daughters. Even Bertie himself worked there for a couple of weeks before he enlisted. And if he – if he's . . .' She stopped as her voice threatened to break. She did not want to shed tears in front of the matron, indeed in front of any of the staff. She was determined to show them that she could keep her feelings under strict control whilst on duty.

Dulcie was still shaking her head. 'I don't like to ask her. It puts me in rather a difficult position.'

'Then please will you give me permission to ask her?' Bridie suggested.

'As long as you make sure Mrs Stokes understands you are asking her in a private capacity and that it is not an official request from me, then yes.'

'Thank you, Matron.'

At that moment, Fred Martin was driving the motor car through Nottingham's dark streets, taking Eveleen to her home.

'I ought to walk home, Fred. It's not far. We didn't ought to be wasting petrol.'

'It's not a waste. You're not walking the streets alone at this time of night, Evie,' Fred said firmly. He was always respectful towards the woman who was now his employer, but he had known her from the time she had first arrived in the city, homeless and looking for work. 'Poor beggars,' he muttered almost beneath his breath as a wounded soldier, leaning heavily on a crutch, stood beneath a gas lamp. The man cast a baleful glare at the motor and then spat into the gutter. Eveleen knew it was because she was riding by in a fine vehicle, when he, who had fought for his country, was reduced to begging in the street.

She glanced back at the man out of the rear window. There was something familiar. Even in the half-light she had seen something in the set of his shoulders, the way his head thrust forward, his bald head shining in the light from the lamp . . .

'Stop, Fred, stop!'

Almost before the motor car had drawn to a halt, Eveleen had opened the door and was scrambling out. 'I know who that is. I'm sure I do.'

'Wait for me, then. Don't go on yer own—'

But Eveleen was already running down the street

towards the man, who had turned and was trying to limp away as fast as he could.

'Wait! Wait!' Eveleen called, whilst behind her Fred levered himself out of the motor and hurried after her.

She caught up with the man and touched his arm. 'Please wait. Let me help you.'

The man turned away, trying to hide his face and mumbling, 'Leave me be. I don't want your help.'

Fred reached them, panting hard, as Eveleen said clearly, 'Maybe you don't want my help, Bob Porter, but you look as if you need it.'

'Porter?' Fred repeated, straining through the dimly lit street to see for himself. 'Bob Porter?'

The man whirled around suddenly, throwing off Eveleen's hand and almost losing his own balance. 'Let me be. Let me rot. It's what you wanted, ain't it?'

Eveleen gasped, almost as shocked as if he had struck her. 'No, Bob, it isn't. It was your own stubbornness. No-one asked you to leave Reckitt and Stokes and certainly no-one asked you to enlist.'

'Well, I did, and now I've lost me leg I'll never work again.'

'We'll see about that,' Eveleen said firmly. 'In the meantime, you're coming home with me and tomorrow Fred will drive you out to Fairfield House.'

'Eveleen, I don't think—' Fred began, but she interrupted, 'Take his other arm, Fred, and let's get him into the car.'

'I ain't . . .' Bob began, but then suddenly he sagged against Fred and would have fallen if Fred hadn't held him upright. 'Sorry,' he mumbled. 'I ain't eaten since yesterday.'

Above his head, Eveleen and Fred exchanged a look in the fitful gaslight, and now Fred Martin argued no more.

Forty-Two

'Let me take him to our place, Eveleen,' Fred suggested in a low voice after they had helped Bob into the back of the motor car. 'My Win'll look after him and tomorrow I'll take him to Fairfield House, like you say.'

'No, he's coming home with me. Cook and Smithers are still with me.' She smiled in the darkness and put her hand on Fred's arm. 'I'll be quite safe,' she whispered and Fred had the grace to chuckle. 'By the look of the poor beggar, he hasn't the strength to try owt. Well, if you're sure?'

'I am.'

At Eveleen's home Fred helped Bob into the house, whilst Eveleen hurried to rouse Cook and Smithers. Only minutes later Bob was sitting at the end of the long table in the dining room, ravenously devouring the dinner that Cook had kept hot for Eveleen's return from work.

'He has more need of it than me,' Eveleen had insisted when the cook demurred. She turned to Fred. 'You go on home now, Fred. Win will be wondering what's happened to you. We can manage. I'm just going to make up a bed in the spare room.'

In a low voice Fred said, 'He's been sleeping rough, Eveleen. He's not fit to . . .'

'Fred Martin, I never thought to hear such words from you.' Eveleen wagged her finger in his face. Whilst she kept her tone amused and almost teasing, there was nevertheless a hint of censure in her voice.

Fred looked ashamed. 'Oh, I know he's fought for his country and all, but—'

'But nothing, Fred.'

'At least let me stay and help you get him upstairs. Smithers is getting on a bit. I doubt he'll manage him.'

'All right.'

'And I might be able to get him to wash an' all,' Fred murmured and Eveleen stifled her laughter, at once seeing right through Fred Martin's ploy.

Half an hour later there was a lot of noise, splashing and swearing, coming from the bathroom.

'Mind me bloody stump. That butcher of a doctor at the field hospital just hacked it off. Could've saved it, I reckon.'

'Well, you'll get it seen to where you're going tomorrow.'

'Where am I going?'

The sound of their voices was lowered and Eveleen only caught brief snatches of the conversation as Fred explained about Fairfield House. Then, once more, Bob Porter's voice was raised in resentment. 'Oh, trust 'er to be playing the Lady Bountiful. 'Er and 'er do-gooding.'

'Let me just tell you summat, mate, afore you go shooting yer mouth off.' Fred defended them. 'They're doing a grand job, 'er and Mr Stokes. They didn't have to bother to set up a home for soldiers and he certainly didn't have to use his own money to do it.'

'Oh aye, money earned off the backs of silly buggers like us who've sweated for him for years.'

She heard another splash and then Fred's voice. 'Well, you can stay there till the water freezes, for all I care, if that's all the gratitude you can show. I wish we'd left you on the streets. I really do.'

There was silence and Eveleen, who had been unable to resist creeping closer to the door to listen, held her breath. There was a low mumble of words, which she could not make out, before Fred said, 'Aye, well, that's better. Come on, let's get you out of there. You've fair soaked me with all your splashing. By, you're an awk'ard bugger, Bob Porter. Still, you allus were.'

Eveleen smiled as she hurried downstairs and by the time she came back up with a cup of hot milk and plate of biscuits, Bob Porter was sitting up in the bed she had made up for him, dressed in an old nightshirt of Richard's. His bald head was pink and shining and his face – and presumably the rest of his body too – was scrubbed clean.

Eveleen set the tray at the side of him and stood looking down at him. 'Is there anything else I can get you, Bob?'

The man shook his head.

'Then I'll say goodnight. Come along, Fred. Thank you for all your help, but I'm sure Bob's tired now.'

As she ushered Fred from the room and was about to close the door, she heard Bob say, 'Missis.'

She pushed the door wider again. 'Yes, Bob?'

'Thanks,' was all he said, but for Eveleen, who knew how much even that one word had cost Bob Porter, it was more than enough.

When Fred arrived the following morning to take Bob to Fairfield House Eveleen said, 'I've decided to come with you. I'm a bit worried they might not have room.

If they don't, I'll have to smile nicely at my mother and Josh again.'

'Oho, you're on a loser there. Josh and Bob Porter never did see eye to eye when they worked together.'

'Things are a little different now,' Eveleen said quietly. 'Josh isn't the sort to harbour grudges, especially when he sees him in this state.'

Fred smiled at her. 'Neither are you, Evie, are you? Here you are, trying to help the man who almost brought your factory to its knees single-handed.'

She sighed. 'Trouble was, Fred, even then I could see his side of the argument, although I couldn't agree with it.'

'Aye well, that's as maybe.' He thought for a moment and then added, 'I must say this for him, he did always seem to have the interests of the workers at heart. I mean, what he did wasn't just for his own ends.'

'No, it wasn't. He resigned on a point of principle, didn't he?'

'Aye, an' look where he's ended up because of it. On the streets, begging for a living.'

'Not any more. He could still do the job of factory manager with only one leg. So, when he's well enough, I intend to offer him his old job back.'

'You do?'

Eveleen nodded but then smiled ruefully. 'But whether he'll take it is another matter.'

They laughed together.

As the motor came to a halt outside the front door of Fairfield House, Bridie came running down the steps.

'Oh, Auntie Evie? Have you brought Mrs Hyde? How did you know? Oh!' The hope on her face died as she saw the man sitting on the back seat. Then her eyes widened as she recognized him.

Eveleen was climbing down. 'I've brought Mr Porter here as a patient. That is, if you've a bed. If not—'

'You'll have to see Matron,' Bridie said promptly and then grasped Eveleen's hands. 'Oh, Auntie Evie, Bertie Hyde's here. You know, Mrs Hyde's son. Does she know he's here? She must come to see him. He's – he's . . .' She swallowed painfully, controlled her excited outburst and added, 'Very, very ill.'

Eveleen at once realized the situation. 'I'll bring her back myself this afternoon, Bridie.'

Bridie hugged her aunt. 'I knew you would. Thank you.'

There was one bed spare in the house. Sadly a patient had died in the night and it had been Bridie's job to strip the bed and put fresh sheets on it. It was not her place to tell her aunt that there might well be a place for Bob Porter, but as soon as the matron had given permission, Bridie helped him up the stairs and into the room he was to share with three others.

'Could I have a word with you, Mrs Stokes?' Dulcie asked.

'I'll wait in the motor, Eveleen,' Fred murmured.

Dulcie smiled at him. 'They're serving elevenses in the recreation room, if you'd like to join the patients. I'm sure they'd love to see a new face.'

'Right you are, Matron.'

As Fred left them, Dulcie drew Eveleen into her office and motioned for her to take a seat.

'Is everything all right? It's not about Bridie, is it?'

Dulcie smiled. 'No, no, she's doing really well. And on the whole all is well here. It's just that we're running awfully short of bandages. It sounds silly, I know, but I hadn't realized we would get so many post-operative cases and patients with such dreadful wounds that won't heal. Do you think Mr Stokes might be able to help, with all his contacts?'

Immediately into Eveleen mind's eye came the picture of the rolls and rolls of three-inch-wide lace stored at the factory, orders that had been cancelled at the beginning of the war.

She smiled. 'I might have the very thing for you.' Swiftly she explained to Dulcie. 'Would it be useful?'

'It'd be wonderful. We've plenty of dressings to go on the wounds themselves, you see. It's just the bandages to hold the dressings in place that we're short of.'

'I'll bring them this afternoon.'

'Oh, there's no need—' Dulcie began and then she saw the look on Eveleen's face and understood. 'Ah, Bridie has told you. You're bringing Mrs Hyde.'

Wordlessly Eveleen nodded.

'Luke, could we make bandages on our curtain-making machines?'

'Bandages?' For a moment, Luke Manning appeared nonplussed, but even as she watched him, Eveleen could see the idea begin to take shape in his mind. 'Bandages,' he murmured again and then added, 'I don't see why not, if we had the right yarn to do it. You'd get the homeworkers to cut the fabric into strips and finish them off, would you?'

Eveleen nodded. 'Or the women in the inspection room. I mean to talk the idea over with Mr Stokes, of course, but I needed to know from you if we could do it first.'

'I'll give it a try myself, Eveleen, and show you.' She felt him watching her, shaking his head.

'What? What's the matter?'

'Nothing, lass. It's just you. You're a little marvel, you are. Always coming up with new ideas, to say nothing of helping Bob Porter – and after all he tried to do to you.'

Solemnly Eveleen said, 'He's hurt, Luke. You could say destroyed. I mean to help him more, if I can.'

'You mean you'd have him back here?'

She nodded. 'I know it would mean you stepping down again, but . . .' She was interrupted by Luke letting out a loud guffaw of laughter.

'Don't you worry about that. I'd be only too glad to hand back the reins to Bob. He's welcome to 'em. I don't reckon too much to being a manager. It's a lot of aggravation, if you ask me.'

'Of course, I don't know if he'd want to come back. He's lost his leg, you know.'

Shocked, Luke stared at her. 'Oh, poor bugger.'

The fact that he forgot himself enough to swear in front of her spoke volumes to Eveleen.

Forty-Three

'You know, I'm so very proud of you, my dear,' Brinsley said, as they sat together in Eveleen's office at the factory. 'Everything you've achieved. Finding new work for the factory and warehouse and even sending workers out to your uncle to keep his little place going. How are things at Flawford, by the way?'

'Fine.' Eveleen smiled. 'I visit as often as I can, which I have to admit isn't as often as I'd like. The women we sent have fitted in very well and my grandmother and my uncle are well cared for now by Mrs Turner, who lives in the village. Bridie arranged all that before she left.'

'Ah yes, Bridie.' Brinsley smiled at the thought of the girl. 'She's a born nurse. You see, my dear, what I mean. Not only did you set up the home for the care of all those soldiers, but you found little Bridie her life's work.'

'That was your idea too. The home, I mean. You made all the financial outlay.'

Brinsley shrugged off her praise. 'It's the very least I could do. Besides, it helps me to feel I'm doing my bit towards the war.' His voice shook a little as he added, 'Helping to keep Richard safe.' He cleared his throat and said more strongly, 'But it was you who made it all happen. He will be so proud of you too, when he comes home.'

Eveleen echoed the words in her mind like a fervent prayer. When he comes home.

At Fairfield House Mrs Hyde sat by her son's bed, holding his hand. She had spoken to Dulcie and had been told the sad truth. Her son had only days, possibly hours, to live. In the bed opposite Field wiped his eyes and could find no words of comfort to say to the mother of his wartime companion.

Bridie's help was more practical. She brought cups of tea, even a meal, but the woman hardly touched anything. The nurses did their best to keep the boy comfortable, but at three o'clock in the morning, with his mother at his side and Bridie wiping his brow, Bertie died. Briefly Mrs Hyde closed her eyes and wept silent tears. Her grief, so dignified and controlled, was more heart-rending than if she had ranted and raved. She kissed her son's forehead and stroked his cheek and then allowed Bridie to lead her up the attic stairs to Bridie's own bed.

'You lie down and rest now,' the girl told her gently but firmly. 'I'm on duty all night, so my bed's not needed.'

Without arguing, Mrs Hyde lay back against the pillows and closed her eyes. 'I shan't sleep. I'll just rest awhile, but I shan't . . .' Her voice faded and already the woman had fallen into an exhausted sleep. Gently Bridie stroked the grey hair back from Mrs Hyde's face and covered her with a blanket.

Downstairs, Bridie went in search of the sister on night duty to tell her of Bertie's death. Only much, much later when she went to her now empty room to sleep during the following day, did Bridie allow herself to shed tears for the poor young boy.

Relentlessly the war continued abroad. At times Richard's letters to Bridie were quite jovial.

> *We decided that everything was too quiet and we ought to liven things up a little by annoying the enemy. The artillery began by strafing his billets, but of course he wasn't going to stand for this and he soon let us know it. Then one of our companies carried out a raid. While this was going on, I was on duty in the support line and the enemy started to strafe the line sending over 5.9s three at a time. We could even see the flash of his guns and he was sending them over about every half minute. It's the waiting for them to arrive that's the worst. It seems ages, though it can only be seconds. Then there's an explosion and you wait again and each explosion seems to get nearer and nearer as he traverses from left to right and back again. It played havoc with the support line, but somehow he missed our little spot.*
>
> *By the way, you'll never guess what we call the sixty-pounders – toffee apples!!*

At home the war had its effect too. More and more women were employed in what were traditionally classed as men's jobs. They were now a familiar sight behind shop counters, working as railway porters, as bus and tram conductresses, postwomen and even policewomen. But most of all they nursed the sick and wounded coming home from the carnage of the Front.

Just before Christmas Richard wrote,

It's raining every day. The trenches are knee-deep in water and caving in, so consequently there is very little shelter and we're wet through all the time. Luckily we can all swim!

From his letters, it seemed as if his life consisted of digging, carrying rations, and spending a few days in the trenches only to return to fatigues once more. Now he gave even Bridie very little news of the shelling and the machine-gun fire. He seemed to concentrate only on the conditions rather than the fighting, the constant noise when under bombardment and the ever-present fear that even the bravest must surely feel.

In late January and early February, he told them,

The cold is dreadful. Eggs and tins of milk are frozen solid and even the tea, brought up in large Thermos-type flasks and hot when poured, has ice on the surface within three or four minutes. Today, as I was cutting up a loaf of bread, each slice sparkled like diamonds . . .

'He never asks about what's going on here, does he?' Eveleen remarked, as once again she and Bridie exchanged their most recent letters, sitting together in the library at Fairfield House to read them. 'I send him long, newsy letters about everything that's happening here. About the factory and – oh, everything. But all he seems to want to talk about is how his feet are.'

'It's understandable,' Bridie murmured. 'We've got patients here with trench foot. It's horrible.'

Towards the end of March, Richard came home again on leave. He had changed again. This time he did not sit, lost in thought. The apathetic look in his eyes had been replaced by a cold and heartless attitude. He visited the factory, striding through the machine shop and then the warehouse, climbing to each floor. He found fault with everything. The girls working in the inspection room were too young. They were idle and their work was not up to standard. The women working in the machine shops were spending too much time chattering and not helping the twisthands properly.

'The place is untidy, too. Get someone to clean it up,' he barked at Eveleen.

'How could you?' she demanded when they returned home. 'You humiliated me in front of the workers. How do you expect me to earn their respect if they hear you talking to me like that?'

Richard, his eyes steely, shrugged his shoulders. 'I only spoke the truth. If you don't keep a tight rein on the running of things, it'll get out of hand. The youngsters will take advantage of leniency. It's human nature. They're not to blame – you are. You should never have antagonized Bob Porter. At least he knew how to run the factory.'

Eveleen bit her lip, unsure how to handle this man, who seemed to have changed from the loving, caring husband she knew into an unfeeling stranger. She went to him, put her hands on his chest and, standing on tiptoe, kissed his mouth.

'I'm sorry. I'll try to do better. Your father's much better these days. Perhaps I can persuade him to come to the factory more often.'

'It shouldn't be necessary. You should be able to handle it. We've given you the authority,' he reminded her harshly. 'You're a director now.'

Later, as they sat together after dinner, she tried to

confide in him about buying Fairfield House. 'Your father agreed. He thought it was an excellent idea.'

'It is,' Richard said. He gave her a tight smile. 'And you got your revenge at last on young Dunsmore, I take it.' There was sarcasm in his tone, something she had never heard from her husband before.

Eveleen felt the colour rising in her face. He had seen straight through her motives, as she had feared he would. 'I feel badly about that now. Especially since he said I was forcing him to enlist.'

'I shouldn't let that worry you,' Richard said with callous nonchalance. 'It was high time he did his bit. He'd have been called up sooner or later anyway.'

His words, which should have brought her some measure of comfort, did not.

Later, in bed, there was no problem of impotency this time, but he took her roughly, selfishly, with no tenderness, leaving Eveleen sleepless far into the night and shedding silent tears into her pillow.

On 6 April, just after Richard had returned to France, the news came that America had entered the war.

'Now we'll show 'em,' Josh beamed. 'Now we've got them on our side, we can't lose. It'll all be over soon now, mi duck.'

But it was not until June that the first American troops stepped onto French soil to be given a heroes' welcome.

At the end of July came Passchendaele and the newspapers were once more full of daily reports of the carnage and loss of life.

And now there were no more letters from Richard.

'I don't think he's there,' Eveleen told Bridie. 'But unless he writes I've no idea where he is. He – he could have been moved,' she whispered. 'He could be there.'

They stared at each other, neither knowing what to say to give comfort to the other.

There was nothing they could say.

Towards the end of August the matron sent for Bridie. Fearing the worst, the girl hurried to her office and only relaxed when she realized the news was not about her uncle.

'We have a new patient arriving tomorrow and I want you to take special care of him. He's a bit of a mystery.' Dulcie looked down at the sheet of paper in front of her. 'He's lost his memory and no-one else seems to know who he is. The authorities have tried to piece together what might have happened. He was picked up off the south coast and at first it was thought he could be a spy. He's been in hospital: under guard, I might add. But now they seem fairly satisfied that he must be a survivor from a British ship that was sunk in the Channel about the time he was found. His uniform – if he'd had one – was ruined by sea water and there was no identification on him.' She smiled up at Bridie. 'But his accent, they say, is pure Lincolnshire. A very difficult one for a foreign spy to impersonate.'

Bridie grinned at the matron. 'Ya right there, missis,' she quipped, deliberately accentuating her own dialect.

'However,' Dulcie went on, 'they're sending him here, hoping that in familiar surroundings his memory might improve. And this is where you come in. They want a careful watch kept on him. They want someone to monitor him closely, to see if he writes letters, sends messages, receives visitors, and so on. At the same time that person must try to draw him out, try – very subtly – to prod his memory. The doctors think that, with rest and care, there is no reason why he shouldn't recover fully.' Dulcie looked up at her. 'I would like you to undertake this, Bridie. You're not only becoming a very good nurse, but you're bright and intelligent. And you'll be able to talk to him – as none of us can – in his own language. Use all the Lincolnshire sayings. You know?'

Bridie's eyes shone and she nodded, unable to speak for excitement. She was thrilled to be trusted with such an undertaking.

'Is he injured in any other way?' she asked.

Dulcie consulted the patient's notes again and shook her head. 'No, no other physical injury apart from the effects of being in the sea for some hours.' She looked up again. 'There is another way of looking at it, of course, and the authorities are fully aware of that too.'

'What's that?'

'That he's swinging the lead to get out of being sent back to the war when he's physically fit again. If that is the case, then it is your duty to catch him out, Bridie. That's the hard part. Can you do it?'

Bridie was silent for a moment, pondering now the full extent of what was expected of her. Slowly she said, 'I didn't agree with the war from the very first. I didn't want Andrew, or Uncle Richard, to volunteer but they did and now I feel as if I'm doing my bit too.' She stared straight into Dulcie's kind and knowledgeable eyes. 'It – it might sound silly, but I feel that if I do everything I can that's asked of me then – then I'm helping to bring them safely home. I've always believed that Andrew is still alive. That – like this sailor – he's lost his memory or – or been taken prisoner.'

Dulcie reached out and touched her in a rare moment of an outward show of emotion. 'My dear girl, I do understand. And, yes, you *could* be right.' She laid great emphasis on the word 'could'. 'And I hope fervently that you are. It does happen. We are going to see that for ourselves. But, my dear,' her tone was soft and gentle, 'it is a rare occurrence.'

'I know.' Bridie nodded. 'But until someone can give me proof that Andrew is dead, I will go on believing – and hoping – that he is alive.'

'And if he isn't? If he really isn't? What then?'

The girl raised her chin defiantly. 'Then I'll cope with it.'

Dulcie patted her hand. 'Good girl,' she said briskly and turned the conversation back to plans for their expected patient. 'We'll put him in that smaller bedroom over the hallway. There's only room for two beds in there and we'll have to pick his roommate very carefully.'

'There's Joe Horton. He's from Grantham.'

The home, though originally for Nottingham soldiers, also took in a few whose homes were in the neighbourhood. Grantham was only a few miles away and Fairfield House was an ideal location for their families to visit. As for the soldiers' families from Nottingham, Brinsley Stokes had organized omnibus outings on Saturdays and Sundays to the home.

'We can't have folks like poor Mrs Hyde not being able to visit their boys,' he said.

Dulcie nodded now in answer to Bridie's suggestion. 'That's a good idea. Ask Joe if he minds being moved. Tell him only that we think he could help this poor man who has lost his memory.'

'We can't tell him everything, can we?'

'No, we can't. There's only you and I who know the full story.'

The mysterious patient arrived the following day. He had been given a new sailor's uniform – his own had been spoilt by sea water. His cap – which might have borne the name of his ship – had been missing, so there had been no clue there.

He was of medium height and thin. He had brown eyes and close-cropped brown hair. A full beard hid the lower part of his face and the visible skin was weather-beaten to a deep tan. And, Bridie suffered a pang at the realization, he was about Andrew's age.

'This is your room,' she announced, flinging open the door and trying hard to put all thoughts of Andrew out of her mind and to concentrate on helping the newcomer. 'And this is Joe. He'll be sharing the room with you.' She turned towards the man already sitting in a chair by the window. 'Joe, this is . . .' She turned back, as if innocently, to say, 'I'm sorry, I don't know your name.'

'Neither do I, lass,' the man said, sitting on the edge of the single bed and bouncing on it a little as if to test its comfort. Then he tapped the side of his head with his forefinger. 'Can't remember owt.'

'So,' Bridie asked, 'what would you like us to call you?'

The man shrugged and said morosely, 'Dunno. Some bright spark christened me "Nelson" at the last hospital. Clever devil.'

Bridie could see from his expression that the nickname hadn't pleased him.

'Well, how about you think of a name and that's what we'll call you here,' she suggested.

'Surname an' all?'

Bridie spread her hands. 'Whatever you like. Doesn't matter. Just one name will do. Just so we have something to call you.'

'Bloody nuisance, more than likely.'

'Oi.' Joe spoke up from his chair by the window for the first time. 'None o' that sort o' language in 'ere, mate. Not in front of this lass any road, else you an' me is going to fall out afore we've even got to know each other.'

The newcomer seemed to take no notice of Joe. He was staring at Bridie now, his glance taking in her young, lithe body, then coming back to rest on her face. He frowned slightly. 'What's your name?'

'Bridie. Bridie Singleton.'

The frown deepened and he repeated her name. Then he shrugged. 'No, it dun't mean owt to me. Pity. I thought for a minute you looked familiar.'

He closed his eyes and lay back, swinging his feet up to stretch out full length on the bed. Bridie stood a moment, watching him. His breathing became regular and she could see that he had immediately fallen asleep. She turned, smiled at Joe and put her fingers to her lips. 'He's had a long journey,' she whispered. 'Let him rest.'

Joe nodded and turned back to looking out of the window.

The newcomer did not mix easily with the rest of the patients, not even with Joe, his room mate. It was not that he was unfriendly or snobbish, merely that he had little to talk about. No memories of his previous life, of his family, of his home, not even of his recent experiences.

'Maybe that's a blessing in disguise,' Dulcie remarked in one of their private conversations when Bridie reported on the progress of her special patient – or rather the lack of it, 'if he's lost all his shipmates. Does he talk at all?'

'He asks a lot of questions, but the others just get sick of answering him all the time. They don't want to be reminded of what happened to them at the Front. And they don't want to talk too much about their families. It just reminds them that they're still separated from them, even those that have regular visitors.'

'Is he asking anything that the authorities might regard as suspicious?'

'I'm not sure I know what that is,' Bridie admitted.

'Well, if he wants details of what regiment, battalion, company the men belonged to. If he wants detailed information of where they were on the front line. The name of their commanding officer. That sort of detail.'

Bridie shook her head. 'I don't think so. Yes, he asks how they got wounded and I suppose he might ask where it happened, but as far as I can tell he doesn't do anything with the information.' She ticked off the points on her fingers. 'He doesn't have any visitors. He doesn't write letters or receive any. How can he? He doesn't know who he is. Or at least he's not supposed to know.'

'Have you any doubts about his loss of memory.'

Bridie frowned. 'I've never known anyone before who'd lost their memory, so it's difficult.'

'Well, I have to admit that, in all my nursing life, neither have I,' Dulcie was quick to say too.

'But if he is having us on,' Bridie said slowly, 'then all I can say is he's a very good actor.'

Forty-Four

'I've had enough of him,' Joe Horton said after only two weeks of sharing a room with Walter, as the mysterious patient had decided he wanted to be called. 'He dun't give a damn about owt. He's forever flirting with the nurses.' He cast a shrewd glance at Bridie. 'Dun't you be teken in by him, lass, will ya?'

Bridie laughed as she plumped Joe's pillows. 'I won't.'

'There's a few here,' the man said gently, 'who'd like you to be their girl. And there's one or two ya'd be safe wi', but not him.'

'I'm quite safe. I'm waiting for someone to come back, you see.'

Joe glanced at her but said nothing. He'd heard the rumour that this poor lass's feller had been posted missing but that she refused to believe it.

'Anyway,' Joe went on, 'this Walter, or whatever his name is, he's a devil with the girls, if you ask me.'

'Now how would you know that, Corporal Horton?' Bridie asked him archly. 'And you a married man.'

Joe chuckled. 'I've 'ad me moments in me time, lass, I've 'ad me moments. Afore I met the wife, that is,' he added comically. 'I'd sooner be back in the trenches than face my Milly if she found out I'd been flirting with you nurses.'

'What do you make of him then?' She couldn't tell

Joe her real reason for asking, but perhaps, unwittingly, he could help her in the task she had been given. 'Do you think he still remembers nothing?'

Joe shrugged. 'Far as I can tell, though there was something the other day.'

'What?'

'Well, we went for a walk. Him not being hurt – physically, that is – and me with only me shoulder.'

Only his shoulder! Bridie thought. Poor Joe's shoulder had been badly wounded. There was still a piece of shrapnel embedded somewhere in it, yet here he was making light of his injury.

'And?' Bridie prompted.

Joe's forehead furrowed. 'It was funny. He seemed to know his way about the place. "We'll go up the hill to the village," he said. Now how did he know there was a village up the hill?'

'You can see the church at the top. Perhaps he just realized that where there's a church there must be a village.'

'Aye, I suppose so. But then, coming back, he brought me back through the fields, through the covert and down to the beck. He seemed to know his way about, if you know what I mean. Mind you, then he stood near the water gazing down at it for so long I got a bit worried.'

'Why?'

'I thought – well, I thought he might be thinking of doing summat. You know?'

For a moment Bridie stared at him, then understanding dawned. 'You – you don't mean you thought he might try to – to drown himself?'

'It crossed me mind, lass. I've heard of some of the lads who've come back from the war, maimed for life, haven't been able to face up to the future. Sad, ain't it, to think they survived the trenches and then are driven to doing that?'

Bridie nodded. 'But you don't think Walter's like that, do you?'

'No,' Joe said firmly now. 'Know why lass?' When Bridie shook her head, he said drily, 'Cos he thinks too much of hissen, that's why.'

In the September of 1917 Bridie was sixteen. She thought that the most that might be done to celebrate her birthday would be tea at Pear Tree Farm or perhaps a day in Nottingham with her aunt – if Eveleen could spare the time. So she was disappointed that by the time she awoke on the morning of the birthday, no invitation from anyone had been forthcoming.

There were no cards or letters in the morning post for her either, but she plastered a cheery smile on her face and went about her work, trying to forget what day it was.

At three-thirty in the afternoon she was surprised to see all the patients disappearing into the sitting room that had been turned into the patients' recreation room. Those who could walk were helping those who could not.

'What's going on?' Bridie asked Nurse Collier.

'Oh, I don't know,' the nurse said vaguely. 'I expect they're having a meeting or something. Look, could you do me a huge favour? There's some sheets need mangling in the wash-house in the yard. The girl who comes from the village didn't show up this morning. Be an angel and do them for us.'

Bridie sighed inwardly, but replied, 'Of course. Do you want them hanging out on the line?'

'Er – well, yes, whatever you like. It's a bit late in the day, but they might dry.'

'I'll ask Jack to put the line up.' Jack Morton, Micky's younger brother, now worked at Fairfield House.

'I don't think he's here,' came the swift reply. 'Just mangle them for now, Bridie. We'll hang 'em out in the morning.'

Bridie shrugged and went down the stone passages towards the back door. As she passed the kitchen, the door slammed shut and beyond it she heard the two young kitchenmaids giggling.

She was tempted to open it and poke her head round to see what they were doing, but then she heard the cook's sharp voice. 'Behave, you two. She'll hear you.'

Bridie smiled. Matron's authority even extended into the cook's domain.

She had finished mangling the sheets and, with little else that needed her immediate attention, she slipped out of the gate from the yard leading into the field and walked down the slope towards the beck, rippling and gurgling in the warm September sunshine. She sat down on a boulder at the edge of the water and slipped off her boots and stockings. Pulling her skirts up to her knees, she dangled her feet in the rushing water. It was cold, but the feel of it soothed her aching feet. She had been rushing around since early morning without a moment to herself. It was such a lovely, peaceful place, she thought, her gaze drifting over the fields. She should bring Walter to this spot. Perhaps its tranquillity would help him. Then she remembered what Joe had told her.

Perhaps it would be safer to keep poor Walter away. It was a strange coincidence, she thought, that the name the man had chosen to be called was the same as Bridie's grandfather, who had died here in the beck. She didn't want to risk something similar happening to him.

She sighed. Here, in the stillness, there was nothing now to keep her mind off what day it was.

Tears filled her eyes. Every year until he had volunteered Andrew had visited her on the Saturday nearest to her birthday. He had taken her on a trip into Grantham, treating her to cream cakes in a fancy restaurant, before taking her to the photographic studio to have her birthday picture taken. True to her promise to him, on her half-day off the previous week, Bridie had gone into Grantham to have her photograph taken. It lay now in the chest of drawers in her bedroom, along with the other two taken in the years since he had gone away. It was almost three years since she had last seen Andrew. Three years in which she had grown up and three photographs that he hadn't even seen.

The view before her blurred as she remembered what he had done with all the earlier photographs. When she could, Bridie promised herself, she would take the new ones to Flawford and stand them on the mantelpiece in Andrew's cottage for him to find when he came home from the war. At the thought, her heart overflowed with love for him. She lifted her face to the sky and closed her eyes, praying as fervently as if she were kneeling in her uncle's chapel.

'Bring him home safely. Oh, please let him be alive.'

'So, this is where you're hiding.'

The voice behind her startled her so that she gave a little cry and turned to see Micky Morton grinning down at her.

'What are you doing here? Shouldn't you be at work?'

He squatted on his haunches beside her. 'I got the afternoon off, seeing as what day it is.'

She gaped at him. 'What day it is?' she repeated stupidly.

'Yeah. Don't tell me you've forgotten your own birthday?'

She glanced away and looked down, tearing at the grass growing out of the cracks in the rock where she was sitting. 'No, I hadn't. But I thought everyone else had.' She smiled up at him. 'But at least you remembered. Thanks, Micky.'

He stood up and held out his hand. 'Come on, then.'

'Why?'

'You'll see.'

She shrugged, but did as he asked. Pulling on her stockings and her boots, she gave him her hand and he hauled her to her feet.

'Race you back,' he said and began to run.

'Hey, that's not fair. You can run faster than me anyway . . .'

Panting, they arrived back in the yard. He turned to look at her. 'The matron wants to see you. You'd better go and tidy your hair.' His glance took in the dishevelled uniform that she had worn since early morning. 'And put your Sunday best dress on.'

'Whatever for?' she asked again.

'Don't argue. Just do it.' He gave her a gentle push. 'Go on. Just for me.'

Muttering to herself, she went up the backstairs to the tiny bedroom she shared with one of the other younger nurses. As she splashed her face in the bowl on the washstand and smoothed back her hair – she hadn't time to replait it – she wondered why Micky wanted her to put on her Sunday frock. Then a thought suddenly occurred to her. Perhaps word had come from Pear Tree Farm. Perhaps she was going out to tea after all.

But as she went down to the hall, Micky was waiting for her and he led her towards the patients' sitting room. He flung open the door and the singing that erupted caused Bridie's mouth to drop open.

'Happy birthday to you, Happy birthday to you . . .' the whole gathering trilled.

All the patients, all the staff and her gran and Josh were there. And standing in front of them all with her arms stretched wide and a broad smile on her face, was her aunt Eveleen.

'Happy birthday, darling. Come and open all your cards and presents and then we'll have tea. The kitchen staff have been so busy. Cook has even made you a cake.' She laughed. 'But they had such a job to keep it secret.'

Cook, large and round and rosy-cheeked, waddled forward. 'She's all over the place, this one. You never know where she's going to pop up next. We had a fright earlier when she went past the kitchen. I was putting the finishing touches to the cake. The girls only just managed to shut the door in time. And then I thought she'd hear them giggling.'

Bridie laughed. 'Oh, so that was what it was all about.' It had not been the matron they had been afraid of catching them. It had been her.

A veritable feast was laid out on a table set at the side of the room. A buffet so that everyone could help themselves. In the centre stood a huge iced cake decorated with pink sugar roses and the words 'Happy 16th Birthday, Bridie' inscribed upon it.

Tears came to Bridie's eyes and she clasped her hands. 'Oh, Cook, it's beautiful.'

The cook beamed happily as everyone murmured their agreement with Bridie's praise. Then Bridie opened her cards and presents, and there seemed to be something from everyone. Little gifts, some handmade, from every member of the staff. But what touched her most were the presents from the patients. There was even a lace-edged handkerchief from Walter.

'You must come and meet him, Auntie Evie,' she whispered, explaining swiftly that they still didn't know who the man was.

She led Eveleen across the room to where Walter was sitting in front of the window, gazing out down the garden. 'He doesn't mix a lot with the other patients. I think it's because he can't hold a proper conversation with anyone. You know, he can't talk about his family, where he comes from and that, like everyone else does. Isn't it sad? He seems so lonely.'

They fell silent as they reached him and Bridie touched him on the shoulder. 'Walter? Thank you so much for the lovely handkerchief.'

He turned, his brown eyes smiling up at her. 'S'all right,' he said in his usual offhand manner. 'One of the nurses said I had to give you something. She bought it.'

'Oh.' Her disappointment was acute. She wondered how many other patients had been coerced into giving her presents. Eveleen moved and put her arm about her shoulders. She must have realized what the girl was feeling because she whispered in her ear. 'He's the only one they had to do that for. Matron told me. He couldn't seem to take in what was happening.'

Bridie nodded, but the lump in her throat refused to go away.

They stood in front of the man looking down at him. He looked up again, glancing from one to the other and then his gaze came to rest on Eveleen. She stared back at him and her heart seemed to miss a beat.

Dark brown eyes, so like her own, stared back at her. The rich, chestnut hair, cut very short, was now flecked with tiny strands of white. His beard hid his wide, generous mouth, yet she would have known him anywhere. Her eyes widened and her hand fluttered to her mouth as a startled gasp escaped her lips. She knew Bridie was glancing from one to the other, looking puzzled.

Deep in the man's eyes, the vacant look began to dispel. Memory forced its way into his damaged mind and fought for recognition.

His lips moved and, as he stretched out his hand towards her, they heard his tortured whisper. 'Evie?'

Forty-Five

Behind them the room had fallen strangely silent as everyone became aware of the unfolding drama.

'Jimmy, oh, Jimmy!' Eveleen cried.

Bridie glanced up and saw Mary weaving her way around the furniture towards them. Realization came swiftly to her. This was Mary's long-lost son. This was Jimmy Hardcastle. And this, then, was her father. Deep inside her she felt a trembling, yet, as she saw the look on Mary's face, Bridie pushed aside her own feelings and moved at once to meet her grandmother, suddenly afraid of what the shock might do to the older woman. 'Gran, wait a minute.'

'Leave me be, girl,' Mary snapped, pushing her away. 'I want to know what's going on.'

Bridie watched as Mary stood before the man whom everyone present knew only as Walter. Then she too cried out, 'Jimmy. Oh, my boy. My baby! Oh, Jimmy.' She fell to her knees beside his chair, clasping his hand and kissing it fervently, tears coursing down her cheek. A look of distaste came into the man's eyes and he tried to pull himself free.

'Gerroff.'

Then Evie began to laugh and cry, almost with a tinge of hysteria. 'Oh, it is you, Jimmy Hardcastle. Now I know it really is.'

Helplessly Bridie looked round for the matron. She

felt suddenly very much out of her depth, worried for her aunt, her grandmother, but most of all for the patient.

Dulcie was hurrying towards them. 'Now, now,' came her soothing voice. 'What's happened?'

'My – my aunt,' Bridie stammered, 'seems to know him.' Could it really be true? she was thinking now.

Eveleen turned, wiping the tears from her eyes, but her voice was steadier now as she said, 'Oh, I know him all right. It's the prodigal son. This is my brother and, Bridie, your father.'

The room erupted then into noise, the news spreading like a stubble fire out of control, whilst Bridie stared down at the man she had longed to meet the whole of her young life. And yet at this very moment, if the good Lord had given her the choice, she would far rather it had been Andrew Burns who had come back into her life than this stranger. He was looking her up and down, appraising her. But there was no warmth in the look, no fatherly interest. She felt suddenly nauseous and took a step back, sick at heart. She felt Josh's comforting arm around her shoulders.

'It's all right, mi duck. Bit of a shock for you an' all. But it'll be all right.'

Bridie, not trusting herself to speak, nodded, yet she could not drag her gaze away from Walter. Jimmy, as she and everyone else must now think of him. Dad or Father, she supposed that was what she should call him, but that would take some getting used to after a lifetime of absence.

Mary was still fussing over him, stroking his hair, kissing his hand and repeating over and over again, 'Oh, Jimmy, my Jimmy.'

Eveleen and Bridie were forgotten, even Josh. Mary

had her son home again and for the moment no-one else in the world existed.

Standing up at last, Mary said, 'He's coming home with me. Back to Pear Tree Farm. I'll look after him now. There's nothing like a mother's love.'

'I'm afraid that won't be possible, Mrs Carpenter,' Dulcie said at once, still hovering nearby. 'Walter . . .' she glanced at the patient. 'I'm sorry, Jimmy, is still under our authority. I cannot possibly release him into your care without the express permission of . . .'

'Nonsense,' Mary said briskly. 'He's coming home with me.'

'No, Mam. Matron is right. He has to stay here . . .' As Mary opened her mouth to protest, Eveleen added swiftly, 'At least until we see what the doctor thinks.'

Now Josh moved to his wife's side and took her arm. 'Mary, love, we'll get a room ready for him at home. I'm sure they'll let him come home very soon, but we must do it properly.'

'This had nothing to do with you, Josh Carpenter,' Mary snapped, shaking off his touch. 'He's not your son.'

She could not have hurt the big, kindly man more if she had struck him across the face.

'Mam!' 'Gran!' Shocked, Eveleen and Bridie spoke out together.

Mutinously Mary glared at them. 'Well, he isn't. He hasn't any children of his own.'

'Not now,' Josh said quietly, his eyes full of ill-concealed pain. 'I had a son once though, didn't I?'

Mary had the grace to look ashamed as she muttered, 'I forgot.'

Years before, Eveleen remembered, Josh had told her he had been married briefly as a young man, but his wife had died in childbirth and their child along with her. She glanced at her own mother in disgust, yet Mary's behaviour was no surprise – at least not to Eveleen. Jimmy had always been their mother's favourite and the years between had made no difference, it seemed.

'And besides . . .' Josh was smiling again now, brushing aside Mary's tactless remark with his usual forgiving nature, 'Bridie has been like my own.' Now he turned to Mary again and, despite his gentleness towards her, there was a note of firmness in his tone. 'Of course, Jimmy must come home to us but only when proper approval has been given.'

'But—' Mary opened her mouth to protest, but Josh had his answer ready. 'We don't want to get Jimmy in trouble with the authorities, now do we, love? They can be very severe if they think there's even a hint of desertion.'

'Desertion? How could they possibly think that? He's sick. Injured. He couldn't remember who he was, not until he saw Evie.'

'He's physically quite fit again now, Mrs Carpenter,' Dulcie put in. 'It was only because of his amnesia that he could not be sent back on active service.' She looked down at Jimmy. 'But if his memory is returning . . .' She left the rest of the sentence unspoken, but her meaning was clear to them all.

Eveleen watched her brother as he pulled his hand away from his mother's clinging grasp. 'I'm staying here. I don't know you,' he said. 'I know Evie. She's me sister. But I don't know anyone else.' He looked up at Dulcie a hangdog expression in his eyes. 'Honest, Matron. I can't remember her . . .' He jabbed a finger at Mary then towards Josh. 'Or him.' Then he glared accusingly at Bridie. 'And I certainly don't remember having a daughter.'

'How could you?' Eveleen said, deliberately making no effort to keep her voice low. No-one had left the room; they were all far too interested in the revelations about the unknown sailor. And now it seemed family quarrels from years ago were surfacing. This was real life drama, far better than the pictures. 'Seeing as you ran away to sea before she was even born,' Eveleen went on, with more than a hint of sarcasm in her tone. 'And since then you've made no effort to find out how Rebecca was or whether you had a son or a daughter.'

Jimmy shook his head. 'Rebecca? I dun't remember no Rebecca.'

'You remember me, lad, don't you? Mr Carpenter from the Reckitt and Stokes factory in Nottingham?'

Jimmy shrugged. 'I've never been to Nottingham.'

Eveleen watched him, her eyebrow arched in disbelief. Then suddenly she leant close to her brother so that only those standing nearby heard her words.

'You might be able to fool everyone at the home here. Even your own daughter. But I know you too well, Jimmy. You're going to have to be very careful you don't get caught out. Very careful indeed.'

Forty-Six

'How could you be so cruel, Eveleen? But, then, I should have known. You and Jimmy never got on, did you?'

Having driven Josh and Mary down the lane back to Pear Tree Farm, Eveleen was obliged to listen to her mother's tirade. They had almost had to drag Mary away from Jimmy.

'I'll make you a cup of tea, mi duck, before you go back,' Josh said to Eveleen and disappeared into the scullery, whilst mother and daughter faced each other across the hearth. Eveleen sighed inwardly, but decided that honesty was the best policy.

'Mam, I've always loved my brother, but he was never the easiest person to deal with. You spoilt him.'

'Well, your dad spoilt you,' Mary countered. 'Jimmy couldn't do anything right for him and you couldn't do anything wrong.'

Eveleen felt the familiar stab of loss as she thought of her kindly, easy-going father.

'If you hadn't been deceiving us in meeting Stephen Dunsmore, your father might still be with us. And all our troubles that followed his death can be laid at your door, Eveleen.'

The old feelings of guilt she thought long buried came flooding back. Whilst she would never quite forgive herself, it came as a shock that her mother still harboured bitterness against her. She had thought, when her mother had found new happiness with Josh, that Mary had forgiven her. Now, it seemed, she had not.

'Mind you . . .' Mary glanced at her. 'You've got your revenge on Master Dunsmore now, haven't you? Good and proper.'

Eveleen swallowed. 'I only bought his house—'

'Oh, you did more than that,' Mary rounded on her. 'You disgraced him in his parents' eyes. He couldn't face them, so he went to enlist. And now he's dead.'

Eveleen felt as if her heart stopped and then began to thud loudly and painfully. Her voice was a strangled whisper. 'What?'

'Oh, aye. Word came last week.'

Eveleen closed her eyes. More guilt was being heaped upon her head. And this was a burden she would carry for ever.

But now Mary was dragging her back to think of Jimmy. 'We had to go to Flawford when your precious Stephen Dunsmore turned us out of our home, didn't we? We had nowhere else to go.'

That Eveleen could not deny. She sighed and sank into a chair beside the table. Heavily she said, 'So it's my fault that Jimmy got Rebecca pregnant and then refused to marry her?'

'They'd never even have met if it hadn't been for you.'

'But they did and he seduced a young and innocent girl. That was hardly my doing. And he had no need to run away. I couldn't have *made* him marry her.'

'Huh! You always got your own way, Eveleen.' Her mother glared at her and Eveleen realized Mary was now referring to the day's events. 'You still do. Jimmy should be at home here. With me.'

Eveleen was thoughtful and then she played her

trump card. 'He's safer there, Mam. If he leaves the home, the authorities will come looking for him. They wouldn't believe his amnesia story. He'd be back aboard ship in a trice.'

Josh, carrying a tea tray into the room, caught Eveleen's remarks.

'She's right, mi duck. He's best where he is.' He glanced at Eveleen and murmured in a low voice so that only she could hear, 'For several reasons.'

Eveleen understood. The last thing Josh would want would be Jimmy living at Pear Tree Farm.

Mary began to weep, sobbing into her handkerchief. 'You're all against me. I want my Jimmy home. Nobody knows how I've missed him all these years. You don't want me to be happy.'

Josh hurried to her side and put his arms around her. 'Mary, love, that's not true and you know it. But Eveleen's right, Jimmy is safer there. And you can visit him every day.'

Mary looked up, her tears drying. 'Can I?'

'Of course you can. Every afternoon between two and three. I asked the matron.'

'An hour? Is that all? One hour a day? Well, she can forget that. I'll go whenever I want to and stay as long as I want. So there.'

Eveleen and Josh glanced helplessly at each other, but said no more.

'What do you think you're staring at?' Jimmy challenged Bridie as she stood in front of him.

'You,' she said simply. 'I've dreamed about meeting my father all my life. Imagined how it would be . . .'

There was a catch in her voice, for her dream had been nothing like the disappointing reality. 'And now I have.'

'Huh! You don't want to believe everything Evie tells you.'

Bridie regarded him, her head on one side. 'How is it you can remember your sister, but not your mother?'

His eyes were suddenly wary. 'Dunno. I suppose me memory's coming back a bit patchy.'

'Do you remember my mother, Rebecca?'

Jimmy glanced away and shook his head, then he laughed. 'But I've had so many girls from here to Timbuktu. Mebbe I've got bastards all round the world.'

Bridie bit her lip, but raised her head defiantly. 'Well, I expect you'll soon be getting to know your mother all over again.'

He eyed her suspiciously. 'What do you mean?'

Bridie grinned. 'If I know my gran, she'll be here every minute of the day visiting you.'

He frowned and stared out of the window. 'Reckon I'd be better off back at sea,' he murmured.

He was not the sort of father Bridie had longed for. However, as the days passed she could began to understand how a young, impressionable girl, starved of affection as she now guessed her mother had been in the strict regime of Harry Singleton's home, could have succumbed to Jimmy Hardcastle's saucy charm. He still flirted with the younger nurses, though now never with her. He avoided his mother's daily visits as often as he could, pleading headaches, sickness – anything to evade her. All the staff had been briefed by the matron that Mary was not allowed to go upstairs to his room.

'We have to afford our patients the right of privacy. If there is someone they don't wish to see, then we must respect that. Whilst I have every sympathy with Mrs Carpenter,' Dulcie went on, speaking now in confidence to her trusted staff, 'I have to admit that she is visiting a little too often. One can also see his side.'

When just the two of them remained in the office, Bridie asked Dulcie, 'Do you believe that he really has lost his memory?'

Dulcie considered before answering. 'I think he did, initially, yes. But how much it's coming back now, I don't think he's telling us. I think he's playing a very clever game.' Then she smiled. 'I'm glad I don't have to be responsible for deciding whether he's fit to return to active service. That's Dr Roper's job, thank goodness.'

'Supposing you were, would you say he was fit?'

'Not yet, no. But I do think he's recovering much quicker than he's letting us know. But there's one thing, Bridie. At least we can be pretty sure now that he's not a spy.'

They laughed together, but then the merriment left the girl's face as sadness clouded her eyes. 'No, I'm sure he isn't. But he's not quite what I dreamed my father would be, either.'

Forty-Seven

The weeks passed towards another Christmas and still there was no word from Richard. Eveleen veered between crippling fear that he was dead and determined optimism that, because she had heard nothing from the War Office, he must be still alive.

'It'll just be that his letters aren't getting through.' Bridie tried to comfort her aunt. 'You'll see. There'll be some simple explanation.'

Their news of the war now came only from newspaper reports. In October the Italian army had suffered a crushing defeat, the enemy gaining many miles of ground. The Allies feared that Russia, with its own terrible internal problems, would pull out of the war when talks began in December between the Bolshevik government and Germany. By March 1918 an uneasy peace existed between the two and, as the Allies had predicted, a great number of the enemy troops that had been deployed in the east were now released to join the war on the Western Front. By the end of that month these reinforcements had helped to deliver a catastrophic blow to the Allied lines in France.

'It must be chaos out there,' Bridie said, scanning the newspaper that Eveleen had brought on her weekly visit to Fairfield House. 'No wonder letters aren't getting through. Let's just hope that he's getting ours.'

They both still wrote each week, but had no way of

knowing whether their letters ever reached their destination.

'How's Jimmy?' Eveleen asked, bravely trying to change the subject.

Bridie pulled a comical expression. 'Much the same. He's not giving much away.' She shrugged. 'I can't guess what he remembers and what he doesn't. You're still the only person he'll admit to recognizing.'

'Not Mam?'

Bridie shook her head. 'Much to Gran's disappointment.'

'What about him going home? To Pear Tree Farm?'

'The doctor thought that it might be a good idea. He thinks that the familiar surroundings might help his memory, but my father flatly refused to go. Gran's tried everything. Wheedling, crying – everything, but the more she pleads, the more he resists.'

Normally what Bridie was telling her would have made Eveleen chuckle, but laughter was difficult when her heart was so heavy with dread. But she tried to hide her fears and summoned a weak smile. 'Poor Mam,' she murmured.

In April Sir Douglas Haig, the British Commander-in-Chief, sent a personal message to the army: *'Every position must be held to the last man: there must be no retirement. With our backs to the wall and believing in the justice of our cause each one of us must fight on to the end.'*

Reading this, Eveleen gave way to tears. It was her darkest time, for now all hope seemed lost for both the war and her beloved husband. Her feeling of hopelessness was reflected by everyone around her. The veterans at Fairfield House were sombre, their cheerful banter silenced. Some of the nurses with relatives at the Front were red-eyed and even Josh shook his head in sadness at the futility of almost four years of carnage, which now threatened to end in defeat. In the city more and more wounded flooded into the hospitals and Brinsley was once more grey-faced and anxious.

Only Bridie, the youngest amongst them, held onto her faith. 'They'll come home. Both of them,' she said, confidently. 'You'll see.'

'Oh, Bridie,' Eveleen mourned, 'if only I could believe you.'

It wasn't until July that news came that the tide of war had begun to turn in favour of the Allies. Suddenly there was cause for renewed hope.

Then came the day when Eveleen received news. She drove recklessly to Fairfield House and ran up the steps. 'Bridie, Bridie, where are you? He's coming home. He's safe. Richard's coming home.'

He had been wounded in the leg and the injury was too severe for him to recover in a field hospital. It was a 'Blighty' wound.

Bridie hugged Eveleen, tears streaming down both their faces. 'Oh, Auntie Evie. He's safe. With a bit of luck, he'll never have to go back. When will he be home?'

Eveleen wiped her eyes, laughing and crying at the same time. 'Next week.'

They both met the train that brought him to Nottingham station and watched as he was carried off on a stretcher, along with other wounded, and put straight into an ambulance. Eveleen and Bridie were not even allowed near enough to him to say 'Hello'.

Bridie grasped the arm of one of the attendants. 'Where are you taking him?'

'The hospital. He's still in the army, you know. He

can't just come home when he decides. Besides . . .' The man glanced over his shoulder towards where Richard lay, silently staring up at nothing in particular. He had not even raised his head to look around for them, though surely he must have known they would come to meet him, Bridie thought.

The attendant was speaking again. 'Poor feller's shell-shocked, I reckon, as well as his injury.'

'Shell-shocked?' Eveleen frowned. 'What do you mean?'

'Putting it bluntly, ma'am, he's not sure whether he's on this earth or the next. I've got to go now, but go to the hospital later. They'll tell you more.'

'Can't he come to Fairfield House?' Bridie asked. 'We're as good as a hospital.'

'Dunno about that, miss. We've got our orders.'

The man turned away, leaving a mesmerized Eveleen staring after him with Bridie standing beside her. Young though she was, she knew better than Eveleen what being shell-shocked really meant. She had seen so many cases of it already at Fairfield House.

Much later they were allowed to see him. They sat on either side of the bed, speaking to him but getting no response. Eveleen kissed his forehead, but he did not look at her, did not even seem to notice.

'Be careful what you say in front of him,' Bridie had warned her earlier. 'Matron at the home says we can't be sure they don't understand everything that's going on around them even though they can't, or don't want to, take part.'

Eveleen had nodded, biting her lip to hold back the tears. 'What are we going to do?'

Bridie considered. 'If they'll let us, I think he should go home or at least to Fairfield House.'

'Oh no, if he's going anywhere, then it's home with me.'

'Will you be able to manage?' Bridie asked her candidly.

'Of course,' Eveleen almost snapped and stood up. Now she kissed her husband's forehead tenderly and turned away.

Bridie too kissed his cheek and whispered, 'You'll soon be well again, Uncle Richard. You're home now. You're safe.'

His eyes flickered and he turned his head to look at her, a ghost of a smile on his mouth, but he did not speak.

Watching, Eveleen was surprised at the shaft of jealousy that seared through her. Richard had responded to Bridie, but not to her, his own wife.

Two weeks later Richard was brought home. Eveleen had everything ready and had even engaged a girl to sit with him during the day whilst she had to be at the factory. Brinsley visited his son daily, though Richard's mother's visits were spasmodic.

'I can't bear to see him like that.' Sophia shuddered. 'When will he be better?'

'We don't know,' Eveleen said and added harshly, 'but his family can all help by being with him and talking to him.'

It was a deliberate reproach to her mother-in-law and Eveleen could see that Sophia recognized it as such, but still she was not prepared to let her sick son interfere with her comfortable existence. She stood up. 'Keep me informed,' she said curtly and swept out.

Brinsley, however, was very different. He could not do enough to help his son. 'Do you think this is the right place for him, Eveleen? I mean, he doesn't seem to be making much progress. He just lies there all day, staring at the ceiling. I haven't heard him speak yet. Have you?'

Eveleen shook her head. They were sitting together in the dining room over a dinner that neither of them felt like eating.

Brinsley reached out and covered her hand with his own. 'My dear, do you think he should go into a nursing home where he could be cared for properly?'

Eveleen's voice was high-pitched. 'You think I'm not spending enough time with him. That I'm concentrating too much on work and not on him.' She felt guilty enough about the fact already, but to have her father-in-law point it out hurt indescribably.

'No, no, my dear girl, I'm not criticizing you. You've done a wonderful job at the factory. But for you the whole business might have gone under. You've kept it going, kept people in jobs. Even kept jobs open for the men to come back to, but—'

'But I'm still neglecting my husband now,' Eveleen finished, her voice flat. She gripped his hand and whispered hoarsely, 'You don't need to tell me. I know.'

'I didn't say that,' Brinsley insisted gently. 'To be honest . . .' He paused, as if knowing what he was going to say would hurt her even more. 'I think he needs expert help that neither you nor I can give him. With the best will in the world we're not medically trained, my dear.'

'No.' Eveleen was forced to agree. Her thoughts turned to Bridie. The girl was not yet a fully fledged nurse, but even she had known how to reach Richard far better than Eveleen had. Eveleen knew it was the sensible thing to do, the right thing to do, but she had always been in charge of her family. It had been Eveleen who had taken the reins after the death of her father, she who had moved the family to Flawford and then later to Nottingham, with the extra burden of an unmarried mother-to-be and coming baby too. Whether everything she had done had been right, she could not say. All she knew now was that she was not ready to relinquish control yet.

'A little longer,' she pleaded with Brinsley. 'Let's try a little longer.'

A week later Bridie came to Nottingham to visit.

'You go to work,' she urged her aunt. 'And you can give the girl a day off. I'll look after him.'

Eveleen eyed her doubtfully. It was not that she questioned Bridie's capability. Far from it. She was being unreasonable, she knew, but she could not help feeling jealous that her niece was far more knowledgeable and efficient at dealing with Richard than she was. She tried, weakly, to protest. 'But it's your day off from nursing. Don't you want to go into the city? See the shops?'

Bridie shook her head. 'I'd sooner stay here with Uncle Richard.'

Eveleen sighed inwardly, knowing herself defeated. 'I'll see you this evening, then. I'll drive you back.'

'No need.' Bridie smiled. 'I've got tomorrow off too. I can stay overnight.' Her smiled broadened. 'If you'll have me.'

Eveleen felt a sudden rush of affection for the girl and guilty for her irrational jealousy. She hugged her. 'Of course. It'll be lovely to have you here.'

When Eveleen returned home that evening, Bridie had wrought a miracle. Richard was out of bed, fully dressed and sitting near the window overlooking the street.

'Go and sit with him, Auntie Eveleen. I must change for dinner,' Bridie urged. 'Just talk to him. Tell him about your day.'

Eveleen felt strangely tense as she sat beside him. This was her beloved husband, the man she had lived with, had been so close to and yet he was a stranger to her now. As Bridie had suggested, Eveleen began to talk to him, haltingly at first, but then the words began to spill out and she was chattering maybe too much in her nervousness. Suddenly she stopped mid-sentence. He wasn't listening. He was staring out of the window, yet he didn't seem to be seeing the street below and the people. As she fell silent, he turned his head slowly to look at her.

His mouth worked as if he wanted to speak, but had forgotten how. 'Where's – ' he mumbled at last – 'B-b-bridie?'

Forty-Eight

'It seems to be you he wants,' Eveleen said resentfully, when she went to find her niece in the bedroom that was always called 'Bridie's' now, even when she wasn't staying there.

Bridie stared at her aunt for a moment and caught some of the tension in her, the acute disappointment that her husband, though physically safely back home with her, was asking for someone else. She crossed the room swiftly to where Eveleen stood in the doorway, her hand still gripping the doorknob. Bridie held out her arms and tried to embrace her aunt, but Eveleen stood stiffly unresponsive.

'It's only that at the moment he looks upon me as his nurse.' Bridie laughed, trying to make light of the situation, but at the same time trying to make her aunt understand. 'We have the same trouble at the home. Sometimes when a patient's family visits, they'll hardly speak to them. Their little world is the home and the nursing staff.'

Some of the resentment left Eveleen's face, but she said flatly, 'Then you'd better go to him.'

'Let's have dinner first. Come on, we'll go down.' She took her aunt's hand. 'Just you and me. Then I'll help him into bed. You can be with me and see what to do.'

Eveleen felt like shouting back, I know what to do.

Haven't I been caring for my family for years? Didn't I care for you from the time you were born?

But for once she bit her tongue to stop the words being spoken as she realized the truth. Eveleen had to admit that she had no idea how to cope with the injured and emotionally damaged man who had returned from the hell of the trenches.

Bridie had to leave the following afternoon, and after she had gone Richard sank back into his silent, lethargic world. Eveleen could not even coax him to get out of bed, other than to visit the bathroom, never mind get dressed. Once more he just lay, staring vacantly at the ceiling.

'Please, Richard . . .' Eveleen took his hand. 'Won't you get up and sit by the window like you did yesterday?' Though the words nearly choked her, she added, 'Like you did for Bridie?'

He did not look at her as he mumbled, 'Bridie. I want Bridie.'

Eveleen sighed, straightened up and turned away. 'I can't cope with this,' she muttered as she left the room. The man who had cared for her and looked after her was now lost to her. Downstairs she pulled on her coat and put on her hat, ramming the hatpin viciously into place, anxious to be gone from the house. At least at the factory I know how to cope with all the problems, she thought. Though there had been difficult times, Eveleen had faced and dealt with them all and now the factory, though vastly changed for the time being, was running comparatively smoothly. She had earned the respect of all those who worked for her.

Eveleen decided to walk to the factory to work off some of the anger boiling up inside her. As she marched along with long, almost manly strides, her head held high, she was unaware of the striking figure she made and the admiring glances she attracted.

Why can't I cope with it? she castigated herself. Is it because I'm so used to him being the strong one? Or is it, she pondered, trying to be completely honest with herself, because after years of coping with my mother's weathervane moods I've just reached breaking point?

She had reached the factory gates and as she stepped through them she sighed. She was no nearer solving her problem, but at least, for a few hours, she could bury herself in a different set of problems, but ones that she was now fully capable of dealing with.

'I want to see my son. You've no right to stop me.'

Mary Carpenter stood in the hallway at Fairfield House, her voice raised in petulant anger, and faced the matron.

'I'll ask Jimmy if he's feeling well enough,' Dulcie said calmly. She turned and addressed Bridie, who was hovering in the shadows near the staircase. 'Singleton, will you inform Mr Hardcastle that his mother is here and wishes to see him?'

Bridie turned and began to run up the stairs, but as she did so her grandmother elbowed the matron out of the way and pushed past her. 'All this nonsense. I've a right to see my son. I don't see why he can't come home with me.'

'The authorities—' Dulcie began primly.

'Damnation to the authorities. What do they care

about my boy?' Mary was climbing the stairs now, almost up to where Bridie stood looking down at the matron, uncertain what she should do.

Dulcie nodded to her, capitulating to the determined woman with a sigh.

'This way, Gran.'

'I know where his room is, girl,' Mary snapped, but Bridie insisted on leading the way along the landing and opening the door of Jimmy's room.

She smiled as she entered and announced, 'A visitor for you.'

As Jimmy, in his chair by the window, turned and saw his mother, Bridie almost laughed aloud at the look of horror on his face. As Mary hurried towards him, her arms outstretched, he cringed back into the chair. But there was no escaping the woman's tender caress, her kiss. As she sat down beside him, she took his hand and though he tried to pull away, she held it firmly in her grasp.

Quietly chuckling to herself, Bridie closed the door.

'So,' Bridie asked Jimmy later, trying to keep her impish smile in check, 'did you have a pleasant afternoon with your mother?'

Jimmy glowered up at her. 'Who ses she's me mam? *I* can't remember.'

'Well, she's positive she is. Besides, you recognized your sister. So, if Eveleen is your sister and Mary's your mother, then I'm your daughter.'

He was suddenly angry. His hands gripped the arms of his chair until the knuckles showed white. He thrust his head towards her, his eyes glittering. 'You can't prove that. No-one can. It could have been anyone. It could have been Andrew Burns. He was like a lovesick puppy, always hanging round her.'

She stood staring down at him as he glared back at her. She brushed aside the implied insult to her dead mother as a slow smile spread across her face. 'So,' she said quietly, 'you do remember, after all?'

Appalled, Jimmy glared up at her. 'You little bastard!' he muttered through gritted teeth. 'You tricked me.'

'Oh, I'm that all right,' she said airily. The horrible name he had called her was nothing new to her. She had grown up with it being called after her in the schoolyard and along the lanes near her home. Bridie the bastard, they had called cruelly after her. Only Micky Morton had ever stuck up for her, earning himself a bloody nose more than once in her defence. 'You saw to that, didn't you? Running away to sea instead of marrying my mother.'

'I told you, you can't prove I fathered you.'

'No, I can't, but from what Auntie Evie has told me about my mother and what I've seen now I've met her father and my great-grandmother I don't reckon my mother would have been the sort to have had a string of fellers.'

His head came up sharply. 'You know them?'

His guard was down now. He was talking to her – really talking to her – for the first time. And now he was making no pretence that he had lost his memory.

Bridie nodded. 'I went to help out. I got quite close to the old lady, but . . .' Her eyes clouded. 'He won't have anything to do with me.' Then suddenly she grinned broadly. 'But I haven't given up yet.'

Jimmy snorted. 'I wouldn't count on him ever coming round. If he can cast his own daughter out, aye and his sister 'afore that, then you've no chance.'

She regarded him steadily, her head on one side. 'I grant you Andrew was in love with Rebecca.' Her voice faltered for a moment. So much in love with her, she was thinking, that he still sees her in me. Pushing aside her own sadness, she concentrated on the man before her now. 'But when you came along, she had eyes for no-one else. So I'm told.'

Jimmy shifted awkwardly in his chair.

'So,' she persisted, 'why, exactly, won't you at least acknowledge that you *could* be my father?'

He raised his eyebrows. 'Oh, I admit I could be your father, but I'm just not saying that I am.'

'Why?'

His lip curled. 'I didn't want to be saddled with a misery for a wife and a howling kid.'

'If she was such a misery as you call her, why did you – want her?'

He shrugged. 'She was there,' he said callously. 'And she was – available.' He smiled maliciously. 'And it was fun to take her away from poor old Burns.'

Bride felt the urge to slap his face really hard. Instead, she controlled her anger to say with icy calm, 'Do you know something? I think it's you that's the bastard, not me.'

Sick with disappointment at finding out just what sort of a man her father was, Bridie turned away. She was halfway across the room before he said, 'I suppose you're going to report all this to your precious matron and have me sent back to sea. Back to the war.'

She stood a moment, her heart beating fast. Then she turned and walked slowly back to him. She bent over him, her hands resting on the arms of his chair. She thrust her face close to his. 'I'll strike a bargain with you. I'll not say a word about any of this.' She paused and then added pointedly, 'At least at the moment. But from now on you treat your own mother with a lot more respect than you treated mine.'

He stared up at her and then there was a brief flicker of admiration in his eyes. 'By heck, you're a hard little bugger, aren't you?'

She stood up, her face grim. 'I can be when I need to be. I wonder who I get it from.'

Forty-Nine

Midway through the afternoon an urgent message from her father-in-law was delivered to Eveleen at the factory that she must return home immediately.

She went at once, knowing that Brinsley would not panic easily. Her heart in her mouth, she hurried home, opening the front door to a cacophony of noise. Jane, the girl Eveleen had employed to watch over Richard during her absence, was standing in the hall in tears and wringing her hands helplessly. The sound of shouting and of breaking glass or pots, was coming from upstairs.

'Oh, madam.' The girl rushed towards Eveleen. 'It's the master. He's – he's gone berserk. I can't do a thing with him. Nor – nor can Mr Stokes.'

Not even pausing to remove her hat and coat, Eveleen ran up the stairs. The door to the main bedroom stood open and a scene of devastation met her eyes. Ornaments, perfume bottles, face-cream jars lay scattered in pieces on the floor, their contents spilled. Clothes had been pulled from drawers and the wardrobe and flung around, even the mattress had been upturned and rested drunkenly half on, half off the bedstead.

Richard stood in the centre of the room, his eyes wild, his arms flailing, his hands reaching for something else to throw. And he was shouting.

'I want Bridie here. Get Bridie.'

Brinsley hovered at the door, his face white with anxiety. 'Thank God you're here, Eveleen. Maybe you can calm him.'

Eveleen stood a moment and watched. 'I doubt it,' she said drily. 'It's obvious who he wants.'

She felt her father-in-law glance at her, but he said nothing. Eveleen stepped into the room and moved towards her husband. To see the loving, kindly man she had known reduced to this was breaking her heart, yet she knew she had to be strong.

'Richard, please . . .' She tried to catch hold of his arms to still them, but his hand caught the side of her face, striking her jaw and almost knocking her to the ground.

'Bridie? Where's Bridie?'

For a moment Eveleen, her hand to her cheek, stared at him. Then suddenly something seemed to snap inside her. All the emotion of the past four years: her ill-concealed anger at his volunteering, the stress of trying to take over the reins at the factory and the antagonism she had faced, and the never-ending worry for his safety. And, though buried deep, the thought too that she would never now bear a child. All of this bubbled up inside her until she felt as wild as the man before her.

With a noise in her throat like a growl, she raised her hand and slapped his face hard. There was sudden silence. Richard stood quite still staring at her. Behind her, she heard her father-in-law's muttered, 'Oh, Eveleen, you shouldn't have done that.' Immediately she was filled with remorse. After all he had suffered, all he had been through, all his loving wife could do was to strike him.

Tears filled her eyes and she held up her arms to him. 'Oh, Richard, I'm sorry. I'm so sorry.'

Richard shook his head and passed a weary hand across his eyes as if waking from a dream, or perhaps a nightmare. Drained, he sank to the floor and Eveleen knelt beside him, cradling his head against her and stroking his hair, rocking him like a child.

Brinsley stepped into the room. 'I think, my dear,' he began, but now there was a firm resolution in his tone, 'you should let him go to Fairfield House.' His eyes held deep understanding. Perhaps he guessed something of what she was feeling because he added, 'I understand how you must feel, but it seems to be what he wants and I think it would be for the best. We can't – ' he waved his arm to encompass the destruction around them – 'have this and he needs proper care. Care, my dear, that neither you nor I can give him.'

It was a gentle reproach, but Brinsley was generous enough to include himself in the failure.

Eveleen closed her eyes and held Richard close to her. Then she kissed his forehead and whispered, 'You're right. It would be the best thing for him.' Though not for me, she was thinking. Aloud, she added, 'I'll take him this afternoon.'

'Will they have a place?'

As she rose to her feet, she nodded. 'I think so. Bridie said that two were discharged last week. One to go home and one to return to the Front.'

'Poor fellow,' Brinsley murmured, saddened by the thought that someone who had already suffered injury should be made to return to that living, dying hell.

There was only one place left at the home; already the other had been filled by a soldier with bandages round his eyes.

'He's been blinded,' Bridie told Eveleen. 'Isn't it sad? He was a watchmaker.'

Eveleen bit her lip. Sorry for the stranger though she was, her mind was filled with her own problems. 'Oh, Bridie, I hit him. I hit Richard. I'll never forgive myself.'

Bridie took her aunt's hands, suddenly seeming the older of the two of them. 'Don't be upset, Auntie Evie. You maybe did the right thing.'

Eveleen stared at her. 'The right thing? How can it possibly have been right to hit him?'

Bridie shrugged. 'It was a kind of hysteria, wasn't it?'

'I – I suppose so,' Eveleen responded doubtfully, still feeling the enormous guilt.

'And it worked, didn't it?'

Eveleen nodded.

'There you are then.' She patted Eveleen's hand, trying to comfort her. 'And I know how you must feel having to bring him here, but you have done the right thing. Honestly.'

Eveleen nodded again, but the tears spilled down her face and Bridie hugged her. 'There, there,' she whispered as if to a child.

Later, after Eveleen had left and Richard was asleep in his room, Bridie confided in the matron. 'She slapped his face. Was that the right thing to do?'

Dulcie pursed her lips. 'I'd sooner she had found another way. I wouldn't allow any of the nurses under my control to use such methods. The furthest I'd go is some kind of restraint.' The matron sighed. 'But I understand how difficult and frightening it must have been for her.'

'She had a bruise on her jaw,' Bridie went on. 'He caught her as she tried to calm him. He didn't mean to hit her, she said. He didn't know what he was doing.'

'He wouldn't. But he's here now and we'll keep him here until he's quite, quite well.' She smiled at the girl. 'And he can be your special patient, along,' she added, her eyes twinkling, 'with Mr Hardcastle.'

The war news was heartening. At the end of September the papers said that the Allies were sweeping all before them along the whole Western Front. On 11 November came the news that the whole country had longed to hear for more than four years. The war was over. Church bells rang out to herald the peace. In the city factories closed and a jubilant workforce rushed into the streets, cheering, dancing and waving flags. At Reckitt and Stokes Eveleen declared a day's holiday, but as Brinsley remarked sadly to Eveleen, 'The fighting may be finished, but the war will never be over for so many. They've another kind of battle to contend with now. We've lost a whole generation of our youth.'

Brinsley visited Richard regularly at Fairfield House and Eveleen came every weekend and on Wednesday afternoons. But Sophia Stokes now refused to visit her son.

Shortly after noon on Monday, the day before Christmas Eve, when Bridie was helping to usher the patients into the dining room for their midday meal and carrying trays to those who could not manage to get down the stairs, she heard the sound of a car in the driveway. Glancing out of a window, she saw her aunt climbing out of the vehicle and almost running towards the front door.

Bridie's heart skipped a beat and then began to thud. Something was wrong. Eveleen had only left the previous evening after her usual weekend visit. And Monday was one of her busiest days at the factory.

Bridie hurried into the bedroom and thrust the tray at the man in the bed. 'Sorry. I've got to go. Auntie Evie . . .' She rushed out of the room again and ran down the stairs.

'Bridie!' Dulcie's voice rang out in the hall. 'Don't run.'

'Sorry, Matron, but Auntie Evie's here.' As she spoke the urgent pealing of the front doorbell began and despite Dulcie's reprimand, Bridie scurried across the polished hall floor and pulled open the door.

Eveleen's face was wreathed in smiles and Bridie felt a sudden relief. There was nothing seriously amiss if her aunt was looking happier than she had for weeks, months – probably years – since this whole sorry war had begun. Standing on the doorstep, she flung her arms wide and cried, 'I've wonderful news, Bridie. The best Christmas present ever. Andrew's safe. He's coming home.'

Bridie smiled and nodded and gestured her aunt to step inside. 'Of course he is,' she said simply.

Eveleen entered the house, staring at Bridie. 'You don't seem surprised.' She glanced towards Dulcie. 'Oh, you've heard already?' The matron shook her head and they both turned towards the girl.

Bridie was smiling happily, but all she said was, 'I told you all along he wasn't dead. I knew he'd come back.' She shrugged. 'I just knew God wouldn't let him die.'

The two older women now glanced at each other, marvelling at the young girl's unshakeable belief. Eveleen put her arm about Bridie's shoulders and her voice shook slightly as she said, 'I wish your grandfather could see you at this moment. Your faith shames even his devotion.' She handed Bridie a letter. 'This is for you. It was enclosed in mine.'

Now the girl's hands were shaking as she took the letter and thought she recognized the handwriting. She held the letter to her bosom for a moment, then, slipping it into her pocket, she murmured, 'I'll read it later.'

'He's been in a prison camp,' Eveleen explained. 'That's why we've heard nothing. Evidently when he went on that raiding party, he was injured and lay out in the open all night. In "no man's land" they call it.' Bridie nodded. She had heard the soldiers talking about it. 'The following day,' Eveleen went on, 'he was found and taken to an enemy field hospital and then to a prison camp. He had no identification on him and he refused to tell them who he was. In fact, he wouldn't tell anyone until he knew he was back in England.'

Bridie brushed away her joyful tears and asked, 'When will he be home?'

'We're trying to arrange that. He's in a hospital in the south of England at the moment, but Mr Stokes is making enquiries – ' Eveleen laughed – 'and pulling a few strings to get him moved here.' Her face sobered and she glanced from Bridie to Dulcie and back again. 'There's just one thing. You'll have to watch both Jimmy and Andrew. There could be trouble. I've no doubt that Andrew has harboured bitterness against my brother all these years.'

'Perhaps it would be best if Andrew didn't come here,' Dulcie said.

'Oh no, please let him come,' Bridie exclaimed at once. 'I'll manage them. Besides, my father is much better . . .' Then she remembered to add hastily, 'Physically, that is. Perhaps he could go to Gran's. It's what she wants.'

Eveleen smiled wryly. 'Ah, but is it what Jimmy wants?'

In the privacy of her room, Bridie opened her letter.

My dearest Bridie . . .

His 'dearest', she thought, clasping the letter to her again. Then she read on.

How long it seems since I was able to write to you, but the worst of it is that you have no doubt been informed that I was 'presumed killed' and I couldn't send word to you that I was all right. How I long to see you again. The thought of you has kept me going all through the long years of the prison camp. We were pretty well treated, but it was no holiday. I have had your photograph with me all the time and look at it every day. I hope you've had a photograph taken on your birthday every year for me . . .

Bridie smiled gently, relieved that she had kept her promise to him.

I'll be home soon as soon as the hospital will release me. All my love, always, Andrew.

All his love, always, she thought. If only he really meant it.

'I aren't going there.' Jimmy glowered. 'I don't know them from Adam. Why should I go and live with strangers?'

Bridie could not argue, for Dulcie was standing beside her. She had no intention of breaking her promise to her father, even though he was glaring at her as if the suggestion that he was well enough to go and live at Pear Tree Farm now had come solely from her.

'Trying to get your own back, are you?' he hissed at her.

'No,' the girl said calmly. 'We thought it might be best. It might help you to regain your memory,' she added pointedly, 'if you were in familiar surroundings.'

'They won't be familiar, will they,' he countered sarcastically, 'if I can't remember them.'

'True,' the matron agreed. 'What Singleton means is that surroundings that should be familiar to you might help jog your memory.'

Jimmy's only answer was a growl.

Ignoring it, Dulcie went on with a tone of finality that suggested the decision had been made for him. 'Besides, we need the bed.'

'Don't tell him who it's for,' Bridie had warned Dulcie earlier. 'Else he'll refuse to go just out of spite, if what Auntie Evie says is anything to go by.' But it seemed that the grapevine within the home had been buzzing.

'Oh, aye. Is it for Burns?' A sly grin spread across Jimmy's face. 'Well, I'd like to be here to greet him. I'd like to see his face when he sees me here.'

Dulcie was staring down at him. Slowly she said, 'I thought you couldn't remember anything?'

'Oh – er – well, I get little flashes now and then,' he faltered and then, as his mind worked surprisingly quickly, he added, 'Besides, Eveleen was telling me. How we had a fight and all that.' He nodded towards Bridie. 'Over her mother.' He grinned broadly. 'I expect I won.'

As they moved away, Dulcie frowned thoughtfully whilst Bridie held her breath. Was she going to be questioned and found out?

'I think he knows more than he's letting on to us, Bridie, don't you?'

'It – it sounds a bit like it,' the girl said, crossing her fingers behind her back and praying for forgiveness for the little white lie. But perhaps now there was no need to keep up the pretence. The war was over and even if Jimmy went back to sea eventually he would not be going back to a war situation. Not now, thank God.

And now Andrew was coming home. Bridie skipped through her work, her heart singing.

Andrew was coming home.

Fifty

'He's here. Oh, he's here!'

Bridie ran down the wide staircase and across the hall. Dulcie appeared in the doorway of her office, but for once she did not reprimand the excited girl. Earlier she had warned her that they had not yet been informed of his injuries. Andrew might look very different from how Bridie remembered him. 'You do know, don't you, that he could have lost a leg or an arm or be blind, deaf . . .?'

Bridie had stood calmly in front of her and had nodded soberly. 'I know, Matron. I don't think there's anything we haven't seen here, is there?'

'No,' Dulcie had said quietly. 'But it's very different when it's someone you – you love.'

Bridie heard the catch in the woman's voice and wondered. But Dulcie had cleared her throat and ended the conversation by saying, 'So long as you are prepared, my dear.'

Now the moment had come and Bridie was pulling open the heavy front door and running lightly down the steps to the ambulance that had brought Andrew and another patient to Fairfield House. The two ambulance men carried off a stretcher case first and Bridie stood on tiptoe, craning to see. But it was not Andrew. This man's face was gaunt and his skin yellow, his eyes closed.

Then she saw another man climbing stiffly out of the back of the vehicle. He stooped a little and leant heavily on a stick as he moved forward. But his hair was fair, not at all like Andrew's.

She glanced again towards the stretcher that was now being carried up the steps and in through the door, which the matron was holding open.

'Private Burns, ma'am,' Bridie heard one of the men carrying the patient say. 'Where do you want him?'

Bridie picked up her long skirt and ran up the steps in time to hear Dulcie say, 'Up the stairs and it's the dormitory to the left. Ah, Bridie, perhaps you will go with them. Show them the way.'

Bridie walked beside the stretcher, gazing down at him. Tears blurred her vision momentarily; to think that she had not recognized her beloved Andrew. Impatiently she brushed away her tears, took a deep breath and led the way up to the long, sunny room on the first floor that had been turned into a dormitory for six beds.

'Please could you put him in the end bed. Has he any kit?'

One of the men shook his head. 'Not much, miss. Just this small bag.' He nodded down to a small bag that looked to contain shaving equipment.

'Nothing – nothing else?'

'Only his wallet and he won't let anyone have hold of that.' The man grinned and nodded towards the end of the stretcher. 'Keeps hold on it, tight to his chest, he does. Here we are, then, mate. Let's have you off this thing and into a nice soft bed. And here's a pretty little nurse to look after you.' He laughed. 'Some fellers get all the luck, I reckon. Ready?' He asked his partner. 'One, two, three, upsy-daisy.'

When the two men had gone, Bridie stood beside the bed. 'Andrew,' she whispered.

His eyes flickered open and for a moment he stared at the ceiling and then he turned his head slowly to look up at her. His face was so thin that the cheekbones stood out. His eyes were dark hollows yet, now she could see his hazel eyes, she knew it really was him. He was blinking at her, as if trying to focus, and for an awful moment Bridie wondered if he was blind. He had not lost a limb, that she could see now, but perhaps his injuries were the sort that were not so apparent at first.

His lips parted and he seemed to speak, but no sound came out.

She found his hand and held it close to her. 'Andrew, it's me. You're safe now. You're home and I'm going to take care of you.'

Though it was strictly against the matron's rules, Bridie leant over and kissed his forehead. 'Oh, Andrew, I do love you so.'

He closed his eyes and she heard his long, deep sigh. 'Oh, my darling,' he whispered hoarsely. 'My darling Rebecca.'

Bridie had known hurt in her young life, but all were as pinpricks beside this. Andrew's undying love for her mother stuck a knife deep into Bridie's heart. He did not even see her as herself, the girl thought. Only as her mother's daughter. Her gran had been right all along. She was determined, however, that no-one should see her torment. She plastered a brave smile on her face and kept her voice as cheerful and gently teasing to all the patients as always.

Fortunately she was now run off her feet helping to care for her three special patients; her father, Richard and Andrew. She had little time to dwell on her own disappointment. They were each demanding her time in very different ways.

Richard called for her constantly, would let no other nurse near him. Andrew lay in his bed, demanding nothing from anyone, yet her love for him brought her constantly to his bedside like a moth to a flame. As for Jimmy, he watched the goings on closely and smiled with malicious relish.

'Does Burns know I'm here?' he asked Bridie frequently.

'Just you keep away from him.' She turned on him, speaking rashly. She bit her lip as she saw Jimmy's eyebrows rise questioningly. She didn't want him guessing the extent of her feelings for Andrew. She didn't want anyone here to know. Only her family knew of her fondness for him, yet even they still believed that it was more of a father–daughter relationship. All her life Andrew had been her surrogate father, a replacement for the errant Jimmy. Sadly Bridie knew that that was how Andrew thought of her too. As the daughter he should have had with Rebecca.

She put her head on one side, her hands on her hips and met her father's gaze. 'I heard about you and Andrew fighting over me mam, so just you keep away from him.' She'd turned it neatly away from herself to the events of the past. But Jimmy was not to be so easily deceived. She felt he was watching her face intently for every fleeting expression.

'Seems to me he's more to you than just one of your mam's old boyfriends.'

With an outward calm she did not feel inside, Bridie said, 'Of course he is.' She leant towards him accusingly. 'He took your place all the time I was growing up. He was like a father to me.'

Jimmy laughed. 'Perhaps he was, young Bridie. Perhaps he really was your father. Who's to know, eh?'

His insinuations brought fresh dread to Bridie's already wounded heart.

'Seems to me,' Jimmy was still watchful, 'that it's my dear brother-in-law, Richard, who's got his eye on you. I'll have to warn poor old Evie that she'd better watch herself.' He laughed. 'She never did have much luck with the gentry.'

Despite her anger at him for his machinations, Bridie couldn't help being intrigued. 'What do you mean?'

He waved his hand and glanced around the room. 'Chap who owned this place. He was her lover.'

'Her – her lover?' Bridie's voice was a shocked squeak. Jimmy's words implied so much more than the innocent romance of a girl and a landowner's handsome son, yet Bridie could hardly believe such a thing of her aunt. She had only witnessed the strong and sure love between Eveleen and Richard, and despite their present difficulties she was convinced that, deep down, it was as steadfastly secure as ever. Once Richard was well again everything would come right for them.

They were alone in the room whilst Bridie changed the sheets on his bed, so Jimmy felt able to speak freely without compromising himself. 'Our parents tried to stop it. Me mam in particular was dead set against it. Probably because of what had happened to her when she was young.'

Bridie bit back the tumult of questions. She would learn more if she kept quiet and let him ramble.

'Anyway, when our father died suddenly Master Stephen threw our Evie over and turned us out of our home.'

'And that's when you went to Flawford and met my mother,' Bridie said pointedly.

Jimmy eyed her suspiciously, aware that she was trying to trap him into an admission. Carefully he said, 'Well, yes, I met her. Of course I did. She was our cousin.'

Bridie arched her eyebrow quizzically, but said no more.

At ease again, Jimmy looked about him once more and laughed. 'Good old Evie. She got her own back on him though, didn't she?'

Now Bridie was puzzled. 'How do you mean?'

'Bought him out, lock stock and barrel, hasn't she?' He pulled his earlobe. 'Oh, this place is a den of gossip, I don't mind telling you. The things I've been hearing. Make your hair curl, lass. It would really. There's a feller in here from Bernby. He used to work on the Dunsmore estate afore he went in the army. He's been telling me a thing or two. After the old man, Stephen's father that is – now what was his name? – Ernest, that was it. Mr Ernest. He went off to London to be an MP and left his son in charge of the estate. By all accounts, Stephen drank and gambled all the money. I bet he was only too glad to get away.' He laughed. 'I expect the Front was a better prospect than his creditors chasing him.'

'Hardly,' Bridie said wryly. 'He was killed.'

Jimmy had the grace to look startled, but it only lasted a brief moment before he said grimly. 'Good riddance.'

'That's a horrible thing to say about anyone,' she cried.

Jimmy met her gaze steadfastly and his expression

was the most serious she had ever seen it. Quietly he said, 'We're a nasty lot, us men, Bridie lass, and I'm probably worse than most. You wouldn't want me for a father, really you wouldn't. You'd best stick with Burns. He's a much better father-figure for you than ever I'd be.'

Bridie, smoothed the pillow on his bed and pulled the counterpane straight before going to stand in front of him. She looked directly into his eyes. Quietly she said, 'We can't choose our parents, can we? But you're my father. I know you are, even if you won't admit it. So it looks like we're stuck with each other, doesn't it?'

Without waiting for a reply, she turned and left the room, leaving him gazing after her. Besides, Bridie was thinking as she collected fresh laundry and hurried along to Richard's room, I've other plans for Andrew Burns, even if, at the moment, he doesn't realize it himself. The last thing I want is Andrew as my father.

Eveleen was with Richard, but the moment Bridie entered the room it was as if she no longer existed. She watched as Richard's face lit up at the sight of her niece. He even held out his arms to her, inviting a hug, but Bridie laughed gaily and said, 'Do you want to get me the sack, Uncle Richard? I'm on duty, you know that.'

She put the clean linen down on the bed and glanced from one to the other. 'Now, how about you go out into the garden or perhaps go for a drive with Auntie Evie, while I get your bed changed and Minnie comes and cleans your room.'

'Can you come with us?' He was pathetically eager and his face fell as Bridie shook her head. 'You know I can't. Now, off you go. It's a lovely morning. Far too nice to be stuck indoors. Why, don't you go to Pear Tree Farm? Gran'd love to see you.'

Eveleen stood up and smiled at her niece, though she found it difficult. She felt as if she were merely stretching her mouth and that the smile did not reach her eyes.

You're being silly, she castigated herself silently. How can you be jealous of your own niece? She's Richard's nurse and he's just leaning on her whilst he's ill. But, the insidious voice persisted, hasn't he always been fond of her? Remember the Goose Fair? The memory still hurt, but that day had been her fault. If she hadn't been so busy, so wrapped up in her own importance, trying so desperately to prove that she could run the factory, then it would not have happened. They would have had a lovely family day at the fair, the three of them.

Perhaps it was all her own fault. Eveleen was never less than honest with herself, even if the truth hurt. If she had devoted all her time to her husband when he had come home from the war, it might not have been necessary for him to have come here. She sighed, but it was too late now. He was here and there was no doubt, however painful the realization might be, that he was improving greatly under the wonderful nursing care at Fairfield House. And, if she was brutally honest with herself, it was mainly Bridie's loving care that was bringing about his recovery.

She moved to Richard's side and took his arm. Trying to make her tone playfully light, she said, 'I think she wants to get rid of us. Come along, darling. We'll go for that drive.'

For a moment, Richard looked disappointed, but then he nodded, tried to smile and said, 'Shall we go to Pear Tree Farm and take Jimmy to see his mother?'

'I don't think he'll come,' Eveleen said.

'What about Andrew then?'

'He's not well enough,' Bridie said. 'Not yet. I'm going to take him for a little walk in the garden later.'

Eveleen saw Richard look towards Bridie, who was already stripping the sheets from his bed. The look in his eyes was gentle as he murmured softly, 'Lucky Andrew.' But Eveleen knew that Bridie, concentrating on her task, had not heard.

Fifty-One

Josh lumbered forward as the car turned in at the gate.

'Oh, this is wonderful. Are you feeling better, Richard? Come in, come in. Dinner should be nearly ready and I'm sure there'll be enough for both of you. Mary, Mary love . . .' He drew them into the house, calling, 'Look who's here.'

Mary made even more fuss than Josh, but then, Eveleen reminded herself with a wry smile, Richard was a man. For Mary that was as natural as breathing.

But the man himself, though polite and smiling, seemed ill at ease, on edge all the time and perpetually glancing at the clock on the mantelpiece above the range.

'Like a walk whilst the ladies wash up?' Josh invited and though Eveleen could sense that he would rather not Richard gave in gracefully.

When they were alone in the house, Mary said, 'He's not himself yet, is he?'

Eveleen bit her lip and shook her head. 'No. I wonder if he ever will be.'

'All he needs is a lot of love and care, Eveleen.' Mary spoke harshly, accusingly. 'A bit of, of – ' she sought for the elusive word – 'tenderness. You've no tenderness in you, Eveleen. You're always too busy doing what *you* want to do. Organizing things, running things. Trying to take the place of a man.'

'We've had to these last few years,' Eveleen was sharply defensive.

'I know all about that.' Mary waved her hands dismissively. 'But they're home now and you should be concentrating on looking after your husband. You've got a good man there, Eveleen.' There was a hint of surprise in Mary's voice as if she still couldn't quite believe how her daughter had captured such a prize. 'If you don't devote yourself to him now, then you'll soon find someone else will.'

Unbidden, an image of Bridie pushed its way into Eveleen's mind's eye.

'Yes, Mam, perhaps you're right,' she murmured.

'Oh, I know I'm right,' Mary said with the conviction of a woman who had always known her lot in life. In her eyes, it was a woman's duty to pander to the man in her life.

They heard the back door open and changed their conversation swiftly, only to have it interrupted by Richard saying, 'Isn't it time we were getting back?'

As they pulled into the driveway of Fairfield House and the noise of the engine died, Eveleen reached across and touched Richard's hand. 'Darling, I've decided. Now so many of the men are back at the factory, I'm not needed there any more. And you seem so much better. You wound is healing nicely. Isn't it time you came home?'

His eyes clouded and he looked about him, almost as if the answer he wanted would come out of the air to him. He stumbled over the words. 'You – ought to – I mean, there's no one to run the place.'

Eveleen laughed. 'Oh, didn't you know? I've persuaded Bob Porter to come back. He's fit enough now. Losing a leg won't stop him managing the factory just like he always did. Besides, now he has men back, he'll be much happier. He can get rid of all the troublesome women. Several have left already of their own accord. Those whose husbands have come back.' Her voice was low as she added, counting herself amongst them. 'The lucky ones.'

'What about the widows?' Richard blurted out, a strange desperation in his tone. Eveleen could sense that he was casting about for an excuse not to come home. 'They'll need jobs. You should keep on as many as you can, Eveleen. It's the least we can do.'

She squeezed his hand. 'Why don't you come home and help me?' she said. 'I – I need you, Richard. I want you to come home.'

He shook his head. 'No, no. I'm not ready. Not yet.'

He climbed out of the motor and hurried up the steps as if he couldn't return to Fairfield House quickly enough.

Eveleen watched him go, her hands gripping the steering wheel and tears blinding her eyes.

In the yard behind Fairfield House, Bridie said, 'Now lean on me, Andrew. We'll walk down the field towards the beck. Cook has packed us a picnic so we don't need to get back for tea and I don't need to be back on duty until six. We've three whole hours.' She hugged his arm to her side, blissfully happy to be alone with him.

'You don't want to be spending your time off with me,' he said, looking at her so fondly that her heart turned over.

'Can't think of anything I'd rather be doing,' she said simply.

He was watching her, as if drinking in the sight of

her, every detail of her face, her hair – everything about her. Since that first day, he had never again called her 'Rebecca' yet she had the uncomfortable feeling that every time he looked at her she felt that it was not her he was seeing but her mother.

'I can't believe how you've grown up. When I went away you were a little girl and now, just look at you. A young woman.' His voice was hoarse. 'A very beautiful young woman.'

Now Bridie laughed, the sound echoing across the fields. 'Thank you, kind sir.'

'Have you – have you got a young man? I bet they're queuing up.'

She didn't answer him at once. They had reached the beck and she found a suitable spot to spread the rug on the grassy bank. When they were sitting side by side, she looked into his eyes, her face deadly serious, and said quietly, 'All my life I've told you that I was going to marry you when I grew up.'

He smiled and touched her cheek. 'All little girls want to marry their father—'

She interrupted swiftly, 'You're not my father.'

'No, no, I know that. But how I wish I had been. And I've always tried to be there for you, haven't I? I did my best to take his place.'

Now was the time to tell him about Jimmy, for the staff had all contrived to keep them apart and to keep the knowledge of Jimmy's presence in the home from Andrew Burns. But they were bound to meet sooner or later. Whilst Andrew had been confined to bed, it had been comparatively easy, but now he was up and about it was impossible to keep them apart much longer.

But for the moment, Bridie had another, far more important issue to discuss.

'Andrew, I've loved you all my life, but not as my father. I want to spend the rest of my life with you, as your wife.'

He was gazing at her but shaking his head slowly. 'I'm far too old for you. I'm almost twenty years older than you.'

'So? What does that matter?'

'It – it wouldn't be right. What would people think?'

'I don't care what other people think,' she cried passionately. 'Hasn't this awful war proved that we have to take our happiness when and where we find it?'

He was silent, avoiding her intense gaze now.

His glance roamed the landscape before them: the beck, the field beyond, where cows grazed placidly, and in the distance the buildings of Pear Tree Farm.

Softly, but with a catch in her voice, Bridie said, 'The truth is that you don't love me in that way do you? You're still in love with my mother.'

Andrew did not answer her.

Fifty-Two

It was as they returned to Fairfield House that they came face to face with Jimmy in the hall.

'Well, well, well! If it isn't Andrew Burns himself,' was Jimmy's greeting.

Luckily Bridie had forewarned Andrew only moments earlier as they walked back across the fields. 'He's here, by the way,' she said casually, trying to make light of it.

'Who is?'

'My father. Jimmy Hardcastle. His ship went down somewhere in the Channel. He wasn't physically hurt, but he suffered amnesia.'

Now the two men were standing face to face for the first time in more than seventeen years.

'Your memory seems to be coming back quite nicely,' Andrew said bitterly. 'Remember Rebecca, do you? And what you did to her?'

Jimmy put his fingers to his forehead and frowned. 'Do you know, I can't remember much about her at all. But then, there have been so many since then.' He laughed. 'A girl in every port, you know.'

'Why, you . . . I'll smash your face in.' Andrew clenched his fists and took a step towards him, but Bridie clung onto him, pulling him away. Andrew was obliged to content himself with shaking his fist in Jimmy's face. 'One day, Jimmy Hardcastle. One day, I'll have you.'

The tension was broken by a voice behind them and Richard came hurrying towards them. 'There you are, Bridie. I've been looking everywhere for you. Where've you been?'

Jimmy turned and, shoving his hands into his pockets, walked away, whistling nonchalantly. Andrew, his face like thunder, stared after him.

'We went for a picnic, down by the beck, didn't we, Andrew.' Bridie sought to divert his attention. 'It's the first time he's been out.'

'I wish I'd known. I'd have come with you.'

'That'd have been nice,' Bridie said evenly. She had wanted to be alone with Andrew, so desperately wanted to declare her love for him. She had even dared to hope that now she was grown up there might be a chance he would return her love in the same way. But those hopes had been dashed.

But at least now she knew the mountain she had to climb and Bridie was never going to give up. Her hope refused to die. Now she said brightly, 'Andrew's tired. I must see him to bed. I'll see you later, Uncle Richard.'

'Don't be long. I want to talk to you.'

As she helped Andrew prepare for bed, he was still smarting from the meeting with his old rival. 'I could quite cheerfully kill him, you know, Bridie, for what he did to Rebecca. And to you, of course,' he added as an afterthought.

Bridie managed to smile. 'He's denying that he's my father.' She paused, wondering if she should continue, but decided that the best course was to bring everything out into the open. She was sure Andrew was strong enough now to cope with it. 'He says it's more likely that you are my father.'

Andrew snorted contemptuously. 'Does he indeed? Well, I can assure you I'm not.' His voice softened, 'Although I have wished all my life that I was.'

She believed him implicitly and, in one way, his words gave her fresh hope. Andrew, though he might have longed for it to be otherwise, was not her blood relative.

'So,' she asked slowly, 'do you believe that he is my father?'

Andrew looked at her keenly. 'I could almost wish it had been anybody else *but* him, but, yes, he is your father.'

He got into bed and lay back against the pillows with a sigh. On the bedside table the last photograph that had been taken of Bridie, crumpled and stained from being carried everywhere through four years of war, now stood in a frame. But Andrew was not looking at her photograph now. He lay staring up at the ceiling, seeing pictures from the past. 'They came to Flawford, your gran, Eveleen and Jimmy, when they had to leave the farm. You know all about that, of course.'

'Well, bits,' she said guardedly, wanting him to tell her all that he knew. She sat down on the edge of the bed, breaking yet another of matron's rules.

'She'd never known other lads, apart from those of us who worked in her dad's workshops. And Harry kept her away from them all as best he could. I don't reckon he ever intended to let her get married. He'd lost his wife and he wanted to keep Rebecca to look after him. Before Jimmy came I thought she loved me and I was going to do it all proper. Keep in her dad's good books, court her, like, but all with his permission.'

'Perhaps,' Bridie suggested gently, 'her father would never have given permission. Not even to you.'

'Mebbe not. But I'd have waited. I'd have waited all me life for her, if I'd known that she really loved me. But then *he* came and it was as if I didn't exist any more.'

Bridie took his hand and held it to her cheek and at last, his gaze came back to rest on her face. 'You remind me of her so much. You look a lot like her, but you're very different in your – your nature. She was quiet and gentle and easily led. I can see that now. Not her fault,' he added swiftly, as if regretting even the slightest implied criticism of his beloved. 'But you're feisty. You're a fighter. I get the feeling you'll get what you want.'

She smiled broadly at him. 'You're right there, Andrew Burns. I never give in until I get what I want.'

It was not a threat, but a promise.

Richard was still hovering in the hallway when she came down the stairs. He hurried towards her. 'Is something wrong? You've been so long.'

'We were talking. About my mother – and my father. He needed to talk.'

'I need to talk to you too.' There was a plaintive, selfish note in his voice. Bridie looked up at him in surprise. This war had changed so many things in so many lives, but she would never have believed that her lovely uncle Richard could be so different. But, smiling up at him, she tucked her arm through his and led him to the patients' sitting room. 'Come along then. It should be quiet in here now. What is it you want to tell me?'

'Eveleen wants me to go home,' he blurted out when

they were seated side be side on a sofa. 'But I don't want to. I want to stay here. With you.'

'Why?' she asked candidly.

'Because – because I feel safe here. I can't – can't cope at home.'

'Why not?' Bridie asked again gently. Instinctively she was drawing him out, getting him to face whatever it was that was troubling him.

'I'll be expected to go back to work. To the factory. She's said as much. She needs me to help her, she says.'

'I'm sure she's only suggesting that because she thinks it's what would help you.'

'Mm.' He sounded doubtful.

'So tell her. Be honest with her. Tell her that you don't feel ready – yet – to go back to work.'

'I don't think she'd understand.'

'Yes, she would. She loves you so much, Uncle Richard. She'll do anything – anything at all that will make you well again.'

'I know,' he said dully. 'That's why it's so difficult.'

There was silence as Bridie almost dreaded to ask yet again, 'Why? Don't – don't you love her any more?'

'I . . .' He stopped and in his eyes she could see that he was appalled at himself at what he was obliged to say. 'She frightens me.'

'Frightens you?' Bridie repeated in amazement.

'I know I shouldn't be talking to you this way. You're only a young girl, yet – yet you seem so wise, so mature.'

'Don't worry about that,' Bridie said softly. 'I don't think there's much I haven't heard, working here.'

Although she was still only seventeen, Bridie felt years older. Was it really only a year since her sixteenth birthday, the day she had met her father for the first time? She had witnessed all manner of suffering during her time as a trainee nurse here at Fairfield House. She had heard all kinds of confessions, listened to so many sad tales, that, whilst never immune to their emotions or unfeeling for their anguish, she had grown strong enough to be a good listener. And in many cases that was all that was needed.

But her uncle was a different matter. She couldn't help but be closely involved. She took his hand. 'Tell me,' she urged gently.

'I can't – make love to her any more. I can't – feel anything. When I was at home she was so loving, so – so giving. I knew I ought to, but I – I couldn't.'

'It happens to an awful lot of you.'

'Really? You're not just saying that?'

Bridie shook her head. 'If I had a pound for every time I've heard a soldier tell me that, I'd be rich.' She leant closer to him. 'You've all been through a dreadful time. How can you possibly expect to step back into the life you had before the war as if nothing had happened? It's changed us all, Uncle Richard. Even though we haven't suffered like you have, it's altered our lives, in some ways probably for ever. But as for you – your problem – well, time will heal that, I promise.'

'How do you know?' he asked gloomily. 'What if I can never . . .'

'You will. When you're fit and strong again. What you've got to do whilst you're here is to work at getting physically well. Plenty of good food, fresh air and walks each day. The rest will come right. Honestly it will.'

He picked up her hand and held it to his cheek. 'Oh, Bridie,' he murmured, 'what would I do without you?'

Beyond him, out of the corner of her eye, Bridie caught a movement in the doorway. She glanced up to look straight into her father's grinning face.

Fifty-Three

'I can see I shall have to warn my sister about that husband of hers,' was Jimmy's greeting the next morning. 'Mind you, it's her own fault. She never could keep a feller for long.'

'Don't talk such nonsense,' Bridie snapped, for once her patience at an end.

He laughed. 'I expect, when all this is over, she plans to come and live here. Play the lady of the manor like she always wanted. Maybe it's all she'll have left.' He winked at her and tapped the side of his nose. 'If her dear husband's got his eye on you.'

To her dismay, Bridie could not stop the colour flooding her face. She was angry, yet knew he would see it as embarrassment.

'Oho,' Jimmy said at once. 'I see I'm right.'

'Nothing of the sort,' she answered hotly. There was only one way she could nip this in the bud. 'Besides,' she added, 'I've got my sights elsewhere.'

But Jimmy only laughed. 'Trying to put me off the scent, eh? Well, I know what I saw last night and I'm sure my sister would be interested to hear all about it. Very interested.'

'You . . .' Bridie began taking a step towards him.

'Is he bothering you, Bridie?' Andrew was coming slowly down the stairs, holding tightly onto the banister. He had not yet fully recovered his strength and the wound in his side, even after years in the prison camp, still refused to heal properly. ''Cos if he is . . .'

'No, no.' Bridie hurried towards him to help him down the last few steps. He stood at the foot of the stairs, panting from the exertion, yet his eyes glittered with hatred as he glanced at Jimmy. The latter, however, just stood smiling superciliously at them both.

'Oh aye, and what do you reckon you could do about it? You couldn't beat me last time, so what do you think you could do now, eh?'

'Will you two just stop it?' Bridie began, but already Andrew was pulling himself free of her hold and stepping towards his adversary.

'I'll swing for you, Jimmy Hardcastle. I'll—'

'Come on, then.' Jimmy adopted a fighting pose, fists raised. 'Let's be having you. Let's see what you're really made of, Burns.'

'Stop this. Please—' Bridie pleaded, but Andrew pulled himself free and lunged towards Jimmy, who landed a punch on his jaw with his right hand and then swiftly followed it up with a heavy blow to Andrew's side. Then he stood back as Andrew groaned and doubled over in agony, crumpling to the floor.

'Whatever is going on?' Dulcie was hurrying across the hall. Bridie turned to her in relief. 'I couldn't stop them. I—'

'Go to your room, Singleton. I'll deal with you later. And you too, Mr Hardcastle.' She glared at him and added sarcastically, 'It seems to me that your memory is returning very quickly now. I shall be calling the authorities to have you assessed with a view to you returning to duty.'

'And as for you.' She looked down at Andrew, writhing on the floor. 'How are we to get that wound to heal if you get involved in fights?' She tutted disapprovingly and beckoned to two other nurses to help her take Andrew back to his room so that she could examine the damage.

'Please, Matron—' Bridie began, but Dulcie only said sharply, 'I told you to go to your room. I'll send for you when I'm ready to listen to you.'

'I can't have that sort of behaviour, Bridie.'

She was standing in front of the matron's desk, whilst Dulcie sat in the chair behind it. The fight had reopened Andrew's old wound and the doctor had had to be called.

Bridie stood silently, her head bowed, taking the blame. She felt Dulcie's gaze on her and heard her soft sigh. 'I know it wasn't really your fault, but it's a mistake to have them all here. I thought it would be helpful to them, Mr Stokes as well, for them to be near you, but it seems I was wrong. I'm sorry, Bridie, but I will have to take steps to alter the situation. I intend to ask Dr Roper, when he calls to see Mr Burns, to send Mr Hardcastle to his mother's.' Dulcie smiled wryly. 'It's what she wants anyway, even if he doesn't. But he seems to be the centre of the trouble. Mr Stokes and Mr Burns have no quarrel with each other, have they?'

Bridie shook her head, but bit her lip. There hadn't been actual trouble yet, but if Jimmy carried out his threat then there very well could be.

'Very well, then. You may go now, but do try to keep them apart as much as you can.'

'Thank you, Matron,' she said in a small voice.

*

That evening, after dinner, Richard was once more hovering in the hall, waiting to waylay her. 'You're right, Bridie. I should talk to Eveleen,' Richard said. 'Perhaps she will understand.'

'Of course she will.'

'But would you – would you talk to her first? Maybe she'd understand better if you explain to her that it – it happens to a lot of men.'

Bridie nodded. 'If you really want me to.'

'I do.' He was pathetically grateful.

But when Bridie broached the delicate subject with her aunt the following Sunday, Eveleen felt humiliated. 'How could he? How could he do that to me? Discuss such a personal matter with anyone else.' Eveleen paced up and down Dulcie's office. The matron had given permission for Bridie to talk to her aunt in private and they were alone in the room. Eveleen whirled around now and faced her niece. 'And to you, of all people. You're only a child.'

'I'm seventeen, Auntie Evie,' Bridie said quietly. 'And believe me, after what I've witnessed here, I feel much older.'

'He should have talked to me.' Eveleen's face crumpled and tears threatened.

Bridie stepped towards her, her arms outstretched. 'Oh, Auntie Evie, don't. It'll be all right—'

But Eveleen pushed her away, beside herself with resentment and jealousy. Richard had talked to Bridie, had discussed an intimate problem with a young girl when he should have talked to her, his wife, about it.

'He's coming home with me. Today. I won't have him stay here another minute.'

'Please, Auntie Evie, listen to me. You mustn't be angry with him. You must treat him kindly – gently—'

'Don't you tell me how to treat my husband,' Eveleen flashed back and Bridie could see that her efforts were hopeless.

Eveleen brushed past her and marched out of the room, slamming the door behind her. Alone, Bridie closed her eyes and groaned aloud. She had tried her best, yet now she feared she had only made matters worse.

Eveleen had enough common sense to see that she must not show her anger to Richard. Though it pained her to admit it, she knew Bridie had been right in all that she had said. Many men returning from the war had great difficulty in adjusting to their home life once more, even to a loving relationship with their wives. Win, ever grateful for Eveleen's help with her son-in-law, Sid, had confided, 'Things are much better between them. He's that sorry, he can't do enough for our Elsie.' She had sighed. 'The only thing he can't do is be a proper husband to her, if you know what I mean.' Win had gone on to tell her that several of the homeworkers, whose husbands had returned from the war, were experiencing similar problems. But knowing this still didn't make it any easier for Eveleen to deal with and to have had it confirmed by Bridie had been more than she could bear. To think that Richard had preferred to confide in the girl rather than in his wife hurt her deeply.

But to Richard she presented a smiling face, a gentle tone and understanding. Only when he asked her, 'Has Bridie talked to you? Has she told you?' did it take a supreme effort to keep the smile on her face and the anger from her voice.

'Yes, yes. We've talked. But everything will be fine, darling. Matron says you must see the doctor first, but she sees no reason why you won't be able to come home next Sunday. And once you're home and we're together again everything will be fine.'

She saw him glance at her, saw his wan smile and knew he was not convinced.

After her conversation with Richard, Eveleen talked to Dulcie and then she went alone to Pear Tree Farm.

'I've got a feeling Fairfield House won't be needed as a home much longer. Several of the patients are well enough to go home now. Even some of the staff have left. And Richard's coming home next week.'

'What about Jimmy?' Mary asked at once.

Eveleen placed her cup and saucer carefully on the table. 'That's partly why I'm here. There's been a bit of trouble between him and Andrew and Dulcie feels that Jimmy is well enough to leave. Once she's had the doctor's approval and possibly that of the naval authorities too, he can be released.'

'He must come here. He must come home,' Mary said, clasping her hands in glee, her eyes shining.

Eveleen glanced towards Josh sitting quietly in the chair near the range. They exchanged a long look of understanding and she heard the big man sigh with resignation. He loved her mother dearly and Eveleen knew he could refuse her nothing, but the prospect of having Jimmy to live with them obviously did not appeal. Mary, however, was too wrapped up in her own anticipated pleasure to notice.

For very different reasons, Eveleen warned them, 'He probably won't stay long, you know. As soon as he's really fit again, he'll want to be off.'

She had a job to stop the laughter bubbling up as she

saw the acute disappointment on her mother's face, but the relief on Josh's. But then Mary smiled. 'We'll see. Once he's tasted my home cooking again, he'll not want to go back.'

'He may have to, Mary, love.'

She spun round on Josh. 'Why? The war's over.'

'But Jimmy didn't join the navy just for the war. He's been a regular for years.'

'So, he can still leave, can't he?'

'It depends how many years he's signed on for.'

Mary thought for a moment and then said confidently, 'Well, they won't want him back if he's lost his memory, will they?'

Eveleen and Josh exchanged another glance as Josh said heavily, 'No, I don't expect they will.'

'Lost his memory? My foot!'

The following Sunday, when Eveleen came to Fairfield House to take Richard home to Nottingham, she was once again in the matron's office. She had never seen the calm, usually unruffled Dulcie so incensed.

'I'm sorry, Eveleen.' The two women had become friends and had been on first name terms in private for some time. 'But that brother of yours!'

Eveleen smiled. 'You don't need to tell me.'

'He's hoodwinked the doctor and the naval people who came to assess him this week. D'you know, he should have been an actor. I wouldn't believe a word he says. He's caused nothing but trouble here since he came. Flirting with the nurses, upsetting Bridie. He won't even acknowledge that the poor child is his daughter. And then that fight with Andrew last week, well, that was the last straw.'

She marched up and down her office. Then she stopped and faced Eveleen. 'There's one good thing, though. The doctor and naval people have agreed that he can be allowed to go home to Pear Tree Farm. The only thing is . . .' She smiled slightly and there was a conspiratorial twist to her mouth. 'He's refusing to go and whilst the home is still open, I can't insist that he should leave. I was wondering—'

Eveleen smiled. 'You want me to tell him that the home is closing and that everyone must leave.'

'Would you?'

'What about the other patients?'

'There's only Andrew, who's not really quite fit to go home without someone to care for him. And *that's* Jimmy's fault, anyway.' She sat down and leant her forearms on her desk, clasping her fingers together. 'The thing is, Eveleen, Bridie is willing to go home with Andrew to care for him. In fact, she's desperate to go with him. But I wondered how you'd feel about it? Would you mind?'

'Me? Why should I mind?' Mind, Eveleen was thinking, I'd be delighted.

'Well, I understand you are her legal guardian. Or is that your mother?'

Eveleen shrugged and laughed. 'It wouldn't make a deal of difference. If Bridie wants to do something, she will, no matter what we say. Besides, I haven't any objection.'

On the contrary, Eveleen thought, it couldn't be a better solution. If Bridie were safely in Flawford, caring for Andrew, perhaps Richard would begin to forget about her.

Her smile widened. 'I think it's a grand idea.'

*

'I'm coming home with you and that's final,' Bridie declared, packing Andrew's possessions into a small trunk. There were pathetically few of them. He was sitting holding the photograph of her. She held out her hand. 'Let's put that on the top and close the lid.'

'Wrap it in something. I don't want it to get broken. It's the last photograph I have of you.'

She smiled at him. 'I've four more upstairs in my chest of drawers just waiting for you to come home. I even went into Grantham this September and got one done.'

'You remembered?' he said softly. 'You got a photograph done each year?'

'Of course,' she answered gently. 'How could I forget a promise to you?'

'Will you have another one done for me on your next birthday?'

'You don't need any more photographs. You've got the real thing now.'

His face clouded. 'Your grandfather won't like you being alone with me in my cottage.'

She grinned at him. 'We'll have to get married then, won't we?'

He shifted uncomfortably in his chair. 'I've told you, I'm too old for you, Bridie.'

She closed the lid of the trunk and straightened up, her face sober now. 'It's nothing to do with age, is it? You don't love me the way I love you.'

'I do love you, my dearest girl. I always have. You know that. You're the most important person in my life. You're the reason I survived the war and then the prison camp for all that time.'

'But . . .' she prompted.

He sighed, but could not answer her. She moved and

stood beside him, resting her hand on his shoulder. Her voice was shaky, but the words had to be spoken. 'You still think of me as a little girl. As Rebecca's daughter. As the daughter that you and she might have had. Don't you?'

He took her hand and held it against his cheek. 'I'm sorry,' he said hoarsely.

Bridie laid her cheek against his hair, the lump in her throat growing so that she felt as if it would choke her. And though her voice trembled as she spoke, her words were full of bravery. 'Never mind. I'm still going to take care of you. At least until you're quite well again. You're – you're not going to get rid of me that easily.'

Fifty-Four

Eveleen had arranged for Fred Martin to take Bridie and Andrew home to Flawford.

'I must stay with Richard,' had been her excuse for not taking them herself.

The yard was strangely quiet as they opened the gate.

'Funny,' Andrew murmured, pausing to listen. 'There's no sound from the workshops.' He glanced at Bridie. 'I thought you said Evie had found him some workers. And some of the fellers should be back home now anyway. Those,' he added soberly, 'that are coming back. Something must be wrong.'

Andrew pushed open the door to his cottage and stepped inside, Bridie close behind him. The whole place felt cold and damp. Thick dust covered every piece of furniture.

'Oh, Andrew, I'm so sorry. When I left here, the whole place shone. I cleaned everything myself.'

'Never mind, love. We'll soon have it warmed up and spick and span.' He put his arm about her waist, trying to chase away the look of disappointment on her face. 'Mrs Turner must have been too busy looking after the old lady and your grandfather to worry about my place. It doesn't matter.'

She bit her lip and nodded. She had imagined bringing him home to a glowing fire and a meal ready on the table. That's why she had written to Gracie Turner last week to warn her of their arrival. Surely she could have done something?

'I'll have to go to the village shop and buy a few things.' She moved to the chair by the range and dusted it. 'You sit down. I'll light a fire first.'

'No, you go and do the shopping. I can manage a fire. I expect there's still kindling in the wash-house and the coalhouse is usually kept well stocked.'

'Are you sure you can manage?'

'Yes. Off you go.'

Bridie hurried out of Singleton's Yard and along the village street towards the shop near the green. On her way she passed Gracie Turner's cottage and paused outside the gate. Then, deciding suddenly, she marched up the pathway and knocked on the door. No-one answered and the cottage had the feeling of emptiness about it. She was turning away to walk back down the path, when the woman in the neighbouring house opened her door to shake a doormat.

'Hello. Looking for Gracie, are yer?'

'Yes.'

'Didn't you know? She's in hospital again.'

Bridie's eyes widened. 'Again? What's been the matter with her?'

''Pendicitis. Rushed in two month ago. All sudden, like. It went wrong and she got – now what do they call it?'

'Peritonitis?' Bridie supplied the word.

'Yes, that's it.' The woman looked at her, marvelling. 'Fancy you knowing that. Anyway, poor Gracie was real bad. She almost died. It were touch and go.'

'Oh no!' Bridie was genuinely concerned now for the kindly woman. 'And you say she's still in hospital after all this time?'

'No. She's in *again*. She came home for a few weeks, but the scar wouldn't heal and they've taken her back in. Last week, it were. Nottingham, she's in.'

Expressing her sympathy and concern for Gracie, Bridie hurried away towards the shop desperately anxious now to make her purchases and get back home. What, she was thinking, had been happening to the old lady and her grandfather if Gracie had not been caring for them for the last two months? She couldn't blame the woman for not letting her know. Obviously she had been taken ill so quickly and so severely.

And Harry Singleton would sooner starve to death, she thought grimly, than ask her, his granddaughter, for help.

'What do you want to do today, darling?'

Eveleen was doing her best, but the days since she had brought Richard home from Fairfield House had been difficult. He was unsettled, ill at ease in his own home. Adamant that he was not yet ready to return to work – he didn't even want to set foot in the factory – he nevertheless seemed to need something to occupy him. Drives into the countryside, visits to his parents' home or sitting at home reading, still did not seem enough.

'I don't know,' he answered her listlessly.

They were sitting together in the morning room, Richard making a pretence of reading the morning paper, whilst Eveleen tried to concentrate on making a list for their cook of meals for the week. They heard the distant peal of the front doorbell and heard Smithers's footsteps crossing the hall to answer it.

'You were lucky not to lose all the staff,' Richard remarked.

'The young ones went. Emily went to work in munitions, but Cook and Smithers were too old.'

The footsteps were approaching the door of the morning room. It opened and Smithers appeared. 'It's a Mr Porter, ma'am, for the master or you. There's trouble at the factory, he ses.'

'Right.' Richard got to his feet and flung the crumpled newspaper to the floor. Eveleen held her breath. For a moment, she thought he was going to take up the reins once more, but his next words dashed her hopes. 'You'd better deal with this, Eveleen. Seems they can't manage without you after all.'

He marched from the room, leaving Eveleen staring after him.

The matter was nothing serious and, in one visit to the factory, Eveleen sorted out the problem. But the incident had shown her two things: that Richard was unshakeable in his resolve about not returning to work, and that Bob Porter could not now cope alone with any kind of crisis, even a minor one.

Eveleen pondered her dilemma. She was determined not to break her promise to stay at home with Richard and yet she could not stand by and see all her work over the past four years slip away because of the incompetence of one man. It was hardly fair to blame Bob. He had been through enough already. And it was no use asking Brinsley. Whilst he was willing, she knew his health would not now stand the rigours of running the factory and warehouse.

But there was one man who could help her, she thought. If only he would.

'Richard, Richard,' she called, running up the stairs to find him when she returned from her brief visit to the factory. 'How would you like a drive out to Pear Tree Farm? It's such a lovely day.'

Fifty-Five

Eveleen had not been inside the farmhouse many minutes before she felt the tension in the air. Jimmy sat idly by the range in the chair that had always belonged to the master of the house. In her earliest memories it had been Walter Hardcastle, their father, who had sat there. When Josh had married Mary it had become his chair. But now Mary's spoilt son had returned and had taken up occupation and, Eveleen suspected grimly, had usurped the place of the rightful head of the house.

'He's so much better. Aren't you, dear?' Mary fussed around Jimmy, stroking his hair as she passed his chair between the kitchen range and the table.

Jimmy smiled at his sister with a look that resembled a cat licking his lips after a saucer of cream.

'And his memory's coming back so well now,' Mary went on. 'I said it would if only he'd come home to familiar surroundings. He should have come home to me instead of going to that place.' She glanced resentfully at Eveleen, as if it had all been her fault.

Josh rose from the table and lumbered outside, slamming the back door behind him. Mary appeared not to notice, but Eveleen saw that Jimmy's smile widened.

'And how are you feeling now, Richard?' Mary now turned her attention to her son-in-law. 'You're looking much better. Is Eveleen looking after you properly?'

After a few moments, whilst Mary chattered happily,

not even requiring answers from anyone, Eveleen slipped quietly from the room and followed Josh outside. He was leaning on the five-barred gate at the end of the yard, watching the sun sink in the west, silhouetting the ramparts of Belvoir Castle in the distance.

'This has always been one of my favourite views,' Eveleen said softly. She forbore to say that it had been her father's too. Standing beside this man, who had in so many ways taken Walter's place, she did not want to cause him further hurt by referring to the past. Mary was already pushing him out of her life. Her days now, Eveleen could see without being told, revolved around her selfish son.

'Josh,' she said quietly, 'I need a huge favour. Would you come back to Nottingham – just for a while – and manage the factory?' Swiftly she explained her problem. 'Mr Stokes's health is not up to it now and Richard is not ready to go back yet. I must give him time and I – I need to be with him. And, to put it frankly, Bob Porter's not quite up to it yet. He's doing his best, but with the men coming back from the war and wanting their old jobs back, it's causing nearly as much trouble as when they went.'

Josh regarded her steadily for a few moments, then he asked, 'Are you sure it's *you* who needs the favour?'

Eveleen smiled and put her hand on his arm. 'I can see how things are. You don't have to tell me. I've lived with it all my life. But he'll go, Josh; sooner or later he'll be off. He's enjoying her fussing over him now, but he'll soon get fed up with it and he'll be gone. Then – ' she nodded – 'she'll be distraught. It'll be Mam who'll need the cosseting then.'

The big man let out a long, deep sigh. 'I hope you're right, Evie, mi duck. Don't get me wrong,' he added hastily. 'I don't like to think of your mam being upset, but . . .'

'I know,' Eveleen murmured. 'I know, Josh.'

They stood in silence for several minutes before Josh said slowly, 'Yes, I'll come. There's plenty of folk who'll give a hand with the work here now. Ted Morton's brood are looking for more work now they're growing up, though we all miss Micky. Still, he's happy at his work in Grantham.'

'How is Ted? I heard he'd come home safely.'

'You know Ted. He's fine. Hardly a scratch and quite his old self.'

Eveleen smiled, thinking of her childhood friend. 'I'm glad he came back, but is there a job for him on the estate?'

'Oh, aye. His dad, Bill Morton, is a fine bailiff for you.'

'I know,' she agreed. 'He should have been bailiff years ago. I hope Ted will take it on when Bill wants to retire.'

'I expect he will.'

There was silence between them as they watched the sun sink lower.

'You know,' Eveleen began haltingly, 'I can't stop feeling guilty about Stephen.'

Josh looked at her in surprise. 'Whatever for, mi duck?'

'Well, I bought his house. I was the cause of him enlisting and then – and then he was killed at the Front . . .'

To her amazement, Josh gave a bellow of laughter. 'Him? Dying a hero? Oh, you've got it all wrong, Evie love.'

'But – but Mam told me he'd died.'

Josh nodded and his laughter faded. 'He was killed all right, but it was in a drunken brawl in the back streets of London.' He cleared his throat, obviously embarrassed. 'Over some woman, we heard. He never got anywhere near a recruiting office, believe you me.'

Though sad to hear that Stephen had sunk so low, Eveleen felt as if the burden of guilt, at least over Stephen Dunsmore, had been lifted away. She leant her head against the big man's comforting shoulder. 'Oh, Josh,' was all she said and knew he understood.

They stood together for some time before he said, 'I'll get everything sorted out here and be with you by the end of the week. Can you sort me some lodgings out in Nottingham . . .?'

'Don't be silly. You'll stay with us.' As he opened his mouth to protest, she raised her hand. 'And I won't take no for an answer.'

Josh smiled. 'I never was any good at refusing you anything, was I, mi duck?'

Eveleen smiled and linked her arm through his as they turned to walk back to the farmhouse. 'No, Josh, you weren't.'

Bridie hurried back towards Singleton's Yard, taking little running steps every so often in her anxiety to get back as quickly as possible.

Already Andrew's cottage felt warmer; a fire now crackled in the grate and the kettle was placed on the hob. He looked up as she entered.

'I haven't seen anyone yet. The place seems deserted. I've been into the workshops. There's no-one there. No-one at all. In fact,' he added worriedly, 'it doesn't look as if the machines have been working for a while.'

They faced each other, their faces grim, whilst Bridie related what she had found out in the village.

'You go to your great-gran's. I'll see if I can find Harry.'

Bridie nodded and was out of the door and along the path towards the far end cottage.

'Great-Gran!' she called hesitantly as she pushed open the door that, as ever, was unlocked. The cold met her just as it had in Andrew's house and this time, it chilled her to the bone. What had happened to her great-grandmother? She climbed the stairs calling out, but there was no answer and, until the moment she pushed open the bedroom door, she thought the house was deserted.

Bridie let out a little cry of shock. The old lady was lying in the bed, her eyes closed, her breathing a rasping sound. The state of the bedclothes and of the whole room was far worse than the first time Bridie had found her in a neglected state. On the bedside table there was the remains of a meagre meal and half a cup of cold tea, but that was all.

There was no fire in the grate. The bedlinen and the old lady's nightgown were soiled.

'Oh, Great-Gran . . .' she began and tiptoed to the bed, but at that moment there was a noise downstairs and she heard Andrew calling, 'Bridie, Bridie, come quickly. It's Harry.'

She touched Bridget's bony hand on the coverlet and whispered, 'I'll be right back.' Then she hurried down the stairs.

Andrew was beckoning her urgently from the doorway. 'It's Harry,' he said again. 'He's in a bad way.'

'What's happened?' she asked as they hurried along

the path in front of the cottages to the one at the opposite end.

'I – I don't know. He's just sitting there in his chair by the fire.'

She stopped suddenly and stared at Andrew. 'You – you don't mean he – he's dead?'

'No, no. He spoke to me, but he – he didn't seem to recognize me. I had to tell him who it was.'

She stepped across the threshold and took a moment for her eyes to accustom themselves to the gloom.

Harry Singleton was sitting, as Andrew had said, in his chair by the range. But here again, as with her great-grandmother's home, no warming fire burnt in the grate. On the table, spread with a crumpled check cloth, was a stale loaf of bread and a butter dish with rancid butter in it. The whole place was even more dirty and neglected than the first time she had seen it.

Now her attention fastened on the man himself. Though he still had a full beard, it was ragged and unkempt and, beneath it, she could see that his face was much thinner and his clothes hung loosely on his body. She moved nearer. 'Grandfather?' she said gently. He turned his face towards her, but his eyes did not focus on her.

'Who's that?' he grunted. 'Who is it? Come over here where I can see you.'

She knew his eyesight was poor, so she said, 'It's me. Bridie. Your – your granddaughter.' She moved closer and touched his hand. 'And Andrew's here too. He's come home from the war. He's not quite fit yet, so I've come to look after him. I'll look after you and Great-Grandmother too.' She paused and then added pointedly, 'If you'll let me.'

The old man pulled his hand from beneath her touch.

'Haven't got a granddaughter and we don't need help from anyone. Specially not from a child.'

A lump grew in her throat. Still, he refused to acknowledge her. Even though he was living in squalor, he would never admit to needing help. And especially not her help.

'How long have you been like this, Grandfather?'

'Don't call me that,' he growled.

Bridie sighed. 'What happened after Mrs Turner was taken ill?'

'Lil from the cottage facing the street has looked after us. We're all right.'

Bridie gave a very unladylike snort. 'Her? Well, that explains it all. Now, Andrew's going to light a fire for you and very soon I'll bring you a meal, but I must go back to Great-Gran. She's . . .' She hesitated, not knowing if he knew that his mother looked in a very bad way. But it seemed he did for he said, 'She's not gone yet, then? I keep expecting to be told . . .' His voice petered away.

'She'll be fine,' Bridie said determinedly, 'now I'm back.' Without giving her grandfather time to protest any further, she turned to Andrew. 'Can you manage? Don't overdo it, will you?'

'I'll be fine, love.' He drew her to the door and whispered, 'Your great-gran? Is she bad?'

All Bridie needed to do was to bite her lip and to nod for him to know the serious state of her great-grandmother.

'I'll get this fire lit and I'll get the doctor. You go back to the old lady.'

Bridie hurried away.

By the time the village doctor arrived, the old lady was lying in a clean nightdress and between sweet-smelling sheets. A fire burned in the grate, but Bridie had been unable to rouse her great-grandmother.

'Is she unconscious?'

The doctor did not answer her until he had examined Bridget thoroughly.

'She's a very sick old lady,' he told her solemnly. 'I'm sorry, my dear, but she may well not last the night. Do you need any help? I can send a nurse . . .'

Bridie shook her head and explained what she had been doing for the past two years. The doctor nodded. 'Very well, then. No-one can do more than you are clearly capable of doing.' He sighed. 'But I'm sorry, my dear, you must expect the worst.'

Fifty-Six

For the rest of that day Bridie seemed to be running everywhere. She made a meal and asked Andrew to take a plateful to her grandfather. 'You'll have to sit him at the table, put the knife and fork in his hands so that he can feed himself.'

'Sit down and get yours while I take it, then,' Andrew ordered. 'You're going to need all the strength you can get over the next few days.' He reached out and took her hand. 'Oh, Bridie love, I wouldn't have brought you here if I'd thought for a moment we were coming back to all this.'

'You couldn't have stopped me,' she said, giving him an all-too-brief smile. There was little to smile about at present. 'Besides, I'm glad you did. At least, I can help grandfather, if he'll let me, even if it's too late to . . .' She said no more, but poured hot milk into a bowl of bread broken into small pieces. 'I'll have a quick bite, but I'm going to sit with my great-grandmother. Will you be all right?'

Andrew nodded. 'Course I will. I'll snooze in the chair here for tonight. We can air the beds tomorrow.'

She bent and kissed his forehead briefly and then hurried back to the old lady's bedside. As she sat down beside her, Bridget's eyes flickered and she made a tiny sound.

Gently Bridie spooned milk between the thin, parched

lips, very slowly and carefully so that the semi-conscious woman did not choke. It reminded her of the time she had spoonfed poor Bertie Hyde. This time, though, she vowed, she would not lose her patient. And then Bridie began to talk. Quietly, but persistently, she was trying to drag her great-grandmother back in to the world of the living. The old lady was hovering between one world and the next, but Bridie's determination would not let her go.

Through the night Bridie chattered on, scarcely knowing what she said, yet instinctively knowing that she had to keep on. She refused to let her great-grandmother die without a fight.

She kept the fire built up, keeping the room cosy throughout the long night. As the pale fingers of dawn filtered through the lace curtains, Bridget opened her eyes. Looking straight into Bridie's eyes, she said, 'Can't a body get a bit of peace? Do you ever stop for breath, girl?'

Then she closed her eyes and slept. But now it was a natural sleep.

Bridie laid her head on the coverlet and allowed the tears of relief to flow.

'How is she?' Andrew tapped on the door only minutes later and tiptoed into the bedroom.

Bridie raised her weary head, but her eyes were shining. 'She's going to be all right. She spoke to me.' She was laughing and crying at the same time as she stood up and flung her arms around Andrew. 'She told me off for talking so much. Oh, Andrew, she told me off. Isn't that wonderful? She told me off.'

Andrew chuckled. 'If you say so, love.' They stood together looking down at the old lady, now sleeping peacefully. 'But now you must come and get some breakfast. I've got it all ready.'

'Oh, you shouldn't have. You'll . . .'

'I'm quite all right. I can manage a few jobs. Though . . .' He winced slightly. 'You'll have to redo my dressing soon. It's starting to hurt.'

'When the doctor comes this morning, I'll get him to take a look at it. And at Grandfather too, if he'll let him.'

'Huh,' Andrew snorted. 'There's about as much chance of that as me learning to fly.'

'Well, my dear, you've worked a miracle. I didn't expect to see Mrs Singleton still alive,' the doctor from the village told Bridie later that morning. 'I'll call each day for a while, but I think she's turned the corner. And as for Harry, well, I think you've arrived just in time to stop him sinking into a similar state.' The kindly man shook his head. 'Dear, dear, I had no idea things had got as bad as this. Someone should have called me.' He looked at her keenly. 'I understand you only arrived here yesterday?'

Bridie nodded.

'Who had been looking after them?'

'It had been Mrs Turner . . .'

'Ah, now that explains it,' he nodded.

Bridie forbore to explain Lil's part; she planned to speak to that particular lady herself very soon. 'But now I'm back and staying, things will be very different.'

'Good, good.' The doctor picked up his case. 'See

you tomorrow. If you have any problems, be sure to let me know and I'll come at once.'

Bridie's meeting with Lil was brief but fiery.

'Well, if that's how you feel, don't ask for my 'elp again,' the slovenly woman said huffily. Her apron was dirty and her hair hung down in unwashed, lank strands. She folded her arms across her ample bosom.

'Don't worry, I won't. I'm here to stay.'

Lil's face twisted into a sneer. 'Oh, staying alone in the cottage with Andrew, are yer? Yer grandfather won't like that.'

Bridie arched her eyebrow and glared at the woman whom she blamed for the sorry state she had found on her return.

She pointed an accusing finger at Lil. 'You mind your business and I'll mind mine. If there was a court of law to put you in for what you've done, I'd do it. As it is, I'll have you thrown out of your cottage if I get any more trouble.'

'Huh!' the woman sneered. 'Harry wouldn't throw me out. I've done a lot for Harry Singleton. Looking after his cantankerous mother, for a start.'

'You call that "looking after" someone? You don't know the meaning of the word.'

'He'll not get rid of me.' The woman was smug as she delivered her final ace. 'I clean his precious chapel.'

Bridie laughed aloud, the sound echoing down the narrow street. 'Is that all? There's plenty of folk willing to do that. And they'd do it a lot better than you, I shouldn't wonder.'

For the first time a flicker of uncertainty crossed Lil's face. 'Who?'

Bridie grinned in her moment of triumph. 'Me, Lil. Me. I'd clean his chapel for him. In fact, from now on I will.' Her face sobered as she said threateningly, 'You keep your distance from me and mine from now on. And remember what I said. I'll have you thrown out on the street if you don't.'

The woman gave a snarl and slammed the door in Bridie's face, but the girl had seen the look of fear on Lil's face. She would not trouble them again.

'Now, Josh, have you got everything you need?' Eveleen asked, as the three of them sat down to dinner in their city home. 'Is your room all right for you?'

Josh cast her a comical look. 'It's fine. A bit too posh, though, for the likes of me, mi duck.'

The three of them laughed together.

'I know what you mean, Josh. I felt just the same when I first married Richard.' Laughing at herself, she added, 'But it's surprising how quickly you can get used to the easy life.'

'Oh, I wouldn't say you've had it easy. Not over the last few years, anyway.'

'We've been lucky, though.' Her voice was husky as she reached across the corner of the table to touch her husband's hand. 'At least Richard's come home safely. The rest is up to us now.'

Richard raised his head slowly and looked into her eyes. He turned his hand beneath hers and gripped it like a drowning man.

Hoarsely he said, 'You're right. It is up to us now.'

Momentarily they forgot that Josh was in the room. For a brief moment, there was no-one else in the world but the two of them. In that instant, a new understanding, a fresh determination to put matters right between them, began to blossom.

Josh cleared his throat, startling them from their mutual reverie. 'Aye, you're right. So many haven't come back or, if they have, they're so badly damaged that their lives can never be the same again.'

'I'm afraid,' Eveleen said quietly, 'that's what you're going to face at the factory. There are so many pleading for jobs and yet . . .' She sighed heavily. 'I don't know whether they're capable of the work.'

'I expected as much. But we'll cope, mi duck. I'll explain it all to Bob, an' all. Make him understand that I've only come back temporary. Just to help out a bit. You leave it to me, Evie.'

The weeks turned into months. At Flawford, Bridie's days were exhausting, yet she was happy just to be with Andrew, content, for the moment, to bide her time. His health improved rapidly and his wound began to heal, so well now that he was champing at the bit to begin some kind of work.

'I'm going to talk to Harry about the workshops. I can't understand what's happened. Why is no-one working there, even if he can't any more?'

'I don't know. Go and ask him.'

'Right, I will.' He moved to the door eagerly and then hesitated. He turned back to her and said, 'Will you come with me?'

'Coward!' she joked, but moved to his side. 'Come on, let's beard the lion in his den together.'

Once, he could have been called a lion, with a fine mane of hair and head of the pride. But now the old warrior was laid low by infirmity.

'It's only us, Grandfather,' Bridie called out cheerfully as she opened the door. 'Me and Andrew.'

'What do you want now, girl?' he asked gruffly. She was still not welcome in his home, but he did now eat the meals she prepared, though she was always careful to make sure that Andrew took them along the pathway to his cottage.

'Andrew's come to talk to you about the workshops. What happened, Grandfather? Why is no-one working there any more?'

'What's it to do with you?'

Bridie and Andrew exchanged a glance, then she shrugged helplessly, gesturing that Andrew should carry on the conversation. She certainly wasn't going to get anywhere.

'I just wondered,' he began hesitantly, 'if you'd like me to get things going again?'

'We were doing all right. The women Eveleen sent did all right. I'll give her that,' he added grudgingly. 'Three of 'em got quite good on the machines and the others did the seaming, the winding or the washing, an' that. But when the war finished, they was off back to the city life. The old feller that was here gave up and the boy went to work in the city an' all. And,' he added bitterly, unwilling to admit failure, 'my eyesight isn't what it was. So, young Burns . . .' To Harry Singleton, Andrew would always be 'young Burns'. 'What do you want to do with my workshops?'

'Get them working again, Mr Singleton. Get this yard back to what it used to be.'

'Then what are you waiting for, young Burns? What are you waiting for?'

Fifty-Seven

Eveleen had not felt so happy since before Richard volunteered. Every day he was improving and the previous night he had made love to her for the first time.

At the breakfast table she could not hide the glow of happiness on her face and she was hard pressed not to laugh aloud at Richard's somewhat sheepish expression as he said, 'It's a good job Josh leaves early for work. I'm sure he'd guess.'

Eveleen giggled deliciously, like a young bride. 'I don't care if he does. Oh, darling Richard, we're going to be all right.' She held him close and he buried his face in her neck.

'Yes, yes. I really think we are.'

Even the letter that Smithers brought in on a silver tray moments later, could not cast a shadow over her new-found confidence.

'It's from Bridie.'

Already they knew about the situation Bridie and Andrew had found at Flawford. Eveleen had visited once, going alone, guiltily persuading Richard not to go. But the atmosphere between aunt and niece had been strained and Eveleen had not been able to bring herself to go recently. She felt ashamed that she had not visited again and therefore eagerly scanned the letter for news.

'Things are much better,' she said. 'Andrew's opening up the workshops.' She looked up briefly. 'Do you know, I hadn't realized the machines were idle, but now I think about it, I didn't hear any noise the day I went.'

'Andrew will soon have things up and running again. He'll find plenty of men coming back from the war who are only too glad of a job,' Richard said.

'Mm,' Eveleen agreed and returned to reading the letter. 'Gran's asking to see my mother.' Then she gave a little gasp of surprise. 'Bridie wants to know if we can arrange it.'

Richard shrugged. 'I don't see why not. Would you like me to take her? It's high time I started driving again.'

'No,' Eveleen's reply was swift – perhaps a little too swift, but Richard did not appear to notice. 'No. I – we'll – go out to the farm this afternoon and see what they want to do. All right?'

'Anything you say, darling.'

Eveleen felt the tears spring to her eyes, but they were tears of joy. His words were simple, but they spoke volumes to Eveleen. Her husband – her husband of old – was truly back home with her.

'Jimmy will take me. There's no need for you to bother. Not that I really want to go, but I suppose I'll have to. Maybe she's dying and that's why she wants to see me.'

Eveleen was appalled at the callous tone in her mother's voice. There had been a lot of bitterness in the past, but surely Mary did not still bear resentment against a frail, sick old lady – her own mother. But Eveleen made no comment, merely asking, 'How are you going to get there?'

Mary waved her hand airily. 'Oh, Jimmy will borrow something.'

'Josh can bring the car home on Saturday. He could take you on Sunday. I don't think it would be a good idea for Jimmy to go.'

'Why ever not?' Mary snapped, defensive at once.

Eveleen sighed. 'He'll only cause trouble with Andrew if he goes.'

'No, he won't. And I want Jimmy to take me. I'll only go if Jimmy takes me. So there.'

Sometimes, Eveleen thought crossly, her mother was like a petulant child. 'Then Jimmy,' she snapped back before she had stopped to think, 'can find his own means of transport, if that's how you feel.'

'It's all right, darling,' Richard said. 'Josh can still bring the car and Jimmy can drive it.' He turned towards Jimmy. 'You can drive, I take it?'

''Course I can. Nothing to it.'

But Eveleen had the distinct feeling that his answer was based more on bravado than actual capability. She knew her brother of old.

Bridie read her aunt's letter with trepidation.

I'm afraid your gran insists that Jimmy should bring her. It's the only way she'll agree to come.

'You will keep out of his way, won't you?' Bridie begged Andrew. 'Please. I don't want any more trouble.'

Andrew's mouth was a grim line. 'I'll not start anything. I'll promise you that much, but if he starts something . . .'

Bridie sighed. It was the best she could hope for.

The following Sunday was bright and warm. *They'll be coming in the morning. Your gran won't want to risk being forced to attend chapel*, Eveleen had written.

Though Bridie still went and sat in the family pew

next to her grandfather, just as she had done before, she could not persuade Andrew to attend the services.

'I've lost me faith, Bridie,' he told her. 'After all that I've seen in the war, there is no God in heaven.'

'Oh, Andrew, it wasn't God who caused the war, but the greed of men. You can't blame him.'

He'd looked away from her, ill at ease. 'I know I shouldn't, but he let it happen, didn't he?'

For the moment there was nothing she could do or say. Andrew would have to find his way back in his own time. In the meantime, her knees became quite sore from praying for her beloved Andrew.

Bridie fussed over the Sunday dinner, acutely nervous that everything should be just perfect. But it was not so much the preparation of the food that caused her concern, but the worry of the trouble Jimmy's mere presence might cause.

They arrived at half-past ten and came to the far-end cottage.

'Where is she, then?' Mary demanded curtly, with scarcely a greeting to Bridie.

'In bed, Gran. She can't get down the stairs now, though she sometimes can manage to sit in a chair by her bedroom window.'

Mary climbed the stairs, Bridie following her closely, torn between being with her great-grandmother during the visit and keeping an eye on Jimmy.

'Here she is, Great-Gran.' Bridie forced herself to say brightly as she opened the bedroom door and ushered Mary inside. 'Here, Gran, sit in this chair by the bed.'

Mary sat down and stared at the old lady in the bed. 'You're looking well, Mother.'

'Stuff and nonsense,' the old lady retorted with asperity and Bridie hid her smile. Old and frail she might be physically, but Bridget Singleton was still quite capable of dealing with a visit from her daughter.

'I'll leave you to it,' she said, confident now of leaving them together. 'I'll call you when dinner is ready.'

Downstairs she went through to the front room to check on the joint, sizzling in the oven in the range.

The room was empty; Jimmy had disappeared.

Bridie ran out of the cottage and along the footpath, bursting into her grandfather's cottage. 'Is he here?'

She glanced round the room, but Harry was sitting alone in his usual place by the range. 'Is who here?' he grumbled and Bridie realized she had awoken him from a nap.

'Oh, never mind.' She turned and hurried out again. There was no-one in Andrew's cottage either.

'I'll be in the workshop. I don't reckon he'll come up there,' Andrew had told Bridie earlier. 'Though your grandfather won't like it if he knows I'm working on the Sabbath.'

'If it prevents trouble,' Bridie had said, 'I think the Good Lord will overlook it this once.'

Bridie ran down the path towards the workshops, tripping on an uneven brick in her haste. She climbed the stone steps and heard their voices in the workroom above her. She paused to listen.

Andrew's was raised in anger. 'How dare you say such a thing about her? It's not true. None of it. I'll smash your face in.'

Jimmy's voice came nonchalant and tormenting. 'If you don't believe me, ask Eveleen. She'll tell you.'

Oh no, Bridie groaned inwardly. Even after all these years, they're still fighting over my poor mother.

Fifty-Eight

'Andrew! What a lovely surprise. What brings you to Nottingham?' Eveleen cried, rising from the sofa and holding out her arms to greet him when Smithers showed him into the morning room. Then she saw the expression on his face. 'What is it? What's wrong?'

At once, she feared the worst. Was it her grandmother? Had the old lady died? But Andrew's expression was not one of kindly concern at being the bearer of sad tidings. It was anger that Eveleen saw on his face.

'Sit down. I'll get Smithers to bring us tea—'

'Don't bother.' His manner was curt. 'This isn't a social call, Eveleen, and when you've heard what I've got to say you'll likely have me thrown out.'

'Thrown out?' Eveleen gave a nervous laugh. 'Whatever could you have to say that . . .?' Her voice petered away and she sank back onto the sofa, feeling suddenly queasy in the pit of her stomach. Andrew remained standing.

'Your mother came to visit last week.'

'Yes, I know about that.'

'Jimmy brought her.'

'Oh!' Realization began to dawn. Once again Jimmy had tried to make trouble. She sighed.

'I tried to keep out of his way. For Bridie's sake. She asked me to. Now I know why,' he muttered in a low voice more to himself than for Eveleen to hear. Louder, he went on. 'But he found me. Sought me out in the workshop. He couldn't wait to tell me.'

There was a pause and Eveleen prompted. 'Tell you what?'

'That your husband and my Bridie are having a love affair.'

The room seemed to spin around her and the sick feeling increased so that she almost wanted to rush to the bathroom. She covered her face with her hands.

'Evie, I'm sorry.' Andrew came to sit beside her and put his arm about her. 'But I have to know. I have to know if it's true or if it's Jimmy up to his old tricks.'

In a low, muffled voice, Eveleen said, 'I haven't any proof, but I had suspected it.'

'You had?' Andrew sounded startled, as if he had fully expected her to refute any such suggestion.

Eveleen dropped her hands and turned to face him. She could see the incredulity on his face. He had clung to the belief that it was all Jimmy's lies and now the shock that it might actually be true was plainly written on his face.

Her voice was flat with defeat as she explained. 'Perhaps it started as long ago as the Goose Fair.'

'She was only a child then.'

'Yes, yes. Oh, I don't mean that he would have – but he might have started to care for her then in a way . . .' She took a deep breath. 'In a way that was not strictly uncle and niece.'

Andrew clenched his fist. 'I'll bloody well kill him.'

'He was always very fond of her, but – but it got more – more noticeable when he came back from the war. He was in a dreadful state. Shell-shocked, they call it. Bridie was the only one who could handle him. Tha was why he went to Fairfield House.' There was a wealth of sadness in her tone as she added, 'I couldn't help him. In fact, if I'm honest, I seemed to make matters worse.'

'Is it still going on? Because I don't see how they can have met up since we've been at Flawford. I've been with her all the time. Unless—'

'Unless what?'

He shrugged. 'Well, I've spent a lot of time in the workshops recently. I can't say that I know what she's been doing every minute of the day. When she's gone out shopping and that.'

Eveleen shook her head. 'I don't know for sure, but we've been together most of the time since he came home from Fairfield House.' There was a catch in her voice as she thought how close they had become once more. Was all that to be torn away from her again? 'But he did suggest,' she went on, her voice trembling, 'that he should drive my mother to Flawford.' They stared at each other as she went on, 'Perhaps – perhaps that was an excuse so that he could see her.'

'Where is he? I want to see him.'

'He's – he's out for a morning walk. He shouldn't be long.'

'Then I'll wait,' Andrew said grimly.

'Where's Andrew?' Harry asked belligerently when Bridie took his dinner.

'Gone to Nottingham.'

'To the lace market?' It seemed that Harry could bring himself to speak civilly to her if it was a matter of business.

'He didn't say.'

Bridie was worried about Andrew. He had been bad-tempered ever since Jimmy's visit last week. Worse still, he had been offhand with her and several times she had found him watching her with a strange expression on his face. She couldn't think what the matter was, other than that he was beginning to believe Jimmy's lies that he, Andrew, might be her natural father. But he had always been so adamant that that was impossible. Surely that meant he had never made physical love to Rebecca.

She had tried to question him, but each time he turned away from her, tight-lipped and uncommunicative. In the end, she had given up trying to coax him to tell her what was obviously bothering him.

'He'll be back,' Bridie said, forcing herself to be cheerful. 'Maybe he wants to surprise us with some good news about the workshops.'

Her grandfather gave a grunt as if he didn't believe it. And, for once, Bridie had to agree with him.

They heard the front door open and close, heard Richard greeting Smithers as the manservant took his master's coat and hat and heard the low murmur of their voices as he was told he was wanted in the morning room. They heard his footsteps cross the hall and then Richard was in the room and coming towards Andrew, his hand outstretched in greeting.

Andrew had risen from his seat, but made no effort to shake Richard's hand. Richard paused in puzzlement and glanced from Andrew to Eveleen and back again, realizing at once that something was dreadfully amiss.

'What is it? Is it bad news from Flawford?'

He moved towards Eveleen to put his arm about her, but she could not bear him to touch her and she moved away to stand near the window, leaving Andrew to broach the subject that was uppermost in both their minds.

'Eveleen?' Richard said, but as she turned her back on him, he looked towards Andrew for an explanation.

Andrew was blunt. 'Are you having an affair with Bridie?'

For a long moment Richard stared at him incredulously, as if he couldn't believe what he was hearing. 'An affair? With Bridie?' Then he began to laugh.

From her place by the window, Eveleen turned her head to look at him, but Andrew, his fists clenched took a step nearer to him.

'It's no laughing matter—'

'Oh, Andrew, Andrew . . .' Richard was reaching out to put his hand on Andrew's shoulder, but the latter knocked his arm away. Richard's face sobered as he glanced from one to the other. 'My God! You actually think such a preposterous idea is true?' He paused and now there was anger in his tone, yet it was tinged with sadness. 'How could you even think such a thing of me? Or of Bridie? Good God!' He was shouting now, incensed at their lack of faith in him. 'And you, Eveleen? How could you ever, *ever* think that about me? She's a child, for heaven's sake!'

Andrew shook his head slowly. 'Oh no, she isn't. Not now. When we went away, she was, but not any longer.' There was sadness in his own tone now as if he mourned a personal loss. 'While we were away, she grew up.'

'You want the truth? Well, you can have it. I do love Bridie – very much.' Now they stared at him and Eveleen gave a little whimper and pressed the back of her hand to her mouth. 'But as my *niece* and, latterly, as my nurse. She was the only one who could help me when I came back from the war. She was the only one who took the time to understand . . .' His words were a direct, hurtful accusation aimed at Eveleen. 'She *cared*.' Now he turned to Andrew and pointed his forefinger at him. 'And you, Andrew Burns, are the biggest bloody fool around. That girl has spent her life loving you. Even as a little girl she always said she was going to marry you. And, as far as I know, now she's a grown woman she still feels the same. Though God alone knows why. And she is a grown woman, despite her tender years, because what she's seen and dealt with in the time she's been nursing is more than you, Eveleen,' he swung round once more to include her, 'have ever experienced in your life and that includes the hard times you had as a girl.'

'Richard, I'm sorry . . .' she began, moving towards him, reaching out to him. But he held up his hands, palms outwards, to fend her off.

He turned on his heel and went towards the door, flinging it open. He looked back over his shoulder and addressed his final words to Andrew. 'I just hope she's got the sense to find someone more worthy than you for all that love she's got in her heart.'

Then he left the room, slamming the door behind him and leaving the two of them staring after him.

'Oh, Andrew,' Eveleen whispered, the tears running down her face, 'what have we done?'

Fifty-Nine

'I'm sorry, Evie.' They were sitting on the sofa, Eveleen weeping against Andrew's shoulder. 'There I go, crashing in with my big feet and all I've done is cause trouble between you and Richard.'

Eveleen hiccuped miserably. 'We'd only just got back to something like we used to be. And now . . .' Her tears flowed afresh.

Andrew hugged her. 'Me and my big mouth. I'm so sorry. I'll go and find him. Explain that it was my fault.'

Eveleen shook her head. 'It won't do any good. He could see I believed it too. Besides, I heard the front door bang. He's gone out again. Oh . . .' she cried. 'I think I'm going to be sick.' She got up and hurried from the room, holding her hand over her mouth. She only just reached the bathroom before she began to retch. When the spasm had passed she went back downstairs to find Andrew still waiting for her in the morning room.

'All right?' he asked, rather unnecessarily, for Eveleen's face was deathly white and she was shivering as if with a fever. But she nodded and sat down, gripping her hands together in her lap.

'What are you going to tell Bridie?'

He was silent for a moment before he answered. 'I'm going to ask her to marry me.' He paused and then muttered, 'If she'll still have me after this.'

She looked up, startled. 'What? But I thought you didn't think of her in – in that way. I thought you loved her, well, more as if she was your daughter.'

He smiled sheepishly. 'I did. Or at least I thought I did. But when Jimmy told me about her and Richard, well, I saw red. I was in a blind, jealous rage, Evie. The jealous rage of a man who's in love with the woman he was talking about.'

He passed his hand across his forehead, still feeling confused. 'I didn't think I could ever stop loving Rebecca. I thought that what I felt for Bridie was because she's Rebecca's daughter. But not now. Not any more. Jimmy's shown me that, even though I could have killed him for saying what he did. And when I got here this morning I could have killed Richard.' He looked Eveleen straight in the face. 'If he hadn't been so obviously telling the truth – and yes, I do believe him – I might very well have throttled him.' He shook his head as if he couldn't quite believe what he was hearing himself say. 'This war's changed us, Evie. We think nothing now of taking another man's life. Isn't that terrible?'

Staring at him, Eveleen nodded slowly.

Andrew stood up. 'If you're sure there's nothing I can do to put matters right, then I'll go.' He looked down at her once more. 'I'm so sorry, Evie,' he said hoarsely.

By dusk Richard had still not returned home and Eveleen lay on her bed, her eyes swollen but now, for the moment at least, she could cry no more. She had eaten nothing since breakfast and now her stomach rumbled with hunger and yet she still felt sick.

And yet, she began to realize, this queasy feeling had

not just occurred today. She had been feeling unwell for several days now, especially first thing in the morning.

She rubbed her stomach, gently over the place where her womb lay. Was it possible? Could she really – after all this time – be with child?

And then, as she realized what terrible damage this day's events had wrought, the tears came again.

In the moment that should have brought her the greatest happiness of her life, she was plunged into the depths of despair.

'Where have you been? I've been worried sick.'

'Oh, Bridie.' Andrew held out his arms to her. 'I've done a dreadful thing today.'

After a moment of surprised hesitation, Bridie went to him to be enfolded in his embrace. He hugged her so tightly he almost squeezed the breath from her body. 'What is it?' she whispered. 'Tell me.'

So, almost as if he were kneeling in the chapel, but instead standing with his face buried against her neck, Andrew made his confession. So, Bridie thought as she listened to him, the quarrel she had overheard between her father and Andrew had not been about Rebecca as she had supposed. It had been about her. She heard him out until the very end and then, gently, she drew back and put her fingers beneath his chin to lift his face and to look into his eyes. 'Why didn't you ask me?'

He could not meet her gaze. 'I couldn't. I was that mad, that – that jealous.'

She shook her head sadly. 'You didn't trust me, did you? You really thought it could be true?'

Shamefaced, he nodded. She uttered no word of reproach, but merely took him into her arms now and held him close for a long time. At last she said, 'Poor Auntie Evie. I must go to her.'

'Oh, Bridie, I shouldn't. I've caused enough trouble.'

'I'm not going to cause any trouble, Andrew. I'm the only one who can sort it all out. I'll go tomorrow morning. I'll leave everything ready for the old folks here. And you,' she tapped him playfully on the nose, 'will have to look after them both.'

Andrew looked askance, but – as Bridie knew full well – he was in no position to argue.

When she was shown into the morning room the following morning, Eveleen ran into her arms with a sob. Bridie held her and patted her back comfortingly. 'It'll be all right, Auntie Evie, I promise. It's not true. Not a word of it. You do know that, don't you?'

Eveleen nodded and they sat down side by side on the sofa. 'I do now, but . . .'

'You mean, you thought for a while that it was?'

'Oh, Bridie, I've been so silly. I don't know what got into me. But – but you seemed to be able to do so much more for Richard than I could. You and he seemed so – so close.'

'I told you,' Bridie said gently, but very firmly, 'it was because I'd seen so much of it at the home that I could understand. Besides, although I love Uncle Richard dearly – *as an uncle*,' she emphasized with a smile, 'I was still able to deal with it rationally. To separate myself just a little. It's very difficult, you know, for families to help their nearest and dearest.'

'Is it?' Eveleen did not sound convinced. 'I thought it should be me, more than anyone else, who could help him.'

Bridie shook her head. 'No, it's not always the case. Believe me.'

'I do,' Eveleen said simply and they both knew that she was not merely referring to Bridie's nursing knowledge.

'So,' Bridie asked, 'where is he?'

'I don't know,' Eveleen said and her voice threatened to rise again into a despairing wail. 'He didn't come home last night. I don't know where he is.'

'Didn't . . .' Bridie began incredulously, but she could see by her aunt's face that it was all too true. More practically, she asked, 'Then where do you think he might be? At his parents?'

Eveleen shook her head. 'I've already sent word to see. He's not there. Oh, Bridie . . .' she clutched at the girl. 'I'm so afraid he might have – might have done something awful. He was so angry. So hurt.'

Bridie shook her head. 'Uncle Richard wouldn't do that. He's just taken himself off somewhere to be alone.' She thought for a moment and then her expression brightened. 'Has he taken the motor?'

Eveleen nodded.

'Can you borrow another motor car from somewhere?'

'I suppose so,' Eveleen said. 'I expect his father would lend me his.'

'Right then. Send Smithers to fetch it and get your coat and hat. We're taking a trip into the countryside.'

'Why? Where do you think he's gone? Flawford?'

Bridie shook her head. 'No. Fairfield House, of course.' She knew that there was still a skeleton staff at the home. 'It's where he felt safe. Where else would he go?'

Sixty

'He wouldn't go to Pear Tree Farm, would he? To have it out with Jimmy?' Eveleen asked as she drove, a little unsteadily, out of the city.

'I hope not,' Bridie said grimly. 'Else there might be fisticuffs again.' They drove a little further and then Bridie asked suddenly, 'Does Josh know about any of this?' She was aware that Josh was staying with Richard and Eveleen.

'No. I avoided him this morning.' Eveleen smiled wryly. 'One look at me and he'd have known something was wrong. I can't hide much from Josh.'

'So, he doesn't know the trouble my dear father's been causing?'

'No. Apart from the fact that he's been the cause of Josh agreeing to run the factory for us for a while. He'd never have wanted to leave my mother if it hadn't been for Jimmy being there. Josh felt pushed out.'

The rest of the journey passed in silence, but as they drove up the driveway of Fairfield House, Bridie said, 'Now, I need to talk to Uncle Richard alone first. You go down to the beck, Auntie Evie, and wait there. If – if everything's all right, I'll send him to you.'

'Why do you need to see him alone?' Was there even yet a faint hint of mistrust in her?

Bridie eyed her, as if guessing. 'It would be awkward with you there too. You must see that. I need to give him some straight talking. I need to tell him how things have been for you while he's been away. Don't you see? These returning soldiers have no idea what we went through back here. Oh, I'm not suggesting that we've experienced anything like they've been through. But it hasn't been easy, has it, suddenly left alone to cope? Especially for us weak and feeble women.'

Bridie was laughing and even Eveleen had to smile. 'Once upon a time, I'd have said I was a strong woman,' she said, 'but not any more. I'm as weak as a kitten.' She turned to face her niece, this young girl of whom she was so proud. If only . . . She pushed the thoughts away. She must begin to trust again and what better moment to start than right here. Right now.

She nodded and climbed out of the vehicle. 'I'll go round the house and through the back yard and down to the beck. But what if he's not here?'

'He will be,' Bridie said confidently. 'But if not, I'll come to you.' She jumped down and set off towards the front steps, whilst Eveleen disappeared round the side of the house.

'He's in the gardens, miss,' the maid, who answered the door, told her.

'Thanks, I'll find him.'

She found Richard sitting on the wooden seat in the rose garden, staring straight ahead at the golden blooms in front of him, yet she knew he was seeing nothing of their beauty.

'Hello, Uncle Richard,' she called as she approached and sat down beside him.

He turned his head slowly as if waking from a dream, or rather a nightmare, to look at her. 'I'm surprised you dare be seen in my company. I'm supposed to have seduced you and we're having this passionate affair.'

She grinned at him, but there was no answering smile. 'Daft, isn't it?' she said.

He sighed. 'From your point of view, yes. But from mine, well . . .' He lapsed into silence.

'Why from my point of view?' she asked.

'I'm old enough to be your father, for heaven's sake,' he said testily.

'So's Andrew, but I'm going to marry him.'

'Are you?' There was a faint humour in his tone. 'Does Andrew know?'

Bridie giggled. 'Oh yes, but so far, he's refused me.'

They smiled together but then the smile faded from Richard's face. 'So what you're saying is,' he said slowly, 'that it's quite possible for other people to have thought that I – that we . . .'

She nodded. 'Of course it is. A lot of older men marry younger women. Now, just you listen to me.' She tapped him on the arm, demanding his attention. 'Look at it from Auntie Evie's point of view. You rush off to war leaving her to cope with the factory and then, when you come back, you're like a mardy child because she can't stay with you every minute of the day and hold your hand. Besides, she didn't know how to deal with you. How could she? You came back a different person from the man who went away. And then the only person you want is me! Just put yourself in her place for a minute. How must she have felt?'

'She should know I love her. That I've never loved anyone but her.'

Bridie leant forward and said gently, 'I know it's none of my business, but wasn't she hurt, years ago, by a young man she thought loved her? Didn't she trust him and he let her down?'

Richard nodded. 'Stephen Dunsmore. He lived here at Fairfield House.'

'How old was she?'

'Seventeen, I think.'

'The same age as I am now,' she said softly. 'But, you see, I'm lucky. I've never loved anyone – in that way – but Andrew. My only sadness is that he doesn't love me in return, but it doesn't – can't – stop me loving him. But don't you think that being let down like that at that age – the first big love of her life and he callously rejected her – don't you think it scars a young girl for the rest of her life? Do you think she can trust anyone completely ever again? Even you?'

He stared at her. 'Why,' he asked slowly, 'are you so very sensible?'

She laughed ruefully. 'I'm anything but sensible if I spend the whole of my life hankering after someone who doesn't love me.'

Richard made a sound deep in his throat – a sound that was suspiciously like a chuckle. 'If I'm not mistaken, Andrew is finding out that he does indeed love you – in that way, as you put it. Why else would he come looking to kill me? There was murder in his eyes yesterday, Bridie. And don't think I haven't seen that look far too often in the last few years not to be able to recognize it.'

'Then maybe I have something to thank my father for, after all. Only don't let his lies come between you and Auntie Evie. She's desperately unhappy. Every bit,' she added, 'as miserable as you look.'

'Where is she?'

'Down by the beck.'

He rose from the seat. 'I'll go to her.' He looked

down at her, then suddenly he bent and kissed her cheek. 'You're a great girl, Bridie. I just hope Andrew comes to his senses and realizes what a lucky chap, he is.'

Bridie giggled and blushed. 'So do I, Uncle Richard. So do I.'

'Are you coming with me?'

'No, no, you must talk to her on your own now. Besides . . .' She too rose. 'There's something else I have to do. I'm going to Pear Tree Farm, but I'll go round by the road.'

She stood on tiptoe and returned his kiss.

Eveleen waited by the beck, scarcely able to sit still on the rock by the flowing stream. Every few seconds she glanced back towards the yard of Fairfield House, praying that Richard would appear. But the minutes ticked by so slowly and she had begun to give up hope, tears welling in her eyes so that the sun glinting on the water blurred her vision. Impatiently she brushed her tears away and glanced up the field once more. This time she saw him coming towards her.

She was motionless, just staring at him, holding her breath. Then, halfway down the field, he held out his arms wide to her. Her heart began to thud and, with a little sob, she rose and began to run up the slope towards him.

Sixty-One

The yard at Pear Tree Farm seemed deserted. Only hens scratched about the place and the noise of pigs scuffling in the sty.

As Bridie pushed open the gate and stepped through it, the back door of the farmhouse opened and Mary came into the yard.

She flung her arms wide and gave a heartrending wail. 'Oh, Bridie, he's gone. My Jimmy. My Jimmy's gone away and left me again.'

Here we go again, Bridie thought, as she steered the weeping woman back into the house, pushed her gently into a chair and scurried between scullery and hearth, making her grandmother a strong, sweet cup of tea.

'There,' she said, placing it on the table at her side. 'Drink this and tell me what happened.'

She poured herself a cup and sat down to listen.

Mary took the cup in both hands and drank thirstily. She placed the cup down with shaking hands and leant back in her chair, closing her eyes and sighing deeply. 'When we got back from Flawford that day, he just disappeared upstairs. I was busy down here, getting his tea, but then he appeared with his kitbag and dressed in his naval uniform and announced that he was off. Back to sea. He said he was fully fit now and that if he didn't report back, the authorities were bound to come looking for him sooner or later, specially now that Fairfield

House had closed as a home. I tried to argue with him . . .' Her tears welled again, but she continued, 'I told him there was no need to go that very minute. I begged him to stay a little longer, but he was adamant. He said he had to go. "They'll come looking for me," he said. "I have to go." '

'Gran,' Bridie said gently, taking hold of her hands. 'I don't think it was the authorities he was worried about. Not really.'

Mary stared at her. 'Why? What do you mean?'

Bridie sighed. 'Whilst you were at Flawford talking to Great-Gran, he went looking for Andrew. He went looking to cause trouble. Again!'

'What sort of trouble?'

'He told Andrew that he thought Uncle Richard and me were having a love affair.'

Mary blinked and stared at her. 'How – why did he think that?'

'When Uncle Richard came home from the war, I seemed to be the only one who could help him. But there was nothing more than that between us. I promise you.'

To the girl's surprise, her grandmother snorted and said, 'Well, I know that, girl. I could have told him that. Richard's only ever loved Eveleen. Everyone knows that.' She thought a moment before saying slowly, 'So you think he believed Andrew would come looking for him?'

'Not only Andrew,' Bridie said wryly. 'Andrew went straight to Eveleen and, sadly, she believed him.'

'Eveleen did? The silly girl.'

'Then Richard came home and Andrew tackled him about it. He was dreadfully angry – and hurt. When Andrew came home yesterday and told me what had happened, I went to Nottingham this morning. Richard didn't go home last night and poor Auntie Evie was frantic. But I guessed he'd have come back to Fairfield House and he had. I've had a talk with him and they're together now.' She squeezed Mary's hands. 'Let's hope everything's getting sorted out between them right this minute.'

Mary nodded. 'Why on earth did Eveleen believe it? She must know how much Richard cares for her.'

'She was hurt years ago, wasn't she? I expect there's still a tiny part of her that is unsure. Always will be, probably. You've been very lucky, Gran. You've been loved by two wonderful men. You've never know what it is to be rejected by the man you love, have you?'

There was a silence in the room that seemed to go on and on until Mary said softly, 'Yes, I have, love. Oh yes, I have. At least, I thought so at the time. Now – well – now, I'm not so sure.'

Bridie had the sense to remain silent. She waited, willing her grandmother to tell her more, yet not wanting to press her. Doing so might have the opposite effect.

As dusk crept into the room and their faces were illuminated by the firelight, Mary began to talk.

'I fell in love with a young man when I was about your age. Desperately in love and, I thought, for ever. But his parents – and mine too, for that matter – did not approve. Then he went away and I found I was pregnant and that, to my family – my father and my brother, Harry – was the worst sin a woman could possibly commit. I thought that my young man had gone away deliberately, that he had deserted me when I needed him most. My family made my life hell and so I ran away. I worked wherever I could and I ended up here, working on the Dunsmore estate.' Her voice was flat and unemotional in the telling of her sorry tale, yet Bridie could feel the tragedy behind her words. 'I gave birth to my child in a ditch at the side of a field with only a gypsy woman to hold my hand. There in the dark and the cold, my baby died. I would have done too, if it hadn't been for your grandfather, Walter Hardcastle, who took me in and cared for me and eventually married me. Walter was a good man, a kind man. If it hadn't been for him, I don't know what would have become of me.'

She fell silent and now Bridie could not help asking, 'And your young man, your first love? Did you ever meet him again?'

Mary nodded and smiled, though the smile was tinged with sadness for her lost love. 'Oh yes, and according to him, he was deceived by his parents. He vows he never knew of my plight. They knew, of course, but he was only nineteen and when they sent him away to complete his education he obeyed, thinking that when he came back he would be of age and no-one could stop us marrying. But when he did return home, I had disappeared and he couldn't find me.'

'Do you believe him?'

Slowly Mary nodded. 'Yes, I do believe him. He's a good man, too. A fine man. Don't you think so?'

'Me?' Bridie was startled. 'How should I know?' She thought for a moment and then realization began to dawn. 'You mean – you mean, I *know* him?'

Mary nodded.

Then Bridie's face cleared. 'Oh, it's Josh. You found each other after all and . . .'

But her grandmother was shaking her head. 'No, no,

it wasn't Josh. Though he's a wonderful man and I'm a very lucky woman. No, my first love was the man who is now Eveleen's father-in-law. It was Brinsley Stokes.'

Bridie walked back to Fairfield House, her mind in a whirl at her grandmother's revelations. She had guessed something of the sort, though only part of it. She couldn't, of course, have guessed about the baby. Her mind reeled at the thought that Mary, of all people, should have had a child out of wedlock. And that Brinsley Stokes should have been the father. She tried to imagine them as young people, innocent and so in love. And the strands of their lives were still entwined all these years later, yet a lifetime of happiness together had been denied them.

She found Eveleen and Richard sitting on the sofa in what had been the patients' recreation room, their arms around each other. They looked up and smiled at her as she entered the room, but they did not move apart.

'Gran's in an awful state, Auntie Evie. My father's upped and gone again.'

'Oh no!' Evie buried her face against Richard's shoulder and then she looked up and sighed heavily. 'I'd better go to her.'

Bridie shook her head. 'I think the best thing you could do, Auntie Evie, is to get back to Nottingham as quickly as possible and tell Josh.'

Eveleen nodded. 'You're right.' She smiled and added pointedly, 'As always.'

As they rose from the sofa, Richard reminded them, 'We've two cars to drive back, you know. And we've to take Bridie back to Flawford.'

Flawford lay to the south of Nottingham and was a little out of the way of their direct route back to the city.

Eveleen thought for a moment and then said, 'You take Bridie and I'll go straight home to Josh.'

She noticed that Richard and Bridie glanced at each other and then they both stared at her.

'What? What's the matter?'

'Are you sure about that?' Richard asked, hardly able to keep the smile from twitching at the corner of his mouth, whilst Bridie grinned openly.

'Oh, you!' Eveleen said and held her arms wide to embrace both of them. The three of them stood together, their arms about each other, laughing and crying together. But now their tears were tears of joy.

It was late when Eveleen reached home, but Josh was still waiting up for her.

'I've been worried all evening. Smithers said you went off this morning very upset. Oh, Evie, it's not Mary, is it? Is she all right?'

'Sit down, Josh, and I'll tell you, but first let me ring for a cup of tea. I'm parched.'

She told him briefly that she and Richard had had a misunderstanding but that everything was fine now. Then gently she took his hands into hers. 'Josh, Jimmy's left and Mam's in a dreadful state.'

He pulled his hands from hers and levered himself up. 'Then I must go to her at once. Poor Mary. My poor, poor Mary. What a thoughtless lad that son of hers is.' He glanced down apologetically. 'Sorry, mi duck. I know he's your brother, but . . .'

'Don't apologize to me, Josh,' Eveleen said, with

feeling and hearing the tone of her voice, Josh looked puzzled.

Eveleen sighed. 'It was Jimmy who caused the trouble between me and Richard. He – he told Andrew that Richard was having an affair with Bridie. And, of course, Andrew came straight here.'

'He – said – what?' For a moment, Josh's face was like thunder. 'It's a good job he has gone, then 'cos at this moment I could break his bloody neck. How could he say a thing like that about our Bridie – or Richard, for that matter?'

'He's always liked causing trouble,' Eveleen said bitterly. 'Even as a young boy. It was like throwing a stone into a pond and watching the ripples, only Jimmy liked to do it with people's lives.'

'But his own daughter? How could he treat his own daughter like that?'

'I know, Josh. I know,' Eveleen said sadly. 'But he won't acknowledge that she is his.'

'Poor child,' Josh murmured but then added tartly. 'Mind you, I reckon she's better off without him, but mebbe she doesn't see it that way.'

'I'm not so sure now,' Eveleen said thoughtfully. 'If anything good has come out of all his lies and trouble-making, it's made Andrew see sense where Bridie's concerned. I don't think we need to worry about her any more. She's going to get what she's always wanted.' Her smiled broadened. 'Andrew.'

Josh smiled. 'That's all right, then.' Then his face sobered. 'But now I must get home to my Mary.'

'Tonight? But it's late, Josh. Won't you . . .' She did not finish the sentence for Josh was shaking his head emphatically. 'No, I must go to her now. Can you get Fred Martin to drive me back? I know it's late, but I'm not much of a driver at the best of times, Evie. I'll pay him, but I must get back to her. She'll need me now.' He needed to say no more. He was in such a state of anxiety himself that he was not safe to attempt to drive.

Eveleen stood up too. 'I'm sure he will. I'll send Smithers to Fred's straight away.' She stepped closer and put her arms as far round the big man's girth as she could. 'Do you know something, Josh Carpenter? I think you're one of the kindest men I know. It was my lucky day when I met you.'

Josh patted her shoulder and his voice shook a little as he said, 'And mine too, mi duck, and mine too.'

As Richard drew the motor car to a halt in the narrow street outside Singleton's Yard, he said, 'I won't come in, Bridie. It's late and I want to get home. But whilst we're alone I want to thank you for all you've done for me and I'm only sorry that my – my dependence on you has caused trouble for you.'

In the dusk, she smiled up at him. 'As long as you're well again and everything is all right between you and Auntie Evie, that's all that matters.'

'Not all, my dear. We want your happiness too, you know. You're very dear to both of us.'

'Well, I'm hoping I might have some good news for you soon. Wedding bells, you know.'

He clasped her hand and leant across the space between them to kiss her cheek. 'Good luck then, my dear little Bridie.'

Bridie climbed down and stood watching whilst he turned the motor around and drove off down the street. And if I'm not much mistaken, she was thinking as she waved him off, Auntie Evie might be giving you a bit of good news too very soon.

Smiling to herself, she opened the gate and stepped into the yard.

Sixty-Two

'I've been a bloody fool. Can you forgive me?'

Bridie wound her arms around Andrew's neck and smiled impishly up at him. 'I'll think about it.'

'So, when are we going to be married?'

'Well!' she exclaimed and stood back. 'If that isn't the most unromantic proposal a girl ever had.'

'Oh, Bridie, I'm sorry.' He ran his hand nervously through his hair.

Bridie chuckled and hugged him. 'I'm only teasing you. Of course, we'll be married as soon as possible. If only to stop the gossips,' she joked.

'Who do I ask for permission? Your grandfather?'

Her smile faded and she straightened up. Sadly she said, 'I wish it was. Oh, how I wish it was. But he still doesn't want anything to do with me, does he?' She sighed. 'My own father won't acknowledge me and nor will my grandfather.'

Andrew touched her cheek and said softly, 'I'll make it up to you, darling Bridie.'

She held his hand to her cheek. 'I know you will . . .' she hesitated.

'But it's not the same for you, is it, love?'

Tears were close as she shook her head and whispered. 'I'm sorry, but no, it isn't. It isn't my father so much. Now I've met him and see him for what he really is, well, he's smashed those particular dreams, but – but – it's grandfather I really care about now. If only . . .'

'Maybe in time, he'll come around.'

'Maybe,' she said, but the doubt was evident in her tone.

'I tried,' Andrew told her later the following day.

'What did he say?'

Andrew bit his lip, reluctant to tell her but Bridie was insistent.

'He – he said the same old thing. That he has no granddaughter.'

There was a lump in her throat as she whispered, 'I expected as much.' But still, deep inside her, there was a little spark of hope that refused to die completely.

Over the weeks that followed she planned her wedding.

'I shall come,' her great-grandmother said. 'Ne'er mind what Harry ses, I'll be there, Bridie. Someone'll have to take me across to the chapel in a bath chair, but I'll be there.'

'I'm counting on it, Great-Gran.'

'Who are you asking to give you away?'

'I – I haven't asked anyone yet. But I suppose it'll have to be Josh, because Uncle Richard is to be Andrew's best man.'

'You're still hoping that old fool will come round, aren't you? Well, don't waste yer life wishing, love.'

Bridie turned away. She knew her great-grandmother was right. They were all right. And yet . . .

*

It was three weeks before the day of her wedding, when Bridie was passing the door of her grandfather's cottage as she returned from the village shop, that she heard a huge crash from inside and the smashing of crockery. At once she dumped her bags on the ground and opened the door to find Harry struggling to get up from the floor. She hurried to his side to help him.

'Grandfather, what happened? Are you hurt?'

His trembling hands reached out in front of him to grasp hold of something – anything.

'Sit down in the chair,' she ordered.

He shuffled backwards, allowing her to guide him now. Then, fumbling, he found her arms and grasped them so strongly that she almost cried out in pain. 'Bridie . . .' he gasped, clinging to her like a drowning man. 'Bridie – I can't see. I can't see anything.'

She stared at him for a moment, but already she could see that his eyes, though wide open, were seeing nothing. He was staring ahead, but he was unable to focus. He could not see her. He could not see anything.

She wriggled from his grasp and then took hold of his hands in hers. 'It's all right, Grandfather. I'll get the doctor. Maybe it's only temporary. You'll be all right . . .'

He shook his head. 'No, no, I won't. My sight's been getting worse and now it's gone altogether.' Tears were now pouring from his sightless eyes, down his wrinkled cheeks and into his beard. 'I'm blind, Bridie, I'm blind.'

She put her arms around the big man and held him close, whilst he laid his head against her breast and wept.

*

Three weeks later Bridie stood in the spare bedroom of her great-grandmother's cottage before the speckled mirror and stared at the stranger reflected there.

Behind her, Eveleen, her voice choked with emotion, said, 'You look beautiful, Bridie. The most beautiful bride I've ever seen.'

'I wish Grandfather could see me today,' Bridie murmured.

Eveleen smiled, determined not to let her brood. Not today of all days. 'Come along. It's time you were going. Andrew's waiting for you. And Richard's with him. They've all gone across to the chapel. Even your great-grandmother, riding like a queen in her bath chair. They're all waiting for you – Gran, Josh, Mrs Turner, even Mr Stokes. They're all there, all except . . .' They exchanged a look and then Eveleen added, 'But I'll be there to help you. I'll be just behind you.'

Bridie nodded, unable to speak for the lump in her throat, willing herself not to cry as she carefully descended the stairs.

As she stepped out of the cottage, she stopped and gave a little gasp of surprise when she saw the man waiting at the end of the pathway; a tall, broad-shouldered man, resplendent in a morning suit, his face turned towards them.

Bridie glanced at her aunt, the question she dare not voice aloud written in her wide eyes. Eveleen was smiling, tears in her own eyes as she said, 'Yes, my darling, he's waiting for you, too.'

Bridie, her knees trembling, walked towards him, the beautiful white lace train of her wedding dress trailing behind her, her trembling fingers clutching the bouquet she carried. As she reached him, she put her hand on his arm and whispered softly, 'Here I am.' And in a voice that was a little unsteady from the joy in her heart she asked, 'Are you ready to give me away?'

'I'm ready,' Harry Singleton said, his voice husky with emotion. 'I'm ready – Granddaughter.'